YOU, MY BROTHER

Philip Burton

You, My Brother

A Novel Based on the Lives of Edmund & William Shakespeare

RANDOM HOUSE NEW YORK

Library of Congress Cataloging in Publication Data
Burton, Philip, 1904-
You, my brother.
1. Shakespeare, Edmund—Fiction. 2. Shakespeare,
William, 1564-1616, in fiction, drama, poetry, etc.
I. Title.
PZ4.B9745YO3   [PR6052.U72]   823'.9'14   73-5009
ISBN 0-394-48478-9

Manufactured in the United States of America
First Edition

To CHRISTIAN

CONTENTS

Book One

1596

ONE

HAMNET WAS DYING. THE PHYSICIAN HAD BLED AND PURGED THE BOY TILL all strength was gone, and the family now awaited the end. Death would come for him in a day or a week. All hoped that it would delay its coming until the father could be brought home to see his son.

Richard had set out for London on Dapple that morning as soon as the sun gave light. Neither he nor his horse had taken such a long journey before, and there was much trepidation at their setting forth, but Richard showed no sign of fear or dismay. He only wished that the family could have spared the money for a succession of hired horses so that the hundred and twenty miles might be done in half the time; old Dapple would be hard put to it to maintain thirty miles a day. Though he would share the bed with as many as need be to sleep cheaply, Richard agreed to the extravagance of sleeping at inns because he was certain that Will would reimburse the family for everything spent to bring him home. His father's concern was that Richard, being a tyro in travel, would lose his money to highwaymen, pickpockets, dishonest beggars, or clever talkers. But Richard had no such fear. What worried him was that he was leaving on Market Day—and the red sunset had promised a fair Thursday. That would ensure a good crowd after such continual heavy rains as had swollen the Avon until it was feared that two days more of downpour would make the Clopton bridge impassable. August was always a good selling month, for then the farmers had money, even in these bad times, and the John Shakespeare gloves were much in favor, especially with the rhyming jingles that went with them when they were intended as gifts; Will had had a knack for such foolishness, and now Ned turned them out indifferent well. He was not good for much else. Richard had wanted him to take charge of the stall for this day—it was high time at sixteen that he became a man—but his mother would not hear of it. And so a whole day's trading would be lost.

Ned had wanted to take Richard's place in going to London to find Will, not from any sense of family duty but because dangerous, crowded, noisy, exciting, wicked London was the lodestar of his dreams. But the family was adamant in its refusal of the suggestion: he was much too young for such a hazardous adventure. Always, as it suited their argument, he was too young or too old. Sixteen was a loathsome age.

So now, practical, trustworthy Richard sped to the best of Dapple's very limited ability along the rain-muddied roads with his sad message to brother Will, and good-for-nothing Ned was deputed to take his eleven-year-old niece, Judith, out of the house where her twin brother lay adying.

It was four o'clock as they came out onto Henley Street, and the sun was so warm that everything steamed from the recent rains. A lively murmur in the distance called to their welcoming ears. Both boy and girl felt impelled to run to join the boisterous crowd, but the proximity of death at their backs cowed and constrained them, and they walked slowly toward the High Cross.

This was the best time of the Market. Most of the trading had been done by noon. Now was the hour for gossip and laughter and scandal and japes. But, Ned sadly reflected, this was no time for enjoyment; Hamnet was dying.

Ned had never known death in the house—his little sister Anne died the year before he was born. It seemed that Death was fought with strange smells—the house was heavy with the scent of herbs and flowers dried and hanging, herbs and flowers distilled on fire. And Death was fought with red colors: Hamnet's room was all red—red covers on the beds, red covers on the windows. Hamnet now lay in his mother's bed, while she lay in the truckle bed, lay but without sleep. For the first time, Ned felt sorry for Will's wife Anne. He had little sympathy for her austere puritanism, but now she was a mother losing her only son, and she might be past bearing another. She could not be older than his own mother was when he was born, but Anne looked too old; to Ned she had always looked too old.

Ned would miss Hamnet. He was a lively little fellow who would always strive at games more mightily than his frail body would allow. It seemed that there was not enough strength for both twins, and Judith was the lustier. Twins were supposed to share a spirit. Would Judith die a little with Hamnet? She surprised his thoughts by speaking.

"Father won't come in time."

"How do you know that?"

"I know."

They were passing the smithy. By this time the shop showed little sign of the great fires of 1594 and 1595, which had destroyed so much of the town. Their own house had miraculously escaped, except for a charring on the west side. Master Hornby, the smith, and two of his sons were busy; two horses were being shod and four were still waiting, tied patiently to the post. Ned and Judith stopped; they could never resist the smell and sparks and clanging of the smithy, and Master Hornby was always loud in friendliness.

"Hello, Ned. How's the lad?"

"He doesn't change for better or for worse," replied Ned.

The smith said, "I saw Richard setting out this morning. He's a brave one to travel to London alone, and for the first time too. But yesterday I gave Dapple four good shoes to go on; not that good shoes are of much use in mud, and that's what he'll have all the way. I've never been to London, and never want to go. 'Tis a Sodom and Gomorrah both, from all I hear."

Ned felt called upon to defend the great city. "The Queen lives there and all the great ones."

The smith was not to be outdone. " 'Tis the heavy price they have to pay for high position. I thank God I was born to be a lowly smith here in Stratford. What say you, sons?"

"You are in the right, Father," said Roger, the elder son, but Francis, the younger, contented himself with a dubious smile. Ned knew that Francis would give much to be rid of both smithy and Stratford. The two had often discussed the borough of their birth, and their comments and conclusions would have surprised and horrified its worthy aldermen and burgesses.

Judith felt that the conversation had wandered away from her and the all-important subject. She waited while the smith raised a hind leg of the patient horse into his leather apron to try the shoe for size. When the sizzling had ceased and she had savored the pungent, acrid smell, she said, "I heard Mother say that Hamnet could not last."

The smith delivered a preacherly comment in appropriate tones. "None knows better than your mother that such things are in the hands of the Lord. Miracles have happened to rebuke man's despair."

Ned was impatient of the sermons and abruptly took his leave of the smith and the smithy, drawing his charge away by the arm. He had been puzzled for some days by the apparent heartlessness of Judith toward her brother's sickness, and he decided to question it openly. "You seem not to be very unhappy about Hamnet. Won't you be sad if he dies?"

Judith puckered her brows for a moment and then said, with exaggerated gravity, "Yes, but it will be God's will."

Ned wondered if she fully understood what was happening. She was not without feeling; she had cried bitterly when her pet pig died from swine fever. Possibly she was jealous of Hamnet because Grandfather, Grandmother, Father, and Mother made too much of the boy. Why did a son seem more important than a daughter? To perpetuate the Shakespeare name meant everything to Ned's father and much to Will, and now it seemed that the hope might be lost. And yet, apart from Will who might still have another son, there were three unmarried brothers, Gilbert, Richard, and Ned himself. Surely among them they could beget a son. But Gilbert didn't like women and was certain not to marry. Richard was a mystery: he said he would not marry until the family fortunes were restored, but in the meantime his ways with women were secret, and this in Stratford, where to have a secret was a rare accomplishment. As for Ned, he had already, at sixteen, lain joyfully in the fields with numerous girls, and some married women, but he was determined against the shackles of marriage and Stratford. First London, and then perhaps he would marry a rich widow and beget a son to please his father.

By this time Ned and Judith were mingling with the crowd at the High Cross. Three sideshows were receiving packed attention: a dancer who performed to his own piping and drumming, a pair of tumblers, and a ballad-singer who told the bloody details of the thirty-year-old murder of Rizzio, now a safe subject with the Scottish Queen Mary dead by the ax these ten years.

It was the singer who most attracted Ned, and it chanced that as he and Judith arrived, the ballad came to its end. There was a stirring among the crowd as those in front quickly moved to another attraction in their haste to avoid putting a coin into the performer's proffered bag. This gave Ned and Judith a chance to squeeze their way to the front for the next performance. Ned wondered if he was doing right to submit the ears of his charge to the probably bawdy and certainly gory song, but he satisfied his slightly troubled conscience with the reflection that perhaps she wouldn't understand what she shouldn't hear.

The singer, who called himself "Robin of London Town," was a tall, ragged, and uncouth young man, who obviously spent more nights in ditches than in beds. Yet Ned envied him. He wore his colorful rags with more pride than graced the sober suits worn by the sober citizens who stood around with eyes and ears agape. Robin was new to Stratford and was bent on ingratiating himself. In an age when most smiles revealed teeth yellow, black, decayed, and gapped, his frequent smile showed teeth white, complete, and regular. Ned determined forthwith to spend vigor and time on rubbing his own teeth with salt and his gums with alum.

Now Robin carefully placed against a post which supported the canopy of the High Cross his crudely made lute. He treated it with the reverence more suited to the Queen's beautiful golden-stringed instrument. Then he took out the contents of the collection bag and showed them to his audience, broadly smiling as he said, "Five farthings, one whole penny, and a pretty button! The button is not meant for such as I, and I herewith bestow it, with my undying devotion, upon this beautiful young maiden."

With a bow that would have graced the most accomplished courtier, he gave the button to Judith. Embarrassed and delighted, she made a bobbing curtsey as she received the gift. Robin then took up his ragged lute and, exaggerating a meticulous care, began to tune its catgut strings. This was but an excuse to give time for his new audience to settle, the while he delivered a preliminary harangue. "Draw near, gentles all," he smilingly invited while pretending to catch the twanged strings in the tiniest deviation from the true sound. "Draw near and listen to the true tale of the murder of David Rizzio, a queen's Italian paramour and a singer like myself, who was done to death by a jealous husband, the Lord Darnley, and his cruel confederates. Never before has this song been sung in this fair town of Stratford, and—this I pledge—never will you forget it."

Having said this and judging the moment to be as ripe as it was likely to be, he launched into his song, which had fifty-six verses,

> "One for each thrust of dagger and sword,
>   That spoiled the Queen's young lover."

The refrain ran,

> "All this did happen as I do tell,
>   In Holyrood in Scotland,
> The blood was spilt despite of Hell,
>   In Holyrood in Scotland."

The crowd delighted in the bloody details, which were delivered to great effect by the singer's vigorous baritone voice and his highly dramatic manner. Ned was soon absorbed in the performance, but was guiltily reminded of the questionable presence of Judith by the verse,

> "Rizzio hid behind the Queen,
>   Now six months big with Jamey.
> Darnley the father was, I ween,
>   But she had lain with Davey."

This verse caused uneasiness in the crowd. Some young folk found it delightfully daring, but their elders held it to be impolitic and even dangerous. Word of it spread around, and several had come to hear for themselves. Robin was well aware of the risks he took but judged them to be worth the crowds they drew. In Coventry they had earned him a night in the stocks, but the collection had been good too. Everybody of earnest persuasion was offended by the song—the majority because of the slur on James, who seemed likely to be the next king of England, the Catholics because of the slur on Queen Mary, of martyred memory, and the Puritans because such a song was clearly the work of the Devil. Robin gambled that when enemies were equally offended, their enmity would prevent them from taking joint action against him, but he was often wrong, and so it seemed it would prove in the case of Stratford.

Very soon a portly draper, Burgess George Badger, appeared, followed by a group of eager citizens confident that a good show was in the making. Robin sensed trouble but continued with his song. He had come to the fiftieth verse, which, in spite of the approach of evidently hostile authority, he delivered with comically impudent ambiguity.

"Lord Darnley was a man right fair,
Of men accounted handsome.
He did beget young James, I swear,
Or Mary's soul's in ransom."

Robin started the refrain for the fiftieth time, but Master Badger, a known Catholic, held up his pudgy hand and imperiously commanded, "Hold!" With no outward sign of his inward quaking, the singer stopped amid-note on a white-toothed smile.

"Who are you, sir, and by whose authority do you perform?" demanded the burgess.

"Robin of London, at your service, a loyal subject of Her Majesty, as my song doth proclaim," retorted Robin with a deep bow. He then added a bold and barefaced lie. "I perform under the authority of my lord, the Earl of Warwick."

Further questioning was interrupted by the arrival of another draper, also a burgess, tall, gaunt Nicholas Barnhurst. Again the crowd gave way, but now with eager and hushed expectancy, as all awaited the inevitable explosion between the two business rivals, Catholic and Puritan, Badger and Barnhurst. The forbidding Puritan came to a halt next to Judith and Ned, and his appalled eyes took note of them. In tones calculated to freeze the marrow he said to Judith, "Your brother dying, and you here to listen to this spawn of Satan!" Judith shrank against Ned, which brought the Barnhurst battery upon him. "This is your doing, Master Edmund. Get you home, and take the child with you, and pray God's forgiveness for both of you."

Had Ned thought he possessed a scrap of justification, he might have hazarded some retort, but the glaring denunciation only echoed his own guilt. There was nothing for it but to take Judith's hand and slink away. He was sure that Robin would go to jail tonight and to the pillory or the stocks on the morrow.

But Ned had not allowed for the minstrel's wiliness. With deferent courtesy he addressed the burgesses, "Worthy aldermen, for such I am sure you must be, allow me but to sing my song that you may fairly judge of its merits, which I protest call for commendation, not condemnation."

"Not a word, sir," barked Barnhurst, "not a note." Then, turning to the crowd, he said, "Fetch a constable, and we will soon have this jackanapes in jail." Everyone was reluctant to leave, for the real fun had not yet begun. "Go you, young Williams," said the angry burgess, fixing his eye on a spindly and pimply youth whose excessive height singled him out for attention. Barnhurst held him with a baleful glare until Williams was forced to hurry in search of a constable.

Now Barnhurst bore down upon his hated rival Badger and said, "I might have known you would be here, a party to this vile ribaldry." This unjust accusation surprised some of the onlookers into laughter, which stung both opponents.

Badger, his hand upraised, shouted, "I call high heaven to witness . . ."

But Barnhurst interposed with, "Be not so blasphemous. Heaven is deaf to the call of idolators."

To this Badger had a reply ready with frequent usage. "And Heaven turns its face from psalm-singing hypocrites."

Under cover of these opening exchanges, and with the conniving assistance of some of the crowd, Robin stole stealthily away. As soon as he was free of the crowd, he ran swiftly down Wood Street to cross the bridge on his way to Banbury. Thus it was that he passed Ned and Judith making their way down to Butt Close to watch the archers.

Ned called. "Robin!"

As Ned drew alongside, Robin said, "I can't stop; they're after me."

Ned volunteered, "I'll help you to hide."

Robin, still walking sturdily, said, "I am grateful, young sir, but could you help me to ride 'twould be more fitting to my need." Then he stopped abruptly and grasped Ned by the arm. "Look! Spindleshanks and the constable!"

"Quick," said Ned, and drew Robin across the street and into the yard of the Crown Inn. While they waited there with as much nonchalance as they could muster, Judith came up to them.

She had understood all, and said, "They didn't see you. It is safe to go."

"Thank you, fair maid," smiled Robin. "I wish I had another button to give you. Fare you well, and you too, young sir."

"Can we not walk with you? 'Twill look better if you have company," suggested Ned.

Robin smiled and said, "I see you are a born knave. Come then."

"I too," said Judith.

"But we shall walk fast," objected Robin.

"Then I shall run," Judith flashed back.

With a shared laugh, they set out. As they walked, Ned said, "Know you my brother, the playwright and player?"

"His name?"

"William Shakespeare."

" 'Tis a good name," mused Robin.

"But do you know him?" Ned insisted.

"I fear me not." Robin saw that both his companions were disappointed by this news, so he added, "Be not down-spirited, for I will confess a truth to you, and that is a mighty compliment, for the truth is something I never waste speech on. I was never in London Town. Though I call myself 'Robin of London Town,' in truth it should be 'Charlie of Chester.' But that has a comic ring to it and suits ill with my quality. Now I am on my way to London, where fame awaits me. It may chance I shall happen upon your William." He said this with such gracious condescension that Ned laughed at Robin's pretensions though he liked him all the more. Here was a player indeed, one whose performance never stopped.

By this time they were on the Clopton bridge, and Robin stopped briefly. "Here we must part," he said. "You to go back to Stratford, a fate for which I pity you, and I to go on to London, to justify my name and to claim my true place in the great world. Farewell to you both, and my thanks for your help and company." He adjusted his rough instrument on his back—he had no other baggage—and was away. Ned and Judith called their farewells after him, and stood to watch him as he went. They waved to him, but Robin did not turn.

As they walked back, Judith said, "He was a liar."

"Yes," agreed Ned, "but a pleasing one."

Judith, with a troubled frown, said, "I heard Mother tell Uncle Richard that all players are liars, that they earn money by pretending to be what they are not, and that is lying. Is that true?"

Ned himself had had this argument with Anne, who was tormented that she lived on the proceeds of playacting, but he could not now undermine Judith's faith in her mother. He said, "Yes, it is true." He couldn't resist adding an argument he had used with Anne. "Even Christ himself used stories, which are a sort of playacting, to teach the truth."

"Then Christ was a liar too."

The blasphemy of Judith's simple logic frightened Ned. Instinctively he looked around to see if anybody had heard it; nobody was near enough. Suppose the child said to someone, "My uncle Ned told me that Christ was a liar." A long imprisonment for atheism would be the least he could expect. He hastened to erase the phrase from Judith's mind, but it wasn't easy. "Judith! That was a terrible thing to say, and you must never use those words again. Christ was God, and God cannot lie."

"But you said . . ."

"I did not. There are all kinds of lies, and some are good ones."

"Is playacting good lying?"

"It can be."

"Is Father's?"

"I think so, but your mother thinks not."

"I think so too, and Mother is wrong."

"You must not say that or think it either. Your mother is a very good woman, and she believes she is right."

TWO

RICHARD WAS NOT TO REACH LONDON UNTIL NOON ON SUNDAY, AND HE could not have managed that if he had not been given a change of mount. At the Crown Tavern in Oxford, his first stop, Richard sought out Master Davenant, the host, for he had heard Will speak of him as a good friend, and such he proved to be. Davenant seemed a saturnine and dour man, but his looks belied him. He greatly admired Will and proudly displayed five books by him, two long poems and three plays. Richard had never seen them before, but he had heard that *Venus and Adonis* was a wicked work. He suspected that Will had given Ned a copy, but, if so, it was a carefully kept secret; they would not wish to give Anne offense. The other poem was about a rape, and that spoke for itself. As for the plays, one was about some character from the ancient world whose name Richard had never heard, and the other two were about a king of England, one of the Henrys. Master Davenant was for reading aloud long passages, but a yawn, which Richard did not try to stifle, reminded him of the condition of his guest, and he bustled him to bed.

Master Davenant joined Richard for breakfast; and it was only then that he learnt of his guest's sad mission. He was genuinely and deeply moved. His own wife lay sick abed because two days before she had been delivered in a long and painful birth of a boy who breathed for an hour and then died. As an expression of his compassion for William, Master Davenant insisted that Richard pay not a penny for his stay. More than that, since speed was imperative he said that tired Dapple could stay in his stable, to be picked up on the return journey, while Richard hastened to London on a fresh mare which he would lend him. He chose for the purpose a mount used to the noise of London, which was so great that a horse strange to it had been known to be frightened into wildness.

Richard worried about his ability to find Will; the family had not been able to help him because not one of them had ever visited Will in London. (For three years Will had rented a large house in Shoreditch near the Theatre, for Anne and the children to join him, but she had steadfastly refused to submit herself, and still more her children, to the manifest evils of the city.) But now Master Davenant was able to help, and he advised Richard that Will might be hard to find: he might be at the theatre; he might be at home; he might be rehearsing somewhere. But his brother Gilbert should be easy to find. When Richard came to the Fleet River, which was just outside the city wall at Newgate, he should turn right and follow the river for about half a mile toward the

Thames, when he would come to a haberdasher's shop with the sign of a blue doublet with a red cape.

Richard would have to spend another night on the road and Master Davenant suggested an inn at High Wycombe for the purpose. He said that the mention of his name would ensure good hospitality—and it did, if sharing a bed with three other men be good hospitality. But without the Davenant name, Richard would not have had a bed at all. After almost empty roads, everything changed a day's journey from London. It seemed the world was bent on getting there on the Sunday, in spite of mud which the hundreds of hooves made deeper.

While his Saturday night host took pains to fit Richard in for the sake of his good friend, John Davenant, he could not spare time for company. This sorted well with Richard's disposition, and he listened as he ate his supper to the hullaballoo of loud chatter about him. Gradually he gathered that tomorrow was to be a great day in London. The Queen was going down the Thames in her royal barge, which in itself was worth traveling many a mile to see, to welcome home her victorious fleet and her gallant commanders, the Lord Admiral and the Earl of Essex. The news of the "Triumph" had only been announced from the Palace of Westminster that morning, but it had spread with the gathering power of a forest fire.

It seemed that there had been a great victory in Spain some weeks or months before. Rumors of it had reached Stratford, but Richard paid little attention to rumors of affairs far off, or indeed to gossip of affairs near at hand. Now he could not choose but listen to vociferous argument about the exact time of the great doings at Cadiz; know-alls, with professions to inside knowledge, claimed that it was scarce a month ago, others that it was more than two months and that the return had been delayed by terrible storms. There was agreement that the Earl of Essex had been the great hero of the occasion and that he had sacked Cadiz. But there was fierce disagreement about how many had been killed, the proponents clearly revealing their own predilections, some glorying in the fact that not a man, woman, or child had been spared, and others equally exultant in the fact that the chivalrous Earl had spared every woman and child, seeing them to safety before their homes were burnt. There was no doubt that the Spanish fleet had been destroyed; not a ship was left afloat, said some, but others had it on the most reliable authority that several of Spain's greatest ships were being brought home to be presented to Her Majesty.

Bewildered by the confusion of sound and argument, Richard betook himself to bed with the aid of a tallow-candle, only to find that one of his bedmates was before him, already fast asleep, smelling high and snoring loudly. Richard decided to lie with his head at the foot of the bed and his back to the odoriferous feet. He had blown out the candle and was about to fall asleep, when the remaining would-be occupants of the bed arrived. They were a well-dressed pair, loud and drunk, and were obviously traveling together—to no good purpose Richard felt. He recognized the taller of the two as the most bloodthirsty argufier during supper and lavish with both money and words. He was a handsome man, but his companion was a weasel, whose upper lip was drawn back in a permanent sneer. Their laughter awoke the snorer, a little old man, who cursed them for a pair of bellowing bulls.

The taller rascal quickly pulled out a dagger and held it to the old man's throat. In a menacing whisper he said, "Go to sleep, Methuselah, or you won't wake up at all."

The weasel chuckled heartily at this, and the old man closed his eyes with a frightened grunt.

Richard quickly pretended to be asleep. He felt a lantern held close to his face and tightly clutched the wallet containing his remaining ten shillings. The tall one said in a voice he clearly meant Richard to hear, "I saw this young yokel downstairs. He said not a word but tried to look wise, and now he affects sleep. 'Tis well. Fear closed his mouth but it may cause his other mouth to bring forth soft utterings." Both the gallants laughed uproariously at this coarse witticism. Then the tall one continued. "Enough, enough. Let's to bed, for we must be up betimes. Great things lie ahead in London." He added, with a conspiratorial whisper, "and rich fruit for the picking."

Richard heard the sound of belts being unbuckled and the grunts and thuds as each took off the other's long boots. Then the lantern was blown out and they plopped into bed, both with their hot and unwashed feet to his head. The short one was next to Richard, and he gave him a vigorous kick in the stomach as he settled down, but Richard refrained from even a whimper of protest; he remembered the dagger. He was in such a nervous state that he was the last to fall asleep, but prayers to God for protection through the night and guidance on the morrow, coupled with travel exhaustion, finally brought him welcome oblivion.

He was dragged awake from a deep and troubled sleep by the old man's repeated cry, "I've been robbed. I've been robbed." Instinctively Richard felt for his own wallet; it was gone. He sprang out of bed. There was no sign of the two thieves. His first thought was that he had no money to pay his bill. He had offered to do so the night before, as he found was customary, but the host, in a gesture of trust and friendship to John Davenant, had told him the morning would be time enough. Richard's distress was nothing to that of the old man, who sat on the bed and wept openly. Richard tried to comfort him with the thought that the thieves had at least spared him physical harm, but the old man refused to be comforted, though gradually he restrained his sobbing so that he could tell his tale. He was a jeweler from Gloucester on his way with some precious stones to his son, a tire-maker, in London. The father was very proud that the Queen herself had worn one of the bejeweled headdresses made by his clever son. In one respect Richard was the worse off of the two victims; the old man had paid his inn bill of six shillings for himself and his horse the night before, and he had but three shillings left for the thieves to take. The jewels were hidden in his belt, but now he realized that his failure to take off his belt aroused the suspicion of the thieves. Richard marveled at the deftness of their fingers.

It was now six o'clock. The thieves had probably stolen away while it was still dark. When the two robbed men told their tale to the innkeeper, he was properly commiserative, though he seemed to Richard improperly tolerant of the thieves. He dismissed the episode as one of the natural hazards of travel "in these unsettled times." As for Richard's bill, he readily took the young man's word that he would pay it on the return journey; again the Davenant name was sufficient guarantee. Richard had shown such compassion for the old man in his loss that the innkeeper took him aside and told him to keep his sympathy for himself. Where had the old man got the jewels in the first place? Almost certainly from pirates who had stolen them from savage men in far-off places. It was a world of thief-rob-thief, and one's concern should be for oneself. Richard set off for London as a lamb being driven toward a den of wolves.

Once within a mile of the city wall, the procession of travelers began to thin, for some riders, and walkers too, turned to the right whenever a road or street gave opportunity. They were making for the bank of the Thames and a good vantage point from which to see the royal progress down the river, which was rumored to start from Westminster at two in the afternoon.

Richard had no difficulty in finding the Fleet River, and, remembering Master Davenant's instructions, he turned right to follow it. In the August heat it was a noisome river, a receptacle for vile-smelling refuse, liberally sprinkled with butchers' offal which screeching gulls claimed.

He had come within sound of the crowd waiting on the Thames bank without seeing his brother's haberdashery shop. He came to a halt by an imposing building, Bridewell Palace, once an emblem of Cardinal Wolsey's pomp and power, but now a prison. Gilbert's shop must be on the other side of the Fleet River. There was a convenient bridge at the northern edge of the Bridewell grounds, and Richard crossed it and made his way slowly back up the river bank, his eyes anxiously alert for the shop sign. And there, at last, it was: the blue doublet with the red cape. The shop was meaner than Richard had hoped, but it was a great relief to see it.

He dismounted, and grew concerned lest Gilbert too might be down on the Thames bank. There was an impressive and shining brass knocker on the door, and Richard, with sickening hope, rapped the knocker hard. He waited. There was no response. He rapped again. This time the top half of the door of the house on the left was flung open, and a gnomelike little man popped his head out like a puppet in a show. He looked questioningly at Richard over the spectacles resting on the edge of his nose. From the number of threaded needles that were stuck in the top of his apron, Richard assumed he was a tailor and could not refrain from an unspoken reproof that he was working on the Sabbath.

"They're not in," chirped the gnome pointlessly. Then, seeing that the visitor was completely at a loss, he added, "They've gone to see the Triumph, with the rest of the addlepated crew."

"Do you know where I might find them?"

"No, and I shouldn't try. People have been trampled to death at such gatherings, but today 'twill be a case of pushed into the water and drowned. If they return alive, shall I give them your name?"

"Yes, sir. It is Richard Shakespeare."

"Ah, the brother. Have you come from Stratford?"

"Yes, but to see my brother Will. I sought Gilbert to help me find him."

"I have seen that William. He is a goodly gentleman, and he prospers too, for he is both player and poet. He will not waste the treasure of his time on such foolishness as the Triumph."

"Know you where I might find him?"

"At home, I judge, writing another play, for they are ever in need of a new one."

"Can you tell me how to find my brother's house?"

" 'Tis in Shoreditch near the two theatres. I once took a suit there from Master Gilbert. You go back up Fleet, turn into the city at Newgate, then through Cheapside into Threadneedle Street—not Lombard or Cornhill but Threadneedle—then you turn into Bishopsgate . . ." The puzzled look on Richard's face moved the little tailor into saying, "Wait. I will come with you. 'Tis clear you are a stranger to London. The preachers say God rewards a good deed done on the Sabbath, but I pay little mind to preachers. They are in love with their own words, which are, for the most part, wind and air."

Without waiting for a response from Richard, the tailor disappeared. Penniless, alone, and adrift in a frighteningly strange world, Richard had become very dejected, but now he was fully restored in spirit by the tailor's kindness. He tried to express his gratitude when the little man reappeared, divested of his apron and with a shapeless old hat to cover his bald head, but his bumbling sentences were set aside with, "Say no more. 'Twill do me good to take the air."

Richard set off with his companion behind him on a horse. As they rode through the streets, Tim the Tailor, for that was how he named himself to Richard, kept up a running commentary, largely a satirical one, on the sights they passed. They took a shortcut through St. Paul's Churchyard, and here Richard was shocked beyond measure. Here were no quiet, churchgoing families taking a stroll in the afternoon. Even to Richard's unsophisticated eyes and ears, it was a place of beggars and ne'er-do-wells, thieves and peddlers, desperate out-of-work men and plying-for-hire whores, men displaying surreptitious goods and apprentices looking for mischief. Tim became eloquent in describing the depravity of the scene, occasionally emphasizing his remarks with a vicious kick at a too importunate beggar who clawed at the riders. As they left the churchyard and moved into Cheapside with its splendid shops, he gave his final withering comment on the St. Paul's scene: "Yes, 'tis bad, a den of thieves; but 'tis worse on other days, for now the gentlemen are at the river, and they are the masters of villainy. That the spire was struck by lightning 'twas surely a sign from God."

At last they left the city by Bishopsgate and came into open country though there were a few streets off the main highway and some scattered houses. A stench hit Richard from a ditch which hugged the city wall and served as an open sewer. There was also a miasma rising from some marshlands. Small wonder that London bred the plague, with such foul smells outside its walls. Anne was right not to bring the children here; it was a hell of pestilence and vice.

As he mused, Tim spoke. "If Master Shakespeare be not at home, 'tis like he will be at the Theatre."

Richard suppressed his horror at this possible desecration of the Sabbath and said, "Have you been to the plays?"

"Yes, but rarely. I saw Master Burbage play the hunchback King when the players came back to London after the plague. 'Twas wonderful to behold. I never shall forget how he called for a horse."

"They have horses on the stage?" asked Richard in surprise, but prepared to believe anything of this devilish city.

"No, no," was Tim's testy reply. "He did but call for one."

At last they came to a round wooden building on the left of the road, some three rooms tall. Richard looked his question.

"No," said Tim. "That is a theatre but not *the* Theatre. That is the Curtain. The Theatre is the one beyond. Do you see it? Master Shakespeare does not live far from it."

They rode on and soon they came to William's house. It was made of timber and plaster, roofed with tile, and was backed by a pleasant garden. But two stories high, it was more like Stratford than anything Richard had seen in the city, where most of the houses had three stories and some were as tall as churches. Nor had he ever expected to see so many glass windows; London was clearly a place of great wealth and great poverty. Whereas Richard had been disappointed by Gilbert's shop, he was pleased by William's home.

Tim said, "I doubt not he will be sitting in the garden." He led the way around the house and there indeed was the man they sought, seated in a pleasant arbor. There was someone with him. Will had on a long, loose gown, for he had been taken from his writing, but his companion wore a fine tunic. Will was not tall, but the other man was shorter. His beard and incipient paunch made him look a little older than Will, though he was in fact a few years younger.

As the group approached, Will stood. He had eyes for none but his brother, for he sensed bad news.

"I'm Tim the Tailor. I live next door to your brother the haberdasher, Master Shakespeare. This other brother came to find him but he was out at the Triumph, so I offered to conduct him to you, for it was you he came to see."

"That was kind of you," began Will, but now Tim had turned his attention to the other man.

"Master Burbage, 'tis indeed an honor to meet you. Your hunchback King was a marvel to behold."

"Thank you, sir," said the player with a professional courtesy which masked his amused observation of the little man.

All this while Richard had been staring at Will, not knowing how to give his news in such company. Will spoke. "You will excuse us, gentlemen. My brother has come a long way to communicate something to me. Be kind enough to wait for me, Dick."

Richard followed his brother into the house. The main room was furnished well but sparsely. There were more books scattered on a table than Richard had ever read, and on the wall was a painted cloth, but of a pagan scene, not one from the Bible. He was so occupied with observing the room that Will had to prompt him.

"Now, Richard. I know what you have to say is important, and I fear 'tis bad."

" 'Tis Hamnet, Will. He is very sick."

For a moment Will said nothing. He moved away. Then he turned back. "Is it the plague?"

"The physician knows not what it is, but the lad wastes away. He cannot eat or drink, and shakes with cold while his body burns."

After another moment of silence, Will said, "We will set out at once. But first I must speak to Master Burbage." He started out, but stopped. "Oh, have you eaten, Richard?"

"No, Will. I was robbed in High Wycombe."

Richard made this confession with such a tone of shame that he could not take better care of himself that Will could not forbear a smile. "You will find bread, cheese, and ale in the larder there. Some fruit too." He went out to the garden as Richard hurried to the larder.

Tim was delivering a long speech to the amused player on the subject of the wickedness of those in high places. Will caught the words "Everything they do lines their coffers . . ." but the look on the face of the approaching Will silenced even Tim.

"Dick," said Will, " 'tis bad news. My boy is very sick."

It was Tim who spoke. "I grieve for you, Master Shakespeare. Your brother didn't tell me. How old is the boy?"

"He's eleven and a half." Will was eager to talk to his colleague alone, but did not know how to deal with this ebullient little man who had brought Richard to him.

"You have other sons?" asked Tim, with the implied comfort that, if he did, one could be spared.

"No, he is the only one."

Richard Burbage spoke. "You must go to him, Will. Do not worry about anything here. In next week's plays you only appear twice, and we can spare you." He said these last words with warm humor.

Tim would not be silenced. "Shall I give a message to Master Gilbert?"

"Tell him what has happened and that we cannot spare the time to see him, but I will do so when I come back."

Tim saw that the two men wished to be alone. "I hope to see you again, Master Burbage. It has been a great honor. You too, Master Shakespeare." The mention of the playwright was a courteous afterthought, and with it Tim skipped away.

Burbage said. "I grieve for you, Will. I know what 'tis, but none of my sons lived to be as old as Hamnet. I pray God he be spared."

THREE

WITHIN HALF AN HOUR, WILL AND RICHARD HAD SET OUT. IT WAS ALMOST three o'clock. Will wanted to travel alone by a series of hired horses, leaving Richard to follow and pick up Dapple at Oxford. But his brother persuaded him of the foolishness of this plan. The weather threatened and seemed likely to make night travel impossible; at best it was dangerous. Besides, what could such haste do? Everything was in God's hands. And whatever awaited him in Stratford, complete exhaustion would not fit Will to deal with it. As if to reinforce the argument, there was a frightening flash of lightning followed quickly by a cannonade of thunder. It was decided to make night stops, as had Richard, at High Wycombe, Oxford, and Compton Winyates, though Will would omit this last stop if the weather permitted. It didn't. Before they had left the city proper, heavy rain began to fall and it accompanied them intermittently throughout their journey.

There was little conversation between the brothers. Of all the family, Richard most shared Anne's puritan values, and Will was well aware of this. He was equally aware of Richard's virtues; he was the most dependable and self-sacrificing of the family; the pursuit of duty drove him as the pursuit of pleasure did other men. Will could imagine Richard's regret at having to forgo Market Day. And their father was of little help. As he thought of him, as he often did, Will smiled ruefully and lovingly. It was nearly twenty years now since that vivacious, energetic man who had risen to be Stratford's leading citizen became so bowed and embittered by misfortune that he had incarcerated himself in the house. In explanation he had said, "The world has turned against me; I turn against the world." He broke his vow never to face the world again only one notable day—to vote for his old friend, John Sadler, for bailiff.

Will had been eighteen at the time. What a year that had been for him! He had lain with Anne, and she had become pregnant with Susanna. Two months later he had married her.

His musings, as his horse jogged through the soaking rain, returned as they always did to his beloved Hamnet. The twins were named for Hamnet and Judith Sadler; that Hamnet had been the nephew of Bailiff John Sadler. (According to some alehouse wags, the death of the bailiff in office some six months after his election had been caused by his surprise that the elder Shakespeare had left the house to vote for him.)

Richard made some attempts at conversation, but did not receive much encouragement. Will, in apology for his taciturn companionship, would make routine inquiries about Stratford, but even these revealed the gap between the brothers. Richard waxed enthusiastic about the new vicar, Richard Byfield. From Will's point of view, the previous one, John Bramhall, had been bad enough—he had described the disastrous Stratford fires of 1594 and 1595 as the punishment by God for the habitual disregard of His Sabbath—but the Reverend Byfield sounded even worse. Will dreaded their inevitable meeting.

When Will broached family matters, it seemed safe to inquire about their sister, Joan. Richard reported that there was now a man in Joan's life. No one knew much about him, he was not a Stratford man. His name was William Hart, and he was a hatter who had opened a shop in Stratford soon after last year's fire, when there seemed opportunity for new enterprise. Gilbert had called on the hatter, from their mutual interest in merchandise, when he was home from London for Christmas and, because the newcomer to Stratford was alone, had invited him to join the Shakespeare family festivities; thus it was that Joan had met him, and he was now a frequent visitor at Henley Street.

"Is marriage imminent?" asked Will.

"I think not," said Richard. "They are cautious."

"Caution is wise, but pleasureless," retorted Will. Richard's face tightened at this remark, and silence fell between them again. Will wanted to question Richard about his own marital future, but dared not. The poet toyed with the conceit that his brother was an oyster no one would ever open, but there was a painful pearl inside.

It was not until late on Wednesday, after dark, that they came to

Clopton bridge. The rain had stopped and a fitful moon showed that the Avon almost topped the arches of the bridge. They proceeded cautiously across the bridge and into the dead town, in which no person stirred abroad and no light showed.

Will took desperate comfort from the darkness of the Shakespeare home. Surely it meant that Hamnet was better and there was no longer need for a night vigil. The two brothers quietly dismounted and led their horses around to the little stable at the back of the house. Will took a searching look at the part of the house which was his; it was a self-contained unit which projected into the yard and garden. There was no sign of light or life. His hopes rose.

They began to stable the horses, giving them some hay after the long journey. As they did so the back door opened and John Shakespeare, in nightgown and nightcap, stood there with a lantern. He called quietly, "William?"

Will left Richard to deal with the horses and approached his father. Before he could speak, his father said, "You are too late, my son. They buried the lad today."

Will noticed that "They." His father had not gone to the funeral. The old man continued, "For a week I have known there was no hope. You could have done nothing. Grieve not that you did not see him. 'Tis better so. You will remember him laughing and lively."

At last Will spoke, but only one questioning word, "Anne?"

The father was evasive. "She is a mother who has lost her only son, and that is beyond even her Christian patience to endure. She does not weep. She does not speak. 'Tis against nature."

They had waited for Richard to join them. When he did, the three men entered the house. Richard carried two leather traveling bags, his own and Will's.

Will moved to the settle, and the other two left him to his grief. The father sat apart in a chair, and Richard moved a stool near him.

"Did you see Gilbert?" asked John in a respectfully quiet tone.

"No," said Richard. "They were out." George Smith and Gilbert Shakespeare were always referred to as "They," as though they were man and wife.

"It was a bad journey for you," said John.

"Yes," said Richard. "I was robbed in High Wycombe."

"I knew it," said his father, unable to refrain from raising his voice a little in this justification of his prescience. "'Tis a terrible world, and I do right to shun it. The lad is happy to be out of it."

Will spoke. "Is Anne asleep?"

"I'm sure not," said his father. "Only the children are asleep, and perhaps Edmund, though he is no child."

"I will go to her," said Will.

Will took the lantern and mounted the stairs quietly. Though the creaking betrayed his coming, Anne had waited with quick-beating heart from the moment the horses had approached the house.

As Will entered the room he was taken aback to find that Anne was not alone. Judith lay fast asleep next to her in the bed, and Susanna was sleeping in the truckle bed. The family had insisted that Anne be not left alone this night. Will was shocked by Anne's appearance, which the lantern light made even ghastlier. She was eight years older than he, but now, at forty, she looked an old woman. The thought leaped into Will's mind, and he frowned with guilt at it, that Anne could never bear him another son.

Husband and wife looked at each other without speaking. Then Will put the lantern down and slowly sank to his knees that he might speak quietly to Anne. His feelings welled up in him: compassion for the bereft mother, grief at his own loss, guilt that he had not been there to share the burden of Hamnet's sickness, and despair at the gulf between him and his wife. All he said was, "Anne."

With a terrifying stoniness she said, "We must not wake the children."

"But I must speak to you," pleaded Will.

"There is nothing to say. The lad is gone."

"I beg you, Anne."

After a short hesitation, she said, "Go downstairs. I will come to you."

Will got up, picked up the lantern and left the room with an ominous foreboding about the scene that lay ahead. Nothing he had known of Anne in the past had prepared him for this reception. He had longed to comfort a grief-stricken woman in the hope that a shared sorrow could overwhelm the differences between them.

Anne, in a dressing gown, came down the stairs quietly. Will held out his arms to her, but she ignored him and moved to sit in a chair. Almost in a tone of command she said, "Sit down, Will." He had no choice but to do so. He chose the stool which was near her rather than the more distant settle.

"Anne," Will began, "I know how you feel . . ."

"You cannot," she interposed. "You never have."

"But your grief now is mine too. God gave us tears to ease our sorrow. Give way to them, Anne, give way."

"Talk not of God. You know Him not. Think you I do not weep because I do not feel? I am empty of tears, Will. They are all shed. I know now why Hamnet died." Will looked at her questioningly. She turned to face him fully. "God took him from us as a punishment for sin."

In exasperation, Will sprang up with the words, "I cannot believe that."

"He is just, and justice is hard on the sinner. Did He not say that He would punish unto the third and fourth generation of them that hate Him? And every feigning player shows by his life that he hates God. I know now, Will, that unless you give up playing and repent and lead a godly life with me and the children here in Stratford, you will be punished throughout the generations. The Lord has given you a sign by taking your Hamnet from you, a sign that, unless you change your ways, no man shall ever bear your name and blood."

Anne's tone in making this dreadful pronouncement had gradually lost its sternness and become almost a desperate plea. Will took advantage of the change to return to sit by her and attempt to reason with her in gentleness. "You are wrong, Anne. Those same words of God which you spoke go on to say that He will show mercy unto thousands of them that love Him, and God He knows that you love Him, Anne."

"I do, and He shows His mercy to me every day, even though I sinned grievously against Him with you."

"I beg you, Anne, not to speak of that any more. If sin it was, then it was mine more than yours."

"No, Will. You were but a boy, and I was a woman."

"Could it be a sin that gave us our beautiful Susanna? And God will bless our union again. He will give us another son."

Now it was Anne's turn to rise. She stood for a moment with her back to Will then turned to him and spoke with a sad finality which nothing could shake. "I believe I am past bearing, Will."

Will jumped up and answered her with the only language she could understand. "Rachel was past bearing but God blessed her womb with Joseph."

"But the father was Jacob, who trusted in the Lord."

"I trust in Him too."

"No, Will, you do not. By the death of Hamnet, God has put it into my heart that I must never lie with you again while you remain a player."

Bewildered and beside himself, Will spoke wildly. "I will cease to be a player. I will play no more."

A look of irrepressible joy came over Anne. "Oh, Will! You mean it?"

"Before God, I mean it."

"And you will cease to pen lies for players to mouth?" At this Will was silent. "Tell me, Will. You will give up the theatre altogether?"

In agony, Will temporized. "That cannot be God's will, Anne. Remember what Christ said about the talents. God has given me the talent of words, and I must use it."

"Then use it for His glory, not for the glory of the Devil."

Will moved to the settle and sank sadly onto it. He spoke almost to himself. "I cannot do it. You ask too much, Anne."

"Not I, but God."

Will made one last plea. "You are my wife, and you have a duty to me as your husband."

"My greater duty is to God. I will be a mother to your children, and bring them up in the fear of the Lord, but I will not be your wife in the flesh any more. It was the flesh betrayed me all those years ago, and I must now forswear it, until you heed the voice of God as I do."

Will stood up and faced Anne. "Your God is not my God, Anne, and never will be." And he hurried out of the house into the rain, which had come again.

FOUR

WILL'S MOTHER WAS THE FIRST TO COME DOWNSTAIRS IN THE MORNING. IT was scarcely dawn and she was shocked to see, in the half-light, her son lying on the rushes which covered the floor, groaning as he tossed about in sleep. She ran to him, knelt by his side, and urgently called his name, shaking him awake. He was dazed, and it took him a little time to recognize her and his surroundings. With a desperately tired voice, he said, "Mother, I'm cold." She hurriedly pushed herself upright and went to the table. It was covered with a carpet of her own making—carpets were much too rare and precious to be placed under foot—and she put it over him. He responded with a weak smile of gratitude.

She said, "I'll fetch your father." But she also went up to wake Richard and Anne.

Richard was the last to appear, from sheer exhaustion—Mary had said, "Richard must help him to bed." While the three waited for him, she said to Anne, "Go and take the children to their own room. They need not get up yet."

As Anne mechanically moved to go upstairs, John asked her, quietly but urgently, with accusation in his voice, "William came to you last night. What happened?" There had never been sympathy between John and his daughter-in-law.

She looked straight at him as she answered. "I do not know. He left me. He went out." And she continued upstairs.

John turned to Mary with muffled fury. "I don't know what happened, but this is her doing."

"We must be patient. It is hard for a woman at her time. And to lose her boy now when she knows she can have no more. It is hard, John."

"And what of William?"

"He has his work and his success," Mary said.

Richard came downstairs and wasted no time in asking questions. Will had lapsed into a semiconscious state but he stirred again and smiled wanly at Richard as he became conscious of the effort to raise him to his feet. Why wouldn't they leave him where he was, with the covering over him? Richard was speaking. "Come on, Will. We have to get you to bed. You are tired and must sleep."

Anne was in the room freshening the bed. She stopped for a moment to look at Will. He returned her look, but neither said a word. She moved aside while Richard helped Will to sit on the bed; then she held her husband to prevent him from toppling backwards as Richard pulled off the riding boots. Will was aware of Anne's solicitude and was grateful, but she went out of the room while his brother and father helped to prepare him for bed. As his hand touched Will, John exclaimed, "He's drenched!" He was, but it was as much from fever-sweat as the night's rain.

Richard left the room to get a rough towel. John could not refrain from asking, "What happened last night, William?"

Will made an effort to answer, struggling between what should be told and what should be hidden, conscious again of the instinct to protect his wife from his father's hostility. "I was tired. That is all. I was tired. So tired." The repetition of the word seemed itself to induce the desire to sleep. That was all that mattered. Sleep. Sleep.

Richard returned with a towel and began a vigorous rubbing of Will's bare back and chest. Will protested feebly while his mind vaguely registered Richard's good intentions.

At last he was in bed, and his father was murmuring words of reassurance, while Richard went in search of more covers. John, as he watched and spoke to comfort his son, was filled with selfish thoughts in spite of himself. Was William to be taken away too? This would be the ultimate disaster. He had deplored Will's life—his enforced marriage to a stiff-necked woman eight years older than himself; his running away and leaving his wife and three children; his choice of a disreputable career. John enjoyed the traveling players he had seen at Stratford, but he was revolted by his eldest son's becoming one. Still, William had made a great success, and his future looked even brighter. He was the mainstay of the family, and if he were taken away now . . . it didn't bear thinking of.

Richard returned with two blankets, and as he covered Will to sweat out the fever, he spoke to his father. " 'Tis Market Day again, Father. I must open the stall. I know what you would say. The funeral yesterday, Will sick, and myself weary from travel, but we cannot lose another day. Ned shall help me."

"I doubt not you would do better without his help."

"He must learn, Father."

Mary entered with a steaming pewter goblet of a medicinal infusion of her own devising, containing sage, parsley, and camomile in hot elderberry wine. While they waited for the drink to cool, Anne came into the room and in a proprietary voice, said, "I will give it to him." Richard willingly relinquished his place, and Will was glad to rest against Anne's breast; it was softer than the spirit it enclosed.

John felt that Anne should be left alone with her husband, that she might make amends for whatever she had done the previous night; never for a moment did he doubt that the fault was all hers.

When they got downstairs, John said, "We must send for the physician."

"No, John. Anne and I talked of it. We would tend him ourselves. What good did the physician do to Hamnet?" This was indeed an unanswerable argument.

It was now almost six o'clock and full daylight. Richard was already in the workshop, which was the front room of the east side of the house, preparing the gloves for market. They were the product of two weeks' work by his father, an excellent craftsman, and one week of his own labor, with some reluctant assistance from Ned, whose skill was restricted to the tawing of leather.

WHEN JOHN SHAKESPEARE CAME FROM HIS FATHER'S TENANT FARM AT SNITterfield more than forty years before to make his fortune in the town, he had years of remarkable success. And the seal was fixed by his marriage with Mary Arden, daughter of his father's landlord. A dominant motive in John's life had been to justify the social prestige of his marriage, and he rose to be the chief citizen and much respected in the thriving township. He bought two houses which adjoined his original purchase, and turned all three into the most impressive home on Henley Street.

Then things went wrong. Not satisfied with his skill as an artisan, he dabbled on borrowed money in numerous commodities. Years of bad trade and bad trading left him a perpetual debtor. The climax of his disgrace was the mortgage and loss of the Asbies estate, his wife's patrimony. Thereafter he never went out and was content to exercise his skill as a glovemaker. Richard now was the businessman, and he was so cautious that he would never make a fortune; but he would not disgrace the family either.

NOW, AS HE JOINED RICHARD, JOHN SAID SNAPPISHLY, "WHERE'S THAT Edmund?"

"He's coming. There's a deal of tawed leather we can take today."

"Let me see it. The best we must keep."

"Ned made some pretty verses for the gloves."

John just grunted while he sorted the white skins.

"He did well to learn to read and write without schooling," said Richard in further defense of Ned.

"He owes that to you and Gilbert and William. And for all I see, reading foolishness never did man good. I never learned to read and write, and never wanted to. But no man could best me at figures."

At this moment, Ned arrived yawning prodigiously. His father said, "Look at him! Still half asleep."

By way of apology, Ned said, "I was late to bed last night, waiting for Will."

Susanna, awake by this time, was genuinely distressed to hear that her father was sick. She had a deep feeling for him; deeper than she seemed capable of, for already she gave the impression of a certain light-tongued superficiality. In a house of divisions she never took sides, but seemed always to echo and support whomever she was with. Her grandfather adored her for her liveliness, her grandmother for her ladylike ways, her mother for her piety, her Aunt Joan for her helpfulness in the house, Richard for her carefulness with money, and Ned for her love of playacting. When Susanna found a husband, she would easily accommodate herself to a fervent belief in his brand of Christianity, just as she at the same time, and with complete conviction, endorsed her grandparents' love of ritual and her mother's loathing of it. Ned had questioned her about this when she was only nine years old, and her answer became part of the family legend; "When I am happy, I like Grandfather's God, and when I am unhappy I like Mother's God."

It was only her sister, Judith, Susanna could not win. She was such a favorite that it was inevitable that Judith should be jealous of her, but there was more to it than that. Judith was open and forthright, and she knew that her sister wasn't. The two sisters had fought in their very different ways for domination of Hamnet and Susanna had usually won. It was Susanna who had chiefly undertaken to teach the twins to read and write, and in rebellion Judith refused to learn. But Judith had her champion too: her grandfather. When others complained of her obstinacy and disobedience, he praised her spirit. Judith alone could make the old man laugh as he had done in his young days.

Today the sad faces of her grandparents frightened Susanna. She insisted on going up to see her father at once, and her insistence was so appealing that they allowed her to. Upstairs, her mother sat upright by the bedside. She motioned Susanna unnecessarily to make no sound. This made the tears well up into the girl's eyes, and she left the room abruptly.

As Susanna flung herself on to the bed they shared, her body racked by sobs, Judith, who was dressing, asked "What's the matter?"

"Father is going to die, I know he is."

Judith was puzzled for no one had yet told her that her father was home. Gradually she learned from the crying Susanna of her father's condition and she said, "I'm going to see him," leaving the room quickly before her sister could stop her. When she came to her parents' bedroom, where she had a hazy recollection that she had been sleeping last night, she found her father and mother as Susanna had told her.

"Is he going to die, Mother?" she asked.

Anne rebuked her as sharply as the need for quiet would allow. "No, child. You must not think such a thing."

"But Susanna said . . ."

"Go child, and pray that your father may soon be well."

Judith hurried back to the bedroom, but it was empty. She finished dressing and went downstairs. There Susanna, no longer tearful, was waiting and Judith attacked at once. "You were wrong. Mother said that Father isn't going to die."

All in the room were shocked. John was the first to speak: "What are you saying?"

As the girls began to argue, John closed the incident with "Whatever Susanna said, we must all pray that your father will be well very soon."

"That's what Mother said," commented Judith.

"And she is right," agreed John, surprised to be caught in agreement with his daughter-in-law.

FIVE

Will made a rapid recovery. In forty-eight hours the fever subsided, and by Saturday afternoon he was downstairs. It was a beautiful day and after a good meal of roast leg of lamb, a treat to mark both his visit and his recovery, he was taken to sit in the garden. There by tacit agreement he was left in the company of his mother, who was thought to be the most restful of the family companions. The three men went to work in the shop, and Joan and Anne, with the two girls, were busy giving the house its weekly dusting and scouring in preparation for the Sabbath, when no work must be done, not even any cooking. Soon Mary would come into the house to supervise the cooking for the morrow. The Sunday dinner, which would be cold, would be at noon, after the return from church. It had been agreed that all—except John—would go to church together, in family mourning for Hamnet.

As Will sat in the sun he only half-listened to his mother's pleasant chatter. His mind was in London and the manifold troubles of the Lord Chamberlain's Men, the band of players to which he belonged. His thoughts tripped on their title; no longer were they the Lord Chamberlain's Men, for that nobleman had died but a few weeks before and the new Lord Chamberlain, Lord Cobham, was puritanically opposed to the theatre. They were now Lord Hunsdon's Men; he was the son and heir of their former patron, but it was clear that he lacked the prestige of his father's office in the inevitable conflicts with the City Council. Then there was the Theatre, urgently in need of repair and refurbishing. Furthermore, the twenty-one-year lease ran out next year, and the owner of the land, Giles Allen, bid fair to be troublesome; already there were vague threats of tearing the building down. Then old James Burbage, now a sick man, had leased a hall in the secularized Blackfriars Abbey and was turning it into an indoor theatre. Did he hope the company would play there in the winter? If it did become their permanent home, Will would have to take note of it in his writing: he had already found, from playing to the Queen and her court by candlelight, that what was effective for a boisterous and mixed crowd on a sunny afternoon in an open-roofed theatre was not always so effective for a sophisticated few sitting in comparative darkness.

But James Burbage was inviting trouble; the city fathers would have a heavy hand for any theatre inside the City walls. Surely James Burbage knew this; it might be that he meant his new theatre for a new company of children. The Boys of St. Paul's had drawn both clever playwrights and a discerning audience, and the distinguished patronage which boy-players gathered protected them from too much interference from the city council. Such a plan by mercenary James Burbage would be direct treachery against his own son, Richard, London's leading player.

Money . . . money. More and more it seemed to dominate men's lives. It was the subject of Will's new play; he was having trouble with it. Very often the characters took on an obstinate life of their own, and the Jew was being particularly difficult. Why couldn't he be as simple as Marlowe's Jew?

These thoughts raced through Will's mind to the accompaniment of his mother's gentle voice. Now she was talking about Hamnet. "So sad to lose him after rearing him so long. I know something of what it is, for my own Anne died when she was eight. Do you remember her, Will?"

"To be sure I do, Mother. I was fifteen when she died. It was my first funeral."

"I cannot keep the years clear in my mind any more. But of one thing I am sure: you knew not my first two little girls, for they were dead before you were born. I trembled when you came, for it seemed certain I should lose you. It was a hot spring, and the plague raged. Death was in every house, and it was a miracle of God's mercy that you were spared."

The plague. Again Will's thoughts flew to London. If this warm sun shone there too, after so much rain, it would bring the plague and close the theatres again. Already they had been closed for one week in July. Perhaps the company would be on tour when he returned. Those dreadful tours: long travel, hard work, beds of lice in rooms sometimes so damp that snails crawled on the walls, small pay. Thank God that during those two terrible years when plague kept the theatres almost permanently closed, the young and handsome Earl of Southampton had been there to help; but that recollection brought its own bitterness to Will.

His mother was now talking about her beloved Ned. ". . . what to do. He is my last-born, Will, and I fear I am somewhat foolish about him. When he came, I thought I was past bearing. It had been six years since Richard was born. I knew from Ned's first crying he would live and be strong. He was born but two weeks after the great earthquake, and surely that must foretell a future for him." This last sentence had been spoken humorously but in partial belief. "You are my eldest, Will, he is my youngest. You are well-nigh old enough to be his father. I beg you to help me with him. His own father lacks patience with the lad. But there is good in Ned, Will."

"What would you have me do, Mother?"

"Take him with you to London."

Will's wandering attention was fully captured. "That cannot be, Mother." Mary was so abashed by the vehemence of his reply that he quickly grabbed at reasons. "I could not look after him. . . . Anne will never come to London, and so I am going to give up my house. . . . And what would he do? He has no skills."

"He wishes to be a player, like you."

Will was shocked into silence. He had always liked Ned, but he didn't know him well; he had left Stratford when Ned was a young boy, not more than six or seven. He was bound to notice and enjoy the growing lad's frank hero worship of him, but at the same time he had tended to take on his father's critical attitude toward Ned's apparent aimlessness. He remembered giving the boy a secret copy of *Venus and Adonis* only last year, with strict injunctions that no one else was to see it. This conspiratorial pact had increased Ned's enjoyment of the gift, though Will often wondered how he managed to keep the book from the eyes of Richard with whom he slept, or from the ever-cleaning women of the household. It was really Anne who must never find the book, though with her slender reading ability she would have to have it read to her.

Finally Will found words to answer his mother. "Did Ned ask you to speak to me?"

"Yes, he did. He thought he should speak to me first; but he did not want to approach his father until he knew you would be willing to take him."

"Mother, this cannot be. I joined the company because I had a gift for words and could patch up old plays quickly. Besides, Ned is in between ages. He cannot play the parts of queens and ladies . . ."

"No," agreed Mary regretfully, "he has a manly voice."

"But he does not yet have a man's years."

"Are there no parts for boys of sixteen?"

"Not enough, and they are all taken by boys who have acted the lady parts until their voices cracked."

A silence fell between them. Will felt guilty, because he knew that all his objections to taking Ned to London were selfish. To have his wife and children to live with him had been a basic desire of his for years; he longingly observed the lives of fellow players, like John Heminge, with their houses full of children. Had Anne shared his bed and the children his board, he would have been saved from some of the amorous complications which loneliness and frustration had driven him to in recent years. But a young brother to look after and to destroy his privacy was quite another matter.

At last he spoke. "The sun is too strong for me. With your permission I will go up to my bed."

"I fear I have troubled you, Will."

Will smiled back at her. "And I fear I have disappointed you."

"One thing more I ask, that you explain to Ned why it cannot be. He knows I have spoken to you."

Will agreed, though he did not welcome the prospect of the scene with his brother. With a feeling of scarcely concealed irritation, he entered the house and went upstairs.

Anne was in the bedroom, doing some cleaning. He smiled at her and said, "The sun is hot. I came to lie down."

" 'Tis hot in here. Could you not sit in the shade?"

"To speak truth, it was not the sun that drove me in; 'twas Mother. She wants me to take Ned to London—to be a player."

"You must not," was Anne's immediate and strong reaction.

"I cannot. I will not. 'Tis only you and the children I want with me."

This was such a closed subject for Anne that she gave no indication that she had even heard it. "I will go and leave you to rest," she said as she left the room.

Will took off his doublet and his slippers and lay on top of the bedclothes. Soon Ned burst in, looking sullen and almost hostile.

"You won't take me to London. Why?"

Ned's aggressiveness provoked Will to an unconsidered retaliation. "Why should I?" he said.

"Because you are my eldest brother and you could help me, but if you don't, it will make no difference. I am going to London to be a player. You went away. I shall go too. It is easier for me; you had Anne and the children."

"But you are too young . . ."

"I know, I know. Mother told me. Too old to be a boy and too young to be a man. I am old enough, and people think me older than I am."

"You don't know what you are saying. It is not easy to be a player."

"I will learn. If you won't teach me, somebody will."

"I did not mean that. It is not easy to get work as a player. There are many in London from many parts who dream of being players, but few fulfill their dreams."

"I shall be one of the few."

"Have you told Mother of your plans?"

"No. I shall tell no one but you. They would try to stop me. And do not worry; I shall not trouble you in London. One thing only I ask: that you tell no one what I have said." And Ned abruptly left the room. Will called after him but he did not return.

Will raised himself to follow the boy, but, after a moment's thought, lay back to consider what he should do. It was infuriating that this additional burden should be piled on him, for the boy seemed determined to go to London whether he took him or not, and once he came to London, Will could not ignore him. He might have a talent for playing. The lad was handsome and manly, and already his voice had a ring to it. Did he have the patience to endure years of menial tasks and small parts? His mother had spoiled him. The company might take him to please Will, but it would be some years before he would earn enough to live on. And all that time he would have to live with Will, for lack of money to do otherwise.

Now that he finally abandoned all hope of having his family with him, Will had decided to give up his house and move into lodgings. He and Ned could have separate rooms; the boy would understand that the writer had to have solitude, and this might stop any encroachment on his private life. If Ned was determined to go to London, it was preferable that Will should take him. It would please his mother, and almost certainly his father. It was probably the father's attitude to the boy that reconciled the mother to losing her last-born to London. But it hardly seemed fair to deprive Richard of Ned's help, however reluctant and inadequate it was. And Anne: it would drive another wedge between her and Will, for she would believe that he was contributing to the boy's damnation. Perhaps he would be doing so, even in terms that Will could understand. Look at Robert Greene, a man of talent embittered by Will's success and dead these two years from drinking and whoring. What would happen to Ned if he failed while his brother succeeded? Hero worship turned sour is a bitter brew.

Will went downstairs to the shop in search of Ned. His father was regaling Judith with a highly colored account of the great days when he had gone to London to represent Stratford in the High Courts of the land, and of the notable victories he had achieved. With a sly look at Richard he was saying, "Nobody robbed me," when he saw Will. "Ah, William," he said warmly. "It rejoices me to see you up and about again. You will be all the better for the rest."

Richard looked up and smiled. He was intent on cutting out some gloves for which he had received orders on Thursday. To his father was left the elaborate adornment.

"Now, William," said his father, "you are come in right time to help us. Edmund is off somewhere—and to no good purpose, I warrant—and we need a poesy for these gloves. John Lane wants to give them as a birthday gift to his wife, Frances. Come now. Show us your quality. Let that Edmund know what a real poet is."

Will obliged with the pat doggerel:

> "Dear Mistress Lane
> My life began
> When you became
> My dearest Fran."

"Excellent, excellent," exclaimed John. "Write it down, Richard. Can you remember it?"

"I can," piped up Judith, and she rattled off the lines.

"Can you write it too?" asked her father.

Judith shook her head shamefacedly, but her grandfather sprang to her defense. "No, she cannot. She is like me in that. She won't need reading and writing to get her a good husband. Edmund can read and write, and what good does it do him?"

Will, without intending to do so, found himself saying, "What say you if I took Ned to London?"

"What would he do there?" asked John.

"He wants to be a player."

Will noticed that Richard, as well as his father, had stopped working.

"A player!" said John. "Think you he could become one? He's good for naught else."

"I know not," said Will. "I have not put him to the test. What think you?"

"The lad is unhappy here. It may be that London is the place for him. But what of his mother? She could not bear the loss of him."

" 'Twas she that first asked me."

This was such a surprise to John that he took refuge in an oft-repeated aphorism. "Women! Women! They are beyond man's understanding."

"What think you of it, Richard?"

Richard was appalled by the prospect of yet another Shakespeare becoming a Devil's emissary, but he would not give offense to Will. He said, " 'Tis not for me to judge. It rests with our father."

"Then I say it rests with William," said John. "But I would warn you, William, that the lad takes handling. His mother has coddled him, and his spirit is proud and rebellious. I will speak truth; the house will be quieter for me without him."

Richard rushed to his brother's defense. "There is good in Ned, Will. It is just that Stratford irks him."

Judith, who had been quiet for an unusually long time, spoke with a poignant appeal. "Father, would you take me to London, too?"

"No, Judith," said Will with a warm smile. "You must stay with your mother. And girls cannot be players."

At this moment Ned entered. Without a word, he moved to his bench to resume his tawing of skins.

"Edmund," began his father, "William has been talking to me."

Ned immediately assumed that Will had broken his confidence about running away, and he flashed an angry look at his brother.

Before John could say more, Judith said, "Let me tell him," and she hurried across to Ned to say, "Father is going to take you to London." She added sadly, "But he won't take me."

Ned looked in disbelief and confusion at Will, who smiled and said, " 'Tis true, Ned. I have changed my mind. We leave together on Monday morning. Now I wish to talk with you. Let us go into the garden."

Ned moved to his father. "Do I have your leave, Father?"

"You do, lad." He added with a chuckle, for now he could afford to relent in his attitude, "And may you prove to be a better player than you are a whittawer. You go with my blessing, Edmund."

"I thank you, Father, and I shall try to make you as proud of me as you are of Will."

"Nay, lad, aim not so high." But Ned barely heard this as he hurried out to Will. Before they could speak, their mother came out of the house, followed by Joan, Susanna, and Judith. All were beaming with delight at the news. Increasingly Ned was becoming difficult, and his relationship with his father was poisoning the home. Now the problem was happily settled. Anne was pointedly absent from the general rejoicing. The women all spoke at once, thanking Will and wishing Ned well.

It was his sister Joan who was the first to be practical. "We must see to Ned's clothes. There is stitching aplenty to be done, and 'tis the Sabbath tomorrow." The three women bustled off, followed reluctantly by Judith.

"When did you decide you wanted to be a player, Ned?" Will asked.

"I never decided. I always knew. Every time the players came to Stratford, I went to see them. Mother gave me the penny, but nobody else knew. When I came home I used to tell Mother all about it, and she used to say my telling was better than being there. Once, somebody saw me and told Father. He was very angry."

"Father used to like the plays himself. When he was bailiff he paid the players what he judged to be their deserving—and he was always right," Will told his brother.

Ned laughed and then made the rueful comment, "Now the Puritans dominate Stratford, and they will even pay the players to stop them from playing." Almost shyly, yet with eagerness, he said, "Shall I speak you some lines?"

Will was both surprised and delighted by this indication of the seriousness of Ned's intent, and said he would very much like to hear him; Ned forthwith embarked upon Will's own *Venus and Adonis*. The choice pleased the author but made him a little skeptical that it was not chosen just to please. But Will dismissed this idea as unworthy. What else could Ned have chosen? He certainly could not have gotten his hands upon a play script.

Ned recited well, with energy and sensitivity. His characterization of Venus was somewhat comical, because he exaggerated what he conceived to be her feminine qualities. When, after some ninety lines, Venus started on her long harangue of the reluctant Adonis, Will stopped Ned and said, "Know you it all?"

"Yes," said Ned.

"It must be over one thousand lines."

"One thousand, one hundred and ninety-four."

"Come to where Adonis speaks. 'Twill fit you better than Venus." And Will smiled.

" 'Tis hard for me to understand Adonis. Venus is the most beautiful woman in the world, and he does not want to lie with her."

"There are men like that," Will observed dryly. "But let me hear your Adonis."

Ned thought for a moment and then recited:

> "I know not love," quoth he, "nor will not know it,
> Unless it be a boar, and then I chase it.
> My love to love is love but to disgrace it . . ."

Ned stopped abruptly and said, "I don't understand that."

"It is good that you should say so; most actors would not confess so much. What it means is that his feeling toward love is that he abhors it. I had never heard it spoken aloud before; 'tis not a good line. Tell me, Ned, how came you to learn all those lines?"

"I liked the poem; not Adonis, but Venus. And I like to speak good words."

"How did you manage to hide the book?"

"There is no secret place in the house, so I keep it in the stable under a pile of old things in a corner, but alas! Will, the rats have begun to eat it."

" 'Tis no matter now that it is in your head, for they cannot get to it there. Come, Ned. I have a new play in my satchel. 'Tis not finished yet, but 'twill serve our purpose." As they walked back to the house, Will continued. " 'Tis hard work in the theatre, a different play each day and a dozen and more new ones in a year. A player must be a quick study and his mind must carry a heavy load of remembered words."

Suddenly Anne appeared and faced Ned. She spoke stern words but there was compassion in her voice. "Ned, I warn you. If you go to London and do as Will has done, God will punish you, as He has punished this family already. I beg you to consider. Punishment must follow sin as day follows night. You will be a wiser and a better man if you follow Richard, not Will."

She walked back into the house, not waiting for a reply, but there was a sad loneliness in her body, even though she walked erect.

"Anne disturbs me," said Ned.

"Then you will listen to her and stay here in Stratford?" Will was not able to conceal his eager hope.

"No," said Ned vehemently. "But her own sadness saddens me. 'Tis catching, like the plague."

"Then forget Anne and think of the hard work that lies ahead in London."

Will had told Ned to forget Anne, but he could not follow his own advice. This climax in their relationship had to be resolved, and the place was the bedroom that night. While he was sick, she had lain in the truckle bed, but tonight she must come back to his bed, that second-best bed of the household—John and Mary shared the best bed—where Hamnet and Judith had been conceived, and which had been the scene of many a fierce encounter, deeply satisfying to both of them.

Throughout the evening Will let most of the conversation of the household pass over him. Much of it was concerned with going to church in the morning and decisions about the mourning to be worn; they knew they would be the cynosure of all eyes. At one point Will made an appeal to his father to join the family at church. This was a forbidden subject and caused some embarrassment, but John himself, who was in a very good mood, took the question lightly. "No, William," he said, "church is the one place I will never go to again, to feel all those wicked eyes on me, after all I have done for this town. Besides, they tell me this new vicar is a mighty nay-sayer, and that ill suits my disposition; I like not canting hypocrites." He added with a twinkle, "There's yet another good reason for me to keep away. There are those who come to church just to catch old debtors for money long lost. I am too cunning an old fox to walk into such a trap. But the lad shall have my prayers nonetheless."

There was some talk about Ned's going away, but, as soon as it began, Anne took her children out of the room on the excuse that she wanted to see what they should wear in the morning. When she did so, John made some sarcastic mumblings, and Will realized how happy a solution it would be for his parents if Anne would move to London. It was unfair to both his father and his wife to coop them together under one roof.

At last, the light faded and it was time for sleep. Will undressed and pointedly lay to one side of the bed, while he waited for Anne. It was almost dark before she came. Neither spoke. Both were in a turmoil of spirit, for Anne had noticed that her place awaited her.

Finally, when she made a move toward the truckle bed, Will spoke. "Anne!" he said with firmness. "This is your rightful place."

Anne hesitated. Will could feel the conflict in her. At last, and without saying a word, she came to the bed and lay down, being careful to avoid letting her body touch Will's.

After a moment, Will turned to her and said quietly, "Anne, I love you and I need you. We need each other now for we share the grief of Hamnet. I beg you not to be hardhearted to me."

Anne said not a word. Then without warning she burst into tears, but she turned away from Will. He tentatively put his arm around her and began to whisper comforting words. Finally he seemed to get through to her, for she turned and clung to him, still sobbing convulsively. As her sobs subsided, she began to murmur. All Will could gather from her sounds was "Hamnet, Hamnet," repeated over and over. Then the litany of sorrow changed to one of appeal. "Will, Will."

By way of response he tightened his embrace.

"Will, I beg you to stay here with me."

He could not answer this, but his left hand slid down to her thigh. His mouth sought hers. Lightly he kissed her. She suffered it without response. Emboldened, he increased the pressure and opened his mouth while his left hand became more intimate. Immediately she pulled away and gasped, "No. I told you, no."

"But, Anne . . ."

"No, Will. Never again. God will not allow it."

Will seized her fiercely, as his own Tarquin had seized Lucrece; he could not resist this shameful image, even in the moment of assault. Anne fought desperately, and in her struggle prayed aloud, "Oh, God, preserve me from this man." These words paralyzed Will for a moment and Anne scrambled out of bed and out of the room. Will called after her with a wild appeal he knew was in vain. He sank back on the bed and gazed blankly up at the darkened canopy and bleakly into the darkened future.

SIX

SUNDAY WAS ANOTHER HOT DAY. THE FAMILY SET OUT FOR THE CHURCH in conventional procession. First came Will and Anne, the chief mourners, then Mary and Richard, Joan and Ned, and finally Susanna and Judith. Sympathetic nods and smiles, together with inquisitive eyes, greeted them in the street. The eight mourners each carried a black-ribboned posy of flowers gathered in the garden on Saturday.

When they came to the churchyard, Anne led the way to Hamnet's grave. There they stood in silence, while people observed them from a discreet distance. In turn, they placed their posies to form a mound on the freshly dug earth. Only Mary and Susanna wept. Then the procession re-formed and moved into the church, which was already fairly full.

Churchgoing was a legal obligation; failure to attend without due reason was liable to fine. But the Sunday morning service was a welcome diversion for most people. The pious found a special joy in it, but even the most worldly-minded looked forward to the neighborly chatter which followed the service. Then there was the sermon, and Stratford had been blessed with a succession of forceful preachers in recent years, men who were not content to read the homilies provided by their bishops, but who thrillingly rebuked sinners, and even took occasion sometimes to comment on events of national importance. The new vicar's performances in the pulpit had already added a fresh zest of anticipation to the obligatory attendance at church.

When the service began, Will looked at old Higgs, the curate, whom he had affectionately pictured in his Sir Nathaniel as "a marvellous good neighbour." Nobody could remember Stratford without him; he had already outworn six vicars and three wives. He it was who as "under schoolmaster" had first drilled Latin into Will; old Higgs was proud of his Latin, making much of little.

Old Higgs was followed by the Reverend Richard Byfield, a handsome middle-aged man with an almost fanatical glint in his eye. As he intoned the opening sentence, "When the wicked man turneth away from his wickedness that he hath committed, and doeth that which is lawful and right, he shall save his soul alive," it sounded more like a threat of punishment than a promise of salvation.

All awaited the sermon, and it did not disappoint. The text was, "Teach us to number our days that we incline our hearts unto wisdom." The theme was that God often speaks to us through numbers, especially of those compounded of the mystical numbers, three and seven, and we should study His numbers and give heed to their teaching. He referred to a recent sermon in which he had proved beyond questioning that 666, the number of the Beast as revealed in the Book of Revelations, clearly pointed to that "harlot of Rome," the Pope, and his "paramour," Philip of Spain. But today he had another number to talk about, 63, which was compounded of seven times three times three, a number fraught with peril for the nation, for this was their Queen's sixty-third year. At this portentous time, God had seen fit to bless her and her country, the champions of true Christendom, by lending His almighty power to the destruction of the Spaniard at Cadiz.

"But," and the ominous force with which he uttered the word thrilled his congregation with its promise of toothsome horrors to come, "the

Queen's climactic year is not yet over, and Satan is at large in our land. Corn is scarce and Satan corrupts the hearts of men to store corn in their barns for higher prices while people starve." Covert glances stole toward some local worthies guilty of offense of this kind. "Satan stirs men's hearts to discontent and rebellion against God's lawfully appointed authorities. But Satan has a new instrument to his hand that grows in power from day to day. Nigh twenty years ago a devout man of God from these parts spoke with the voice of God when he wrote," and here the preacher held an opened pamphlet at arm's length, to accommodate his longsighted eyes, " 'Satan hath not a more speedy way to bring men and women into his snare of concupiscence and filthy lusts of wicked whore-dom, than those places and plays and theatres are; and therefore it is necessary that those places and players should be forbidden and put down by authority.' " At this point, he slowly raised the pamphlet above his head, thus calling on God to witness his next words. "And here I pledge before God my utmost endeavor that no such plays be ever again seen in Stratford."

Will could feel the concealed glances on him, but most of all he felt the agony in Anne; the embarrassment in the other members of the family he could discount. It was this vicar who had buried Hamnet, and at that time he must have learnt of the imminence of the father's arrival. But now he had passed on to lash another group of Satan's ministers, the wicked idolators who chose to pay fines rather than come to a church newly purged of all false gods.

At last it was over, and the mourning family kept their order as they walked into the open air. Will was glad to see and speak to a few old friends. First were Hamnet and Judith Sadler, for whom the twins had been named. Hamnet was genuinely glad to see his schoolboy friend, and he mumbled some deeply felt words of sympathy. When Will inquired how he was doing, he became evasive; gradually it emerged that he was having difficulty in restarting after the previous year's fire which had destroyed his bakery and all he possessed.

While Will was talking with the Sadlers, another school friend breezed along. It was Richard Quiney, and he oozed prosperity and good fellow-ship. Already he had been bailiff of the town and would be again.

As he suddenly remembered the reason for Will's visit, he muted his approach. "Will," he said, "it rejoices me to see you but I regret the occasion. Hamnet here and I know how you feel, but 'tis your first loss. With us 'tis common. I have lost three and Hamnet here five."

"Six," Hamnet corrected him. At this, Judith, his wife, hurried away, fighting back tears. In explanation Hamnet said, "Another child is sick."

"Enough of such sad matters," said Master Quiney, resuming his habitual manner. "Let us walk home together, as we did all those years ago; though then, I fear, we ran." He found this observation very funny, and to his loud guffaw, they started off.

Richard Quiney launched into an account of his brilliance in negotiating help at the Queen's Court in London for Stratford, stricken by fire those two successive years. Nudging Will vigorously in the ribs he hinted broadly that he had looked after Quiney affairs too, and at the town's expense. He would be coming to London again, and he would be certain to call on his old friend, Will. It could be that they might be able to discuss matters to their mutual advantage, for he was given to understand that the theatres prospered and Will might be glad of the advice of someone with shrewdness and skill in investment of money.

Although Will found Richard Quiney amusing he would much have preferred to spend the time with Hamnet Sadler, whose quiet unhappiness sorted more with his own mood.

As they passed "New Place," which was already a hundred years old, civic-minded Quiney stopped dramatically and with a full gesture said, "Look at it. The best house in Stratford, built by a Lord Mayor of London, the same great man who gave us our beautiful bridge, and look at it. A disgrace to the town. Generation after generation of neglect, and this Underhill is the worst." Here he became very confidential. "I hear he means to sell it, but it needs a man with money to restore it to its first splendor. A man like you, Will." He laughed again and this time bestowed one of his painful nudges on Hamnet Sadler. "What say you, Hamnet? A man with money, eh? Our vicar told us this morning that Will does the work of Satan, and Satan always rewards his own." This remark convulsed Quiney.

They stopped briefly at the Sadler home. Will and Hamnet both voiced conventional hopes that they would see each other again before Will left Stratford, both knowing that they would not, but each feeling the other's warm friendship beneath the words. Master Quiney brought their leave-taking to an end by grabbing Will's arm and pulling him away, facetiously calling out to Hamnet, "Watch your scales, Master Baker. Give good weight. And mind your manchets have only the whitest flour. We have our eyes on you." As soon as they were out of hearing, Richard Quiney whispered to Will, "A poor man that. No spirit. The fire destroyed more than his home."

Will remonstrated. "He's a good man. I feel deeply for him."

"So do I, Will. So do I. He's a good man, but such goodness is for Heaven, not earth. Here a man must be his own best friend."

As soon as Will was free of Master Quiney, his sister hurried along to introduce William Hart. The first impression Hart made was of a neat, trim little man of about thirty, eager to please. He said he was very honored to meet Master Shakespeare; he had heard much of him from Mistress Joan. Nervous pleasantries continued for the further two hundred yards home. Will's private judgment was to hope the marriage would take place; Master Hart seemed inoffensive and gentle, and would need a woman like Joan to make a man of him, which making Joan would enjoy. And it was high time Joan got married. She must be . . . twenty-seven. Most women were tired with childbearing by that time.

When they got inside the house, it was immediately apparent that hostility and hurt were in the air. Without thinking of the implications, Mary had told John how mortified she had been by the vicar's denunciation of plays and players. John was volubly irate because he rightly assumed that the "vile-spirited Puritan" had been prompted by William's presence and had deliberately aimed to disgrace the Shakespeare name publicly. He had then turned on the taut but silent Anne and accused her of applauding the preacher's words. Anne had retorted, in spite of her determination to suffer in silence, "The preacher spoke truth."

"Read your Bible, woman," shouted John, "and learn what St. Paul says of the duty of a wife."

Anne knew her Bible better than ever John would. "I know my duty to my husband, but there is a greater duty to God."

"God's will is that you serve your husband and tend your children."

Mary, as usual, tried to calm John. "Now John, you know that Anne is a good mother."

John snorted and turned away, only to become aware of Richard who had sat silently during the row. He too suffered conflict between his duty to the family and his feeling that the vicar and Anne were in the right. John challenged him. "What thought you of Master Byfield's malicious words?"

Richard caught a pleading and accusing look from Anne. "The preacher spoke what he thought was truth, but he may be wrong."

"That is most certain," John said.

Richard looked at Anne. "The Queen approves the players, and she is a godly woman."

"You say right again, Richard." John mellowed at this unexpected support, and could now afford to moderate his tone to Anne. "In the Bible it says that we should dance and make a joyful noise unto the Lord."

Anne, stung by what she considered Richard's temporizing and desertion of the truth, said, "The Bible says, 'Thou shalt not bear false witness,' and such is playacting."

John was about to begin another explosion when the rest of the family came into the house. A moment's awkwardness ensued which Mary broke. "Everything is ready, so if you will all wash your hands we'll have dinner. Oh, I see the two Williams have met. Now, how shall we make difference between you?"

Laughter at this problem eased the situation.

The second William volunteered a solution. "My mother oft called me Willikins."

"Then Willikins it shall be," said Mary. Only a sharp look from Will stopped Ned from bursting into laughter.

The dinner was cold in viands and spirit. Mary strove hard to keep frothy conversation going about trivia, but an occasional reference to the dead child rebuked her. Willikins felt called upon to break one silence, and he used a conventional gambit to do it. "The sermon was a good one, was it not?" Even as he said it, he remembered the offending passage, and his question petered out in acute embarrassment. The others felt it was too dangerous to reply to the question and a worse silence than ever resulted.

Again it was Mary who broke the impasse. "Tell me, Will, have you seen any of these newfangled forks in London Town?"

"Yes, I have seen them but never used one."

"A knife and fingers are all man needs. These foreign habits will ruin England. Next they'll be drinking ale with spoons," commented John.

This caused a deal of laughter, which was both dutiful to the head of the household and a relief from the atmosphere he had engendered. "Everything is changing, and not for the better," he continued. "All the changes make man less manly. Take chimneys. My father could not abide a fireplace in the wall that took away the smoke. He said a hearth in the center of the room waas God's way to cure timbers, hams, and men."

This too was greeted with laughter, which John acknowledged by licking his greasy fingers, taking a mighty swig of ale, and emitting a reverberating belch. "When I was High Bailiff—you were but a toddling child at the time, William—I took you with me into New Place. Master Underhill had just bought it from that rascal, Bott. Ten rooms had fireplaces! I could not believe my eyes. Ten rooms! If all had fires in them at one time, think of the smoke escaping to cloud the heavens!"

From this point on, the conversation was determinedly pleasant. While it flowed easily about him, Will found himself thinking of New Place, and when an opportunity occurred he spoke to Richard and said he would like to take a walk with him in the afternoon.

John was out to impress his prospective son-in-law. "Do you see that crossbow on the wall?" The question omitted any name of address; "Will" was ambiguous and nothing would ever induce John to use "Willikins." "That crossbow was carried by my great grandfather at the Battle of Bosworth Field, where our Queen's grandfather overthrew the tyrant and took the throne."

"As you know—er—" he went on without using a name at all, "Mistress Shakespeare, my wife, is an Arden, and the Ardens are the best family in Warwickshire. The Forest of Arden is named for them and has carried that name for longer than man can remember."

While she enjoyed her name, Mary was always embarrassed by her husband's parade of it, for she came from one of the less illustrious branches of the family. She said, "Enough of that, John. I am now a Shakespeare and have been this many a year, and I am proud to be so." She turned to Master Hart, "Ned goes to London with Will tomorrow to be a player."

William Hart, to whom this information was like telling him that Ned was going to the New World to become an Indian, smiled vaguely and said, "That is very good. I wish him well."

Practical details for Ned's departure were discussed. Since no work could be done on the Sabbath, they would have to get up very early in the morning, but Ned decided privately that, Sabbath or not, he was going to try to find out about a horse he had heard needed to be taken to London. Ned was determined to be as little a financial responsibility as possible to Will. Already he began to resent the obligations he would have to his brother. Perhaps it would be better if he ran away on his own. That is what Will himself had done.

Throughout the meal, Anne remained almost completely silent, speaking only a few times to the children; twice she quietly reproved Judith for laughing too loud at her grandfather's jokes.

As soon as the meal was over, Ned disappeared, but soon afterwards Will and Richard set out on their walk down to the church and home by way of the river.

Will began their talk by thanking Richard for coming to London to fetch him. Then he went on to say how much he appreciated the way in which his brother, who was ten years younger than he and at an age when most men had eyes only for themselves, was bearing so much of the family load.

Richard took the thanks and praises awkwardly. There was little compatibility between the two, and though he was glad to hear Will speak like this, and with such genuine feeling, he was embarrassed to have to hear it. He said, "I do my duty; I should not be happy if I did not."

Will went on to speak of Ned and to explain that he had only agreed to take him because the boy had threatened to run away.

"He meant it," Richard said surprisingly. "Just as surely as Stratford is the right place for me, it is the wrong place for Ned."

"And you do not mind his loss?"

"No," Richard allowed himself a smile. "The house and the shop will be quieter places. Nothing I could say would alter Father's opinion of Ned."

"Father! It is of him I most want to speak. I am going to tell you something that I long to tell him, but dare not for fear it may not come true. Twenty years ago he applied for a coat-of-arms."

"I know."

"You do? But it was a dark secret, because he failed. You were only a babe at the time."

"The day before I came to London, I went out to the stable in the evening, and there was Father all alone, just sitting and weeping. He said many things to me, and yet not to me. He just spoke, and I chanced to be there to hear him. One thing he said was, 'I hoped the lad would have been born a gentleman to bear the Shakespeare arms. They robbed me of that as they robbed me of everything else.'"

"I have applied again, and this time I think we shall be successful. The last time, Father's affairs were falling apart. Besides, he had not the money to pursue the claim. Now it is different, and I have good friends in London. The family motto will be *Non sanz droict,* 'Not without right,' and 'tis fitting, for Father deserves his crest."

When they arrived at New Place, Will said, "Know you Master Underhill of New Place, Richard? Does he have family?"

"I have seen him in church and in the street, but not for some time. He has two sons, Fulk and Hercules. Both are near Ned's age."

"Richard Quiney told me that Master Underhill wants to sell the house."

"I have heard so. But who would buy it? It is so large and in great need of repair."

"I might buy it, Richard, though if ever there was a secret, this is it."

As they walked, Will became serious and sad. "Richard, I have hoped for some years that Anne would join me in London. I know now she never will. But she cannot stay at home; Anne and Father should not be under the same roof. She and the children must move. I must have a home of my own here in Stratford. And why not New Place? What better way to restore the Shakespeare name?"

"But, Will, the money!"

"I am not without it, Richard, and expect to get more. 'Tis a strange world. I write better than I play, but playing makes the more money, and I find that money can make itself without man's help. I want you to find out quietly if New Place is for sale and what price is asked and how much it should cost to put it into repair. Unless we play for the Queen at Christmas, I shall come home, and you can tell me then."

As they were turning from Church Street into Churchway, they saw Ned, coming down Bull Lane on a beautiful, lively chestnut stallion. Ned reined the horse to a halt near the two watching men and dismounted.

"Isn't he a beauty?" said Ned with joyous enthusiasm. "His name is Cut because his tail has been docked. He belongs to Richard Field in London and has been here for stud. I told them you would know where Master Field lives, Will."

"Yes, I know," said Will. Richard caught a certain reservation in his tone, but Ned was too excited to notice such subtleties.

"It was he who printed *Venus and Adonis,*" Ned said, forgetful in his soaring mood that the subject was not one to be mentioned in the hearing of Richard. Nothing could prevent Ned from voicing some lines from it he had been mouthing to himself as he rode along. He delivered them with a flourish which both impressed and startled Richard.

> "So did this horse excel a common one
>   In shape, in courage, color, pace and bone.
>   Round-hoofed, short-jointed, fetlocks shag and long,

Broad breast, full eye, small head, and nostril wide,
High crest, short ears, straight legs and passing strong,
Thin mane, thick tail, broad buttocks, tender hide.
Look, what a horse should have he did not lack,
Save a proud rider on so proud a back."

" 'Tis apt and fitting but that his tail is cropped," smiled Will.

"True; and now he has a proud rider on his back." And Ned laughed, mounted, and rode off. He wanted to learn the manage of the horse before the long ride began in the morning. As they watched horse and rider disappear, Richard, with unaccustomed wit, said, "There goes a well-suited pair. You will have to learn the manage of Ned too, Will."

"Will it be so difficult?" asked Will, as they continued their walk.

"I fear it may."

Richard guessed that the poetic description of the horse, which seemed innocent and true, came from *Venus and Adonis,* which he heard whispered was lascivious. Now he learnt it had been printed by Richard Field. This was very confusing because Master Field was well known as a pious and godly man; he was also known to have married a pious and godly woman, the widow of a refugee French Huguenot, to whom Master Field had served as apprentice in the printing trade. To judge between good and evil was becoming increasingly difficult for Richard, especially in the light of all he had learnt on the walk.

They went to the churchyard to look once again on Hamnet's grave. Moved by a new feeling toward his brother, Richard haltingly expressed his deep sympathy. Will was instantly aware of the change in Richard's attitude, and, as they walked on toward the river, he wondered if his brother could help him with Anne. He said, "Richard, I know you share Anne's feelings about my work. You think I do the Devil's work, but in my own way I think I do God's."

Richard felt he had to say something, and he had to be honest. "Will," he began hesitantly, "I no longer know what I think. 'Tis not for me to judge. It is true that I have felt with Anne and thought you should come back here to live with her and the children. But all men are not alike; God made some to wander and others to stay at home. You and Ned could not be content here; I could not be content anywhere else. For the playing, I know not. Once only did I see a play and there was much lewdness in it. That was most certain not God's work. But Father told me he saw many plays that told Bible tales and others better than sermons. There is good and bad in everything. I cannot think, Will, you would work evil for money."

Never had Will heard such a long speech from Richard, and he was moved by his brother's desire to think well of him in spite of deep prejudice. If only Anne could even have Richard's new uncertainty!

"Will you speak to Anne, Richard, and try to get her to look at my work with less severe eyes?"

" 'Twill do no good," said Richard with a sad smile. "She will think I have listened to the Devil."

"At least it is good to know I now have but one enemy in the family. 'Tis hard it should be my wife."

"She loves you, Will," Richard expostulated.

"She loves the man but hates the player, and they are one person."

Susanna and Judith had been clamoring for the return of their father, for he was going to leave them again in the morning. As soon as they saw him, they captured him and took him out to the garden. Susanna wanted to talk; Judith wanted to hear all about London. Will made shrewd judgments of the children as he enjoyed their chatter: Susanna could deal with whatever life afforded, but Judith could be hurt. In marriage Susanna would make a good and careful match, but Judith might make a rash and wrong one. Susanna might bring luster to the family, but Judith might not. And all the time in Judith he saw his lost Hamnet.

To his surprise, Anne came to join them. It may be that she felt compelled to keep up the appearance of family unity in the eyes of her in-laws, but Will was glad that she came, and smiling too.

As they saw their mother coming, the girls knew they must not speak of London. Susanna instinctively steered the conversation to a safe place. "I was telling Father about the beautiful clothes you have made for us."

Anne, with a determined effort, made lighthearted talk about the girls. She even laughed at some of Judith's escapades, and this on the Sabbath and while she still grieved for Hamnet. Will knew the effort involved, and he was grateful.

In the bedroom that night he made no attempt to leave place for her in the bed. When she came in the room, she saw and was relieved. It enabled her to speak gently to him. She said, "I hope you and Ned have a good journey to London. I shall pray for you both. Let not Ned be a burden to you; there is wildness in him that must be tamed."

"Time is a sure tamer," said Will.

Before she went to her truckle bed, Anne came to Will and kissed him gently on the forehead. She had forgiven him for last night's assault, for she had often felt in herself the urge which had driven him to it. Will neither moved nor spoke.

SEVEN

IF HIS MOTHER HAD HER WAY, A PACKHORSE WOULD HAVE BEEN NEEDED TO carry Ned's things to London. The house was ransacked for things he might need, including a goodly stock of herbs and ointments. For once John and his youngest son were agreed in belittling the mother's excessive concern for her last born. But Will indulged her to the extent of adding to his own horse's load several articles intended for Ned's well-being. One thing he stealthily stowed away, after Ned had angrily rejected it, was a package of carefully garnered and very precious specifics against the plague. They had been dearly bought from Master Philip Rogers, the wise old apothecary in the High Street, wise in the ways of merchants as well as in medicinal lore. The package contained six wax candles in which the wax had been mixed with mysterious herbs whose burning would purge the air of pestilence, and a precious vial of the powdered horn of a unicorn mixed with oriental spices of magical efficacy. These must have long been in the house, for only in the days of Master John Shakespeare's prosperity could they have been afforded, and Will smilingly mused that they had not been given to him when he first faced the perils of the plague in London. All gave Ned some parting token, but Richard's was the most welcome—money.

Tears were shed by all the women at the parting. Will was warmed to see that even Anne wept. His own farewell to Richard had the old, conventional words, but there was a new quality to them; the brothers looked at each other with the depth of shared secrets and a fresh respect. After a barrage of repeated last-minute injunctions, embracements, and farewells, the two brothers set off.

It was eight o'clock and a beautiful day. In sharp contrast to the rain and mud of the journey from London, the return was blessed by blue skies and warm sun. Francis Hornby was on the street. He ran by Ned's side and pressed into his hand an amulet with the figure of a delicately handbeaten brass bull, Ned's zodiacal birth sign. When Will was shown it, he said, "That is a work of love. You have a good friend. . . . Taurus is my sign too." Ned took this as a guarantee of assured success in the theatre.

Both horses were rested and in good fettle, and both riders were eager to get to London, so they determined to press on to Oxford for the night. They finally got to the Crown Tavern just as the sun was setting. Master Davenant was delighted to see Will and, after expressing his commiseration for the loss of Hamnet, gave a cordial welcome to Ned, who was much impressed by the respect in which his brother was held and was determined to win it for himself some day.

That night Will and Ned shared a bed for the first time in their lives. In spite of the hard day's journey, Ned was in no mood for sleep. He was full of questions about London and the theatre and the players, but Will's answers became shorter and hazier and sleepier and finally ceased. Ned was annoyed for a moment and then conceded that he must make allowance for his brother's tired old body; after all, he was thirty-two, twice Ned's age.

The next day's journey was more leisurely. It would have been impossible to get to London, for it was much too dangerous to travel at night. So again they broke their journey, at High Wycombe. The inn was as crowded as on the night Richard had been robbed, but this time most of the travelers were leaving London. The plague had broken out again and more seriously than in July. Will wondered where the players would be. Cuthbert Burbage would tell him, and Will would follow them. Cuthbert was the brother of the actor, Richard, and now managed the Theatre in the sickness of their father, James Burbage, who had built it twenty years before. Will would leave Ned in London; it would be much easier in his absence to discuss his joining the company. But was it wise to leave him alone in his first experience of the city? Then he thought of their brother Gilbert; he would ask Gilbert to take charge of Ned until the company of players returned to the city.

It was too early to go to bed, and Will said he wanted to do some work on his new play. While this was true, he also wanted to make it quite clear at once to his charge that he was going to need privacy, and a lot of it. He had not counted on the fact that Ned would welcome the opportunity to be free in a strange place.

In spite of the crowding, the innkeeper, Master Harry Lockett, had found them a private room, for Will was a valued customer and paid well. While Will went up to the bedroom, Ned went out into the yard where there were some young ostlers of his own age tending to the horses of the travelers. Cut was by far the best-looking horse, and Ned ostentatiously walked over to him in a proprietary manner. A rough lad of about Ned's age was rubbing down a horse stalled next to Cut; the horse was sweating and exhausted because the rider had spurred it for the last miles in order to reach the safety of shelter before nightfall.

The ostler eyed Ned shrewdly and said, "Is that horse yours, young sir?"

If the light had not been fading, Ned might have caught a glint of mischief in the question and the questioner, but he answered with simple pride, "Yes, he is."

"You are very young to have such a beautiful animal. Are you a lord, sir?"

"No," said Ned, but doubtfully, as if to suggest he was not far from that aristocratic distinction.

"A gentleman, at least."

Ned couldn't even claim this rank in the social scale, but he certainly wasn't going to acknowledge that. He said the truth but his tone made up for the meager facts. "My mother was an Arden of Warwickshire, and my father was High Bailiff of Stratford."

"Stratford! I remember now. I knew I had seen this horse before; not many like him come to our stables. A boy from London was taking him to Stratford for stud. But he said the owner of the horse lived in London."

The young groom had been working during the conversation, but for that last sentence he stopped and addressed Ned in a tone of merry challenge.

Ned was caught. He did not try to bluster his way out. Instead, he used a ploy that was going to be overworked during his life. He smiled an ingratiating smile which complimented his questioner for astuteness and said, "You say true. 'Tis not my horse, alas! He belongs to Master Richard Field, who was a friend of our family before he left Stratford for London."

"Do you sleep here in the stables with us?"

"No," said Ned, outraged that his social position had been so misread. "I sleep with my brother. We have a private room. He is a famous player and poet."

"I humbly beg your pardon, sir." And now the young ostler, for his own purposes, assumed an exaggerated tone of respect. " 'Tis clear to half an eye that you do not belong to the likes of us horseboys. Your brother must be rich to have a private room when the inn is so crowded. His name?"

"William Shakespeare."

"I envy you, sir, to be the brother of such a famous man. His name is on every tongue." This was so far from the truth that probably not one tongue in the inn that night had ever uttered it, save that of the host to whom it meant a frequent and profitable guest. "Might I be so bold to inquire your name, sir?"

"Edmund. Edmund Shakespeare."

"It has the ring of fame about it too. But now I must go help serve the ale, for there are many callers tonight. Mayhap you will be one of them."

"Mayhap," said Ned, who had not previously thought of being so.

"Do but call on me, and I shall be honored to answer."

"What is your name?"

"Giles, sir. And should you need tobacco, I can find some, and even a wench."

Here was heady stuff indeed. Ned had never smoked; it was a vice of the wealthy. His father denounced it as a foreign evil, fit only for the savages who had begotten it. London had not even seduced Will into smoking. When Ned once dared to question him about it, his brother said he wanted nothing to dull his wits; but he admitted that lofty ones of great wisdom sometimes smoked. Pipes and tobacco could be obtained from Master Rogers, the apothecary of Stratford, who assured people it was a specific for the quieting of troubled spirits, but not till Giles of High Wycombe offered it did it seem desirable to Ned. As for the wench, he assumed that the offer implied hire; he had enjoyed many girls and women, and looked forward to doing so again, but never would he bemean himself to buy what his charm and body could get for nothing.

But tobacco could not be seduced. With the leering assuredness of a man-about-town Ned told the stable boy, "I pay for no wench, but for tobacco and good spirits, that is a different matter. Could you bring me pipe and tobacco and some ale out here?"

"Nay," said Giles. " 'Twould be too dangerous. We dare not have a flame near all this hay. But I will find you a quiet corner and there I will bring you pipe and tobacco, and some aqua vitae, for ale is but a poor drink for such as you. Come."

Ned followed Giles docilely, fearful that if he betrayed hesitation his manhood and his superior status would be impugned. Giles led him to a rough shed in the yard, near the pigpen. He explained that there wouldn't be a seat in the tavern, and one had to be seated really to enjoy a pipe. He hurriedly disappeared giving Ned no time to demur or even question.

As Ned settled down on a rough stool, he wondered how much his pipe and drink would cost. Richard had given him ten shillings, his father had surreptitiously added two more, and his mother even more surreptitiously had given him a further shilling. He himself had saved nearly five shillings, so he had in his pocket the lordly sum of nearly eighteen shillings, which would be enough to support many a Stratford family for two weeks and more. He had heard that Apothecary Rogers charged threepence for pipe and tobacco, but he did not know what aqua vitae cost. Up to this point in his life his acquaintance with strong drink had been restricted to ale of his mother's monthly brew and an occasional goblet of canary wine at times of celebration. Aqua vitae was a drink of whispered potency. He must be careful not to get drunk.

Giles was soon back with a small jug, and smoking a pipe. He explained that he had had to fire the pipe indoors, but would bring another when the first was smoked out, and he hoped Master Edmund would condescend to drink from the jug, as no goblet was readily at hand; he had never known the inn to be so busy. And now he would leave the young gentleman if he would be so good as to give him one shilling for commodities and service. Ned thought the price was exorbitant but felt that to cavil about such matters of peasant concern was to risk losing the respect of this pleasant and obliging menial. As though he were paying a farthing, he gave Giles a shilling, and then, as the groom was hurrying away with words of thanks, he put a hand on his arm to detain him, and with a gesture of magnificence gave him an additional penny. Giles was appropriately overwhelmed by such truly gentlemanly generosity and promised to return with another pipe anon.

Ned first applied himself to the pipe. Gingerly he puffed it and fell to coughing mightily. To stop the coughing, he took a substantial swallow from the jug, which left him gasping. But when he had recovered, a pleasant daze suffused him so that he could not forbear taking a second drink, but a more cautious one. Then, in concern that the fire in the pipe might go out, he puffed again, but again his inhalation of the smoke was so inexpert that he was forced to cough, which caused recourse to the jug again. And so the cycle of activities continued, becoming more mechanical with each round as Ned slipped progressively into a state of pleasant unawareness.

It was more than two hours later when Will stopped writing for lack of ink. His eyes were aching from strain in the light of a poor candle. He had done some good work and felt happily tired with accomplishment. He suddenly thought of Ned, with immediate concern for his well-being and guilt if anything had gone wrong. Will put his papers away and hurried downstairs. By this time most of the travelers had betaken themselves to bed, but a few groups remained, some noisy in good-fellowship or argument, and some drifting into somnolence. There was no sign of Ned. Will went to the host, who, yawning himself, was waking some sleepers to persuade them to go to bed. In reply to Will's questions, Master Lockett said that he remembered Ned but had not seen him since supper. He tried to still his guest's troubled questioning with the easy assurance that Ned was old enough to look after himself and would turn up in the morning none the worse for his night out. But Will's distress was too deep for such facile comfort, and with great reluctance the innkeeper agreed to make a search of the yard and stables.

The tired host took a lantern, and he and Will went outside. The stables revealed some boys fast asleep in the hay, but no sign of Ned. They began a search of sheds and outhouses, for Master Lockett said that when the inn was crowded, all kinds of mischief took place in dark corners. Finally they came upon Ned, lying in a dead stupor on the ground in his own vomit near an overturned stool. There was no sign of either pipe or jug which had conjoined to bring about his condition. Will was repelled by the stench of vomit and urine.

The two men tried to rouse Ned, dragging him away from the mess he had made. He began to stir and as he returned to consciousness he was aware of acute discomfort; with no warning he belched forth a flood of vomit over himself and the hands and the sleeves of the men who held him. At this, a tide of anger overwhelmed the guilt which Will had been feeling, and he flung away from his infuriating brother. Master Lockett, with no hint of irritation, went beyond the light of the lantern and returned with a small bundle of straw. He put it on the ground and gave a handful to Will to clean himself, then set to work to clean Ned, leaving his own cleaning up to the last. Ned slowly gathered what was happening and began to make muddled attempts to help, muttering sorrowfully, but unintelligibly.

With most of the inadequate cleanup accomplished, the innkeeper said, "Up you get . . . Lend a hand, Master Shakespeare." With Ned's clumsy assistance the two men got him to his feet.

The mention of "Master Shakespeare" had drawn Ned's attention to Will, and, as he hazily focused on him, he began to mumble an apology and explanation; there was much about "Giles" and "tobacco" and "aqua vitae." During this monologue Master Lockett had been taking off Ned's belt and doublet. As he gave the garment a final rubbing with straw he broke into Ned's monologue, " 'Tis time for bed now. You'll sleep it off and all will be well come morning. Here Master Shakespeare; take these and get him upstairs. I must do some more cleaning up."

Will thanked the innkeeper for his help, and the two brothers began to move slowly and awkwardly away. They had gone but a few paces when Ned said, "Stop! My purse. It's gone. That Giles has stolen it. All my money." Turning back to the innkeeper, he said, "That Giles of yours. Where is he?"

"I know not. He is not asleep in the stable, where he should be; I saw that when we went searching for you. I knew then he was up to mischief."

"Then in the morning I will front him."

"I doubt that, lad. If he has money, the inn won't see him in the morning. Put him and your money from your mind; they are both gone. 'Tis a lesson you've learnt this night; never forget it." He had had much the same sorry comfort for Richard ten days before.

Will said, "Come. Let's to bed. Good night, Master Lockett, and I thank you for your help and kindness."

Not another word did Will say to Ned that night, but coldly received his apologies and vows of recrimination against the thief. The shared bed served but to strengthen the barrier between the two brothers. Nothing could keep the younger one awake for long, and Will even resented Ned's easy ability to fall asleep. At the same time he was suddenly struck by his own excessive reaction to an escapade characteristic of a spirited lad; he himself had made many a worse blunder; with which more compassionate reflection he too at last found sleep.

EIGHT

BY THE MORNING WILL WAS SWEETENED BUT NED MORE SOURED. IT WAS now Ned's turn to receive his brother's attempts at conversation with a surly silence. Ned's healthy appetite forsook him in the face of breakfast and the prospect of being shaken up and down on the journey filled him with foreboding. For once he was quite content to hold the horse to a measured walk; there was enough time, so Will made no attempt to force the pace; nor did he make any mention of the night's escapade.

Gradually the morning air blew away from Ned's head and stomach the noxious fumes of the night, but he became increasingly obsessed by a sense of his own folly and a desire for revenge against the world in general. His hostility became focused on his brother; he interpreted Will's friendly approaches as coming from a smug superiority. Thus when Will, chancing on what seemed to be a safe subject, asked if he had brought his copy of *Venus and Adonis* along with him, Ned snapped, "No. I left it for the rats." The truth was that he had forgotten it in the excitement of leaving, but this was no time for truth.

Will began to explain his plans: since the plague was certain to have closed the Theatre, the players would be on the road somewhere and Will would have to follow them. In the meantime Ned could stay with Gilbert. Ned received this intelligence with noncommittal silence. He had never been comfortable with Gilbert and his instinct was to demand to go with Will and join the players without delay. His poisoned attitude made him sense the truth: Will was shelving the burden of his young brother as long as possible.

Around noon, Ned became unbearably hungry, and to appease his stomach it became necessary to soften his attitude to his brother. Ned made an indirect request. "Are you not hungry?"

Will was tempted to reply that he had had a good breakfast, but this would have been too pointed a reminder of Ned's folly. He contented himself with saying that there was an excellent tavern about a mile further on. On hearing this, Ned spurred his horse to a trot. Will followed, smiling; the breach would be healed over the meal.

As Ned began to gobble up his slices of cold chine of beef and crisp, fresh manchet, Will dared to caution him to eat slowly as his stomach might be still somewhat unsettled. Ned obeyed, and then ventured a tentative smile toward Will, who determined to make no reference to the previous night. He said that they would first have to deliver Cut to Richard Field, then they could put all the baggage on Will's horse and walk to Gilbert's, which was not far away. Ned asked how long he would have to stay with Gilbert, and Will said it would depend upon the duration of the plague. In the meantime he would give Ned some books to read and perhaps even a precious playscript or two; he explained that not even the actors were given a whole script because they might get a copy made and sell it to a rival company.

The sign that most impressed Ned of their approach to the fascinating but dangerous city was the Tyburn gallows, where three cadavers hung motionless in the hot air, unregarded by the passersby except for an aversion of the head and a holding of the nose against the stench of putrefying flesh.

"What had they done?" asked Ned.

"One of a hundred things, or maybe only the plotting of one."

"But the priest. What of him?"

"He is lucky that he was but hanged. Priests are usually hanged for treason, and 'tis customary that they be drawn and quartered too. 'Tis almost certain this one died for plotting to overthrow the Queen."

"But why? She is good and great."

"Not to one whose allegiance is to the Pope. For most of my lifetime and all of yours she has been excommunicate, and her life in danger. For King Philip of Spain the overthrow of our Queen is a religious crusade blessed by the Pope. You cannot serve both Queen and Pope, though some good men try, in torment of soul."

"And you, Will? What think you?"

Before replying, Will looked at Ned and weighed his words with a smile. "I trouble not myself with such high matters, and you would do well to do likewise. Right and wrong are not always easy to judge, but goodness is. And God is greater than Queen or Pope. One thing is certain: we players have many enemies who would triumph over us, were it not that the Queen is our friend. I tremble at what may happen to us when she dies, as die she must. She is older than our father; but she defies age as she does her other enemies. She still dances and loves to laugh."

"I would I might see her."

"'Tis most like that you will, for she is not shy of showing herself to her people. Besides, if you join our company, you may even play for her."

"If I join! There must be no if, Will." There was anger as well as fear in Ned's voice.

"The say lies not alone with me. There must first be a place in the company, and others must decide on your fitness to fill it. Would you have it otherwise?"

"I care not how I become a player, for I will prove a good one. You must make them take me."

"No," said Will, still smiling, "it is you who must do that, but I promise to plead well on your behalf."

And with that Ned had to be content. He did so the more readily that the nearer they came to the city the more there was to absorb his eyes. At one point there was a great press of traffic, all bent on giving a certain house a wide berth. All its windows were firm shuttered and on its closed door was a red cross to warn of the presence of plague in the house. When they had got past the crush, Ned said, "That was a wooden cross nailed to the door. When there was plague in Stratford, they just painted a white cross on the door."

Will explained, "So they used to do here, when first I came, but painted crosses are easily washed off, and people wanted to bury their dead in a churchyard, not in a common pit, so they wiped out the stigma of the plague."

"When I die," said Ned airily, "I care not what they do with my body."

"But those who are left may care," replied Will. "It will be a sad judgment on your life if they do not."

When Will said they were within ten minutes of Richard Field's house, Ned was full of questions. Field had been born in Stratford some two years before Will. Like many an ambitious apprentice, he had married his master's widow and inherited a prosperous printing business, which he proceeded to make even more prosperous.

With some hesitation Will said, "You must not expect Master Field to be very friendly with me."

This took Ned completely by surprise. "Why not?" he asked. "He printed your two long poems."

"True, but I wrote no more, as he wished me to do. The poems sold well, and Master Field is a shrewd merchant. But he frowns upon the theatre. If he had his way he would close all playhouses and jail the players."

"Then I like him not, and he deserves not this lusty stallion," said Ned forcefully.

"Nay," said Will, "he is a good man, and deserves well."

When Ned and Will arrived at the printing shop of Richard Field, they found him to be a compact, reserved, no-nonsense man, with a good deal of authority. Master Field greeted his fellow Stratfordians with politeness but little warmth, and when he learned that Ned had come to London to become a player, he looked accusingly at Will.

Then he said in a very abrupt tone, "I am told that Master James Burbage is trying to set up a theatre in the Blackfriars Abbey. He will not succeed. There are men of title and substance in this neighborhood who will see to it that he does not. I also hear that he has not long to live. Tell him to prepare to meet his God. He perils his immortal soul by spending his last days in the work of the Devil. And mark you that too, Will."

Ned, whose anger had been mounting, stalked out of the shop followed by his elder brother who was smiling wryly.

As they neared Gilbert's, Ned hoped strenuously that he would not have to stay with his brother for long, not only because every day away from the theatre was a day lost, but because he accorded ill with Gilbert, and despised him for his notorious subservience to George Smith. In Stratford Ned had heard his brother snickeringly referred to as "Master Smith's spaniel." And yet Gilbert had much to commend him: he was honest and good-natured and had such a quick head for business that his father often contrasted plodding Richard with clever Gilbert and lamented the latter's going to London.

As for the relationship between George Smith and Gilbert, Will was much more tolerant than Ned. He had himself known the enslavement to masculine beauty, but preferred to lie with women. Abiding love and lasting devotion were so rare and precious that they were to be commended even in a home made by two men, and it seemed that the bond between George and Gilbert bid fair to endure, for they had been together now in London for nearly eight years; they had left Stratford soon after Will himself, not the first congruence in the lives of George Smith and Will Shakespeare, for they had been born in the same week.

When the brothers arrived at the shop, they found Gilbert busy fitting a young gallant with a splendid new doublet, but the customer was full of complaint that George was not there to fit him, as Gilbert had "a better head for numbers than figures."

Both Gilbert and his customer, Master Francis Barnes, who turned out to be a wealthy student of law at the Inner Temple, were delighted to see Master Will Shakespeare, for they were both avid patrons of the Theatre. Then Gilbert remembered what Tim the Tailor had told him, and he inquired after Hamnet.

Will said, "We were too late to see him." To cut off further conversation on the painful subject, he said to the law student, "This is my brother, Edmund."

Master Barnes smiled at Ned, his junior by only two years, and said, "Are you a player too?"

Without qualification, he simply replied, "Yes."

Gilbert was taken aback by this exchange but decided to postpone comment. He merely said, "Would you take Ned upstairs, Will, and I will be with you anon."

As the two brothers mounted the stairs, Master Barnes delivered a parting quip, which he would relate with gusto and embellishment for the rest of his life. "It was good to see you without your gray beard, Master Shakespeare. Play younger parts; the gray hairs will come all too soon."

Ned was much impressed by the furnishings of the living room which was as impeccably neat and clean as if it were cared for by a house full of women. Three things most drew his eyes: a fine tapestry which depicted the shaving of Samson's locks by Delilah, a shelf full of beautifully bound books, and an exquisitely inlaid lute which hung on the wall.

As Ned moved to inspect the books, he said, "Are any of your plays here, Will?"

"I hope not," was the surprising answer. "So far I have written thirteen plays—this play of *The Merchant* is the fourteenth—and four have found their illicit way into print, in form so mangled that I am angered to look at them. But I think you will find the two long poems there—and well preserved from rats." This last was said with a smile.

Gilbert came hurrying up the stairs. "I'm sorry to keep you waiting, but that young popinjay is demanding. He would have kept me longer if he did not know that you were waiting for me." He crossed to sit by Will on a colorfully cushioned oak bench. "I grieve for you, Will, in the loss of Hamnet. I know how much he meant to you—and to Father too. Pray God you will be blessed with another son."

"It's Ned I want to talk about, Gil. He has come to London to be a player."

"Can he act?" asked Gilbert, as though Ned were not present.

"Yes, I can," interposed Ned aggressively.

"How do you know?" said Gilbert, turning his attention to his young brother.

"How did Will know he could write? How did you know you could be a haberdasher? How do you know anything about yourself? You just do."

Gilbert again turned his attention to Will. "Is there a place for him in your company as an apprentice?"

"I know not," replied Will. "I must talk to my fellows about it, but I fear the plague may have driven them from the city."

"It has. A customer told George that yesterday."

"Then this is it. I must go to join them, and, while I am gone, it would be a kindness to Ned and me if he could stay with you."

Gilbert could not hide a surprise of embarrassed reluctance. He stammered, "I would . . . it would . . . let me speak to George about it. For myself, I would be happy, but it may be that George . . ."

Annoyed at being a troublesome family burden, Ned burst out, "Let me go with you, Will. The sooner they see me the better. Let me plead my own cause with them."

"It will be better if I pave the way for you," said Will.

"To be sure it will," said Gilbert. "What else do you have to recommend you but Will?"

At this moment the shop-door bell rang, and Gilbert hurried downstairs. It was George, and in a bad mood; he had arrived too late to purchase cheaply some pirated Spanish velvets. The brothers upstairs heard him proclaim, "This place is a pigsty. Will you never learn to put things back in their places?"

There followed a deal of whispering by Gilbert; and then George was heard to say, "Here? But that is not possible. Why did you not tell them so? You behaved like a frightened rabbit as usual."

But when he came up the stairs to greet the visitors, George almost fawned upon Will, for whom he had genuine admiration. He was a handsome man, and his carefully cultivated, pointed beard and trim moustache gave his face a very aristocratic cast, which his bearing complemented. His usual arrogance made his respectful attitude to Will all the more impressive. His clothes, both in themselves and in the way he wore them, were a splendid advertisement for his profession. Ned took a dislike to the man, all the more because he saw much in him to envy, and he despised Gilbert for being what he assumed to be the lackey of such a creature. He had not the experience to know that Gilbert's subservience was as necessary to George as George's dominance was to Gilbert; each knew exactly how to work his will with the other, and there was a bond of true affection between them.

When Will introduced his young brother to George, Ned was conscious of a piercing scrutiny which made him ill at ease. Then George awarded him a dazzling smile and surprised everybody by saying, "I understand you are going to stay with us for a short time and that you have come to London to be a player. It will pleasure me to know that a future Burbage spent his first night in London under my roof, and i'faith you start with advantage over the famous Richard: you are much more handsome."

Ned mumbled his thanks to "Master Smith."

"Nay, 'tis George I wish to be to you; through Gilbert we are related."

Will too expressed his thanks and said he should be leaving as he had much to do. Gilbert told George about Hamnet and this led to appropriate commiseration which George capped by saying, "We bachelors have an advantage over you married men: not to beget a son is to miss the pain of losing one."

Then George turned to Ned and said, "Well, Master Edmund, we must do something about your clothes. To be a player you must look like one. Now you reek of Stratford, not the stage."

"He is travel stained," ventured Gilbert in his brother's defense.

"Indeed he is," said Will, and the ghost of a smile played between him and Ned.

The shop-bell broke the conversation. George, now all affability, told Gilbert to attend to the customer while he went to the third floor to prepare Ned's room. Just before he left, Will gave Ned ten shillings. He said it was a gift to welcome him to London; no mention was made of the loss of the money at High Wycombe. Ned was grateful for the gift and the tact, but would have wished that neither had been necessary.

George took pleasure in introducing Ned to the house. Behind the living room was a neat room which served as kitchen and dining room. Again it seemed made to be looked at rather than lived in; even the smoked hams and dried herbs that hung from the beams were decorative, and the pots appeared never to have been used. The silver and pewter ware on polished shelves seemed to shout, "Don't touch me!"

George led the way up to the third floor. There the front room was dominated by a magnificently carved and canopied oak bedstead, amply big enough for two people to sleep together without being aware of each other. Everywhere, on walls and furniture, Ned was dazzled by ornately patterned velvets and brocades, made doubly dazzling by reflection in a handsome mirror, placed so that people in bed might ogle themselves.

Ned was to sleep in the back room, which was furnished rather more daintily as a boudoir. It contained a daybed which seemed much too slender and feminine for Ned's sturdy body. The boy had become increasingly impressed by the obvious display of wealth in the house which completely belied its rather modest exterior. He put his luggage down in a corner where it would be least obtrusive.

George pointed to a basin and a ewer filled with water. "You will need to wash and change," he said, "and then, if you are not too tired, we might take a walk. It will pleasure me to show you the town, though I fear the plague has robbed it of its rarer delights. But 'tis not a bad visitation this time, so have no fear."

"This is the best wearing I have," said Ned, with a mixture of shame and defiance.

"The best? Then spare my eyes the worst. I will see what I have downstairs. Let me see you." He grasped Ned by the shoulders, and then felt his frame to the waist and the thighs. "Turn round," he said peremptorily. Ned reluctantly obeyed. George felt and appraised his back and his buttocks. "Yes," he mused, "a goodly frame to hang beautiful clothes upon. Now get undressed, wash well, and put on a clean shirt." With that he disappeared, leaving Ned in a turmoil of embarrassment.

The boy began to undress hurriedly, determined to be washed and in his clean shirt before George returned. He had been proud to uncover his nakedness to women but knew it should be shrouded from George. But it was Gilbert who returned with the clothes; again George had been detained by a customer, who wanted to gossip with the witty haberdasher, whose retailed bon mots had done much to ensnare new customers.

Ned's eyes goggled at the clothes Gilbert carried: royal-blue, velvet trunk hose slashed with panels of crimson silk, a dark-red, brocaded doublet with sleeves of light blue slashed with silk of yet another red, and a decorated and stuffed codpiece the color of burnished copper. Only once had Ned seen such clothes before; a visiting player had worn them on the stage in Stratford, and it was the would-be player in Ned that now responded to them with delight; Will's Adonis should wear such clothes. Oh, if only they would fit! They did, well enough, and when he was fully dressed, Ned hurried into the bedroom to preen before the mirror. Gilbert followed him with pride; with George's approval of Ned, he would now be free to be happy in his brother. Almost imperiously Ned said, "It lacks a hat and a cloak." Gilbert was enraptured by Ned's tone and hurried away to supply the lack.

As Gilbert again climbed the stairs, he heard his brother speaking. He stopped to listen. Ned was declaiming lines like any seasoned player. Gilbert recognized them; they were the words of Will's Adonis. Beaming with pride, the elder brother bore his gifts in to the younger. Gilbert almost worshiped actors, and Ned was going to be a fine one, much more dashing than Will, who usually played men old enough to be his father.

The cloak was of dark-blue, brocaded velvet, lined with silk of the palest pink, and it was fastened with cords of gold thread. The hat was made to match it; the crown being of the same pink and the underbrim of the dark blue. The hat was decorated with a plume of white flecked at the edges with black and fastened to the hat with a gold-plated buckle. As Gilbert adorned Ned with the cloak and hat, the while the wearer admired the effect in the mirror, he prattled endlessly. "I'm so proud of you, Ned; so proud. I know you will be a fine player, the talk of London; and I'll be able to say, 'He stayed with us when he first came. He's my youngest brother.'"

When they went downstairs, George was in lively colloquy with a young exquisite whose bright plumage outdid Ned's in several particulars: he wore a single, jeweled earring and three jeweled finger-rings, and his codpiece was decorated with a silken bow, fastened with a gold pin. The brothers were in time to hear the tag end of George's quotable brilliance: ". . . so jealous that his water was green." This was greeted with a peal of high-pitched laughter, which was broken off at the sight of Ned with the remark, "What have we here? Where have you been keeping this? And where did you find it?"

Ned fumed. Gilbert was quick to sense an imminent explosion and said, "Permit me to introduce my brother Edmund, my lord." The title effectively stifled Ned. George completed the introduction: "You are new to the town or you would recognize Lord Marshfield. Not to know him is to be ignorant indeed."

"You flatter me, George," said his lordship, "but I must confess I am known to too many, and most of them it were better I had not met."

"I hope I am not counted among those," said George.

"Nay, George. You brighten my days. Those it were better I had not met have brightened my nights." And here the nobleman accorded his own wit a peal of laughter, which was dutifully echoed by Gilbert and accorded a faint snigger by George.

Lord Marshfield now gave his full attention to Ned, whom he regarded appraisingly. "I see you have been in town long enough for George to dress you, Master Shakespeare, for I warrant that garb was not made in the country. But you should take Master Smith to task for the fit is not perfect. Or do I detect the careless eye and clumsy hand of Gilbert? Be advised, young man, trust not your brother to dress you. He is a sorry bungler compared with the master." This was accompanied by a slight inclination of the head toward George, who received the compliment with a flourish and low bow.

Gilbert seemed not to be offended by this treatment, but Ned was incensed on his behalf and could not forbear saying, "My lord, I am but newly arrived. These clothes were not made for me."

Before Ned could continue, his lordship interposed with "Then take them off. I am sure the result would be most pleasing to all three of us."

Gilbert quickly stood in front of Ned, pretending to adjust his cloak. He looked him earnestly in the eye, pleading with him silently to restrain himself. Luckily, at that moment another man entered the shop, a smelly ruffian, carrying a bundle. Only George seemed not to be put out by his appearance. Lord Marshfield's face was distorted with disdain, as he exclaimed, "Master Smith, what patrons you serve! This creature reeks of Moorditch, and I have not my pomander with me. I must away on the instant or I shall swoon." He made for the door, making an ostentatiously wide circuit of the newcomer, who cringed away from offended nobility.

George glanced at Gilbert, who was quick to take the hint and suggested that he and Ned should go upstairs. He knew that the bundle contained some stolen rich cloths, and Ned should not be present at the ensuing transaction.

To distract Ned, he began to talk about his career as a player. Not for a moment did he doubt that the boy would join Will's company, for their reputation depended more and more on Will's plays, and so they could deny him nothing. He suggested that Ned should read aloud to them after supper, to show his quality and exercise his voice. But Ned would better that; he would recite the whole of *Venus and Adonis*. Gilbert was delighted by this prospect, as he was sure George would be. When Ned asked if he might have free access to the books, Gilbert was certain that he might, and recommended the most imposing of the tomes, Raphael Holinshed's *Chronicles of England, Scotland and Ireland,* for Will had already written six plays about kings of England, and doubtless more were to come.

George came bounding up the stairs in high spirits; he had struck a good bargain for excellent treasure trove. Now it was time for him to take Ned for a walk while Gilbert prepared the supper. He explained that, when they entertained guests, a cook, a kitchen-help, and a serving-man were hired for the occasion, but Ned had taken them by surprise; in addition, he was a member of the family, and hardly ranked as a guest. But he hoped that Ned would be present on a great holiday occasion, when he would see what true feasting was.

He asked what Ned would most like to see in London.

"The Theatre," was the answer.

"Nay, 'tis closed because of the plague, and 'tis too far to walk. We shall go to Paul's and come home by way of the river."

While it retained the same raucous admixture of hucksters, beggars, and whores, the St. Paul's that George introduced Ned to was very different from the one Richard had seen, for now it abounded in young gallants who had been drawn away by the Triumph on the former occasion. George knew many of them and introduced Ned as "my young friend," which invariably resulted in a quizzical raising of eyebrows. The implication was not lost on Ned, and he was quick to explain that he was staying with George and Gilbert until his brother, Will Shakespeare, returned to town. He was impressed to observe that all the men George spoke to admired Will, and were eager to see his next play, whatever it was.

Ned wanted to see the bookstall with the sign of the White Greyhound, for his copy of *Venus and Adonis* had told him that that was where it was sold. He was astounded by the number of bookstalls, which spilled out beyond the churchyard walls, each of them containing more books than he had ever seen together. When George introduced the brother of William Shakespeare to the proprietor of the White Greyhound bookstall, that foxy old fellow begged the young man to persuade his brother to write another *Venus and Adonis,* for it would be a certain success; a fourth edition of the poem had been printed a few months ago, and already it was almost all gone. In his opinion, *The Rape of Lucrece* was a better poem, but that might be the taste of an old man. No, he didn't go to the theatre; it was the enemy of books, only good for people who couldn't read, or were too lazy to read for themselves. Wouldn't the young gentleman like to buy a book? At this point, George pulled Ned away and took him inside the cathedral; that it was open showed that the plague had not reached dangerous proportions.

The first thing that struck Ned under the sacred roof was the din of talk. The place was a mart. George warned him to keep close as the aisle was a den of thieves. Young gallants swaggered by, vying with one another in gaudy display. George was quick to notice every quirk of new fashion. He took Ned to one of the huge pillars on which were posted innumerable notices, most of them offering the services of men of all trades. Most of the men were illiterate and their notices had been written by scriveners. Now they stood by the pillar hoping to attract the attention of possible employers. They were a motley crew: maimed soldiers from the wars, country men adrift in the city, younger sons of younger sons with no patrimony but good breeding, unemployed craftsmen, and a good sprinkling of confidence men seeking to gain a man's trust in order to betray it.

"Let us take a look at Humphrey's," said George. In reply to Ned's unspoken query, he added, "Duke Humphrey's tomb. Some say Humphrey of Gloucester is buried elsewhere, but no matter; 'tis called Humphrey's whatever corpse it contains, and it makes no difference to those who gather there. They too seek employment, but would not bemean themselves to stand by the pillar, or advertise themselves in written words. They would be taken for gentlemen, and some of them doubtless are, but cast upon the world for reasons best left unknown. Had you not Will to help you, it is at Humphrey's you would stand, dressed as you are; dressed as you were a few hours ago, your place would be the pillar."

George's tone was friendly, but yet Ned bridled at the remark. When they came to Duke Humphrey's tomb, Ned would have accounted the twenty or so men who stood there all noblemen, such were their clothes and demeanor. They chatted in groups, but their eyes were stealthily on the passersby. Two stood apart and alone, a distinguished gray-bearded man of about fifty, and a handsome young courtier in his middle twenties. George decided to question them, that his charge might still further be initiated into the ways of London.

Approaching the older man first, George questioned him directly. "Your name, sir? And what do you at Humphrey's?"

Ned was amazed that this was not resented, but the man seemed to expect it, and he answered in a tone that blended independence with deference. "My name is Roger Banks and I was Master of the Household to my Lord of Granston."

"He that now lies in the Tower for treason."

"Even so, sir, though I dare swear his innocence. But his goods were confiscate, and my Lady can no longer maintain the castle. I seek employment, and should be grateful if you could recommend me to some noble house."

"How long have you been at Humphrey's?"

"Every day for nine weeks."

"And where stay you?"

"In a mean place, sir, that befits my shrinking purse, but I am every day here at Humphrey's."

"I will bear you in mind," said George with a patronizing grandeur that embarrassed Ned; it was clear that Master Banks was more a true gentleman than Master Smith would ever be.

They passed on to the young man, and in response to George's same direct question received the answer, "My name is Walter Furze and I was a member of the company of players called The Children of the Chapel."

"But that must have been a long time ago."

"True, sir, but I am still proud that I acted in Master Lyly's *Sapho and Phao* and his *Campaspe*. To act again is what I most yearn to do."

"Then you should haunt the theatres and the taverns where the players gather, and not Humphrey's."

"I have tried and tried, sir, but to no avail. Now I seek what employment I can find, I care not what, so it befit a gentleman who was schooled at Oxford. Know you any who could help me?"

It was Ned who answered with a blurted out "Yes." He was prompted by a desire to help the young man with whose need and ambition he had been in sympathy, and also by the impulse to display the influence he felt he had.

But George quickly reproved him. "Be not so certain that you can help another player, Master Edmund, until you become one yourself."

"You are a player, and so young?" marveled Master Furze.

It was George who answered. "He would become one, and I think he may, for he is brother to Master William Shakespeare."

"Then he is fortunate indeed." He turned to Ned. "But tell me, how comes it that Master Shakespeare is a poet and writes plays on scholarly subjects and yet did not go to the university?"

Again it was George who took upon himself to answer, and with some acerbity, for it rankled within him that he lacked the blood and education fully to play the part in life he had designed for himself. "How comes it, sir, that you who did go to the university are not a poet and do not write plays? Nature has her poets as she has her gentlemen. Come, Ned." And he moved away like a ship in full sail.

As Ned made to follow, the young man grasped his arm and with desperate urgency said, "Speak for me."

Ned said, "I will. I promise." Reluctantly he caught up with George. Both maintained a silence until they were in the open air again, and then George, deliberately closing the Humphrey chapter, said "And now the river." Ned, who felt he had been humiliated by George, said nothing. But when they got to the Thames, the sight of the activity was so exciting that he soon forgot St. Paul's. The Thames was the true highway of London. It seemed a miracle that the many boats that plied for hire did not collide; some nearly did and the curses of the boatmen added to the raucous cries of those at the bank who scraped their throats with cries of "Eastward ho!" and "Westward ho!"

Ned was dazzled by the sight of a noble barge making stately progress upstream, propelled by eight boatmen in colorful livery. The passengers were out of sight under an ornate canopy, but George, who was well versed in such matters, said, "That is the barge of Lord Howard, the Lord Admiral. He is almost certainly on his way to the Palace of White-hall." As the barge passed, many of the boatmen and their passengers shouted "Hurrah!" George explained, "That is for the great victory at Cadiz, but you would hear a greater shouting if it were the barge of Lord Essex. Oh, that I could dress that man!"

George pointed out, a half-mile to their left, "one of the wonders of the world," London Bridge, with five and six storied buildings atop its twenty sturdy arches. George said that few boatmen and fewer passengers would dare the currents and tides beneath the bridge; most travelers landed on one side, walked to the other, and took another boat.

When they arrived back home, supper was waiting: cold mutton with peas, a green salad decorated with leaves of rosemary, meslin bread made of unsifted wholewheat flour with some rye added, and Spanish Alicant wine sweetened with sugar.

Ned was hungry and the food was good but the meal was an ordeal for him. George, always striving to be among the first in fashion, had introduced forks into the household some months before. By now he and Gilbert were proficient in their manipulation, but Ned had never even seen one before. Gilbert was patient in explaining the use, but at the first attempt Ned's forked meat skidded off his pewter plate and onto the rushes on the floor. In embarrassment he picked the treacherous meat up with his fingers, brushed off some pieces of rush, and ate it, which George made quite clear was not comme il faut. George was adamant; if Ned couldn't learn to use a fork, how could he hope to use a sword, and every player had to be an expert swordsman.

After supper Ned came into his own with his spirited recital of *Venus and Adonis*. When he came to the final lament of Venus for her dead Adonis, the effect of his first audience on him was such that he forgot his artificial impersonation of the feminine goddess and was so transported by her grief that he moved his brother to tears. Gilbert's joy was only partly due to happiness at Ned's talent, for it was clear that even George was impressed. Gilbert had feared his usual witty dissection of a player's performance.

And so Ned went happily to bed on his first night in London, but he was careful to bestow his clothes more neatly than ever before. Since it was a warm night, he slept naked. As he sorted out his jumble of first impressions, the many unpleasant ones now mellowed by the afterglow of his successful performance before a critical audience, someone came stealthily into the room. In the moonlit darkness he saw it was George. Ned pretended to be asleep, but George sat on the couch and gently roused him by shaking his shoulder. Ned's fake waking was not very convincing and did not deceive George, who said quietly, "Be not alarmed. I just wanted to wish you a private goodnight and to tell you that I think you have true quality as a player, and that on the stage you will excell your brother Will. Now that should give you happy dreams." He leaned over and kissed Ned on the cheek. The boy neither moved nor spoke, and George left as quietly as he had entered.

It was some time before Ned could get to sleep. He listened intently to the next room. The door had been left open to ensure a cooling draft. There was a good deal of muffled talk and some muted laughter. Gradually his ears could distinguish a few words. He heard Gilbert say, "No; Ned's still awake." Then George said, in a volume that may have been deliberately judged to let Ned hear his words, "I hope he is. The sooner he learns about us the better." Then words ceased. There was silence for a time, but soon there were sounds of physical pleasure; the voice was that of George. They continued for some minutes, then they stopped for a short time and were replaced by the voice of Gilbert, but now the sounds were of pain, enjoyable pain. Then there was silence.

NINE

IT WAS WEDNESDAY WHEN WILL LEFT NED, AND IT WAS SUNDAY BEFORE
he returned. During that time the boy was kept busy. While George and
Gilbert were in the shop he read hungrily, but it was difficult to please
both of his hosts, for while Gilbert urged Holinshed's *History* upon him,
George insisted on an immediate acquaintance with Sir Thomas Hoby's
translation of Baldassare Castiglione's *Il Libro Del Cortigiano* and
George Pettie's translation of Stefano Guazzo's *Civile Conversazione.*
George rolled the Italian names on his tongue with great gusto, though
he spoke no Italian. He explained to Ned, "First a gentleman and then a
player, and there are none who know the ways of gentleman so well as
the Italians." Ned fulfilled the rival requests by reading history in
private and manners aloud after supper, though he found that this latter
became a performance which needed preparation.

Then there were the sights to see, and George and Gilbert alternated
in showing them, George choosing those he wanted most to talk about
and Gilbert those he thought Ned wanted most to see. Thus it was with
Gilbert that he saw the Theatre and the Curtain, though they failed to
get inside either of them. It was with George that he first took a boat on
the Thames to see the beautiful gardens of the noble houses that lined
the banks on the way to the Palace of Whitehall. It was also with George
that he walked across London Bridge. The end of this latter expedition
was a cautionary tale, for on top of the southern gate of the bridge were
displayed the severed heads of "traitors." George said, "You see it is wise
to bridle your tongue, for ears are quick to catch echoes of heresy or
treachery, and I have already noted that you are glib of tongue and quick
to anger."

"But you are yourself sometimes scandalous in speech," Ned ventured.

"Scandalous but witty, and always on petty matters."

In addition to the reading and the sightseeing, Ned's wardrobe was
overhauled. The costume that had been improvised for him on the first
day was made to fit him by Tim the Tailor, who did most of the shop's
tailoring. He was also provided with a more workaday outfit, but even
this would have made heads turn in church on a Sunday morning in
Stratford. Ned was reluctant to accept the gifts, but George insisted they
were but investments in the brilliant theatrical future of Edmund Shakespeare; he added that one suit was from him and the other from Gilbert,
and he was sure that Ned would have no doubt about which was which.

When Will came on Sunday afternoon, he was struck by the change in

Ned. Not only was he a new man in appearance, but even his accent had begun to reflect that of George; Gilbert still sounded of Stratford. George was proud to relate that Ned had drawn many an eye and questioning whisper in church that morning.

Will had much to tell. When he went to seek him, Cuthbert Burbage had already left for Canterbury to tell the players that since there was no sign of sufficient abatement of the plague—theatres were closed when there were more than forty deaths a week in the city and its environs—arrangements were being made for a tour to Oxford, Gloucester, and Bristol, with the hope that they could then return to London. After a quick visit home for a change of clothes, Will too had set out for Canterbury where he arrived on the Thursday evening. There the principals of the company had gathered in a room of the inn—Richard Burbage, Augustine Phillips, Thomas Pope, Will Kemp, John Heminge, Richard Cowley, George Bryan—to hear Will read the new play, *The Merchant of Venice*.

As they listened to the play, the actors characteristically had ears chiefly for the parts that they hoped would be theirs, but, as sharers in the company's profits, they all were anxious about the chief comic part; for Will Kemp, a popular favorite, had been showing dissatisfaction of late; the last really good part Will had written for him had been that of Bottom in *A Midsummer Night's Dream*. Now there was general relief as they listened to Launcelot Gobbo, and knew what Kemp would make of him, especially in his first scene where he had the stage to himself. There was general enthusiasm about the play, though Burbage had half-playfully wished that he had been young enough to play Portia.

Will was aware that his two brothers and George were fascinated by whatever he chose to tell them of the working of the company, but he knew it would be cruel to postpone reporting on what he had been able to do in the matter of Ned.

In the happy atmosphere after his reading of the play, Will had taken occasion to broach the question of his young brother to some key members of the company. Now he was able to report that, provided he passed muster at an audition to be held for Augustine Phillips, Ned was to be accepted as an apprentice on probation; Will did not mention that he was to be personally responsible for the boy's board and lodging and upkeep during the period of probation.

The company had returned to London with Will, but was to set out again the following day. Phillips had suggested that the audition could wait until the end of the tour, but Will, knowing what agony this would mean to Ned, persuaded his friend and fellow player to hear the boy that night. Both George and Gilbert were quick to say that Ned should speak the end of *Venus and Adonis;* it had moved them so much that it could not fail to gain the boy a place in the company.

Ned was full of questions about Master Phillips, in whose hands his fate seemed to lie. George and Gilbert began with praise of him as an actor. George, hoping he would be quoted, said, "He has the grace of true nobility and adds luster to his profession." Will said that Master Phillips, if he were satisfied with Ned, would undertake his training, and that would be great good fortune, for none exceeded him as a teacher of acting.

Gilbert was eloquent about Master Phillips as a musician; there was no instrument he could not play, and well too. George added that he was also something of a composer. Last season he had written a jig for Will Kemp to dance, wearing his floppy slippers which no one else could walk in, much less dance, and the melody had caught the town. It was said that the Queen herself had danced to it.

But there was more news in regard to Master Phillips. Will was going to relinquish his house and move to live in the Phillips home, south of the river. Ned would live there too.

"Not if he won't take me as a player," Ned quickly interposed.

"Let us wait to make that decision," Will said gently. "If all goes well tonight," he added, "you will stay there, and I will join you in a week or ten days. I have some changes to make in the new play and to see to the copying and get everything ready so that rehearsals can begin as soon as we are all settled in London again."

Gilbert looked nervously at George, hoping he would suggest that Ned could stay with them until Will was ready to move. George understood the look but pretended to ignore it; the boy was well enough, but already Gilbert was giving too much thought and care to him.

"When you move, will we have to share a bed?" asked Ned somewhat fearfully, not from mistrust of Will but from need for privacy.

"No," said Will with a smile; "not even a room. It is a large house. Mistress Phillips has children of her own but there is always an apprentice in the house. Sam Gilburne is with them now; he is a little younger than you and excels in lively young female parts, though his voice has begun to crack. Come. We have much to do, and Master Phillips has invited us to supper."

There was much advice about the care of Ned's new clothes and an abundance of thanks and good wishes, but at last they were away. They went first to Will's home, which Gilbert had pointed out to Ned on their expedition to the Theatre.

Ned was impressed by the inside of the house. "It was for Anne and the children, but now . . ." Will left the sentence unfinished. In a matter-of-fact tone he added, "I shall have to sell most of these things before I move." Ned made no comment but thought how Judith would have loved the house.

Ned had been wearing his splendid costume—"On Sunday," George had said, "you should dress in your finest, in honor of God,"—but Will suggested that it would be more fitting if he dressed more modestly on his first visit to the Phillips home. The boy said he would feel more like Adonis in the noble suit, but Will tactfully pointed out that Master

Phillips could the better judge his talent if he were not distracted by outside grandeur, so Ned donned Gilbert's gift.

As the brothers rode across London Bridge, Ned's excitement mounted. He was coming to the Bankside. Here was the Rose theatre, where the Lord Admiral's Men played, led by the great Edward Alleyn. Here too was the grand new Swan theatre, where the new company, the Lord Pembroke's Men played, the Paris Gardens, a place of bullbaiting, cockfighting, and bearbaiting, and where the strange wonders of the world, brought back by sailors, might be seen. This, Ned felt, was his part of London. If Master Phillips rejected him tonight, this was where he would find work, this was where he would live, but not in the Phillips home.

His first impression of the Phillipses and their home, which was between St. Saviour's and the Bear Garden, was very favorable. Augustine Phillips, who looked to be about Will's age, was all that George had described, but there was a warmth in him that Ned had not expected; he had a gentle dignity it seemed nothing could ruffle. Mistress Phillips, on the other hand, was a bustling, lively soul. She was several years younger than her husband, and appeared made and ready to nestle a houseful of children. Already she had two, both girls, one a new baby in arms who clearly revealed the delicacy of the father and the other a toddler, who showed the robustness of the mother. The house never lacked an apprentice, whom Mistress Phillips enjoyed mothering as much as her husband enjoyed teaching; and now the house might have two, with the additional prospect that Master Shakespeare himself would soon be under her roof. All this would have dismayed many a woman, but Mistress Phillips rejoiced in it. Ned was startled to hear Master Phillips address her as "Anne." So Will was to live with a perpetual reminder of Stratford.

The supper was a happy occasion. The boy player, Samuel Gilburne, was present. He looked younger than his years, and had the persistently merry twinkle of a mischievous little boy. He was obviously sincere in his hearty welcome of Ned, and seemed to assume that they were going to be fellow lodgers; they were to share a room, but not a bed. Ned was keenly disappointed that he was not to have a room of his own.

The supper conversation was almost entirely confined to the two men, who talked of a novel program which had been decided upon for the first week after the return of the company to London. The excitement generated by the Cadiz victory had resulted in an extraordinarily patriotic reception in Canterbury of the new *King John,* which had exploded, by Burbage's speaking of the final speech, into such a display of approval as neither man had ever witnessed. It was this that had given Burbage the idea of presenting Will's six plays about English kings in their historical order on six successive afternoons. At this point, the master of the house asked his pupil Sam if he could name the plays in their correct order. (Ned didn't even know their names.) After a moment's thought, Sam rattled them off: *"King John, Richard II,* the three parts of *Henry VI,* and *Richard III."*

Then Augustine brought up a subject which had obviously been discussed in Canterbury; the company wanted more historical plays from Will, for there seemed to be a tireless demand for them. Burbage longed to play that great hero among English kings, Henry V. But Will was reluctant to attempt it because such a hero, whose exploits were hallowed by generations of memory, was hard to bring alive as a human being. At that time he had revealed that he had already started on a play about Henry when he was the attractively dissolute Prince of Wales; that was easier. "Gus" begged for some details, but Will politely refused to break his rule not to speak about a play until it was finished.

To compensate for Gus's disappointment he told a secret that those at the table were the first to hear, though they were warned that they must not blab it, for the "sharers" rightfully assumed that they should be the first to hear of any new play by Will. He was beginning to think of a new comedy which would give Will Kemp his best part since Bottom. This was such good news that Gus urged Will to whisper it to Kemp, for the secret would flatter him as much as the promise would please him. Will said he might do so if rehearsals for *The Merchant* went happily.

Ned wondered how much he was to share in all these exciting plans, when he would get a good part, or whether he would ever get one at all.

Mistress Phillips commented on Ned's silence, attributing it to his growing nervousness at having to recite for Master Phillips. She begged him be of good cheer for he had much to commend him: he looked well and spoke well; she had expected him to be pure Stratford, but already he was a London man.

As soon as the meal was over, Will asked to be excused. He wished the others good night and Ned good fortune.

The audition took place in the music room. Musical instruments were everywhere; hanging on walls, lying on shelves or on the floor, resting against a bench or stool; there was an exquisite lute, a cittern, a bandore, several recorders, a treble viol, a bass viol, a flute.

Observing Ned's wonder, Master Phillips said, "Your brother has some beautiful lines about music in the new play. He has a true ear for sweet sounds and delights in them as I do. But 'tis the music of words I wish to hear now. Come, Master Edmund. Be not afraid that you are nervous. All players are so. 'Tis a good sign."

Thus encouraged, and placed as far away from his host as the room would allow, Ned explained what he proposed to speak, and Master Phillips nodded approvingly. Almost before his hearer was aware of it, Ned had spoken the opening line: "As falcons to the lure, away she flies." Even as he spoke them, Ned knew the words were empty, and too high in volume and pitch. Master Phillips stopped him and told him to take time and start again; first he should use his imagination to see Venus and hear the "merry horn" that startled her. The teacher continued to speak until the pupil was calmed and his imagination stimulated. Then Ned started again, and as he spoke, his concentration on what he was saying overwhelmed his concern for the result.

Augustine Phillips's chief reaction was one of relief. Had the boy not been good enough to encourage, his task would have been difficult. Will had insisted that his judgment be as impartial as he could make it, but the boy showed real promise, and his personality was of the kind that could charm an audience.

When Ned finished there was a silence. Only then did the boy realize that his future was to be settled in the next minute; his concern for Venus had temporarily obliterated his concern for himself. His anxiety showed in his face. Master Phillips smiled and said, "Welcome to our company, Master Edmund Shakespeare."

In his relief, Ned could scarcely keep back tears. He managed to mumble, "Oh, thank you, sir, thank you," and he flopped down on a stool, thereby knocking down a cittern that leaned against it. Master Phillips was quick to jump up and rescue it and, as he assured himself that no harm had been done and to Ned blamed himself for being so careless in the placing of his instruments, his words were overlaid by a torrent of apologies from Ned. They realized that both were speaking and neither was listening. They stopped and laughed together, and ease was restored.

Then Master Phillips talked practical details, all of which had obviously been thought out in advance. To begin with, Ned was to attend every performance the first week after the return. On Monday he would be accompanied by Will, who was being excused from all playing that he might get on with his writing; on Tuesday he would go with Mistress Phillips; and thereafter he was to mingle on his own with the groundlings, whom the player described as "our best friends and worst enemies." During the weeks the company was away, he was to work on a speech that would be assigned by Master Phillips, who would work with him as time afforded; what with a different play every day, in all of which Master Phillips was involved, and rehearsals every evening for *The Merchant of Venice,* Ned would have to be patient. He hoped to get permission for the boy to attend some of the rehearsals, where he would learn a great deal. He would also be given some books to read, notably the first three books of Edmund Spenser's *The Faerie Queene;* Master Phillips had not yet obtained the remaining books, which had just been published. He would look forward to hearing Ned read aloud from Master Spenser.

Ned wanted to know what play speech he should first commit to memory. Master Phillips said they would choose parts, even though they were unsuited to Ned's age, which he had himself played, for thus there would be no difficulty in securing a copy of them. "Let us begin with the speech of King Philip of France to the citizens of Angiers, which, God willing, you will hear me speak that first afternoon of our return. It begins, 'When I have said, make answer to us both.' "

It was clear that Ned wanted to ask a question but was hesitant about it. Master Phillips read his mind and smilingly said, "You want to know when you will first tread the boards." Ned nodded eagerly. "Maybe in *The Merchant;* attendants will be needed, and there is a scene in a court of justice."

"But will I speak?"

"Speak? The first time you appear? Nay, lad, that must wait a while."

Wait, wait, wait! Ned's impatience showed.

Augustine Phillips explained. " 'Tis not now as when we started. Now much is expected of us, and we dare not trust a beginner with even one line, for during that one line he must hold the stage, and to do that with ease he must first learn to be at home on the stage. Be patient, lad; you are very young."

"But Sam Gilburne is younger."

"And is already a veteran player. He has been playing since he was ten, and is a great favorite with both lords and groundlings. Soon he will have to relinquish his feminine roles, and will find himself in small parts again. At last he may become a hired man, and years from now perhaps even a sharer, but for that he will have to wait until one of us dies—and so will you."

There was a kindly understanding in the voice and Ned responded to it gratefully. "I am glad I am to live with you, Master Phillips."

"You will see more of Mistress Phillips than of me, but she will be a good mother to you in absence of your own."

Ned mumbled something about payment and it was Master Phillips's turn to show hesitation; Will had made it quite clear that Ned was never to know that he was taking charge of all costs until the new apprentice proved his worth.

"Master John Heminge will explain about money to you," said Master Phillips, adding with a chuckle, "as he does to all of us." He continued, "I will take you to see him that first Monday morning, when we meet to prepare for the afternoon. And now 'tis growing dark and time for bed, for we must be up betimes. Come."

They climbed to the third and top floor, where Ned's luggage had already been carried. Sam was lying atop his truckle bed and, by the light of a candle, was going over the lines he had to speak in *King John*. This was a rule that had been rigorously inculcated by Master Phillips; with a different play every day it was wise to rehearse tomorrow's lines the night before, no matter how well you thought you knew them. The rule still obtained, even though the performance was still three days away in Oxford.

Sam set aside his "part" in order to talk. Ned had never seen a part before and he asked if he might look at it. With comic exaggeration Sam said he would be severely punished if he allowed anybody to see the part; they were as jealously guarded as the master copy itself and, like that precious document, always had to be kept under lock and key. Then he relented laughing, and with a mock judicial air said that since Ned was the playwright's brother, he would venture to let him see the family property.

The part was three sheets of paper filled with close writing and pasted together to form a scroll attached to two rolls of wood. Ned couldn't understand it. Sam explained that the part was that of Arthur and contained all the speeches, introduced with the cue lines. "It's one of my favorite parts," said Sam; "not very big but plenty of meat. There's a wonderful scene with Hubert—that's my jailor and I love him—and there's a good death scene too; I have to jump down from the balcony to try to escape, but the fall kills me. They all gasp when I jump, but it would be easy if you could land properly. It's the having to fall badly so that you die that's difficult. Master Kemp taught me to do it; although he's fat and getting old, he's very nimble and tumbles well. You will see me. Mistress Phillips told me that you are to see all the plays that first week. On Tuesday I'm to play the Queen. It's Gough's part, but he is to be free to learn Portia with your brother. And I've played the Queen before when Bob was sick. On Wednesday I play Joan, the witch of France; that's even better than Arthur, but different. On Thursday, it's easy: young Clifford and an apprentice. Friday it's the Earl of Rutland; oh, his name is Edmund, like yours. Then on Saturday it's a lot of nothings."

"Nothings?"

"Nothing to say, but in and out all the time in different clothes. It's hard work changing all the time, especially on a hot afternoon."

As soon as Ned lay down, Sam blew out the candle and, with a cheery "goodnight," soon fell fast asleep. But Ned lay awake an unusually long time. He had passed the test and was now on his way to be a player. He should feel elated, but he didn't. The words that kept hammering at him were "Wait. Wait. Nothings. Nothings."

TEN

By morning Ned's depression had lifted, for the day in prospect was full of excitement. The boys were awakened at dawn by Master Phillips and urged to be quick in washing and dressing as there was much to be done. He suggested that, while Sam washed, Ned should begin copying out the speech from *King John* he was to learn; Master Phillips had brought with him the scroll and pointed out a scholar's desk which was provided with pen, ink, and paper. Master Phillips would have to take all his parts with him on tour.

Ned was eager to start but found it hard to concentrate as Sam was making strange noises with his voice, part singing, part shouting, part hard breathing; he explained he did it every morning to "clear the pipes." Once or twice he was exasperated when his voice cracked. He said, "You are lucky, Ned. Your voice is settled. You are a full man. It is better to start with nothings, like you, than to go back to nothings, like me."

Sam was very businesslike about tidying his bed, his clothes, and the room, and Ned did his best to emulate him. Before they were finished, the voice of Mistress Phillips came from two floors down bidding them make haste, as their porridge and milk were ready. Ned had long left behind such a child's breakfast; like most adults he was content to begin the day with a pot of ale; but to Mistress Phillips all apprentices under her roof were children.

Sam descended the stairs with great care for he carried a jordan full of the night's urine; he made it quite clear that from now on the unsavory task was to be undertaken alternately by the two boys. Ned did not object; at home it had been his daily task to carry down Richard's water as well as his own. George had talked much of Sir John Harington's invention of the water-closet; it was rumored that the Queen was going to try one; in the meantime, George's jordans and privies were supplied with aromatic herbs whose sweet scents were released by infusion with urine.

Ned had toyed with the idea of wearing his George costume, but was glad he had not when he saw how workaday both Master Phillips and Sam were dressed; and yet there was an air about them that lent distinction to the most ordinary apparel; what George affected came naturally to them: the assured authority of their mock kings and princes had become a part of the players even when they were offstage.

After breakfast, Ned had to accompany Sam to get water from the public conduit. Mistress Phillips was delighted that she now would not have to buy from the waterman, for with each boy bearing a bucket and a ewer, she should have enough water for the day. As the boys lined up at the fountain, Ned was envious that Sam was well known; most of the men and women hailed him happily, some insisting that he and his friend take their places. A few knew him as a player, and were eager to know where he was going during the plague and when Master Burbage was going to play Richard Crookback again, but there were some men and women who held themselves severely aloof from the din and chatter; Ned would have recognized them anywhere; they were Puritans like Nicholas Barnhurst back home.

With the water fetched, the next part of the daily routine was a visit to the "jakes" in the garden. When Ned said that he did not need to go, Mistress Phillips said that often the need did not meet with an opportunity, and that a daily morning visit would at last teach the belly its proper manners.

Master Phillips found time to take Ned through the speech he had to learn, explaining the circumstances which produced it and answering Ned's questions. The boy should be able to speak it without script by the following morning. Ned was set to finish writing out his own copy of the speech.

Master Phillips, catching Ned's sad and envious look, stopped his packing and instructions to his wife to talk to the boy. He said, "You would like to come with us, would you not?" Ned nodded sadly, knowing from the tone of the question that it could not be. "We never take any extra men or boys on tour. We have to watch every farthing, and even then we sometimes lose. We cut the plays to the bone to do without hired men. If you came, it would be a special favor, and that you would not want." Master Phillips had already sensed Ned's fiery independence. "You will not have to wait long, and you have much to do. One more thing: it sets my mind at ease that you are here to take care of Mistress Phillips."

Ned was not deceived by this last argument. He knew who was going to do the taking care of, and he resented it in advance; the milk and porridge breakfast still rankled.

Master Phillips interrupted his thoughts with an unexpected question. "Do you play the lute?"

Shamefacedly Ned shook his head but quickly added, to show that he was not a complete barbarian, "But I read music and can sustain my part."

"Mistress Phillips does passing well on several instruments; it is yet another bond between us. She will teach your fingers some skill so that we can have a consort of four when I return."

At last came the moment of departure, and Mistress Phillips wept unashamedly as man and boy waved their goodbyes from the backs of their horses.

When they were out of sight, Mistress Phillips bustled back into the house and set to work immediately to rid the place of the signs of packing, saying as she did so, "I cry when he goes, I cry when he comes back. I'm a crying woman."

Soon Ned was hard at work in the music room, learning the speech from *King John*. It was the beginning of a full and happy three weeks. Mistress Phillips won him over completely until he was eager to join her on expeditions to market, to church, to friends' houses. She in turn enjoyed teaching him the lute, being his audience while he read aloud, and taking him sightseeing. Somewhat reluctantly she took Ned to the Paris Gardens and the Bear Garden, but he could not persuade her to let him see bullbaiting and bearbaiting. "I could not abide the blood and the cries and the death, but worst of all I could not abide the cheers and laughter of the men." He had to be content to watch the sideshows of tumblers, magicians, dancers, and ballad-singers; everywhere he looked for the minstrel, Robin of London, but never saw him.

George and Gilbert came for him occasionally, and it was easy to persuade them to take him to the baiting of the animals. During that first week the plague death roll was so minimal, only twenty-five, that all public entertainments were in full swing; Lord Hunsdon's Men need not have left town. Ned had thought both his brother and George might have had the same reaction to the baiting as Mistress Phillips, but they were as eager for the gory spectacles as he was, so he was not surprised to find the audiences a compound of the elegant and the rough, the well dressed and the ragged. At the bearbaiting he found the sympathies of the audience were entirely with the bear; there was one blind bear that was an especial favorite, and when he managed to claw or bite a dog to death he received mighty applause, but when he was himself in imminent danger the bear wards were quick to enter the ring to rescue him. The bullbaiting left Ned with an unsavory memory which Mistress Phillips said was a just punishment; the bull tossed a gored and gory dog right out of the ring and into his lap, where the animal died as it landed. Ned's reaction of distaste and embarrassment created the best laugh of the afternoon. Some nearby spectators eagerly grabbed for the carcass and threw it back into the ring. George's vexed comment was, "Oh, why didn't you wear Gilbert's costume!" for Ned was indeed dressed in all his finery. They left at once to expunge the blood with soap and water.

During the last of the three weeks, Will arrived to take up his lodging at the Phillips home, but Ned saw little of him. His room, a large one on the second floor, had beeen furnished to serve him as bedroom and study. He did not come down in the morning until Mistress Phillips sent Ned to fetch him to dinner. During the meal he generally seemed preoccupied, but was always genial. Mistress Phillips longed to question him about the new play he was writing about Prince Hal, and about *The Merchant of Venice,* and about a host of subjects, but she had been warned by her husband that a poet, "wrapt in the mystery of creation," was a delicate creature to be protected from the small concerns that filled her life.

After dinner every day Will left the house, presumably for the theatre. One morning, when Ned went to take his ewer of washing water to him and to bring down his jordan of urine, he was not there, nor had his bed been slept in. Ned, puzzled and slightly worried, hurried down to tell Mistress Phillips. She seemed embarrassed but not perturbed, and said, "Master Shakespeare told me he would not be home every night; he sometimes works very late on theatre matters." Ned suspected that the urgent matters were more fleshly and wondered how and when he could emulate his brother, for there was a growing urgency in him too.

The company returned on the Saturday. Sunday was to be free for the players but not for the stage staff who had much to do to prepare for the week ahead. All were in high spirits because the tour had been unusually successful, and this confirmed them in the wisdom of the novel repertory in the week ahead, for they had played nothing but Will's histories, and their reception had repeated that in Canterbury.

All three players returned to the Phillips home with their parts in *The Merchant of Venice*. It had been decided that Will should play the part of the Duke, since the rehearsals would keep him away from his writing in any event. Sunday was to be devoted to a study of the new parts, for the first reading would take place the following night at Richard Burbage's, chosen for its proximity to the theatre.

Dutifully all five went to church in the morning, but for Ned the great event of the day was that he was to be "heard" in the afternoon by Master Phillips; the occasion was made more exciting because the other three members of the household were invited to be present.

He began with *The Faerie Queene,* and after a nervous and somewhat faltering beginning soon was himself absorbed by the glory of the language. After about fifteen minutes, when he was well launched into the terrors of that "bold, bad man," Archimago, Master Phillips suddenly stopped him and said, "I'm sure you know what Styx is, but what is Cocytus?"

Ned, put out at being stopped in full flood, had to confess somewhat testily that he didn't know.

Master Phillips said, "You can never act properly what you do not understand. Words themselves are not enough." Seeing that Ned was upset he added, " 'Tis a worse fault to pretend knowledge than to confess ignorance. Often I have to ask your brother here what his words mean."

To complete the restoration of ease to Ned, Will added, "And often I do not know myself until I am forced to explain."

Sam, also eager to help, said, "I know not what Cocytus is."

"It is one of the six rivers of Hades," said Master Phillips. "I too had to ask somebody the meaning."

"And I can guess who that somebody was," said Will. "Gabriel Spencer."

In explanation to Ned, Master Phillips said, "He is a hired man who has been to the University at Oxford."

Will could not resist adding, "He thinks Latin and Greek and all who wrote in those languages are his personal property, and he keeps jealous guard over them."

Mistress Phillips doubted the propriety before Ned of Will's wryly critical tone and she quickly added, "He is a very good actor, and handsome beyond compare. Truly an Adonis."

Ned wondered why such a paragon of learning and looks should be only a hired man and determined to question Sam, but Master Phillips broke the digression about Gabriel Spencer by saying, "Now, Ned, try that stanza again."

Ned did so, and all went well from there on. Many a time the mentor wanted to check and correct the pupil, but decided against it; it had been a mistake to invite the audience. When Ned delivered the memorized speech of King Philip to the citizens of Angiers, his assumption of regal dignity and royal threat were almost comic in their exaggeration, but no one smiled. Master Phillips could not commend it and yet he felt it unwise to criticize as it deserved, until he was alone with his pupil. It was his wife who resolved his dilemma by saying, "Master Phillips, you must look to your laurels. Were Ned old enough, he could supplant you in that part." During the laughter which greeted that remark, she went on to say, "Now, Ned, the lute. Show them how well I have taught you."

Nervously Ned took up the lute. While proud and assured in his acting, he was dubious about his quality as a musician. He was wrong in both judgments, for in his present stage he was a better singer and a worse actor than he knew. Accompanying himself inexpertly with a few chords, he sang Will's "Who is Sylvia?" and provoked loud applause, as much to comfort as commend him. Then Mistress Phillips heartily suggested that they should make music together, and soon four instruments were being harmoniously blended to accompany Ned's voice. The afternoon ended with the first tentative attempts at some music Augustine Phillips had composed, while on tour, for the final scene of *The Merchant of Venice*. Again he praised Will for the beautiful lines he had written about music, which were to be spoken by Lorenzo while the music was played.

"Who plays Lorenzo?" asked Mistress Phillips.

"Gabriel Spencer," answered Will.

That name again. As soon as they were alone in the bedroom, Ned questioned Sam about him.

"Keep away from him," said Sam. "He likes to hurt people. But he is a good actor."

"Since he is such a good actor, and so learned and so handsome, why is he only a hired man?"

"Because he will never have the money to buy a share in the company. He drinks all he earns, and has a heavy reckoning at all the taverns. He is ill-disposed when sober and dangerous in his cups. Yet he sometimes can be gracious and friendly. He took upon him once to teach me some new feints and thrusts in fencing."

Ned's first day in the Theatre dawned bright but chilly; it was the Monday of the last week in September. As the four players set out on their two-mile walk, Master Phillips suggested that Sam should tell Ned the story of *King John,* which he was to see that afternoon. Sam presented the story from the point of view of Arthur, the part he himself played and Will was gently amused.

Then Master Phillips began to prepare Ned for his experience of the inside of a theatre and the men who worked in it. He told him of the bookholder and his assistant, who would be very busy now, preparing the book of *The Merchant of Venice;* then there was the tireman and his assistant, who would be readying the clothes for the afternoon, making minor repairs always necessitated when the company had been traveling, and beginning to think about clothes for the new play; finally there was the stagekeeper, who, with his assistants, would be cleaning the stage for the afternoon and getting ready such properties as the throne, drums and trumpets, the furnace to heat the irons with which to put out Arthur's eyes, the chair and the cords to bind him to it, and the waxen and bloody head of the Duke of Austria.

Ned wanted to know if there would be a rehearsal of the afternoon's play. He was told that there would be no need for a full rehearsal, since they had played the play a few days before, though in a simpler version suitable for traveling with a smaller company. He might see some of the company walking the stage and trying out speeches, and he would certainly see the stagekeeper and the bookholder assembling the hired men to ensure that they knew the positions and movements in the scenes of court and on the battlefield.

When they arrived at the Theatre, they went in through a back entrance, and Sam was deputed to take Ned immediately onstage. It was nine o'clock and a bright morning. As Ned walked into the sunlight and looked around at the surrounding galleries, he felt an exhilaration hard to contain; this was his world and he must conquer it soon. He was only partially aware of Sam's torrent of explanation, but he was forced to take note of the balcony from which Sam would jump that afternoon. The stagekeeper was harassed; one of the hired men was late for rehearsal. Sam explained that this was a heinous sin; if a player was late for an entrance, he lost a day's pay; if he missed a performance, without prior warning, he lost a week's pay. The hired man they awaited came hurrying onstage; he was unkempt and unshaven, and had in fact spent the night in the stews where he had been drugged and robbed by a whore. But he was a good actor and usually reliable, so the stagekeeper contented himself with a reprimanding mutter and a scowl; besides, this man was important in *King John* for he played First Citizen, together with some nothings.

The stagekeeper looked at Sam meaningfully, and the boy plucked

Ned by the sleeve, whispering that they had to leave the stage so that the rehearsal could begin. They went to the tiring-room and there were hailed by Augustine Phillips, who was talking to Will, and a tall, robust man who turned out to be John Heminge. The three had been discussing Ned: his training, his usefulness, his cost. Master Heminge extended his hand to Ned. "Welcome, Master Edmund. I hear promising news of you from Master Phillips here. 'Tis good to have another Shakespeare in the company. You and I must talk soon, but not now; I have much to do this morning." He turned to the others. "And I must do it at once, or I shall be late for the play. Fear not, Will. This *Merchant* of yours will cause no trouble." He left waving a leather pouch which contained the master copy of *The Merchant of Venice*. Ned later learned that he was on his way to the office of the Master of Revels, who had to sanction the play before it could be performed.

Augustine Phillips suggested that Sam should ask the tireman for two foils and take Ned out on the ground of the theatre and give him some preliminary instruction. They could also try some tumbling and dancing. Ned felt like a nuisance that had to disposed of, and Will, sensing this, explained that he should seize on every minute to equip himself and that he could learn a great deal from Sam.

Ned was amazed by Sam's skill and versatility and soon forgot that he was being taught by a junior. Sam began not by teaching but by displaying his skills with a youthful exuberance; he turned back somersaults, walked on his hands, danced intricate steps to the rhythm of his own handclapping, and parried with elegant ease Ned's untutored thrusts with the foil. Ned was embarrassed by his own ineptness and then realized that this was exactly what Master Phillips had expected and hoped for; he had to learn how much there was to learn so that his impatience might be curbed. Ned was occasionally aware of amused eyes from the stage, and this put him in a bad temper. He longed to show his superiority in some field, but all he had was his greater physical strength, and to use that against the smaller boy would be cowardly. Sam seemed to read his mind for he said, "Let us wrestle." Ned was reluctant to do so because he might hurt the boy, but Sam persisted. Ned had done a deal of rough-and-tumble wrestling and decided that this was his chance to show off; he would lift Sam high above his head and threaten to dash him to the ground, only to set him down gently. They grappled, and, even while he was maneuvering for a firm grip, he found himself sprawled on the ground, with Sam standing over him and laughing. The laugh was echoed from the stage. Ned's humiliation was complete, and he longed to steal away. Then somebody jumped down from the stage and came to him. Later he discovered it was Richard Cowley, a tall, pale, cadaverous man with a gentle manner.

As Ned scrambled up in confusion, Master Cowley said, "Be not ashamed, Ned . . . Yes, I know who you are. There has been much talk of you, and we welcome you. Young Sam here is nimble and quick, but you may yet be a better actor than he." Then in fairness to Sam he added, "Though he excels in that quality too, as you will see this afternoon." He turned to Sam. "You now have to prove that you are a good teacher, and you will only prove that when you have taught somebody else to be better than you are. Now start with the foils. Teach him the stance and some thrusts. You will have succeeded Sam, if his brother is proud of Ned when he comes for him. And you, Ned, be patient, and I warrant that, within a month, you will parry all of Sam's thrusts. Now, to it."

Richard Cowley stood by until the boys were totally absorbed in the lesson to the exclusion of all observers, and then he quietly returned to the stage. By the time Will came to stop them, he was indeed proud of his brother's progress; Ned had a greater agility and aptitude for games than Will had ever possessed, and he was already wielding the foil as a natural extension of his own arm. But it was Sam's praise that was sweetest: "One week and you will score a hit on me."

At the Angel Tavern Ned was privileged to sit at the table of the eight sharers. This was unusual, in compliment to Will, and thereafter Ned would sit with the apprentices, who had a small table to themselves. The stage staff too sat separately, as did the hired men. Occasionally, to celebrate a birthday or a birth or a marriage, an employed man was invited to join the table of his employers.

Ned was placed between Will and Gus Phillips; opposite him sat Richard Cowley, but Ned's attention was focused on the famous Richard Burbage, who sat at the head of the table on Will's left. The conversation was largely about *The Merchant of Venice*. The first company reading was to take place at seven o'clock that night. Only the sharers, with the addition of Robert Gough, Sam Gilburne and Gabriel Spencer would be present, all other parts being read by the bookholder. It was aimed to give the first performance of the play in three weeks' time.

"Our patron, the new Lord Hunsdon, is beginning well. I hear from Nat that we can expect two trunks of clothes from him. He likes color more than did his father, so it mayhap that Bassanio will be new and well suited." This was said by Burbage. "Nat" was Nathaniel Tremayne, the tireman. "But it would be well if he were Lord Chamberlain, like his father. This Lord Cobham likes not plays."

"I have a mind to remember that," said Will quizzically.

"Take care," said Will Kemp, who sat on Burbage's left. "It is wise to offend only those without power. You should leave such dangerous things to me, for I do it without words."

"You sometimes do too much without words for Will's liking," ventured Cowley, but jocularly.

"I make them laugh, and that is what they want," said Kemp lightly. His superfluous clowning was a sore subject and Burbage took a quick look at Will, begging him not to take up the challenge.

Will was content to say, "There is some laughter that even I want. Make them laugh as Launcelot Gobbo and I shall laugh too."

"I cannot fail, Will; I cannot fail." He added generously, "Never man wrote better for me than you," but he tempered this tribute by adding, "when you remember that I am in the company."

Burbage changed the subject and graciously spoke to Ned. "Master Phillips has asked if you might come to the rehearsal tonight. Would that please you?"

"Oh, yes sir," said Ned with unbounded delight.

"I fear you may be disappointed; we will be like inexpert skaters, trying the ice. But this afternoon should give you pleasure. And I understand that Will is to take you. That is an honor indeed, for I know nothing else that would draw him from his writing."

Richard Cowley said, "We shall suffer much for you, Ned, for your brother's eyes and ears miss nothing. When we knew he was going to be there, we all went back to our parts and read them over again." This was greeted with guilty laughter.

Will smiled and said, "Pay no attention, Ned. 'Tis no such matter. Once they are out on the stage, they forget everything."

"Including the author's lines," added Will Kemp to more laughter.

Burbage gave the signal for the breakup of the gathering. They would now take an hour's rest before preparing themselves for the afternoon. During the rest hour, Will had further conferences with the bookholder to ensure that all was ready for the reading that night. He suggested that Ned should wander around the theatre, looking at the stage from every vantage point. Ned did a circuit of the stage from each of the three galleries. The sun was warming the air and he immediately saw that the eastern side of the theatre, being in the sun, would be the more desirable today. But for him the best place was standing on the ground, full-facing the stage; the benches were only in the galleries, leaving the open ground for those who could not afford to sit. He had learned that the most expensive seats, which only the wealthy could afford, were at the side of the stage, in the first gallery. They were separated by a wooden barrier, and there was a door to backstage from each side, which certain noble and constant patrons were allowed to use, both coming and going, thus enabling them to avoid contact with the rough, raucous, and stinking commoners. As the Earl of Southampton had said, "Were there a roof to the theatre, we could not live through a performance, for we should all die of the poisoned air. As 'tis, I spend a king's ransom on perfumes when I go to the theatre, else I should swoon."

As one o'clock drew near, Ned was aware of the sounds of a gathering crowd outside. Exactly on the hour a flag was hoisted by one of the stagehands from the roof of the backstage building. It was large and colorful enough to be readily seen by possible patrons on the north bank of the Thames, and signaled a play that afternoon. Then from near the flagpole appeared another stagehand with a trumpet. He blew a long and loud call, heralding to the world the birth of a performance in an hour. His call would be repeated every quarter-hour, the last, at two o'clock, being longer than the others to secure the attention of the waiting audience. His first call was greeted with cries of welcome from the people outside; at the second call they would be allowed inside to scramble for what they thought to be the best places. The first sound of the trumpet prompted activity inside the theatre too; people gradually emerged from backstage and moved to appointed places. There was the doorkeeper and his assistant, then there were the gallery-keepers on each side, readying themselves with their boxes to receive the extra payments necessary for seats in the galleries. It was clear even to Ned's inexperienced eye that the system was subject to much pilfering, and he was not surprised to find a man of obvious authority going to every station where money was to be collected, ensuring that the positions were manned and the boxes were padlocked. Later Ned discovered that this important gentleman was Cuthbert Burbage. He it was who looked after the interests of his father, the owner of the building. John Heminge guarded the interests of the players.

Some sturdy young men appeared, heavily laden, and took their places just inside the main entrance. They were the vendors of refreshments: nuts, apples, ale, and sweetened water. Those with the drinks were the most encumbered, for they carried a spigoted barrel on their shoulders and an array of metal cups attached to their belts.

Cuthbert Burbage, who knew about him, approached Ned, who was looking on at the mounting activity from the side of the first gallery. He suggested that Ned should get to his seat in the front row of the second gallery nearest backstage. Will would unobtrusively join him later. Ned was disappointed; he had hoped to sit in the first gallery in one of what he later learned were called the "lords' rooms."

The second trumpet sounded and the doors were opened, but only wide enough for people to come in two at a time.

Ned looked down from his seat and was fascinated by the people pouring into the theatre. They seemed to be in a holiday mood. News of the company's patriotic plan for the week had spread fast, and many of those who had already seen the play, shown for the first time that summer, were coming again to be part of the excitement they knew it would engender. By the time of the third trumpet, there were some hundreds milling about on the ground and maneuvering for a better view. They were talking and laughing happily. Above their voices could be heard the cries of the vendors in competition for attention; the winner was easily the one who cried: "Apples here. Rosy pippins. Two a farthing." As yet few people were in the galleries, apart from a fair sprinkling in the top which was the twopenny one.

Ned wondered how so many people could be free on a Monday afternoon. Many were middle-aged and soberly dressed husbands and wives, artisans and small merchants. In sharp contrast were the young men, some of them extravagantly and colorfully dressed; and others almost ragged. Two sharply defined kinds kept in their distinctive groups: some were of wealthy families, up in London for legal training after completing their years at the university, while others came of lowly families and were apprentices to a skilled trade. There were a few soldiers and sailors too and several ruffianly individuals of the kind Ned had been made wary when he had seen them in St. Paul's. There were several pairs of young women who had obviously come to be seen rather than to see. They disported themselves flirtatiously with the apprentice lawyers; few of them had eyes for the more humble apprentices.

The fourth trumpet found the galleries well occupied, but the lords' room opposite Ned was annoyingly empty; he could not see the one below him.

Ned had been keeping a place for Will. Now a ruddy-faced citizen with a voluptuous woman, whom Ned suspected was not his wife, asked him to move over. Ned said he was keeping the place for his brother.

"I care not for any brother," said Red Face aggressively. "Move over."

Loud enough for many around to hear, though he had not meant this, Ned said, "He is Will Shakespeare, he that wrote this play."

This provoked a flurry of excited comments and Red Face somewhat abashed, said, with a bludgeon attempt at wit, "If he wrote it, why does he want to see it?"

This quip earned a few titters but more demands that he sit down. His companion sat down and pulled him down after her. Red Face finally muttered to Ned, "If there be no brother you will answer for it." As the final trumpet gave its long signal that the play was about to begin, Will arrived, almost stealthily, through a small door which led backstage. He sat on Ned's left. His appearance caused much excitement in his vicinity and a ripple of heads turning, fingers pointing, and tongues wagging passed along the gallery. But as the trumpet ceased, all attention went to the stage, for to everyone's surprise Cuthbert Burbage came striding on with arms upraised to command silence.

"My noble lords, gracious gentlemen, and kind ladies," which beginning was by way of flattering compliment rather than accurate description.

Ned whispered to Will, "Where are the lords?"

Will replied laconically, "At court."

Cuthbert continued. "I have great news. Our performance this afternoon will be honored by the presence of that beloved hero of our nation, the noble Earl of Essex!"

At this thrilling intelligence, a surge of noisy excitement grew, but Cuthbert's arms were raised again; they were tired before sufficient silence had been restored for him to continue.

"We have received word that the noble earl is already past the Bishopsgate and will be here in minutes." This piece of information caused many near the door to try to get out to watch the arrival. Angry words resulted because the doorkeeper insisted that it would cost them another penny to come back in. Cuthbert quickly realized what was happening and called out in a spirit of generosity prompted by the patriotic excitement, "Let them go." He quickly added, "But remember their faces."

There was no great rush to the door, most people being determined to use the waiting time to win a better vantage point. The question which was in all minds was spoken by Red Face in a loud voice. He leaned over the gallery rail and shouted, "Where will he sit?" This problem had been causing Ned great agony of mind; suppose he should sit in the "room" below. He thought a prayer: Oh God, please make him sit in the room opposite. As if in answer to his prayer, Cuthbert, without a word, dramatically flung out his left arm. Ned would be facing the great man!

Now began such a bustle and pushing to Ned's side of the theatre as would have capsized the building had it been afloat. A few, very few, pure theatre-goers resolutely stood or sat their ground, superior to such vulgar excitement; some of them, indeed, did not approve of Essex's growing power at court and in the land. Some were loyal to Raleigh whom Essex seemed determined to supplant; rumors had begun to spread that there had been great dissension during the astonishing adventure of Cadiz; it was whispered that Essex had tried to assert authority even over Lord Admiral Howard. But there was no denying the man's courage and attraction.

There was a great deal of pressure to squeeze the people around Ned into the wall. Now he was grateful to Red Face, who spread himself firmly and refused to budge; gallantly he seized an opportunity to change places with his companion to protect her and her dress.

At last two trumpeters, in brocaded tabards, appeared on the stage and blew a brilliant fanfare to the offstage accompaniment of drums. The Earl of Essex entered with his lady, famous in her own right as the beautiful widow of Sir Philip Sidney. In the entourage were other dazzling young noble lords and ladies.

At the appearance of Essex, those standing pressed toward him and all those seated stood; he would have been a foolhardy man who did not stand. The applause and shouting were thrilling to Ned, and he joined in lustily. Will, too, joined in with enthusiasm. Essex acknowledged his reception with happy smiles, waves of the hand, and gracious bows. He did not doff his hat, but behaved with the decorum of a monarch. At last he raised his hand in signal that the play should begin, and he and his party sat on their velvet-cushioned benches. It took some time for the hubbub to subside sufficiently for the players to make their first entrance, and for a few minutes they had to struggle to make their lines heard, but with the entrance of Richard Burbage as the bastard son of King Richard the Lion Heart, Essex was forgotten and the play was all.

Even before Burbage's entrance, Ned had spotted the player who was undoubtedly Gabriel Spencer. He played Chatillon, the French Ambassador, and when with haughty disdain he used the phrase "borrowed majesty," Ned almost thought he caught the slightest shadow of a glance in Spencer's eyes toward the Earl of Essex, but he decided he must have been mistaken; nobody could have been so impudently daring.

After the capture of Arthur, Will quietly left his seat and went backstage without a word of explanation. Soon Ned knew why. As Robert Gough, in the character of Constance, went wild with grief for the loss of her son, Ned remembered Hamnet. Will could not now bear to hear the words so descriptive of his own hidden sorrow; Hamnet too was to him, "My life, my joy, my food, my all the world!" Tears came to Ned's eyes, for Constance, for Arthur, for Will, for Hamnet. There was guilt in the tears too; he had been forgetful of Will's grief. Only now did he realize why Will had been so withdrawn and silent. A part of his life had ended with the move to Bankside.

But Will was back in his seat for the final great public moment. As Burbage spoke the words,

> "Now these her princes are come home again,
> Come the three corners of the world in arms,
> And we shall shock them,"

he turned full to the Earl of Essex. His further and last sentence was not heard, for bedlam was let loose. It was a unique experience for everybody there. Fifteen hundred people had become one multivoiced creature with waving arms and a vast undulating body. Ned found that he was jumping up and down, gesticulating wildly, and shouting. He turned to the lady on his right who was similarly transported. With mutual impulse they embraced each other, and Red Face seemed not to mind, he was so intent on proving by mass and volume that he was the most patriotic person there. Ned turned to Will; he had gone again. Ned was momentarily stunned—how could Will choose to miss this great experience which his words had conjured up?—but then he abandoned himself again to the wild ecstasy.

By this time the whole company of players was on the stage, including the bookholder, the stagekeeper, their assistants, and Cuthbert Burbage. Several of the younger groundlings also climbed up onto the now crowded stage. Concern flashed through the mind of Cuthbert lest the timbers of the galleries and the stage might not be able to endure the strain now being put upon them.

After basking in this orgy of adulation for nearly ten minutes, the Earl of Essex gave a farewell wave and moved toward the stage door. This was the signal for a general dash to the main doors which were now flung wide open; everybody wanted to see the procession, and those with horses hurried to get mounted to follow its progress back to Essex House. But news of the earl's presence had already spread, and the vicinity of the theatre was crowded; it was a struggle even to get to the hitched horses.

Ned was about to follow the general move to the main entrance, when he suddenly realized his new privilege, and he hurried through the little stage door. A few people nearby saw his move and debated whether they dare follow him. Only Red Face had the temerity to do so, and he pushed past his lady and dragged her unwillingly after him. They found themselves facing a darkly shadowed and narrow stairway down which Ned was fast disappearing. The lady was timorous of the descent, but Red Face settled that by pushing her in front of him.

They were not the only people to venture backstage. Those who had already invaded the stage sought to follow the players, and this alarmed the sharers and Cuthbert Burbage; there were things lying around, asking to be stolen. They began to impede the invaders, and soon a scuffle was taking place. A quick-minded assistant hurried backstage and soon returned with an armful of cudgels which were quickly seized and used unsparingly by other assistants and the hired men; by some unspoken code, the players in regal garb were felt to be above the use of such menial weapons, though Richard Burbage managed to draw his sword and use the hilt to good effect. One young legal apprentice was heard to shout in high glee, "Burbage hit me!" He hoped for a lasting scar which would give him a story for the rest of his life.

Word of the fracas was brought to the earl, who said that he would wait a while until his "friends, the players," were free to receive his commendation of their excellent performance. Thus, Ned was enabled to observe the great man from a discreet distance.

What impressed Ned most was the number of fine noblemen and elegant gentlewomen who seemed to pay court to the Earl of Essex. They had not all been with him in the theatre. Then he realized that the lords' room, which had been below him and which he had not been able to see, had also been occupied, and apparently to capacity. Red Face seemed to be knowledgeable about them, and Ned, while striving to appear not to do so, strained to catch the hoarse whispers of information aimed at the lady. Ned caught the name of Lord Mountjoy, and gathered that his companion was Lady Rich, the sister of the Earl of Essex. The particularly splendid young man was the Earl of Southampton, but the beautiful lady with him was unknown to Red Face.

The players were now flocking backstage in triumph. Sam, still in the apparel of Arthur, spotted Ned and came over to get him. When he saw Red Face and his lady, he said, somewhat imperiously, "Who are these?" Ned quickly disavowed knowledge of them, and Sam, who seemed years younger than his near sixteen, spoke with an authority that amazed Ned and cowed Red Face. "You have no right to be here. Go." He pointed to the nearest stage entrance, and the lady pulled her escort toward it. He followed meekly, muttering something about puppies; he had been aware of the struggle on the stage, and did not want to draw the cudgeled wrath of the players on his head. Ned wondered how they would get down from the stage; vaulting seemed not to be within the compass of either of them. He had no time to investigate the amusing possibilities, for Sam drew him into the group gathered near the earl.

The players faced the earl and the noble folk backed him. He was complimenting the company on their patriotic and timely repertoire for the week, and wished he could be present every afternoon, but alas! affairs of state forbade that. He promised to tell Her Majesty of the plan; she would be much gratified by it. Then the earl said, "But where is our poet? Where is Master Shakespeare?"

It was Augustine Phillips who took upon himself to reply. "He did not play this afternoon; he is at home writing."

This openfaced lie astounded Ned; but all the players seemed to accept it without embarrassment. Ned could not forbear a questioning look at Sam; he was rewarded with a very knowing look and a subtle glance toward the Earl of Southampton.

Essex said, "Convey him my thanks for a memorable afternoon and bid him show us more of England's kings. There are greater ones than have yet appeared on your stage."

Then the earl turned to leave, with his lady on his hand. The entourage followed, according to their position in the hierarchy, and behind them pressed the theatre men eager to see the scene outside.

There the earl's private bodyguard waited, some three dozen of them. Eight on each side of the lane, with pikes grasped horizontally to form a barrier, kept a way open for the procession to the two carriages; there were also several fine horses, held in check with difficulty by straining grooms. The rest of the bodyguards were closely massed in two groups, the one to form a battering ram to force a way through to Bishopsgate Street, and the other to afford protection at the rear of the procession. Some of the players wanted to join the crowd, but John Heminge, supported by other sharers, peremptorily forbade it. They were still in their stage finery; besides, much remained to be done, and there was a rehearsal that night.

As they went back inside, Cuthbert Burbage spoke to Ned. He had a message from Will, which he had been unable to deliver sooner. Sam was to bring Ned over to Richard Burbage's house where they would have supper before the rehearsal. Soon Sam, still in high excitement, came for Ned and, as they walked the mile or less to the Burbage house, Ned questioned him about Will's disappearance.

Sam stopped before answering and looked appraisingly at Ned wondering how much he should tell him, how much he would understand. They resumed their walk slowly as Sam began to speak, but in an intimate tone, very different from the uninhibited one he had been using.

"All I know is theatre gossip, but it does make sense. When he was only twenty years old, the Earl of Southampton was Master Shakespeare's patron, and was kind to him when the plague closed the theatre for so long. Your brother stayed with the earl for months."

Ned sensed Sam's reservation and was quick to show he had some knowledge of the situation. "Will dedicated his two long poems to the earl."

Sam hinted mystifyingly, "There are wicked whispers of other poems too." Ned's complete bewilderment made Sam decide not to pursue that story. "The two men were very close, so far as a commoner can be close to a nobleman, and an older man to a younger."

"Do you mean they slept together?" Ned asked, as if he had no personal involvement in the answer.

Sam was nonplussed by this bluntness. "I did not say that, and I do not believe it, whatever others say."

Pleased with the success of his tactic, Ned pursued it further. "Have you been to bed with a man?"

The younger boy had now completely lost his sophisticated initiative. Pleading for understanding he said, "I was a boy player. But now I know my pleasure will be with women. As Master Shakespeare's is."

"And mine," added Ned.

"They say it was a woman that came between Southampton and your brother. I think it was something more than that, for there is lasting bitterness between them."

"Who was the lady with the Earl of Southampton?"

"Mistress Elizabeth Vernon." Sam stopped again to whisper the name impressively. "They are said to be very close, though to speak of it is a dangerous matter. The young earl is much favored of the Queen, and she will admit of no rival."

"Much favored? Does that mean bed too?"

Sam was truly appalled. "That is a hanging matter, Ned. The Queen is an old lady and is still as virgin as when she was born. Handsome young noblemen can win her heart, but even kings have failed to win her body." Sam decided it was high time he became the embarrassing questioner. Abruptly he changed the subject. "But tell me of your brother. He is a secret man. We hear of a wife and children, but never see them."

Ned did not want to discuss Anne, so he smoothly turned his answer to speak of Hamnet. He added, "This afternoon you were Hamnet, and Will could not bear to sit and hear a mother's grief, uttered in words that he had written." He went on to talk on the safe subject of the other children, Susanna and Judith, and, before Sam could get to any troublesome questions, they were at Burbage's house.

Will greeted them warmly and introduced them to Mistress Winifred Burbage, a woman permanently saddened by the death of several children and overawed by the already great and yet still growing reputation of her husband. She hovered in waiting for the company, whom she would greet graciously and then disappear. Waiting for the boys was bread, cheese, fruit, and ale served by a hearty widow, Mistress Long, who was indispensable to the Burbages. She lived nearby in a cottage with six children, the eldest of them ten years old; her husband had been lost in the wars.

"They say he was killed," she said cheerfully and frequently, "but I never saw his corpse, and he was not one to run into danger. When he's tired of roaming, he'll come back home. I've got a whip waiting for him, and he'll be glad to go back to the wars."

Between whiles of seeing that the boys filled their stomachs, Mistress Long helped Tom Vincent, the bookholder, to prepare the room for the reading. Will had decided that Ned should sit with the apprentices on the farthest bench.

On the side of the refectory table was an array of flagons of ale, leathern bottles of sugared Spanish wine, tankards, and goblets.

Apart from Richard Burbage, who had gone to call upon his sick father, the company arrived together; they had eaten together at their favored tavern and were still full of excited talk about the afternoon. Will took the bookholder to his place at the table and entered into an earnest colloquy with him. At one point they seemed to be talking about Ned, for he caught them looking at him. Master Vincent, who was some years older than Will, was a stern man with a permanent frown. Not even Will Kemp had ever succeeded in making him laugh.

Ned was fascinated by Gabriel Spencer, who kept himself aloof and apart; he was the only hired man present. He caught Ned looking at him and bore down on him, carrying a tankard of ale.

"You are Master Shakespeare's brother, are you not?" There seemed to be accusation in the simple question.

"Yes," said Ned, feeling his reply inadequate.

"How else could you be so privileged as to be here? You are a fortunate young man. And you wish to be a player. Be warned. 'Tis all glitter, like hell itself, but it is the home of the damned." He spoke with a handsome smile that seemed to belie his words, and walked away.

Ned was shaken by this encounter, which to others in the room, who saw the movement but had not heard the words, looked like a kindly greeting. The boy was reminded of a sermon he had heard about Satan, the fallen prince, who retained all his princeliness, though fallen.

At ten minutes to seven Richard Burbage arrived and took the place which had been reserved for him at the bookholder's right. Next to him sat Thomas Pope, a portly player whom Ned had much admired as the papal emissary that afternoon. He was to play Shylock.

The reading began with the bookholder's reading of the cast list. This was a mere formality, for the parts had already been distributed. John Heminge, ever mindful of the money, asked if they couldn't do with four hired men, but both Will and the bookholder insisted that it had to be five. But Master Heminge was not satisfied. Since Dick Cowley was doubling Old Gobbo with Tubal, why couldn't he double something with the Prince of Morocco? It would be so easy to wash off the dark make-up and be a different character. Richard Burbage said the matter could be decided later, but Ned felt that Master Heminge would have his way.

The bookholder was using Will's manuscript of the play. The master copy was with the office of the Master of the Revels. John Heminge would call for it in a week's time and would then be told of any passages to be excised or amended; no such instruction was anticipated in the case of *The Merchant of Venice*.

What surprised Ned most about the reading was the difference in the facility of the actors; some, like Augustine Phillips who was to play Antonio, read as if the words were already theirs; others, like Richard Burbage, read as if they scarce knew how. Both the boy-players, as Portia and Nerissa, read easily. There were frequent stops to elucidate a word, and it was often found that the copyist had made an error; Will made a note to check them in the master copy. The bookholder read all the parts of the missing actors, and did so as if they were so many bills of lading.

The never-to-be-forgotten moment for Ned occurred when the bookholder stopped as he was about to say a line and said, "There's a line here for a servant of Antonio; just one line. Will wondered if his young brother over there might do it, and Gus thinks he could." Will Kemp, full of good will because he was already enjoying himself as Launcelot Gobbo, said, "Let the lad read now and prove his quality." Several of the company caught the infection of good spirit and urged Ned to go to the table to read, and Master Vincent beckoned him, but with an expression that made the table a gallows. The script was turned toward him and the line indicated by the bookholder's long and scrawny finger.

Richard Burbage spoke kindly. "Be not afraid. I am sure you are a better reader than I. Read it to yourself first, and make it yours before you read it to us."

Ned took the book up. After reading the words to himself as carefully as his nervousness would permit, he read them aloud, and, in doing so, unconsciously imitated George. "Gentlemen, my master Antonio is at his house and desires to speak with you both."

There was some unnecessarily hearty applause, colored with amusement. Richard Burbage said, "That was well spoken, Ned, and the part is yours."

Ned mumbled his thanks and walked back to his seat in triumph. As he did so, Will Kemp said, "Look to your laurels, Master Burbage. This young man's servant is more noble than your king," which sally was greeted with laughter and the reading resumed.

It was past ten o'clock before it was over and the goodnight drinks had been drunk. It was agreed that Burbage, Pope, Gough, and Gilburne should be at the theatre at eight in the morning to work with Will on their parts; the others were to be free until ten, when they would all meet to prepare for the afternoon's performance of *Richard II*.

And so they ventured out into the moonlit night. They went in close groups for protection.

Ned was too excited to pay much attention to the homeward conversation. There was much talk about the new play, and how different Will's

Jew was from Kit Marlowe's. This and much else would have been beyond Ned's understanding even if he had listened carefully. But all he could think of was that Master Phillips had said he would have to wait and wait before he was given a line to speak on the stage, and here he was going to speak in his first play! "Gentlemen, my Master Antonio . . ." How did it go? My master Antonio. That would be Master Phillips.

ELEVEN

THE FIRST PERFORMANCE OF THE NEW PLAY WAS THREE WEEKS AWAY, BUT Ned was not to become involved until the last week. His first week was dominated by playgoing and the most notable experience was Burbage's performance of *Richard III,* on the Saturday.

The Theatre was at its fullest, and Ned found mixing with milling groundlings exciting in itself. Will had warned him to wear his Stratford suit and to carry no money.

A half-hour before the performance began there were already some five hundred people crowded into the ground and hundreds more in the galleries. Ned had entered with the boxholders and vendors before the doors were opened. As long as he had easy mobility he moved about and listened to the spectators. There were those who boasted how many times they had seen the play and those who were seeing it for the first time. There were visitors up from the country, some of them looking nervous, and foreigners who spoke little or no English. Some seemed to have come to eat, for they had large packages of food on which they feasted, hungrily observed by a host of birds flying over them or watching them from the surrounding roof. Then there were the pickpockets who spotted a stranger as unerringly and eagerly as the birds spotted a crumb. One of these, misled by Ned's suit, thought he might provide easy if slender pickings; sometimes these country boys had money and were foolish enough to carry it on them. He smiled and said, "Were do you come from?"

"Stratford-on-Avon," said Ned. The questioner, about whose motives the forewarned boy had no doubts, reminded him of Robin, the ballad-eer; there was the same proud wearing of tattered clothes, and the same hearty yet condescending friendliness.

"I know it not," said the con man, thus dismissing the town as of no significance. "Is it far?"

"Three days' journey on a good horse in good weather."

"Have you been long in the city?"

"Some two and a half weeks."

"Are you alone?"

"Yes."

"Have you seen much of the city?"

"Yes."

"The women?"

Hesitantly Ned replied, "No."

"Then you have seen nothing. To a lusty young gentleman like you, there is no sight like that of a London woman, and I can show you the best of them. But it will take a full and open purse, which I dare swear you have."

From the first mention of women the conversation became intimate. It was made more so by the man's putting his right arm around Ned's right shoulder and bringing his mouth to Ned's left ear, the while his left hand skillfully felt Ned's jerkin in search of his purse which must be hidden there since there was none at his belt.

"I have no money; it is at home," said Ned.

"And where is home?"

"On the South Bank."

The angler paused for a moment, assessing the further possibilities, and decided to throw this unpromising fish back into the sea. With a twisted smile, which commented on his wasted time, he gave Ned a perfunctory pat on the back and moved off to cast his line elsewhere.

At the fourth trumpet, Ned wormed his way through to a group of well-dressed students, some years older than he, who stood in a good position, fairly near but to the right of the stage. Ned wondered why they did not sit on the most expensive gallery benches, not knowing that it was a fashionable affectation, while students, to be groundlings, though some of them sat in a lords' room when their noble parents came to the theatre. As he reached the group, the student nearest him turned and regarded him steadily and suspiciously. Embarrassed and angry, Ned said, "I am no thief, sir." The young aristocrat deigned him no word, but turned back to his fellows. It was not Ned's fingers he had suspected but his ears, for one of the group was talking about the play they had come to see in reckless and treasonable words; nor was he speaking with guarded volume. Ned heard him say, "He was a Welshman, and I hate all Welsh-men, as they hate us. His grandfather stole the widow of that great monarch, Henry V, and he himself stole the throne of England from Richard III, as you will see this afternoon. But Richard was not the monster we shall see in Burbage. That is the fiction of that arch liar, Thomas More, now made doubly a lie by this man Shakespeare."

The young man who had examined Ned said, "Take care, Nutleigh. You speak of the Queen's blood."

" 'Tis twice tainted, from her father and her mother."

Two of his companions were so angered by this that they roughly seized Nutleigh. A struggle ensued and others became involved, trying to separate the quarrelers. Notable among the interveners was the thief whose fingers moved profitably everywhere. Ned denounced him and tried to detain him, but his voice was lost in the growing din. A well but dirtily aimed blow doubled Ned up in pain, and the scoundrel made good his escape.

The confused row did not cease until the final trumpet announced the beginning of the play. Most people there knew or had been told that the play began with a solo appearance of Burbage, and magically the noise gave way to a hush of expectancy.

Burbage waited backstage until the only sound was the twitter of birds. Then he entered. As he limped down to the edge of the stage, a crescendo of applause greeted him. While he waited for it to subside, his Richard Crookback slowly scanned the audience surrounding him on three sides, with an air of enchanting devilry. At last he spoke.

Ned had seen Burbage play every afternoon that week and knew that to be an actor like him was the greatest thing in the world, but he became so absorbed in Burbage's King Richard that he forgot all personal ambition. When the misshapen body lay finally slain, Ned's sympathies were much more with the villainous dead than with the virtuous living. But his speculations were checked by words from the stage:

> "Abate the edge of traitors, gracious Lord,
>   That would reduce these bloody days again
>   And make poor England weep in streams of blood."

Ned felt a great desire to see Burbage after the performance, but the press of people made it impossible to make straight for the stage. He had to float out with them and go around. When he got to the dressing room, his transports of adulation were rudely checked: the kings and nobles were ordinary men again, laughing over the mistakes of the afternoon, none of which Ned had noticed, and a few of them were congratulating themselves on having Sunday free while others had to rehearse *The Merchant* at the theatre. Burbage himself had his tunic off, thus exposing his fake hump, and he was taking a mighty swig of ale. He caught Ned's eye and said, "Were you out there?" Ned just nodded; he could not speak. "Did you like it?" Like it! What feeble words! Ned contented himself with "Yes, sir," and, with an embarrassed smile, moved away.

During his second week in the theatre, Ned was given sundry tasks backstage, helping the tiremen and the stagehands. He longed to see the plays, for they were all different from the week before, but he realized that he never would see them now, for never again would he be out in the audience.

It was in the third week that the excitement really began, for then every morning, from eight to ten, full rehearsals of *The Merchant* took place onstage.

On the Monday morning the action was sketched out by the bookholder, with Will standing by to amplify the instructions and answer questions. Ned was rather bewildered by it all, but gradually he gathered that he would play three different people—only one was a "part" because it had words to say—which would mean that he had three different costumes, and five appearances to make, two as one of the attendants of the Prince of Morocco (John Heminge), two as the servant of Antonio (Augustine Phillips), and one as an attendant at the court of Venice. It seemed that everybody was being pressed into service to "dress" the court, which would be presided over by Will, who was to play the Duke; later, if the play proved successful enough to be added to the repertory he could be replaced to return to his writing. There had been painful instances when a new play had died on its first day of life, for the audience passed judgment swiftly and ruthlessly; there even had been a few cases in which they had noisily refused to hear the play to its end.

Ned was disappointed to find that for his first speech in the theatre he would be clad in a suit of sober gray, as befitted the servant of the melancholy Antonio. He had a very colorful costume as a member of the train of the Prince of Morocco, but two stagehands would be similarly garbed; furthermore, not even Gilbert would be able to recognize his darkened face. (It had been arranged that Gilbert should be there for his debut. Secretly, Ned would have preferred George, but both could not be away from the shop, and George had decided that Gilbert's was the prior claim. George would try to come to the second performance—if there was one.) In the court scene he would be lost to sight under an academic gown, a hat, and a heavy bunch of gray facial hair, which would hang from his ears by wires. Since he had not to open his mouth, not much fastening with gum would be required, and after the court scene he would have to make a fairly quick change back to being Antonio's servant.

Ned had sensed that Richard Burbage was not enthusiastic about the part of Bassanio. He mentioned it to Sam, who said, "I don't blame him. It's *Romeo and Juliet* all over again; the lady's is the better part. Bobbie Gough is lucky. He always is. I wonder if women will ever be players."

This idea shocked Ned. "I hope not, for then nobody would look at the men or listen to the play. But it can never be. The city fathers and the preachers speak out against the theatres now. What would they say if a woman walked onstage? All theatres would be closed at once."

The Sunday which was the eve of the planned first performance of the new play was an exhausting one, and it seemed to Ned that the bewildering activity could never be shaped into a play in time. The bookholder had posted a plot of the play which gave the players some idea of the sequence of the action. Several times people missed entrances because they

were not quick enough in changing costumes. On three occasions the rehearsal was stopped by a brief shower of rain, but when the company was
thus driven indoors they spent the time in solving the problems that had
already arisen. Augustine Phillips seized every opportunity to rehearse
the musicians who had much to do in the play.

Ned was assigned to cue Robert Gough, whenever there was time. As
Portia, Gough had much the longest part and his nervousness seemed to
increase as the opening day approached. Now he started to act the part to
Ned in odd corners, and words which he had gabbled with confidence
fled when he gave them full voice. Unlike Sam Gilburne, Robert Gough
was a secret boy, hesitant and quiet offstage, but transformed into beautiful, witty, and assured queens and ladies onstage.

There was no break for dinner on that Sunday. They all ate what they
could when they could. It was nearly four o'clock before it was decided to
try an all-out run-through. The hired men and extras took a last look at
the plot sheet to make certain that their changes of costume were in the
right order. The stagekeeper checked that all was ready, the bookholder
gave the signal, Augustine Phillips walked out on the stage with two
hired men, and the play had begun.

Ned, feverishly darkening his face, heard the words from the stage,
muffled by curtains and distance. There were so many players in need of
the mirror, which was shared by hired men and apprentices, that Ned
never had long enough at it to ensure an even coloring. Gabriel Spencer,
handsomely garbed as Lorenzo, said in passing, "You are supposed to be
a colored man, not a dirty boy." This increased Ned's nervousness and he
smeared his beautiful costume, making matters worse by trying to rub it
off with his already browned hand. Before he was ready, the bookholder's
assistant was there urgently whispering "Morocco!" Ned hurried to his
place behind John Heminge, who looked imperiously magnificent in
purple and gold. The fanfare betokening a royal entrance sounded and
Ned was walking out onto the stage. As the Moroccan group entered
from one side, Portia and Nerissa, with two attendants, entered from the
other. Ned could not take his eyes from Robert Gough, who was astonishingly beautiful and desirable as Portia. A quick flash from his Stratford
upbringing made Ned feel that there was something morally wrong
about his reaction, but then he recalled the diffident boy he had cued.

During the casket scene, Ned let his attention wander out into the
theatre, and there, sitting alone in the second gallery above the main
entrance, he saw Will, already dressed as the Duke. He thought Will
caught his eye and he felt guilty, because his attention should have been
onstage.

In no time at all, Ned was back in the tiring-room harassed by his first
quick change. He found that the clothes were not the problem, but
getting the color off his face. He had not had the foresight to provide
himself with a piece of rag, and, seeing Ned's desperate plight, one of the
attendants generously let him use a corner of his own rag. Unbelievably

soon, the stage assistant was there with his imperious whisper: "Tubal!" This was the key word used to designate what Ned thought of as his scene. With a last desperate wipe with the rag, which left his face with piebald streaks of sun, he donned his tunic and fumbled with the buttons as he awaited his cue. There it was, from Shylock: ". . . it shall go hard but I will better the instruction . . ."

Ned's words took the three men on stage by surprise, for he was on and speaking loud and clear before Tom Pope had finished his sentence. Antonio's servant received such an angry glare from Shylock as well befitted his Jewish hatred of Christians. Even as he was speaking, Ned realized that he was making all the mistakes possible: too soon, too quick, too loud. But within fifteen seconds he was offstage and glad to be. Salanio and Salarino made the same exit with Ned, and, as they did so, one of them whispered, "Don't worry, lad. 'Tis but a rehearsal, and 'tis better to be early for an entrance than late."

This was but cold comfort for Ned, and he had time to wallow in misery while he changed for the court scene. He went to the mirror and the sight of his streaked face added to his agony. He applied water and drying rag in masochistic fury. Then he faced his next problem in the spirit of assured disaster: the beard. Suppose it fell off? And while Master Pope was speaking? He seized a container of gum and practically bathed his face in the forbidden substance, until a stage assistant snatched the phial from him, reminding him how expensive it was and that he had yet another change back to being Antonio's servant.

Quickly he tried to wipe off some of the gum, but there was no hot water and the rag tended to stick to his face. The long wait had suddenly became a very short one. He strung the hairy adornment over his ears and tenderly patted it into the gum in a few places. Then he tentatively moved his jaws. There was no doubt that the gray beard and moustache were stuck. He contorted his face; the false hair followed every contortion. He knew now that during the long trial scene he would be thinking of but one thing: how could he get the beard off quickly without ruining the expensive appendage?

He had forgotten one thing: Will was presiding over the trial scene, and Ned had never seen him before as an actor. The boy had thoughts of nothing else. It became clear why Will had been chosen, or had chosen himself, for the part. There were others in the company who radiated more imperious authority, but none who had the same combination of quiet command and gentle dignity, so essential to this mercy-loving Duke. Will's concentration on the action was complete, for not only was the Duke hearing a case but the poet was watching his play. Ned's attention wandered far from the play to the hidden life of his brother.

As Ned followed Will in procession from the court, his mind reverted to the beard and the last quick change. He hurried to his place in the tiring-room, unhitched his beard from his ears, and began to pull gently at it. The gum held firm, and Ned began to panic. Other beards around him were coming off with ease. With desperation in his voice he begged a fellow magnifico of Venice for help. Laughing with carefully subdued heartiness, that now clean-faced worthy lent a hand. He warned Ned that it would hurt and began to pull the beard away from the face, being much more careful of the false hair than the real skin. His final wrench caused Ned to emit a squeal, which he quickly managed to muffle.

"Ultima" came the whispered call for the last scene, and Ned was not ready. Augustine Phillips was looking for him as he awaited his cue with Richard Burbage and George Bryan. The cue came and the group walked on. Bassanio and Portia were already talking by the time Ned arrived for his entrance, his face blotched red and with stray hairs attached. He decided to get onstage as unobtrusively as possible. As he did so, Bassanio was saying of Antonio, "Give welcome to my friend." Had there been an audience, there would have been howls of laughter. As it was, George Bryan, Sam Gilburne, and an attendant could not repress a stifled titter. Ned suffered a torment of humiliation, not so much from the laughter as from the slight curl of the lip he had seen on the face of Gabriel Spencer. This was not theatre as he had dreamed of it. This life was not for him. None of these now onstage could ever have been as awkward and inept as he. Now he longed for the play to be over that he might escape from it all.

At the end of the scene, the whole company came onstage as the daylight was beginning to fade. A rehearsal was called for 8 A.M. and all but the sharers and Gough and Gilburne were dismissed; that select group was going to have supper together and iron out some of the rough places revealed by the rehearsal. No one said anything to Ned about his glaringly bad contributions to the afternoon. He would have felt better about it if they had. It was as if he was so bad as to be beneath their criticism.

Ned went to the tiring-room consumed by anger and despair. After the whispered atmosphere of the rehearsal, he was now surrounded by lively chatter and laughter. Was he the joke? In a seething silence he changed into his own clothes. A glimpse of his patched face in the mirror confirmed his mood; viciously he pulled off every disfiguring hair. While he was engaged in this painful activity he saw the reflection of Augustine Phillips as he approached. "Ned," he said in his usual friendly tones as though nothing had happened. "Nick Dodman will take you home. Tell Mistress Phillips I shall be late." Ned could not trust himself to do more than nod, and his mentor walked away, unaware of the hostility he left behind. He needed nobody to take him home; he was no child. And Nick Dodman was the attendant of Bassanio whose hilarity at Ned's late entrance had been most apparent. Ned had no intention of walking home with him or anybody else.

Nick Dodman, an ebullient hearty, swaggered up to his assigned charge. "Hurry, lad. 'Tis getting late, and I have a wife waiting who is getting angrier by the minute. She never believes my tales of late rehearsals—and most times she is right."

Now all Ned's wits were bent on eluding his escort. He finished dressing with deliberate slowness, and surreptitiously kept his eye on Dodman. At last his opportunity occurred; the bookholder came for Dodman and two others who were needed onstage for some change in positioning. Quickly Ned hurried away and out into the lane on which the stage door gave. He felt a heady sense of freedom. He had to get away from the theatre quickly, lest he should be seen and hailed.

As he became aware that daylight was fading, his exciting feeling of escape began to give way to one of danger, but it was titillating rather than frightening.

As he walked down Bishopsgate Street toward the city Ned met but few travelers, and no solitary one on foot like himself. Most were mounted and traveling north, going home in groups for safety after paying Sunday visits in the city. Occasionally a single rider would gallop by, a posthaste courier. Once a noble carriage passed on its way to the city; it had outriders with torches already lit; Ned wondered who was hidden inside the coach; George would have known.

It was dark now; the sky was clouded and there was little moonlight. He was fearful of passing Bethlehem Hospital, where Bedlam mad folk were kept. He crossed to the left side of the road to give the place a wide berth. His apprehension increased his awareness of an eerie silence, but, just as he passed the infamous institution, an unearthly scream rang out, which was taken up by others. It seemed to Ned as if they had been occasioned by sight of him. He broke into a pell-mell run, and did not stop until he was within the city walls. There he paused to recover his breath and his wits, and, as he stopped in the shelter of a darkened house, it began to rain. While he crouched into the wall for further shelter, four men with a lantern approached; two had pikes and two had cudgels. They were the watch.

They stopped at sight of Ned and the leader questioned him. "What do you here?"

"I'm going home. I'm a player coming late from rehearsal."

"That is no occupation for an honest man. Where are your fellows?"

"I left them in the theatre."

"Left them? Why?" Before Ned could think of an acceptable answer to this, the leader went on. "Anyone walking alone at night is on mischief bent."

One of the others said, "Let us give him to the press and make some pennies. He would make a stout sailor for the Queen's navy."

A sense of real danger overtook Ned. He had heard scaring tales of the pressing of young men into the navy, where they were lost without word for years at a time, and sometimes forever. He must escape. But how? There were four of them, and armed.

While one with a cudgel guarded Ned, the other three were having a mumbled discussion as to what to do with him. Ned moved. His guard put a restraining hand on him. Consciously imitating the blazing authority of Richard Burbage as he confronted the halberdiers in *Richard III,* Ned said, "Unhand me, villain. Unmannered dog! Knew you but whom you dare to touch, you would tremble." The manner of Robin of London, George's speech, and Burbage's performance were all in this.

The leader began to growl his authority, but Ned overrode him. "Speak not to me. I come of a noble house whose name would have you in awe, chose I to speak it. If I dress in mean attire and walk alone for may own purposes, 'tis naught to you." He had been sufficiently impressive to make the watch hesitate. Quick to spy his advantage, he decided to add a note of gracious condescension. "But you are good and worthy men, and but do your duty and do it well." He now addressed the leader directly. "Your name, that I may tell it to my noble father."

Almost mechanically the man said, "Thomas Upham."

"Thomas Upham. I shall remember it. And now I beg that you forget that you have seen me, for I will whisper my secret: I have been wenching in Shoreditch, and the drab took all my money, but not quite. I have yet a few pennies and I would bestow them on you that you might drink to the health of Her Majesty and our noble house." Here he took out his few coins and gave them to the leader who received them almost unconsciously. Nothing Ned could have bought with them could have matched the pleasure he received from the effect of his manner on the men.

As he bade them, "Goodnight, good men," he stalked off into the pouring rain with as stately a gait as he could muster. His instinct was to run as soon as he was clear of the watch, but now it was as important to him to maintain his act as to escape. He walked slowly and never looked back.

When he came to Gracious Street many people were abroad, in spite of the darkness and the rain. The Bull Inn, the Cross Keys, the Bell Inn, and the Boar's Head were all inviting with warm laughter and happy chatter. But Ned plodded past oblivious of all but that every step was nearer food, dryness, and bed.

At home, Mistress Phillips was all solicitude for the wet and miserable lad who needed warmth and comfort. She told him to go upstairs, and put on a dry shirt and a woolen robe which she gave him. In the meantime she would heat up a mutton stew; this was no night for a cold supper.

Ned was silent and morose as he ate his meal. Mistress Phillips questioned him about the rehearsal, and she attributed the brevity of his answers to tiredness, but Ned was in misery because he had added to his folly onstage the foolhardiness of his walk home. And tomorrow there would be awkward questions to face.

The following day dawned bright, and the boys were awakened at first light. Ned was dragged up from a nightmare in which he was drowning at sea while Master Phillips and Will looked on from the deck of a ship and laughed at his cries for help. And there above his waking eyes was the face of Master Phillips, stern in accusation.

"Good morning, sir," he said. His pretense was going to be that he was quite unaware of any concern he had caused or danger he had run.

Master Phillips did not return the greeting. "Why did you not wait for Nick Dodman?"

"I thought he might be a long time and I was hungry."

"Then why did you not tell me or someone else?"

"I did not want to trouble you, sir, because everyone was busy with the play, and I knew the way home."

Sam, who was dressing, had eager ears for the conversation, but Master Phillips turned to him. "Hurry downstairs, Sam. I wish to speak to Ned alone."

As soon as Sam was gone, Master Phillips resumed his inquisition. "Ned, you are not telling me the truth. You knew you should not walk home alone and in the dark. Why did you? Did something happen in the rehearsal that upset you?" Ned kept silent. "Players have delicate spirits; what others would laugh at makes them angry or makes them weep. It was your first full rehearsal and it may be you were not ready for it. I noted you were late for one entrance."

Thus encouraged, Ned finally blurted out his whole sad story. Master Phillips listened and smiled with indulgent understanding, and then said, "Rehearsals are there for us to learn from our mistakes. You will see that this afternoon will be different, especially after another rehearsal this morning."

And it was. The sound of the gathering audience began to grow, and at five minutes before the final trumpet, Cuthbert Burbage came back to say that the house was full for a Monday, especially the first gallery, which was the most expensive, and that both lords' rooms were taken; Sir Walter Raleigh was with company in one, and in the other some gentlemen newly come to knighthood on the battlefield of Cadiz. But Cuthbert had bad news too: a few black clouds threatened rain.

As the last trumpet signaled the start of the play, Will, already dressed as the Duke, came to Ned and said, "This is the beginning, Ned. Today you become a player. 'Tis a good calling, and I am glad to welcome you to it."

Ned could do no more than smile his gratitude. All the morning he had been grateful for Will's silence about yesterday.

Even the usually garrulous quipster, Nick Dodman, was restrained. All he said was, "You went home alone then. You must have gotten wet." Only a strict injunction from Master Phillips—or Will—could have caused such restraint.

As Ned waited to make his entrance with the Prince of Morocco, he could feel the difference in the occasion. "They" were out there, eager to enjoy, to praise, to damn. They were even now in the act of judging whether this new play should live or die. So far they had delighted in Portia and Nerissa, approved of Bassanio and Antonio, reveled in Gratiano, and been somewhat puzzled by Shylock. Shylock had seemed at first sight to be the typical, villainous Jewish usurer, but the audience already, in his first scene, was feeling a difference, a difference which Pope emphasized in a way he had never revealed in rehearsal: you could certainly count on this Jew to be ruthless and cruel, but he had suffered cruelty too, and at the hands of the good and gentle Antonio. The audience was puzzled and intrigued. They shared Bassanio's troubled doubts when he said, "I like not fair terms and a villain's mind."

This was almost the Moroccan cue. As Ned listened to it, the Prince, John Heminge, turned to Ned, smiled, and patted him on the shoulder. The fanfare sounded; they were on. The splash of color and pageantry as both parties entered was greeted with gasps of delight, and Ned felt an ecstatic glow that he was a part of it.

When they came offstage, Ned did not go the tiring-room, for he had no change to make before his next entrance. The bookholder understood his excitement and gestured him an unobtrusive place to stand. Others who were not changing also found places to hear the audience's reaction to Will Kemp's first scene.

Launcelot Gobbo appeared, and there was a gleeful roar of welcome as he clumped in his clownish shoes down to the limit of the stage. The audience was delighted to find that he was alone, because this promised a typical Kemp diversion, and they were not disappointed. Ned was amazed by the transformation in Kemp. He had given little indication of his skill in rehearsal, but now, when it seemed to Ned that the audience had laughed themselves dry, he was surprised by a louder burst than before.

During the second Moroccan scene it began to rain preliminary drops that threatened worse. Ned was eaten by the fear that he might not be allowed to make his speech. The audience would endure light rain, and the players would shrink their scenes back under the canopy, but heavy rain frequently forced abandonment of a performance.

While Ned washed his face of "the shadowed livery of the burnished sun," and changed into Antonio's servant, his ears strained to catch the sound of the rain. It became clearer and clearer and though the performance continued, the actors were raising their voices to be heard above the rain.

The "Tubal" call came and Ned was ready. He took his place behind Shylock whose entrance was a couple of minutes before his. Pope was fuming and cursing the rain under his breath for it was going to spoil his favorite speech. Now there was movement in the audience; some of the groundlings were leaving, others were pressing against the galleries for cover, those in the front rows of the galleries were trying to find places further back.

Shylock was on. The three players were bunched close under the canopy for the wind had begun to send the rain in search of them. Angered by the elements and the movement of the audience, Pope put such venom into Shylock's speech on revenge that it became a memorable moment for all who heard it. Then Ned entered and made certain that everybody heard his line, but at sight of an insignificant servant the audience, momentarily caught by Shylock, was released to the rain again. In spite of valiant efforts by Pope and Cowley, the performance gradually petered out into complete inattention and was abandoned at the end of the scene.

Thus Edmund Shakespeare, at the age of sixteen years and a few months, became a player, but his initiation filled him with frustration and disappointment, and he began to wonder if the theatre was the right place for him. His spirits were not cheered by a passing remark of Gabriel Spencer: "You brought us bad fortune."

TWELVE

As THE PHILLIPSES AND THEIR LODGERS SAT AT SUPPER, MUCH OF THE CON-versation was aimed at consoling Ned for the afternoon's disappointment with the assurance that he had acquitted himself well. There was talk of Pope's Shylock. Mistress Phillips, like most members of the audience, had been puzzled by it; she felt unsettled at feeling some sympathy for a villainous usurer, but it seemed that Will had been pleased by Pope's Jew, insofar as he could judge from backstage. He did not clarify the ambiguity by saying, "Villains too are men."

They were discussing the weather prospects for the morrow—the rain had already stopped—when there was a clamant knock on the door, so urgent as to be startling. Mistress Phillips made to answer it, but her husband restrained her and went himself. He opened the door to reveal John Heminge and a hired man, Henry Condell. Master Condell was a handsome, quiet man, who seemed always to be reading. Sam, who had supplied Ned with pithy and often scandalous biographies of most of the company, had had little to say about Condell except that he was hard put to feed and clothe a large family, though it was not as large as Master Heminge's who seemed to be breeding a whole company of players. Heminge and Condell were friends and lived near each other in Cripplegate.

Heminge was obviously disturbed. Without more ado he said, "It's Spencer. He's in prison. He has killed a man."

Once the shock of this bald announcement was absorbed, Master Phillips said, "Let us go into the music room." It was tacitly assumed that the "us" referred to the four men, and as they left the living room, Mistress Phillips and the two boys felt cheated. They immediately fell to conjecture and surmise and Sam was ready with tales of Spencer's quick temper: he always carried a sword and there were rumors that he had used it. As for the afternoon, all Sam knew was that Spencer had been suffering from toothache, a common enough affliction and scarcely one to lead to murder. He had probably been drunk again.

Mistress Phillips kept repeating what a pity it was that such a good actor and such a handsome man should be so taken with the devils of drunkenness and bad temper. Suddenly she saw the significance of the coming of Henry Condell; he was to replace Spencer as Lorenzo the following day, and he had been brought to work with Master Shakespeare. Abandonment of the performance of a new play because of rain always led to a second performance the following day. "Let me see. He played one of those people in the beginning of the play. Does he have a name?" asked Mistress Phillips.

"Salanio," said Sam.

"I don't remember that."

"Nobody calls him it, nor Salarino. Only Salerio is named, but you didn't hear that either, because the rain came too soon."

Ned felt it was time he showed that he was in the play too, so he said, "It's a joke in the tiring-room. They are called the three Sals, but it's the costumes that have the names, not the men."

During the conversation, their attention was really on the door of the music room, and at last Master Phillips reappeared. He looked grave as he spoke. "You will want to know what happened. So far as Master Heminge has found out, Spencer went to a barber's to have a tooth drawn. It was in Cripplegate, near Master Heminge's house. That is why he was sent for. It seems that Spencer cried out in pain, and one who was waiting to have his beard trimmed laughed. On the instant Spencer was up and with his sword out. In blind rage he attacked the man who had laughed, who seized a brass candlestick to defend himself. Spencer ran him through and killed him. Spencer escaped, but the hue and cry is out and doubtless he will be caught, if he has not already been. 'Tis a woeful happening, and one that brings disgrace on all players."

"What will you do tomorrow?" asked Mistress Phillips.

"That is it I come about. Master Condell will play Lorenzo, and we wondered if Ned here could replace him as Salanio." Ned's head spun. "He is ten years too young, though he does not look it." He allowed himself a smile as he added, "But I'm sure he feels it is not ten minutes too soon for him. Come, lad."

In a daze Ned followed Master Phillips into the music room. The three men already there regarded him critically as he entered. It was John Heminge who spoke. "Sit down, Ned. Think you you can learn Salanio by tomorrow?"

Henry Condell interposed, as if to assure him. " 'Tis but some fifty lines."

Fifty lines. Were it five hundred, Ned could have learned the part with ease. Why did they not let Condell keep his fifty-line part and let him play Lorenzo? But all he said in answer to Master Heminge's question was, "Yes, sir."

"Think not this is usual we do. 'Tis a counsel of desperation for a lad your age and an apprentice so new to be given such a part, but you are a comely lad with a good voice, and a handsome beard will give you years—though we can scarce expect you to grow one by tomorrow afternoon." All greeted this with laughter, in which Ned joined uncertainly. "When we debated who we could get at this hour for Salanio, it was your brother who suggested you might play it." Ned wished it had been Master Phillips so that he would not have to owe everything to Will.

"It seemed good to us, for Master Condell has the part with him and can help you," John Heminge continued. "He will stay here the night to work on Lorenzo with the author, and if the author is willing to entrust you with his Salanio, why should we have doubt? But now I trifle precious time. You all have work to do. We meet at the theatre at nine o'clock." They all rose as he said, "I wish you all a goodnight. May God bless your labors and curse the man who made them necessary."

As soon as John Heminge left, Will took charge. Mistress Phillips and Sam were sent off to bed, Master Phillips was to go with Ned into the music room to begin work on Salanio while Will and Henry Condell worked in the living room on copying the part of Lorenzo from the original manuscript.

Ned received the part from Henry Condell and went into the music room, his mind a jumble of hopes and fears about the morrow. If he played Salanio well, would he get other parts and, perhaps, become a hired man, the youngest there had ever been? If he did, people would say it was because he was Will's brother. He owed Salanio to Will. Ned blessed and cursed his brother in the same thought.

Now he was reading the part carefully, preparatory to reading it aloud to Master Phillips, and the very first speech contained words that rang true for him:

> And every object that might make me fear
> Misfortune to my ventures, out of doubt
> Would make me sad.

It was past midnight when Ned finally got to bed. He had never been up so late before. His eyes ached from strain of candlelight and he was chagrined that, although the part of Lorenzo was three times as long as that of Salanio, Condell had learned it in half the time Ned had taken for his part. He wasn't even certain that he would know it in the morning. Master Phillips had told him to keep saying the lines to himself as he undressed and was falling asleep, and they would be safely his when he awoke. Ned was determined to wake early to go over them once again, but this he failed to do; in fact, Augustine Phillips had much trouble to shake him awake, and this in spite of the fact that he had let both boys sleep a half-hour later than usual.

The day was clear and crisp with no threat of rain. As they washed and dressed and made their beds, Sam bombarded Ned with talk about Gabriel Spencer—Had he been caught? Would he be hanged? They argued about what should happen. Sam wanted Spencer hanged to prevent him from killing more men. He said, "He may have a scholar's tongue, but he has a murderer's heart."

But Ned said he felt some strange sympathy with the dangerous man, even though he had suffered his hostility.

"As well feel sorry for a viper," Sam replied.

"I do. God gave him his poison."

Before they left for the theatre, Will cued Condell, and Master Phillips cued Ned. The boy had great difficulty with the speech in which Salanio reported the distress of Shylock; he got "daughter" and "ducats" mixed up. When he told this to Will, his answer was, "Don't worry. Shylock got them mixed up too."

All the offstage talk at the theatre during the morning rehearsal was of Gabriel Spencer. He had been easily caught, "too drunk even to escape." Now he was in prison, awaiting trial. Much to Ned's surprise, there was general agreement that Spencer would not hang. Dodman said cynically, "Scholars and gentlemen always get off."

"But he was a player too," objected another hired man, "and if he comes before a Puritan justice, that will go hard for him."

"The hanging verse will save him," said Dodman.

While the tireman was finding a suitable costume for the new Salanio, Ned asked him about the "hanging verse." Nat Tremayne, who was in a good humor because of Ned's wide-eyed enjoyment of the finery he was to wear, was pleased to expatiate. " 'Tis called 'Benefit of Clergy,' and comes from ancient times when few but the clergy could read. To hang a man who could read and write was a loss of a precious person. So for a first offense, the convicted cleric was given a verse from the psalms to read, and thus his life was spared. And so 'twill doubtless be with Gabriel Spencer, though he is more acquainted with heathen authors than with his Bible."

"And will he come back to the company, think you?" asked Ned with as much nonchalance as he could muster, for his stake in the answer was great.

" 'Tis to be doubted, though he is a good player. Maybe when memories are dulled, he will come back."

"But how will he live?"

"How does any player live who is not a sharer? Not all are brothers of Master Shakespeare." This last was said innocently, but it hurt. All the morning Ned had been too aware of covert glances from hired men and assistants; he was certain that they were making sarcastic remarks about an apprentice, and a raw one, being promoted to the part for which a new hired man should have been brought in.

While the tireman was looking for a suitable beard, Will came to say he had sent a messenger to Gilbert to tell him Ned's news. The boy was overwhelmed with gratitude to his brother for such thoughtfulness, gratitude made all the greater by guilt for the resentment he had been feeling.

The bits and pieces of rehearsal had gone fairly well in the morning. Apart from the fitting in of the new Lorenzo and the new Salanio, a lugubrious stagehand was commandeered into taking the various nothings that had been Ned's. He was not at all excited about having to speak a line, and it was very dubious that it would ever be heard. Nick Dodman whispered to Ned that that was their best hope, for if it were heard, it would cause the biggest laugh of the afternoon; it sounded exactly like an invitation to a funeral.

It was a cool, bright afternoon, with no chance of rain. The first trumpet sounded all too soon for Ned. He dressed with nervous hands and Nat the tireman gummed on with great care the beard and moustache which exactly suited Ned's own fair hair. He treated the boy as a painter would his canvas, and the subject was surprised and delighted by the Salanio who looked back at him from the mirror. Nat crept up behind and as a final touch attached a dazzling earring to Ned's left ear.

By the fourth trumpet the sounds of the audience were loud and lively. Ned was ready, his opening words running through his brain over and over again. Several people came up to wish him success. He noticed that they did not do the same to Henry Condell, but then he was just doing another day's work. What Ned had no time to realize was that Condell would have new parts every day; there was little sleep for him in the weeks ahead, for he was taking over all the Spencer parts, whereas Ned would revert tomorrow to a backstage assistant; not even nothings for him for some time.

Just before the last trumpet sounded, Will came to Ned, who was already lined up with Augustine Phillips and Nick Dodman to go on. He grasped Ned's hand and said, "I know you are going to do well and I'm proud of you." Then he added, "Gilbert and George are in the audience; they closed the shop." Not for a moment did Ned doubt that he was the cause of their being there, not the first performance of an important new play by Will. He did not even wish Will well.

Suddenly he was consumed by nervousness. He could not go on. He could not remember the words. He would make a fool of himself. And there was the last trumpet, sounding doom, not the beginning of the play. The hubbub began to subside. They were waiting, waiting to laugh at him.

Augustine Phillips sensed the young actor's panic and inwardly commended it as a good sign. He was far from being in a state of calm assurance himself. He put his arm around the boy and hugged him hard. His smile and the understanding in his eyes made words unnecessary. Then they were on.

The performance was a complete success. Even the lugubrious manner and funereal delivery of Antonio's messenger were taken to imply the imminent danger of his master and added a spice of suspense that not even Will could have anticipated. Yet, was there anything that surprised Will? In the theatre—or in life? These thoughts had been prompted in Ned by hearing Augustine Phillips say to the bookholder, "You were against it, but Will knew what he was doing."

"He always does," said Tom Vincent, but coming from his sour mouth it did not sound like a compliment.

After the performance there was a great air of triumph backstage. Pope made history with his Shylock. His Jew provoked the laughter and the hisses expected of the stock character, but there was something more which crystallized into an uncomfortable sympathy. Gough was radiant as Portia; no real woman could have looked more beautiful or been more captivating. Burbage could do no wrong, but he had made something remarkable out of Bassanio by showing how the dashing adventurer changed into an adoring lover. For Kemp the play was an excuse, some of it tedious, for him to display his brilliant, clownish skill, and he was and would be buoyed up for some hours by the waves of laughter he had caused; he even later tried to persuade Heminge and other sharers to repeat the play the following day, an unheard of procedure. Quiet Condell was wreathed in smiles; not only did he get through an ordeal, but he made something memorably exquisite of the speech about music; this speech was beautifully enhanced by the offstage musicians, and it was to them that both Augustine Phillips and Will Shakespeare went with their thanks and congratulations immediately after the performance.

And Ned? It had all been so wonderful that Signor Salanio was very reluctant to change into Edmund Shakespeare. Mistress Phillips was there to greet him in the tiring-room; she had come through the door from the second gallery while the company was still receiving the vociferous plaudits of the crowd. Her face was wet with tears and she was beyond words, but she crushed Ned to her bosom, and happily sobbed into his ear. Then Gilbert and George were there, shaking Ned's hand and patting his back, both gushing compliments. They sought Ned out first, before even going to congratulate Will. George was bubbling with delight, particularly about Ned's appearance and showered compliments on Nat when he came to remove the fragile beard. George himself was more handsomely arrayed than had been Burbage in Bassanio's wooing costume, and he caught all eyes in the tiring-room, but particularly those of the connoisseur, Nathaniel Tremayne. The two adorners of peacocks were indeed happily met, and as they twittered together, Ned was filled with distaste. Gilbert sensed it and suggested to George that they should go to see Will.

All the company had supper together, and it was a hearty one with much drinking. By tacit agreement there was no talk at any table of Gabriel Spencer. Ned sat with the apprentices and was amazed to find that the glorious and witty Portia was again the diffident and monosyllabic Gough. Their table was dominated by a battle of wits between Sam Gilburne and Will Eccleston, who had played Jessica, but Ned listened to it very little, contenting himself with an occasional obligatory guffaw; the silence of Gough was much more to his liking. He decided that the world was divided into loud and silent men, and the most silent of all, the most secret, was his own brother Will. He looked toward him at the top table. There he was, smiling gently as Kemp continued his clowning. As if in response to Ned's look, Will turned to him, and his smile broadened into one of happy approval. Never had the brothers been so close.

Book Two

1598

THIRTEEN

Ned's eighteenth birthday had been the happiest in his life, for on that day he became a hired man in the company of the Lord Chamberlain's Men. (The players had resumed their old title a year before when their patron, Lord Hunsdon, had like his father been appointed Lord Chamberlain.) It was true that Ned's salary was only the minimum of six shillings a week which did not go far in London, but he was his own man at last. All the more so because on the day after Ned's birthday, one month before, Will had left for Stratford and the date of his return remained indefinite. Will had purchased New Place the year before, and Anne and the two girls now lived there. Some mysterious business about the house had caused Will's hasty departure, and he had seemed a troubled man when he left.

Now it was a beautiful Monday morning in early June. With the other members of the company, Ned was in the Curtain Theatre preparing for the afternoon's performance. Some difficulties about the lease of the ground on which the Theatre stood had closed that building to the company temporarily; there were underground mutterings that they would never get back to it. The Curtain was unsatisfactory because it was too small; it could not take enough money and the players were cramped, both on and off stage.

The play that afternoon was *The Merchant of Venice*. It had proved to be a firm favorite and was a sturdy item in the repertory twenty months after its first performance, though there had been some changes in the cast. John Heminge, happy to save a salary, doubled the Prince of Morocco with the Duke of Venice, and a vibrant and dashing actor, William Sly, had replaced George Bryan as Gratiano. Master Bryan had abandoned the false pageantry of the stage for the real pageantry of the Palace; he had always been dazzled by the pomp of the great and had finally decided that "it were better to be a groom in earnest than a duke in jest." His place as a sharer had been bought by Henry Condell. He had been helped in the purchase by a loan from his friend, John

Heminge, who had been motivated in the transaction not solely by friendship but by the interests of the company; Henry Condell was a handsome and reliable player, but, almost more important, he was a shrewd judge of a script and had become the principal reader for the company.

The most notable change in the cast of the afternoon's play was that Portia was now played by Christopher Beeston. Robert Gough had out-grown the women's parts. Ned was amazed at how well the boy had taken his relegation to small bits and nothings after being a leading player for several years. Gough had bounded into manhood with a will, and was already devotedly in love. The girl who had caught his eye and his heart was Elizabeth Phillips, the sister of Augustine Phillips, as much younger than her brother as Ned was younger than Will. Both Ned and Sam had tried to attract the beautiful Elizabeth, but she was put off by Ned's air of experience and Sam's flippancy; in Robert she had found her perfect mate.

Sam too had lost the part of Nerissa, and in *The Merchant of Venice* was now playing the one-line servant and the sundry nothings for which Ned had originally been cast. Sam still took some female parts, older women with tart tongues, but was beginning to be best known for the impudent youngsters he played; to see him was to smile in preparation for some cheeky witticism.

As Ned was dressing in his favorite costume as Salanio, an assistant came to tell him he was wanted in the bookholder's room.

Ned was surprised to find several of the sharers crowded into the tiny room, apparently waiting for him. It was John Heminge who spoke.

"Ned, we want you to leave for Stratford tomorrow." Ned's immediate reaction was a confusion of reluctance and eagerness; he did not want to leave London, but he had not been home for nearly two years. "You will take three letters for Will with you, one from Master Cuthbert Burbage, one from Master Richard Burbage, and one from me." An immediate question formed in Ned's mind which John Heminge's next sentence answered. "If that were all, we could send them by a carrier, but we want you to talk for us to Will too, and for that purpose we must first talk with you. Tonight Master Phillips has invited four of us to supper and after-wards we will give you our thoughts and words to convey to your brother." Master Heminge continued in a solemn tone, "We are putting out trust in you Ned, and that is an honor for one so young. At first it was thought that I or Master Phillips should make the journey, but consideration told us that you might make the better messenger. And it is easier to replace you in the company while you are away, and besides, it is high time you returned home to show them that the boy has become a man. You shall have a good horse and ample money for comfort on the journey. What say you?"

"If you wish it, I shall be happy to go."

As Ned went back to the tiring-room, one of the assistants who was standing in as nearly a remote corner as the Curtain would allow called to him with a commanding "Hsst!"

The caller said, "Here, take this. The gentleman said that nobody was to see me giving it to you." He thrust a piece of paper into Ned's hand and was away.

Ned moved to where there was sufficient light to read the message. It said, "Dear Master Edmund Shakespeare: I must see you after this performance. I shall wait for you at the main entrance. I shall not keep you long, for it is better that the others know not that we have met. I shall know you, if you know not me. Anon, anon, sir. One who hopes you will befriend him that he in turn may befriend you. Ben Jonson."

Jonson's cryptic, "Anon, anon, sir," filled Ned with pleasure. It referred to his performance as Francis, the tavern drawer, in Will's *Henry IV*. The play had first been given the previous summer and was immediately established as one of the greatest successes of the company. Pope's Falstaff, Burbage's Prince Hal, and Sly's Hotspur had all found enthusiastic acceptance, but Ned, in a tiny part, had caught the fancy too, and his harried, "Anon, anon, sir" became a catch-cry of the town; Ned was hailed with it by friendly strangers on the street. It was even rumored that, after the Queen saw the play at her Palace of Whitehall during the Christmas festivities, she laughingly used it the following day to the Earl of Essex when he dared to show some impatience at being kept waiting. And now here was the much-talked-about Ben Jonson using it again.

Throughout the performance that afternoon Ned kept thinking about the man who, it was said, would someday rival Will. Jonson was as public a person as Will was private, and a better player offstage than on, where he had failed to cut much of a figure. A year before *The Isle of Dogs*, a play by him and Tom Nashe, had been performed by a new company, the Earl of Pembroke's Men, at the splendid new theatre, The Swan. Though Tom Nashe had escaped, three players had been caught and taken to prison for performing a piece so scurrilous and seditious that the city fathers had ample excuse to close down all theatres for the whole season. One of the captured players had been Ben Jonson; another had been Gabriel Spencer.

Spencer's learning had saved him from the noose for his barbershop murder, but the Lord Chamberlain's Men had thought it discreet not to rehire him. However, he was such a good actor that he readily found employment in the new company, and his venomous delivery added poison to the offending text of *The Isle of Dogs*. Indeed, one wag had said, "Ben Jonson was imprisoned for his bad acting, and Gabriel Spencer for his good acting."

Ben's promising reputation as a playwright was based upon two comedies, both entirely of his own making, *The Tale of a Tub* and *The Case Is Altered*, but it was the scandal of *The Isle of Dogs* that Ned had heard most about, necessarily so because the play had affected the lives of all the Lord Chamberlain's Men, and not least his own. The closing of the theatres for the whole summer had sent the company out on the road, but it was a skeleton company and Ned had been left behind. He was given a full program of self-improvement and a vague assignment to assist Cuthbert Burbage when called upon, but he had plenty of free time. He made the most of it and in the process London had become his very own city.

Bulking large in tales of Ben Jonson had been his rows with Gabriel Spencer. It seemed that Ben had an inordinate love of Latin and Greek authors and prided himself on knowledge of them, acquired without benefit of university. Gabriel Spencer scorned the amateur and baited him on occasion, so subtly that only Ben's sensitivity could feel the barb that was unnoticed by others. Ned's sympathies were entirely with Ben, for he too had felt Spencer's cruel innuendoes.

After the performance, Ned went around to the main entrance of the theatre. There were still some people standing in groups outside. Several recognized Ned and some acknowledged him with a smile and a wave. A man approached him; there was no doubt that it was Ben Jonson. He had an assertive rather than a commanding figure, was of middle height, and looked older than his twenty-six years by reason of an untrimmed beard and a drinker's paunch. There was about his face an unsettling irregularity that was lost in the broad smile with which he greeted Ned. He said, "Your fellows call you Ned, and I would be one of them. I pray you will honor me by calling me Ben. Come; we must talk much in little."

Without saying a word, but already well disposed toward his new companion, Ned followed him. It was soon clear that he was expected to listen, not to speak.

"I would take you to a tavern, but taverns have long ears and long tongues. Moreover, you must waste no time in getting home, so I will bear you company as long as need be, and some other time we will pledge our friendship in good canary. You have a meeting tonight that means much to me. That is why I sought you out."

Ned could not resist interrupting with, "How did you know about that?"

"Because I shall be one of the subjects they will talk about or, to be more true, a play of mine. It is a good play, Ned, a new kind of play, a true play about men and women we all know. Not about kings and princes and battles of long ago fought by ridiculous armies of two or three stagehands smeared with buckets of blood from a slaughterhouse. I have known real battle and real blood and 'tis a shameful sham to mimic them on the stage."

Jonson pulled himself up. Such implied criticism of Shakespeare's histories was not likely to commend him to the author's brother. "My play is different. 'Tis called *Every Man in His Humour*. I had expected that Master Henslowe would seize upon it for his Admiral's Men, but he is afeared to put on anything as new and fresh as this play of mine. I have taken it to the Lord Chamberlain's Men, but their counsels are divided. It rests with your brother to make the judgment, and you will carry the play to him. He and I have not met, but we will. We will. Of that I have no doubt. Tell him I admire him, and that is not empty flattery to gain my way. He is older than I, and much in his mind and his pen are foreign to me. But in his last play, *Henry IV*, the tavern scenes are kin to my muse, and I would give much that his Falstaff were mine.

"I will be honest with you, Ned. I have a wife and children, and the larder is thin. But I beg not charity; only honest reward for work of merit. Yet I would be helped if I were given a part in my own play. There is one that fits me, body and soul: Signor Giuliano. I made no mention of it to Master Heminge, but tell your brother. One thing more: there is a good part for you too—the son, Lorenzo. Speak well for me and my play, and I will do as much for you and your part. When next we meet, may you be my Lorenzo. Farewell, good friend."

Without waiting for a reply, Ben strode off and entered a nearby tavern without a backward glance.

Ned stood for a moment, benumbed by the impact of the forceful Ben and his long monologue. As he resumed his way, the dominant thought in his mind was that Ben's new play had a "good part" for him. But why had Philip Henslowe refused the play? It must be a poor one; or a dangerous one. Perhaps all the sharers were against it and had merely used Will as an excuse for dealing with Ben, who Ned surmised could be mightily persistent.

CONVERSATION AT THE SUPPER TABLE, AS IF BY AGREEMENT, AVOIDED THE reason for the presence of the four guests: Richard and Cuthbert Burbage, John Heminge, and Henry Condell. There was talk of the afternoon's performance; of a strange new book said to have been dictated by the ghost of Robert Greene, the notorious and dissolute writer now six years dead; of a recent disturbance at Oxford, in which students had clashed with armed citizens; of the deterioration of the neighborhood in which Heminge and Condell lived, by the division of good houses into poor tenements; of the health of the hostess who was happily six months pregnant again, eager for a newcomer to replace the baby who had only lived a year. They were waited on at table by Letty, an orphan whom the Phillips household had rescued from poverty and mistreatment.

As soon as the meal was over, the sharers retired with Ned into the music room. They began by delivering to him the three sealed letters which had been mentioned in the afternoon.

John Heminge took upon him to open the dialogue. He said, "We each of us have something for you to convey to Will, though Gus is here as our host and to see to it that you are well prepared and provided for." Ned was flattered by the intimacy. This was the first time anyone had spoken of Master Phillips as Gus to him. "Each of us will restrict ourselves to one subject to prevent confusion, though we all are interested in all of them. I will begin with William Kemp, a sore subject." There was some slight but meaningful laughter. "Tell Will his promised *Much Ado About Nothing* is urgent. For nearly two years Kemp has been kept dangling. Now he is threatening to leave. You know how bad-tempered he has become. If he should join the Admiral's Men, it would be a grievous loss to us."

Augustine Phillips interjected, "He would never do that. He barks and threatens, but 'tis no more."

Richard Burbage added, "It's the *Henry IV* that has soured him. There was nothing for him in that, and now he knows that Will is working on another *Henry IV* play, and that he can expect nothing in that."

Henry Condell said, "He told me the other day that Will hates clowns, and maybe he will write no more such parts."

Heminge retorted, "That is nonsense. There will be other comedies and other parts for Kemp, but Will must prove it by giving us *Much Ado,* and giving it soon. Tell him, Ned, how Kemp is behaving."

Ned now felt confident enough to add his own observation of Kemp. "This afternoon when he was taking leave of Jessica, he kept coming back and crying more and more; he had soaked a kerchief in water."

Heminge quickly changed his mind. "On second thought, Ned, don't tell Will that or anything like it. It will but determine him never to write for Kemp again. Tell him rather that the whole town awaits his new comedy."

Richard Burbage now spoke with a quiet seriousness. "My message is about the next *Henry IV* play. I know Will is finding it difficult. He told me 'twould be impossible, because the story must be the same in essence —another conspiracy against the King. Tell him what matters is how the wicked Prince became the good King, and let the people have more and more of Falstaff; they cannot have too much. Beg him to persevere. Hint that the Queen would like to see the new play this coming Christmas, because she enjoyed the first one so much last Christmas."

Heminge now turned to Cuthbert Burbage, who began to speak with an air of troubled mystery. "I cannot tell you, Ned, all I would tell Will, for there is a secret brewing that none but a few of us must know. Nor is it in that letter of mine you carry. That but begs Will to return, for we need his help and counsel. Since our father died last year, Richard and I have had a burden to bear that is too heavy for us. Richard is a player and has no mind for aught else. And I am not the adventurer my father was. But Will is poet, player, and man of affairs too, and it is the man of affairs whose help I need now. You know that the Burbage lease on the

Theatre ran out last year and a new one is not settled yet. The landlord, Giles Alleyn, gets harder and harder. That is why we play at the Curtain. But 'tis not good enough for us, and now we have a plan. I can say no more. Just entreat your brother to return. Tell him that when I speak to one of the sharers about the plan, whoever it is, he always asks, 'What does Will say?' "

Finally, Heminge said to Condell, "And so we come to you, Henry, but before you speak, I want Ned to know that there is difference between us this time. So far, Ned, we have been as one in all you have heard, but now we are divided."

Condell indicated a leather pouch as he spoke. "I have a play here which I want you to carry to Will. We need his judgment. It is by Ben Jonson. I like it greatly and think we should do it, but I am alone in my liking of it."

Heminge said testily, " 'Tis not the play I mind so much as the playwright. Look what his last play did. Jonson fell in his own shit, and he still stinks from it. I hold that till the stench fades, 'tis not wise to go near him. For the play itself, some of us like it more than others, but we have all agreed to abide by Will's judgment. 'Tis true we could do with a new comedy, but we would all wish it to be *Much Ado About Nothing.*"

Phillips smiled and said, "Two comedies would not be amiss, Will's *and* Jonson's."

Heminge ignored this and gave his final injunctions to their messenger. "Take good care of the script, Ned. I know not what Master Jonson would do if you lost it. And take good care of yourself too. Gus has wherewith to provide you for the journey."

When the meeting broke up, Ned was eager to get to his room, or rather Will's room which he occupied in his brother's absence. He was itching to read Ben's script. The hostility toward Ben that he had felt among the sharers only confirmed him in his loyalty toward the maligned man. Ben was a good man, and if Henry Condell said his play was a good one, it most assuredly was.

Ned quickly thumbed through the script for the part promised him by Ben, the son Lorenzo. It was in several scenes, and there were long speeches! Most of the play was in prose, but in the very last scene Lorenzo Junior had a long speech in verse! "As deep as Barathrum." What was that?

While Ned was puzzling his way through "his" last speech, he heard footsteps coming up the stairs and toward his room. Quickly he returned the play to its pouch and made as if he were preparing for bed. Gus entered carrying a steaming mug.

"No dawdling tonight, Ned. You must get a good sleep. Mistress Phillips has prepared this posset of hot milk with some wine and good spices in it. I know it brings sound sleep. Here, drink it. But take care, 'tis hot."

Both sat down while Ned began to sip the hot drink. He found it unpleasant, which was probably why Gus was determined to stay until every last drop was drunk.

"I shall take this script with me and give it to you in the morning; I want to refresh my mind about it. Besides, you might be tempted to read it, though I think the posset would soon made you nod." As he looked at the pouch containing the playscript he continued. "I wonder what Will knows about Ben Jonson. One thing is certain: if Will had been here, he would have met him ere this; Master Jonson would have seen to that. I think he has talked in private to most of us." Here Gus smiled. "He is a most persuasive gentleman." Ned was disappointed and hurt to find that he was not the only one who had been approached privately by Ben, but he said nothing to Gus, who continued speaking. "Now about tomorrow. Are you confident in traveling alone?"

"Yes. In good weather like this it should be easy."

"You have only made the journey once. Will you remember the way?"

"I think so."

"Don't try to do too much and, above all, don't travel in the dark. You will have ample money for the journey both ways. And, Ned, try to bring Will back with you."

FOURTEEN

THE SUN WAS HOT AS NED MOUNTED THE BEAUTIFUL HORSE MASTER PHILLIPS had provided, and he set out on his journey home, full of manhood and importance.

As he rode across the Bridge and through the city, he felt that London was his true home and he would be eager to return to it. All went well on the day's journey and he was at High Wycombe well before dark. He rode into the yard of the Stag, and a young boy ran to hold his horse. Ned, careful to carry with him the double pouches draped across his horse's back, went in to confer with the host, Harry Lockett, whom he recognized at once; he hoped that the recognition was not mutual, for he was still filled with shame at the memory of his foolish night. When he asked for a room, the host was about to say something when he stopped and looked at the would-be guest appraisingly. Then he walked away saying he had to make an inquiry. Ned was made nervous by this strange procedure, but soon the innkeeper returned and said there was a room, which he would have to share, though not the bed. As casually as he could, Ned asked if Giles still worked there.

Master Lockett's manner became surly and suspicious. "What do you know of that one?" he asked.

Ned decided to be blunt. "He robbed me when last I stayed here."

"Small wonder. He's a bad 'un. A month since, they took him for the Irish wars, but he left with a bag of my money. He'll end on the gallows, that one, unless the wild Irish catch him, make a stew of him, and eat him up; even then, he'd poison their guts. I doubt the army will ever get him to Ireland; he'll give 'em the slip. He was born for the gallows, and there he'll end, and I'll take my oath there'll be many a one there to cheer when they pull the cart from under him."

Ned paid in advance for his night's lodging and then went to see to the disposal of his horse. Afterwards he was shown to a small but comfortable room. Some luggage already lay on the better bed, and its quality betokened a man of substance; Ned was relieved to judge from it that his room companion was unlikely to threaten his money. Curiosity prompted him to take a closer look at the leather pouches and cases; some of them bore an engraved seal. He picked up a large wallet for a closer look. At the same time he heard a footstep and a voice. "What are you doing, sir? Put that down."

Ned had turned, still holding the wallet. Guiltily he returned it to the bed and stammered, "I meant no harm. The coat of arms attracted me. I wondered if I knew it."

"Do you?"

"No, sir."

"Then I shall not enlighten you."

As the speaker strode toward him, Ned backed around to his own bed. The stranger was a handsome young man in his early twenties. He had the looks and bearing bred of centuries of superiority. His clothes were elegant and exquisitely tailored; George would have been proud of them. And yet there was something a little wrong with the picture; something not quite English. The nobleman, if such he was, ignored Ned and sat on a chair, taking upon his lap the wallet Ned had handled. He opened it and carefully examined the books and papers it contained as if to assure himself that Ned had not taken any. Ned was mortified but felt the procedure was justified, for if the circumstances had been reversed, he would have done the same. He himself made a pretense of checking his own possessions, the while he made a surreptitious but careful examination of the stranger. Suddenly he realized the flaw in the picture; there was no doubt about the genuineness of the canvas, but the frame was a little frayed and tattered, though great pains had been taken to conceal the blemishes. The beautiful clothes had been worn too long and should have been discarded; the long traveling boots were down at heel, and the creases in the leather legs were becoming cracks for lack of care. And why would such a nobleman be sharing a humble room in a common inn? That was it: for some reason he had become impoverished.

The stranger caught the sidelong glance of Ned and returned it frankly. Ned was embarrassed to be caught in a further act of prying, and was surprised when the challenging look changed into a warm smile, and was still further surprised by the words which were addressed to him. "I beg your pardon for my suspicions. Your curiosity was innocent. I dare be sworn you are an honest man. My family has suffered much from hostile suspicions."

"It is I who should beg pardon. I meant no harm, sir."

"Since we are to share a room, 'tis well we should be acquainted." He stood and offered his hand, which Ned was happy to shake. "It will suffice that my name is Clement." Here he paused a moment, as if expecting a reaction, but the name obviously meant nothing to Ned. "May I ask your name?"

"Edmund Shakespeare. They call me Ned."

"I knew I had seen you before. You are brother to the playwright and you made me laugh with your 'Anon, anon, sir.' It became the fashion of the town."

Ned was so happy that he was eager to take up arms against all those whose evil suspicions had done harm to this wonderful man's family. He said, "They say that after the Queen saw the play at Christmas, even she said, 'Anon, anon, sir!' "

At mention of the Queen, a shadow clouded the stranger's smile, but he quickly recovered. "Shall we sup together?"

"I should be honored, sir."

"Not 'sir,' Ned. Clement. I care not to eat in public. I will go see Master Lockett and he will send our supper to our room. Will you take wine or ale?"

Here was a dilemma for Ned. He knew that private service in a room was expensive, and he wondered if he should afford it, especially wine, which he assumed the stranger would choose. But if the stranger lacked means, why was he so extravagant? As these questions rushed through his head, he said, "I shall be happy to abide by your choice."

"That is a gentlemanly answer. I would I could persuade you to do so in more important matters." With which enigmatic words he left the room.

As soon as he was alone, Ned was tempted even more than before to examine the stranger's belongings, but he resisted the temptation. His plan for the evening had been first to deal with Giles—in what way he had not determined—and then to read Ben Jonson's play. This unlooked-for encounter far outweighed his disappointment at missing Giles, and the play could wait until the next night, at Oxford.

When Clement returned, he brought with him a pitcher of wine and two goblets and said, "This will stay us until they bring our meal. I took a glass of this wine with Master Lockett. 'Tis stolen from the Spaniards, of course, but tastes none the worse for that."

"Better," ventured Ned, in an attempt at wit.

"Think you so? Then I see you are a loyal Englishman. But come, let us drink to the success of our ventures, whatever they be." As Ned was about to raise his goblet, Clement added. "It lacks sugar. I cannot abide the English habit of spoiling good wine with sugar. Why must we English take so much sugar? Is it to cover something sour in us? But to your success!"

"And to yours," said Ned. To him the wine was so bitter that he longed to spit it out, but he swallowed it with concealed distaste and good grace in imitation of Clement's genuine enjoyment.

"Like you it?" asked Clement.

"I must confess I am used to sugar." The truth was that Ned was little used to wine, with or without sugar; ale was his drink. "But I will soon grow to like it, and 'tis good I should."

"Well spoken. Now tell me, if you will, what brings you from London, for our host reports that your company of players is not here."

Ned explained, without any detail, that he was conveying messages to his brother, Will. Clement plied him with questions about the theatre, and his questions proved that he was an enthusiastic and knowledgeable playgoer. Ned had warmed enough to relate some amusing descriptions of his fellow players. Soon a sumptuous supper arrived, borne by a maid and two young men. Ned inwardly quaked at the cost. There was enough to feed a whole company of players, and they had notoriously unappeasable appetites. There was capon, ox-tongue, veal, lamb, and venison, with a rich assortment of salads, sauces, and relishes; in addition there was pickled and jellied fish of several kinds. Ned saw a profusion of fruits and cheeses, but no tarts and cakes and sweetmeats, which were his favorite part of a meal; it was clear that Clement abominated sugar. Ned was on the point of asking for some comfits at least—was he not paying for his share of the meal and should he not have what he wanted?—but he lacked the courage. The maid retired, but the servingmen remained, one to carve and the other to serve. They addressed Clement as "M'lord."

During the meal Clement said, "I told our host I was melancholy this evening and that I should welcome company of the right kind. I am happy that he found you."

"I am happy too," said Ned gallantly. He was consumed with curiosity about his mysterious companion, but he did not know how to satisfy it. Clement ate hugely, yet with slow delicacy. He said it was his first meal of the day because he felt it only right to preserve his appetite to do justice, if that were possible, to the fare he knew Master Lockett would provide. Ned deduced from this that the young man had been expected.

The meal took some two hours and was spiced with pleasant conversation, from which Ned gathered little more about his fellow guest than that he was traveling from London to Oxford, where he would stay with friends.

At the end of the supper, the servingmen cleared away the remains of the meal—and most of it remained, though everything had been tasted. As the servants disappeared, Ned wondered about the payment, but did not know how to raise the subject. He decided he would settle with the host in the morning, and resolved that he would practice drastic economies for the rest of his journey to make up for what he was sure would be the most expensive meal he had ever eaten or was ever likely to eat.

When they were alone, Clement said, "My friend, for such I judge you to be now, I have questioned you much and told you little. 'Tis for your safety that I act thus, for many would think it dangerous to know me, and yet I mean no harm." He went on speaking with a deep sadness. "I will tell you something of myself if you choose to know, though nothing that might put you in danger if the Queen's officers should question you."

Ned's apprehension of danger was lulled by the wine, whose taste was no longer unwelcome, and he said he would be honored by any confidence of Clement's.

"First, then, I must question you, and your answer may at once stop my tongue. What is your religion? I know you are not a Brownist or any kind of Puritan, or you would not be a player."

Dulled though his senses were, Ned immediately judged that Clement was a Roman Catholic. He knew there were Catholics who managed peacefully to serve both master and mistress, the Pope and the Queen, yet there was something different about Clement.

"You hesitate. Is it because you are reluctant to tell me?"

"No. I go to church every Sunday because it is the law and the custom. I never think about it."

"You have no religion, my friend. I have little else, and yet I pity you. I was born a Catholic and shall die a Catholic."

Suspicion and hostility began to grow in Ned. "Are you a traitor to our Queen? Do you plot her death?"

"No. Rest easy. I am no traitor, but I cannot belong to her church; it was made by man, not by God. Every day I pray that she will be brought back to the true faith, and her people with her. If prayers be treachery, then am I a traitor."

"'Tis not right that Englishmen should bow down to an Italian in Rome."

"Then 'tis not right that Englishmen should bow down to Christ, for the Holy Father is his representative on earth."

Ned was out of his depth and floundering. Clement smiled at his discomfort and said, "Let us not argue, for 'tis clear that you have thought little about it. Do you still wish to hear my story?"

Somewhat more reluctantly, Ned said, "Yes."

"I will only tell you what the Queen's officers know. I said I traveled from London and that was true, but to London I had come from France. I was taken there more than ten years ago by my mother, when my father was arrested and placed in the Tower on charge of treason. There he has been ever since."

"He must be a traitor," said Ned truculently.

"No, if treason means plotting harm to the Queen. It is true that some men sought refuge with us, for we had a priest who could give them confession and the mass. They were captured and hanged for plotting with Spain to kill the Queen. Perhaps they were guilty—I do not know. But my father was innocent. All his property was confiscated and my mother and I went to live abroad on the kindness of friends. I came back to see my father and to tell him that my mother had died of grief. My father too longs for death. Soon I shall return to France, for there is nothing left to me here."

Ned was overwhelmed by the tragic tale. He mumbled some indistinct syllables of sympathy.

Clement continued. "Now you can understand why I needed company tonight. I feel better for having spoken to you. Thank you."

Ned's wits returned. "There are Catholics, recusants, who live well in England. Why not you, since you say you mean no harm to the Queen?"

"An uncomfortable thing called conscience that would not let me rest." Clement refilled their goblets. "Enough of my sorrows. Tell me more of your life and your brother and the other players. What is Richard Burbage like? To me he is Richard Crookback."

The rest of the evening passed pleasantly until it was time for bed. Ned was first in bed and he watched Clement, while trying to seem not to do so. He was embarrassed to see his companion go down on his knees, take a crucifix from around his neck, kiss it, and hold it in his hands as he prayed. Ned was puzzled about himself too; why did religion mean so little to him, while other men died for their beliefs?

In the morning he was shaken awake; the unaccustomed wine had given him a longer sleep than usual. Standing over him was a severe-looking man in dark clothes. Behind the stranger stood Master Lockett, who appeared harassed. There was no sign of Clement, nor did his bed seem to have been slept in.

Even before Ned was thoroughly awake, the sober-suited man started questioning him. Ned glanced a pleading look on the host's face, and pretended to be sleepier than he was in order to prepare his answers. Should he deny having seen Clement? That was too dangerous, for the servingmen and maid would talk, if they had not already done so. And if he had been alone in the room, why had he not slept in the better bed? Clement had said that all he had told him was known to the Queen's Officers. Ned decided, for his own safety, to be truthful. He was ready for the inquisition.

"What was the name of the man who slept in the other bed?"

"I do not know. He told me to call him Clement."

The questioner gave a slight guffaw, a gentlemanly one. "You believed that?"

"Yes," said Ned, puzzled.

"Clement is the name of his master, the Pope. He said that to test you. I believe you are truly innocent, innocent as a babe."

Ned was insulted by this, even though it spelt safety for him. He was about to object—he knew a boy in Stratford whose name was Clement and the family were Puritans who thought that the Pope was the Devil Incarnate—but he was stopped by the complete surprise of the next inquiry.

"You had supper together in this room last night. Tell me what mine host here provided for you."

Ned looked for guidance to Master Lockett, but his face remained impassive for the questioner also had his eye on him. Ned stood by his determination to speak the truth, and he gave as complete a picture as he could remember of the sumptuous supper.

The officer, for such he must be though he was not in a military uniform, seemed to be happily satisfied. "That was a test of your truthfulness, Master Shakespeare—oh yes, I know your name and much else about you—for I had already heard of the meal from the servingmen. Now, were you not surprised by such a meal?"

"Yes, I was."

"Did it not mean that Clement was expected here?"

"I never thought of it," lied Ned.

"Did you pay for your part of the meal?"

"No, not yet. I was going to settle with the host this morning. I paid for my bed."

"And how much, Master Lockett, are you going to charge this young player for his part of such a meal served in a private room by three servants?"

After some hesitation, during which Ned awaited the reply nervously, the answer came. "Three shillings."

This was more than six times what Ned had intended to pay for his supper, but he had sadly to agree with the officer's comment. "A fair price for such a banquet, but I judge it to be beyond the means of a young player who has just begun in a profession where only the few become wealthy, and that after many years."

"I can pay," Ned said defiantly, and he reached for his purse and counted the three coins into Master Lockett's hand.

"Done like a gentleman, Master Shakespeare. And now I'll let you get dressed, for I have more questions to ask Master Lockett. But I want to speak to you again. Perhaps you will join me downstairs in a pot of ale—and be my guest. Be at ease; you have nothing to fear."

Left to himself to dress and pack, Ned was, first of all, relieved that he himself was free from suspicion. But Master Lockett? It seemed clear that he was a Roman Catholic supporter of Clement, and was probably suspected of involvement with him in some plot. Clement had said that he meant no harm to the Queen, and Ned still believed him. Now that the officer seemed to trust him, dare he try to speak in behalf of Clement?

When Ned went downstairs, the officer ordered breakfast from the same young man who had served the private supper the night before.

"Now, Master Shakespeare," said the friendly inquisitor, "I want you to try to remember every word that passed between you and the young nobleman. First: did he mention the name of John Gerard? 'Father' John Gerard?" and he added a thick layer of sarcasm to the priestly title.

Again Ned was taken aback. His puzzled no was patently truthful. He remembered the Gerard sensation; everybody had talked of it, about a month before last Christmas. Gerard was a notorious Jesuit priest and, with another Roman Catholic, had made a daring escape from the Tower, climbing hand-over-hand along a rope which had been fastened to a cannon in the Tower and to some object on the other side of the moat. Since then the hue-and-cry had been out for him, but he had not been caught. The sympathies of Ned, like those of most men not inhibited by genuine religious belief, had been with Father Gerard, especially when it leaked out that he had left behind him a document declaring that he had no treasonable intent against the Queen and so was justified in escaping from wrongful imprisonment.

Having satisfied himself about John Gerard, the officer plied Ned with bread, cheese, ale, and further questions. He seemed to share Clement's enthusiasm for the theatre, and Ned was particularly pleased to recount the "Anon, anon, sir," story.

"When did you last give that play?"

"About a fortnight ago."

"Our Catholic friend could not have seen it then for he was in France. His last visit of which we have record was two years ago. Could he have seen the play at that time?"

Reluctantly, for now he saw he had been trapped into giving incriminating evidence, Ned said, "No."

"When did you first give the play?"

"Last summer."

"And several times after that. It was popular, was it not?"

"Yes." Ned was having some difficulty in swallowing his food, for his answers were strengthening a suspicion.

"You have been frank with me. I will be equally so with you, for I think you are a loyal subject of the Queen. We believe that your friend of last night played a leading part in arranging the escape of John Gerard, for which purpose he stole into this country without our knowledge. We further believe he is on his way to John Gerard now, to smuggle him out of the country. They are brave men and, apart from their popish beliefs, good men. For myself I think that Gerard will refuse to leave England, for danger means little to him, and there are Catholics to minister to in secret. But 'tis not for me to pass judgment; he is an escaped prisoner of the Queen, and we must catch him. Master Lockett, a Catholic who manages to keep on this side of the law, knows no more than you where Lord—I was about to give him his title but he has been stripped of it—where Clement has gone; to 'friends at Oxford.' Clement was wise not to imperil you with further knowledge. Now we must be on our way. May both our journeys end in success."

Ned merely said, "Thank you, sir, and for the breakfast too."

As Ned was mounting his horse to leave, Master Lockett approached him, smiling happily: the officer and soldiers had already left. He handed Ned back his three shillings. "You were both my guests last night," he said. Ned began to protest, but Master Lockett continued. "You gave him a few hours of happiness; that is more than money. Besides, your brother always pays me well. And so shall you another time. And now may God be with you."

Ned rode out of High Wycombe, pondering the force of a religion which gave men the strength to die for their beliefs. In the past fifty years Catholics and Puritans had died by ax, fire, and halter in equal hundreds and with equal courage. For him, religion had been the cause of largely meaningless family quarrels occasioned by Anne's zealous puritanism. His parents had been born into Henry VIII's newly established Church and so had known no other, yet they both had a liking for vestments and ritual and were opposed to the drabness of Protestant austerity, which was gradually assuming dominance in Stratford. Mary, his mother, treasured a jeweled crucifix which had been given her by her mother on the day of her confirmation, but in the interests of domestic peace she kept it out of sight of her daughter-in-law to whom it was a pagan idol.

And what was Will's religion? In this, as in all else, he was a secret man. By law and custom, he went to church every Sunday, but that could mean much or nothing. What had he said when they saw the hanged priest at Tyburn? "God is greater than Queen or Pope." Ned remembered that, when he himself was having trouble in learning his catechism—he could learn the lines in plays easily enough—his mother had held up Will as a shining example: "When he was your age, he knew the Prayer Book and the Psalter better than the vicar."

When he got to Oxford, Ned found that the Crown Tavern was closed. Upon inquiry of a yardboy, he learned that Mistress Davenant had died that day in her last fruitless childbirth. Ned debated whether he should seek out the widower to offer his condolences but decided against it; the man might insist on accommodating him and he had no fancy to spend a night in a house with a corpse, two corpses; besides, words of condolence would be awkward on his tongue.

The Crown Tavern shared a yard with the Cross Inn, and Ned had no difficulty in securing a bed there.

Ned was hungry and he fed full on the supper's cold mutton and apple pie. As he ate, he mused on the title of Ben Jonson's play: *Every Man in*

His Humour. Since last summer there had been much talk around town of the "humours," for the scholarly George Chapman had written a play called *An Humorous Day's Mirth.* The Admiral's Men had made a big success of it, though George had thought it was "much ado about little." The upshot of the play had been that the "humours," previously a subject for the erudite, became a fashionable topic in the mouths of the ignorant. All Ned knew about the subject was that a person's character and disposition were supposed to be determined by the balance of fluids in his body. Once, when he had given vent to a blaze of anger in the theatre because a costume he needed for a quick change had been moved, one of the company had said, half jokingly, "The trouble with you, Ned, is that you have too much yellow bile." Another time, as he walked to the theatre in a high euphoric state after a glorious evening with a rich merchant's beautiful young wife, Augustine Phillips, who had surmised the reason for his condition, said, "Your blood is too rich, but if you have to have one of the four humours, the sanguine is the best."

When he settled down to the Jonson play in his room, Ned soon forgot the title and any implications it might have. He did not know quite what to make of the play, except that there were some funny parts in it, but he had no doubt that he wanted to play Lorenzo Junior, largely because of the size of the part. Before he fell asleep, Ned rehearsed the subjects of his mission to Will: *Much Ado* and Will Kemp; the second *Henry IV* play; the problem of the Theatre (and the secret brewing that could not even be mentioned in Cuthbert Burbage's letter); and Ben Jonson's play. Now he was eager to get home. He decided he would make an early start in the morning and get to Stratford in the one day; he had done it, coming with Will, and he would do it, returning without him.

FIFTEEN

NED FAILED TO WAKE AT DAWN AS HE HAD INTENDED, AND HE WAS TWO hours late in setting out. He was still determined to get to Stratford that night, and decided not to stop for a meal anywhere. He took with him some bread and cheese to eat by the wayside when it became necessary to give his horse a brief rest. He pressed the horse to make time, and she responded well, but darkness turned the end of the journey into a nightmare ride. He met no one but thought he met many; any movement caused by the wind or an unseen animal convinced him of imminent attack by highwaymen. Time and again the horse strayed off the road, in some places little more than a path. And once the horse stumbled so abruptly that Ned was thrown into a ditch.

At last Ned knew where he was; he never thought he could be so grateful to be near Stratford again. Even the baby moon seemed to shine brighter and laugh at his recent fears.

It was past one o'clock. For a moment he wondered whether he should go to New Place but decided to abide by his original plan to go home. After he had seen to his horse, he carried his luggage to the back door, which, to his surprise, was open; his father always made a ceremony of locking it at night. Quietly Ned went inside, debating whether he could get to bed without waking anyone. Since Will's family had moved out, he did not know how the sleepers were disposed.

He had just decided to sleep on the floor with his coat for a pillow, when he was aware of some movement overhead. Someone was coming stealthily down the stairs. It was Richard, and his first whispered question assumed that only trouble could have brought Ned home without warning and in the dead of night. Assured that all was well, he explained that their father had been abed in fever for a week but that the worst was over and he was mending. Richard prevailed on Ned to share his bed, and they were gathering together the luggage to go upstairs when their mother appeared. Her joy at seeing her favorite child was muted because of her overriding consideration that her husband should not be awakened: all else could wait until the morning. So the three of them quietly went up to bed.

In the morning John seemed to be considerably better—his breathing was less stertorous than it had been for days—but he was still sick enough to be content to lie in bed. Something of his old manner returned when Mary told him of Ned's late and unexpected arrival. "Why did he ride through the night?" he asked accusingly.

"He has been away so long that he was eager to get back to see us."

"I don't believe it. Did he not have money for an inn? Has he come back in poverty to live on us in idleness again?"

"No, John, he is a fine young gentleman now. You will be proud of him."

In reply to this her husband snorted, bringing on a heavy fit of coughing. As soon as the paroxysm was over, Mary gave him a herbal draught, in readiness by the bedside. John was spent and breathing in quick gasps. It was better that he lie still, so Mary stole from the room lest her presence provoke him into further spirited comments on Ned.

Richard was in the shop and at work; he had got out of the shared bed and dressed without causing a murmur or movement from Ned. Joan was downstairs, busy with the day's chores. Her mother had already told her of Ned's return when he appeared.

He had been at pains to present himself to the family in daylight at his proudest and best. The mother's eyes sparkled with pride and love, and the sister's with surprise and admiration. The difficult boy had returned a confident gentleman; it was hard to believe that he was only eighteen and from Stratford. The more than ten years Will had been away had not caused such a transformation in him as had the less than two years in Ned. Mary was eager for John to see him.

Although Ned said it was imperative he should see Will as soon as possible—he made the most of the importance of his mission—Mary insisted that his first duty was to see his father and also that he should have some breakfast. Joan said that she would walk over to warn Will that Ned would be seeing him within the hour. She hoped Will would be in a good mood; he was very tetchy these days because the worries of the house were interfering with his writing. That house was nothing but a worry; what did a family of four want with such a big place?

As Joan was leaving the house, her mother said, archly, "I doubt not that you will stop by to see your own Willikins too."

Joan's reply was a coy smile, and as soon as the door was closed, Ned asked in amazement, "Are they never going to get married?"

His mother sighed and said, "Next year they say. 'Tis high time. She is in her thirtieth year. But come; your father."

The approach of Mary and Ned woke John from a doze. Their first sight of each other surprised both father and son; both seemed years older than at last sight, a fact which aroused compassion in the son and admiration in the father, reluctant feelings in both men.

"You look well, lad," said John, somewhat grudgingly.

"You too, Father," lied Ned.

"Why did you come by night?" challenged John.

"Because my business with Will is urgent and important, and a day counts."

"What is it that is so important?"

"They are matters of the theatre that you would not understand."

Mary was quick to interpose with a question which it was surprising that she had not yet asked. "How long will you stay, Ned?"

"A few days; no more. I am needed back in London." This last was said for his father's ear, and there was no one by with knowledge to laugh at his presumption.

"Have you come to take Will back with you?" asked Mary.

John did not wait for an answer. "He cannot leave Stratford now. He is a man of property. A house with ten fireplaces cannot be left to a woman and two children. Besides, he is making many alterations. Also, he has some profitable enterprises in hand. London has seen the last of him. He is my eldest son and must take my place in Stratford. Now he is the son and heir of a gentleman, and that is not only an honor but a responsibility."

Ned followed the direction of his father's look and saw for the first time a painting of the new Shakespeare coat-of-arms, with its falcon and two spears. He remembered it chiefly as the butt of sarcasm. Several other members of the company had acquired coats-of-arms in their endeavors to gain respectability for a profession generally regarded as vagabond. Spencer made frequent remarks on the theme that they aped their betters offstage as well as on. "Blood, not parchment, begets blood," he had said.

Mary, who had been watching her husband closely, said, "You must rest, John, and Ned must go to see Will. Come, Ned."

She went without waiting to be obeyed. Ned hesitated, because he wanted to say something more to his father, something kindly to the ailing man. John sensed the impulse and said, with a warm smile, "I am glad to see you, Edmund. It is clear that you prosper."

"Thank you, Father," said Ned, and then followed his mother. While he ate breakfast, Ned asked for news of Will, to prepare himself for the meeting. His mother could not tell him much. Her husband's illness had kept her indoors for two weeks, so she had been unable to go to church where she could count on seeing Will, Anne, and the children. Will was too busy to come over often, although Judith came every day to see her grandfather. New Place had been in such a bad state when Will took it over that it was taking a deal of money, time, and worry to restore it. And now there was other, great trouble about the property—but Will would tell him. Mary was afraid that Ned would not be welcomed by Anne or the children if he had come to take Will back to London. Yes, Will seemed to be settled; he had been home for fully three months now. But Ned would see and judge for himself.

When Ned came to New Place, the sight of it staggered him. Now it deserved its name once more. Never before had Ned realized how large and imposing the house was, and when he thought how much there was behind this imposing front—two barns, two gardens, two orchards—it gave him the thrill of personal possession to know that it belonged to his brother.

He was about to raise the brass knocker when the front door opened. Will had been watching for him from an upstairs window ever since Joan had brought the news, and his growing impatience at delay was expressed by the energy with which he hurtled downstairs to greet his brother.

Ned was delighted by his reception, although he knew that it was London that was being greeted as much as a brother. Will hugged him, which Ned did not remember his ever having done before. Behind Will stood Judith, one huge grin as she eagerly waited to fling herself into her old companion's arms. Waiting too was Susanna, now at fifteen beginning to blossom into ladylike womanhood and anxious to make as big an impression on this newly handsome young uncle as he was making on her. Anne was not there. Will said she had taken some delicacies to a friend who was sick.

When the greetings were over, father and daughters took Ned on a tour of the house. There was a bewildering number of rooms—most of them empty. Four bedrooms were furnished, though sparsely. A guest room had the newest bed in it, and Will, supported by the girls, insisted that Ned should be its first occupant. After all, there was no separate bed for him in Henley Street; and he had come to see Will. Ned said that their mother might be hurt if he did not sleep at home; it was Susanna who assured him that all would be well.

In the gardens and orchards, two workmen were trying to repair many years of neglect, and another one was at work on one of the barns. Ned had already noticed that some of the stones and bricks of the house were new, and at the back of the house was a large pile of old discarded stones and bricks which Will said he had sold to the town council. He kept repeating two themes: it was all costing more money than he had antici-pated and he was not going to furnish more rooms until his title to the property was free and clear. Two sons had inherited the Underhill estate. The elder, Fulke, had been found to have poisoned his father and had been hanged for it. Now Will would have to wait four years, until Her-cules, the youngest son, came of age, before the transfer of New Place would be completely valid.

They went into the barn that was not in need of repair, and Ned was surprised to find that there was a deal of corn there—malt mostly, Will explained; eighty bushels of it; the price was bound to go up, and he needed every penny he could make. There had been much outcry against the hoarders in the present time of scarcity, and Ned had learned to think of them as the villains of the commonwealth. And Will was one of them! It was a consummate irony that Ned had heard them described as the "Shylocks of the crops." Will sensed his brother's unspoken criticism and said, half sadly, "I am a man of Stratford now and do as others do."

Anne was there when they returned to the house. She welcomed Ned correctly but suspiciously. He thought she looked like an old woman; at forty-two her face and body were set in hard lines. His staying there had obviously been discussed, for she said, "Will would have you stay with us. Will you do so?"

"Thank you, Anne," said Ned. "I shall be honored to be your first guest."

"Now, Ned, we have many things to talk about," said Will. "Let us go into my room."

"Dinner will be at eleven o'clock," said Anne as they moved away.

"My room" had little in it beyond the necessities for Will's writing: a table, a chair, an armchair, some shelves for books. It looked out on the gardens and orchards.

Ned gave Will the letters from Cuthbert Burbage, Richard Burbage, and John Heminge. When he had read them, Will said, "Why did you, and not a carrier, bring these letters?"

"Because it was thought you might have questions I could answer." Ned told of the briefing he had received from the sharers, and he ended by saying, "And there is one matter about which there is no letter. It is this." He handed Will the pouch containing Ben Jonson's play and told him of the division of opinion about it; he thought it wiser to say no more than that at the moment.

Will said, "There is much I must ponder before I even ask you questions about these letters, and I must read the play before we talk about it. Tell me, have you read it?"

Somewhat guiltily, Ned said, "Yes,"

"Your reading was uninvited?"

Ned nodded and smiled.

Will smiled in return and said, "How could a player be expected to carry a playscript and not read it? Tell me now of the company and London and you. I am hungry for news."

Ned enjoyed appeasing his hunger; it was gratifying to find their roles exchanged, and to be the one to bring news of the great city. This sharing of a life so foreign to their surroundings seemed to weld them together as never before; their embrace at meeting had been the greeting of a prisoner to a visitor from the world of freedom. They laughed together at the foibles of the company—at the hired men's complaints of the discomforts of the Curtain ("Nick Dodman says we're so cramped together that he put his leg into his neighbor's breeches"), and at Will Kemp's growing disgruntlement ("You can tell when *Henry IV* is going to be played by his sour face the day before"). They passed on to court gossip, and Ned reported rumors of growing conflict between Lord Burleigh and the Earl of Essex; the old lord could not last much longer, and all the talk was of who would succeed him as the nearest confidant of the Queen. Most people were certain it would be her favorite, the earl, but there were some that were equally certain that the old lord had prepared the way to the Queen's ear for his crook-spined son, Robert, who was already serving her brilliantly as Secretary of State.

During dinner, the conversation turned to Stratford matters and Stratford men.

Anne asked, "Will you be here on Sunday to join us at church, Edmund?"

Ned looked to his brother for a reply.

"I think so," said Will, "and I hope so. It will take me a few days to prepare considered messages for my friends in London."

Ned had long realized that the main purpose of his mission was to persuade Will to return with him to London, and now it looked as if he had failed before he had begun. Immediately he felt the embarrassment of his report to the sharers in London. Anne's reaction was that now she could afford to be more gracious to her young brother-in-law and to feel guilt for her previous inhospitality.

"While Will considers his replies, Edmund, why do not you take the girls for a walk this afternoon? They will enjoy your company."

"And I theirs," said Ned, replying in polite kind.

Judith was disappointed that it had to be the "girls"; she wanted Uncle Ned to herself; Susanna always spoiled things.

Their walk took them to Henley Street. Ned had anticipated difficulty with his mother about his sleeping in New Place, but there was none. Mary was proud that her handsome Ned should be the first guest in the fine new bed, but she stipulated that he had to come over for a long talk every day and that the whole family should come back to dinner after church on Sunday; she even hoped that John would be well enough to get up for it.

When Mary brought Ned up to see his father, she broke the news of his move to New Place as if she had arranged it all.

"Have you seen New Place since Will bought it, Father?" asked Ned, knowing full well that he hadn't.

Withdrawal had become such a habit for John that he now found excuses for it where before he had found reasons. He said, "Not yet. I told Will I would wait until it is finished, and, from all I hear, that will be a long time."

It was not until after the early evening meal that Will and Ned got down to their crucial talk. Both were nervous about it. Will took great care to ensure that the door of the study was securely closed as Ned made garrulous chatter about how everything was the same in Stratford. Will busied himself with making Ned comfortable and pouring ale for both of them. At last, after complimenting Anne's brewing, Ned fell silent and waited. Will went straight to the heart of the matter.

"The answers to the letters and Ben Jonson's play can wait. The all important question is whether I am coming back to London." So it still is a question, thought Ned, and his attention quickened. "I must and can be frank with you, for you are my brother and now a man. What is more, you are a player, and only you can understand. If I could be content to write poems, as Richard Field would have me, I would not need London, but my plays are my life, and the people in them sometimes more real to me than my own flesh and blood. Plays need players and a theatre, and only London has those. To be a player myself now matters little to me, but to be a playwright is all. Still, I am a man too, with a wife and children, and now a big home. I often wonder why I bought New Place. It's true that Anne needed a home of her own and away from Henley

Street. It's true too that I wanted to restore the family name in Stratford. But more and more I think what really drove me was to give myself an anchor here so strong that I could not get away to London. Ned, I am already dragging at the anchor."

"Anne and the children should come to London with you," said Ned hotly.

"Should? You think so, I think so, but Anne's God does not. I admire and even envy her strong and simple faith, Ned. I have told her that I have abandoned London, else she would not come to bed with me. Sometimes I make her listen to a few lines I have written, lines which I know she will approve, and I blush to my bones with shame when I do it, for it is an evil seduction with lies. The Lord Chief Justice in my new *Henry IV* pleases her, and she is right. I admire him too, but I love my Falstaff."

"Everybody loves him," said Ned.

"No, Ned, not everybody. Only wicked sinners, like you and me." Will said this with a smile, but then added with a sad seriousness, "But there comes a time when Prince Hal and I must forsake him. London is my Falstaff, full of lively companionship, enchanting lies, and beguiling vice. There will come a time when I must forsake it. I thought it had already come. But now my spirit cries out, 'Not yet, not yet.' "

"Then you will come back with me?" asked Ned eagerly.

"I don't know, Ned; I don't know. I will let you know tomorrow. If I decide to stay in Stratford, there is much that you will have to do. I will have to go carefully over every word of the new *Henry IV* play with you . . ."

"Then it is finished?"

"Yes, but it has been hard, Ned, hard. The King—and I too—had to renounce Falstaff, and it was not easy for either of us."

"Why did you not let him die? He's an old man, bloat with many sicknesses. His death would be natural."

"But that was a coward's way out for me—and the King. No, the play is ended and Falstaff is alive and rejected. If I come not to London, you must see the play copied and so you must understand every word."

"But the rehearsals? And all the questions? What of them?"

"Let my fellows think of me as dead."

"No, Will. You must come. Tell Anne 'tis only for a time, to arrange your affairs. Tell her you will not act again. Tell her anything."

"Anne sees through my lies."

"Then tell her the truth."

"That would be cruel, and it would be the end between us, and for me that too would be a kind of death. And there are the children. They mean much to me. I still mourn my lovely Hamnet. Every day my heart is wrung for him, because I see the boys going to school across the way and then coming home with laughter, and I see and hear my Hamnet among them."

Will turned away in pain and, when he spoke again, it was of other matters. "We must talk of the letters. John Heminge can be happy: *Much Ado About Nothing* is also finished—and it was a relief to work on it when I was having difficulty with Falstaff and the Prince—and Will Kemp will be dancing for joy; Dogberry will be his best part. But a word in John Heminge's ear: I am tiring of writing for such clowns as Kemp. I have a fancy for a jester who causes laughter with his gibes. A play is aborning in my head for such a one; it is begotten of the struggle within me between Stratford and London, but it will be a merry comedy. It comes from Tom Lodge's *Rosalynde,* which I have read with enjoyment many a time."

"Is any of the play written yet?"

"In my head only. 'Twould be better to write it in London, for then Stratford would seem the more golden."

"Another reason for returning with me."

"I need no reasons. What moves me to stay and to go are both stronger than reason."

"What of Cuthbert Burbage's letter?"

"There is no message you can convey in reply to that, for the purport of his letter is to beg me to return to London. It seems that he and Richard have some plans brewing for another theatre, but I cannot think what I should have to do with it. Did he give you any message for me?"

"None; it was all secret. They have again been refused a license for the Blackfriars."

"And so the boy players may thrive there while the men players starve." Ned smiled. "I exaggerate. 'Tis a poet's privilege. And that is a good cue to talk about Ben Jonson's play, for in holding up the humours to ridicule, he exaggerates indeed."

"You like not the play?" Ned's disappointment was obvious.

"Why do you so much want me to like it?" asked Will in some surprise.

Ned told him the whole story and about wanting the part of the young Lorenzo. "Only Henry Condell was strong for the play," Ned said in conclusion.

"And that to me is a very powerful argument in its behalf. I like the play too, and my counsel is that we should do it."

"We?" said Ned slyly.

"I cannot think of the company as 'They'; I doubt I ever shall."

"What of Ben Jonson? There is a feeling he is troublesome. Do you know him?"

"I have never met him, but from his play I feel I know him, and what I know I like. I do not fear the trouble he will give. If Philip Henslowe is afraid to put his play on the stage, he will be grateful to us for having the courage. Not that it takes courage; the play is a harmless delight. And there is a part in it for Will Kemp, so that should make everybody happy."

"Which part?"

"I think Cob, the water carrier."

"And my part?" asked Ned with an anxious smile.

" 'Tis a big part for a new hired man," said Will, failing to hide a smile.

"But I can do it, and Ben Jonson said he wants me to do it."

"That will not be a very powerful argument with some of the sharers," observed Will wryly.

"And you? What do you think?"

"That you can do it and do it well. But it is not for me to say so, nor would you want me to be the one to press your claims. I have known all along how you have resented owing so much to me." Ned began to expostulate, but Will overbore him. "No, no. There is nothing wrong with that. There have been times when you have been grateful too, and that also I have known. Lest you think I have caught you in a great wickedness, it is only fair that I should say there have been many times when I have resented you and wished you back in Stratford. Only a saint can accept an obligation of giving or receiving with perpetual grace, and neither of us is a saint. There now; that has cleared the air of two years between us, but it will cloud and fog many a time again. We are brothers, and that is a bond. There are times when we are grateful for the strength and comfort of such bonds, and there are times when we strain to break them." As he spoke that last sentence, Will seemed to be talking to himself, and Ned sensed that he was thinking of his wife rather than his brother. Will again focused on Ned. "As for Lorenzo Junior, 'twill be more politic to get Gus Phillips to press your claims to the part, though I promise to have a word in his ear."

"All the time you talk as if you were coming back with me."

"Because all the time I want to."

"But will you?"

"I don't know. Today is Friday. With or without me, you must start back on Monday morning. I would say Sunday, for our fellows in London will be watching for you every day, but that would hurt too many people here: Mother because it will pleasure her to have all the family but Gilbert to dinner with her after church, and Anne because to travel on Sunday without dire need is to break the Sabbath."

"When will you make up your mind, Will?"

"Maybe tonight. I don't know. It all depends on Anne. She is in torment too. To her you are the great tempter. You have brought the smell of London into this house and she fears it will be stronger to me than the smell of the corn in my barns. She has learnt not to trust my fine words, and I have learnt it too, and yet I think they are true when I say them. She will search my heart tonight and I don't know what she will find there."

SIXTEEN

NED WOULD NEVER KNOW WHAT PASSED BETWEEN WILL AND ANNE THAT night, but by the morning the issue was decided: Will was to return with him to London on Monday morning. Ned himself had found difficulty in getting to sleep but then slept well in the fine and virgin bed. He had been awakened by Will whose blear eyes and drawn face betokened that he had had no sleep at all.

Will apologized for waking Ned but explained he had to give him the decision before he chanced to see Anne, who, as had been expected, was taking it very badly. Ned immediately saw the impossibility of staying on at New Place and said he would return to Henléy Street that morning. Will made no attempt to stay him; instead, he said he would accompany him for he had much to ask of Richard in connection with New Place.

Ned asked if he should see Anne before leaving but Will decided it would be wiser if he did not.

But Ned did see Anne. As he came downstairs, she was crossing the hall. She stopped and stared at him with loathing. Uncomfortable under her silent glare, he continued to descend and when he was level with her, he felt he had to say something. All he managed was, "I'm sorry, Anne."

"You lie," she snapped. "The Devil always gloats over his victories. You came to take him away from his wife and children, and you have won. But you will both be made to suffer for your wickedness, and I shall have no pity for you."

"Come with us, Anne, you and the children," Ned pleaded hopelessly. "Will needs you."

Anne did not deign to reply. She turned abruptly and walked away. Ned did not see the children. Will was giving them the news, emphasizing, as he had done to Anne, that he would be away but a short while to attend to matters of business. They believed him; Anne didn't.

As the brothers walked together to Henley Street, Will was greeted with deference by several citizens; wealth apparently commanded respect, even though it was considered to be ill-gotten. They talked about the family dinner on Sunday and decided they would be grateful for the presence of Willikins. Will was certain Anne would come; she would feel it to be her duty and that would overrule all else. Furthermore, she always made great efforts to hide from the children the deep rift between their parents; he was even certain she would confirm his story to them of the necessity of his departure. It was God's commandment that children should honor their father and their mother, and Anne would say nothing that might hinder them from obeying that commandment.

Will told his mother his news and then went upstairs to his father. To his mother the news was not unexpected; her chief concern was the effect it would have on her husband and daughter-in-law. She need not have worried in the case of her husband, for Will was employing a tactic with guilty cunning.

"Father, my money comes from London. I have to go there to make more of it, and I can; much more. But you know you cannot trust others to do things for you; you have to be there yourself."

"But what about New Place?"

"Things there are settled now. Anne can manage, with Richard's help. And I expect to be back in a month or so."

"What does Anne say?"

"I need not tell you. I wish she would understand, as you do."

"She's a stiff-necked woman, William; stiff-souled too."

"She's a good woman and a good mother, and would be a good wife if I were different."

"If you were a sniveling, psalm-singing hypocrite, you mean."

In replying to this Will spoke with genuine fervor. "She is not a hypocrite, Father. Sometimes I wish to God she were. She has the faith that would go to the stake."

Both father and son were silenced by embarrassment after this outburst.

Will's next conversation was with Richard in the shop, and it was a pleasing one. Ever since that Sunday walk at the time of Hamnet's death, a slow change had been taking place in Richard, and it was accelerated by Anne's removal from the house. He had become proud of his brother's success and happy to be in his confidence, for Will entrusted him with all details of his affairs in Stratford. When he had an occasional twinge of doubt about the origin of Will's money, he would still it by doing some service for Anne or the children. He admired Anne's unshakable convictions, though they were tottering in himself.

Richard was not upset by Will's going to London—a man must do what he must—and there was a part of him that was gladdened by the news. It meant that he again would be the fount of power and authority in all affairs relative to New Place: he would supervise the workmen and see to their payment, he would receive the deference now accorded to Will, and it was to him that Anne would turn in case of need. All that was very welcome to a serious young man of twenty-four on whom the family honor depended, for he was the permanent citizen; Will was but a visitor whose natural habitat was London, not Stratford. As for the glove-making, he would not let that suffer; besides, whatever he did for Will would be but repayment for Will's many kindnesses to the family.

There were nine Shakespeares and one Hart at the Sunday dinner table. John was downstairs to greet the churchgoers as they variously arrived. All commented on how well he was looking, but he would have been better pleased if they had congratulated him on his fortitude in assuming his duties as head of the family in spite of his obvious sickness. Anne commented that God had answered her prayers for his recovery. John had no satisfactory answer to this, for, while he had to be grateful to God, he almost resented Anne's intercession; she was altogether too familiar and proprietary in her attitude to the deity for his liking.

To Ned's amazement, conversation at the dinner table was almost monopolized by William Hart. No longer was he a nervous visitor but an established member of the family, and a garrulous one. To Joan he was the fount of all wisdom, but to everybody else at the table he was a rather foolish little man. Still, today they were grateful to him because, from ignorance, he kept away from the subject that was uppermost in all their minds, Will's imminent departure. Mary had suggested to Joan that he not be told until the meal was over and Anne had gone home. It was natural that he should ask Ned when he was leaving.

"Tomorrow," Ned said without further elaboration. Judith looked pointedly at her father but managed to remain silent.

There was no awkward hiatus in the conversation, for Willikins was away again, this time in a disquisition on London, with particular phrases aimed at particular ears. "Ah, London! A great city, I have no doubt, but one I suppose I shall never see; Stratford is world enough for me. I should be afeard of London. I lack the boldness of spirit of a Shakespeare, for I had not such a man as Master John Shakespeare for my father. Three sons out to conquer the great world, and succeeding, succeeding. They say it is a place for a man of my talents, and indeed I fear that Stratford may prove a sorry place for a hatter, but I feel there are other things for me to pursue than the wealth of London, other more precious things, and they are all to be found here in Stratford, and I shall find them, with the help of Mistress Joan."

At one point, in an effort to draw Anne into the conversation, Mary asked what seemed to be an innocent question, but even before she had completed it, she realized it had dangerous implications. "Anne, when are you going to brew next?" With Will going away, there would be no need of brewing, for neither she nor the children drank ale.

Anne replied diplomatically, "I have enough ale for some time."

Willikins took up the cue. "I'm sure the New Place ale is among the best in Stratford." He had never been invited to the house, and longed to be. "Writing, I'm sure, is thirsty work, and, from what I hear, the New Place barn is filled with malt, but perhaps that is to be turned into money rather than ale." There had been a deal of gossip about Will's hoarding, and the hatter was angling for an item for his customers, but he was not to be rewarded. Indeed, John took it upon himself to rebuke him, and not for the first time; Master Hart was not yet married into the family—though it was high time he was—and while he remained a suitor he must not be accorded the privileges of a son-in-law.

John said, "Master Hart,"—he could not bring his tongue to "Willi-kins"—"the affairs of New Place are my son William's, and not even I pry into them."

Judith, who had been bored with her own long silence, spoke with sudden unexpectedness. "I hate brewing day; the smells are so bad."

John quickly forestalled a reprimand from Anne by saying, "The worse the smell, the better the taste. Remember that, my child." Pleased with his aphorism he went on to spoil it by elaboration. "The harder the toil, the sweeter the rest. The longer the work, the greater the reward."

Not to be outdone, and seeing an opportunity to get back to the subject which had provoked the original rebuke, Willikins said, "And the fewer the goods, the higher the price."

Susanna, who was beginning to glory in her reputation for a ladylike wit, felt that here was an opportunity to top the exchange memorably; a rhyme would do it. "The louder tongues confound, the more do lies abound."

This was greeted with general approbation. Even Anne indulged her clever daughter with a warm smile. Willikins, in self-protection, was the loudest in applause. John said, with enthusiasm, "There you are, Rich-ard. There's your new rhymester for the gloves. Like father, like daughter."

The rest of the meal and the rest of the day passed peaceably. Will was fully occupied with preparing for his departure. In spite of his assurances, even to himself, that he would return soon, he knew that he probably would not. Only to Richard had he mentioned this possibility.

Ned spent a pleasant day with his mother and father. Both of them were glad to welcome him back under their roof, though they both deplored the reason for his return, John vociferously. Lying in bed again, he delivered an angry homily to Ned on the duties of a wife and advised him on the qualities he should look for in choosing a mate. "Let her be healthy so that she may bear you children that live, comely that she may warm your body, industrious and cleanly that she may keep you a good home, quiet in speech and rich in laughter that she may be a pleasing companion, but above all, let her have no opinions about God or man that are other than her husband's. Look at Will and his wife and beware. And then look at your mother and me, and in your marriage seek to follow us. You have always been her favored son, Edmund, so you know how good a mother she has been, but only I know how good a wife."

SEVENTEEN

THE JOURNEY TO LONDON WAS UNEVENTFUL. THE FURTHER THEY GOT from Stratford, the more did the oppression of it lift from Will's spirit and the more was it replaced by the excitement of London. Ned was full of questions and, in answering them, Will formulated the suggestions he would make to the sharers.

There were three new plays to be done. Will thought they should put *Much Ado About Nothing* into rehearsal immediately. That would mollify Will Kemp when they followed it with the new *Henry IV* play. Then they should do Ben Jonson's play. Ned wanted to know if Will would act in any of the plays.

Will replied with a smile, "You are not really interested in whether I play or not. What you long to know are what parts there are for you."

"Do I play Francis again?"

"No, there is no Francis. I could not use the 'Anon, anon, sir' jest twice. But there may be even better things for you. Time and the sharers will tell."

"And in the comedy?"

" 'Tis better I say nothing so that you will not be disappointed, but you have brought me and three new plays back to London, and for that they will want to reward you."

" 'Tis not I that brought you back."

"Your presence was a more powerful persuader than any letter could have been."

They arrived in London on Wednesday. Will had wanted to get to the theatre before the afternoon performance was over. The weather was still fine; there had not been a drop of rain for more than a fortnight. It was the kind of weather in which the plague flourished, but there was no talk of any.

They got to the Curtain, a half-hour before the end of the play. It was *Titus Andronicus*, which Nat Tremayne, the tireman, called *The Slaughterhouse*, because it needed more pints of animal blood than any other play, and the sight of the blood, and on a warm day like this the smell of it too, nauseated him. But his discomfort was as nothing to that of those players who had become corpses, tormented by flies which their blood-spattered clothes had attracted.

The welcome extended to Will, muted though it had to be while the performance lasted, was very gratifying to him. This world of make-believers was the only true one for him.

Ned too had his welcome, for he had become a popular member of the company, though he was suspiciously sure that the friendliness shown to him in some cases was due to his being Will's brother. But there was no doubt about the genuineness of the greeting from Sam Gilburne as he came off stage from grieving over the death of his grandfather, Titus Andronicus.

It was decided that the sharers who were present should eat together and then repair to Richard Burbage's house. William Kemp, who was not in the afternoon's play, should be sent for to meet with them there, it having been learnt to the great relief of the others that *Much Ado About Nothing* awaited him.

Ned, on their way home, had much to tell Sam, but Sam in return had something very exciting to tell Ned. There had been a great row in the theatre that morning during rehearsal, between Ben Jonson and Gabriel Spencer; they had even come to blows and had had to be separated. Ben Jonson had come to the theatre each of the previous three mornings to find out if Ned had returned. This morning Gabriel Spencer came too, looking for work, Sam supposed, "but in such a manner as if he were seeking to bestow a favor, not to receive one." As soon as the two men saw each other, it was "like linstock to gunpowder." They had grown to dislike each other during *The Isle of Dogs,* and their shared imprisonment which followed it had turned the dislike into a settled hate.

Sam had seen and heard it all that morning. "Neither of them was carrying a sword, or one of them would be a corpse by now, and I fear it would be Ben Jonson, for he looks clumsy, and Spencer is deadly with the rapier. Spencer called him an abominable player and an ignorant scribbler. Jonson said that Spencer was so full of poison that his breath reeked, and that he hated everybody because he thought they were as vile as himself whom he best knew. Then he spouted Latin which I could not follow—I have to see it, with a dictionary at hand. Spencer sneered at him and said, 'Quote not Juvenal to me, you classical parrot.' That was when Jonson hit him, and hard too. Spencer went staggering into a rack of costumes and Nat Tremayne screamed. Spencer rushed back at Jonson and went straight for his throat. The tireman's scream had brought everybody running, and soon the fighters were separated and held."

"Did Master Heminge see the fight?" asked Ned.

"Yes, and he was as furious as either of the two quarrelers," replied Sam. "From such a fray, he said, ill-wishers could talk of riot and get the theatre closed. He told Ben Jonson to go to the bookholder's room and wait for him there. Jonson was about to spit some last words at Spencer, but Heminge said, 'Enough. Go.' And Jonson went like a lamb. Then Master Heminge told Spencer never to come to the theatre again, for there would be no place in the company for such a cantankerous fellow. Spencer stopped struggling and said, like a king, 'Unhand me!' And they did. Before he left he said to Heminge in that proud, sneering way of his, 'I warn you, Master Heminge, if you have aught to do with that man

Jonson, you will rue the day.' And he walked out, like Richard II turning his back on Bolingbroke."

Ned and Sam were both abed and asleep when Will and Gus came home. The two men were in a happy mood. The meeting had gone well. Will's suggestions had all been adopted. On Thursday evening he would read them *Much Ado* at Richard Burbage's house, and they would have a preliminary discussion of the casting. The following day Will would set the copying in train. On Sunday afternoon they would all go to the Phillips home where they would discuss further the casting of *Much Ado* and Will would read them the new *Henry IV* play.

The only disagreement had been about *Every Man in His Humour;* in spite of Will's eloquent praise, there was still considerable doubt about it, occasioned by the playwright rather than the play. Heminge reported his conversation with Jonson after the morning's fracas, and his counsel still was to have nothing to do with the man: he had caused trouble before; he would cause trouble again; he would always cause trouble. None of the sharers doubted that Spencer had been the prime mover in the quarrel, but those who had witnessed it reported that Jonson had temper and tongue to match his opponent.

Heminge recalled that, when they were alone, the fiery Ben had said, "Spencer is an evil man and he will die a violent death; I pray to God it may be my sword that spits him." But when he had quieted down, he had been alternately suppliant about his play and arrogant in his claims for it.

The sharers finally decided, some of them still with reluctance, to do Jonson's play. With two provisos: Will was to meet with him and test his amenability to changes that might be necessary in his script; and Will was to take a part in the play to ensure his presence at rehearsals in case Jonson should prove difficult and troublesome, for it was felt that the fledgling playwright would accept the authority of the established one. Will contested the second proviso because he said he was eager to start his own new comedy which was becoming ripe in his head for the pen. As soon as he mentioned "comedy," Kemp's eyes brightened, but Will would say no more about it. The anti-Jonson forces used the news as a further argument for not doing *Every Man in His Humour;* therefore Will, in his regard for the play and sympathy for the playwright, ultimately agreed to both provisos.

As they walked home together, Will leading his horse, Gus raised questions about the new comedy. What was it about? Why had Will been so secretive about it? Will replied that there would be no part in it for Kemp. This was very distressing news to Gus, as it would be to the other sharers. What would they do with Kemp? "Find another writer for him, perhaps this Jonson," testily observed Will; and he added, "but from all I hear, I doubt fiery Ben would be as tolerant of Kemp's clownish tricks as forbearing Will. In truth, Gus, I long for a fool whose wit is in his head, not in his feet."

"Do you have such a one in mind?"

"Yes; one who learnt his trade under Tarlton. I saw Tarlton play at Stratford once. He was so ill-featured that to look at him was to pity him or to laugh, but he did not pity himself and so we laughed. His tongue was daring and impudent, and he made many squirm. But they laughed to hide it. And now he is gone these ten years."

"It was the year of the Armada," mused Gus. "Do you remember the ballad?

> "Our Queen doth grieve to lose her fool,
>   As Philip doth to lose his fleet.
> 'Tis harder for her now to rule
>   For Tarlton made her laugh so feat."

Will said, "Tarlton is gone, but the one he nurtured in his skill lives."

"You mean Robert Armin," said Gus in amazement, for there would be no room in the company for both Kemp and Armin.

"Yes, Armin is the one I want to write for, yet he writes well enough for himself."

"But . . ." Gus began to expostulate.

"But Kemp. Yes, but Kemp."

"He's a sharer."

"The more's the pity."

"The people idolize him. He has but to appear and they laugh and applaud."

"The more's the pity."

"Will, put it out of your mind. Apart from Burbage, there is no more important player in London than Kemp."

"Would he would leave London."

"Forget Armin, Will. 'Tis impossible."

"Then my new play is impossible."

AT BREAKFAST THE FOLLOWING MORNING BOTH NED AND SAM WERE EAGER FOR news of the sharers' meeting, but neither dared ask anything; they had to be content with what they could glean from the conversation of their elders and with what scraps were vouchsafed to them. They gathered that Will was to have two important meetings that day, one with Ben Jonson and the other with Cuthbert Burbage.

Ordinarily Ned would have been reluctant to go to the theatre for a morning rehearsal of *The Comedy of Errors* because all he had in it was a couple of boring nothings, but he went eagerly on that Thursday because he hoped to see Ben Jonson to be the first to whisper to him the good news. He intended to do so in such a way as to suggest that he was at least in part responsible for it. He was overjoyed when John Heminge gave him the task of looking out for Master Jonson and taking him to the bookholder's room to meet Will, who would be carefully going over the script for copying of *Much Ado*.

When Ben saw Ned, who had stationed himself where he could not be missed, his face brightened with greeting, but his words showed that his welcome was less of Ned than of the possible significance of his return. He said, "Has he come?"

Ned nodded energetically, and his smile showed that the news was good.

"He likes my play! I knew he would; he is a man of discernment."

"I like it too."

"You read it?" asked Ben in surprise and with a slight note of disapproval. It should have been kept from prying eyes until it was registered and publicly performed. He should have sealed the package. Too late now, and the lad seems honest enough.

Ned in his eagerness to impress Ben chose to hear pleasure rather than suspicion in his question. He said, "Yes, I read it before Will did and I told him I liked it. I long to play young Lorenzo."

"And I to play Giuliano, but Master Heminge says no." Here Ned could not miss the implication that the no was expected to apply to Ned's ambitions as well.

Somewhat dashed in spirit, Ned said, "I am to take you to see my brother. Come."

When Ned introduced the two playwrights, there was a moment of silent appraisal between them. Ben could not but be envious of Will's success and power, and there was only eight years between them, much too little for the mantle of Elijah to pass to Elisha. While he had contempt for the crudity and lack of scholarly standards in much of Will's work, he had nothing but admiration for parts of his *Henry IV* play, and now there were rumors since yesterday of another soon to be offered. Previously, Ben had only seen Will on the stage and had thought him lacking in theatrical presence; he seemed to regard the stage as a private room, whereas to Ben it was an arena, and when he played he entered like a gladiator. Face to face, Ben found that very quality of quiet ease and poise which he had thought to be unsuited to the stage was the outcome of an inner strength and mystery. Will Shakespeare did not wear his heart on his sleeve as Ben did.

For his part, Will immediately saw in Ben the man he had heard about, the man who from rough honesty would cause trouble. But he saw more in him too, the sensitive and skillful man who had written a good and different play. When Will had set out in the theatre, he had written in imitation of others and what was in demand—a Roman farce, a bloody tragedy, an English history. Not this Ben; he was his own man, and he expected the theatre to come to his terms. Yet in spite of his blustering confidence, he was frightened that it might not.

Will introduced Ben to Tom Vincent, who received the introduction as though it were yet another affliction about to be added to his already overburdened back.

"When it comes to copying my play, there will be no difficulty, Master Vincent," said Ben. "I write with care. Have you seen the script yet?"

"No," curtly replied the bookholder, with a tone of forlorn hope that he never would see it.

"Now, Tom, Master Jonson and I must have conference. Perhaps you could find a nook somewhere to decipher more of my scrawl."

Ned would have liked very much to hear the conversation between Will and Ben, but the bookholder held the door for Ned to precede him and then carefully closed it after them.

As Will gathered together the papers of *Much Ado,* he invited Ben to sit where the bookholder had sat.

Inquisitive about the papers, Ben asked, "A new play?"

"Yes, a comedy."

"But I heard last night of a new *Henry IV* play," said Ben in surprise, suddenly realizing that this miraculously prolific Shakespeare might have two plays ready.

"And you heard true," said Will, and he smiled, for he sensed the doubts and fears that were racing through Ben's brain. He quickly added, "But I have advised that we do your play too."

Ben, his confidence shaken for only a moment, did not express thanks or appreciation to Will; he merely said, "When?"

Will was somewhat taken aback. He said, "Let me see. 'Tis now mid-June. Let us allow a month for each of my new plays, assuming the theatres remain open the whole summer . . ."

"You fear another *Isle of Dogs.* There will never be one from me."

"No, Master Jonson. I was thinking of the plague."

"Your pardon, Master Shakespeare. I am too sensitive. Whenever I meet a player for the first time, I think he sees *Isle of Dogs* like the mark of Cain on my forehead."

"To return to our arithmetic. London should see *Every Man in His Humour* by mid-September, if . . . ," and Will paused significantly.

"There is an 'if'?" asked Ben in genuine surprise.

" 'Tis best I be frank, Master Jonson, for so I would wish you to be with me. You know the sharers are divided in the matter of the play."

"Unfairly so. 'Tis that *Isle of Dogs* again. There is no harm in this new play."

"None whatever. But 'tis not only the play. There are those who believe you are a troublesome fellow." Ben's mouth dropped open. "That may be because you are a blunt and honest man who disdains the smooth courtesies that oil the wheels of society. Although I have recommended that we do your play, 'tis not yet so decided. All depends on the outcome of this conversation." Ben was now floundering in speechlessness. "Would you be prepared to make such changes in the play as I thought necessary?"

This released the challenged author into speech. "But 'tis written with great care. Every word is weighed and placed."

"But words carefully weighed and placed on a page often change their value in the mouth of a player."

"Then the player must be taught to speak them as the author intended."

"Players too are men, not machines. Then there is the audience which cannot be controlled. Thus, when they know the play is coming to a close, the sooner 'tis over, the better. In your play there is a long speech at the end on the nature of true poetry."

"A fine speech, Master Shakespeare, and a necessary one when so many harlot words masquerade under the false name of Poesy."

"True, Master Jonson, but I fear the audience would find it tedious."

"They must hear what is good for them to hear."

"For that they are made to go to church. In the theatre we must woo their pennies away from the bearpit."

"I know they will listen to that speech and like it. It makes a worthy man of the young Lorenzo. Without it, he is just a worthless scamp who deceives his father."

"Your young man and his father are but the scaffolding of your play. 'Tis your gulls and braggart and jealous husband and scheming servant that give life and color to the building. You have a rare gift for comedy, Master Jonson, and you will best teach your audience when they most laugh."

Much mollified, Ben said, "Master Shakespeare, I trust you, but I beg you to rehearse the play as now 'tis written. If then the lines on poetry prove tedious we will cut them out, and any others that prove not worthy."

" 'Tis better to make some changes before we start, for it is harder for players to unlearn than to learn."

"I beseech you to retain young Lorenzo's speech; it matters much to me." Then he added, "I think your young brother might speak it well."

Will looked quizzically at Ben to estimate what had prompted the reference to Ned. He said, "There is time enough to allot the parts, and it will be done by agreement among the sharers."

"And the author, Master Shakespeare, for he knows best what his characters call for." Ben had spoken this with some spirit. Hitherto his tone had been reasonable and, when he had differed, pleading. Now there was a hint of the belligerence that had soured his reputation.

Will replied quietly but firmly, "And only the sharers know the qualities of the players. But we shall most surely want you to read your play to us and answer our questions. Your reading will give us much pleasure, of that I have no doubt, for you are a player yourself."

"And wish to play in my play, Master Shakespeare, but your Master John Heminge . . ." The need for tact stemmed the words that were rushing to Ben's lips, and he hesitated.

Will was quick to seize the hesitation to utter a warning. "John Heminge is a good friend, a good colleague, and a good judge of plays and players."

"But he has not seen me play. I was a rare Hieronimo."

"I do not doubt it," said Will with a smile, for he could see the fiery Ben lashing himself into a lather of sorrow and rage to make the groundlings gape and shudder.

Unpredictably Ben reacted to Will's smile with a chuckle which grew into a loud laugh, for he suddenly saw himself with Will's eyes, ranting and raving in an old play which he despised.

"Why do you want to act?" asked Will. "For myself, I feel that every hour on the stage is one stolen from my pen."

"But you are older than I, and the stage has had time to stale. Besides, Master Shakespeare, I need the money; I have a wife and children."

"So have most of our present hired men, and they have no ability with the pen to support them. You must accept the fact, Master Jonson, that, if the Lord Chamberlain's Men perform your play, it is most unlikely that you will have a part in it. That being so, would you prefer to sell your play elsewhere?"

"No," said Ben sadly. "There is no other market for it that can pay the price. You know that I have worked for Master Henslowe and the Admiral's Men, and he paid me some money for the play while I was in jail, but now that he has read it, he likes it not. My play of the humours is too new for him. He is a fearful man, with an eye for pennies, not poetry."

At the midday meal in the tavern, Ben was Will's guest at the sharers' table. Out to ingratiate himself with the company, he became a bounding source of wit and good fellowship, and every tankard of ale he took loosened his spirit and his tongue still more. Soon he and Will Kemp were trading stories, and at last even the suspicious Heminge was relaxed and laughing. Occasionally, too, Ben would give a revealing glimpse of himself which in its honest self-awareness was beguiling. Thus, when the subject of wives came up, he said, "There must be only one tongue in my house and that is mine. But my wife's is longer and louder. I know that is hard to believe, but 'tis true. Still, an admirable woman. I love her the more the further I am away from her."

Ned, from the table of the younger hired men, kept looking toward the sharers' table, as from time to time did most other people in the room, especially when peals of laughter drew their attention. It was clear to him that *Every Man in His Humour* was to be bought by the company, and he longed to talk about it to Sam and the others but decided that this would be indiscreet. He was pleased that Ben seemed to be winning over those sharers who had been opposed to him.

The dinner company broke up in some haste, for their laughter had delayed them, and the bookholder had been fluttering about for some time like a worried hen over wandering chicks. Fortunately *The Comedy of Errors* was a short play, though it was customary for Will Kemp to use that as an excuse for lengthening his clowning.

The meal over, Ben was anxious for a private conversation with John Heminge in the hope of acquiring at least an advance payment on his play. Heminge told him that he was in haste to prepare for the afternoon's performance and would see him the following morning. Ben's efforts at dinner had been chiefly aimed at winning over John Heminge, and now he sensed in Master Heminge a return to something of the former attitude.

When his companions had left, Ned still lingered, but nervously, for he was on at the opening of the play as an attendant of the Duke. He had to have a word with Ben, and, as soon as John Heminge strode out, he hurried across to him. Ben, who had been the funmaker at the table, was now suddenly disconsolate, but he made an effort to brighten as Ned approached him.

"All is well?" queried Ned.

"Well enough," replied Ben, but, when he saw that the implied qualification puzzled and dashed his questioner, he quickly added, "I mentioned you for the young Lorenzo to your brother."

"What did he say?"

"That the choice lay not with him alone. He's a good man, your brother, an honest man. I would he were my brother."

"I must hurry. Goodbye."

As Ned ran out, Ben called after him, "I come to the theatre in the morning and hope to see you then."

As soon as the afternoon's performance had begun, Cuthbert Burbage came to the bookholder's room where Will was poring over the script of *Much Ado*, making more legible some of the words that Tom Vincent had questioned. Will had expected Cuthbert, but was unprepared for the hushed secrecy of his greeting. Cuthbert, who compensated for his lack of opportunity on stage by a dramatic approach to everyday life, whispered that what he had to say could not be spoken where other ears might hear; they should take a walk in the fields; he would not venture to speak of this even within the walls of his own home. Amused and mystified, Will followed the comically cautious man out of the theatre, but Cuthbert forbore speaking until they were alone in the fields. Then he began, and by this time his speech was well rehearsed for he had already delivered it to five other people with a cumulative effect of secrecy.

"It's the Theatre, Will. Giles Alleyn is a Shylock, but I will not give him his pound of flesh. I have now abandoned all hope of renewing the lease of the land for any reasonable sum. And the Curtain is not good enough; not good enough for players, sharers, householders, or audience. We must have another theatre, Will. My father had hoped it would be the Blackfriars, but try as we may, we cannot get a license to play there."

"But the children play there to your profit," observed Will laconically.

"What would you? We must live. But to return. We must have another theatre, and outside the city walls. Where, Will, where?"

" 'Twould be convenient for many of us if it were on the South Bank," said Will with amusement.

Cuthbert stopped dramatically and, clapping Will hard on the back, said, "You have hit it, William, you have hit it."

"So have you, Cuthbert," commented Will wryly as he eased his back from the blow. But Cuthbert ignored such facetiousness.

"Bankside! I am negotiating with the utmost care and caution to lease some excellent land from one Nicholas Brend, right across the way from Henslowe's Rose; as you might say, right under the nose of the Rose!" He tried this quip every time he delivered the speech, but his hearers never laughed as heartily as he did. Cuthbert collected himself and swept on. "And for thirty-one years, not twenty-one as my poor trusting father did with that despicable Giles Alleyn." While Will might agree with the epithet applied to Giles Alleyn, he certainly had reservations about those applied to the departed James Burbage, who was known to have been lacking in trust and was reputed to have been lacking in scruple. "And for seven pounds, five shillings a year, less than three shillings a week, a reasonable sum with money losing its value all the time."

"And you and Richard will build a new theatre for us on Master Brend's land," said Will, still failing to understand the need for all the secrecy.

"New and yet old," Cuthbert said mysteriously, enjoying Will's puzzlement.

"I understand not the secrecy nor why it concerns me," said Will, some irritation beginning to creep into his voice, for he had much work to do.

"Bear with me, William, bear with me and all will be made clear. Yes, Richard and I would build a theatre on Bankside. But we have not the money." And he said this with a most inappropriate note of triumph. Will jumped to what was coming and became both interested and cautious. "Our plan is that we bear half the cost, the other half to be divided equally between five carefully chosen sharers, who would thus become householders as well."

"And I am one of the chosen ones?"

"The first."

"The others?"

"John Heminge, Augustine Phillips, Thomas Pope, and William Kemp."

Will had hoped that last name would not have been included, but had feared it inevitably would be. He asked, "Have they all been sounded?"

"Yes, Will. You were the first to be chosen but your absence made you the last to be told. The others have all agreed, and I might say agreed eagerly, as I am sure you will."

Instead of the eager agreement which Cuthbert confidently expected, Will said, "Now riddle me your 'new and yet old.' "

"Ah! That is the pearl in the oyster, the jewel in the crown, and that too is the secret of all secrets. The land the Theatre is on belongs to Alleyn but the building belongs to the Burbages. Our plan is to move it pillar by pillar and plank by plank to Bankside! We must prepare for this with care and stealth, for, if Alleyn caught a whisper of it, he would burn the Theatre to the ground rather than let us take it."

"When is this, this theft to take place?"

"Theft? You speak like Alleyn. You cannot steal your own."

"He will bring force to stop you."

"We will have greater forces."

"He will bring suit against you in court."

"Let him. He will not win. We shall give him his land back as we found it. What say you, William? Is not the plot masterly?"

"As good a plot as ever was laid. A good plot, good friends, and full of expectation."

Cuthbert missed the irony of Will's quotation from his first *Henry IV* play, for Hotspur's "excellent plot" had ended disastrously.

"And you will become a partner, and a householder in our new theatre?"

To become the part owner of a theatre was highly desirable, but there were great risks in this venture. Will temporized. "I must first know what money is involved, for my purse is much stretched by my new house in Stratford. I will talk to John Heminge and Gus Phillips."

"There is time, William, there is time. First, I must get the lease from Brend, and it will be winter before we move the Theatre, for then Alleyn's watchdogs will be asleep. But I beg you, William, when you speak of this, to be wary of prying ears."

Will, his mind now reverting to the immediate task, the copying of *Much Ado About Nothing*, replied in his Benedick's words: "I can be secret as a dumb man."

EIGHTEEN

The reading of Much Ado About Nothing at Richard Burbage's that night was a great success but it led to a crisis. All had been agog to hear the Kemp part and they were not disappointed. Kemp himself was ecstatic, and when they took a break for refreshments at the end of Will's reading, he kept repeating with great gusto the line that he knew would take the town: "Oh! That they had writ me down an ass." He hugged Will with joy and gratitude, but Will caught the eye of Gus Phillips, and they both remembered their conversation about Robert Armin.

It was when they settled down to a preliminary discussion of the play and the casting that the trouble occurred. It was clear that Verges had been written for skinny Cowley, and to Will it was equally clear that Claudio had been intended for Richard Burbage, but, when it was mentioned, Burbage said, "No."

"But . . ." said Will, Heminge, and Phillips all together, and the spontaneous chorus relaxed the gathering into laughter, a welcome relief to the immediate tension that Burbage's plain no had caused.

"Claudio is all work and no play," explained Burbage. "Be honest with me, Will. Beatrice and Benedick are your own invention. They are the characters that gave you most delight. Am I not right?"

"Yes," Will had to admit.

"And to make room for the Claudio-Hero story you had to curb Beatrice and Benedick."

Will nodded with a rueful smile, because he sensed that Burbage's argument was going to take him back to a decision he had made regretfully during the writing and which he was now going to be asked to unmake.

Burbage addressed the room. "My suggestion is that we postpone *Much Ado* to enable Will to reshape it, to shake off the shackles of the story and follow his true inspiration." Will Kemp was looking sour, and Burbage tried to mitigate this as he proceeded. "Dogberry and Beatrice and Benedick can set the town alight with laughter."

"What say you, Will?" said John Heminge.

All looked toward Will. After a moment he spoke, but slowly, as if to himself. "Dick is right; but the plot needs the space. It will be hard to cut it down to give Beatrice and Benedick more room. I debated it before and thought there was no other way. Claudio must have time to prove himself worthy of Hero."

"If Henry plays him," quipped Burbage, "everybody will know he is worthy," and they all looked at Condell and smiled and nodded warmly.

Will came to a decision. "Let me brood on it till we meet on Sunday. There may be a way; for one thing, Hero's mother might go, and that would give more space."

Phillips objected, "But she is a strong character with powerful lines."

Will smiled and said, " 'Tis easy to give powerful lines to mothers of wronged daughters."

Heminge took charge. "Then 'tis settled. We shall delay the copying of *Much Ado* and see what Will's brooding hatches by Sunday. If it's a live chick, we'll wait for it to grow and put the new *Henry IV* into rehearsal instead."

"You haven't heard it yet," said Will.

His tone gave Heminge pause, and he asked rather fearfully, "Nothing has happened to lessen Falstaff's part, has it?"

Pope looked very anxious as he awaited Will's reply.

"No. He has more of the play than before."

"Then all is well." And Heminge and Pope exchanged a beaming smile. "So we will do the new *Henry IV* first, and then *Much Ado.*"

"That gives me little time," said Will. "The rehearsals of the new *Henry IV* are going to keep me busy."

"While we play in the afternoon, you write," said Heminge. "Beatrice and Benedick will flow out of you with ease. I'll wager that by Sunday you will already see them full grown."

Henry Condell spoke. "If there are difficulties, Will, we can do the Ben Jonson play after *Henry IV;* that would give you another month."

"I still care not if we never do that play," grumbled Heminge.

"But Giuliano is a good part, John, and one made for you," Tom Pope said slyly.

"It must be a good part. Ben Jonson told my brother Ned he had written it for himself," commented Will.

"He told me so too," said Heminge, "but I held out no hope to him. If now I play the part he wrote for himself, he will pray for my sudden death."

With the laughter that greeted this remark, the meeting broke up, everybody, except Will Kemp, telling Will how much they looked forward to his reading of the new *Henry IV* on Sunday.

Ben was early at the theatre the following morning, and Master Heminge, striving hard to hide his reluctance, paid him three pounds, half the price of his play, the other half to be paid when the play was put into rehearsal.

"And when will that be?" asked Ben.

" 'Tis in some doubt," said John Heminge, and would not be drawn further.

Ben sought out Ned for explanation, but Ned could offer none, much to his own exasperation. As he left, Ben was a little worried, though considerably comforted by the chink of coins in his purse.

Rumor was rife among the hired men, apprentices, and assistants backstage in the next two days. All that was known for certain was that the copying of *Much Ado About Nothing* had been halted. Ned was appealed to as the most probable source of private information but all he could report was that his brother stayed all the time in his room, where his meals were taken to him by Mistress Phillips, who spent much of the rest of the time in enjoining Ned and Sam to be quiet.

For some unspecified reason, Augustine Phillips on several occasions during that Friday and Saturday urged Ned to practice his singing. When Ned pointed out that it was impossible to make music and keep quiet at the same time, Master Phillips said, "Sweet music does not disturb Will. His muse thrives on it. But keep the door closed." And so, after supper on both evenings, Ned repaired to the music room, closed the door, took up his lute in the use of which he had become pleasingly proficient, and, in a voice now matured into a smooth robustness, sang some of the many songs he had acquired since coming to London. One of his ambitions had always been to sing on the stage. Was this injunction of Master Phillips a hint that there might be a singing part for him in one of the new plays?

On Sunday morning Gus went up to Will's room to tell him it was time to prepare for church. Will looked tired but excited; the rewriting of *Much Ado* was going well, and he was happy that he had undertaken it. Already there was no doubt that the revised comedy would be ready to follow *Henry IV*.

The prayer for "moderate rain and showers" was said in church that morning, and it looked as if God was going to answer it, without paying any attention to the adjective. A flash of lightning followed almost immediately by a nearby thunderclap sent the congregation scurrying. Mistress Phillips's pregnancy slowed the Phillips party, but they got home just as the heavens opened. In no time at all, the path outside the door was beaten into mud. There was general agreement that the rain was too heavy to last long and would not interfere with the meeting of the sharers, due some three hours hence, to hear Will read his new *Henry IV*.

While Mistress Phillips and Letty prepared the table for the cold Sunday dinner, Master Phillips suggested that the men should make some music.

As they settled down in the music room, Will said, "My mind is full of Benedick; he cares not for the lute. This morning I wrote a new line for him: 'Is it not strange that sheep's guts should hale souls out of men's bodies?' "

"Dick will enjoy that," laughed Gus.

"I was thinking of him when I wrote it; he could willingly live without music."

"But not Will Shakespeare; and not Ned either. Come, lad. Give us a sample of your quality. One of Will's songs."

"On the Sabbath?" said Ned with mock alarm.

"Tush!" said Gus. "This storm will keep people indoors, even prying Puritans. Come."

And Ned again sang his favorite among Will's songs, "Who is Sylvia?", for his most satisfying conquest to date had been a Sylvia, a rich old merchant's bored young wife. There was one epithet that Will gave to his Sylvia that was most certainly not applicable to Ned's; she was not "holy."

Will was surprised and impressed by Ned's performance, and immediately guessed what Gus had in mind: Ned to play the songster, Balthasar, in *Much Ado*. And why not? Will was made guiltily aware that his brother and charge had been blossoming into full manhood without even his notice; as he listened to the song he was shocked to realize that he had been only about three months older than the boy that was now singing of love when he had himself begotten Susanna. But there was a great difference between Ned in London at eighteen and Will in Stratford at the same age. Ned had already completely left Stratford. A large part of Will never would be able or want to leave it, and that part needed a wife, children, and a home. Ned's happiness would lie in pursuing women and evading a wife. He had doubtless found his way into many beds already. Strange to think of it.

Will was warm in his praise of Ned's singing, and his obvious genuineness delighted both pupil and mentor.

During dinner there was much discussion as to the better room for the reading, and the living room finally won out over the music room. Mistress Phillips could lie down for the afternoon, and Ned and Sam could go for a walk if the weather permitted.

The rain stopped some time before the sharers were due, and the weather resumed its recent sunny brilliance. The young men were cautioned to don their long boots for their walk, as they would have to plough through mud and rivulets. They were not questioned as to where they intended to walk. Both the Phillipses regretfully assumed it would be to view the coarse delights of the Bankside and Paris Gardens.

Mistress Phillips was distressed that the floor had had its monthly change of rushes the day before; rushes were rapidly becoming an expensive luxury. Gus suggested that the men of the household should collect slippers for the six expected guests; then the wet and muddied boots could be discarded and left at the door. In fact the change of rushes had been advanced by a week because the heat had bred fleas and other irritating insects in the old ones, and the host and hostess wanted to spare the guests excessive itching and scratching.

The first visitor was Richard Burbage, anxious to know the result of Will's days of isolation. He was delighted with the report and still more to be told that Will was grateful that he had been persuaded to sacrifice the plot he had borrowed to the characters that were the beloved children of his own invention.

Burbage, Heminge, and Condell arrived on horses; Pope, Cowley, and Kemp on foot, for they lived close by. Kemp arrived last and was obviously in a bad humor. Apart from his disgruntled lack of interest in the *Henry IV* play, he was an addicted smoker. Not only was it impolite to bring the fumes of tobacco into a house you were visiting but it had been established a long while that no smoking was to take place during a reading, and particularly during the reading of a whole play by one voice. Will had once said that to read a play aloud in a small room filled with smoking men would be a particular torture reserved for him in hell. To cap Kemp's discomfort it was discovered that the last pair of slippers was too small for him, and he did not take kindly to Cowley's joke that now he understood that Kemp's grotesque stage slippers were really his natural size. The sour clown kicked off the too-small slippers and decided to walk about in his nether stockings.

Ale was liberally dispensed, and the sharers sat around the long table to listen to Will's new play. But he had an announcement to make which altered their tentatively revised plans: not only was he going to be happily able to do the suggested rewriting of *Much Ado About Nothing*, but, if he could be given a week of unworried isolation, it would be completed, which meant that their original plan of doing the comedy first could be adhered to with just a week's postponement. This was enthusiastically agreed to, and Kemp's grumpiness disappeared, especially when he had been assured that the rewriting would not in any way diminish his part.

In reply to a question by Will, John Heminge took it upon himself to say that no further reading of *Much Ado* to the company would be necessary and he thought they should discuss the casting forthwith, before their minds were full of the new play Will was going to read to them. According to Heminge's calculations, they would be able to do the play without employing more than the permanent hired men; that was, of course, if Will would play a part. As Will began to demur, Heminge overrode him with his usual argument: Will would have to be at all rehearsals, so he might as well play a small part—"that Friar, for instance"—thus saving a salary. The part could go to a hired man later.

Will did not argue overmuch, because he had an unusual suggestion to make. It had been assumed for some time that young Sam Gilburne had outgrown ladies' parts, but he wanted him to play Beatrice, for he had the right spirit for the part, and Beatrice was no young girl, no Juliet. Richard Burbage welcomed the suggestion. With Benedick and the author strongly for it, the doubts of some others were stifled, and thus Sam, who was at that moment being prevented by Ned from succumbing to the blandishments of a diseased harlot in the Paris Gardens, was elected to the part of the witty lady who was born under the sign of a dancing star.

Heminge grumblingly supposed that they would have to hire a minstrel to sing the songs.

It was then that Gus pressed the claims of Ned, and the idea was heartily welcomed by all. Gus was the arbiter in all matters musical; Ned was liked, Will would be pleased, and another salary would be saved.

Before Will started to read the new play, it was decided that they would break off at half-past four and take a walk, to enable Mistress Phillips to prepare supper. During the meal there was to be no discussion of either new play, but, after a plea by Gus Phillips, it was agreed that the boys should be given their good news with the understanding that they were to keep it to themselves, an understanding that the men who made it were sure would not be kept. They all knew the sore temptation of the tongue to blab good news about oneself and bad news about others.

Will's small audience settled down eagerly as he began his prologue with the words:

> "Open your ears, for which of you shall stop
> The vent of hearing when loud Rumour speaks?"

At that same moment Ned and Sam were listening with great excitement to a ragged balladeer in Paris Gardens. Ned had at last found Robin of London. The unmistakable voice and manner had first caught Ned's ear. He had often told Sam about the minstrel, and now here he was. He lived up to Ned's tales. He was as flamboyant as before, but more gaunt and wild-eyed; London had brought him neither fame nor fortune. A motley crowd of some thirty or so was gathered around him, some of them so poor and desperate that they would have stolen his tattered lute, given the slightest chance. Robin was standing on a rock and luring his audience, who stood on the muddied grass.

"Draw near and listen to a tale you will never forget. A true tale and a new tale. As God is my witness, I was there and saw it all." Some very sober burghers were joining the audience, and Robin was quick to counter their possible hostility. "This is a Sunday, the Sabbath, the Lord's Day, and it is fitting that my tale be true and that it preach a lesson that warns us of mortal dangers to our souls, for this is a tale of God's vengeance against wicked people, people with hearts of stone, and of His mercy toward poor people, poor in the eyes of the world but blessed in the eyes of God." And Robin, with the hastily assumed fervor of a Savonarola, launched into his song.

> "List to the tale of Twyford Town,
>   Twyford is in Devon,
> Twyford Town was all burnt down
>   With corpses forty-seven.
>
> Full forty-seven were smoked and charred
>   But they went not to Heaven.
> 'Twas Hell received those hearts so hard
>   With fire seven times seven.
>
> Seven times seven hotter far
>   Those fires so stoked by devils.
> Eternal punishment they are
>   For men and all their evils."

The song was a long one and told of how a poor woman had nothing for fuel but cast-out straw which she collected and dried, but the lighted straw soon set her cottage ablaze and the fire enveloped the houses of the rich who had scorned the hungry poor from their doors. But God had worked a miracle.

"An almshouse stood amid the flames
    Where lived the poor and needy,
Not one was scorched, for God thus tames
    Those fires so fierce and greedy.

And thus He made it plain to see
    That Heaven will be forever
For those who give in charity
    And works of like endeavour.

So when you see a wretched wight
    Remember Twyford fire.
Bestow upon him pennies bright
    To escape from Hell so dire."

As he sang this last verse, though Robin looked the most wretched of all wights, very few felt their chances of immortal salvation would be greatly increased by bestowing their pennies upon him. This new song was generally so unprofitable that he was determined to discard it from his repertoire after today. Even before he had finished, most of those with the means to reward him had begun to drift away. He stepped down from the rock to move among the crowd. A few gave him a measly coin or two, which were hungrily regarded by those with no coins at all; Robin kept a tight grip on his frayed collection bag.

Ned and Sam approached Robin, and Ned hailed him. Whenever he heard his name called, Robin's instinct was to run, and he began to do so, but Ned grabbed his arm and, in a tone so friendly that it stayed the balladeer, said, "I'm Ned Shakespeare. Stratford-on-Avon. Long ago. Nearly two years. My sister and I helped you to get out of town. You gave her a button."

Robin had not the slightest recollection of the incident—there were so many towns he had had to get out of, with or without help—but he was prepared to remember it, and vividly, for a price.

Ned continued. "This is my friend, Sam Gilburne. We are players. The Lord Chamberlain's Men."

Robin's wary look began to dissolve.

"Don't you go to the theatre?" asked Sam.

" 'Tis rare that one performer has time or opportunity to watch another," said Robin rather grandly. "Besides, I have not been much in London. As you have just seen, they have no taste here for men of my quality. They revel in the gore of bearpits and bullrings." Robin should have been grateful for this fact, for his nimble fingers had gained him richer pickings inside such places than ever his voice and lute had gained outside.

"Where do you live?" asked Ned, with the friendly object of offering to accompany the singer home.

Robin's honest answer would have been, "Wherever the night happens to find me." Instead, he said, "To be truthful, I seek a new lodging this night. I was ill content with my last one. The bed was lousy and the food nigh poisonous with age." The mention of a bed, though he had not slept in one of any kind for a long time, reminded him of the presence of some lice which still found his undernourished body palatable, and he began to scratch vigorously.

"I wish I could offer you a bed with me, but alas! that cannot be. The house is not mine, and this night it is full of guests."

Sam who saw Robin much more clearly than did Ned, was relieved to find that his friend realized the impossibility of introducing the filthy vagrant into the Phillips household.

"But let us have a pot of ale together," said Ned.

"With, mayhap, a bite of bread and cheese?" queried Robin, striving to hide the urgency of his stomach.

"We are expected home to supper," said Sam.

"But drink without food is like the sea without ships, only good to drown in," said Robin, proud of his impromptu apothegm.

And to bathe in, thought Sam, who had become very conscious of Robin's stench.

"So I will eat for all three of us," concluded Robin, implying a generous sacrifice on the altar of good friendship.

The haze of memory had not completely blinded Ned to Robin's unsavoriness, and, as they began to walk along, he found it difficult to decide which tavern was best suited to their purpose; it had to be one where Robin's appearance would not make him unwelcome and yet one where he would not be ashamed to take Sam. As he mulled over the problem, he made conversation. "Did I not tell you, Sam? Has not Robin a good voice?"

Sam thought that Ned must be deaf as well as blind in the matter of his hero, for whatever voice he might once have had was already scraped raw with ill usage. He evaded an answer by saying, "Ned has spoken much of you, Robin."

The balladeer, with a meal and perhaps more in sight, lied liberally. "And I have often thought of him and his sister, to whom I gave a button in remembrance." In remembrance of what? Had she been an older and desirable sister who had satisfied his carnal needs?

Ned had suddenly thought of the right tavern, a respectable one, The Bunch of Grapes, with two rooms, one for the well-to-do and the other for laborers and artisans. In his relief at solving the problem, he became dangerously generous. "Sam, we must introduce Robin to Master Phillips. Perhaps he could become a minstrel for the company."

Sam was appalled by the prospect, but at the same time his funny bone itched to be present at the meeting between Robin and Master Phillips. He was spared having to comment on Ned's suggestion, for Robin, his imagination ablaze with possibilities, jumped in.

"This Master Phillips. Who is he?"

"A player and a musician, and a sharer in the company. It is at his house that Sam and I lodge. My brother Will too."

Three lodgers, mused Robin. Maybe more. Probably a wealthy man. This brother Will. Another musician? His thoughts were jolted by a surprise statement from Sam.

"I take it you read music."

"Does a cat lap milk?" responded Robin after a moment's hesitation, for indeed he read neither words nor notes.

Ned had a further inspiration. Tomorrow's play was the first *Henry IV*. Robin should see him as Francis.

"Tomorrow you must come to the theatre, Robin, and after the play I will introduce you to Master Phillips."

"Which theatre is it?"

"The Curtain," said Ned in a tone of surprise, as though everybody should know that.

Robin realized he had made a mistake and laughed away his temporary ignorance. He had heard mention of the Curtain, but had no idea where it was; his knowledge of London was restricted to the South Bank. He had ventured across the Bridge once, lured by tales of St. Paul's, but he soon retired in defeat, for he lacked the clothes to present the necessary false face, and he scorned being a plain beggar. He decided he would have to inquire his way to the Curtain tomorrow. It might be worthwhile to gamble a precious penny for entrance. He had never been inside a theatre but he assumed the cost would be the same as at the Rose and the Swan, where he had sometimes mingled with the crowd waiting admittance, but had only once been able to filch a purse and that had proved to be empty. His ragged appearance made his purpose so apparent to possible victims that they eyed his approach warily and took firm grip of their wallets.

At the tavern, where Robin offended the eyes and noses of even the humblest laborers, he kept his promise to eat for all three, but, though he ate with a wolfish gusto, he did so with an engaging flourish.

As Ned drank and watched him, another problem presented itself, one which had immediately occurred to Sam. Robin could not be introduced backstage looking like this.

Robin seemed to divine Ned's concern for he said, "Think not I shall present myself to Master Phillips attired like this. I assume this guise when I perform the Ballad of Twyford the better to move men's hearts for the wretched wights of this world."

Even as he told his lie, Robin was scheming. Monday was washing day in most homes, so it should be easy to pick up a drying shirt and hose from a hedge or a line.

Sam became restless. It was time to go home to supper. He wanted not to miss a minute of the meal, for all the sharers would be there, and although they would be carefully discreet, one or more might drop a morsel of information.

Ned had the same expectations of the supper. When Sam made him aware of the need to hurry, he quickly paid the four-pence-ha'penny that their refreshments had cost and bade a bustling goodbye to Robin, who openly picked up the unconsumed bread and cheese, saying that he would give it to some beggar, for the Twyford ballad always made him think of the poor. Feeling guilty at his hasty departure, Ned said that they would have supper together tomorrow.

As they squelched through the mud which feet and hooves had as yet prevented the sun from drying, Ned and Sam were silent on the subject of Robin. Ned suddenly realized that he had promised to help Robin to become the company minstrel when he himself might be given that role; why else would Master Phillips have gotten him to sing for Will? And that recollection started an even worse dilemma: it was the custom for the beauteous Sylvia to come to the theatre whenever he played Francis, and if her husband was going to be away that night—the wool trade often took him away to East Anglia—she would send some token backstage. Now he had engaged himself for supper with Robin, whom exasperation showed him in a revealing flash to be a tatterdemalion, stinking vagabond. The realization put him into a bad temper.

Supper had already begun by the time they got home, and both were annoyed by the thought of what they might have missed. There was abundance of good humor around the table so they judged that the new play had found favor.

"Shall we tell them, gentlemen?" asked John Heminge with ponderous patronage. There was a chorus of ayes, and the good news was given.

Sam was stunned into incoherence by his unexpected good fortune. Ned had more than half expected his, and his reaction was spoiled by the thought of Robin.

Master Phillips suggested that while Sam helped Mistress Phillips and Letty to clean up after the meal and restore the room for the resumption of the reading, the gentlemen should listen to Ned in the music room.

Ned acquitted himself well to the delight of the sharers; once he strummed his lute, the pride of the performer overwhelmed his private woes. Master Phillips asked Will if he could remember the words of Balthasar's song, that Ned might savor the joy in store for him. Will obligingly recited, "Sigh no more, ladies," and it elicited several witty and approving comments on the line, "Men were deceivers ever."

When the reading was resumed, Ned went to Sam's room to share in his joy. They could now discuss Robin frankly. He could not understand how memory had so cheated him; even the teeth that had been so memorably white were now a dirty brown and jagged. Ned and Sam discussed stratagems for dealing with Robin, and Ned hinted at the possible amatory complications.

The new play was full of surprises for the sharers. This was no echo of the first *Henry IV,* but was almost totally different in spirit; there was sadness, death, and solemn duty in it. Hal, the prankster, became Henry, the dedicated king, and Richard Burbage welcomed the transformation. When it was his turn to comment at the end of the reading, he urged that Will could no longer put off writing a Henry V play; it was his duty, which he could no more escape than could Prince Hal the crown. Thomas Pope could scarcely believe his good fortune; this Falstaff gave him even greater opportunities than the first, because it was more varied. Justice Shallow was the wonderful surprise. Will Kemp yearned to play it, but Will had made it perfectly clear by the physical descriptions that it was intended for Richard Cowley, to whom a major part was long overdue; no other member of the company could carry the description, "the very genius of famine."

Augustine Phillips took his pregnant wife carefully into his arms that night to gloat in her receptive ear over the wonderful death scene Will had written for him.

NINETEEN

Breakfast the next morning was a hushed occasion at the Phillips home: Master Shakespeare was working and would probably be doing so for the rest of the week. Letty had fetched down his jordan of urine and taken up his ewer of water. Both times Will seemed completely unaware of her.

Ned was glad of the morning quiet because he was preoccupied with thoughts of Robin and Sylvia. He told Mistress Phillips not to expect him for supper, and that he might be staying out late. His first staying out late had led to one of the rare arguments between husband and wife. Both of them had correctly assumed that Ned was "dallying with a wench." Gus had thought that this was right and proper, and that Ned could look after himself better than most young men of his age, but Mistress Phillips had been deeply concerned about the dangers to their charge, especially since his brother was away in Stratford at the time. She had remained fitfully awake throughout the night but failed to catch the return of the furtive Ned and was very surprised when he came down with Sam in the morning, looking even fresher than usual. She had reported the matter to Will on his return and was reassured by his amused acceptance of it with the words, "Boys will be men." Now the occasional late homecomings of both Shakespeares caused no concern. When Ned made his announcement that Monday morning, Mistress Phillips caught a pathetically envious look in the eyes of Sam and wondered how long it would be before he too would be out at bedtime.

At the theatre, with a quarter of an hour to go before the play began, Ned did indeed receive the token he awaited. It was a red rose. The excited anticipation which Sylvia's tokens usually aroused in him was complicated this time by thoughts of Robin. It was customary for Sylvia to wait for him in her curtained coach near St. Leonard's Church. He would be delayed by Robin, if no worse. There was no way to get a message to Sylvia. Suppose that, on account of a worthless vagabond, he lost her. He began to loathe Robin, and yet faint glimmerings of justice in his rapidly clouding judgment made him admit that Robin had done nothing to deserve such harshness.

All the while the object of Ned's loathing was resolving his dilemma for him, but unintentionally. After a good night's sleep under a Thames wharf, free from the usual pangs of hunger, Robin finished the remains of last night's supper, which had been carefully wrapped in his ragged jacket to deny it to the rats. As he yawned awake, he took stock of the promising day ahead. He had threepence-farthing; only the penny for the theatre needed to be spent, for he foresaw a prodigious free supper after the play. First, he must find where the Curtain was. That would be easy. He would set out at once for it so that he would have ample opportunity on the way to collect a clean shirt and hose.

The first person he questioned concerning the whereabouts of the Curtain Theatre took one quick look at him and hurried away. The second one stopped and deluged him with suspicious and hostile questions, declaiming aloud that such vagabonds should be sent to the wars or locked up; this time it was Robin who hurried away. He was very careful in his choice of the next man he spoke to. It was a young apprentice who was blithely whistling as he went on his way. He was friendly to the appearance of the wandering minstrel and his lute. Moreover, he not only knew where the Curtain was, he had seen a play there.

The two young men met on London Bridge where congestion made conversation difficult, so the apprentice turned around to accompany Robin for some distance. He was very impressed when he learned that Robin was going to the afternoon's play at the invitation of a player with whom he was going to have supper afterwards. He himself was apprenticed to a goldsmith and was on an errand for his master. "Gold" and "errand" aroused Robin's quick interest but it was soon dashed when probing discovered that the errand was the delivery of a bill. Charlie, as the apprentice soon declared his name to be, would love to be a player; there was precedent for it. Robert Armin had been apprenticed to a goldsmith. Robin was glad to hear that the Curtain was only a little over a mile away from the end of the bridge, and about half a mile beyond the city walls; the open country should make the filching of clean linen easier. Robin got rid of the friendly Charlie with a few perfunctory words of thanks and farewell.

Once he had passed Bishopsgate his hopes rose. It was now midmorning, and the more industrious housewives would already have had their laundry out drying for some time. A path to the right looked promising. He followed it, and soon a perfect opportunity presented itself: a high trimmed and thick privet hedge which hid him from the house, and on it a fine display of linen. Most of it was bedware and night gear but he soon espied a beautiful white cambric shirt. Having assured himself that there was no one around to see him, he reached up and very slowly made the shirt his. He waited. There was no outcry. Next he aimed at some light blue hose; these were more difficult because they hung just outside his reach; he would have to jump. He did so and grabbed the hose, but this inevitably resulted in his having to jerk them down. The sudden movement must have caught attention, for a harrowing female shriek rent the air, and it was soon followed by the clamor of several approaching voices. Robin ran hard and made for the cover of some trees a couple of hundred yards to the north. From his hiding place he heard the housewife's loud laments about the wickedness of the world.

After removing his lute from his back, he threw himself down on the ground to gain his breath and enjoy his spoils. His fingers were savoring the texture of the shirt when he heard someone approaching. Quickly he put the stolen garments under the inadequate cover of the lute.

Two men stood over him. Robin appraised them. Both were sturdily made and a few years older than he; roughly bearded and better but soberly dressed; both carried daggers. These were dangerous men; not colorful highwaymen so dear to the folk imagination but workaday villains; they were careful to dress simply and respectably that they might not readily be remembered and recognized.

"You run well," said one whose three-fingered left hand rested on the hilt of his dagger.

"What do you want with me?" asked Robin with a strength that surprised him. He began to scramble to his feet; but the second man pushed him back down roughly with his foot.

"To begin with, that shirt and hose, and then anything else you may have filched," said Three Fingers.

"I have nothing," said Robin.

"No money?"

"Nothing."

Three Fingers gave a slight look toward the silent one, who with astonishing speed was on his knee with the point of his dagger at Robin's throat.

"No money?" reiterated the now smiling questioner.

Robin, unable to speak, shook his head vigorously.

"None?" The word was said with a drawled menace; the intention was unmistakable.

"Threepence-farthing," Robin said weakly.

" 'Twill do to slake our thirst."

"But I didn't steal it," pleaded Robin. "I earned it by singing."

"Your voice is not very profitable," sneered Three Fingers.

A slight pressure from the dagger point caused Robin to search out his coins hurriedly.

"I beg you to let me have one penny, just one penny," said Robin with desperate urgency. How was he to get into the theatre?

"Sing for it—but not to us," laughed Three Fingers as he walked away with the shirt and hose under his arm.

The silent one indulged himself by kicking Robin viciously in the stomach before following his companion. Robin gave a gasp of pain and doubled up. He retched to throw up, but couldn't.

By the time he was able to get to his feet, the robbers were well lost to sight. Painfully he began to walk in the direction where he thought Bishopsgate Street, the road to the Curtain, lay. As he walked he took stock of his sorry condition. How could he get into the theatre, and how dare he present himself to Master Phillips looking as he did? He was tempted to turn back to the city, but then he would miss his supper. If all else failed, he could wait outside the theatre until Ned came out and then say he had been too busy to change and go to the play, and it would be better to wait to see Master Phillips another time. Gradually his habitual optimism asserted itself, and, as the pain in his stomach wore off, his jaunty step returned.

When he got to the theatre some thirty or so people were already gathered outside although there was still half an hour before the doors would be opened. The sight of a group of people standing around was always an invitation and a challenge to Robin. As if by instinct he was soon with his back to the theatre wall, tuning his lute and giving his luring speech, but this time his audience was already captured, so he changed his speech to offer a selection of his wares.

"What would you have, gentles all? The Murder of Rizzio? The Twyford Fire? The Sack of Cadiz? The Lopez Plot with the Hanging of the Jew? What would you have?"

Most of the people were pleased at this unexpected diversion to while away the waiting in the hot sun. A group of apprentices thought that the vagabond minstrel might prove fair game and one of them called out, "It's murder we want, with plenty of blood."

"You shall have it, young sir. The Murder of Rizzio, who was done to death with fifty-seven gory stabs."

To their own surprise the apprentices were held by Robin's performance, and after the fifth verse they began to join in the chorus:

"All this did happen as I do tell,
      In Holyrood in Scotland;
The blood was spilt despite of Hell,
      In Holyrood in Scotland."

With each succeeding refrain more of the spectators joined in, and the audience swelled as more people arrived for the play. A few maintained silence lest their participation should betoken approval of sentiments that might be considered dangerous, but by the time Robin was halfway through the ballad the lusty chorus could be heard for some distance. It drew the attention of some of the lesser players returning from dinner to prepare for the afternoon performance; the principals were already back-stage before Robin had begun. Among the laggards was Ned, and the remembered chorus told him that his problem had arrived. Neither he nor his companions stayed more than a minute with the crowd, for they had begun to be recognized, and it was a strict rule that the players should not mingle with their patrons. As Master Phillips had said: "They pay to see us as kings and lords; 'tis better not to remind them that we are but men, and some of us a sorry lot."

When news of the balladeer was taken backstage, Cuthbert Burbage, who was making preparations for the doors to be opened, was consider-ably annoyed; this scurvy minstrel might inveigle pennies that were intended for apples, nuts, and ale. He stalked out to put a stop to the unlicensed encroachment on the theatre's perquisites.

He got to the crowd as the fiftieth verse was started, and so he did not have a singing chorus to battle his way through. But as he began to remonstrate with Robin upward of a hundred voices drowned him. With growing exasperation he waited, looking for and failing to find some-thing on which to stand; how could he speak to the people unless they could all see him?

Robin started brazenly to continue his song, but Cuthbert, having failed with command to silence him, tried to take his lute from him. Some of the nearest in the crowd, notably the apprentices, immediately championed the singer; he whom they had meant to taunt was now their cause. Voices were raised in mounting confusion. The information spread that the spoilsport was Master Cuthbert Burbage, and when this perco-lated through the front ranks, it was decided to give him a hearing. It was not every afternoon you met the brother of a famous man.

The chorus which had made Cuthbert wait had also given him time to think of a telling argument; he dared not speak the mercenary truth. "This is an unlawful assembly," he began, "and I do not need to tell you who love the theatre that there are those, and powerful ones too, who do not. This would be enough to enable them to close the theatre; they have done it for less." Fortunately nobody pressed him for proof of his last statement. "I have naught against this young man—'tis clear he has found favor with you—but I dare not countenance his unlicensed performance."

"Let me but finish my ballad," begged Robin who had entertained growing hopes of a good collection.

Several voices took up his plea, but they were silenced by the raising of Cuthbert's imperious hand. " It cannot be. Even now some informer may be in our midst." People eyed their neighbors with suspicion. "But you can all bear witness that I, Cuthbert Burbage of the Curtain Theatre, left my duties to come outside to uphold the law."

A diversion now took place, as welcome to Cuthbert as it was unwelcome to Robin: the second trumpet sounded and the theatre doors were opened. There was a quick movement to the entrance; many who had enjoyed the ballad were grateful that Master Burbage's interference had prevented their being asked to pay for it.

Cuthbert waited until he was alone with Robin and then he said with a quiet emphasis, "If you come near this place again, you'll go straight to jail—or the navy." Cuthbert left no doubt as to which he considered the worse fate.

"But I was robbed. I only sang for a penny to go to the play." In desperation he added, "I know Ned."

"What Ned?"

Robin couldn't remember the surname. "The player," he said. Then he recalled something. "He plays Francis this afternoon." A further detail came back to him. "Stratford-on-Avon," he said with cryptical triumph. "Ned wants me to see the play. Afterwards he will introduce me to Master Phillips and we shall go to supper."

Cuthbert hesitated. The story sounded circumstantial but it was hard to believe.

Robin sensed the weakening in his opponent. "Master Burbage, if you had not come I should have had many pennies; I need but one. It is true, sir, that I was robbed." It was rarely that Robin had truth to plead, and he made the most of the unusual experience.

"Come with me," said Cuthbert curtly. "I will pass you in. But no more singing near the theatre. I warn you."

And thus it was that, lacking a penny, Robin still found himself inside a theatre for the first time. Several people recognized him and some apprentices soon had him under their wing. They urged him to complete his ballad, just quietly for their private benefit, but he was wary enough to know that all his hopes now centered on seeing Ned after the play. He must do nothing that might jeopardize that.

Robin began to move around and take in all the wonders of this new world.

But almost against his will his roving eye sought out an easy purse to filch. And then his ear caught words he had paid no attention to in the general din. "Rosy pippins! A farthing a piece." The price had doubled since Ned first heard that call, but the voice was the same; it belonged to a cheery young man whose cheeks rivaled the bloom of the polished apples he sold. Robin watched as the caller approached. He was doing a thriving trade. Crosswise around his neck were hung on one side a rapidly diminishing bushel of apples and on the other a gaping wallet of coins. It was temptation beyond endurance. Robin awaited his opportunity; congestion was the essence of the necessary situation. Happily three or four people at once wanted to buy. Robin with well-practiced skill pretended he had been pushed, stumbled against the seller, and, as he turned, fulminated against the awkward and aggressive burgher whom he accused of pushing him. Thus turning the attention of the bystanders to that innocent and protesting citizen, his hand dipped greedily into the purse. But he had reckoned without the seller, in whom long experience of attempted depradations had given to his wallet the sensitivity of an exposed nerve. His hand fastened with the grip of a bulldog's jaws on Robin's wrist and his salesman's voice was used to its utmost efficiency with its cry, "Thief!"

Public assemblies in London bred pickpockets as the open sewers bred rats, and this ever-present menace had resulted in an excessive hostility on the part of the potential victims. Young and old, men and women, belabored Robin with blows as he ran the gauntlet toward the doors. It seemed that everybody there strove to hit or kick him, and among his most enthusiastic punishers were the apprentices who previously had championed him. Worse to Robin than the blows was the fact that his precious lute was torn from his back and broken to irreparable fragments on his head and shoulders.

To complete Robin's ill-luck, Cuthbert Burbage had returned from backstage to the doors, waiting to greet some prosperous patrons who were expected. It gave him a grim satisfaction to find that the object of the people's wrath was the balladeer. He watched with righteous justification as the thief, with a final outburst of violence, was thrown into the roadway. Conscious of approving eyes, he strode over to stand above the luckless miscreant. He waited a moment until Robin was sufficiently recovered to hear him, and then he said, "I knew you for what you were. Never try to enter any theatre of mine again. Mark him, Master Doorkeeper, mark him. If ever you see his filthy visage, send at once for a constable." He bent down to speak words that others were not to hear. "And I will convey your respects to Master Ned Shakespeare, your dear friend. Liar!"

At that moment Cuthbert espied the merchant for whom he had been waiting, and whose good offices he hoped to use in one last effort to get Giles Alleyn to be reasonable about renewing the lease of the land on which stood the Theatre. Like David returning from slaying Goliath he walked across to the merchant. The spectators lost their interest in Robin, who slowly picked himself up and stumbled away.

With ten minutes to go before the play began, Cuthbert came to Ned.

"Know you a vagabond balladeer, a ruffian, and a thief?"

Startled, Ned said, "Why?"

"He said he was to see you and Master Phillips, but I know the fellow is a born liar."

"Where is he?" asked Ned.

"Gone with his tail between his legs like a beaten dog, and the dog was well beaten, for the groundlings caught him thieving, and that they cannot abide. You did not want to see him, did you?"

"No," said Ned.

"Some rascal from Stratford, I dare wager, presuming on your family name. He'll not worry you more." Cuthbert walked away with the satisfaction of a job well done, and Ned was free to envisage his evening with Sylvia without complications.

The afternoon's performance of *Henry IV* went well. Both Pope and Burbage brought a new fullness to their roles in the light of what they knew lay ahead for them in the second play; their comradeship was more precious because they knew it had to end. Ned's Francis was greeted as an old friend, and there were some in the audience who chimed in with his "Anon, anon, sir."

Ned had managed during the afternoon to tell Sam what Master Cuthbert had said about Robin and had charged him to find out what had happened, as he himself had to hurry away after the performance. Sam watched with envious admiration as he transformed himself from Francis the drawer to Edmund the lover. His haste was not unremarked by other members of the company, who exchanged leering smiles and salacious innuendoes. As Ned was leaving, Nick Dodman called after him, "Ned, you have forgotten something," and he held out Sylvia's rose. Rejoicing in his amatory reputation, Ned quipped, "Wear it in your codpiece; then it will contain something to attract a lady." This provoked hearty laughter; he was a rare one, this Ned, not like his brother at all.

The coach was waiting discreetly in a side lane by the church. The coachman, whom Sylvia rewarded well for keeping his eyes open and his mouth closed, saw the approach of Ned without seeming to do so. As soon as Ned was inside, the coach moved off with a jolt, but the uneasy movement of the springless vehicle served but to intensify the embrace of the lovers, which had begun before Ned was even seated.

Sylvia was a lively young woman, not yet twenty. In spite of her fine clothes and jewels she still was the ruddy-cheeked Suffolk lass who had been bought for his bed by Sir Gerard Barstow. He had bought most things in life, including his title. True, Sylvia had been little loath to be called Lady Barstow. She was Sir Gerard's fourth wife. He had worn three into the grave, but Sylvia could not fail to do him a similar service; he was more than thirty years older than she. By his first wife he had two children, a son, Kenneth, and a daughter, Elizabeth, both older than Sylvia, though Sir Gerard insisted on their calling her "Mother." Sylvia pouted with becoming misery when her husband had to leave her and always beamed with welcome on his return, a welcome not wholly false for he invariably brought her some dazzling trinket; besides, in spite of his lascivious intentions, he was often so tired on his return that he was asleep before getting into bed. Not that she objected to his connubial embraces; he was still lusty and astonishingly agile in spite of his protuberant belly and flabby breasts.

Elizabeth, the daughter, was now twenty-two and so plain, heavy and dull that it would take all her father's money to find a husband for her. The son, Kenneth, a dashing young man, had regarded his new "mother" with far from filial eyes, and she had found such regard not unwelcome. Sir Gerard had sensed a scandalous danger, and had promised his son a fine house and the money to sustain it, in return for a daughter-in-law in three months and a grandson in a year. It was four months before Kenneth had gotten a wife, but he had bettered the second part of the bargain, for the grandson had been born six months after the marriage. Now the new family was safely ensconced many miles away, in Devon.

Sylvia, whose eyes had first been taken by Ned when she saw him in *The Merchant of Venice,* had hit upon a daring stratagem to insinuate Ned into the Cheapside house. Taking a hint from *The Taming of the Shrew,* she had said she was most eager to acquire the ladylike skill of lute-playing, and a certain player had been recommended. To kill any suspicion in her too readily jealous spouse, she had said that Elizabeth should join her in the lessons. Poor Elizabeth! As well expect her to caper gracefully in a galliard. By chance it happened that this highly recommended master of the lute, being a player, was only free on an occasional evening and so he had to be fetched from the theatre, take supper with the family and, after the lesson, be taken back home. Sir Gerard had had serious doubts about letting a mere player eat at the family table but his objections had been overborne by Elizabeth who took more delight in sharing a supper than a lesson with the teacher. Still further to dull any suspicion, Ned had been deliberately invited to the house on one occasion when Sir Gerard was present, on which occasion he had behaved so circumspectly and had catered so expertly to the merchant's self-esteem and to his concern for Elizabeth's happiness that Sir Gerard had actually offered him a permanent place in the household, at which both Sylvia and Ned almost betrayed themselves by laughter and took great pains to avoid each other's gaze for the rest of the meal.

By this time the evening's procedure was well established. Behind the curtains of the coach, which the driver had orders to drive slowly to avoid excessive jolting, Sylvia and Ned had some twenty minutes or so of private titillation. When the coach came to a halt at the splendid house, there was a pause before the door was opened, to allow the occupants to repair their appearance after the dishevelment consequent on the journey. Elizabeth was always there to greet Ned at the head of the staircase which led from the business rooms on the ground floor. Each time she tried to outdo her previous appearance, with grotesque results whose absurdity was only equaled by Ned's praises of them. The meal was always surpassingly good and Ned looked forward to it as an integral part of the evening's delights. During the meal he told tales of the theatre to Elizabeth's wide-eyed ravishment. Fortunately Sir Gerard's few visits to the theatre had led him to the conviction that it was no place for the tender susceptibilities of his daughter—when she was married, an increasingly unlikely eventuality, that would be a different matter—and so Elizabeth never had the disillusionment of contrasting Ned's minor roles on the stage with his major roles in his stories, and the taller his tales the more did Sylvia enjoy them too. Elizabeth soon tired of her lute lessons, and by ready agreement she abandoned them. However, it was decided by all three conspirators that her father was not to be told of her defection. Sir Gerard had some ear for music and had determined in advance never to submit himself to the torture of Elizabeth's playing and singing. But Sylvia proved an apt pupil and was soon able to please him with her voice and fingers. After supper, all three always repaired to the music room, which contained a beautifully inlaid virginal that nobody in the house could play. Elizabeth would listen for a while to Sylvia's lesson but would soon become bored and beg permission from her "mother" to go to bed. The lesson would continue for such time as it would take for Elizabeth to be soundly asleep, and then the real purpose of the evening was undertaken. There was no appropriate couch in the room but there was a sufficiency of cushions to make the floor comfortable, and there was not the danger of telltale rushes, for in this wealthy house they had been replaced by coarse matting.

On this particular warm evening in mid-June, after the first erotic embrace the couple pulled apart; the necessarily closed curtains of the coach made the confined space too hot. Besides, Sylvia had something to say. For Ned's return journey through the night the coachman always insisted on being accompanied by a house-servant, one Joseph Biddle, for guard and company, and this Joseph was now in the habit of taking impudently knowing glances at his young mistress. She had chosen loftily to ignore them, but she was worried. When Ned asked what they could do about it, she said that he should come more frequently when her husband was at home so that it was clear to all that his presence was approved, and on their private occasions he should leave at nine instead of ten o'clock; that would still give them enough time.

Ned doubted the truth of this story. He suspected it was the sign of Sylvia's cooling off, though apart from the slight to his amour propre, this was not unwelcome to him. The original ardor had subsided and the varieties of excitation which each had been able to contribute to the other's already extensive experience had been exhausted. Repetition was already leading to routine, accompanied by a deadening sense of duty and obligation.

Later that evening, as if determined to prove to each other that there was no waning of desire, they made a play of almost tearing each other's clothes off, at the same time being shrewdly careful not to do so in fact. The tonguing of tongues, the biting of nipples, the licking of bodies, the fondling of parts had a pristine freshness, and Ned was almost persuaded that he had been mistaken in his doubts, but when he started a third round of foreplay, Sylvia drew away and stood up, reminding him of the "agreement" that he should leave an hour earlier than usual.

They both dressed and put the room to rights in silence. Then Sylvia flung herself into Ned's arms assuring him of her undying devotion, and while her face nestled against his breast they indulged in a parting dialogue that deceived neither.

TWENTY

Since he had received no token for a month, Ned put Sylvia out of his mind. He did this the more easily that the success he had confidently expected as Balthasar had brought him in favor with two beautiful damsels, a result he had also confidently expected. One was Katherine, the daughter of a knight who danced attendance on the Earl of Essex, and from whom he received fascinating bulletins of the state of affairs between the Queen and the Earl. There was one memorable day when he brought to his fellows backstage the news that there had been a great argument about Ireland between the Queen and the Earl, in the presence of some of the great ones of the land. The Earl had turned his back on her, whereupon she had slapped him in the face and he had laid his hand to his sword! Thereafter Ned was pressed for daily news of the temperature between the Queen and the Earl, most of which he had to supply from his imagination.

His other amatory conquest, Mary, had been a ward of the Queen ever since her parents were lost at sea on their way to Denmark as part of the English representation at the marriage of James VI of Scotland to Princess Anne. Mary was eleven at the time and had been brought up to believe that the storm which had drowned her parents was the result of witchcraft; indeed, witches were burned in both Scotland and Denmark as being responsible for the storm which had prevented the Princess from coming to Scotland for the marriage and for that which had overtaken the King on his way to Denmark. Mary, now twenty years old, imprudently and dangerously whispered to Ned that her life was shadowed by another witch, Queen Elizabeth. Ned was terror struck by the words, however intimately whispered. Mary had been royally promised in marriage to a "loathsome old goat" who lusted after her. The wedding was to take place the following spring, and in the meantime she was determined to enjoy herself. Ned was an integral part of that plan; she found no difficulty in coming to the theatre, for many a young gallant was eager to escort her when a nobleman's party was organized to occupy a lords' room.

Sometimes Ned had difficulty in accommodating both Katherine and Mary, but the excuse of rehearsals was often useful, and during the rehearsals of the new *Henry IV* play, which began almost as soon as *Much Ado About Nothing* had opened to great popular acclaim, the excuses became genuine reasons, for he was frequently prevented from answering the calls of either the languorous Katherine or the spirited Mary because he was busy with three parts: a drawer (but not alas! Francis), Mouldy (a comic recruit which necessitated his reviving, with some difficulty, his long since buried Stratford accent), and Humphrey, Duke of Gloucester, Prince Hal's youngest brother.

It was clear during the later rehearsals of the second *Henry IV* play that the people would clamor for more and more Falstaff, and Will was persuaded, against his instinct, to write an epilogue in which he promised yet another play about the lovable old rascal. But this would mean the *Henry V* play, which Richard Burbage was always urging and Will was always avoiding. Under pressure, Will got the idea that a comedy might solve the problem of the paragon king, and it might be possible to write such a comedy around the wooing of Princess Katherine of France. And so, all too glibly, his hastily written epilogue promised such a play. Will was also persuaded by John Heminge to apologize for a disastrous new play by a tyro author, which had been put on when Will was in Stratford, and to make quite clear that no slight had been intended in Falstaff to the Lollard martyr, Sir John Oldcastle, which had been the fat knight's original name. Altogether, the epilogue was a hodgepodge which Will wrote unwillingly and was to regret bitterly.

As the rehearsals for the new play progressed—the company called it *Falstaff* to distinguish it from the first *Henry IV* play, though this did not sit well with Richard Burbage, who insisted on referring to it as *Part Two*—Will's normal, quiet self-control frequently gave way to bouts of moodiness which could erupt in most surprising outbursts. Sundry people had sundry explanations for this unusual irascibility in Will. Augustine Phillips assumed it was caused by the persistent nagging of Burbage and Heminge which resulted in the epilogue. He knew too that Will longed to be free to write his new comedy, and was secretly tormented by his desire to rid his pen of the necessity of writing for Kemp. Ned was certain it was largely occasioned by Will's guilt about his family left in Stratford and by that part of him which yearned to be there; he noticed that his brother was at his moodiest after receiving a letter from Richard—Anne had never learned to write. All members of the company knew that Master Shakespeare's growing exasperation was due, at least in part, to the increasing frequency with which Ben Jonson haunted the theatre as the time for the rehearsal of his play approached. Ben had little respect for a "history" as a form of play, and had little regard for the fact that it was a complicated form to make stage-worthy, and that this particular history was a particularly complicated one; he would seize every possible moment to buttonhole a leading player to discuss the parts in his own play and to suggest casting. Feeling that Will's was the most sympathetic ear, he laid siege to it most frequently until even Will lost patience. What neither Ben nor the company knew was that Heminge had wanted to bar the pestering playwright from the theatre, and it was Will who had argued against it; he should be allowed to observe the players in rehearsal so that he could get to know their quality. "Observe!" commented Heminge. "He is blind to all but himself."

Without meaning to do so, Will had become Ben's champion against Heminge, and the climax occurred as rehearsals of *Every Man in His Humour* became imminent, the same time the rehearsals of *Henry IV* were in their final chaotic stages. Heminge held to his insistence that Will take part in the comedy so that he would have to be present at rehearsals. Will was particularly infuriated by the unctuousness with which Heminge concluded, "It will do you good to rest your pen a while and stretch your acting limbs again." Small wonder that Will lost patience with Ben the following morning, when he was lamenting the inadequacy of certain players for his characters. Will said, "You should play all your parts yourself, for that will be the only way to satisfy you, and you will not be a part of the audience to see how badly they are done."

For a moment it had looked as though the Jonson temper was to be fired, but he checked himself and with ominous control said, "So. You too. Now I know where I stand." And he had stalked out, brushing aside Nat Tremayne whose mouth was full of pins which he almost swallowed.

Heminge had watched Jonson's exit and crossed to say to Will, "I didn't hear what you said, but whatever it was, it was good."

Will loathed both Ben and Heminge, but still more himself.

Henry IV, Part Two was as great a success as *Much Ado About Nothing*, but to the distress of the author the line which provoked the loudest applause was the Epilogue's promise of a further play about Falstaff; the audience chose to ignore the threatened possibility of the fat old knight's death. The exhaustion consequent on opening two new plays in rapid succession caused rehearsals of the Jonson play to be postponed for at least a week. The respite from rehearsals gave an opportunity for Ned to renew contact with Katherine and Mary, but neither was available. Katherine was confined to her home because of the estrangement of Essex and his faction from the Queen. The situation was complicated by the death in early August of old Lord Burghley, and now, when the Earl of Essex should be at the Queen's side to ensure his place as her supreme confidant in affairs of state, he was not even at court. Small wonder he was sick and his adherents despondent. As for Mary, her "loathsome old goat" had decided that he could not wait until the spring, and was insisting on a September marriage. Elaborate preparations were keeping his bride-to-be fully occupied.

Thus robbed of the company of both ladies, Ned wondered where and how best to cast his rod anew. He left the theatre after a performance in *Much Ado,* sending word with Sam that he would not be home for dinner.

His desire for a woman was imperious, and though he had never lain with a whore, the recklessness of such an adventure suddenly appealed to him. He would go to a notorious tavern not far from the Phillips home; he did not want to risk too far a walk through dark streets late at night. He checked his money; he had only eightpence. It was not enough. He was hungry, and even the most raddled old whore would want sixpence, and at that price he might have to pay with the pox. When he remembered the ravages of that disease which had been pointed out to him, he decided to pocket his money, and go home.

When he arrived, the household was just settling down to the table. He was prepared for some comments on his unexpected arrival in time for supper, but instead Master Phillips said, "We are glad you came, Ned, for we have good news for you, very good news. Tell him, Will."

"It's the Ben Jonson play, Ned," said Will. "You are to have the part you wanted, young Lorenzo."

Ned's despondency and disappointment lifted from him. He glowed with delight; this would be his biggest and best part.

"But that's not all," said Gus. "Go on, Will."

"I have been persuaded to play in it too. I am to be your father."

This intelligence had convulsed the table at first hearing, and they laughed heartily again. Ned joined in for good company but wasn't certain why it was funny; Will was old enough to be his father.

WHEN BEN JONSON READ HIS EVERY MAN IN HIS HUMOUR TO THE SHARERS, he put on a most energetic performance, and its reception both disappointed and secretly infuriated him. The players felt that the author's attempt to impress them as an actor was misplaced, and to the discerning the more Ben gave of himself in the reading the less did they want him as a fellow player. His reputation as a roarer and ranter was deserved. The play ended with a line of Latin: *"Claudite iam rivos, pueri; sat prata biberunt."* Ben delivered it with smug authority and then said, "There may be some of you who do not profess Latin, so I will translate it: 'Cut off the streams now, lads; the meadows have had enough to drink.' Some of you, I'm sure, will recognize it as the final line from the Third Eclogue of Virgil. It is a most fitting conclusion, I think."

Most of Ben's hearers, whether they professed Latin or not, felt that the stream should have been cut off much sooner, for the end of the play dragged. John Heminge lost further stock with Ben by saying at the end of the evening, and with no great enthusiasm, that he was sure they could make something out of it. But at least he paid Ben the remaining three pounds, which was a considerable comfort to the perpetually impoverished man, in whose hands money melted as he held it.

The rehearsals of the play were dire in portent. The first company reading took place on a Saturday evening in August at the house of Richard Burbage. The following day was to be free for private study of parts and the first theatre rehearsal was called for 8 A.M. on Monday.

During that Saturday there was news of a major disaster to the Queen's forces in Ireland. It was, indeed, the worst defeat sustained by her army anywhere during her reign, and rumor made it even worse. In an attempt to relieve the siege of Blackwater, the army had been skillfully ambushed by the "rebels." In this and a subsequent engagement, the Queen's Marshal, Sir Henry Bagnal, and his second, Sir Thomas Wingfield, were killed, together with other officers and some two thousand men, but rumour left not a man alive.

The play that afternoon was the new *Henry IV*. The voice of Rumour, with which it opened, "stuffing the ears of men with false reports," was not warning enough to dispel the gloom which had infected the audience. As the newly dedicated leader of his people, Henry V, emerged in the play, many men in the audience felt the need for such a leader to avenge the Irish disaster, and most of them thought of the Earl of Essex. Those younger men in the audience who had no fixed occupation felt a personal danger in the news; there would undoubtedly be a fresh impressment of new soldiers, and most of them wondered how best to evade it.

As the company gathered for the reading at Richard Burbage's that evening, the talk was still of Blackwater, and the attempt was to sift out the truth from conflicting stories. The only one present who had had some military experience was Ben Jonson, and he made much of it. He asserted, "The Queen's troops must have been ill-chosen, ill-trained, and arrant cowards, led by incompetent captains, else how could wild Irish barbarians have prevailed against them when my fellows in the Low Countries were more than a match for the finest soldiers Spain could put into the field?"

Henry Condell quietly suggested that the difference might be that the Irish were fighting on their home ground whereas both English and Spanish in the Low Countries had been in foreign fields.

"No field is foreign to a good captain," countered Ben.

When the company settled down for the reading, all thought of conflict abroad gave way to a sense of conflict in the room. Everybody knew that the author had been deeply hurt by being left out of the cast and that this hurt had been compounded by the fact that his most outspoken opponent, John Heminge, had been given the part Jonson himself coveted, Giuliano. Will had not had the time, energy, or strength of purpose to insist on the changes in the play he felt were necessary, and it was going into rehearsal exactly as Ben had written it.

After the ritual reading by Tom Vincent of the cast—was there a slight hint of defiance in the way he said "Giuliano—John Heminge"?—Will began, in the character of Lorenzo, Senior.

Whenever a tentative reader like Richard Burbage fumbled his way through, Ben became increasingly restless, and whenever anybody hesitated or mistook a word, Ben was quick to jump in with it before the bookholder could open his mouth; it was terrifyingly clear that the author knew every word of his play without having a copy in front of him.

John Heminge too was getting restless and when he himself stumbled over a word and was corrected by the author, he laid his part down, glared at Ben and said, "Master Jonson, our bookholder has a copy of your play and can read."

"Better than you, I hope." Even as he said the words, Ben regretted them.

With iron control John Heminge addressed the sharers, "The presence of this man makes rehearsal impossible, and I for one will no longer endure it." He stood up and walked to the door. Everyone was so startled that no one made an attempt to stop him. At the door he turned and spoke. "I warned you how it would be, and now I tell you this: if Master Jonson is present at any future rehearsal, I shall not stay in the theatre."

Master Jonson, all caution gone, jumped to his feet and shouted, "Go and be damned! There is a better Giuliano here than ever you would make." To leave no doubt as to whom he meant, he thumped his chest.

John Heminge left the room. Henry Condell rose quickly and followed him in the hope of pacification.

Ben, still on his feet, blustered in self-defense. "He was my enemy and the enemy of my play from the beginning. I beseech you to proceed without him and let me play Giuliano."

Richard Burbage spoke with that quiet authority which had often thrilled an audience. "Sit down, Master Jonson." He waited to be obeyed. Like a momentarily quelled but still dangerous animal, Ben sat. Burbage continued. "I will be plain with you. There was much debate about doing your play. It was Master Shakespeare who turned the scales in your favor. But rest assured of this, without Master Heminge in the part of Giuliano, it will not be done by the Lord Chamberlain's Men."

There was silence in the room and during it Henry Condell returned. All looked at him. He sat down and sadly shook his head.

Not only was the fate of Ben and his play in the balance, but that of

Ned too. Was he going to be robbed of his first big part? He looked at Will, who saw and understood.

"Master Jonson," said Will. "I shall try tomorrow to change Master Heminge's mind, though I doubt I shall succeed. He is a man of strong will and purpose, and for that the Lord Chamberlain's Men have often been indebted to him. You are a playwright, and a good one, but you and I are helpless, like beetles on their backs, without a stage and players and an audience. I beg you to entrust your play to us. There will be things we shall do with your words which will disappoint you, yet I know from experience that there are other things which will bring you unexpected pleasure."

"Am I not to be midwife to my own play?" asked Ben, bewildered but still belligerent.

"Healthy babies have been born without the presence of a midwife," said Will. "I promise to seek you out when we have questions that need your answers."

"Will you promise me too that no word will be altered?"

Richard Burbage broke in with irritation. "That cannot be. Words have to be tested in rehearsal, to fit the tongue and the character and the action. Master Shakespeare is forever altering to improve."

Ben exploded. "But how can I alter to improve, if I am not to be in the theatre?"

"You can leave that safely to Master Shakespeare," said Augustine Phillips with warm gentleness.

"Never!" said Ben, and he thumped the table and stood up so precipitately that the other people in the room expected further violence. "It is my play and they are my words, each one chosen with care and craft, and tried on the tongue. Rather than see them mauled and maltreated by another, be he ne'er so skillful, I would burn the pages and starve. But I should not starve. I was once a bricklayer and can be so again. 'Tis an honorable profession, and I begin to fear that playwrighting is not." He stormed out, much to the distress of Mistress Burbage, who was upstairs and already much upset by the shouting.

Ben's exit was followed by a frozen silence, broken by Richard Burbage. "This calls for a meeting of the sharers." He added with a smile, "Those who are left. So I will bid you a goodnight, gentlemen."

William Sly, who was to play Musco, asked the question that was in all minds. "Should we spend tomorrow studying our lines and come to the theatre at eight o'clock on Monday morning?"

Richard Burbage looked for guidance to some of the other sharers. It was Will who spoke. He said, "I judge not. This is no slight trouble. If we can settle this amicably tomorrow, we could rehearse on Monday morning."

"But we cannot study our parts until we have completed the reading of the whole play; we know not how they fit," objected William Sly, who was the usual spokesman for the hired men.

"Could we not finish it now?" suggested Richard Cowley.

"Without Master Heminge? I think not," said Burbage.

"And it would be too confident a presumption, which might tempt Fate to mock us," said Will.

"I feel assured 'twill prove much ado about nothing," observed Augustine Phillips.

"But without Dogberry," said Will Kemp. "This part of Cob is well enough, but 'tis no Dogberry."

Feeling that the discussion was beginning to wander and that time was awasting, Richard Burbage said, "Then this is it. There will be a notice at the theatre by five of the afternoon tomorrow, either calling or canceling another reading here at six o'clock. And now the sharers must meet, so again I bid the others of you a goodnight."

Within a few minutes the sharers had the room to themselves. It was first and unanimously decided that the company really wanted to do the play. In spite of the bad atmosphere at the reading, it had promised well. Then it became a question of reconciling Heminge and Jonson. Henry Condell and Will were deputed to attempt this difficult task. Henry would almost certainly see John Heminge that night, but Jonson was a great frequenter of taverns and it was thought wiser that Will should not seek him out until the morning. If the individual missions were successful, perhaps all four men could meet at Henry's house in the early afternoon.

There was a basic difference of opinion among the sharers about the desirable terms of reconciliation. Burbage stood firmly by Heminge in wanting the troublesome author barred from the theatre during rehearsals, but Will thought this was unreasonable and unfair. "And we might need his help," added Will.

"I feel sure, Will," said Augustine Phillips, "he will fight tooth and nail against changes. To him, his words are the laws of the Medes and Persians."

"*His* words?" jeered Kemp. "He ends with a Latin tag. Only Gabriel Spencer would know where that's from, and I thank God he's not here to tell us."

"Let us not forget one thing: we all want the play to go on, and Ben Jonson more than any of us," said Will.

As Augustine Phillips and Will walked home together after the meeting, Gus said, "I am surprised that you would strive so hard to help Ben Jonson. Were we to abandon the play, you would be free to write your new comedy and the play you have promised the public about Henry V and Falstaff."

"I should be glad of anything that postpones the writing of both plays. Will Kemp stands in the way of the comedy, and now that Hal has become king it will be as hard to contain him and Falstaff in one play as Heminge and Jonson in one theatre; nay, harder."

"Have you hope of controlling Jonson?"

"I think well of his work and that is a sure way to an author's esteem. We bade fair to be good friends until I became childishly irritated with him one morning, but maybe I can win him again."

Ned and Sam were already in bed by the time the men got home, but Will rightly surmised that Ned would not be asleep and he went up to see him. He was reading the Lorenzo part by the light of a candle. He was grateful to Will for coming to see him. Waving the part, he said, "Shall I get to play this?"

"I hope so, Ned, but I don't know yet." And he told him of his mission on the morrow.

"Master Heminge was wrong, Will. Ben was overanxious, that was all."

Will noted the friendly partisanship of the "Ben." "Master Heminge was right, Ned," he said. "He did what he did because he foresaw worse trouble ahead with Master Jonson, and he wanted to forestall it."

"But, Will, you would not let anyone alter your plays, would you?"

"I think I am readier to alter my own plays than is Master Jonson."

"I am sure he will make changes that are seen to be necessary."

"I wish I were assured of that. Perhaps it is you, not I, who should go to see him." Will said this guilelessly, but Ned illogically took umbrage at it and spoke strongly.

"I feel sorry for him. He is alone. You are many and you are all against him."

Will was provoked into spirited reply. "That is nonsense. The play is all that matters, and your Ben may prove the worst enemy of his own work. Already I begin to wish I had given my voice against it." And he turned and left the room without even saying goodnight.

The young men were allowed to sleep until church time, and Will had already left the house when Ned came downstairs. Will had left word that he would be back in plenty of time to let the three players know if there would be a reading that night.

Will took a horse that day because he might have much traveling to do. His plan was to go straight to the Jonson home, the address of which he had been given at the sharers' meeting. It was in Blackfriars, not far from where George and Gilbert lived. If all went well the two authors might go to church together and afterwards travel the mile north to Henry Condell's home.

The Jonson home was the ground floor of a house which had been divided into three tenements. As Will approached the front door, open for ventilation, he heard three voices raised in competition: a child was crying to the full extent of his powerful lungs, a woman was loudly berating it for doing so, and Ben was trying to shout the woman down in defense of the child. As Will made his surprise appearance, the noise gradually stopped; even the child, a boy aged two, subsided into sniveling. Ben took up his son and introduced his wife. She was a robust woman on the verge of slatternliness, an impression strengthened by a six-months' pregnancy. From her attitude to Will, it was clear that she knew about him and was hostile.

"I hope you have come to make amends to my husband, Master Shakespeare," she said. "I told him to expect no help and comfort from you, for his talent is a threat to yours."

"There is ample room for both of us," said Will. "And I am here to try to help and comfort him."

"This is a matter for us men, Anne. Let us talk outside, Master Shakespeare." Will was grateful for the suggestion, for what he saw and smelled of the home was not inviting. As Ben carried the child outside and moved from the door to where the horse was tied up, Will's gaze was on the child. Hamnet had been about that age when he had first left him behind in Stratford.

To gain time for the proper opening to a difficult conversation, Ben used the child's interest in the horse to still the residue of the crying spell and soon he had the little boy smiling and patting the horse. "Equus, equus," said Ben, intent on the child's acquiring Latin with English, and the child echoed him with a delighted sense of achievement. "It's never too young to learn, Master Shakespeare. The Latin masters are my joy and solace, and they shall be my Benjamin's too."

Will smiled and warmed to the man. He reflected that the father's still greater joy and solace was his son, as Hamnet had been his, but oh! the fragility of such happiness. He had an instinct to warn the man, but dismissed it as foolishness. He had come for a purpose, and must begin. "Master Jonson, I should have wanted to seek you out this morning, but I am here at the request of my fellows."

"Master Heminge too?" Ben asked quickly.

"No. He did not come back last night. But Henry Condell is speaking to him for all of us, as I am speaking to you. We want to do your play; you want your play done. Nothing must be allowed to stop it. Not John Heminge. Not Ben Jonson. Were you dead, the play would still clamor to be brought to life."

"But I am not dead, Master Shakespeare, and while I am alive it must be brought to life as I see it."

"Or strangled at birth by the father?"

"Which would you choose, Master Shakespeare: a misshapen child or none at all?"

"I could not bring myself to kill my own."

At this moment, Mistress Jonson appeared. She had brushed her mass of unruly black hair into some semblance of order, had donned a shawl and a bonnet, and was ready for church. Other people were emerging from houses and making their way to St. Anne's, beckoned by the tower and called by the bells.

" 'Tis time for church," said Mistress Jonson.

"We cannot both go, with Benjamin to look after," explained Ben. "This morning it is Anne's turn."

"Has he come to make amends?" Anne asked her husband.

Ben hoped that Will would answer, but he didn't, so Ben said with some slight hesitation, "Yes." Will was careful not to derive too much comfort from this admission, because he rightly assumed that its main purpose was to send Anne on her way.

"Hm," she remarked complacently. "Take good care of the child, and clean him as soon as you smell him; 'tis going to be a hot day. I shall pray for you—both." And she marched off smugly.

"Let us walk down to the river," said Ben.

"Why not give the little one a ride on my horse?" suggested Will.

Ben looked gratefully at Will and then masked the look; he was not going to be trapped into acquiescence by such easy tricks. "He has never been on a horse," he said. "It might frighten him."

"They seem to like each other. Come, let us try. With you on one side and me on the other, he will feel safe."

And so Benjamin Junior took his first ride supported by the two poets, and all three were happy. The sight brought warm smiles to the faces of many church-bound families.

Separated by the horse and concentrating on the child, the two men were gratefully obliged to postpone further talk on the subject for which they were met. Will's pleasure in the child prompted Ben to question him about his own family, and eventually he learned about the death of Hamnet and the refusal of Will's wife to live in London. How could any man bear such sorrows without their marks being apparent to the world? And for what was he deprived of family? Poetry? The muse was a jealous and demanding devil. And yet this man had even forsaken her this morning to come to help another poet. Ben, ever quick to jump to extremes, was filled with admiration, compassion, and gratitude.

After they came to the river and had joined in little Benjamin's pleasure in the swans, luxuriating in the comparative Sunday peace of the Thames, Ben said baldly, "What would you have me do, Will?"

The assumed intimacy of the Christian name, without a by-your-leave, and the ready openness of the question, completely won Will; it was so patently honest and simple.

"Trust us to do your play, and be patient."

"It's you I will trust. Patience is not in my nature, nor ever will be, I fear. Am I not to be allowed to be at rehearsals? That would be hard to bear."

Will smiled. "Perhaps the rehearsals themselves would be harder, and then what would you do? That is it which troubles my fellow players."

"If I promise to contain myself and speak only to you?"

"Is that possible?"

"I don't know, but I would try. If I were playing Giuliano, it would be very much easier for me."

Will refused to be drawn on that subject; he knew it was a closed one for the sharers. "I think you should have a distraction while your child is being born," he said. "I find the best one is to be working on a new play."

"I have another one in mind."

Will was genuinely interested. "How much is written?"

"Not a word yet. I need the encouragement of success, Will. Besides, I have not your magical facility. Words seem to tumble out of you. With me, every one has a hard birth."

"Will the new play be a comedy too?"

"Yes, of much the same kind as *Every Man in His Humour*. If your players give me a success, I thought of calling the new play *Every Man Out of His Humour*."

"Be warned by me, Ben. A few years ago I wrote a special play for a courtly audience. To the surprise of all of us, the town liked it too, and we still play it."

" 'Tis *Love's Labour's Lost* you mean; a very witty invention."

"I was persuaded to write another in the same vein. I called it *Love's Labour's Won*."

"I have heard of it."

"But have never seen it, nor ever will. It was so clever and witty that even I would have difficulty in unraveling it now."

They laughed heartily together and the child, who all this while had been absorbed by the life on the river, looked up at them and laughed with them. Now he clamored to be set on horseback again, and the happy trio made their way back to the house.

Ben said, "I would I could ask you to dinner, but I fear our fare is not worthy of this occasion. Besides, it calls for canary, which we lack."

"Then let us seek it together," said Will.

"Excellent i'faith. Thus are good friendships born."

"And afterwards we will seek out John Heminge."

"I shall find him harder to swallow than the canary."

"It will be easier than you expect."

Ben drank with unusual caution at the meal in the tavern. Beneath the surface of their genuine new friendliness both men were preparing for the meeting with Heminge, for both realized that no promises had been made. The subject of *The Isle of Dogs* came up during the meal, and that led to discussion of a man they both knew: Gabriel Spencer. Will said of him, "He is a lost soul. He has a great talent for playing, but he despises it. There are times when most players of substance do. But with Spencer it is permanent. He hates himself and so hates all the world."

"And most of all he hates me, and I know not why," said Ben.

"Love and hate give no reasons," commented Will.

" 'Tis strange," said Ben. "The man has so much. He is handsome, well born, talented, cultivated, a true man of the university, and yet it all breeds poison in him."

"Pity him, Ben. The man who feeds on poison has a sour diet."

Will paid for the meal without any demur from Ben who seemed to expect it as his due and was only perfunctorily grateful; in Ben's code, effusive thanks were extended to strangers, not to friends.

They walked to Henry Condell's. As they arrived the Heminge and Condell children, normally shepherded by their father, were being mustered by their mothers for the Sunday afternoon walk. Most of the children—and there seemed to be upward of twenty of them—knew Master Shakespeare and they clustered around him in welcome; he ached for his own Susanna and Judith, and, even more, his Hamnet. He managed amid the children's clamor to introduce Ben to their mothers. The women had both heard of the difficult man and now found it hard to reconcile their husbands' descriptions with this friendly and warm creature. Mistress Heminge was fond of saying, "Children and dogs can tell a man as soon as they sniff him." There were no dogs to sniff at Ben, but the children soon made much of him, even deserting Will to do so.

The fathers emerged upon the scene from the house, and a quick exchange of glances between Will and Henry signaled that they had both achieved some success in their missions.

John Heminge took the initiative. He waded through children and extended his hand to Ben who shook it warmly. "I'm glad you came, Master Jonson; we must talk." Then, before Ben could make any comment, he spoke to the chattering assembly. "Now be off with you, and be not unruly. Give good heed to your mothers." Away they fluttered, quite unimpressed by the imperious voice that called after them. "Stay close to the houses. Stray not into the streets. Beware of hooves of horses."

As they watched the two proud hens and their happy chicks move away, Ben said, "A goodly brood, Master Heminge."

"They are not all mine," said John. "That would be scarce possible."

Henry Condell took advantage of the friendly laughter which greeted this remark to suggest that they should go into the garden. When they had been supplied with tankards of Mistress Condell's ale and were seated in the shade of a copper beech tree, John Heminge took the initiative. "I was too hasty last evening, Master Jonson."

"And I was too sharp-tongued. 'Tis a fault in me," magnanimously conceded Ben.

"Players are ever nervous in the presence of their poets."

"And poets in the presence of their players."

"Then thus it is. Give us one week without you, to find our way through your play without being always aware of your disapproving eye, and then you will be welcome in the theatre."

"Welcome?" said Ben in comical disbelief.

John Heminge laughed. "Provided you have lost your tongue," he said.

"When that is so, you have my leave to say 'Ben Jonson is dead.' "

Again John Heminge laughed heartily, while Henry Condell and Will looked on with approving smiles, proud of their morning's work.

The rest of the meeting avoided the dangerous subject of the play and was one of banter, good fellowship, and Christian names. It was even with some reluctance that John Heminge finally broke it up to go to the theatre to post the notice of the evening's reading. As they were bidding their farewells, he said, "We shall miss you this evening, Ben—I'm happy to say."

"And I am happy that I shall see you a week tomorrow, John, though I doubt I shall be happy to see your Giuliano," countered Ben.

The atmosphere was such that even this sally was greeted with loud laughter by John, but neither Will nor Henry believed that the laughter would continue right through rehearsals. Still, the important thing was that the company was now committed to the play and nothing would be allowed to stop it.

At the reading of the play that evening, the company was amazed and amused by the unusual affability of John Heminge, and the mood it engendered lent sparkle, gaiety and promise to the unusual play.

Ned, who had spent the day in studying his part, hoping dauntlessly for the reading that night, acquitted himself so well that any doubts the sharers might have had about his fitness for such a large part were dispelled. Will was relieved. He and Ned both regretted their altercation of the previous evening, but had not had an opportunity to speak to each other privately since. As they walked home with Augustine Phillips and Sam, Gus said, "How does it feel to be your brother's son, Ned?"

"Good and fitting. Will has been both father and brother to me," said Ned.

TWENTY-ONE

THOSE EARLY DAYS OF SEPTEMBER WERE TROUBLED ONES IN LONDON. Disaffected and lawless men had begun to band themselves together and gather arms, even firearms. They had been driven to this by want and near starvation. There were numerous clashes with the forces of law, and several lives were lost on both sides. Martial law was proclaimed, and the gallows were kept busy with summary executions.

The atmosphere of terror infected the theatre. Not only did the fainthearted stay away, but the magistrates, always prone to regard theatres as places of dangerous assembly, kept an even more vigilant eye upon them with spies and informers.

As if to ensure that business would be bad for the theatre, the weather turned foul. Rain and threat of rain reduced the performances in the first week of September to two, and those badly attended, so the rehearsals of *Every Man in His Humour* were difficult and dismal. Will was begged by Heminge and Burbage to keep Jonson away from the theatre on the second Monday, but he refused.

"But we are not ready for him," objected Heminge.

"I doubt you ever will be," countered Will with unusual testiness.

The morning on which Ben was to see his play on the stage for the first time dawned black with storm. The heavens lowered all the morning and the heat was oppressive. Ben was early at the theatre and conscious of the eyes of the gathering players. He was determinedly friendly but very relieved when Will came. The two men greeted each other warmly. Ned hurried across to shake Ben's hand, radiating friendship and esteem.

Will took Ben aside and told him of the difficulties of the previous week. Ben was well aware of all of this and eager to make allowances, so much so that when Heminge came across to greet them, it was Ben who made the excuses in advance for what he was going to see.

Ben expected to sit on the stage, but Will suggested he should sit in the first gallery over the main door. There he sat and watched with increasing dismay the tentative flounderings on the stage; all but a few of the actors still carried their parts. In spite of his good intentions, Ben's face began to mirror the threatening sky. Every five minutes or so such action as there was on stage would stop and the players would confer about their grouping and movements. Will seemed to be the court of appeal on these occasions, and Ben fumed because it was not he. It further increased his frustration that he often could not hear the discussions. They were being pitched low to avoid his ears; from his own experience, this was not how rehearsals were normally conducted. At last he could bear it no longer. He stood up and called in a voice of ominous clarity, "What troubles you?"

All on stage stopped and turned to him, petrified into momentary statues, but before anyone could find voice, the sky did; a frightening flash of lightning was followed almost immediately by a deafening crack of thunder which seemed to be right over the theatre. Then the flood of rain came as though sluice gates had been opened. There was a dash for shelter from the open stage, but Ben stood still watching the flight with satisfaction as though he had caused it.

From the shelter of the canopy, Will and a few other players stopped to watch Ben. He was now thoroughly soaked. Deliberately he left the gallery and came down to the open ground. Then he slowly strode toward the stage, oblivious of lightning, thunder, and rain. And it was no ordinary storm. Later it was learned that the lightning had burned men and buildings. As the onlookers watched, Ben stopped in the middle of the ground and looked up to the heavens as though defying them to do their worst. Then he came to the edge of the stage and glared through the sheet of rain at the cowering players. Will and Ned both made an involuntary move toward him, but they were stopped by the firm grips of their fellows. It was doubtful that Ben could have seen their movement of sympathy. He made no attempt to get onstage. Instead, he turned round abruptly and walked away to the main door. There he raised the great locking bar, flung the doors wide open and disappeared into the storm.

The players slunk backstage in guilty silence. John Heminge called an immediate meeting of the sharers, while the others waited. Ned longed to seek out Ben to comfort him.

As soon as the door of the bookholder's room was closed behind them, John Heminge said, "Will he come back, think you?"

Richard Burbage said, " 'Tis better for him and for us that he do not, and for his play too."

"I fear what may happen to him," said Will. "He is desperate with grief. He feels his child has been torn from him by callous hands."

"But 'tis not so," said Augustine Phillips. "The success of the play means much to us too."

"He knows that," replied Will, "but foster parents can be loving to a child while being cruel to its real father. One thing we must do to make amends. The child must be exactly as he begat it; not a word must be omitted or altered, unless he sanctions it, and I doubt he will do that."

"But already we know that . . ." Richard Burbage began to object.

"Not a word, Dick," said Will with unusual firmness. "As soon as may be, I will go find him and make that promise. He is a good man and a good poet, and he has given us a good play. We must nurture all three."

"I hope he finds shelter from this storm," said Richard Cowley. " 'Twill harm him else."

John Heminge took charge. " 'Twill be best for Ben Jonson and for us that we set to work. We cannot go onstage, but we can run our lines." He added with heavy wit, in reference to Will's dictum about the inviolability of Ben's work, "And maybe we can find some way of saying those lines we hoped to avoid saying."

The company gathered in the tiring-room, and before they settled down to work John Heminge addressed them. "This past week was a bad one; bad outside the theatre and, as a necessary consequence, bad inside it. It has affected our spirits and our work. Pray God this storm will clear the air in all ways. Let us work with a new will on this play. We have but half an hour before we get ready for the afternoon, if there be a performance."

There was a performance, under blue skies, but the roads were streams and the ground of the theatre a pond of mud. After conference with Cuthbert Burbage, it was decided, in the interests of both ground and groundlings, to allow the penny entrants to gain admittance to the third gallery, the total proceeds to be divided equally between house and players. The normal arrangement was that all the groundlings' pennies went to the players and the gallery receipts were divided equally between house and players, but from the players' part of this came all the costs of costumes and furnishings.

The play for the afternoon was *Much Ado About Nothing*. The audience was expectedly sparse, but there was relief in the air after the storm and stress, and both players and audience rejoiced in a new lightness of spirit.

Will left in search of Ben Jonson. He rode on a horse borrowed from the Burbages, and, as the horse splashed through the storm water, he was warmed by the laughter which spilled out of the theatre. He mused on the crisis of the morning. The theatre was a place of crisis, every one of which must seem to the outsider much ado about nothing; children quarreling at play.

Mistress Jonson was surprised to see Will. No; Ben was not at home. Had he not come to the theatre? Was something wrong?

Will assured her that all was well but that it was important he see Ben, and Anne suggested with heavy disapproval that he was certain to be in one of his taverns, adding to the debts he could ill afford. She named a few of his haunts and Will left to make the rounds, promising to bring Ben home.

It was in the third tavern that Will found him, so bedraggled that his skin seemed as sodden as his clothes. He was shivering feverishly and was belligerently half-drunk. The landlord and two tapsters, who knew Ben well and liked him, were trying to get him on his feet and set him on his way home. At sight of Will, Ben stopped struggling and glared malevolently. Then he said thickly, "Why have you come?"

"To take you home," said Will. "I have a horse outside."

The compassion in Will's voice must have penetrated to Ben's befuddled brain, for he suddenly went limp and with chattering teeth muttered, "I am cold. I am cold."

"Help me to get him on my horse," said Will to the others.

Will did not have on riding boots—he had walked to the theatre that morning—and he balked at squelching through the flooded streets, so, after Ben had been precariously hoisted, he mounted behind him, took the reins in his right hand, and put his left arm firmly around the shivering man. The horse at first objected to the unaccustomed burden but was soon under control.

It was not far to the Jonson home. As they arrived, Mistress Jonson came hurrying out with young Benjamin toddling after her. She had been working up to yet another row with her prodigal husband, but sight of him drove all such thoughts from her mind. Will dismounted carefully, fearing to lose hold of Ben. Anne helped to get him off the horse, but he could scarcely stand now and was muttering incoherencies. The child began to cry, but even this seemed not to affect the doting father.

Will and Anne managed to get Ben to the bedroom, an untidy though clean room where Ben apparently worked, for there was a table littered with papers, and there were shelves with books. They eased their burden onto the bed. Ben's mutterings were now punctuated with moans. As he began the difficult task of stripping the inert body, Will said, "Get a towel and some strong hot infusion."

As she hurried out, Anne said, "I have some excellent herbs."

Finally, Ben was dried and under extra blankets. It was a hot day, but he continued to shiver. With difficulty he was persuaded to swallow the fever potion, for he protested at every sip. The child had come into the room. He stood as far as possible from the bed, looking on in wide-eyed fright.

There was nothing more that Will could do. He assured Ben's wife that he would be back the following afternoon, and moved to little Benjy, intending to take him up in his arms to comfort him, but the child shrunk away from him, as if blaming him for the strange state of the father who lay restless and mumbling and moaning in bed. Will left, heavy at heart.

His instinct was to return to the theatre, but he decided against it and made straight for home; he was in no frame of mind to discuss Ben or his play. At that moment the isolation of Stratford seemed very desirable.

When he got home, the place was in an uproar. Neighborly women he had never seen before were clacking all over the place. It seemed that Anne Phillips was terrified by thunderstorms, and today's had induced her to give birth to yet another girl some few weeks before its time. All was well with both mother and child, and it was made abundantly clear to Will that the best thing he could do was to get out of the way, which he was glad to do, merely saying that he would like to see Master Phillips when he came home.

On the return of the three from the theatre, Gus assured himself that his Anne was in no danger and managed to convince her that he was not unduly disappointed that once again he had been cheated of a son; then he went up to Will's room. In response to Gus's urgent questioning, Will told the story of his discovery of the sick Ben in the tavern. The reaction of Gus foretold that of most of his fellows, a guilty relief that the problem of the rehearsals was now solved, and the justification that Ben had brought it all on himself; it was this latter that he emphasized in an attempt to stir Will from his doldrums. He said, "Your Ben has given me a punning line to say to you in his play. 'Let him run his course; it's the only way to make him a staid man.' "

"If Ben became staid," replied Will, "he would be no longer the Ben that matters, and that's the man that has it in him to write many a good play. Besides, he may be stayed indeed, stayed unto death, for he is grievous sick."

"Think not so. He is young and hearty, and will flick off fever like a fly."

Will suggested that, to celebrate the new birth and to solve a possible downstairs difficulty, they should go out to supper, taking Ned and Sam with them. The supper was a happy but hurried one. All felt the need to work on their parts in a new desire to carry out John Heminge's injunction of the afternoon, and they all felt it would be the best way to show their concern for the author. Only Sam, in the small part of Piso, had no heavy burden of memorizing. Ned warmed to Will when he declared his intention of visiting Ben every day until he was well enough to return to the theatre.

The rehearsal the next morning went with a new verve, and the play began to take a lively shape. Backstage the talk was no longer of lawlessness and disaster; the gallows had halted the one and the Queen's forces would undoubtedly redress the other; instead the talk was of "the scandal of the age": the Earl of Southampton had secretly married Elizabeth Vernon, a ward of the Earl of Essex, in order to give a legal name to the child that was about to be born. There was much speculation as to what the Queen would do, for she jealously guarded her prerogative of consent to noble marriages. There was general agreement that the child would be born in prison, especially since the Earl of Essex was no longer at court to plead the cause of the clandestinely wed.

Ned carefully watched Will's reaction to the Southampton rumors. He seemed untouched by them and wholly absorbed in the rehearsal. Whatever the truth of the mystery about Will and the Earl of Southampton, it was strange that they should both have begotten a child before marrying the mother. Ned did catch some words of Will to Gus, but he was not certain that they referred to the gossip. " 'Tis well; the end of an act in an old play."

That afternoon Will found Ben weak, and sick with self-pity and self-derision. He greeted Will with a wan smile and a weak gesture. Will told him of the good rehearsal and of his vow that not a word of Ben's should be changed without his express approval. As Will was leaving, he forced some money on the reluctant Anne to provide "strengthening meat" for her husband, her child, and her child-to-be. Will mused wryly that every Anne he met was pregnant except his own.

THE REHEARSALS PROCEEDED WELL AND APACE, AND THE AUGURIES WERE good. The Earl of Essex was back in town and it was confidently expected that he would soon be back in favor. It was true that Southampton and his new countess had been briefly detained in the Fleet Prison, but, after that gesture of disapproval, the Queen had accepted the situation.

Excitement ran high as the opening day of Ben's play approached and was climaxed by the news that the Earl of Essex had indeed been restored to favor, had taken his seat in the Council, and intended to grace the opening of the new play.

Cuthbert Burbage between whiles of praying for fine weather spent his time in gloating anticipation of the receipts, for first performances commanded double prices.

Will was exhausted from having to fight for the integrity of Ben's text in spite of his own instinct for changes, having to supervise rehearsals, having to learn a part, and having to maintain his promise of daily visits to Ben. Even Augustine Phillips in the part of Doctor Clement, the Justice, had pleaded for some changes. In particular he wanted to cut the Latin tag which he spoke to end the play, but Will would have none of it. He said, "Those who don't understand it will clap loudest to prove that they do."

It was not until two days before the projected first performance that Ben was well enough to come to the theatre, and then on a hired horse. He was warmly welcomed even by those who wished he hadn't come. Will's welcome was genuine; apart from anything else, it meant the end of the daily journey to the sickbed. Ben was solicitously made comfortable onstage with a stool and a cushion, and there he sat beaming approval for an hour. Even when things went wrong and the offending players could not refrain from glancing at him with nervous apology, he continued to smile understandingly.

During his convalescence Ben had decided that, come what may, he must ingratiate himself with the Lord Chamberlain's Men. Besides, Will's concern for him, his daily visits, and his protection of the play had won Ben's heart. He wanted to like all he saw and heard, and was relieved to find that this was not difficult. He even went out of his way to commend John Heminge's Giuliano.

Ben arrived in time to see the last part of the play, and Ned longed for his approval of the speech on poetry. He hung around while the sharers spoke to Ben. Will remained after the others had left. Aware of Ned's hovering, he called him over and said to Ben, "What think you of my new son?"

"He does well; you can be proud of him."

"Liked you my long speech?" asked Ned eagerly.

"Well enough, but give it more vinegar. There speaks the true Ben Jonson, and he speaks strongly. I hate these arrogant scribblers who treat the fair maid of Poesy like a harlot;

> "Nor is it any blemish to her fame
>   That such lean, ignorant and blasted wits,
>   Such brainless gulls, should utter their stol'n wares
>   With such applauses in our vulgar ears;
>   Or that their slubbered lines have current pass
>   From the fat judgments of the multitude,

> But that this barren and infected age
> Should set no difference 'twixt these empty spirits
> And a true poet."

Ben delivered these lines of the young Lorenzo with such venom that Ned longed to imitate him, and yet his rapidly developing theatrical instinct told him that such a spirit injected into the end of a merry comedy would come as an unsettling surprise, especially with the implied insult to London audiences.

Ben looked to Will for approval both of his sentiments and of his spirited delivery of them, but Will only smiled and nodded. The author had just supplied the most cogent argument for cutting the lines but Will was determined that Ben should have his way, though it be to his own detriment.

On their way to the hitching post, Ben surprised Will by saying that he would not come to any further rehearsals unless he was wanted. Hiding his delight at this decision, Will agreed that Ben would do well to build up his strength to stand the excitement of the first performance. Ben assured Will that he was almost a full man again and would be twice himself in two days' time. Will made the smiling comment, "To be twice Ben Jonson would be a rare wonder to behold."

When Will came to the tavern where the players were dining, the news that Ben had decided to come to no more rehearsals was received with joy by all at the table. All they needed for the play now was fair weather.

And they had it. There was a nip in the early morning air of that September day, but no sign of rain. Most of the excitement in the Phillips household centered around Ned, about to play his first big part. Mistress Phillips had made a quick recovery from the birth of the new daughter and she insisted on going to the performance. Apart from the play and her four players, she wanted to see the Earl of Essex and there was even a chance that the new Countess of Southampton might be present; nobody knew how far gone she was in pregnancy.

Anne Jonson also insisted on accompanying her husband to the performance, although Ben feared that the press of the expected crowd might strain her pregnancy; but when Anne had made up her mind, not even Ben could change it. So Benjy was left with a neighbor, who also lent Anne some finery so that she could make a brave show as the author's wife; indeed she made such unusual efforts with her appearance that for once Ben was as happy to walk with her by day as he was to lie with her by night.

Cuthbert Burbage oozed good fellowship when he greeted the Jonsons backstage. They had arrived before the public doors were opened, though Cuthbert had decided to open them even before the second trumpet. Never could he recall such a crowd so early. Whether it was the play or anticipation of another *Isle of Dogs* sensation or the expectation of seeing the Earl of Essex and the Earl of Southampton with his new countess, there had been such a demand by the nobility for seats that the lords' rooms could not accommodate them. Some stools had been placed onstage, a practice that was in growing disfavor both by the actors and the groundlings; the actors disliked it because all too often the stools were commandeered by young gallants who came to be seen rather than to see and to be heard rather than to hear; the groundlings objected to it because the view of those on the sides of the stage was obstructed. But today was a special occasion, and the sight of well-dressed people sitting on the stage would add to the festive air. Besides, the people on view would be oddities: foreigners. Persistent application for good and worthy seats had been made by a court official on behalf of some Frenchman who had recently been presented to the Queen, and who wanted to entertain a group of his friends from the Continent, including some Germans and Italians. He was willing to pay a princely sum for the privilege. Cuthbert had conferred with John Heminge, knowing full well that such wealth would not be turned away. He left it to John to inform the players. Will's comment to Gus Phillips was, "Now you know why we must leave in the Latin; those will be the only lines the foreigners will understand."

The Jonsons were seated in the second gallery with a whole phalanx of sharers' wives and friends. With a burst of unusual generosity, Cuthbert made the Jonsons the guests of the house but all other friends and relations of the players had to pay, and at the double rate too.

At the penultimate trumpet, the splendidly attired French nobleman and his distinguished company were led onstage by Cuthbert Burbage. The previous sight of the stools had warned the audience of their coming, but the vision of elaborate splendor which now appeared onstage did much to silence any protests. Most of the Frenchmen known to Londoners were the sober-suited immigrant Huguenots; this peacock dazzled some to admiration and others to laughter.

The theatre was packed. All now awaited the arrival of the Earl of Essex and his glamorous party. They came at five minutes before the final trumpet and the audience went wild. With the earl and his lady were the Earl of Southampton and his new countess, who was beautifully gowned but with no attempt to hide her pregnancy. To get a better and a level view some groundlings on the far side began to clamber up onto the stage; if these foreigners could be up there, why not true Englishmen? The foreigners were forced to stand to protect themselves, and Cuthbert Burbage with the stagekeeper and some assistants emerged to clear the stage of the intruders. The final trumpet failed to restore order. Only Essex himself could do that, and at last he did. Gradually the pandemonium ceased, the groundlings left the stage, and the foreigners were restored to their positions and their stools amid the profuse apologies of Cuthbert Burbage.

All was now ready for the first entrance of Will as Lorenzo Senior when an outcry took place on stage. A fat and wealthy German merchant, a member of the French nobleman's party, was standing, shouting, and gesticulating wildly. He seemed to be executing an absurd dance as he screamed, *"Raüber. Man hat mich beraubt! Meine tasche. Gestohlen. Dreizen hunderdt kronen. Alles gestohlen."* A confusion of tongues broke out: French, German, Italian, English. Most of the audience callously enjoyed the spectacle and din. The gestures of the distraught German made clear that he had been robbed during the invasion of the stage. There was little sympathy for the rich foreigner; he obviously would not starve for what he had lost.

Wailing to the heavens, and with the reluctant aid of a compatriot, the robbed one was finally persuaded to leave the stage. At last Lorenzo Senior entered and was greeted with loud applause, born of the general excitement of the occasion and a welcome and increasingly rare sight of London's leading playwright. None was warmer and more genuine in approbation than Ben Jonson. The Earls of Essex and Southampton were both seen to clap vigorously too. Lorenzo Senior had to call for his servant several times before the audience settled down to enjoy the play. Many a young man nodded vigorously when Will said:

> "For youth restrained grows impatient,
> And, in condition, like an eager dog
> Who, ne'er so little from his game withheld,
> Turns head and leaps up at his master's throat;"

and many a much-married man sighed with approval at Richard Burbage's words:

> "What meant I to marry?
> I that before was ranked in such content,
> My mind attired in smooth silken peace,
> Being free master of mine own free thoughts,
> And now become a slave?"

But it was the fun that held sway that afternoon: Will Kemp's water-carrier, Richard Cowley's country gull, and, above all, Thomas Pope's strutting braggart, with the face of a lion and the heart of a mouse, Bobadilla.

Ned made a good impression. His Lorenzo Junior was a handsome and appealing young man. More than one young lady eyed him with promise. But as the laughter mounted throughout the afternoon, Ned was more and more troubled about that last speech which he had wanted so much to deliver. Now he knew what others, wiser in theatre than he, had known all the time; it did not belong at the end of this play. He had toyed with the idea of surprising the company by speaking it with the venom that the author had wanted, but instead determined to give it as the earnest plea of a true and unregarded poet, thus gaining sympathy for his Lorenzo. But something unforeseen spoiled his speech and the end of the play.

When he spoke the lines,

> "such lean, ignorant and blasted wits,
>   such brainless gulls,"

the unmistakable voice of Gabriel Spencer rang out, "And that's Ben Jonson." He was standing in the second gallery, right above the room which contained the Essex party, and he was pointing an accusing finger across at Ben. Ned tried to continue his speech, but it was impossible, because of the abuse that Spencer and Jonson hurled at each other and the din of disapproval which began to grow in the audience. Spencer was heard by some to shout a challenge at Jonson and then he disappeared backstage through the private door. In spite of attempts by his wife and others to restrain him, Ben followed suit through the door on his side. Will and Ned were left adrift on stage, but as the audience settled down, Will addressed them.

"My lords, and gentles all, 'twould be foolish to resume the play, for it was almost at an end. I commend it to your favor, for I believe that, in spite of all, it has given you pleasure. I beseech you to bestow your blessing on its author, Ben Jonson."

The audience gave vent to a roar of approval, and the players came on to bask in it, Augustine Phillips happy to be spared the line in Latin. All turned and bowed to the Earl of Essex which renewed the vociferous applause; the earl stood to share in it. Only the author was absent.

He and Gabriel Spencer were with difficulty being restrained from tearing at each other. Cuthbert Burbage, the stagekeeper and a cluster of assistants were hanging on to them and dragging them apart. At last the two combatants ceased struggling and contented themselves with spewing out verbal hatred. Then Spencer repeated, but this time with unavoidable clarity, his challenge to a duel that would end for all time Jonson's "odious pretensions." Cuthbert Burbage, spurred by his fear of such lawless conduct and a new respect for Jonson as a potentially valuable playwright, blustered in condemnation of such an outrageous idea. But Ben was a man to welcome any challenge. Gladly would he rid the world of such a vile encumbrance; Spencer had but to name the time and place. Cuthbert pointed out to Spencer that he was taking undue advantage of a sick man, and that was arrant cowardice.

"Then let your sick man name the time and place. I will wait to dispatch him when he is in full health to die."

"Give me but three days to set my things in order and I will attend you," said Ben.

"The time and place?" asked Spencer.

"As soon as it is full light, say seven o'clock, here in Shoreditch Fields." Now Ben looked first at Cuthbert Burbage and then at all the men who surrounded them as he added, "And let no man bruit it abroad, for Master Spencer and I have had this date with death for a long time and no man must interfere to prevent it. Loose him, and me too, for we shall not touch each other here."

Somewhat reluctantly the restraining hands were taken off the two men. With a deadly calm they spoke to each other.

Gilbert Spencer said, "Until my blade meets yours."

"So be it," said Ben.

After a final glare of consuming scorn, Gilbert Spencer turned abruptly and left. Spent by the violence and the passion, Ben suddenly felt giddy, and he staggered. Willing hands grabbed him and helped him to a stool.

All this while the ovation had continued in the theatre, but now the players came hurrying offstage eager to know the upshot of the Jonson-Spencer confrontation. Soon word of the impending duel was whispered around. As Ben stood up, some of the leading players surrounded him with enthusiastic assurances of the success of his play, which had not been dimmed by the untoward incident at the end. And then came the Earl of Essex and his noble following. He was lavish in his compliments to Ben, who had given London a "new and fresh delight." Then he turned to Will and said, "You must look to your laurels, Master Shakespeare. But now I bethink me, your pens have a different quality and need not vie with each other." Still addressing Will he said, "I long to see the play you have promised about Henry V. How much of it is done?"

"None yet, my lord."

"Then have at it, Master Shakespeare. 'Tis high time. These are stirring days and 'tis well to be reminded of a heroic king."

"Henry," said Essex, turning to the handsome Earl of Southampton, who was now twenty-five years of age, "you were our poet's patron when he was yet but little known. 'Tis you must urge him to fulfill his promise; he cannot but listen to you."

"Will Shakespeare is his own man; he always was; he always will be," said Southampton, and there was respect and admiration in the voice.

"A poet is never his own man, my lord," said Will.

Many listeners, and none more than Ned, had been quick to speculate on possible implications of this exchange, and they were frustrated when Essex brought it to an end by saying, "Fail us not, Master Shakespeare, and you, Master Jonson, make us laugh with another play of the humours." This was the signal for the departure of the nobility.

The company kept at a respectful distance from the group, and behind them pressed the players' families, who had taken some time to make the awkward descent from the second gallery. Anne Jonson was irritated that she could not stand by her husband's side at this illustrious moment in their lives, but she was unknown to the players who stood in front of her, and they had no intention of letting anyone break through their ranks. She could not understand why Ben had been so strangely subdued; he had not said a word. As all but a few swirled past him to watch the Essex procession leaving the theatre, she fastened on to him and said, "What ails you? You must not let that devilish Spencer trouble you. Tell him." She appealed to the bystanders.

John Heminge took charge. "Wait here, Mistress Jonson." He had never met her before, but there was no doubt who she was. "We must talk to Ben in private."

Still in a daze and thinking only of the appointment he had made with possible death, Ben allowed himself to be led into the bookholder's room by Heminge, Condell, and Will.

John Heminge emphasized that Ben must on no account meet Spencer in a duel; the man was deadly, and Ben's life was precious. To prevent it, he would have the fellow arrested for breaching the peace in the theatre that afternoon.

At last Ben spoke. "No, John," he said with firmness. "You cannot prevent the meeting; you can but postpone it. I beseech you to do nothing and say nothing. Spencer and I cannot both live in this world."

"But his rapier is as sharp as his tongue, and both are evil in intent," said Henry Condell.

"I am no novice with a blade," said Ben with a return to his customary manner. "I have dispatched my man on the battlefield."

Will surprised them all by saying, "I will second you, Ben," but Heminge and Condell insisted that Will dare not be a party to such a flagrant breach of the law. Ben agreed with them but was deeply grateful for Will's offer.

Now Ben's thoughts shifted to the waiting Anne, and he begged the three men to give her no hint of the duel. Deliberately they changed the subject to the success of the afternoon, and as they emerged from the room they surprised those who were waiting by the heartiness of their laughing good-fellowship. Those who knew about the duel could not understand the change of mood. Anne had gathered nothing definite from the hostile shouting in the theatre. She was only grateful that the players had succeeded in cheering Ben. She was made doubly happy when she and Ben were invited to join the company at supper in celebration of the success, especially when it was whispered to her by Anne Phillips that it was a unique privilege for a woman to be present at the sharers' table. The invitation had been extended by John Heminge after a quick and quiet conference with a few other sharers; the presence of Ben's wife would be the surest way to banish the subject of the duel from the supper board.

There was general understanding among the players that if the duel resulted in death or even serious hurt, the consequences could be dire; since both men were players it would give excuse to hostile magistrates to say that all players were violent and dangerous, and, in the light of the recent disorders, they might be enabled to close the theatres.

Ned had been caught in a whirlpool of thoughts and feelings since the interruption of his big speech. He felt that somehow he should have dominated the moment, quelling Spencer into silence by the assurance of his stage authority; wasn't this what Burbage would have done? Before he had had a reluctant regard for Spencer; now he hated him. Then Ned felt a furious disappointment that the excitement at the end of the performance had robbed him of the praise he longed for. Only Mistress Phillips had been really warm and sincere, and he discounted her words because, even if his performance had been bad, she would have said them to comfort him. Not a word from Will, who was too occupied with Ben; but surely he could have found time for a word.

It was not until Will came to see him in his room that night that Ned was appeased, for there was no mistaking the genuineness of the praise and the pride. Will also was able to relay golden words of commendation from unexpected sources, even from Richard Burbage. He ended by saying, "You are going to be the player of the family, Ned."

Ned felt an admiring love for his brother when he learned that he had offered to be Ben's second, but he quickly agreed with John Heminge that Will could not be allowed to take such a risk.

Suddenly Ned remembered George and Gilbert. If they had been at the performance, why had they not come backstage afterwards?

Will explained that, because of the presence of the Earl of Essex, no member of the public had been allowed backstage.

"Then why did they not come after the earl left?"

"Because the sight of us as father and son could not vie in George's eyes with that of the Earl of Essex returned to glory and favor."

"And that of the Earl of Southampton and his new countess," added Ned, hoping to draw Will.

All he got for his angling was, "Southampton is but the moon to the sun of Essex. The moon is but a faint shadow in the light of day. By night it waxes and wanes, but it is always beautiful. And now goodnight, my brother and son. You should sleep well and have happy dreams."

When he was alone, Ned's thoughts reverted to Ben. Since Will could not be there to second him, he would. But he must tell nobody, not even Will; not even Sam.

TWENTY-TWO

EVERYMAN IN HIS HUMOUR HAD BEEN SUCH A SUCCESS THAT IT WAS DECIDED to give a second performance that same week. The day chosen was

Friday, the day of the threatened duel. Perhaps the sharers hoped to prove by this conjunction that the Lord Chamberlain's Men were ignorant of the unlawful event or to persuade Ben to ignore Spencer's challenge.

By discreet inquiry, Ned found out the hidden place in Shoreditch Fields where the duel was likely to take place; it was not far from the Curtain.

Ben did not come to the theatre during the intervening days. More than one of the sharers, but most notably Will, wanted to visit him, but it was decided in conference that it would be unwise to have any contact with him. A letter was sent to inform him of the second performance of his play and to invite him and Mistress Jonson again to be the guests of the company, since their enjoyment of the first performance "was marred by the untoward and regrettable incident at its end, which we all hope you have already forgotten. We look forward to the privilege of presenting further works of your pen, and trust that nothing may occur to impair a partnership which, for our part, has been so happily begun."

This last sentence was the nearest John Heminge thought they dared go in hinting at their hope that the duel would not take place; it had the further meaning that the initial difficulties between author and players was now to be forgotten and not allowed to prejudice their future relations. All the sharers signed the letter.

Ben's letter in reply was grateful and cordial. He said that he and Mistress Jonson would be happy to attend the second performance of his play, and he added a conventional clause, now ominous: "if I be alive and well."

When he got to the theatre on the morning after his first appearance as Lorenzo Junior, Ned found a letter awaiting him. It was written by Gilbert, but parts had obviously been dictated by George, and it was signed by both. It contained flattering praise of his looks, his clothes, and his performance—"more than ever are we sure that you will be the successor to the great Richard Burbage, and you are much more handsome than he ever was"—and it explained how they had been prevented from delivering their congratulations in person by "an impudent varlet of a doorman, who forbade us entrance as though we were groundlings striving to push past him to catch a glimpse of the nobility inside." The letter begged Ned to take supper with them that night to enable them to "repair the omission that was much against our will."

Ned was still too fresh to the experience not to seize every opportunity to bask in adulation; he gave Sam a message for Mistress Phillips and Will, and this time he could be explicit about the reason for his absence from supper.

Ned was a little surprised to find that the supper at the haberdashers' was to be a party, but he was immediately reconciled to the situation when he learned that all six men who were present had seen him the previous afternoon as Lorenzo Junior. He was effusively greeted as though he had scored a signal triumph. He never learned the surnames of the other four guests, but he slowly gathered that Henry was a wig-maker and Clarence was a lawyer. Henry was about forty, the oldest in the room, and strove desperately to look and behave as young as his handsome, pouting companion, Tommy, who was half his age. Clarence was a quiet onlooker, about Will's age, with a permanently sarcastic twist to his mouth; his companion, Jamey, was a young law student, who tried to make every utterance brilliantly memorable, always looking to Clarence for approval and getting nothing for his pains from the face which, like a mask, seemed capable of only one expression—faintly amused superiority.

When they moved into the dining room, the table was a marvel of gleam and color, so satisfying to look at that it seemed an act of vandalism to spoil the display by eating and drinking. Only Ned seemed taken aback by the sight; it exceeded anything he had ever seen. The cold meal itself was not as sumptuous nor as satisfying as any with Sylvia, but for elegance the meal was unsurpassed; and to complete the picture, the serving man, Michael, was so handsome that Ned noticed that a speaker whose words were addressed to the table would have his eyes and mind on Michael. There was no woman in evidence; the female cook, hired like Michael for the occasion, had been dismissed some hours before.

Gradually Ned was irritated to find that he had been invited not so much to be congratulated on his performance as to supply information about the outcome of the quarrel between Ben Jonson and Gilbert Spencer. He was determined to say nothing, not only because he was pledged to do so but also because it was good to starve such greedy ears; at the same time it was gratifying to adopt a lofty pose of "I could tell you much if I chose to do so."

It was clear that Spencer's challenge hurled across the theatre had been heard by those near him, in spite of the surrounding noise. George had promised his guests that Ned could and would supply them with the information which they craved in order to whisper it abroad to intimates who would be duly impressed by their access to backstage sources. And now Ned would not cooperate. It was infuriating.

Discussion turned to the ethics of dueling. George firmly upheld it as "a gentleman's way to settle differences." Clarence made one of his rare comments in reply: "If differences were always settled in that way, we lawyers would die of starvation." Henry said, "I long to see a duel, but I should swoon at the sight of blood."

The three satellites were pressed for their opinions. Gilbert said, "Anyone who deliberately kills another man, no matter what the rules, is a murderer." Tommy said, "If two men both want to kill each other, let them, say I," and he relapsed into his pout. Jamey had been trying all the while to compose an aphorism which all who heard would quote. When his turn came he adopted an oracular pose and said profoundly. "Dueling is war in little. War is natural to man and so is dueling. 'Twill be time to outlaw it when war is outlawed, and that will never be."

Jamey was abashed when George said, "Oh, this is all so tedious," but when Gilbert said, "Ned has not given his opinion," all looked expectantly at Ned, who had been so annoyingly enigmatic. He said, "I have no opinion. I have not seen a duel yet."

George could not let it go. He said, "Nobody at this table has seen a duel, but I wager you will see one soon, young man. It is clear that you will not trust us with the when and where of it—you must have taken some oath of secrecy, and I suppose you must honor it—but when it is all over and Ben Jonson is dead, you must promise to tell us every detail of the how of it." George paused momentarily for Ned to make the required promise, but he only smiled and said nothing, so George swept on. "And now let us talk of pleasanter subjects. I have not yet found out who that Frenchman on the stage was, but his costume and accoutrements surpassed anything my eyes have ever beheld. My beloved Essex and my adored Southampton were to him but crows to a peacock."

Ned longed to get away and, as soon as he politely could, he made the excuse that he had work to do in preparation for the next day, and he left, leaving behind him a residue of unflattering comments, which again Jamey felt behooved to sum up. He said, "Players are ever dull dogs in themselves. That is why they are players, pretending to be what they are not."

When he got outside, Ned had a strong impulse to visit Ben Jonson, whose house was near, though he was aware that no sharer was to see Ben before the duel. This clearly also applied to all members of the company, but it had not been so spelled out. Ned, therefore, felt no compunction about going to see Ben, and he felt Will would approve of the visit when he ultimately knew.

It was almost dark by the time Ned got to the house. There was no light, and when he knocked at the door there was a long wait. He knocked again and louder. After another wait, a woman's voice spoke to him through the closed door.

"Who is there?"

"Ned Shakespeare. Will's brother. Is Master Jonson in?"

"No; he isn't. And I've gone to bed."

"Can you tell me where to find him?"

"In some tavern somewhere."

"Please tell him Ned Shakespeare came."

"I will. Tell me, were you young Lorenzo?"

"Yes."

"I liked you. Ben did too. Goodnight."

"Goodnight, Mistress Jonson." That scrap of praise from an unseen woman meant more to Ned than the fulsome adulation of George and his fellows. He was glad that he had come, even though he had failed in his purpose.

When Ben came home and to bed, strangely sober, Anne told him that Ned had called. She added, "I told him you would be in some tavern."

Ben said nothing. He had not been in a tavern. He had been borrowing a good rapier and practicing to get the heft of it. He had also been searching out a man to second him, a difficult task, because every friend who said no might consider it an act of friendship to inform the authorities of the projected duel and so stop it. He had chosen his man with care and insight, an old comrade from the wars in the Low Countries, Jack Goodman, a man whom Ben had taught to read and who was employed by a printer. The rapier had been borrowed from a player friend who belonged to the Admiral's Men. He had tactfully asked no questions about Ben's need for the weapon, but had been happy to try several bouts with him and had promised to have more on the following day. Ben would leave the rapier with Jack Goodman on the night before the duel so that Anne would have no knowledge of it.

THE FATEFUL FRIDAY DAWNED CLOUDY; THE LIGHT WAS NOT GOING TO BE good. Ned had persuaded the maid Letty to wake him at first light. He assumed, and rightly, that she was the first to stir in the household, but he never paused to wonder how such a young body could wake without help. He had warned her that she must be careful not to wake anybody else nor tell anybody that she had waked him. She obeyed him fearfully but heartily disliked being a part of some plot of which she was certain her mistress would disapprove. She shook him by the shoulder, and, as soon as he stirred, she disappeared. Ned moved quickly and quietly and was out of the house before anybody else was downstairs.

When he came to the appointed place, the four men were already there. His approach startled them; they feared he might be an officer come to stop the match. When Ben recognized Ned, he greeted him happily. Gabriel Spencer also recognized him and said, "You are a friend of Master Jonson I see, and have come to take leave of him. Had the light been better, you would have been too late." Then he turned to his second and said something which nobody else could catch, but it caused that gentleman, for such his appearance and manner proclaimed him, to guffaw.

Jack Goodman was expostulating with Ben that the match was uneven for his rapier was almost a foot shorter than Spencer's. He was begging to be allowed to arrange a later date with equal blades, but Ben would have none of it; he could not live longer with the threat; the morning must end it. To cut off the argument, he turned to speak to Ned. He said that Anne had told him of his visit, and he thanked him for coming now, especially since it was a foolhardy thing to do.

Spencer's second approached. He addressed the three men, studiously avoiding a straight look at any one of them. "The light is good enough for us now. How is it with you?"

" 'Tis well," said Ben.

"There is no judge since you both have intent to kill, and nothing less will satisfy you. Master Spencer suggests that we do not even take the customary pause at a hit but carry straight through to a quick end."

"I am content," said Ben. Jack Goodman tried to intervene, but Ben silenced him.

"To your prayers then, and let us have at it." He strode back to Spencer who was practicing thrusts and recoveries.

Ben gripped Ned's hand tightly, but neither said a word. Ned could not speak; in spite of himself, tears were trickling down his face. Ben shook his second's hand and said, "Now stand aside and leave me to my God." As his friends moved a few yards away, Ben closed his eyes and clasped his hands in prayer around his rapier. After a few moments his prayers were interrupted by a peremptory call from Gabriel Spencer: "Now, sir. On guard."

From the first clash of the blades it was abundantly clear that Ben's was shorter. Ned found it hard to stand his ground for the outcome seemed inevitable. Spencer had a devilish glee in the fight; he seemed to be playing with Ben to exasperate him. He even made comments as he thrust and parried. Thus he said, "Your sword is as awkward as your pen, Master Jonson."

But to Ned's surprise, Ben was wielding his rapier, especially as a defensive weapon, with considerable strength and skill. Or was Spencer just tormenting him?

The end came quickly. Ben misjudged a clever feint of Spencer's, and the return thrust got him squarely in the sword arm. Spencer recovered to deliver the final blow at will and, sure of himself, turned to give a smile of triumph to his second. But, after the momentary spasm of pain, Ben had not lost the use of his arm, and, taking quick advantage of his opponent's careless sense of security, he made a strong thrust. Spencer was too late to parry, and it penetrated deep into his body.

A look of utter surprise overcame Spencer. He muttered, "Thank you, but I could have wished . . ." and he dropped to the ground. All four men gathered around him, Ben pressing the wound in his own arm to stanch the blood which was now pouring out. Spencer did not say another word. All efforts to stop his bleeding were useless, and in less than a minute he was dead.

With astonishing calm the gentlemanly second said, "Gilbert expected to die from this encounter, but he thought it would be by hanging. You saved him from that shame, Master Jonson, but he may have thought that to die by your hand was a greater one." Looking at Jack and Ned, he said, "If you would help me, we could get Gilbert's body to my coach behind those trees."

"First we must tend to Ben's arm," said Jack belligerently. "The dead can wait."

Both seconds had provided themselves with salves and bandages. Now Jack stripped Ben's shirt sleeve and proceeded to doctor his arm. The wound was in the fleshy part, but the rapier had not gone right through. A liberal application of a waxy ointment dried up the blood flow and the arm was tightly bandaged.

All three men were so astonished at the outcome of the match that it took a little time for them to feel the full happiness of relief, and instinctively they muted its expression in the presence of the corpse. Ben said, as his arm was being doctored, "I shall go home to tell my wife what has happened, and then I shall surrender to an officer, for I must stand trial for this death."

The other second said, "If need be, I shall testify on your behalf, for Gilbert would have wished it."

"I thank you, sir," said Ben.

"Know you in which prison you will be kept to await trial?" asked the second.

"The most likely one is Newgate," said Ben. "Your friend that now lies there and I were in the Marshalsea together last year, but that is not for men of blood as, by his death, I have become. Now it will be Newgate for me, I fear."

As they carried the body to the coach, Ned said, "I will go home with you, Ben, and to the officer."

"Nay, lad. 'Tis much that you have come this morning. Jack will be my witness. None must know that you were here. But it will be a great kindness if you visit me in prison."

"I shall, Ben."

"Then be off with you now. Whisper to Will what you have seen, but to nobody else, and be surprised when you hear about it, as you soon will, I doubt not."

When Ned got home there was much speculation as to where he had been. He explained that he had been unable to sleep and had gone for a walk, but in the privacy of Will's room Ned told the whole story. Will made no comment on Ned's foolhardiness, but instead seemed pleased by his friendly championship of Ben. He confessed he had slept badly because of fears for Ben's life, and he found Ned's news an astounding relief. As for Gilbert Spencer, he was so soured by life that Will doubted he would regret leaving it. But now the two brothers must enter into a conspiracy of silence, and, when Augustine Phillips came up to tell them that it was time to leave for the theatre, they were busy cuing each other as Lorenzo, father and son. Gus said, "I am troubled about Ben Jonson. I fear he is no longer alive."

TWENTY-THREE

WILL AND NED VISITED BEN TOGETHER ON THE FIRST SUNDAY OF HIS imprisonment in Newgate; he had been there for two nights. Some of London's prisons were under the jurisdiction of the City and others under that of the Crown. Newgate was the chief City prison and was used almost exclusively for people awaiting trial on criminal charges. Accommodations in all prisons were determined by the ability to pay, which made the keepership of a prison a very desirable post. Ben had not the money to secure comfort and good food, but he was not so destitute as those who depended upon charity for food and often starved to death when the basket-man, who went around the streets crying, "Bread and meat for the poor prisoners," came back, in times of dearth or plague, with an empty basket.

The two Shakespeares found Ben lively in spirit and deeply stirred about a discovery he had made. He did not want to talk about the duel or about his forthcoming trial. He did not even seem to be much interested in the glowing account they brought him of the success of the second performance of his play. When Will began tentatively to suggest that perhaps the time had come to attempt some improvements in the text of the play, Ben amazed them by saying, "Do what you will; it matters little." Seeing the expression on their faces, Ben smiled and added, "When you are face to face with death, as I was with Gilbert Spencer and as I am here, you learn what is truly important in life. Look at that man over there, the handsome, tall one talking to the bald, short one." He pointed to two men talking quietly together on a bench some twenty feet away. "His name is Philip Kenton and he is my bedfellow. The man with him is a secret priest of the Roman faith who brings him the courage to die when he could live, if he chose to. He is accused of complicity in a murder and helping a murderer to escape. They are all Roman Catholics with a faith I envy. Philip has chosen to die by *'la peine forte et dure.'* "

Will, in spite of Ben's obvious seriousness, was inwardly amused by his characteristic use of the French and legal term. Ned did not understand, and between them they explained that it meant "pressing" to death. Ned had heard of this but was not clear why a man would choose it, and Ben took upon himself to enlighten him. Indeed, for much of the visit Ben talked to Ned as though Will were not present; his unexpected appearance at the duel had endeared the young man to him.

"Philip refused to plead either guilty or not guilty," said Ben, "and so they cannot bring him to trial. He does this to save his estate for his wife and children."

"But he might be found innocent," objected Ned.

"Never," said Ben. "They know he is a Roman Catholic, and that is enough."

"But did he not aid a murderer?" asked Will.

"Yes," agreed Ben, "but how could he do other? It was his wife's brother, and a man he respected and admired."

"But the murder?" queried the puzzled Ned.

"I don't know the rights of it," said Ben, "but they were harboring the famous Jesuit, Father John Gerard." Ned's mind flashed back to Clement, with whom he had spent that memorable evening at Master Lockett's inn just three months ago. "An officer and some soldiers who were pursuing Father Gerard closed in on the house." Ned wondered whether it could be the officer who had questioned him. "In helping the priest to escape, a struggle took place, and the officer fell down a staircase. In the confusion, the man, as well as the priest, escaped. It seems the officer was killed. And now Philip has chosen to die."

"But this pressing," said Ned. "It is to make men speak. Master Kenton may cry out under the pain and so be brought to trial."

"Not Philip. He has the strength of soul to die in silence."

"His courage will shorten the torture," said Will. "The jailors know he does it for his family, and they will put a sharp stone or piece of wood under his back so that it will enter his body as the weights on his chest are increased."

"The thing that amazes me," said Ben, "is that Philip sleeps peacefully and I do not. His thoughts are already in another world and mine remain stubbornly in this. I would give much to have his faith."

"The Puritans too have equal faith," said Will, "and would die for it with equal fortitude." Ned knew he was thinking of his Anne.

"Talk not of them," said Ben with a return to his old spirit. "Their faith is a torment to them, Philip's is a grace."

Philip Kenton stood up and, with his companion, approached Ben. Introductions were made, and the disguised priest was introduced as "Master Peter Kirby, a librarian in a noble house." Master Kirby was a jolly man who made amusing comments on some of the forty or so prisoners who stood or sat in groups around the room; they all belonged to the middle class and could afford some comfort. "This prison life is a costly one," he chuckled. "You pay to come in, you pay to go out, and you pay for everything in between."

" 'Garnish' is the word," said Philip Kenton, who seemed to have caught the infection of his companion's gaiety. "Garnish for food, garnish for drink, garnish for bed, garnish for the slightest privilege, like the freedom of this room."

"But Philip," said Master Kirby, "jailors too must live. It may be hard to believe, but they too are men with wives and children." He turned to

Ben. "Philip tells me, Master Jonson, that you killed a man in a duel. I'm sure you had good cause. Did he die well?"

"He thanked me."

"I wonder why," mused Master Kirby. "For leaving this world, or for entering the next?"

"I doubt he believed in the next," said Ben.

"Poor soul! He must have been a very unhappy man, to be grateful for leaving this world when he thought there was no other."

"He said something else too, but he never finished it. I think it was, 'I could have wished . . .' but I know not what it was he wished."

Master Kirby abruptly changed the subject. "I hear you are a scholar and a poet, Master Jonson. That means you should be saved from hanging by a verse of Latin, and a very good thing too; the world can ill spare scholars and poets. Know you the verse?"

"Not all of it, but I shall be able to read it. It begins, '*Misere mei, Deus, secundum magnam misericordiam tuam.*'"

"And it goes on, '*et secundum multitudinem miserationum tuarum dele iniquitatem meam.*' You see, I am well prepared to save my neck should I have the ill fortune to kill a man." He thought this was a huge joke, as indeed it was in light of the geniality of the harmless little man, and all laughed heartily. "There is a verse in that psalm that I particularly cherish. I give it in English from the Queen's Psalter." Did he do this to allay the suspicions of strangers? "'But lo, Thou requirest truth in the inward parts; and shalt make me to understand wisdom secretly.'"

Both Will and Ned could not help but contrast the happiness of this utterance with the gloom with which it would have been spoken from the Stratford pulpit. "'Truth in the inward parts.' 'Tis well said. You and I must talk further, Master Jonson. I shall visit Philip here every day. I doubt not the hanging verse will spare you, but you will be branded with the mark of Cain—not on your brow but upon your left thumb." This too seemed to him to demand a chuckle. "T for Tyburn, to show how narrowly you missed the gallows, and to prevent you from claiming benefit of clergy when next you kill a man. But let the T stand in your mind for something else. What, Master Jonson, what?"

"Truth?" suggested Ben.

"Excellent i'faith," exclaimed the merry man with the excitement of seeing a point in a game brilliantly scored. "Excellent. That truth in the inward parts, which we must find or die even while we live." And he said this with a new seriousness, though his note had a wistful sadness rather than a forbidding solemnity. "And you, Master Shakespeare, you too are a poet, and a famous one." He had returned to his light manner. "Alas! I cannot see your plays, for I live in the country and my time is all taken in the care and study of my lord's books." None of his hearers missed the ambiguity in this remark, and all approved the sprightliness of his mind. "Yes, I am a librarian, but I have read your two long poems over and over, and never without profit and enjoyment. In your *Rape of Lucrece* there are two lines which are so sadly true of most men. Let me see if I can recall them. Oh yes, I remember what I read when it is worthy to be remembered.

> "The aim of all is but to nurse the life
> With honor, wealth, and ease, in waning age."

Ned was puzzled. The truth of the lines was obvious, but why was it sad?

" 'Tis true that you go on to say that in seeking them they are often 'all together lost,' " the little man continued. "But consider Master Kenton here. He has chosen not to see his waning age, so that honor, wealth, and ease may belong to those he loves, but he has found something greater than all those things, and that is peace of soul which comes from certainty of truth in the inward parts. But I sound like a preacher, and I have not the solemn face for the part, so I will bid you all a good day for I must have some more words in private with my friend, Philip." He walked away and Philip Kenton followed him.

The three who were left had all been overwhelmed in their various ways by the rotund librarian who, as a priest in fact, dallied with danger every moment of his life. Ned was the first to recover. He felt that something had to be said on the side of the law, on the side of the man whose death had brought Philip Kenton to his present jeopardy; he was now convinced that the man who had died was the one who had questioned him about Clement. He had not been an evil man, but one doing his duty. He said with some force to Ben, "But is not Philip Kenton a traitor to our Queen?"

"I think not, Ned. He would fight for her against all who would harm her, but he will not go to her Church."

"What think you, Will?" asked Ned.

"I admire strength of faith wherever it is found," said Will thoughtfully, "but I fear it too. Men of religion have shed much blood for their faith, and on both sides. God's most precious gift to man is life itself, even though it is often full of pain and sorrow, and I cannot think it right to shed a man's blood to save one's own soul. But enough of such matters; we are here to cheer and comfort Ben."

"And Master Kirby is here to cheer and comfort Philip Kenton," said Ben, "and he does."

Ben's face lighted up at the approach of his wife and son; possibly two sons, for Mistress Jonson could not be far from her time. Little Benjy was obviously scared by the strangeness of the place and the people, but at sight of his father his face brightened. He started to run to him but tripped on the unevenly flagged floor, and fell down in a fit of loud crying. Ben hurried to comfort him, and Anne took the opportunity to speak to Will and Ned.

"Is not this shameful, Master Shakespeare?" she began. "Ben in prison again, and now for killing a man. I thank God that monster, Gilbert

Spencer, is dead, but mark my words, Master Shakespeare, there will come others. Ben gathers enemies as a sweaty horse gathers flies."

"He gathers friends too," said Will.

"Enemies do more harm than friends can remedy," she said.

"Ben will escape hanging, Mistress Jonson," said Ned helpfully.

"Mayhap this time, but not the next," said Anne, refusing to be comforted. "Ben will only be safe from harm when he is dumb, crippled, and unable to swallow canary wine."

By this time Benjy was comforted and his father joined the conversation of which he had not heard a word. "What has my beloved wife brought to sustain me in my durance?" he asked lightly.

She answered bluntly, "Rough bread, strong cheese, good ale, but no canary wine."

" 'Twill serve," said Ben, refusing to be baited. "Above all you have brought me my Benjy to gladden my heart."

"I would have left him with neighbors but he cried so to come. 'Tis not right that children should see the inside of prisons."

Will saw a glint in Ben's eye and realized that a family altercation was about to explode. Quickly he said his goodbyes, with promises to come again, and he and Ned left.

When they got outside, Ned said, "The next time I shall bring Ben some canary wine." Will nodded and smiled.

Since their houses lay on the way home, Will said he would call on John Heminge and Henry Condell. He did not suggest that Ned should accompany him. And so the brothers parted, but Ned wondered whether indeed Will was going to visit his fellow sharers or whether there was some woman to provide Sunday solace. Which reminded him that his own dashing young Lorenzo had not yet caught any attractive fish.

Rain canceled performances on Wednesday and Thursday. Friday morning was dry but black and threatening, and just after the first trumpet the rain began again. Ned had come to the theatre with a cape and boots, and he decided to visit Ben in spite of the downpour.

In fine weather, Ned could have done the walk in about three-quarters of an hour, but what with stopping to buy a flagon of canary, pressing against walls and under overhanging roofs for shelter, avoiding deep puddles, stepping gingerly through water-covered streets, the walk took twice as long.

As on his previous visit, Ned was searched at the prison gate. He had not noticed it particularly before; it had been an empty ritual. But this time the flagon of canary caused trouble; after all, good canary was sold in the prison, for a price and a garnish; this was taking food and drink from the ever-open mouths of the wives and children of the jailors. Exasperated, Ned was tempted to leave the wine at the gate and take it home with him, but, remembering Ben, he reluctantly offered a penny garnish. The searcher stared at it but didn't take it. The implication was clear. With mounting fury, Ned added another penny and the searcher gave a sad smirk of acceptance, picked up the coins with grubby fingers and waved him on with a flaccid gesture.

Ben was deeply depressed. He even disappointed Ned by his reception of the wine. He was grateful for it, but set it aside wearily. Philip Kenton had been pressed to death that morning.

"Was the priest with him at the end?" asked Ned.

"No. Philip wouldn't allow it; it was too dangerous. He saw him for the last time yesterday afternoon. He wouldn't even allow his wife and children to visit him here, because they would be too much distressed. But he wrote to them every day and the priest carried the messages and brought back answers. Yesterday he brought a little gold crucifix that was the wife's. Philip held it tightly in his hand as he went to his death. The executioner was kind. He brought it back to me to return to the widow."

All the while Ben had the sacred symbol hidden in his hand. He held it out to Ned, who looked in awe at it but did not touch it. Suddenly Ben was racked with sobs and tears welled in his eyes. Ned felt inadequate and helpless. To his great relief he saw the priest approaching, smiling as ever.

"What is this? What is this?" he said as he came to them. "Have done, Master Jonson. This is no time for tears. Your friend's tribulations are over, and he is at peace. Here, I bring you a message from Mistress Kenton, and you cannot read it with bleared eyes."

He held out a folded but unsealed piece of paper. Ben roughly wiped his eyes and as he read the message, Master Kirby said to Ned, "She thanks him for helping Philip in these last days."

Ben looked up from the paper. "But I did nothing," he said.

"It is when we think we do nothing that we often do most. Tell me, did Philip pass a good night?"

"Yes," said Ben in amazement. "He slept well and had to be waked. It was I who could not sleep."

"That bespeaks a warm heart in you."

"The executioner brought me this," said Ben as he held out the crucifix.

"Then he was a good man doing an evil task. Mistress Kenton and her children after her and their children after them will treasure this. Did the executioner tell you how long Philip suffered?"

"He said he made it as short as possible because he knew Philip would never speak. He said Philip's eyes were closed and his lips were moving in prayer all the time, but, when he realized what the executioner was doing, he opened his eyes and smiled and said, 'Thank you.' "

The little man voiced what the other two were thinking. "The man you killed and Philip Kenton both said 'Thank you' for death, but I fear there was great difference in their meaning, all the difference between heaven and hell. But now," he said, having spied the flagon of wine, "let us drink a toast to the memory of a good and noble man; he would not have us mourn."

"I have no goblets," said Ben.

"Then let us drink from the bottle and pass it around; 'tis an act of good fellowship," said Master Kirby.

"Then do you begin," said Ben, uncorking the flagon and passing it to the priest.

He held it in the air and said, "May the memory of Philip Kenton sustain us in times of doubt and weakness," and he drank deep. He passed the wine to Ben, who drank in silence, as did Ned in his turn.

Ned soon got the impression that Ben and Master Kirby wished to talk privately together, and, when he suggested going, neither of them pressed him to stay, though Ben was warm in gratitude to Ned.

The rain had stopped. Ned walked home in a deep fit of depression, not so much because of the death of Philip Kenton as because a new fear was being born in him: from the companionship and example of Philip Kenton, and what he was sure would now become the daily visits of Master Kirby, Ben might be converted to the Roman faith, and that could only mean more trouble. There were followers of the Pope who practiced their faith in secret and dissembled in public, but Ben would not be of that kind; what he believed, he would shout from the house-tops. Behind his concern for Ben there also began to stir in Ned's mind the first vague questionings about religion. He could not have done what Philip Kenton did, but then he would never have been in such a situation. Religion really meant nothing to him. He would have been as comfortably a Roman Catholic under Queen Mary as he was a Protestant under Queen Elizabeth. But was this right?

Ned wanted to tell Will about his visit to the prison but he was working in spite of a fever he could not shake off, and was not in a good mood either. He was beginning to rough out the promised play of Henry V and Falstaff and was finding it impossible. Falstaff could not appear; he must die.

Ned misinterpreted Will's surliness as being caused by annoyance at being disturbed. He briefly reported the death of Philip Kenton, which provoked no comment from Will, and he left abruptly. Will was content to let him go, even though he sensed that Ned had come because he needed to talk.

Throughout the next day, Saturday, Ned could not clear his mind of Ben and Master Kirby. He longed to see them again and yet dreaded to; he didn't want to be troubled by the questions they would raise. The weather was clear but beginning to turn cold; the play was *Much Ado About Nothing*. It had not been given for some time and Ned had done no singing, and so he spent an hour in the music room before going to the theatre.

The performance that afternoon was a good one; it always was after days of rain and a closed theatre. The autumnal nip in the air imparted a sprightly vigor to the actors, so that the dance which ended the afternoon never went better. Everybody onstage and in the audience was in a happy mood, and the cloud lifted from Ned.

The next morning, Sunday, Ned decided he must visit Ben, and before Master Kirby came, as come he certainly would. If his absence from church were noted, he would find some excuse.

The air was brisk, and the walk cleared Ned's head so that he was in fine fettle by the time he reached Newgate. Ben was surprised and glad to see him so early; he now did not want any visit to coincide with that of Father Kirby, which had become the center and purpose of each day.

Ben had news for Ned: he was to come to trial the following Friday. He did not seem at all anxious about the result; Gilbert Spencer's previous hot-tempered slaying of a man would tell against him, a friend would testify about the disturbance he had caused at the first performance of *Every Man in His Humour,* and Jack Goodman would describe the fatal match.

But it was not so much indifference to his fate that prompted Ben's casual account of the forthcoming trial as a new excitement about something far more important: the fate of his soul. As Ned had feared, Ben was becoming converted to Roman Catholicism, and the zeal of the convert was already strong within him. Ned felt menaced. He could not and did not want to argue with Ben who could easily overwhelm him with learning and logic. All he pleaded was the danger of the decision. But Ben said he would be careful, a quality Ned felt him incapable of. "Did not Christ tell His disciples to have the wisdom of serpents?" asked Ben. "I shall protect my wife and children, never fear. I shall go to the church every Sunday, though I will not prostitute my soul by partaking of their Holy Communion. Mark my words, Ned, the day will come when Christ's vicar on earth will again rule over the church in this land."

In his excitement Ben forgot to moderate his voice and these treacherous words made Ned look around fearfully. Ben said triumphantly, "You look troubled, Ned. That's your conscience. It's a good beginning. I have a warm regard for you, for you have been a good friend to me. It would do my heart and soul good to bring you back to the true faith. Yes, back, Ned, back; for that's where we all were until that monster of Satan, Henry VIII, led us astray to serve his evil lusts."

The words horrified Ned. Was this what Ben meant by being careful? There was only one way to stop such wild utterances and that was to leave, which he did so precipitately that Ben was amused, interpreting it as a sure sign that Ned was troubled in his soul, a necessary first step on the way back to the bosom of the true Church.

To counteract the dangerous fever to which he had just been exposed, Ned stopped at St. Paul's Cross on the way home, to listen to one of the famous Sunday sermons, which always drew a large, open-air crowd. Only the most powerful and persuasive of the Church's orators could hold such an audience, drawn from all sections of the city and the country. The preacher was Mr. Tolson, of Queen's College, Cambridge, renowned for his fulminations against "popish idolators." This day his text was from the second commandment: Thou shalt not make to thyself any graven image. Mr. Tolson was brilliantly and strongly persuasive. He mocked the pagan superstitions of those who prayed to statues and clutched rosaries like lucky charms and kissed crucifixes and thought that the crumbling bones of men long dead could heal them of diseases of the body. Ned remembered the little crucifix that had helped Philip Kenton to die. His reverie was suddenly stabbed into awareness of the preacher, for he was using the very words that Master Kirby had used: "God requires truth in the inward parts." Ned was puzzled to exasperation. How could they both use the same words to mean such different things? Some words of Will's came to mind: A plague o' both your houses.

Ned couldn't stand it any longer. Fortunately he was standing on the outskirts of the crowd. Even so, his moving away provoked some sternly disapproving looks.

It was a great relief to Ned that the company was enabled to play every day of that week, and so he had good reason for not visiting Ben in prison any more, for the trial took place that Friday and the outcome was the expected one. The only thing that surprised those in the court who knew Ben was the way he read the Latin verse; they expected an orotund performance of it, but instead they heard a simple and pious reading worthy of a devout cleric. It was true that he was branded with T for Tyburn on his left thumb, and his meager estate was confiscated. He was left the bare necessities of living, but these did not include his books; the only one left him was his Latin Bible.

Confident of the result of the trial, the Lord Chamberlain's Men had announced *Every Man in His Humour* for that Saturday. When the expected news was received at the theatre during Friday afternoon, a messenger was sent to invite Ben and his wife to the Saturday performance and to join the sharers at a celebratory supper afterwards.

The Jonsons brought a friend to the performance, Master Peter Kirby, and asked if he might accompany them to the dinner. The next request was a little frowned on by John Heminge but reluctantly agreed to; it was that Will, who was feeling better but still not well enough to go out, should be represented at the sharers' table by his brother, "my good friend, Ned." And so it was that for the second time Ned found himself at the privileged board; he wondered if he would ever sit there by right.

Ned had brought a sealed message to Ben from Will. After Ben read it, he handed it to Ned. It was a warm and friendly message. There was a reference to Ned in it; Will was gratified by his brother's genuine concern and regard for Ben. There was also a reference to Master Kirby with a cryptic addendum: "When next you see the little librarian, as I am sure you will, commend me to him. I shall long remember him. I beg you to bear this in mind always, Ben: it is God's will that you serve your Muse, for it is not granted that she speak to many men."

After the supper, when he was rosy and garrulous with wine, Ben was called upon to speak. He thanked everybody profusely: the players for their perfect performance of his play, the sharers for their hospitality, his wife for her patience and long-suffering, his good friends, Master Peter Kirby and the two Shakespeares "one, alas! absent, but the other happily present." He announced that good fortune had already begun to replace ill for him. "This morning some mindless officers of the law robbed me of my library, but Master Kirby has already promised to replace it." This was greeted with great applause, and the librarian, made even happier than usual by the wine, beamed and nodded.

Ben became suddenly and disconcertingly serious. "We are brought here by the death of a man, a man I killed, Gilbert Spencer. May he at last find that peace in the other world which he failed to find in this one. *Requiescat in pace.*" And Ben crossed himself. Nobody, not even Master Kirby, followed his example. There were reactions of embarrassment, consternation, apprehension, puzzlement, skepticism, and even outrage, but Ben swept on to a memorable and dramatic peroration. His left thumb had been bandaged since the branding the day before. He chose this moment, in spite of protestations particularly from his wife, to unwind the bandage and display the mark of the murderer, which was still red and fiery. Several winced at sight of it.

"Gilbert Spencer was not the first man I have killed, for I have been a soldier in the field. Killing is not always murder, and I cannot think I am a murderer, and so this T stands not to me for Tyburn. Only Master Kirby, Will Shakespeare, and Ned here know what it means to me." And he sat down abruptly and in silence.

After a moment, Will Kemp restored the happy atmosphere of celebration by calling out, "T for Teller of Tall Tales." The game was taken up with a will, and T was called out as standing for Terrible Temper, Tantalizer, Tiger, Tunbelly, Tightfist, Tyrant. It was all in mocking good humor, but Ned thought he heard Traitor too.

As they broke up after the meal, Ned was besieged by questions about the mystery of the T, but he pretended that he did not know what Ben was talking about; he would say anything in his cups. When he saw Will that evening, he told him the story and of his Sunday visit to the prison and St. Paul's Cross, hoping for some solace for his troubled mind. For Ben's conversion, Will smiled and said, "Ben must always rebel until age sobers him. Now he has found a new and defiant red banner to wave. I wager there will come a time when he will grow tired of carrying it." When Ned pressed him about the dilemma of finding truth in the inward parts, when opponents were equally certain that they had found it, Will said, "I know not the answer. For myself, I doubt I shall ever find that peace that was Philip Kenton's, nor will Ben, for if we did we would cease to write, and for that we were both born. Men I grow to understand from my own knowledge, but God I accept from the knowledge of others. It may be, Ned, that it will be different for you."

Book Three

1601

TWENTY-FOUR

THE FIRST WEEK OF FEBRUARY WAS COLD AND MADE COLDER BY HIGH AND piercing winds, but there had been no rain or snow and the Globe staged a performance every afternoon. It was now nearly three years since Cuthbert Burbage had conceived the bold plan of removing the timbers of the Theatre and transporting them across London and over the river to build a magnificent new theatre. During the Christmas holidays of 1598 a band of some dozen brave, hardy, and armed men had accomplished the daring feat to the dismay of the grasping landlord, Giles Alleyn, who was still thundering lawsuits. Among the adventurers had been Ned, hugely enjoying himself as he swung an ax against the timbers and menaced with it some of the landlord's men who had tried to interfere. But by this February of 1601 the escapade was largely forgotten, and the Globe had been in successful operation for nearly eighteen months; there seemed little doubt that Master Alleyn would have to be content with the retention of his empty land.

All Cuthbert's plans had worked out except that it was now four sharers who had a stake in the Globe and not five. Will Kemp had left, edged out by Will Shakespeare's refusal to write more parts for him. This clever Robert Armin was well enough, but Cuthbert had always enjoyed Kemp's clowning. And there he was now in Switzerland, making a fool of himself by dancing his way across the Alps. What money was in that?

The play on Friday was *Henry V,* and Will was playing the Chorus as he had at that first exciting performance at the Curtain in the spring of 1599. But this afternoon he did something which took the audience and the company completely by surprise.

There was particular interest in *Henry V* now that London was seething with fearful whispers and alarming rumors about the Earl of Essex. This play had always been associated with him. Indeed, Will had introduced a specific reference to the earl, for the play had received its first performance when Essex was in Ireland, gone to reduce the rebels to submission once and for all, and to return in glory as he had from Cadiz.

In describing the reception the citizens of London had accorded to Henry V on his return home after the astonishing victory at Agincourt, Will had compared it to that which awaited the Earl of Essex on his return from Ireland. He had written:

> As, by a lower but loving likelihood,
> Were now the General of our gracious Empress,
> As in good time he may, from Ireland coming,
> Bringing rebellion broached on his sword,
> How many would the peaceful city quit
> To welcome him!

But the words had never been spoken in the Globe, for soon after the new theatre had opened Essex had returned in disgrace, and he had continued in disfavor all this while. Gradually men had gathered to his support, some for noble and some for base reasons. Daily they gathered in the courtyard of Essex House on the north bank of the Thames, and there were rumblings of rebellion, of forceful seizure of the aged Queen and her Council. And this afternoon Will spoke the lines which had been deleted so long.

Was it a slip of the memory or deliberate? He had shared in his quiet way the adulation of Essex. Were the forbidden words spoken to remind people of their high hopes? Or were they said to please some adherents of the earl who occupied a lords' room? Certainly they delighted these noblemen, who applauded, and their applause was taken up by some of the audience, though most remained silent in consternation.

As Will came offstage most of the young men of the company greeted him with wide smiles of admiration for his courage, but John Heminge was exasperated by his foolhardiness, and puzzled too. "Why did you do it?" he whispered fiercely, careful that his voice should not penetrate to the stage.

Will looked at him steadily for a moment, considering his answer. Then he said, "I don't know. I found myself saying it."

After the performance the noble followers of the Earl of Essex, eight of them, came backstage and were effusive in their appreciation of Will's memorable contribution to the afternoon, but gradually it became clear that they had come with a deliberate purpose. Sir Gelly Merrick, the steward of the Earl of Essex, was the spokesman. He said they wished to speak in private with the leaders of the company. This request made John Heminge very cautious though he had to accede to it.

With Sir Gelly Merrick, Lord Mounteagle, Sir Charles, and Sir Joscelyn Percy, the eight sharers went into the bookholder's room. Soon after the door was closed, Cuthbert Burbage appeared. Normally he would have been backstage to greet the noblemen, but he had been delayed by a boxholder whom he had discovered skillfully conveying to his own pocket coins intended for the sealed box. When he learned that all were awaiting the outcome of a meeting now taking place, his dilemma was amusing to the company. It was clear that he wanted to join the meeting but doubted the propriety of doing so; the building was his province, not the plays or players.

Cuthbert's dilemma was resolved by his brother, who opened the door of the bookholder's room and called him to join the meeting. When Cuthbert entered the room, he greeted the four visitors becomingly but with caution, for he sensed disagreement among the sharers. It was Richard Burbage who explained the position. That in itself was significant, because the normal spokesman would have been John Heminge, who now sat glumly silent. Richard said, "These noble gentlemen want us to play *Richard II* tomorrow instead of *The Merry Wives.*"

Reasons flashed through Cuthbert's mind, all dangerous. The play told of the deposing and killing of a monarch. Even in calmer days they had never been allowed to play the actual deposition scene, the best in the play. Was the Queen to be another Richard II and Essex the rebellious Bolingbroke? Besides, their patron, the Lord Chamberlain, was opposed to the Earl of Essex, though the earl was a staunch supporter of the players.

Lord Mounteagle took upon him to explain, but his speech hid the real intent. "There is word of new and dangerous preparation in Spain. England must be aroused. We would have you play all your histories before Lent is upon us to close the theatres."

Sir Joscelyn Percy said, " 'Tis some time since we saw *Richard II,* and we like it mightily."

Henry Condell, who shared his friend Heminge's reluctance in this venture, said, " 'Tis stale in the playing, and we would have difficulty in preparing it by tomorrow."

"What think you of that, Master Burbage?" Sir Charles Percy asked Richard. "On your memory the burden falls. I'll be bound you could recite us the whole part now."

"I think not, Sir Charles," said the actor.

"But by tomorrow?" his questioner persisted.

" 'Tis possible," agreed Richard somewhat reluctantly.

John Heminge spoke. "We have thought fit to seek your counsel, Cuthbert, because there might well be danger to the building if we agree to this proposal."

Lord Mounteagle jumped in. "Danger? What danger? We do but ask you to play a play you have performed many times before, one so well known and well loved that it has been printed in several editions. We do not ask you to perform a new and unlicensed piece. Come sir; what danger?"

Cuthbert would have liked to know how the players were divided. His own doubts were resolved by Sir Gelly Merrick.

"The house was small this afternoon," he said.

" 'Tis the cold weather, sir," said Cuthbert. "All this week it has kept the people away."

"Then we would remedy that. *Richard II* will bring you a profitable house."

"The earl will be here?" asked Cuthbert, with a mixture of eagerness and apprehension.

"No," replied Sir Gelly, "but many of his friends, and all of them good friends of England, will be present. Yet it is not that which I meant when I spoke of a profitable house. For this favor to us, we would pay you, in addition to what you get from your boxes, the sum of forty shillings, and here it is."

Cuthbert's eyes were fastened to the leather pouch which Sir Gelly threw upon the table with a tempting clink of coins.

Augustine Phillips spoke. "My lords, you see we are divided in this matter, and we would beg permission to speak together in private."

Sir Gelly was irritated, but did his best to hide it. "Then be quick about it for we have much to do."

As he was about to pick up the bag of money, Lord Mounteagle said, "Nay, Gelly, let it lie there to speak for us. Come."

When the four noblemen emerged from the room, all looked at them expectantly. Lord Mounteagle said, "The players wish to confer in private. 'Tis their privilege. But I doubt not we shall have our way."

And he was right. Within a few minutes the sharers came out, but it was Augustine Phillips who made the announcement, for John Heminge had refused to countenance it. He had quickly cut short the discussion, which had promised to develop into a political one, by calling for a vote, saying that he would abide by the majority decision, even to the playing of his part, the Duke of York, but his voice was full of dire warning. All but Heminge and Condell had voted in favor of the proposal. Augustine Phillips had shown the most enthusiasm. He would have done so without the forty shillings, for he still held the high hopes which all of them had once held that the Earl of Essex would prove the rock on which the country could depend during the storms which would be inevitable upon the death of the Queen, a catastrophe which could not be much longer delayed. Robert Armin had expressed the more general view of the majority when he said, "I vote we accept the money as a protection against the cold."

Augustine Phillips said to the company, "These lords have requested that we play *Richard II* tomorrow, and we have agreed to do so."

Cuthbert Burbage held up the moneybag and quickly added, "In consideration of an additional forty shillings, already paid to us."

Now it was not clear whether the applause which followed was motivated by loyalty to Essex or to money, and John Heminge was grateful for the ambiguity, but not one person in the room missed the implications of the lords' request.

As soon as the noblemen had left, John Heminge took charge, with no sign now of his dissent. "Tomorrow we meet to rehearse at eight, not ten, for the play is stale with us. 'Tis too late tonight to set up bills about the change of play, but we will prepare them now and set them up in the morning. And so to home, gentlemen, and to the study of your parts."

On the short walk home, Gus, Will, Ned, and Sam were full of the morrow's play. No longer did the two young ones have to hold their tongues and listen to their elders, for they were both fully fledged hired men. Neither had a heavy responsibility for study that night. Ned would play Aumerle, the king's "tender-hearted cousin," a small part he loved, and in which he had no difficulty in weeping on cue; Sam played the gardener's assistant and some nothings. So both of them were more concerned with the possible implications of the performance than with their parts, and both were enthusiastic supporters of Essex, who they felt was kept from favor and power by a hostile cabal around the Queen. They were convinced that, if the Essex faction took to arms, its sole purpose would be to rescue the Queen from evil counselors. Gus Phillips shared their opinions and enthusiasm.

Will, too, had been an admirer of the Earl of Essex since he had first met him those many years ago through the Earl of Southampton, but now he seemed to observe the excitement of his three companions with a wry detachment. When pressed for an opinion, he said his sole concern was to commit the part of John of Gaunt to memory. It had been George Bryan's part, but Will had agreed to play it. All the sharers were to be involved; Robert Armin was to play the small part of the gardener; he was much more versatile than Will Kemp had been.

By choice, Will was doing more playing these days. In the past two years he had written five plays: *As You Like It* and *Twelfth Night,* with large parts for Armin, the promised *Henry V,* which he had been forced to follow with *The Merry Wives of Windsor* to still the clamor which had arisen over the death of Falstaff, and *Julius Caesar.* All had proved successful, but now his pen was engaged in secret and long labor on a play which possessed him as none other had; it was based upon an old play which had been performed occasionally during Will's early years in London. He had decided to retain the old title, *Hamlet.* All knew he was working on a play, but he refused to talk about it with anybody, and to avoid persistent questioning he acted frequently, the assumption being that if he were earning his share by regular playing, he could not be pressed to write as well.

Mistress Phillips was both excited and troubled by the news of the impending performance of *Richard II.* As a dutiful wife she echoed her husband's sentiments about the Earl of Essex, but she was fearful of his getting embroiled in dangerous partisanship. She wanted to be present at the performance, but her husband strongly forbade it, and this only increased her anxiety.

The following morning, Will, who had had little sleep, was still nervous about his lines. Richard Burbage too was heavy-eyed, but the bustle of the stage and working in the cold air lent them vigor. It was soon clear that none of the principal players would be able to afford time for dinner in the tavern; they would have to be content with snatches of bread, cheese, and ale in the theatre.

From ten o'clock on, Cuthbert Burbage added to the mounting tension and excitement by joyful reports of the requests for seats brought by messengers of noble lords and gentlemen. The patrons would spill out well beyond the lords' rooms into the first gallery; never had there been such a noble audience, save for a command performance for the Queen at her royal palace. The significance of the parallel was unintended by Cuthbert, whose sole thought was that the take of the afternoon bid fair to outweigh the total of the other five performances of the week, but it was not lost on several of the sharers. Some of them had been keenly disappointed that the Earl of Essex himself was not to be present, but now they began to be relieved that the man who more and more openly challenged the government would not be there to excite his followers. Perhaps John Heminge had been right; he usually had been proved to be.

At eleven o'clock an ominous development took place. An officer of the Queen's Council, with some half-dozen armed soldiers in attendance, came to the theatre and demanded to see the man or men responsible for the afternoon's change of play. Cuthbert blustered ineffectually; instinctively he forbore any mention of the forty shillings. When he said that the change had been made by decision of the sharers, the officer wanted to see them or their representative. When Cuthbert said that they were busy at rehearsal, the officer brushed him aside and stalked onstage, followed by his soldiers.

The appearance of the law in the person of a forbidding officer and armed men brought the rehearsal to an abrupt and fearful halt. The interrupted scene involved Augustine Phillips as the new King Henry IV, John Heminge as the Duke of York, Will Eccleston as the duchess, and Ned as their son, Aumerle; Will, with the bookholder, was onstage, observing the rehearsal.

Without apology or explanation, the officer said, "Who of you will speak in this matter?"

Nobody pleaded ignorance of the matter implied. Eyes turned to John Heminge, but he maintained silence, and it was Augustine Phillips who stepped forward.

"Why did you change the play?" demanded the officer.

"Our histories are popular, and audiences have been small this week," Gus said with a gentlemanly assurance and courtesy that commanded the admiration of his fellows, most of whom had now come quietly onstage to form a background to the scene.

"Was it not prompted by Sir Gelly Merrick and others?" asked the officer with the trace of a sarcastic smile.

After only a moment's hesitation, the company's self-offered spokesman said, "Sir Gelly Merrick and some other lords were here yesterday afternoon to see our *Henry V*. They suggested we should play more histories."

"They paid you to play *Richard II* this afternoon," was the blunt retort.

"I do not deny it," said Phillips, still all gracious affability, "and in February players cannot afford to refuse money for pursuing their vocation. But the play is no secret matter. It is well known and has been often seen."

"Is there not seditious matter in it?"

"No," said Will strongly, drawing all eyes to him. "It is now six years since it was first allowed by the Master of the Revels and has been often played without offense since that time. 'Tis true that Master Tilney forbade us to speak some hundred and seventy-five lines showing the actual deposing of the King, and we have never spoken them, nor shall we do so this afternoon."

"Then since your play is so allowed and innocent, why do the rebellious followers of the Lord Essex seek to have you play it?"

"It cannot foment rebellion, for 'tis a warning against it, as all our histories are," said Will.

John Heminge now spoke, and it was a relief to all the company that he did so, for nothing had been more worrying than his persistent disavowal of the decision to play *Richard II*.

"Master Shakespeare speaks truly, sir," he said. "One of the parts that Thomas Pope here shall play this afternoon is that of the Bishop of Carlisle, and he will speak terrible words to describe the effects of all uncivil strife, all rebellion against lawfully constituted authority. Speak those last words, Master Pope."

Pope addressed the officer directly as he spoke:

> "Disorder, horror, fear and mutiny
> Shall here inhabit, and this land be called
> The field of Golgotha and dead men's skulls.
> Oh, if you raise this house against this house,
> It will the woefulest division prove
> That ever fell upon this cursed earth.
> Prevent it, resist it, let it not be so,
> Lest child, child's children, cry against you, 'Woe!' "

John Heminge quickly commented, "Let all who come this afternoon but listen to those words, and the safety of the realm is assured." Then he went on to say, "And when I play the Duke of York, I shall speak these words directly to the lords' rooms this afternoon:

> My lords of England, let me tell you this.
> I have had feeling of my cousin's wrongs
> And labored all I could to do him right.
> But in this kind to come, in braving arms,
> Be his own carver and cut out his way,

To find out right with wrong, it may not be.
And you that do abet him in this kind
Cherish rebellion and are rebels all.

Now, sir, are we not loyal subjects of the Queen and her ministers? She
has favored us richly, and we are ever mindful of her favors and seek ever
to deserve them."

Never had John Heminge been more impressive, and the officer was
momentarily nonplussed; then he resumed the threat of the law. "I warn
you all that you will be held responsible for the keeping of the peace this
afternoon, and there will be men here to report on all that happens." He
turned sharply and left the stage, followed by the soldiers.

As soon as they had gone, players crowded around John Heminge to
congratulate and thank him, but he was annoyed at having been trapped
into defending an action of which he disapproved; still, the appreciation
could not but be pleasing to him. He said, "Enough. Enough. The rehearsal was interrupted, and we must play well this afternoon."

Ned noted with irony that the scene the officers had interrupted was
one in which John Heminge, as that same Duke of York, denounced his
own son as a traitor, not to the lawful king but to Bolingbroke, who had
seized the throne; many would see Bolingbroke as a parallel to the Earl
of Essex.

The presentation of a play at such short notice, when it had not been
done for some time, occupied the company in preparations almost to the
last moment, but they could not be unaware of the mounting excitement
in the gathering audience, especially as Cuthbert Burbage hurried backstage from time to time, happily harried by the problem of satisfactorily
seating so many nobles and gentlemen. But he also reported, and with
some dismay, that among the groundlings were many lowly supporters of
the Earl of Essex, who were loud in their praise of him and in their
ridicule of the Queen's ministers, particularly "crook-backed Cecil"; it
was also certain that there were many spies for the Queen in all sections
of the audience. "But they have all paid," chuckled Cuthbert, "they have
all paid. It's the best house since the first performance of *Julius Caesar*
last summer."

As they waited to make their first entrance, Richard Burbage (Richard
II), William Shakespeare (John of Gaunt), Augustine Phillips (Bolingbroke), Thomas Pope (Mowbray, a part he doubled with that of the
Bishop of Carlisle), and their attendants were in a state of nervousness
far surpassing that which was natural to the beginning of a performance
on special occasions.

While there was general sympathy for the plight of the Earl of Essex,
he had lost his heroic stature in the eyes of most people as a result of his
failure in Ireland. Will hoped that his play would serve as a warning to
the Essex followers rather than as an encouragement to rebellion which
would be bound to fail, for the Queen was no self-indulgent and ineffec-

tive Richard II, nor was Essex a coldly calculating and self-sufficient Bolingbroke. As he moved out onto the stage and sensed the tensely expectant audience, Will felt there was a tragedy in the making.

The performance was not marred by any undue incident. It was true that there were unusual bursts of applause and smiles of smug satisfaction whenever a line seemed to echo the arguments and sentiments of the Essex group, but stronger approval grew of those lines which condemned rebellion against God's anointed ruler. Lord Mounteagle and his friends chose to ignore this. They had planned the performance to bolster their own resolution and to test the sympathies of Londoners, but they succeeded so well in the first that they were in no state to make a true estimate of the second. Oh, if the earl himself had only been present! bewailed Sir Charles Percy. But that part of the original plan had been unwittingly foiled by the Queen's Council, which had commanded the presence of the earl to answer charges that he sought to seize power by force. The earl had pleaded sickness to excuse himself, but dared not then be seen in public. Sir Gelly Merrick had chosen to stay with the earl; he was certain that the Council would make another move and he wanted to be there for it; privately he hoped that the move would be so unequivocal as to precipitate the earl into action.

After the performance, the Essex adherents flooded onstage and backstage. They were drunk with excitement and their high spirits were infectious; most members of the company were caught up in it, a victory celebration before the battle had been fought.

One very lively supporter of Essex pushed his way through the tightly milling crowd in search of Ned, who failed to recognize him until he had announced himself as Robin. The rapscallion balladeer it was indeed, transformed by prosperity into fleshiness, an expertly trimmed beard, and handsome and well-fitting clothes. He dragged the bemused Ned toward the door to a lords' room, opened it and pulled him in. There they could talk, but the happy babble was such that they still had to raise their voices to be heard.

"Be not amazed," said Robin in the fullness of his old manner. "I have at last come into my own, and greater things lie in store for me when my Lord of Essex triumphs. You follow him, do you not?" This last question was asked perfunctorily as though it were an unnecessary question.

"I admire him and I want him restored to favor," said Ned.

"That can only be when the Queen is rescued from her evil counselors," said Robin with the ready familiarity of an oft-repeated formula.

"But tell me," said Ned, "how came you to this new prosperity?"

"At last my true quality was observed and noted. While the earl was in Ireland I sang a ballad about him and it came to the ears of Master Henry Cuffe, his secretary. Since then, I sing in the earl's service. Now my patron is Sir Christopher Blount, a bountiful master. Every day more and more men come to Essex House and my ballads put heart into them for the great enterprise that lies ahead."

"What great enterprise?" asked Ned, half fearfully.

"Nay, I cannot betray our innermost counsels, even to a friend," said Robin, pretending to knowledge he most certainly did not possess. "But come you tomorrow and you will see for yourself. Ask for me and say you come to hear the sermon of the Reverend Abdy Ashton; he is my lord's most favored preacher and tomorrow he will likely preach some three or four times. I promise he will be mighty eloquent."

The stage was clearing. The Essex party was leaving and Robin hurried to join them. His parting words were "Come early tomorrow. I shall expect you."

Ned determined to accept Robin's invitation. What harm was there? He was only going to hear a sermon, which was his duty on a Sunday. All the same, he would tell no one of his intention; he would leave early to avoid questions.

TWENTY-FIVE

NED WAS AT ESSEX HOUSE SOON AFTER EIGHT O'CLOCK. HE HAD LITTLE difficulty entering the courtyard with the many who were crowding in, but there were numerous citizens who stood outside and watched the arrivals curiously. Some guards at the gate asked him his business, but the mention of Robin and Master Ashton's sermon easily satisfied them. One of the guards surprised Ned by saying, "You are unarmed, but Robin will provide you."

The courtyard was filled with a bustling and noisy crowd, some hundreds, Ned judged. They were of all stations in life: gentlemen, merchants, artisans, apprentices, and a few plain ruffians; most of the men were under thirty. Prompted by the guard's remark, Ned noticed that all the assembled men bore arms, if it were only a strong staff. Ned moved apprehensively through the excited crowd looking for Robin, but he failed to find him.

Gradually the attention of the waiting men was drawn toward a balcony. There stood a man in a black cassock, his arms high upraised. It was Master Abdy Ashton, chaplain to the Earl of Essex. Ned sensed at once that this was a cleric of whom Will's wife would heartily approve.

Suddenly his voice rang out. "Be still, and know that I am God." The clamor was hushed, for the quotation from the Book of Psalms had sounded like the voice of God itself. The preacher waited until the silence he had created was felt by all. Then he rebuked them for desecrating the Sabbath by their worldly din. No one dared whisper, stir, or cough; his tall, gaunt presence had total command of them.

He said, "This is the eighth day of the month, and I shall read to you the first psalm appointed for this morning. I charge you to let every word search your hearts." He began to read with penetrating deliberation, pausing after every verse. During the last verses of the psalm a change came over the listeners. Thoughts turned from contemplation of their own sins and misfortunes to the man in whose name and for whose cause they were gathered: the Earl of Essex, who sat somewhere inside listening with them to the preacher.

"I have required that they, even mine enemies, should not triumph over me; for when my foot slipped, they rejoiced greatly against me." A murmur of approval came from the crowd, and it grew as a response to each verse. "But mine enemies live, and are mighty; and they that hate me wrongfully are many in number." After he had spoken the last verse, "Haste thee to help me, O Lord God of my salvation," the preacher uttered a thrilling Amen, and it was taken up three times in a mighty shout that was heard far and wide and brought people out of doors in the neighborhood of Essex House.

But the preacher's sermon was yet to come, and it surprised everyone who heard it for he bade them examine their consciences to find out what had brought them there. Was it idle curiosity? Hope of some selfish gain? "And you that bear swords, beware, for our Lord said that he that takes the sword shall perish by it. Pray to God that justice may triumph. Remember, vengeance is mine; I will repay, saith the Lord."

The men who were gathered around the Earl of Essex in the room behind the balcony were incensed by this development in the sermon, but the earl bade them be still; not the least of the mysteries in this enigmatic man was his deep and abiding regard for his chaplain, who continually impressed upon him that to make peace with his God was infinitely more important than to make peace with his Queen.

The morning collect which Master Ashton chose to end his service was one for peace, but it contained words which did much to atone in the eyes of the men in the room for his previous lapse. "Defend us thy humble servants in all assaults of our enemies, that we, surely trusting in Thy defense, may not fear the power of any adversaries."

After Master Ashton had left the balcony it took but a little time for the earlier excitement in the courtyard to return, and he and his words were soon forgotten. Ned continued his search for Robin. He decided to make his way back to the gate, where Robin might be looking for him. It was there that he found him, but coming through the gate. Robin greeted Ned in happy friendship, embraced him, then drew him into a nook where they could talk with some privacy. He explained that he had overslept and was glad that he had done so for he thus had missed one of Master Ashton's gloomy sermons.

"But you told me . . ." began Ned.

"So I did, to give Master Ashton as an excuse, should you be questioned. Mark me, Ned; to hear him once is good for the soul, but more is bad for the body."

"Whence do you come this morning?" asked Ned.

"From my new home. Did I not tell you yesterday that my patron is Sir Christopher Blount? Be it whispered, he is a good Catholic and they are better for balladeers than good Puritans."

"Does Sir Christopher Blount follow the Earl of Essex?"

"To be sure he does, else I should not be here."

"But . . ."

"The earl affects the Puritans, you would say. Witness this Jeremiah, Ashton. But men of all kinds and colors of opinion follow the earl."

"But how can papists and Puritans both follow him?"

"For love of the man and a desire to redress their own private wrongs. They love not one another, but they believe the earl's enemies are theirs too. When he comes to power, he will be hard put to it to reward both sides."

"When he comes? You have no doubt?"

"His following grows and grows. At a signal, the city will rise as one man behind him, and his enemies will flee without a fight."

"Yet you carry a sword," noted Ned.

" 'Tis but a gentlemanly adornment, like the plume in my hat. I confess to you, Ned, I do not wield it well, and I hope never to draw it. But come, you must meet some of my friends."

Together the two young men pushed their way through the assemblage stopping frequently for loud and laughing introductions. It was highly gratifying to Ned that he was recognized; many had seen him in several parts and all had seen him the day before as Aumerle. It was pleasing too to find that Robin was well known and well liked. One group besought him to sing them a bawdy song, to take the taste of Ashton out of their mouths. In reply, Robin tried to make a joke on "Ashton to Ashton and dust to dust," but it eluded both him and his hearers.

Finally Ned asked Robin a question that had been puzzling him all the while. "What do they all wait for?"

"The signal," said Robin dramatically.

"What signal? And for what?"

"You will know when it comes. Day after day, more and more come and wait. It cannot be long now. The play yesterday was the first sign. Oh, if only the earl had been there!" Here Robin became as confidential as the circumstances would allow; he whispered loudly into Ned's ear. "Last night Sir Christopher said the earl has become too hesitant and cautious. 'Where is the man of Cadiz?' he asked. 'The pot is coming to the boil,' I told him. 'The lid will lift.' "

The lid was indeed lifted that morning, but from outside. About ten o'clock everyone became aware of loud voices shouting, "Make way! Make way!" A small group of men was pushing its way through to the house; it was clear that they carried news of great portent. Then the crowd became aware that the great doors were being closed and strongly barred; the wicket door too. What was coming?

An expectant hush fell over the courtyard. This was the moment for which they had been waiting, but in many hearts fear began to replace confidence. Soon a loud banging was heard on the great doors and a voice called for all to hear, "Open, in the name of the Queen!"

As if in answer to the call, at the other end of the courtyard the Earl of Essex appeared, attended by numerous lords and gentlemen. Normally his appearance would have been greeted with loud cheers, but the moment was too dramatic for anything but silence. The earl said something to Sir Gelly Merrick, who was at his side. The steward moved down the steps, and the crowd squeezed to open a path through to the main doors.

Sir Gelly called, "Who is there?"

Everybody strained to hear the answer. Those nearest the doors heard "The Lord Keeper of the Great Seal," but the whispered passing back of this to those farthest away blurred the hearing of the other impressive names, though "The Lord Chief Justice" was heard and passed back by some. When Sir Gelly Merrick spoke again, all whispering stopped. He called out, "What would you?"

It was Sir Thomas Egerton, the Lord Keeper, who replied. "We come from Her Majesty to speak with the Earl of Essex."

After a slight hesitation, Sir Gelly said, for all to hear, "My Lord of Essex would do no offense to Her Majesty. If you come in peace, he would speak with you."

"We come in peace," came the answer.

"Then the wicket shall be opened for the four of you, but all those with you must remain outside."

This time the hesitation was from the Queen's men, but soon the reply came. "So be it."

Sir Gelly gave some orders to the guards, who placed themselves to resist should more than the four noblemen try to enter through the door, which was only big enough to allow one stooping man to enter at a time.

The wicket door was opened, and the noblemen began to come through it. The Lord Keeper was the first to emerge. As he stood and waited for his companions, he surveyed the motley and hostile crowd with severe disapproval; his worst fears were clearly confirmed.

Again a path opened up to the steps of the great house, where the earl and his friends waited. As the deputation passed through the crowd, there were whispers of identification. The second couple were said to be the Controller of the Queen's Household, Sir William Knollys, and the Earl of Worcester, who was rising in royal favor.

Ned and Robin had been ill placed to hear the colloquy at the doors, but now they congratulated themselves on being near the steps to hear the dramatic encounter with the earl.

The Lord Keeper found it hard to control his anger as he first looked back from the steps at the crowded courtyard, then at the more than twenty men of title that formed a background for the earl. Finally, he looked straight at Essex and said, "We are here at the express command of Her Majesty to learn the cause of this threatening assembly, and to promise that if you have any just grievance, you shall have just remedy."

The earl, ever a creature of whim and unconsidered impulse, had not anticipated this encounter, but felt now that his moment had come. His impetuous answer was aimed more at the courtyard than the keeper. Words burst from him in a wild torrent. "I have enemies who seek my life. They would poison me at my board, they would murder me in my bed. They tell lies about me to the Queen, they show her counterfeit letters that they say I have written. They are traitors to Her Majesty and to me. I alone am the true friend and defender of the Queen and her realm."

With every sentence came a roar of support from the crowd, and the hostility to the Queen's ministers became open and dangerous; all brandished aloft whatever weapons they carried. Some even cried, "Kill them. Kill them all." Ned was disturbed to notice that Robin was amongst the wildest with such shouts, but he knew that Robin was only playing a part to impress those around him. He wondered how many of the others were similarly shallow in their shouts. The earl was so carried away by his own words and the crowd's response to them that a few of the more cautious and influential of his noble followers moved to him to beseech him to restrain the crowd lest all be lost. With a sudden change to reasonableness, he held up both arms to command silence. There was an eager response in expectation of the earl's signal for action. But it was the Lord Keeper who spoke, and to the earl.

"Let us speak within and in private that we may hear your complaints and the names of your enemies."

It was Robin who shouted loud and clear, "You are enemies." But to everybody's surprise Essex snapped at him before his cry could be taken up, "Be silent." The crowd was disconcerted. Could they never count on their leader? If he shilly-shallied, there was no hope of victory.

Sensing this unease, the Lord Chief Justice addressed the crowd. "On your allegiance to the Queen, I charge you to lay down your arms and depart in peace."

This provoked a few shouts of "Never," which served to bolster again the hostility in the courtyard, but again Essex held up his arms. Then he said, "Let us speak within," and he stood aside for the four representatives of the Queen to precede him. All the gentlemen on the steps followed the procession inside.

Left to themselves, the disaffected men resumed their angry shouts. Words of advice predominated, in the hope that they would penetrate the walls to the ears of the earl. "Be not deceived." "Imprison them." "Kill them." "Now is the time."

Ned had done no shouting and Robin turned on him. "You say nothing. Are you a traitor to my lord? A spy for crooked Cecil?"

"No," Ned replied angrily, as he roughly grabbed hold of Robin, "and take back those words."

"Then declare yourself," blustered Robin, frightened by Ned's intensity but having to keep face before the bystanders who were taking a lively interest in the quarrel.

"Words are nothing," said Ned, equally determined to justify himself to the immediate audience. "Put us to the test and we shall see who will first falter."

"You have no sword," said a well-dressed youth who had delighted in Robin's ballads. "Not even a stick. When the battle comes, how will you fight?"

"What good are swords and sticks against muskets?" retorted Ned.

"There will be no muskets," said a cynical-looking older man, "for we now have four important hostages. All we need is a show of force. Here, to prove you are with us, take my dagger. I will be content with my rapier." He took his dagger from its sheath and held its handle toward Ned, who took it reluctantly. "Can you use it?"

"I am a player," said Ned proudly, resenting the aspersion on his professional skill.

A lively discussion ensued as to the best use of the Queen's ambassadors. It was occasioned by the shouts in which Robin had joined of "Kill them." The cynic, who was addressed by his young friend as "Geoffrey," said, "Those are wild and foolish words, my friend." Robin was immediately abashed. "I grant you our earl is as variable as a woman, and often more bold than shrewd, but he will know that with prisoners in your hand, you can bargain, but not with corpses. They end all bargaining and cry out only for revenge."

"What think you the earl will do next?" asked Ned.

"Send an embassage to the Queen," said Geoffrey, with unequivocal assurance.

"And we? What shall we do?" asked Andrew, the young man.

"Wait, as we have been doing all this while. Just wait."

But he was wrong. The earl emerged on to the top of the steps. With him were most, but not all, of his noble followers. The Queen's messengers did not come out. It was clear that the hero of Cadiz was again alive in the earl. He drew his sword and called out, "We march!"

A great roar and waving of weapons greeted the decision. This was the moment for which they all had waited. Again a path was cleared to the great door and the earl walked down it purposefully, followed by his titled followers. A happy and excited hubbub broke out, full of questions and speculations, as the crowd fell in behind their leaders, in irregular procession. The consensus was that they were going to Whitehall Palace to "rescue the Queen from the earl's enemies."

As the noisy and armed men came through the doorway, they seemed much more than their number, which was about two hundred. The attendants who had been waiting for the Queen's ambassadors were dismayed and gave way without challenge.

Many citizens lined the way, and more and more came to watch. Their attitude was crucial. Everything depended upon public clamor in support of the popular earl. His followers called out, "Come join us. Get weapons and join us." But nobody did. They had come to watch a spectacle, not to join a rebellion.

Almost immediately the march came to the Strand, and here the earl raised his hand to call a halt. He was going to speak to the citizens. They quickly gathered into a dense knot to hear him, and his followers also pressed forward to listen.

"Men of London. The hour has come to save our Queen and her people from the many dangers that beset us. There are wicked men in high places, and they must be brought low. They seek my death, for I alone can frustrate their evil designs. I beseech you to take up arms and follow me. I go to the sheriff's house, for he has at his command a thousand men to join us. All London will be with us. Let us march."

And he moved to the right toward the city. This in itself was a surprise to most of his followers, for they had expected him to march to the left, to the Queen's Palace at Whitehall, and to have taken her into his protective care. They felt that the very boldness of the move would have succeeded. Now this long delay would allow time for counter moves, especially if Sheriff Smith did not support the earl.

The response of the people to the earl's speech had been an alarming disappointment. Not one man joined the marchers. Several times on the mile-and-a-half march the earl stopped to appeal for help, and his pleas became more and more desperate, so that, in spite of the cold February air, his shirt was soaked with sweat. Now fear began to overwhelm some of those whose courtyard shouts had been loudest, and, when opportunity occurred, they slunk away. Robin and Ned would have followed them, the one from natural cowardice and the other because it had been no purpose of his to become involved in rebellion, but they were each reluctant to appear craven in the eyes of the other; besides, they were both shamed and infected by the example of men like Geoffrey, whose resolution mounted as the odds against them increased.

By the time they had arrived at the Fenchurch house of the sheriff, the ranks had been diminished by about a third. All now depended upon the response of the sheriff, who was known to be well disposed toward the earl. Hopes rose when Essex and some of his most notable adherents gained ready access to the house.

As the men waited outside the house, bad news and worse rumors arrived in wave after wave: the earl had been proclaimed traitor; a strong force to seize him was on its way from the Palace; another force was coming from the Tower; many noble names were bandied about as being in charge of these forces. All this was relayed to the earl, who was desperately seeking counsel from his friends, for his main hope had proved frail; the sheriff, warned of his coming, had stolen away to take refuge with the Lord Mayor. It was quickly decided that the best course was to make their way back to Essex House, put it in a state of siege and make the best possible use of the hostages; the Lord Chief Justice should be allowed to return to Whitehall to treat with the Queen.

When the earl came out of the house, although he made no mention of the defection of the sheriff, his harassed look betrayed him. He said, "We go back to my house," and he set off at a rapid pace. Certain that all was lost, many more men dissolved away, but a hard and defiant core remained, now less than a hundred men, and most of these grouped themselves around nobles to whom they had some special tie. Thus it was that Ned, being close to Robin, found himself marching with Sir Christopher Blount, a handsome man in his early thirties, who in turn stayed close to the earl.

As they hurried along, fearful all the time of encountering a hostile force, Burbage's famous line came unbidden to Ned, "My kingdom for a horse!" and he was grateful for the private smile it brought him.

At St. Paul's, more than halfway home, the way was blocked by a strong chain drawn across the street. Behind it was a line of men with muskets raised, and behind them a line of men with pikes. Though altogether they were less than half the Essex force, the frightening difference was that they had muskets. The hurrying march stopped, some twenty yards away. Robin, now an expert in the matter of liveries and badges, whispered fiercely to Ned, "It's the Bishop of London's men. Trust the bishop to be the first in a fight. May he roast in Hell with all others of his cloth."

After a moment's hesitation, the earl drew his sword and advanced, calling on his men to follow him. They did more than that; they raced in front of him, and Sir Christopher Blount's group was in the van. Ned rushed along, brandishing his sorely outmatched dagger, but finding himself seized with a wild desire to grapple with an enemy, and venting this desire in mad and wordless yells. Then the muskets exploded, and almost every one found a mark.

Men screamed in pain and dropped to the ground. Sir Christopher Blount was wounded in the left shoulder. He managed to get to the chain where he was quickly seized. The earl had his hat shot from his head, but was uninjured. The men behind the chain made no attempt to cross it, and the friends nearest Essex bade him urgently to flee. He must get to his house, and the best way was by the river from Queen Hythe. Essex bowed his head in agreement and was content to be led away. It was Sir Charles Danvers who called out to the leaderless and lost men, "Look to yourselves."

Ned had been shot in the right forearm, but the ball had not lodged in it nor broken the bone. Robin had been fatally wounded in the stomach. He lay screaming and crying as the blood gushed out. Other men were helping their wounded friends to safety, and though Ned wanted to do the same for Robin, he was unable to because of his own wound. He grabbed Geoffrey and begged for help. That gentleman, infuriated by what he judged as the pusillanimity of Essex, took one look at Robin and said, "Leave him, he is spent; as are we all. Our hero was a man of straw." Ned hovered helplessly over Robin, whose cries were now becoming faint. He was mumbling occasionally. Ned caught only the word "no" said over and over.

Suddenly Ned became aware of movement at the chain. Some men were lifting it and coming under it to capture him, for he and Robin were now alone. Instinctively Ned dropped his dagger and, still clutching his bleeding arm, turned and ran, leaving Robin to die alone in a pool of blood.

Ned's instinct was to get home. Never for a moment did he consider trying to get to Essex House; he cursed the impulse that had taken him there in the first place. He did think of seeking shelter with Gilbert, who lived ten minutes away—it would take him half an hour to get home and he was already weak in body from loss of blood and in spirit from utter despondency—but he felt reluctant to implicate Gilbert. Though it was true that George had been among the most vocal of the earl's admirers, Ned was cynically sure that George would be equally vocal in pointing out flaws in the defeated hero. Of that defeat Ned was also sure, whatever might be happening at Essex House, and he had not the slightest curiosity to find out what that might be; his sole concern was his own safety.

He zigzagged down eerily deserted side streets, feeling that he was being watched every step of his way. Almost succumbing to a faintness, he leaned against a wall, his torn arm bleeding, his tunic covered with blood. If he attempted to cross the Bridge, he would certainly be stopped and almost certainly imprisoned for taking part in an armed rebellion. For that crime there was only one punishment: death. He decided that he must cross the river by boat, and, fighting off his faintness, he made his way slowly to the wharves at Queen Hythe.

There were a dozen wherries waiting for hire and several larger boats. The swans had undisputed possession of the Thames which was as ominously empty of traffic as the streets. All the boatmen eyed Ned as he approached. They had watched the hasty departure of Essex and his friends in two of the large boats, and they now connected Ned's bloody appearance with the rebellion. He was obviously in flight.

Normally the boatmen would have vied with one another in shouting for Ned's patronage, but not one of them spoke. Ned chose a man who seemed a little less ruffianly than the others, and moved to step into his boat, but a hand was raised to stop him and a harsh voice said, "How much?" The fare was fixed by law at a penny, but it had been so fixed years before and was now patently insufficient; at least twopence was expected even on normal occasions. Ned, with as much hauteur as he could command, said, "Threepence." This was greeted with coarse laughter from those who heard it, and, when it had been relayed to those who didn't, they too laughed. Ned stood, a helpless and pitiable object of ridicule, too weak to feel anger. He said, "I only want to cross the river."

The boatman he had chosen to speak to said, "You are a rebel trying to escape the hangman. Would you have me put my neck in the noose too?"

Drained even of the will to reply, Ned turned away slowly and began to move, but a voice stopped him. "Stay. How much do you have?" Ned turned back. The man who had spoken seemed to be the oldest there. With an effort Ned mustered his memory to reply. "A shilling," he said.

"For that I'll take you," said the old man.

This drew ribald comments from the other boatmen, who called him "Poxy." He took it all in rough good part, saying, "My neck is tough, my ears are deaf, and my purse is empty. Come." And he helped Ned, who was near to collapse, into the boat. Coarse laughter and comments followed him as he pulled away from the wharf.

As they left the protection of the land, the cold east wind caused Ned to shiver uncontrollably. The boatman asked him if he had far to walk. It took a little time for the question to penetrate Ned's clouded mind, and the exhaustion in his no made Poxy forbear from voicing the further questions he wanted to ask.

The unrest in the city had spread to the south bank, and so the boatmen there were idle too; nobody seemed to want to venture abroad. All eyes were on the solitary boat as it crossed the river. Conversation which had been full of speculation about the men who had been seen to go up river in the two boats died down until Poxy came near enough to be bombarded with questions. He chose to say nothing. When the bloody Ned became visible, some of the boatmen became cautious, others hostile, and one, a friend of Poxy's, saw a chance of reward from the Queen's officers. But Poxy had become protective of his pathetically helpless passenger. He himself had two sons who had been pressed into the Queen's service, and he had never seen them again. To help Ned, he had decided to concoct a story. He threw a rope to his friend, "Frenchie," and called "Give me a hand."

As Frenchie tied up, he asked, "Who have you got there?"

"An unlucky young man. He's an apprentice here in Southwark and he was visiting his mother and father in the city, to go to church with them on a Sunday morning, as any good Christian would. He ran into a musket ball."

Frenchie was not to be so easily robbed of the reward he had envisioned. "Is that what he told you, Poxy? Don't you believe it. He's a rebel."

"Then where's his arms?" challenged Poxy.

"He dropped them and ran."

Now it became a matter of pride with Poxy to convince not only Frenchie but the whole of his skeptical audience. "It so happens that I know his mother and father. They are good friends of mine. The father's a tapster, at the Mermaid Tavern. His name is Simon Hunter." Poxy had such a friend who was so prolific in progeny that one more son would not be noticed. "Now give me a hand with him."

Ned had only a hazy understanding of the dialogue, but he did realize that Poxy was trying to shield him. When he stood on the wharf, he began to fumble for the shilling he had promised. Poxy, to prove the authenticity of his story, said, "No, lad; no money. If I can't help the son of my friend, may God rot me." The boatmen were convinced. Dazed, Ned mumbled a thank you and staggered away.

The coldness had helped the bleeding to stop, and the effort to walk had stimulated Ned into awareness again. He was near the Globe and decided that, if it were open, he could tend to the wound there and change his bloodstained clothes.

Nat Tremayne was at the theatre and with him his beloved assistant, Martin, an agreeable young man who ministered to Nat's comforts both in bed and at board.

Ned had been a favorite of Nat's ever since the time, now more than four years ago, when the boy had been so delighted by the Salanio costume. He was horrified by the sight of him on this Sunday morning. He and Martin peppered Ned with a volley of questions the young man was too exhausted and confused to answer. They helped him to a seat and gave him a drink of wine.

Gradually the wine and a growing sense of security enabled Ned to give a sketchy account of what had brought him to his present plight. As he displayed his damaged arm, squeamish Nat turned away from the sight, and Martin took it upon himself to deal with it. There was always a supply of salves and bandages backstage, for accidents were frequent, particularly from the swordplay on stage which had to be dangerously realistic to satisfy the appetite of the audience. While Martin dealt with the wound, first cleaning it out with lint and causing it to bleed again, Nat went to find a change of costume for Ned, wondering what he should do with the telltale apparel. As he chose a costume which would render Ned as unremarkable as possible on the street, Nat congratulated himself on having insisted, at the cost of some harsh words, that Martin should not go to Essex House that morning; he, like Ned, had been earnestly invited by an Essex adherent the previous afternoon.

By the time Ned was changed and refreshed it was still not yet noon, and he could get home in time to join the family at dinner. He had decided to tell the table the whole story of what had happened—indeed, he looked forward to the excitement of doing so, for he could count on the sympathy and understanding of everybody there—and so he saw no reason for not taking with him the bloodstained clothes; Letty would enjoy cleaning them. At the same time he was grateful for Nat's caution in wrapping them in some old sacking. After bandaging the wounded arm, Martin had fashioned a sling for Ned from a scarf, and he was about to set out like a hero returning from the wars, with a bundle under his left arm, when he was stopped by a new arrival at the theatre. It was the same officer and soldiers who had interrupted the rehearsal the previous afternoon.

"Who is in charge here?" the intruder asked abruptly.

Nat as the oldest man present fearfully took it upon himself to reply. "No one. There is no sharer here. We do not play today. I am the tireman. We are here but to work on costumes."

"And you," said the officer, addressing Ned, "what is in that bundle?"

"A costume which I take to be laundered," replied Ned, confronting the officer with a boldly innocent look.

"And your arm?"

"I was wounded yesterday in a stage fight," lied Ned with consummate effrontery.

"It often happens," ventured Martin in support.

The officer accepted the tale with some unwillingness. He turned to Nat. "I come with an order from the Queen's Council. This theatre is closed sine die, and I leave it to your charge to see to it that the order be obeyed." He turned to go but stopped and turned back to say, "I warned you yesterday that ill would come of it if you followed the Essex faction, and it has. Now your principals will be called to answer for it, and I promise that all of you will be made to suffer for your part in this day."

Ned said, "But what has happened, sir?" His question was prompted not merely by an assumption of innocence but by a desire to know the outcome of the events in which he had become embroiled.

"The Lord Essex has tried to take the city by force of arms, but his shameful rebellion has failed ignominiously, and he and all his followers will be punished with the full severity of the law. I doubt not we shall find that all you players come within the compass of that punishment."

When the soldiers had left, Nat was torn between admiration for Ned's coolness—"When you asked him what had happened I thought I should have swooned"—and fear of what lay ahead for the company—"We'll never open again; I feel it in my bones." But practical considerations soon took over; they had to convey the officer's message to the principal sharers. It was decided that, because of the dangers abroad, it would be enough to let Master Phillips and Master Shakespeare know and leave the rest to them.

"I can tell them," said Ned. "There's no need for you to come."

"That cannot be," said Ned rather pompously. "The duty was laid on me and I must discharge it."

"Besides," added Martin, " 'twill be better if we accompany you, Ned, for you are still weak from loss of blood. Here, give me that bundle. We will go together."

There had been great anxiety about Ned at the Phillips home. When the congregation had come out from church that morning, they had been greeted with wild exaggerations of the Essex uprising, and Will, Gus, Anne, and Sam had all jumped to the conclusion that Ned's absence was associated with it, so the sight of him safe and free brought great relief, but this feeling soon gave way to concern about his wound, until he assured them that Martin had taken good care of it. Ned was urged, particularly by Sam, to give a full account of what had happened, but he insisted that Nat be listened to first. Nat made the most of his story, emphasizing Ned's courage and the dire prospects for the company. It was decided that Master Phillips would ride with the news to Master Heminge and Master Shakespeare would ride to Master Burbage.

The Phillips household had just been finishing their cold Sunday dinner when Ned and the others had arrived, and Mistress Phillips now insisted that, before another word was said, the three men should join them at the table.

Will cut up Ned's meat for him, and then he managed well enough with his left hand. Worried lest his involvement might cause trouble for the players, Ned gave an apologetic account of the morning, but Gus was quick to assure him that they were proud of what he had done.

Will had said very little since Ned arrived, and now Gus pressed him for approval both of Essex and Ned's sturdy championship of the earl, though Ned had made it quite clear that circumstances rather than deliberate partisanship had brought about his wound. Rather sadly Will said, "These are dark times. The world is no longer simple. What served at Cadiz in 1596 will no longer serve in London in 1601. I feel sure the earl is a good man and means well, but he has failed, and it will be judged that he meant ill. I fear for him. As for Ned, he has hurt nobody but has himself been hurt, and he has seen a friend killed at his side. Today he came of age."

TWENTY-SIX

THE NEXT TWO WEEKS WERE DARK INDEED. DURING THE FIRST WEEK THE principal subject of muted conversation was the Earl of Essex. His surrender had been inevitable and now he was a prisoner in the Tower, awaiting trial; with him were several of his highborn followers, most notably the Earl of Southampton. There were wild whispers of attempts at rescue, but when he heard them from Sam, Ned was cynical. "Those who talk loudest do least," he said. "All London was going to be on his side, but when Essex called for help, no one came; they just stood and watched, or stole away."

There was much argument about the attitude of the Queen. In spite of their differences in recent years, she could not have lost all her affection for the earl; it had been too deep. He had committed treason and the punishment for that was death, but she would not let him die. And yet there were extraordinary stories of her behavior during the day of the rebellion. Twelve hours had elapsed between the time when the earl had emerged from Essex House at the head of his armed band and the time when, on bended knee, he had delivered up his sword to the Lord Admiral. Throughout that day she was said to have betrayed no sign of fear or even of deep concern.

The theatre was closed, but most of the players found their way to it almost every day. Their fate too was in the balance. Several of them pinned their hopes on their patron, the Lord Chamberlain, who had long been an open opponent of the Earl of Essex. They hoped this would counterbalance the action which had closed the theatre, the special performance of *Richard II*. Ned was infuriated by the ambivalence of this attitude, for the very players who now relied on the enemy of Essex had proclaimed themselves as being his supporters before the fatal Sunday.

People seemed to pour into the city during that second week of February, many of them dissolute and disaffected men. Had they come to cause an upheaval or to profit from one? They crept into every nook and cranny, and citizens were hesitant to go abroad, even by day. Crowds gathered at the Tower, most of them curious but some of them menacing. On Sunday, the fifteenth, a proclamation was issued which ordered all strangers without legitimate business in the city to leave it on pain of death. This was interpreted as a harbinger of fateful and imminent events.

Wednesday, the eighteenth, was to be the crucial day for the players, for on that day their representative had been called to be examined in the matter of the specially commanded performance of *Richard II*. Ordinarily John Heminge would have answered the summons on behalf of the company but Augustine Phillips insisted that it was he who should go, for he held it to be manifestly unfair that Master Heminge should be called upon to justify an action to which he had been opposed.

On Tuesday evening, Gus had a long talk with Will. That afternoon the news had leaked out that Essex and Southampton were to be brought to trial on Thursday. Now it was clear that Gus's deposition would be used in evidence at the trial.

"I can but tell the truth," Augustine Phillips said sadly.

To comfort him, Will said, "There is little you can tell them that they don't already know, and it is for his actions on Sunday that the Lord Essex will be condemned, not for our play on Saturday."

"I shall feel like Judas, though our price was ten pieces of silver more than his."

" 'Tis wrong to feel so. If you lied to the hilt it would not save the earl, but the truth may save us."

"How comes it so?"

"We but played for hire. Had we played for love of the earl, we should be in a parlous state. But those at court believe that players would sell their souls for money and that all their principles lie in their pockets. Therein lies our salvation now."

"But I would have played *Richard II* without the forty shillings to please the earl."

"So would I, Gus, but that is our secret. To bruit it abroad now would do him no good and us much harm."

"Think you the Queen will let him be executed?"

"Yes, because she is more queen than woman, and has been for more than forty years. I condemn her with one breath for it, and thank her with the next."

"And Southampton. Think you he too will die?"

The question was innocently spoken, but with it Gus had probed unthinkingly into Will's past. The answer was a little while in coming, and was accompanied by a sad and cynical smile. "I doubt it. If they condemn Essex, they must condemn him too, but I doubt he will follow his leader to the block. I wager Southampton will win the hearts of those who pass judgment on him. There never was a more winning man, or boy rather, for he is boy eternal, generous and loyal—but for a day only."

The next day the company gradually assembled at the theatre to await the return of Augustine Phillips from the examination. He had little to tell them. He had gone prepared to make an eloquent defense of the play, such as was made to the officer who had interrupted the rehearsal, but he had been cut short. All that was wanted was facts and names. When he was reluctant to give the names of those who had requested the performance, Master Phillips was told, "He who would hide traitors is himself guilty of treason." Consoling himself that there was nothing he could say that was not already known, he had made a bald statement of the facts of the transaction, had it read back to him by the clerk who had copied it, and signed it. Then he asked if the theatre might be opened again. The impudence of the question momentarily stunned his examiners.

Then one of them said, " 'Twould be well for the peace of this land and the immortal souls of the people if it were never opened again." Another said, with a more gentle sarcasm, "For you Lent begins a week early this year, and lasts for seven weeks, not six." It was true that Ash Wednesday was only a week away, which would have begun the Lenten closure of the theatres.

Ned was by turns saddened and infuriated by the selfish reactions of most of the company. Provided the theatre was allowed to open, it mattered not that their erstwhile hero and others with him stood in danger of an ignominious death. Gradually his fortuitous involvement in the rebellion became, even in his own mind, a deliberate act. After all, he could have avoided the ultimate confrontation as others had. He began to feel a moral superiority over his hypocritical companions and to be proud of the scar on his arm.

At supper that night he sat silent and morose as Augustine Phillips gave another and more detailed account of his examination. Mistress Phillips said, " 'Tis well that you have the Lord Chamberlain for patron, for the whole world knows how disaffected he is toward the Earl of Essex." This was bitter gall to Ned, and Will noticed his reaction.

Gus said cheerfully, "Now, Will, you have nothing to hinder you from your writing. We cannot play till Easter, and by then 'tis certain that these troubles will be over."

Ned could not contain himself. "You mean that the earl will be dead and forgotten."

This outburst took everybody but Will by surprise. Although Ned was almost of age and had long been accepted by all in the house as a full man, propriety dictated that he should still conduct himself at table with something of the reticence of the apprentice he had been, not intruding upon the conversation of his elders.

But reproof was not as easy for Master Phillips as it had once been. Apart from the fact that Ned was no longer a boy, the honesty of his angry comment had touched the conscience of Master Phillips, who had himself been disturbed by the general lack of concern for the earl's fate. He looked to Will to deal with Ned's criticism, but Will said nothing. It was Anne Phillips who spoke. She said, "We all feel sorry for the earl, Ned, but what good can we do him now?"

"We can at least think of him and not of ourselves," Ned retorted.

Later that night, Ned, in the darkness of his room, thought of the Earl of Essex awaiting the next day's trial. The world of the theatre with its jealousies, its enmities, its crises seemed trivial. He had first been struck by this thought when Philip Kenton had died so nobly for his faith. And now the Earl of Essex probably faced death. How would he face the moment of execution? Bravely, Ned hoped. There flashed into his mind the last words of Gabriel Spencer, "Thank you, but I could have wished . . ." and his thoughts went to Ben Jonson. It would seem that Ben would have been happy as a defiant supporter of a forlorn hope, though his new Catholicism certainly could not stomach preachers like Master Abdy Ashton. A traditional Catholic like Robin's patron, Sir Christopher Blount, could be more tolerant temporarily, in the hope of concessions when the Earl of Essex came to power. Sir Christopher, like other titled followers of the earl, was now in prison, his fate dependent upon that of his leader. And poor Robin, whose only principle was that of survival, had died for nothing. Ned felt guilty anew at his desertion of his dying friend; but what could he have done?

The following morning Ned woke with the rather chagrined realization that he had had a deep and dreamless sleep. He decided he would go out and stay out for the day. He would make a pilgrimage to the spot where Robin had died.

When he came downstairs, everybody was about except Will, who was working in his room. All greeted him tentatively. Master Phillips said, "You are the last down. I'm glad that you slept well."

Ned bristled and answered, "It was late, very late, before I could get to sleep."

Gus said, "I thought you would have been up to watch the earl being taken from the Tower to Westminster."

The thought had never occurred to Ned, and he was now furious with himself that it had not. He covered up by saying, "What good would it have done?"

"To show him support might have given him courage in his ordeal."

"Then why did you not go? And you, Sam?"

Gus answered for both of them. "We had not had the courage to declare ourselves for him as you had done. In us it would have been but idle curiosity."

Ned was much mollified by this speech and readily accepted Mistress Phillips's offer of ale, bread, cheese, and a well-kept apple. At the same time he determined that, idle curiosity or not, he would post himself where he could watch the earl being returned to the Tower.

With the admiring Sam to accompany him, Ned set out, well wrapped up against a cold day. Sam was thrilled to hear where they were going. He too had been enormously impressed by the transformation in Robin, and he was deeply moved by Ned's account of his death, which deliberately made a hero out of Robin. They walked across the Bridge, turned left into Eastcheap and went on into Watling Street. Everywhere there was a sense of apprehension and foreboding. People walked with eyes downcast or looking straight ahead; there were no cheery greetings or full-faced looks. Even in the yard of St. Paul's the usual bustle and noise were subdued, but the conversation was all about the trial that was taking place at that moment.

One rough old codger who had lost his right leg was haranguing a group of about twenty. "I was with him at Cadiz," he said, "and I left a leg there, so I have a right to speak. He lost and he'll be found guilty and he'll die; there's no other way for it. If he had won, the others like Sir Walter Raleigh would have been found guilty and they would have died. What difference would it have made to men like me? Whoever is in, we are out. The great ones of the land use us and then throw us aside. The Bible says, 'To him that hath shall be given, and from him that hath not'—and that's me—'shall be taken away even that which he hath'—and that's my leg. Even if they kill him, he won't hang like a poor man. No. He'll go to the block, and the ax will finish him neat and quick. It's those I pity that are going to Tyburn." He pointed to a list that was posted on a wall.

Ned and Sam went over to look at the list. Three men were to be hanged, drawn, and quartered at eight in the morning on Saturday for conspiring against the life of the Queen and the safety of the realm. The first name on the list was that of Peter Kirby.

Ned was so shocked that for a moment he became dizzy; then he wanted to scream, No! That gentle, jovial priest who had helped Philip Kenton to die could not be guilty of anything whose punishment was death.

Sam noticed with amazement Ned's reaction and asked, "Do you know any of them?"

"Yes," replied Ned. "Peter Kirby. Let us sit down." He led the way to the steps of St. Paul's Cross, and there he told Sam the whole story that resulted from his visiting Ben Jonson in prison. He ended by saying, "I don't understand any more. If the Earl of Essex dies, I shall understand; he had personal enemies whom he sought to destroy, and he failed. But Master Kirby? He would not harm anyone."

Mindful of where he was sitting, Sam looked up at the cross behind him, and said, "Christ was crucified too. It's a wicked world; it always was and always will be. Will you go to see Master Kirby hanged?"

The nauseating spectacle of a man hanged, drawn, and quartered was more than Ned thought he could stomach, but he had a strange compulsion to be near Master Kirby at the end. His answer was yes.

It was eleven days since Robin had been killed, and there was nothing to mark the spot. Ned had fearfully expected to find stains of blood still in the roadway, but they had been obliterated by rain, feet, and hooves. He explained the "battle" positions to Sam, ignoring the passersby. A dark-suited, middle-aged man came on to him and said in a friendly manner, "Were you here when it happened?"

In spite of the questioner's friendliness, Ned was wary. He said, "Unless I had been with the Bishop's men behind the chain, I should have been a fool to return here, wouldn't I?"

"Were you behind the chain?"

Fearing that he might be caught in a lie, Ned said no.

"Then how do you know so much about what happened?"

"One who was here told me."

"One of the earl's followers?"

"Yes."

"His name?" The eagerness of the question revealed the true motive behind the friendly facade.

"I know not. He was in a tavern, and his tongue was loose. Come, Sam." And Ned boldly walked away followed by an admiring Sam.

They dawdled the afternoon away, never wandering far from the streets through which the earl would have to be taken back to the Tower. As the day waned, more and more people lined the streets. They stood talking quietly, though the talk was not without the excitement of rumors: the Queen had intervened to stop the trial; the Earl of Essex had attacked and severely wounded Sir Walter Raleigh; a rescue was being planned for the earl; his lady had forced her way into the Queen's presence to beg for mercy.

Ned and Sam stood together near the Boar's Head in Eastcheap, so that they would not have too far to walk home. It was past six o'clock when they saw the somber procession approaching, half an hour after the news of the result of the trial had arrived: both earls had been found guilty of treason and sentenced to death. Essex had appealed for mercy, but not for himself; for Southampton.

The procession was led by Lord Thomas Howard, the Constable of the Tower, and Sir John Peyton, his lieutenant. These were on horseback. All others were on foot. Between two lines of armed warders and soldiers walked the two noble prisoners.

The result of the trial was obvious from the mien of the Earl of Essex; he walked with head drooped, never raising his eyes. By contrast, the Earl of Southampton looked appealingly from right to left at the people who lined the route. His handsome appearance seemed to say, "Cannot you see I am innocent? I meant no harm. Must a man die for loyalty to his friend? I am not yet twenty-eight years old." His companion was but four years his senior, but he looked much older. Ned's sympathies were more with the downcast Essex than with the pleading Southampton.

All conversation died as the condemned men approached, only to be resumed after they had passed. But there were no demonstrations for or against them. It was as though the actions which had brought them to this pass had had nothing to do with the lives of the onlookers.

Then, when the earls were passing near to Ned and Sam, a robust burgher, who stood with his stout wife a few yards to Ned's left, called out, "Head high, my lord. She won't let you die." The Earl of Essex, without changing pace, looked up in the direction of his comforter. He smiled sadly, and his smile both acknowledged the kindness of the thought and denied its validity; no one knew the Queen better than he; at most she would be reluctant to sign the death warrant, but she would sign it. Ned would long remember that smile. It would be his last sight of the Earl of Essex.

TWENTY-SEVEN

DURING THE FRIDAY, THE TALK WAS ALL OF WHETHER THE QUEEN WOULD stay the execution of the earls. There was much whispered discussion of her previous relationship with Essex. According to the company, it varied from the political through the social to the bawdy. Strangely enough, even in tavern conversations about the royal bedroom, there was general agreement that the Queen had preserved her virginity. As one wit put it, "Even naked she was a Queen. She would never let a man use her, but she might use him to pleasure herself. His hands were tied, but hers were free." There was also general tavern agreement that, whatever the earl had meant to her in the past, it was long since over; she was now past sixty-seven years old, twice the age of Essex. She surely must have lost her delight in dalliance, and yet they say she still took pleasure in dancing. Certain it was that she was not as other women. One thing only could be depended upon—and thank God for it—she would do what she thought best for her country.

Ned found the speculations about the Queen tedious, for his mind was full of the execution of Master Kirby on the morrow. Time and again he decided he would stay away from it, only to find that there was in him a deep desire to be there, not a morbid curiosity, but what it was he could not determine.

As they all gathered for dinner, Ned contrived to tell Will that he wanted to talk to him in private. Part of the impulse behind Ned's request for a conversation had been to question Will about the Earl of Southampton, but once they were together in the room, he realized he could not do so; it would be gross impertinence, especially to disturb Will's writing for such a purpose. He began by asking about the new play Will was working on, but the answers were evasive.

"I never like to talk about my plays as they are being born, but this one least of all. This is one that will be written almost in spite of me. The world seems no longer young. That may be because I am no longer young. I doubt I shall ever write another *As You Like It,* because the world is no longer as I like it. But come, Ned. Enough of my gloom. What is it you would say to me?"

But Ned had seen a way to the Earl of Southampton. "Is it the Earl of Essex that troubles you, Will?"

"That and much else."

"The Earl of Southampton?"

Will looked directly at Ned and said, "Is that what you came to talk to me about?"

Ned answered, "No. I too am troubled, Will."

"Essex?"

"Partly that, but I am not a friend of his as you were of the Earl of Southampton."

"My friendship with him is long dead. I am grateful to him for many kindnesses. He was a good friend when I needed one, but there must be equality between friends, and there was none between us. When only one is young and wealthy and noble, the other must be hurt, though I think I could meet him now without pain. But you, Ned, what is it besides Essex that troubles you?"

"Do you remember Master Peter Kirby, Ben Jonson's secret priest?"

"Oh, yes," said Will. "A short, fat, bald man, always smiling."

"He dies at Tyburn tomorrow."

After a moment's silence, Will said, "The Lord Essex will die for his belief in himself, and the priest Kirby for his belief in God, yet those who condemned them will see little difference; they will both die because they have been adjudged to threaten the state. Why did you not say this at the dinner table, Ned? Why to me alone? They would all have been sympathetic."

"To speak truth, I know not. To me it is very private; again I know not why. My thoughts are full of death these days. It makes my life seem petty and without meaning. What does it matter what one does, if the end is death?"

"You are young to have such thoughts, Ned, but they come to most men at some time. There are those who say that the best of life is learning how to die. I am sure that the priest tomorrow will show no fear at the end."

"I am going to Tyburn."

"You feel you owe it to the man?"

"Yes," said Ned gratefully, for it was a better reason than he had been able to formulate for himself.

"Then be prepared for a horrible spectacle, and bear it as bravely as the little man will bear his long and cruel death. The hangman is more skilled in prolonging death than the surgeon in prolonging life."

Without a warning even to himself, the growing confusion in Ned suddenly found voice. "Will, I am lost. You have your writing, but I have naught but my playing—and playing small parts—and it is not enough. Sometimes the theatre seems to me silly child's play, and all the disasters and the triumphs, the jealousies and the friendships just something to smile at, as we do with children. The world is bigger and more terrible."

"Much more terrible. This morning I felt that deeply and I called it 'a foul and pestilent congregation of vapors.' Yet there are times when one sees it otherwise. But despise not the theatre, Ned. It can help men to see themselves and their world, the good with the bad, the saintly with the devilish. I'm glad you are going to Tyburn tomorrow, for you will see a man defeat the evil of the world, and it is that which gives us hope. As I speak to you, I suddenly want to be there too. May I come with you?"

"It would please me very much. Sam wants to come too, but perhaps he won't wake in time."

"You will wake him?"

"No," said Ned conspiratorially, and it bred a warmth between the brothers.

"I'm glad I have spoken to you, Will. Thank you. And now you must write."

" 'Must' is the word, Ned. Don't envy me my writing. It is a hard taskmaster that has taken my family from me."

"But that is only because Anne is a Puritan," Ned protested.

"Any wife would be made to suffer. I am glad that Anne has her God to comfort and succor her."

During the supper, Will spoke of the plan to go to Tyburn in the morning. Mistress Phillips, and to a lesser extent her husband, was horrified by the plan, but both were won over by Will's explanation that he and Ned had met and admired Master Kirby and wanted to honor him. Sam made the lame excuse that he too admired the priest from what Ned had told him.

Snow had fallen during the early hours of that Saturday morning but had stopped before it was time for the long walk to begin. By the time the three men were leaving the city at Newgate, dawn light had begun to filter through. They were still less than halfway there, and Ned urged the other two to hurry; he was eager to be near the dread scaffold to catch any last words Master Kirby might say.

"You said there were two others to die. Our man may be the last. It will be past bearing if we have to watch three executions," Will warned.

Sam did not want to miss one, but he knew he dared not be so honest. Instead he said, "If Master Kirby is the last, it will be easier for you to bear if you have had to watch two others die first."

When they got to Tyburn at half past seven, they were disgusted to find a noisy crowd of some hundreds already there. Most were in a holiday mood but some, obsessed by a fanatical hostility toward "popery," were there to exult and gloat. A knot of zealots was gathered around one man who was crying aloud in triumph against the "whore of Babylon" and quoting from the Old Testament some of the vehement passages in which the God of the Israelites had vowed fiery vengeance against all idolators. He was standing on a little mound about twenty yards from the scaffold, and many of the spectators, for want of anything better to do until the main event began, were attracted to him, less for the substance of his remarks than for his vivid performance. This enabled Ned, closely followed by Will and Sam, to insinuate himself quite near to the scaffold; true their position was on the side, but they would surely hear anything that was said and see more than Will and Ned wanted to. Already on the scaffold a rough and dirty-looking young man was tending a brazier of burning coals.

At last the cart with the three condemned men arrived. It was accompanied by the executioner, his two assistants carrying bags containing tools and the necessary equipment, a clergyman, and six guards with halberds.

Ned was dismayed by the appearance of Master Kirby. It was only two and a half years since he had last seen him, but now the priest looked twenty years older and forty pounds lighter. His jolly face had become lined, but still he smiled. Of his two companions, one was middle-aged, tall, and gaunt, and the other was less than thirty and very handsome. All three wore cassocks. They gripped the sides of the cart until it came to a stop. The young man closed his eyes and clasped his hands in prayer. The tall priest stared steadfastly and fiercely ahead, but seemed to see nothing. Master Kirby looked benignly out over the crowd; he seemed to be looking for some one. At last he saw him, and his smile broadened as his lips moved in a Latin blessing and he made the sign of the cross. Ned strained to see the object of the priest's search. Many others turned around too. Fortunately they were the irreligious and merely curious. If they had been militant Puritans, they would certainly have denounced and probably attacked the blessed man, especially if he had had the courage to cross himself in acknowledgment of the blessing. Even when the crowd's attention had returned to the cart, Ned kept looking for the man, and his instinctive knowledge was confirmed when he finally saw Ben Jonson. Quickly he whispered the name to Will, but an excited surge of the crowd hid Ben from sight. Ned felt certain that Ben would have boldly crossed himself in response to the priest.

Two of the prisoners were taken down from the cart. Master Kirby was left. He was to be the first to die.

The executioner and one of his assistants had already mounted the scaffold on which the gallows stood. The other assistant and the clergyman got up into the cart. The crosspiece of the gallows hung out from the scaffold so that the noose dangled above the cart. While the assistant tested the rope, the clergyman spoke to Master Kirby. The crowd became very quiet, straining to hear. Often times the imminence of death caused in the condemned hysterical breakdowns, fierce denunciations, violent outbursts, all of them deeply gratifying to most of the onlookers.

"Pray for forgiveness of your sins," began the clergyman; he had a wheezing chest which was exaggerated by the cold February air.

"I do—and for yours," replied the priest in a manner that Ned remembered vividly. In spite of appearances, this was the same man.

"Remember that Christ died for you."

"And I rejoice that I die for Him."

"Confess your evil designs against the Queen."

"That I cannot do, for I never had any. I pray for her in the moment of my death as I have throughout my life."

"You have been found guilty of serving her enemies."

"To be found guilty is not to be guilty. You waste your breath and my time, and both are short, Master Parson. Have done, I pray you." In further dismissal of the clergyman he turned to the executioner on the scaffold. "Come, sir. I am ready and have been this many a year. Show us your skill."

He clasped his hands in prayer, but kept his eyes open as if he wished to challenge the full agony of his death. The clergyman got down from the cart. As the assistant made to put the noose around the priest's neck, he unclasped his hands to bring the rope to his lips; then he made the sign of the cross over it, and began to recite aloud the twenty-third Psalm in Latin, the hands again clasped. The noose was placed around his neck and tightened. The assistant jumped down. The man at the head of the horse was given the signal, he pulled at the bridle, and the cart was drawn away, leaving the priest hanging, his hands still clasped, his mouth involuntarily opened, and his eyes bulging. Soon some angry voices in the crowd shouted, "Down! Down!" They did not want him to die so easily and thus rob them of the gory delights for which they had come. The executioner's expert eye carefully studied the hanging man, and, at the moment before the victim would sink into the release of unconsciousness, he gave the signal for the rope to be rapidly loosened, thus plunging the priest to the ground.

The assistant who had placed the noose around the neck took it off, and, with the help of two soldiers, heaved the tortured man up onto the scaffold. And it was now that the executioner came into his own; he was an experienced performer playing before a demanding audience.

First, to hasten the recovery of the hanged man, a bowl of cold water was thrown in his face. It was usual at this juncture for the victim to struggle violently, knowing full well what lay ahead for him, and many times a strong man given added demonic strength by his approaching ordeal had done serious injury to one or more of his torturers. This always provoked loud applause from the spectators; it gave them satisfaction akin to that in the Beargarden, when a favorite blind old bear chanced to kill a baiting dog. But Master Kirby was a disappointment. He made not the slightest struggle, and his astonishing passivity began to make some of the audience uncomfortable.

The next step was to strip the victim stark naked. This was usually a time for coarse banter from the crowd, but not a single remark came. There was no struggle, no need to tear off clothes. When the body was naked, almost hairless and very white except for the angry red welt around the neck, the executioner took up his knife. He flourished it with the maximum dramatic effect, for his audience seemed apathetic. The three assistants, for the original one was now released from tending the brazier, held down Master Kirby, but their efforts were unnecessary. There was one on each arm, and the third held the legs apart, contriving to obstruct the crowd's view as little as possible.

The surgeon-killer knelt down ponderously on one knee, took prim hold of the penis and with a neat slash cut it off at the base. Master Kirby winced and uttered a suppressed cry of pain. The penis was displayed for all to see, but it was neither large enough nor small enough to provoke the usual ribaldry. In disappointment the butcher threw the pathetic piece of blood-dripping flesh on to the coals of the brazier, where it quickly scorched and shriveled. He wondered what he could do to win the approval of this lifeless crowd. From now on he could count on one advantage: his hands would be covered with blood.

The climactic act in his display of surgical skill was to disembowel the victim without killing him. This one might even remain conscious, which would give his butcher particular satisfaction, for his unnatural stoicism had already spoilt the ceremony and thereby incurred the ill will of the celebrant. The red and knowing hand roved over the belly finding the right place for the incision. He turned to look at the priest with a challenging grin as if to say, "Cry out this time, damn you," but the gaze of sorrow he received disconcerted him, for the sorrow seemed to be for the killer not the pain, and he stabbed angrily and inexpertly into the flesh. He was rewarded with a loud cry from the priest of *"Domine, in manus tuas . . ."* but the rest of the commendation of his spirit into the hands of God was lost in a spurt of blood from his mouth, and he mercifully lost consciousness, thus depriving the executioner of public approval. The assistants relinquished their token holds on the priest, and their chief called for their help to finish with this carcass as quickly as possible; now all his hopes were pinned on the agonies of the young man who would be kept to the last so that the tortures of the two before him might terrify his spirit before he was even hanged.

Quickly and savagely the intestines were cut out and borne by the assistants to the brazier in a shapeless and dragging bundle showering blood. A loud sizzle resulted and the smell of burning flesh, which the wind wafted to the side where stood the Shakespeares and Sam.

Ned had closed his eyes and winced at most of the horrors. This last smell was more than he could bear, and, without referring to his companions, he turned and stumbled away, though they were glad to follow him closely, and people were glad to let them pass for their going gave a better view of the more promising horrors yet to come. Even Sam was eager to get away.

As soon as he was clear of the crowd, Ned could contain his stomach no longer and it exploded. As he threw up, Will tended him solicitously. Sam took the opportunity to take one last look back at the scaffold. The executioner was holding up, for all to see, the bleeding heart of the priest.

As soon as Ned had recovered sufficiently, they walked on without a word, and then saw, waiting for them, Ben Jonson. It was an embarrassing moment, for they had not seen him for well over a year, and Ben's parting from the company had been a stormy one, after the failure of his play, *Everyman Out of His Humour*. It was he who first spoke.

"I saw you from afar in the crowd. I was glad you came. That you are leaving now proves that you came, as I did, but to pay honor to a good and brave and holy man. He looked for me there and saw me. He gave me his blessing, and I felt truly blessed in having known him. I could wish that he had seen you, for that too would have pleased him."

"He would not have remembered me," said Will.

"Oh, but he did," said Ben. "We often spoke of you. You too, Ned."

"Did he wish to convert us?" asked Will with a smile.

"How could he not so wish? 'Twas his vocation. But we talked of you as a poet and a man, for we both admired you. Let us find a tavern to drink to the memory of Father Kirby, and, if it offend not your beliefs, to the repose of his soul."

As they walked along, Ben took notice of Sam. "And you, sir, were you not Piso in the first *Humours* play, and Fido in the second?"

"Yes, sir."

"I remember you pleasantly. You made beguiling little bricks with almost no straw."

"Thank you, sir," beamed Sam, for such praise from grudging Ben was very sweet.

"Will, Will, *Everyman Out* was out indeed, so no more of that. I thank God that *Everyman In* is still in, if only infrequently. I fear the Lord Chamberlain's Men have ears and tongues for your words only. I say that not to disparage them but to praise you. I bear no ill will, and I hope you do not."

"None," said Will.

"Then I may yet bring you another play." All three looked at him with surprise and some dismay. "Nay, be not alarmed. I have no such play in prospect. But I promise you, Will, that if ever the miracle happen that Master Heminge look upon a new play of mine with kindly eyes, I for my part will listen to your counsel."

Listen, thought Ned, but not take it. The remembrance of the insult to the Shakespeares which Ben had inserted in the printed version of *Every-*

man Out of His Humour still rankled deep in him; Ben had made fun of the motto on the family coat-of-arms, *Non sanz droict,* with the phrase, Not without mustard. Ned was in no mood to succumb to Ben's old friendliness, and he hoped that the Lord Chamberlain's Men would never again buy a new play from him.

Aware of Ned's morose silence Ben said, "Why are your thoughts so sad, Ned? Is it from bad memories of me or good memories of the father?" Ned looked at him and away, but did not answer. "Let not the death of the father sadden you, for he died gloriously that he might enter upon a richer life. To such a man the death of a martyr is welcome. But I fear that it is my presence that sours you."

"And not without right," quipped Will, quoting the motto which Ben had travestied.

"Oh! 'Not without mustard.' Is that it? I assure you there was no malice in it," said Ben.

"And but little wit," said Will, smiling.

"I grant you, I grant you," laughed Ben.

Ned felt that Will had scored well in the exchange, and his attitude to Ben gradually became less hostile. Over drinks in the tavern, Ben regaled them with tales of Father Kirby, whom he fervently admired for his learning, his wit, his warmth, and his assured spirituality. At one point he expressed what Ned had been feeling. He said, "Whenever I think of him, it makes all I am and all I do seem worthless. When I used to tell him of my difficulties in the theatre, he would laugh and make me laugh too. He said once, 'Ben, you have to fight to prove that you're alive. Be certain that you fight for something worthy.' And I don't."

Ned managed to bring the conversation around to the Earl of Essex, for he was intrigued to know why Ben had not been notable in his support.

"When he was a man of action, I admired him, and would have followed him wherever he led, but when he made an ignominious truce with the rebels in Ireland, he lost me and many more. Since then he has pouted and grumbled like Achilles in his tent, and such inaction robbed him of the power to act. Besides, I met Father Kirby, and men like Essex could no longer command my allegiance. Only the unhappy and disaffected flocked to him. Then there was that forbidding chaplain of his, Abdy Ashton. Had he ever had his way, it would have gone even worse for us of the true faith. So the Earl of Essex will die. He failed because he is no longer the man he was, and failure in the game he played is death."

Ned was distressed by this apparent callousness. He said, "Have you no sympathy for the man?"

"We all must die, Ned. I shall pray that he dies well." Seeing that Ned was still disturbed, he went on. "What would you? That he live in perpetual imprisonment and disgrace? I think well enough of him to believe he would not want that. Think too that he will be spared the tortures of

Father Kirby. It is true that the priest died happy, for he died for his faith; the earl dies only for himself. In that I feel for him."

Ned was still not satisfied. Without being certain of his brother's attitude, he said, "Will does not feel like you about the earl."

Ben looked to Will for confirmation. The response was, "The earl stirred the hearts of men, mine among them. When he dies, something will die in many men. In grieving for the earl, I grieve for the times in which we live. I have a feeling that an age is dying."

"Only to give birth to a new one, Will. When your age dies, mine will be born." This last was said jocularly, but Will was quite aware of the aspiration in Ben which prompted it.

Sam was bored with the high-minded conversation, and he took advantage of a brief lull to blurt out, "I never thought a man had so many yards of guts in him."

After a shocked surprise, Ben burst into hearty laughter, slowly joined by Will and Ned, though less heartily. The rest of the meeting was a merry one until the irruption into the tavern of a breathless man with news—or rumor. The Earl of Essex was to go to the block in the Tower on Wednesday morning.

"What about Southampton?" somebody asked.

"Not a word," was the reply.

"She'll pardon him, you'll see," said a grimy wiseacre. "He's harmless, and she knows that, and handsome, and she likes that. A few years of rich living in the Tower, that's all he'll get, you mark my words."

Ben said soberly, "So he goes to it on Ash Wednesday. I pray that his last thoughts will be of Easter Sunday."

Somberly, all hastened home to their dinners, and Will, Ned, and Sam found the Phillipses waiting for them in high spirits. A messenger from the Queen's household had come with an invitation, really a command, to play a comedy before Her Majesty at her Palace of Whitehall after supper on Shrove Tuesday.

The Phillipses had not heard the news of the Earl of Essex. The macabre juxtaposition of the comedy on the eve of the execution struck everybody. The public gesture of pardon to the players for their implication in the Essex rebellion was partly a punishment too. Let them prove their innocence by making the Queen laugh, when she might otherwise be brooding in sorrow for having signed the death warrant of her once beloved Essex.

TWENTY-EIGHT

THE COMMAND PERFORMANCE MEANT THAT THE PLAYERS WERE FREE TO open their theatre on that Monday, but heavy rain prevented a public performance. Ned took deep satisfaction from this, because he had become increasingly infuriated by the heedless joy of the players at having the embargo lifted, by their delight at the prospect of playing before the Queen, and by their lack of concern for the fate of Essex.

To complete his disgust, it was widely circulated that at the vehement importunity of Mr. Abdy Ashton who had "ploughed up his heart," the earl had made a confession before Lords of the Council of his traitorous intentions against the Queen; that he had indeed aimed at capturing her person and forcing her to appoint a new council of his choosing. Admitting to himself that all this may have been true, Ned would have preferred the earl to maintain a strong silence. There was worse in the confession; the earl had denounced certain of his chief followers and members of his staff as having base ambitions and exerting an evil influence over him.

The play chosen for the Shrove Tuesday performance was *As You Like It*. In it Ned played Amiens, the singing role early in the play, and William, a small but delightful part in which he used a peasant Warwickshire accent. It always made Stratford more desirable than he had found it to be in fact. The whole play, contrasting as it did the delights of country simplicity with the dangers of courtly intrigue, seemed to mirror Ned's disillusionment. He knew that life was not as simple as that, for there was perfidy and intrigue and even murder in Stratford, and life in the Phillips household was much happier for him than in his Stratford home, but never had he himself been so implicated in the cruel contradictions of men as now.

The sharpest contrast in the company to the troubled Ned was the single-minded Christopher Beeston who played Rosalind. Ned both envied and disliked him. For young Master Beeston—who was about seventeen at this time, with a body young for his age and a mind shrewd for any age—nothing existed but the theatre and his place in it. To him the Essex rebellion was only an unforgivable nuisance which had closed the theatre, like bad weather or the plague. He was not a person to whom loyalty meant anything, and everybody knew this. People's opinion of him, except as a player, did not disturb Christopher at all, but he was a very good player, and he knew that too. There was nothing underhand or devious about him. He made it quite clear that he intended to be a leading player when he had ceased to play the heroines, and since he was unlikely to achieve this with the Lord Chamberlain's Men, he was already determined to have his own theatre and his own company.

Ned's part in the rebellion had become generally known in the company—how could it be otherwise when such loose tongues as Nat, Martin, and Sam had known about it?—but it had been assumed that Ned had deliberately taken up arms for the earl, and he had not chosen to diminish his heroic stature by telling the truth. Those in the company who had sympathized with the Earl of Essex had a vicarious participation in Ned's injury, though there were also those who thought he had been pointlessly foolhardy and a few who resented his action as possibly implicating the whole company. Among these last was Christopher Beeston, who quite illogically felt that Ned was partially responsible for the closing of the theatre. Although he was junior to Ned in the company, his attitude to him was one of easy equality; he reserved his respect for the sharers.

During the Tuesday morning rehearsal, Christopher came upon Ned as he was practicing his song for the night. He said, with his usual empty friendliness, "You are not in very good voice, Ned. 'Tis a punishment. Essex loses his head and you lose your voice." Ned managed to restrain himself, and Christopher went on. "I am certain you condemn the Queen for wanting to laugh tonight while the earl awaits death in the morning, so why not stay away? Your poor voice will give you good reason." Ned had not even thought of this, and it suddenly became such an attractive possibility that his resentment against Christopher faded, but he had more to say. "I had forgotten. You also play Will'um, and a cold in the head will be good for him. If your nose runs, he will be even funnier."

The players had been in the theatre since nine o'clock. During a run-through of the play, Will had been very aware that there was something wrong with Ned. It was not only that his voice was in poor shape. Gus Phillips noticed it too, and took opportunity to speak to Will about it. They both guessed the real reason for his depression but were careful to avoid mentioning it, even to each other; they too felt unease about playing a comedy on the eve of the execution of a man they had admired for years. They decided to speak to Ned at the end of the rehearsal. But they could not find him.

Ned's torment had grown during the morning until he just had to get away from the theatre, and he left without even waiting until the end of the rehearsal as he should have done. He had no plan of action, but suddenly he knew that he must go to the Tower. It would be a satisfying act of homage to the unhappy and already forgotten man who lay inside the forbidding walls, waiting to be killed. Furthermore, he must go by river and he must find a boatman who would shoot the Bridge.

He had no difficulty in finding such a boatman for extra pennies, but some innate caution made Ned declare his destination as Billingsgate rather than the Tower itself, which would be a short walk away.

Shrove Tuesday was the busiest day of the year for Billingsgate. Never had Ned seen so many boats crammed together nor smelt so much fish. Many men seemed to be spending most of their efforts in beating away with long sticks the audaciously thieving seagulls, whose angry calls added to the din of the dock market.

Ned was hungry. He went into a crowded and noisy tavern and finally found an end place on a bench at a long table. Most of the men at the table were buyers of fish, either for taverns or great houses. They were having what seemed to be a ritual meal of oysters and ale before returning home with their purchases. Ned had never eaten an oyster, but was in the mood for initiation. He had heard much of the oyster lore, about the way they added to sexual potency—not that he was in the need of such help— and of the pearls to be found in them. He discounted this last as being on a par with that foolishness about toads. What did Will say about it in the play?

> Which like the toad, ugly and venomous,
> Wears yet a precious jewel in his head.

The quotation brought Ned's mind back sharply to *As You Like It*. By this time they must have found that he was missing. His speculations were cut short by a raucous serving wench who shouted to make herself heard above the babel, "What's your will?"

"Oysters and ale," said Ned, as casually as he could.

As he waited, he noticed that the man facing him was alone, and watching him. All the others at the table seemed to belong to a fraternity of long standing and to be engrossed in loud discussion of affairs. The man opposite was good looking, probably in his early thirties. His dress was quiet but came from a good tailor; he had a stylish beard. Ned saw that he opened his oysters expertly with his dagger, which like his dress was expensive. Ned had neither dagger nor knife. A quick glance down the table revealed an assortment of privately owned implements.

The serving wench came with a bowl of oysters and a tankard of ale. Before she could move away, he caught her arm and said, "I have no knife. Could you bring me one?"

"No, sir. No knives. Borrow one." And away she went.

The man opposite smiled and said, "May I be allowed to help?"

Ned stammered some embarrassed thanks, and the man did more than lend him his dagger; he took the bowl of oysters and with skill and expedition opened all the shells before returning the bowl. While Ned was very grateful for this help, he wondered if in some way he had betrayed that he was a neophyte with oysters and forthwith determined to prove, by his practiced swallowing, that he was not; he had made good observation of the oldtimers at the table.

With aplomb he took up the first shell and got its contents into his mouth with no difficulty. Out of fear of what a bite might disclose, he swallowed. It was easy. The sensation was pleasant enough but he decided that it was the famed medicinal potency rather than the taste which made oysters such a desirable delicacy. And he could not forbear looking for the pearl.

The helpful stranger said, "Have you been here before?" Ned shook his head and the stranger continued, "What brings you here? I doubt it is just the oysters."

Ned rather resented the question but he had a ready answer. "I had heard that Billingsgate was a sight to see on Shrove Tuesday."

"It will be such a sight every day but Sundays throughout Lent, except when storms keep the ships at sea, or stop them from putting out."

Ned quickly got in his own question. "Do you come here often?"

"Yes. I come for the oysters." But the smile which accompanied the answer made it quite clear that oysters were not the reason for his frequent visits. "May I ask your name? Mine is Jack Barnet."

"And mine Edmund Shakespeare."

"Are you not a player?" asked Jack.

"Yes," said Ned, delighted to be recognized. "Have you seen me play?"

"I go but rarely to the theatre, though I did go recently to see *Richard II*."

"I played Aumerle in that."

"Then I must have seen you, though I must confess to have been more interested in the audience than the players. Are you having more oysters?"

"No," said Ned. His hunger was far from appeased, but one dozen oysters was enough, in addition to which he had begun to feel the company of Master Jack Barnet a little disquieting.

"Then let us pay our tally and walk together. You are a stranger in Billingsgate and I am not. I have time to spare, for I came here to meet a man who has disappointed me."

When they were outside, Jack asked, "Where were you going?"

Some instinct warned Ned not to mention the Tower. He said, "No place in particular."

"Then let us go to the Boar's Head; a dozen oysters are not enough to stay your stomach."

Ned agreed halfheartedly. Jack Barnet must have sensed Ned's caution and reticence, for instead of asking further questions he began to talk about himself. He had a tragic tale to tell, but he told it with a curious detachment, and he stopped frequently to point out something by the way.

"My name was not always Jack Barnet," he began. "I was born in Paris, and I was christened Jacques Bernet. You have heard of the St. Bartholomew Massacre?" Ned said that he had. "My mother and my father were both murdered then. A nurse saved me and smuggled me to England. I was three years old." Here he paused to point out a house. "I call that Hell House. It is a brothel for sailors and filled from floor to floor with the French disease. 'Tis a fitting name. I hate France, but more than that, I hate all followers of the Pope." His words of hate were coldly spoken. He added quickly, "Oh, I hope you are not a Roman." Ned assured him he was not. "More innocent people were massacred on that terrible day than there are in Norwich, or Bristol, or York, and the Pope ordered a Te Deum of praise and thanksgiving to be sung in honor of the deed . . . Look at those rats; they will grow fat during Lent."

"Are you a Huguenot?" asked Ned.

"No. They are admirable people but too solemn for my liking. I owe them much. It was a Huguenot family that took me in and reared me, and sent me to school and Cambridge. They were weavers and prospered. I am not truly religious, Master Shakespeare. I go to church because it is the Queen's. She is my religion, and I serve her."

"And when she dies?"

"For me she will never die. While she lives, I live for her, and when she is dead, I shall live for her memory." The tone of this declaration of faith was still matter-of-fact.

They were now near the Boar's Head. Jack caught hold of Ned's arm and surprised him by saying, eye-to-eye, "Did you follow Essex?"

Ned was so taken aback that he was incoherent in his reply, but there had been no hostility in the question.

"It boots not to deny it, Master Shakespeare. I saw you in the courtyard on that Sunday morning. Yes, I was there. I am wherever the Queen is threatened. But you came without a weapon. Yes, I saw that too, and it told in your favor."

Although Jack's manner was now almost friendly, Ned was thoroughly alarmed. Was this man one of Cecil's paid spies?

"Believe me, Master Shakespeare, your Queen deserves your loyalty ten thousand times more than an ambitious man like Essex. She knew him better than anybody did, and she loved him, but for the safety of her people she signed his death warrant. She alone is the bulwark against seas of blood like that which robbed me of my parents. Any man that threatens her must die." Ned thought of Father Kirby; what threat was he? And yet there was that Pope's Te Deum. "Tomorrow Essex will die. Tonight the Queen will see a comedy. Think not that is heartless of her. She will laugh to prevent crying. She will laugh to show that there is something greater than the love of one man, and that is the love of many, her people."

In the Boar's Head both men took ale, but only Ned needed more to eat. Gradually the distance between them diminished until they were calling each other by their Christian names, when a question from Jack again surprised Ned and took him off balance. "Why are you here instead of preparing the play for the Queen tonight?"

Ned's answer was at first too hesitant and then too emphatic to be convincing. "I cannot play. I have a fever in the head. I cannot sing."

"Then why are you not at home and in bed?" Ned said nothing. "Is it that you have quarreled with your fellows? I hear that players are quick to fall out." Still Ned said nothing. Then came the biggest surprise of all. "I shall be in the Great Chamber tonight. You must be there, Ned." It sounded like the earnest request of a friend, and yet Ned sensed something of a threat behind it. "You may not see me, but I shall see you, and after the Queen has left the Chamber I shall come to you. And now, before we part, let us have a cup of sack together, warm and with honey it it, for that is good for the voice."

As Ned was walking back to the theatre alone, his slightly befuddled brain had much to wrestle with. He would probably get back just in time for the procession, the prospect of which he loathed; they would be passing through some of the same streets through which he had followed the Earl of Essex, and the same people would be lining the way and with the same motive: to see a spectacle. This cynical reflection on the citizenry of London made him examine his own attitude. A sudden stab of honesty made Ned realize that for the past two weeks he had been playing a part, the solitary loyal adherent of the earl, a part which he had grown to believe in because it was satisfyingly heroic, whereas the fact was that it was mere curiosity which had taken him to Essex House in the first place, and, if he had not been with Robin, he would have run away.

By the time Ned got to the theatre, the cart was waiting at the stage door and the numerous tethered horses that would carry the players were being decorated by ostler boys. A little fearful of his reception, Ned went inside. He had a lie prepared.

John Heminge thundered, "Where have you been?"

"I had a head fever, so I went to an apothecary and he gave me too potent a sleeping draught."

"Where did you sleep?"

"At home."

Apparently John Heminge swallowed the lie, for he said, "Hurry. We are about to set out."

Quickly Ned sought out Will, who was working with Sam on the part of William. It said much for Sam that he was almost as glad to see Ned as Will was. In his newly acquired Warwickshire accent, he said, "Where 'ast tha bin, lad?"

"I fell asleep," replied Ned, looking full at Will with an unspoken plea.

Will merely said, "Sam would have made a good William. Come; we must find Gus."

Ned was glad that Will was accompanying him. They had no difficulty in finding Gus, for Fred Ansell's voice guided them; he was practicing the songs of Amiens, and Ned was happy to note that his voice was unsuited to them; it was not lyrical enough.

Will repeated Ned's lie to Gus, whose pleasure at seeing Ned infuriated Master Ansell, who glowered but dared say nothing. He was dismissed by Gus with, "You must work hard on your voice, Fred; it comes too much from the throat alone; it lacks support from the chest." Then Gus said, "Now, Ned. Let me hear you. I pray God your head has cleared."

Will walked away, smiling happily. As he did so, he heard Ned beginning to sing. The voice was better than in the morning, though not at its best. He passed Nat Tremayne, all fuss and feathers, hurrying to confirm the report that Ned had returned and mightily exercised about the costume that would best become him in the procession.

Mounted on a splendid and spirited horse, and dressed in a handsome costume, the actor in Ned asserted itself. As he rode through the streets he could not forbear displaying horse and rider to their best advantage to elicit audible delight from those spectators whom a part of him despised. Then he was momentarily awed by the fact that it could easily have been he that was killed and Robin wounded; what amazed and puzzled him was that he had never before thought of this possibility.

Once they had arrived at the Palace, Ned was overwhelmed, as always, by its spaciousness and magnificence. And at the heart of it all sat an old woman, the most powerful in the world, and one before whom great nobles trembled; truly a great Queen, gifted in languages, learned, witty, and wise, whose hand in marriage princes had sought, but who had chosen to belong to no one man so that she could rule over all. Ned felt ashamed of the disloyalty he had felt toward her.

The flurry of the theatre men as they made their preparations contrasted sharply with the calm and unhurried behavior of the Palace staff, as they trimmed lamps, set candles and checked flambeaux. After artificial trees had been placed, there was a rehearsal of the actors' entrances and movements. The rehearsals at the theatre on the Monday and Tuesday had all been geared to making changes to focus the action on one person, the Queen, and these were now finalized.

The actors were ready well before eight o'clock. As they waited in the anteroom which gave on to the back of the chamber, their nervous excitement increased. It was an excitement different from that which they felt at the first performance of a new play. There was even a difference in the chatter and laughter of the waiting audience. Apart from the fact that there were no cries of vendors, the sound was amplified by being indoors yet muted and polite in quality.

Richard Burbage was particularly nervous. He played Orlando but knew he was too old to do so, and he feared being the subject of one of the Queen's memorable witticisms. While the others had eaten, he had spent the time in trying to disguise his age and to restrain his paunch; he wondered now if the stays were not perhaps too tight for that wrestling match.

There was a distant trumpet. The Queen was on her way. At the first sound, the players all trooped out into the Great Chamber and stood in line, waiting. Ned was always stunned by the sudden sight of the brilliant silks and velvets and brocades, the flash and sparkle of jewelry, all made doubly impressive by the hundreds of lights, but on this night, when the Queen had special reason to be distracted and entertained, all her court seemed to have outdone themselves in splendor. They filled the gallery above the canopied thronelike chair and there were brocaded chairs and velvet-cushioned benches and stools on both sides of the Queen and halfway along both side walls. There were some dozen chairs nearest the Queen's which were reserved for the immediate entourage, who would enter with her.

A second, nearer trumpet sounded. At the third she would enter the Chamber. Now Ned longed to see if she would betray any sign of the distress she must be feeling. Oh, how he yearned to sing well for her tonight! But he knew his voice would not serve; to quote his yokel, William, 'twas but so-so. Then he would concentrate on the words of the songs. As he thought of his favorite song in the play, he was struck by how appropriate the Queen might think the words as describing her relation to the Earl of Essex, to whom she had given more favors than to any other courtier in her long reign.

> Blow, blow, thou winter wind,
> Thou art not so unkind
> As man's ingratitude.
>
> Freeze, freeze, thou bitter sky,
> Thou dost not bite so nigh
> As benefits forgot.

And now she was feeling the winter wind of old age, and the freeze of death could not be long delayed. By the time she would appear tonight, Ned would be among her most loyal subjects.

The trumpeters on each side of the doorway sounded, and the air thrilled with an excited adoration as the Queen approached. And then Gloriana entered on the arm of Robert Cecil, the brilliant hunchback, as devoted and shrewd a servant of the Queen as had been his father, Lord Burghley. At sight of their Queen all the men bowed and the women curtsied in deep obeisance and remained so until she was seated. When he straightened up, Ned, who was standing in the second row of players, took a quick look at the Queen before he had to leave for the play to begin. She was a dazzling sight. Her long V-shaped bodice was of a lustrous white silk, her skirts and pouched sleeves of white velvet, all trimmed with blue flowerets. Over this she wore a sleeveless purple velvet robe trimmed with ermine. Around her wrists was most exquisite starched lace, and around her neck stood a high ruff of layers of the same lace trimmed with pearls. She wore ropes of pearls and over her heart was a large diamond pin. Her face was a waxen white, but even by candle-light her eyes sparkled with a penetrating vivacity. Her head was crowned with a dark red wig in which large jewels flashed, and that in turn was topped by a chaplet of precious stones. It seemed incongruous that such a vision of regality should be famous for her laughter and dancing.

It was appropriate that the play should begin with the Queen's favorite player and her favorite playwright, who played Orlando and old Adam. When they were alone on the floor, Richard Burbage and William Shakespeare bowed again to the Queen. She acknowledged this by a smile and a slight and slow inclination of the head; it was a signal that the play was to begin.

It went well. The Queen was observed to smile frequently and to laugh outright a few times. She was known to take delight in Robert Armin. Touchstone was the first part that Will had written for him, and with it he had made the play his.

The Queen usually commanded that one or two players, as representatives of the company, should approach her at the end of a royal performance to receive some commendation, but it was generally felt that she would omit this graciousness on this occasion in order to remind the players that she was still displeased with them for their *Richard II* performance. When the whole company came out at the end of the play, the eyes of the audience and the players were on her as the general applause subsided. The Queen turned to speak to an attendant and he came down to the players to summon Master Shakespeare and Master Armin to the presence. All strained to hear what the Queen would say. First she spoke to the playwright.

"Master Shakespeare, are we the 'You' in the title of this play?"

"It would honor me, your Majesty, if you were."

"Then we are."

Will bowed low in appreciation of such a well-turned compliment.

To Robert Armin she merely said, "We thank you, Master Armin, for making us laugh." Armin, famous for his extempore wit, had hoped to be given a chance to display it, but since the Queen had asked him no question, he had to be content with silence and a bow. The players walked backwards to regain their places with their fellows.

The Queen stood up, and with her the whole assembly, the trumpets sounded, and she moved out as she had come in to deep obeisances.

As soon as the Queen was out of sight and hearing, chatter began tentatively and quickly grew in volume. Several of the lesser notabilities, and particularly the younger ones, came to congratulate the players. One of the first to get to them was Jack Barnet. He came straight to Ned, who was astonished by the change in his appearance, which was that of a fashionable courtier; George would have been proud if he had dressed him.

With Jack were two young ladies, who were introduced as Lady Cynthia Beldon and Lady Jane Hargreave, the one lively and the other quietly observant. It soon became clear that Lady Cynthia was Jack's particular friend and that Lady Jane was her friend and unattached, at least for the evening.

Jack took charge. " 'Tis Shrove Tuesday until midnight, and we must make the most of it; still a full hour and a half before the dismal chimes bring in sober Lent. Let us four make merry in my rooms. Come, Ned. Waste no more time. Doff that country garb. This is not the Forest of Arden, but the wicked court."

"And you are no melancholy philosopher, like your namesake in the play," quipped Lady Cynthia.

"But did not the duke upbraid him for having been a libertine? It is age that made him melancholy, as it may do me. Quickly Ned, while we talk to your brother and Robert Armin." And he swept the two ladies away.

As Ned changed from his William costume, he was dazed and excited by the turn of events. He was glad that the only clothes he had to change into were the splendid ones he had used in the procession. When he was ready, he went to explain to Will that he would not be going home with him and the others. Will was ironically amused and pleased by the change in Ned's spirits; it seemed that he had forgotten about the execution of Essex the following morning. It had been on Will's mind the whole evening, but he had no intention to remind Ned of it. He said, "I knew you were going to a last-hour Shrovetide party, and here in the Palace. The gentleman with the two ladies told me."

Before more could be said, the mysterious Jack came to take Ned away.

Jack's rooms accorded well with his rich dress. The party had been prepared for with an abundance of wine, fruit, and sweet confections, and in attendance was a discreet young servingman, James. Ned listened carefully to hear how James would address his master, but it was never anything but "sir."

Ned had carefully and correctly addressed each of the young women as "My Lady," until Lady Cynthia said, "That title is for Lent, not for Shrovetide. Tonight I am Cynthia, and she is Jane. You are Ned at all times, which is much easier, and Jack . . ."

Jack quickly interposed. "I am Jack at all times. Jack Barnet." He said the surname as if he were spelling it out.

Both ladies looked at him quizzically for a moment, and then Cynthia laughed and Jane smiled. Gradually Ned gathered that the ladies were some sort of assistant ladies-in-waiting to the Queen; in his vocabulary they seemed to be apprentices.

Jane said, "Please sing for us, Ned."

"I beg you to excuse me. My voice is raw. I have somewhat of a fever."

"A fever?" echoed Jane fearfully.

To reassure her, Cynthia said, "It cannot be much. He sang well enough in the play."

Jack said, "Come, Ned, you must sing, else Jane will fear you have caught the plague. Here is a well-tuned lute. I asked James to have it ready."

Ned resented this indication that he had been brought there just to entertain the others. Jane, now ashamed of her frightened reaction to the word "fever," said, "That song you sang in *Much Ado About Nothing* is my favorite."

"You saw me in that?" he asked, pleased.

"More than once. I have not seen it since William Kemp has gone. It cannot be the same without him."

"I am the same," said Ned, with an inviting smile.

"Then sing 'Sigh no more, ladies.' That's the one Jane wants," said Jack.

"How do you know that? You told me you don't go to the theatre," said Ned.

"I said 'rarely,' " replied Jack, smiling at Ned's challenge.

Ned sang his song, and was pleased to note that his voice sounded better than in the theatre; perhaps, he thought, the wine had mended it, or dulled his standards. His three hearers were loud in their appreciation and begged for more.

Ned glowed with their approval and gave several songs, interspersed with tales of the theatre, egged on chiefly by Jane whom he had originally thought to be but a shadow of the lively Cynthia. But it was Jane who could not hear enough of the theatre and even made the outrageous suggestion that it was grossly unfair that ladies were not allowed to be players.

Cynthia was shocked. Completely ignoring the presence of Ned, she said, "Ladies! It would be shameful if women, even harlots, displayed themselves on a public stage, but ladies! Why, not even a gentleman would stoop to be a player."

Ned was speechless with fury, the more so that neither Jack nor Jane seemed to think that anything amiss had been said. He stood up and, with a cold hauteur worthy of Burbage as Richard II, said, "I beg you will excuse me. I cannot sing or speak more tonight."

"Are you sick?" asked Jack with genuine concern.

"I fear so. It would not be wise for me to stay longer in this room. My ladies—sir—I bid you all a goodnight." He turned and left abruptly, leaving his audience completely puzzled.

Then Jack saw an explanation. "He must have drunk too much. He had been drinking earlier in the day. I see it now. He wanted to spare us the sight of him vomiting. That was thoughtful of him. He's a good fellow—for a player."

There was very little light on the stairs, but that did not prevent Ned from racing noisily down them. There were guards in the courtyard and they directed him to the stable where his procession horse was waiting.

Mechanically he asked questions for direction and answered questions about his identity. All the time he was seething and, once outside the Palace grounds, he sped his horse angrily homeward.

His mind was in a turmoil. He had actually been speculating on the real likelihood of getting to bed with Jane in the near future, but, if he had succeeded, even in the act of submission to his body, she would never have regarded him as her equal, much less her master; he would always have been to her a player, a male whore. He thought back to the other ladies whose beds he had shared. Had they all felt the same way? Now he understood why so many of the sharers tried to acquire a coat-of-arms and the title of "gentleman." He had been scornful of their silly pretensions. He wondered whether Will had got the Shakespeare coat-of-arms to please his father or himself.

He arrived home at the darkened house, stabled the horse, and got to his room as quietly as possible. As he undressed in the dark, he began to shiver uncontrollably.

TWENTY-NINE

A FEVER KEPT NED IN BED FOR TWO WEEKS. ANY FEVER WAS FRIGHTENING because it might be the plague, but no skin eruptions or swellings occurred. Mistress Phillips took it upon herself to cure him without the help of apothecary or surgeon. Whether it was because of her medications or in spite of them, Ned began to improve in the second week, though he was in a considerably debilitated state, for the main result of the potions had been to empty his bowels and his stomach, and to do so frequently. The first sign of his return to health was to refuse any more purgatives and to beg for some solid food.

Will, now completing his *Hamlet,* came in often to see Ned but soon hurried back to his room. When Ned began to take interest in the world again, it was Sam who brought him news. The Earl of Essex had died bravely, with words of forgiveness to his executioner. It was said that all the nobles and gentlemen who witnessed the death were so moved by the earl that they wept. Even the executioner lost his expertness for it took three blows of the ax to sever the head. As he left the Tower he had been set upon by a crowd and would have been beaten to death if the sheriff's men had not rescued him.

Ned's comment was, "They did more for the earl dead than they had done for him living."

Sam reported that the ghost of the earl had already been seen at the place of execution. A few days ago several of the lords who had followed the earl had been tried and all condemned to death.

"Sir Christopher Blount?"

"Yes," said Sam.

"He was wounded and captured at Paul's. 'Twould have been better had he died then, like Robin."

March was a month of executions, both at the Tower and Tyburn, the place of death being determined by the social status of the condemned man. Thus Sir Charles Blount was beheaded at the Tower, proclaiming at the end that he was a Roman Catholic, and Henry Cuffe, who was generally considered to be a baneful influence on the Earl of Essex to whom he was secretary, was hanged at Tyburn, being spared further torture and mutilation.

There were strange vagaries of justice. At the plea of Sir Robert Cecil, the life of the Earl of Southampton was spared, but he remained a prisoner in the Tower. Ned's comment was, "What is the secret of that man? Even his enemies find excuses for him." And the two Percy brothers, Sir Charles and Sir Joscelyn, who had been prominent in the group that had secured the special performance of *Richard II*, were even released from prison and committed to the safekeeping of their brother, the Earl of Northumberland.

With the theatre closed during Lent, Ned had time to ponder the experiences which had overwhelmed him in February, and out of the welter only one man had emerged as being free from the sordidness of the world and the perfidy of men, and that was Father Kirby. But it said little for this world if the only way to live in it was to believe in another and unseen one. While he admired Father Kirby, Ned knew that that would not be the way for him. He belonged firmly to this world, and would be his own man in it, even if it had to be his own unhappy man.

The contempt for players which Jack, Lady Cynthia, and Lady Jane had shown festered in Ned. Never again would he fool himself. Perhaps it was in this way that the Earl of Southampton had given deep hurt to Will. In his fury on that ride from the Palace Ned had decided that he would never again bed a woman of blue blood, but reflection made him want more than ever to lie with Lady Jane and to arouse in her such a fever of sexual need that his contempt for her dependence on his body would equal her contempt for his birth. He was certain she had been disappointed by his sudden disappearance, and there was little doubt that her genuine love for the theatre would bring her back to see him.

Ned had gone unshaven during his illness and the resultant growth had made him decide to cultivate a beard in honor of his twenty-first birthday which would take place on April 30. The beard added a few years to his appearance and was envied by Sam, who made an attempt to emulate it, but with laughable results.

The theatre opened again on Easter Monday, April 13, which was an appropriately beautiful day, full of the bright promise of spring. It had been decided to open with *As You Like It*, to be followed by *Twelfth Night*, *A Midsummer Night's Dream*, *The Taming of the Shrew*, *The Merry Wives of Windsor*, and *Much Ado About Nothing*. The hope was that the comedies would be welcomed as an attempt to dispel the gloom of recent months.

Will was to appear himself only on the Monday. Now he was caught in a fever to finish *Hamlet*. He was rarely out of his room at home and ate most of his meals there. Prompted by Anne, Gus had pleaded with him to slacken his industry, for the intensity of his concentration had begun to take its toll of his body; he looked pale and had neglected his appearance.

Gus said jocularly, "You look like a man in hopeless love."

"I am," replied Will. "This Hamlet has captured me as nothing else ever has. I cannot contain him, Gus. His play will be the length of two plays, but it must be one. He speaks for me, for you, for all of us in these puzzling times. Something is going out of life, Gus."

"Yes," said Gus. "We are living for today instead of tomorrow. The future does not welcome us; it threatens. Maybe it's just that we are getting older."

"It's more than that. Ned feels it too. It must be that soon the Queen will die, and with her will die more than herself. In some strange way I feel that with Essex died the promise of our times."

"But he confessed that he . . ."

"I know, and he spoke truth. That is the greatest sadness of all. It may be that in affairs of state there is nothing and nobody in whom we can put our whole trust. The honest man is a lonely man; such is my Hamlet. But he cannot withdraw from the world as I can and someday will; he has a solemn duty to perform."

"When shall we hear him speak?"

"In a week or two."

Excited anticipation about Hamlet grew during those weeks. But Ned had other and more personal things to occupy him. On the Saturday of Easter Week the Lady Jane came to see *Much Ado About Nothing*, and he was certain that this time it was to see him rather than the play. As soon as he walked onstage in the first scene as an attendant on Don Pedro he scanned the lords' rooms and found her. With the group was also the Lady Cynthia.

Eight of them came backstage after the performance, and a loud-voiced exquisite among them was heard to exclaim, "Oh, how we miss Kemp as the constable!" The remark was not calculated to endear him to Robert Armin.

The Lady Jane was not long in leaving her companions and finding Ned. He had delayed beginning to change, confident that she would come. He ached to seize her roughly, but amused himself by behaving with an exaggerated deference.

"Your voice is fully restored, Ned. You sang beautifully," she began.

"Thank you, my lady."

" 'My lady!' Nay, Ned. Are we not friends?"

"It pleases you to say so, my lady."

"And does it not please you?"

"I would not presume so far, my lady."

"I beg you to call me Jane."

"That would not be fitting, my lady. Not here."

That last qualification was a deliberate suggestion which she seized on. "Then elsewhere," she said. Ned said nothing, so she went on. "Tomorrow is Sunday; you do not play. In the morning there is church, but we could meet afterwards."

"For dinner?"

"No; that would be too difficult. I must dine at the Palace. Meet me at two o'clock at Charing Cross, and we will ride into the country." So it was assumed he had a horse; so be it. "And Ned, come as you were dressed at Shrovetide, and no one will see anything amiss, for you will look indeed like a gentleman of title." This was said innocently, with no knowledge that it could offend, and not by a flicker did Ned betray that it had hurt, but it hardened him in his resolution to humiliate this naturally arrogant lady.

Anticipation of the Sunday afternoon filled Ned's thoughts that night and, regrettably, during the church service the following morning. Will had readily agreed to lend him his new horse, a beautiful chestnut, but the subject of the right dress gave him much thought. He finally decided to dress plainly. This would serve to disobey her, to disappoint her, and to test her desire for him. It would be the beginning of her humiliation. It might be that the sight of him would make her ride straight back to the Palace, but he did not think so. April showers in the morning foiled part of his ultimate plan: the grass would be too wet to lie on.

Ned deliberately arrived at Charing Cross a little late, determined to make no apology for his tardiness, but she was not there. Had she refused to wait for a player? Chagrined, Ned was about to ride home when he saw her riding along at a leisurely walk. She had won the first trick without even knowing that she was playing a game.

As she came up to Ned, her face showed her disappointment at his plain appearance. "Why did you dress like this, Ned? You look like a servant." Not a word about being late, but then he had intended not to say a word either. Yet there was a difference; with him the omission would have been deliberate; she did not see the necessity for it.

His reply had an outer deference but an inner irony, even a note of courtly gallantry. He said, "Today I am not a player and do not dress like one, but I am ever your servant."

Jane herself had chosen to wear her least ornate cloak. Even so she drew many eyes as she sat proudly sidesaddle on a magnificent horse which she commanded with easy skill. "Let us ride," she said.

She led the way north, past St. Martin's in the Fields, and headed toward Hampstead Heath.

"Where are we going?" Ned asked.

"I have a place in mind. Follow me." She spurred her horse into a gallop, riding superbly, and Ned had much ado to keep up with her. When they came to a slight gradient, his horse lagged behind, and she waited for him to catch up with her.

Smiling at him, Jane said, "I set too hot a pace for you. Do you lead; 'tis the man's place." Was she speaking simply or in parables? And the now oversensitive Ned noted that she said "man," not "gentleman."

The horses walked abreast for a time, so that conversation was possible.

"Where are we going?" asked Ned again.

"To an inn where we will be well received. It belongs to Mark Grimsby and his wife, Esther. She was my suckling nurse. Two years ago I gave them money that they might buy this little inn, so they are bound to me, and discreet to boot. I have spent many a pleasant hour there."

Ned began to wonder who was going to win this game of humiliation he had set out to play. It seemed he was just a stallion picked up for an afternoon's pleasure.

Jane said, "You say nothing, but you think much. I will answer the questions you dare not ask. Yes, I have gone there with other men. A few; not often. But this is the first time with a player."

"I am honored, my lady."

" 'My lady' again. That is false on your tongue, Master Shakespeare. It is a mock deference. You are a proud man, else you would not interest me."

It began to rain, though the sun continued to shine; another April shower. Ned made for the shelter of a nearby oak tree, but Lady Jane called after him. "Nay, 'tis not far." Again she broke into a gallop and Ned had to follow her.

By the time they got to the little inn, the Hargreave Arms, they were both thoroughly wet, but Lady Jane found this amusing. She said, "We shall be here long enough to have them dried before the fire. I always keep clothes here, and I'm sure Mark can find something for you."

The host and hostess were more like brother and sister than man and wife. They were both happily overweight, and their attitude to the Lady Jane was born of true devotion. They seemed not at all surprised by the unheralded arrival of the couple. Ned was introduced as "my friend," and he could not but think it was because he lacked a title. Yet, in reluctant fairness, he had to admit the possibility that the Lady Jane might prefer to keep even her titled companions anonymous.

There was great concern over the rain-soaked condition of the young couple. "Come, Esther, and help me to change," said Lady Jane as she moved to go upstairs. She turned and spoke. "And you, Mark, find something for the gentleman. He has just recovered from a fever, and we must not give him another."

Ned was taken into a cozy back parlor and told to take off his wet things, while Mark went to find him something to wear. A log fire crackled a welcome as Ned took off his cloak and doublet. He also took off his riding boots and warmed his legs before the fire. Mark returned with a handsome velvet robe, obviously not his own, and a tankard of mulled ale, hot and spicy. "That'll warm your insides, sir. No fever can match that," he said as he bore the wet clothes away.

Soon the Lady Jane joined Ned. He had expected her to be dressed seductively, but she might have been a wealthy merchant's wife, making herself comfortable for a quiet Sunday afternoon indoors.

Ned was sitting in the room's only cushioned chair. He rose to give it to the lady and moved to the hard, high-backed inglenook seat on the opposite side of the fireplace.

"Now, Ned, amuse me," began Lady Jane.

This command to play the court jester increased Ned's hostility.

"How, my lady?" he asked.

She stood up irritably and paced about as she replied. "A plague on 'my lady.' It was 'Jane' in Jack's room, and I wish it to be so now."

"Then I had drunk too much, and my tongue slipped its guard."

"Then drink too much again, for, sober, I fear you are a dull dog. Why cannot you be the man you are onstage?"

"There I play a part; here I am myself."

She crossed the room to stand over him before she said with mocking emphasis, "You lie, Master Shakespeare. Here you play a part too, and not well; you even dressed for it, the part of the humble servant. But there is no humility in you." Ned said nothing. She sat by him and placed a hand on his knee before continuing in a gentler tone. "I know not whence your bile comes, but I beg you to digest it and be plain man with me."

For answer Ned looked deliberately at her hand on his knee. She took it away. He turned to look directly at her. In some embarrassment she looked away, got up, and moved back to the chair. Once she had regained her composure she said, "Still you say nothing."

With open challenge, Ned said, "Why did you ask me here?"

Excited that she had ripped away his mask, Jane looked straight at him and said with provoking ambiguity, "To amuse me."

"How?"

"You belong to a world that fascinates me. I want to hear all about it."

"There are others who know far more."

"They are older—and married."

"How do you know that I am not married?"

"Jack told me. He knows everything."

"Then he would make a better companion for a Sunday afternoon than I."

"That may well be, but he has his Cynthia. Besides, you are much more my age. With Jack I feel I am a girl. With you I feel I am a woman."

She rang a bell which was on a little table by the side of her chair. Almost immediately the host entered.

"Some wine and comfits to stay our stomachs till supper." Mark grinned broadly and bowed repeatedly as he received the order and left. "The wine may help to loosen the bridle on your tongue," she said with a smile.

Determined to call the tune, Ned said, "I cannot stay until supper," though he had originally been prepared to stay the night.

In wide-eyed surprise she said, "Nor I." Again she had won the trick. "Now tell me what new play you prepare." She said this as though the subject had been the sole purpose of their meeting.

"My brother writes a new one. 'Twill soon be ready. 'Tis called *Hamlet*."

"*Hamlet*. I know the name. 'Twas an old play before I came to court. My father spoke of it, and of a ghost in it that cried, 'Revenge!' It is from my father that I get my love of theatre. He would have made a good player, but alas! his birth prevented that. And I am prevented both by my birth and my womanhood."

Never before had Ned been struck by the limitations of noble birth, nor was he much impressed by them now.

"I saw many plays in the castle when I was growing up, for my father entertained many bands of traveling players. Will you have a handsome part in the new play?"

"I know not yet."

"A gentleman, I hope. It becomes you better than the yokel."

"They are both parts I play, for I am neither gentleman nor yokel."

"Nor very good companion," she said irritably. "I know not why you came."

Ned had no answer for this but was prevented from having to make one by the entrance of Mark with a flagon of wine, two goblets and a platter of tempting sweetmeats. There was silence while he laid down his tray and served the wine.

Feeling that some attempt at gallantry was necessary to restore the possibilities of the afternoon, Ned stood and made a toast. "To a beautiful and gracious lady, who thinks well of players."

Mark's eyebrows rose at the astonishing revelation that the gentleman seemed to be only a player. He was eager to impart the news to Esther.

As soon as they were alone again, Jane looked at Ned over the edge of her goblet as she drank and smiled her acknowledgment of his toast. Then she said, "That's better. Now I will come and sit with you again."

"Nay," said Ned, "stay on your cushions and I will come and sit at your feet."

As Ned moved to do so, she said, "Is this another part you are playing?"

"If it is, do you not find it a more pleasing one?"

"Vastly," she said, as she drew his head to rest against her knee. "If one sip of wine makes this change in you, what will the flagon do?"

"Whatever you would have it do," said Ned as he moved his head up her thigh.

By the time the flagon of wine was finished, both were thoroughly aroused. Ned's stratagem had been to excite and then deny her until the lady groveled before the player and begged for satisfaction, but he had not allowed for the fact tht he himself would become so excited that to remain objective was impossible.

As Jane made a move to join him on the floor, Ned said fearfully, "The door!"

With some return to her mocking tone, Jane said, "Are you ashamed to be caught with me? Fear not. No one will come in unless I ring the bell, and that I am unlikely to do."

In the moment of comparative detachment which this exchange had created, Ned, remembering his original intention, decided he would at least treat her body roughly and thus show his contempt for her nobly born flesh, but even here he was foiled, for the more brutal he was the more ecstatic she became, and she dealt with him in kind, drawing blood from a bite in his shoulder. It was a memorable conjunction such as Ned had never before experienced. He was dazed by the revelation of the abandoned animal in the fine lady. And when it was all over, and they had lain side by side for some minutes in happy completion, she said brightly, "I knew I was right about you. Now repair your appearance, and we'll have another flagon of wine."

This was the first of several lustful Sunday afternoons. Each meeting seemed only to increase in both of them the hungry anticipation of the next. Ned soon laughed at his original motives of social revenge. He was amazed and a little ashamed to find how satisfying was the mutual violence of the sexual encounters with Jane.

At their third meeting he told her that on the previous Thursday he had become legally a man; it had been his twenty-first birthday. Jane's comment was, "The law is late, as ever. You are such a man as I have never met before." On the following Sunday she brought him a present: a beautiful diamond ring. He wore it with pride and it provoked many questions at home and in the theatre, but no answers. Will had seen to it that the important birthday had not gone unregarded at home or in the theatre, but nothing gave Ned such delight as Jane's ring.

But on that fourth Sunday he had to tell her that it would be four weeks before they could meet again. *Hamlet* was about to go into rehearsal and would occupy the next three Sundays. Jane wanted to know all about Ned's part. She asked, "Are you a gentleman?"

The change in Ned was clearly indicated by the fact that he took no offense at the question. He was merely happy to please her by saying, "Yes; a courtier. A friend of the prince, but a false friend. His name is Rosencrantz. He's a spy for the king. Like Jack."

This reference to Jack had been deliberately casual, as if the fact were well known. But Jane asked with apparent surprise, "Is Jack a spy?"

"Is he not?"

"I do not know. It may well be. It would explain much."

"Does Cynthia not know?"

"I think not. When Jack is away—and he is away often—he merely tells her that he is on the Queen's business, and she must not ask more. Now you too are going away, and for four whole weeks. Let us not talk more, but make this meeting one to be remembered." And they did.

Hamlet was such a play as the company, or any other company, had never before performed. To begin with, it was almost twice as long as was the custom, and there began the trouble. When Will first read the play to his fellows, they all knew they were hearing something extraordinary. The story in its broad outlines they knew—indeed several of them had played in the old *Hamlet* play—but the central character had a power and a depth and a mysterious appeal which was so exciting that they would never forget that evening. There were moments when the unknown and unknowable Will seemed to be baring his own heart.

He closed the manuscript after he had been reading for nearly three hours. There was a long silence, which became embarrassing. All looked to Richard Burbage, for here was surely his greatest part. Finally, he spoke, and sadly, "Am I not too old and fat for it, Will?"

"No," replied Will vehemently, "you are my Hamlet. I saw and heard you in every line." He added with a smile, "But with your permission, I will add a line I had in mind, but did not write. When you are breathless in the duel, the Queen can say you have grown fat."

This relaxed the whole company into laughter, and John Heminge could say what had irked him for the last hour. " 'Tis too long, Will. It must be cut."

Richard Burbage said quickly and strongly, "I will not lose a word."

And so the great argument began, which went on through the first three weeks of rehearsal. Every day a new cut was proposed by some sharer, but usually of scenes in which he himself was not involved, and always the reason was, "It's not necessary to the plot."

It was Richard Burbage who, in final exasperation, burst out, "Plot! Plot! Speak no more of it. 'Tis the least of this play."

But it was Will who finally stilled the clamor. On a morning in the third week of rehearsal he came in with a suggestion for a major cut: the words of the Murder of Gonzago, the play within the play, could be entirely omitted, retaining only the dumbshow version of it. John Heminge spluttered in dismay, for he played the Player King. That ended all demands for cuts. No one, not even his brother, would ever know whether Will had been serious in his suggestion or merely clever. Ned was so overwhelmed by the play that he looked upon Will with new eyes. He wondered what went on in Will's soul that could produce the torment of Hamlet.

When it was clear that the new play was going to last more than three hours, Cuthbert Burbage had an inspiration: why not make much of the fact that this was like no other play? People paid money to see giants and dwarfs. This was a giant play. Posters would proclaim the fact and say that it would start half an hour earlier than any other play.

This, coupled with the excitement of the players which had traveled through their friends to the play-loving public, created such eager anticipation that the first performance was bound to be sold out, and at double prices too, if only the weather was kind.

And the play opened on a beautiful June day. The first performance of *Hamlet* was a forever memorable occasion to the more than two thousand people who saw it. Even before it began there was an unusual excitement in the audience and in the company, as if they knew they were about to be joined together in the birth of something remarkable. It had been decided to give the performance without a break and the audience sat or stood spellbound for well over three hours. Had the play had only the unrelieved tension of tragedy, the long strain would have been unbearable, but it was lightened throughout by unexpected laughter, not only by Pope's Polonius and Armin's Gravedigger but even by Burbage's Hamlet, whose mordant wit was delightful. Even the players themselves were amazed by Burbage. Rehearsals had given but a faint promise of the astonishing quality of his performance; he was like a man possessed. In the scenes between Rosencrantz and Hamlet, Ned found the emanations from Burbage almost frighteningly unpredictable; this was not the man he knew offstage but another being. It was somehow fitting that Will played the Ghost of Hamlet's father, for just as the father had laid a duty upon the son, so had the poet on the player; son and player performed their duties superbly.

When the players took the stage at the end of the performance, they were rewarded by such an ovation as they had never known. Burbage seemed bewildered by it all, especially when his fellows on stage joined wildly in the applause. Ned found himself crying, and he was not the only one. Burbage looked around for Will and brought him forward. It was impossible to hear what he said, but he bowed low to the author, who was still clad in his ghostly majesty. Ned was bursting with pride that he too was a Shakespeare.

Everybody in the audience, even the sedate burghers and their wives, was standing and shouting and clapping. Ned looked for Jane who had promised to be there. He wanted to share his joy and pride with her, but he could not see her. His high spirits were momentarily dashed but he decided that there must be some simple explanation for her absence, and he gave himself again to the celebration of *Hamlet*.

The supper for the company which followed the performance was unique in several ways: it began later and lasted longer (There was no rehearsal in the morning, for everybody had been so certain of the success of *Hamlet* that the unprecedented decision had been made in advance to give it for three successive days); it was entirely paid for by the parsimonious Cuthbert Burbage; and some usually abstemious players, from exhaustion and elation drank themselves into a pleasant stupor, and among these, to Ned's surprise and delight, was Will.

Because of Jane's odd absence at the theatre, Ned set out on Will's horse with even more than his usual eagerness for the next Sunday rendezvous at Charing Cross. She was not there. At first he was annoyed that Jane had not shared his eagerness, but annoyance gave way to anxiety when he had waited a full half-hour. Something was amiss and he had to find out what it was. The Grimsbys might know. After waiting for nearly an hour, he set off for the Hargreave Arms at a gallop.

To his worried surprise he found the front door of the inn locked. He knocked on it, but had to do so three times before there was any answer. Then he heard some bolts being drawn and a heavy key turned. The door was opened cautiously, just enough to reveal a partial sight of the host, who showed no signs of allowing Ned to enter.

Mark Grimsby said, with a surliness of which one would have thought him incapable, "We expected it might be you."

Taken aback, Ned said, "The Lady Jane. Is she here?"

Without answering the question, Mark said, "She does not want to see you; now or ever again."

"But is she here?" Ned insisted.

"Be on your way, young man."

Mark made to close the door, but Ned, becoming desperate, pushed fiercely against it, forcing Mark to stumble back. Once he was inside, Ned looked around wildly, now convinced that Jane was somewhere there and, for some inexplicable reason, hiding from him. Pushing the now frightened Mark out of the way he strode to the back parlor, which he thought of as belonging to him and Jane. It was empty, nor was there a fire in it. Returning again to the main room he saw that Mark had been joined by Esther, and they were both barring his way to the stairs. Mark had armed himself with a meat cleaver, which he held aloft menacingly. It was clear that Jane was upstairs, but Ned could not imagine why he was being prevented from seeing her. She must be sick. Was it the plague? The very thought stopped him from making an impetuous dash to the stairs.

"What ails her?" Ned asked, fearful of the answer, but he received none. "Answer me. I must know."

Esther said, "Be gone, young sir, and never come back."

Ned thought he detected a sad, almost sympathetic note in the voice, so he decided to play on it. Ignoring Mark, he said, "God knows I wish her no harm. Let me but see her. She would wish it."

"It cannot be," said Esther.

It was an impasse. Mark took a threatening step toward Ned, which released him into action. The agile younger man made a deft grab for the wrist of Mark's cleaver arm, and a confused struggle began. Esther hurried down the stairs to join in. She seized Ned's hair, trying to pull him loose from her husband. There was a noise of curses, grunts, screams, and squeals, but suddenly Esther cried out in alarm, "My lady!" The men stopped their struggle as they became aware of the apparition at the top of the stairs. There she stood in a nightgown, pale and weak, her long, fair hair loose about her shoulders, her hands grasping the banister for support.

"Let him come up," she said faintly.

"But my lady . . ." began Esther, but Ned was already climbing the stairs. He supported Jane back to the bedroom which she indicated silently. Esther was close behind, clucking piteously.

Soon Jane lay exhausted on the bed, the covers over her. Ned looked on dumbfounded as Esther whimpered words of disapproval on the edge of tears. Finally a gesture stopped her as Jane said quietly, "Tell him."

"No, my lady," expostulated Esther. "Nobody must know."

"Tell him," repeated Jane, and Esther had no choice but to obey.

In great distress Esther told her story. "She was with child by you. It could not be. Even with a lord it would have gone hard for her with the Queen, but with a player, it would have meant long imprisonment for her and worse for you. We dared not to tell anybody, so we could not ask for help. I gave her potions I knew about, but they did not avail. At last I . . . I . . ." Esther broke down completely.

Not knowing what else to do, Ned put his arms around Esther to comfort her. Out of her muffled sobs he heard her say, "I nearly killed her. I could not stop the bleeding. I know not what harm I have done her."

Jane, now somewhat recovered from the effort which had taken her to the stairs, said, "Leave us, Esther. Leave us."

Esther was loath to do so, but a smile and a slight movement of the head from Jane assured her that she should go. She went, drying her eyes with the back of her hand. She left the door open but Ned closed it.

When he moved back to the bed, Jane greeted him with a wan but warm smile. All he could find to say was, "I'm sorry. I'm sorry."

"Nay," she said. "If fault there was, it was mine as much as yours." Then she added with some approximation to her old sparkle, "Perhaps more."

"I wish we could have had the child," Ned said impulsively, taking her hand and falling to his knees.

"That could not be. We could never marry." Ned flinched. "That irks you, but so it is. And now I am tired. You must go."

"I shall come again next Sunday."

She smiled and nodded faintly. He kissed her hand, then rose and left the room.

The Grimsbys were waiting for him at the foot of the stairs. He strode out without a word and, as he mounted his horse, he heard the door being bolted and the key turned.

THIRTY

IT WAS RAINING HEAVILY WHEN NED RODE OUT TO THE HARGREAVE ARMS the following Sunday morning; he had not waited until the afternoon. By the time he arrived, he was drenched. He was pleased to find that the door was not locked. He opened it and went in.

There were some half-dozen travelers there who had come in for shelter from the rain and to have a leisurely dinner. Mark Grimsby was busy, but Esther was not in sight. Instead, a strange woman was doing the cooking.

Knowing the necessity for secrecy, Ned did not stop to question Mark, but started to go upstairs. Mark called out to him, "Wait." The tone had been urgent but not offensive. Ned waited until Mark had finished serving some ale and wine. Then Mark came to him, took him by the arm, and guided him to a private corner.

"How is she?" asked Ned fearfully.

"She's gone," said Mark.

"Gone?" echoed Ned blankly, assuming the worst.

"Yes, and my good wife with her." Ned was completely mystified. "They've gone back to the castle. They started out yesterday in a coach. 'Tis a long journey; far, far away in the north. She left this for you."

He gave Ned a piece of paper, folded but not sealed. The message was printed to hide her handwriting, and it was not signed. Dazed by the news, Ned opened the paper slowly and read, "I shall remember you. Remember me and fare well."

" 'Tis better like this, young sir," Mark said with compassion. "You are wet. There is a fire in the parlor. Go dry there." But Ned walked out into the rain and rode away.

It was late August before he heard word of Jane, and by then he could accept it with a smile: she was to be married, with the Queen's approval, to Lord Berkeley. The news came from George, who was excited to be tailoring his young lordship for the wedding. Ned was able to be generous enough to hope that Jane had found a worthy bed partner, and that Esther's bungling surgery had not robbed her of children.

On Friday, September 4, Stratford again thrust itself into the lives of the three Shakespeare brothers in London. Twice or three times a year Will received a letter of family news from Richard which he shared with the others. But it was not a letter which arrived on that first Friday in September; it was Richard himself. He had gone straight to Gilbert's house, and together they had come to the theatre.

The play was *Hamlet,* now given in a shorter form. After the excitement of the first performances, the one-thirty opening had led to much confusion; there was a memorable day when the play had been stopped by a fight between late-comers and those already absorbed in the play. But even now the play lasted for two and three-quarters of an hour.

Richard had arrived at Gilbert's house just before two o'clock and wanted to go to the theatre at once, but Gilbert persuaded him to wait until the end of the performance. They could get there very quickly by boat; the Globe was just across the river from Blackfriars. In the meantime, Gilbert could make his own arrangements with George to accompany his brother back to Stratford.

Not knowing what play was being given that afternoon, Gilbert assumed it would be over soon after four o'clock and arrived accordingly. He had much trouble to get the doorkeeper to let them in backstage before the performance was ended, but threats of Will's displeasure finally gained the brothers admittance.

Richard was both excited and scared by the strange world he found himself in: boys dressed as women, courtiers and peasants hurrying quietly about, a world of urgent whispers and muted confusion; and in the near distance voices whose words he could not distinguish, but which brought laughter from a large unseen crowd.

Both Will and Ned had finished their performances, and very soon the four brothers were closeted in the bookholder's room where they were free to talk above a whisper. As soon as the door was closed, Gilbert told Will and Ned the news: "Our father is dying."

Ned felt guilty at his reaction; though he was sad, he should feel more. But death was natural, and his father was old; not as old as the Queen, but still old.

Will was talking to Richard. "There is no chance that he will live?"

"None. Even now he may have gone." Richard felt somehow embarrassed to be talking about death to Will who was dressed as a ghost.

"We must all go home. Pray God we may be in time. It would please him to have us all with him at the end."

"Can we leave now? We have finished onstage," said Ned.

"No," said Will. "We must wait until the end. It won't be long. There are arrangements to be made. I may be away a long while." Ned noted that Will had said "I," not "we." Will continued: "We must start at first light in the morning."

"The morning?" Ned said in surprise. "We are four. It would be safe to set out tonight. We could get miles out of London before it was really dark." Ned's eagerness to start was to compensate for his sense of guilt at not being appropriately affected by the imminence of his father's death.

Richard said, "Will is right, Ned. If we get an early start and ride hard, we need spend only one night on the road."

"You can stay with us, Richard," said Gilbert, feeling sure that, in the emergency, George would not object.

After the performance, Will told Ned to go home as his own meeting with the sharers would take some time. This puzzled Ned. A minute or two with John Heminge and Tom Vincent would surely have been enough.

The sharers were equally puzzled to be called together. When one of them had to be away for some time, and only sickness or urgent family affairs made that necessary, it was enough to let John Heminge and the bookholder know.

When they had commiserated with Will on his reason for leaving, there was a moment of awkwardness. Will clearly had more to say, or he would not have asked for the meeting. "This news about my father serves but to strengthen a resolution that has been growing in me. I may stay in Stratford."

"For good?" said Gus Phillips, expressing the consternation of all of them.

Will smiled. "I doubt that. But for some time. If my father dies, I shall be the head of the family, and there will be much to do."

This last reason did not sound a very convincing justification for a long absence. Richard Burbage asked, smiling, "Is it that you want peace to write another *Hamlet*?"

"No," replied Will, also with a smile, "*Hamlet* drained me. I feel no other play in me. Not yet."

"I beg you, Will, another comedy," said Robert Armin with such clownish pathos that they all laughed.

"Above all, I feel no comedy in me, Robert. It may be that Stratford will give me one. If it does, I shall come post haste back to London with it."

"Will Ned stay with you too?" asked Gus Phillips.

"No," said Will definitely. "Stratford cannot contain him. But then he has no daughters to see, as I do. I doubt not he will be back as soon as may be. Now we must part. The company is waiting, and they will be straining at the bit."

Will had asked Tom Vincent to hold the company so that the substitutions for himself and Ned could be announced for the casts of the forthcoming plays. Speedily the other sharers bade Will farewell and hoped he would be in time to see his father alive. Nobody expressed the hope that he might find him on the road to recovery; it was generally assumed that his time of death had come. After all, Will himself was a middle-aged man of thirty-seven.

Will was up more than an hour before dawn, and Ned was annoyed with himself that Will had to wake him.

They rode over the Bridge at first light. Ned's mount had been hired from a local stable at two shillings for the first day and one and a half shillings for every day thereafter. This arrangement pleased Ned, for it put a premium on his quick return.

Gilbert and Richard were waiting for their brothers, and they set out together at once, Richard riding with Will and Gilbert with Ned. Richard had found his night's stay embarrassing. While George had welcomed him to the house and been properly sympathetic about his father, Richard was aware of George's deep resentment that Gilbert was going away indefinitely. There had been frequent variations on the theme: "I shall have to get someone to take your place. It will not be difficult. London is full of young men eager to earn some money, and willing to do anything for it. So don't feel in any hurry to come back, Gilbert."

During the times when the horses were held to a walk, conversation was called for. Ned wanted to talk about his father and the possible consequences of his death, but Gilbert's taciturnity made it clear that he had other things on his mind, and finally he blurted out, "Ned, George is sometimes cruel, very cruel." It was the beginning of a long recital, but Ned's early sympathy soon faded when he realized that Gilbert was enjoying his suffering. Ned was grateful when the leading pair spurred their horses into a gallop. But then, in a flash of self-knowledge, he realized he should not condemn Gilbert, for he himself had enjoyed a similar self-righteous martyrdom in the weeks following the Essex rebellion.

Will and Richard, when the pace of their horses allowed it, talked of Stratford. The tie between the two brothers had become strong. While Richard, who was now twenty-seven, would still have preferred his eldest brother to have become a respected citizen of Stratford rising in time to be bailiff like his father before him, he could not fail to be impressed by Will's ever-growing reputation and affluence, exaggerated accounts of which were always current in the town. Richard, too, as the representative of his absent brother, was treated with an increasing respect, though he had no desire to turn this to his own advantage. Once, when his mother had suggested he might one day become a burgess, and then an alderman, and finally bailiff, Richard had only smiled and shaken his head. His father had laughed the idea to scorn, "What! Richard!" he had said. "He doesn't belong in a council chamber. He would sit there mumchance among all those prating knaves, and because he said nothing, they would think he had nothing to say. 'Tis as well there is a man of few words in the house to balance me, who am a man of too many." John had laughed uproariously at his self-criticism, and Richard had not been at all offended by the description of himself.

But John was not the only garrulous man in the Henley Street home. William Hart had married Joan two years before and now lived there. John still held his son-in-law in some contempt—"He prefers talking to women to talking to men, and what kind of man is that?"—but he was glad that Joan was married, especially since she was thirty before that desirable event had occurred, and a grandson, now more than a year old, had brought great joy to John and Mary. He was christened "William," and in reporting that fact in a letter to Will, Richard betrayed a surprising sarcasm. "The baby is named for his father, but I dare swear that his parents rejoice that it is also the name of his rich uncle."

Will's questions to Richard on the ride were nearly all about the Henley Street household. After he had been assured that Anne, Susanna, and Judith were all well, New Place was scarcely mentioned between them. Richard told Will that their father had had great difficulty in breathing for some months and then, a week ago, a seizure had bereft him of movement and speech. He still struggled to speak and was obviously infuriated that his family could not understand him. Mary pretended that she could, just to appease him.

By hard riding they got to Oxford that night. John Davenant was lugubriously delighted to see them. The expression of his face and the tone of his voice expressed little difference between his joy in welcoming them and his sorrow in learning the reason for their journey, but both feelings were genuine. He was still looking for a second wife, but was taking his time, to be certain of finding a healthy one who could give him a son that would live.

The brothers were determined to be away again at dawn and to make the long ride to Stratford by nightfall, so they went to bed almost immediately after supper and were glad to do so; they were tired and sore.

Will woke first and lit a candle to dress by. The light woke Richard, who went to the room where the others slept, to wake them. John Davenant, who considered himself more friend to Will than just taverner, was downstairs before the brothers and preparing a large breakfast for them; he said that this would save them time as they need not then make a long stop for dinner.

Even so it was past seven o'clock and almost dark before they crossed Clopton Bridge. After a momentary thought of going first and briefly to

New Place, Will decided to go directly with his brothers to Henley Street; it would be too ironic if, after this strenuous effort to arrive in time to see his father alive, he would be cheated by an unnecessary half-hour's delay.

The sounds they made in stabling their horses brought Will Hart out of the house. He was so overjoyed because his prognostication that they would arrive that night had been fulfilled that they had some difficulty in learning from him the state of their father. It seemed that he was still alive, but barely. "He breathes and his heart beats, but no more."

"Is Anne here?" asked Will.

"No," replied Will Hart. "She took the children home about an hour ago."

The first sight that greeted the brothers when they entered the house was a poignant picture of life, not death. Joan was suckling her baby son at the fireside. In his mind's eye, Will saw Anne nursing Hamnet in that very place.

Joan welcomed her brothers with a smile and a quiet word; it was the sleeping baby rather than the dying father which muted her speech.

Without more words, the brothers went quietly upstairs. Their mother heard them coming and was standing to receive them when they entered the bedroom. She hurried into Will's arms first and broke into quiet sobs. As she quietly greeted the others, Will looked across his mother to the bed where his father lay. The rosy and well-fleshed man had become gaunt and gray. His breath was fast and labored, his mouth open, his eyes staring and lifeless.

Mary begged Will to speak to his father, and when he seemed doubtful she said, "He may be able to hear us. I have been talking to him all the time."

Will took his father's cold and unresponsive hand. He bent over him and spoke quietly but with the care one uses in speaking to the deaf. "It's William, Father. I have come from London to see you. It's your son, William. Gilbert and Edmund are here too." He spoke the full names because his father had always frowned upon abbreviations. He used to say, "That is not the name he was given in church. It is not the name God knows him by, nor is it the name that I know him by."

While Will tried to make his presence known to his father, Richard spoke to his mother. "When did he last take food?"

"Not since Wednesday, and then but a little gruel."

"No water even?"

For answer Mary sadly shook her head. Then she took up the attempt to reach her husband with words, grasping his other hand.

"John, your sons have come home to see you. It's a long time since all our children were home together. And John, Edmund is a full man now. We have not seen him since he became twenty-one."

Will thought he detected a flicker of life in his father's eyes. Could it be that jealousy for his wife's love of their youngest born could reach him when nothing else could?

Richard insisted that his mother should go downstairs with the others for a short rest while he stayed with his father, and she reluctantly consented to be led away by Will.

Downstairs she suddenly caved in and became a very tired, very sad, old lady. Joan made her take some bread dipped in hot meat broth; the three broken stumps of black teeth, which were all she had left, made mastication difficult.

When Will Hart returned from New Place, where he had gone to tell of Will's arrival, Joan insisted that she and her husband would sit with her father. But after Will had left and her three other sons had been made to go to bed, Mary joined the Harts. Then they too went to bed and she was alone again with her dying husband.

Thus it was that it was only Mary who was with John when he died during the night. The end came with one brief struggle for breath and a rattle in the throat. Mary was calm at the end. She did not cry out or call for the others. Pressing on his head and his chin, she closed his mouth, then kissed him gently on the lips. She closed his eyes and kissed them, adjusted the bedcovers neatly and crossed his hands on his breast. After making the sign of the cross over him, she knelt by the bed and prayed for the repose of his soul; she knew that Puritan Vicar Byfield would not do that.

THIRTY-ONE

IN SPITE OF HIS TIREDNESS, RICHARD WAS THE FIRST TO WAKE. HE WENT straight to his father's room. Mary had nodded asleep, and his approach woke her. She said, "He's gone, Richard. He went in the night." Seeing dismay on her son's face that he had not been called, she added, "You were very tired. You all were tired. There was nothing you could do. And now it is I who am tired. I think I will go and rest for a while. You should go and tell Will. He is the head of the family now. If the others are still asleep when you come back, you can wake them then."

As Richard walked to New Place, the world was beginning to stir. Cocks were crowing lustily, pigs were grunting for food, and one or two travelers were already setting out on long journeys. It was Monday morning, the first workday of a new week. Richard's mind was full of the practical things to be done. He could leave it to Joan to prepare the mourning bed for the widow, but he would have to make arrangements for the coffin. Then he would go to see the vicar. The burial would be the next day, Tuesday. His father would have liked music and crosses carried in procession, but the vicar would have none of that; it smelt of popery and idolatry. But the bailiff and aldermen and burgesses must be told; perhaps some of them would come to the funeral, though few of them knew his father; it had been fifteen years since he had been disgowned for nonattendance at Corporation meetings, and it was years before Richard was born that he had been bailiff. Still, some of the Corporation might come as a favor to Will; it was he who should ask them. Then there was the funeral feast which could safely be left to Anne. She would have the help of Susanna, now, at eighteen, an impressive young lady of marriageable age. Judith, two years younger, was going to be heartbroken at the loss of her grandfather; they had always been very close.

When he got to New Place, he was not surprised to find that Anne was already up and at work in the kitchen. She had expected that John would die in the night. Her concern now was for the widow who had spent herself in caring for the sick man. Yes, she would see to all the funeral baked meats and sweetmeats and ale, if Richard would see to getting the wine. Now he should go up to wake Will.

Will was so fast asleep that Richard was reluctant to wake him. When he did so, Will took a little time to know where he was.

When Richard gave the news that their father was dead, Will was silent for a moment and then said, "Mother will miss him very much. I thank God she has you."

Richard smiled and said, "I think she will find more comfort in Joan's baby."

Richard outlined the funerary duties of the various members of the family as they appeared to him. Will was grateful that his brother was taking so much upon himself; Richard was assuming the main burden of his father dead as he had of him living. Will agreed to approach the bailiff about official representation of the Corporation at the funeral.

"Who is it now?" he asked.

"Richard Quiney has just been elected again."

"Then it should be easy," observed Will wryly. "He thinks I have more power in London and money everywhere than I have. Oh, how I wish Father could have been buried in the chancel of the church! It would have meant so much to him, a final thumbing of the nose at the men he felt scorned him."

"That cannot be; we have no tithe land."

"Then I must see about acquiring some," said Will jocularly. "To justify Father, some Shakespeares have got to get buried inside that church."

The two sisters were finishing dressing when Will went in to see them.

Anne had been before him with the news, and, in anticipation of the inevitable, she had already provided dresses of mourning black for them. Neither of them was crying. Susanna was playing the part of mature comforter, pointing out that their grandfather had been spared to live longer than most men. When the girls saw their father, Susanna, as the elder, was the first to embrace him. She did so warmly and genuinely, but spoke conventional and neatly chosen words of sorrow for her grandfather's death. Judith hung back. When Will held out his arms to her, she saw the understanding in his face and rushed into his arms, where she broke into convulsive sobbing.

Later that morning Will sought out Richard Quiney and found him outside the Guildhall, and in an unusually bad humor. With a soured face, he said, "Ah, Will. I thought you might be here. Were you in time to see the old man alive?" The news of John's death had spread fast.

"Alive, but beyond speech and hearing."

"He may have known you. I hope he did."

"You are bailiff again, I hear," said Will, wanting to get quickly to the subject of his visit.

"Not if the Lord of the Manor has his way. Sir Edward Greville opposes my election. Sir Edward!" This last was said with blistering sarcasm. "All those knighthoods that were impudently granted by the traitor Essex should be revoked. He's an evil man, Will, an evil man, this Greville. His blood is bad. Was his father not pressed to death for murder? And did he not himself kill his elder brother?"

"But that was an accident with bow and arrow," Will interposed.

"Accident! So it was given out, but the father said it was the best shot his son had ever made."

"Why does he oppose you now?"

"Because I stand for the rights of the citizens of Stratford, which he would buy up and trample on. Earlier this year I led men to tear down the fences when he tried to enclose still more of our common land. I shall fight him here and in the courts of London. You are a man of property here in Stratford, and you are a man of standing in London too. You must help us."

"How?"

"I know not how, but when the need arises I shall call on you. I have tried to see Sir Edward Coke, the Attorney General, and I have good reason to hope that he will stand us in good stead."

All this while men were decorating the Guildhall with bunting and flags. Will looked at them and then questioningly at Richard Quiney.

"Know you not what day it is, and you from London too?" queried the bailiff in disbelief. He continued in response to Will's shake of the head. " 'Tis the Queen's Birthday. Her sixty-eighth. A remarkable woman, Will. We are blessed in her."

Will remembered now the discussion among the sharers of how best they should honor the occasion; it had been decided to present *A Mid-*

summer Night's Dream, which contained Will's boyhood remembrance of the great water pageant at Warwick Castle on the occasion of the Queen's visit. Will had been taken there by his father, then a prominent and prosperous citizen, who had already been bailiff some years before. And now the Queen was sixty-eight and his father was dead. These thoughts brought Will back to his purpose. He said, "My father once was bailiff of this town."

Something in the abrupt change of subject or Will's tone made Master Quiney wary in his answer. "A long time ago, Will, when I was only a boy. Had you even been born then?"

"Oh, yes. I was four years old. I remember sitting on his lap in the Guildhall when he graced the players who had come to town. He was wearing his robe. I can feel the fur trimming now."

"That's one thing no bailiff of Stratford will ever do again, be patron to players, for no plays will be allowed here again." This was said with a puritancial earnestness which showed that Richard Quiney was a politician who reflected the mood of the community. Will remembered when Quiney had rejoiced in the players; but he thought it wiser not to remind him of that now. Instead he said, "It would please my father and put me in your debt if you came to the funeral tomorrow, and in your bailiff's gown."

"That is impossible, Will," Quiney blustered. "It cannot be. To begin with, I have not been confirmed as bailiff, and your father had become an enemy of the Corporation. He said vile things about us. And even after you had cleared him of his debts and gained him a coat-of-arms, he still would not be seen in town, or even come to church."

"But he is dead, and while he lived he hurt only himself. It was his pride that caused him to suffer. He was a good man, Richard, and did much good for this town until he felt the town had turned against him. Be generous and do him honor; if not to please him, then to please me."

"But I am not yet confirmed in my office."

"The town cannot be without a bailiff, and who is he, if not you? It is Sir Edward Greville that stands in your way, but it cannot be for long; the Corporation will be behind you. Besides, to wear your gown and chain of office in public will be an act of courageous defiance. Will you not wear them today to honor the Queen?"

"Yes," conceded Quiney reluctantly.

"Then wear them tomorrow to honor my father, and I shall be ever grateful."

"The vicar will frown upon it, and your word will not weigh with him at all, for you are openly the Devil's man, a player."

"It is my brother, Richard, who will speak to the vicar. And if I am the Devil's man, my wife is still more surely God's woman. Besides, is not this vicar Sir Edward's man?"

"Yes," replied Quiney angrily, "and that is not right. It is the Corporation that should name the vicar."

"My father agreed with you. Before he retired from public life, he was a staunch supporter of town rights. I beg you, Richard, to remember that and honor him tomorrow. Besides, this Sir Edward lives not in Stratford but in Milcote, across the river. And does he not spend much of the time in London?"

"Yes. He is there now, but his men and his spies are here, and none is more his man than Vicar Byfield."

"But the vicar must be mindful of his congregation too, and of none more than Richard Quiney. He needed Sir Edward to become vicar, but he needs the support of his parishioners now."

Will read in Richard Quiney's face that he had still not succeeded in his mission, so he decided to tell him something he had not even told Anne yet. As he did it, he despised himself. "Richard, I am not returning to London this time. Perhaps I never shall. The time has come for me to take my rightful place here in Stratford. It may well be I shall need your help in some affairs I have in mind. But the name of Shakespeare must stand high again in people's opinion. As a sign of that, you must walk in my father's funeral tomorrow in your bailiff's gown, and you must be accompanied by as many aldermen and burgesses as you can muster. If Stratford denies me this, I am no longer its friend."

In that last sentence, Richard Quiney correctly read his own name for that of Stratford. After a moment's further hesitation, he smiled broadly, grasped Will's hand and said, "It shall be done. 'Tis right and proper that the Corporation should honor a former bailiff. I care not for Greville or his vicar. I am no craven."

WHEN WILL GOT TO HENLEY STREET, HE FOUND THE HOUSE TRANSFORMED into a place of black gloom. The Harts had slept little during the night, for there was much to do to prepare the house of mourning. It was a matter of pride that there should be black everywhere, and Joan saw to this. Her husband's main function was to prepare the corpse, which he washed and shaved and shrouded, and placed on a truckle bed awaiting the coffin. The focus of the black display was the widow's bed, which had been the conjugal bed and from which Mary could now look on the dead body of her John. Anticipating the inevitable, Joan had collected by buying, borrowing, and searching through the family cedar chests an impressive assortment of black coverings, pillows and decorations in which her mother now lay in a black nightgown. When Will saw his mother, he was filled with a compassionate love for her, she looked so frail and old, yet she seemed strangely at peace.

Soon the house was filled with a muted buzzing of coming and going.

Most of the visitors seemed more desirous of a word with Will than with his mother. He was a phenomenon to goggle at, a successful adventurer from the strange, dangerous and wicked world of London. It may be that he did the work of the Devil, but it was said that the Queen herself had favored him. Although Will knew that as head of the family it was his duty to stay and receive condolences, his patience began to wear thin. He was glad when Richard returned home and the two brothers could excuse themselves and go into the shop. Richard had completed his missions of the morning: the coffin would be delivered in the afternoon, and the funeral would be at eight in the morning.

"What did the vicar say?" asked Will.

"He said it took death to bring Father back to the Church again."

"Will he speak at the graveside?"

"But briefly, he said. He was so churlish about it that I paid him no more than I had to."

"He will be surprised when he sees the bailiff and some members of the Corporation there." Richard was delighted by Will's account of his conversation with Richard Quiney. "Think you the vicar will come back to the house after the service?"

"Yes, because he is partial to Anne's cooking. He is a valiant trencher-man, though he has no paunch."

"I have noted in many Puritans that they inveigh against all pleasures of the flesh except that of the stomach."

Richard laughed aloud, but stopped abruptly when he realized that his levity might be heard. Will was surprised and pleased by the revelation of a new lightness of attitude in Richard; a few years before he would have been as incapable of criticizing the vicar as of criticizing God.

"Richard, I want to talk to you about this house. While Mother lives, it is hers and all that is in it; but what then? More than to anyone it should belong to you, and, if you get married, it must be yours."

"I doubt I shall get married, Will. I am content with my life as it is."

Will longed to probe into this statement, but respected Richard's privacy. He said, "Then this is it, provided you approve. The house should continue as it now is, with Mother, you, and the Harts all living in it."

"I thought nothing else." Richard added, with a smile, "Will Hart would have trouble providing another home for his wife and child."

"Is life in the house with him easy?"

"He talks a lot but there is no ill will in him. It was Father's voice that used to fill the house. Now it will be Will Hart's. But there is a big difference. Willikins does not mind if you don't listen."

When the coffin was delivered, Will took his mother into the Harts' bedroom while the corpse was being transferred. They sat together on the bed, and Will put his arm around her. He had often marveled at the close-ness of the bond between his parents. He knew that the widow's tears would come in her lonely nights and was glad that Joan's little boy would occupy his grandmother's days.

When they went back into her room, Mary stopped to look at John in his coffin. She bent down and kissed his forehead. The smell of death was countered by aromatic herbs. She said, "I hope his spirit can see his funeral tomorrow. He would be proud and happy."

When the last of the condoling visitors had gone, the whole of the family with the exception of the little grandson gathered in the bedroom. Nine people crowded around the bed, though all were careful not to obstruct Mary's view of the corpse. It seemed that John was part of the circle, the grayness of his death look emphasized by the flickering, black funeral candles. In spite of the herbs, the stench of decay was now strong in the room; for the young people there, it was the first time they had ever experienced it, and they would never forget it.

Most of the conversation was practical, about arrangements for the morrow. Mary was concerned about what Ned would wear, but Gilbert had brought two mourning suits with him. Judith said that she and Susanna had picked evergreens for the mourners to carry. Joan wanted to sleep with her mother that night, but Mary would not hear of it. She said, "This is the last night that your father and I will sleep together in this room."

One by one they kissed her goodnight, and she asked them to do the same to their father and grandfather. Judith was the last, and, when she kissed the cheek of dead flesh, she burst into wild tears. Her father took her in his arms to comfort her, but she cried all the way home.

THIRTY-TWO

RICHARD QUINEY KEPT HIS WORD, AND JOHN WOULD HAVE BEEN PROUD OF his funeral procession. It was led by the bailiff in his gown and chain, preceded by the leather-uniformed Sergeant-at-Arms bearing the silver mace. To protect himself from criticism, Quiney had managed to persuade three of the fourteen aldermen and six of the fourteen burgesses to follow him in the procession. They had been garnered at the Queen's

Birthday supper the night before, when, in the atmosphere of good fellowship, tales had been told about "old John Shakespeare" which found laughter in remembering him as cantankerous and opinionated but a good citizen. "He would have stood no nonsense from Sir Edward Greville. We could do with more of his kind today."

The morning was clouded, but it did not rain, and a goodly number of friends and neighbors laid aside their tasks for an hour to do honor to the family. Will was glad to see his old friend Hamnet Sadler among the bearers. He did not know all of them; Richard had made the arrangements.

Ten members of the family walked by twos behind the coffin: Will with his mother, Gilbert with Anne, Richard with Ned, Joan with her husband, Susanna with Judith. Each of the mourners carried a spray of yew or rosemary. As soon as the procession left the house, some neighborly women set about preparing the tables of food and drink for the return.

Vicar Byfield met the procession at the lich-gate. He had learned at the Queen's Birthday supper of the intention that the Corporation should be represented at the funeral and he had argued vigorously against it, but he had been overborne by Richard Quiney with the words, "This is something you cannot understand, Vicar. You are but five years come to Stratford. John Shakespeare was bailiff more than thirty years ago, and a good one. He did much for this town."

"I know that the vicar at that time was William Butcher, and he was dismissed for popish practices," Vicar Byfield had snapped. "It is likely that this John Shakespeare had kindred leanings. Certain it is that he came not to church when it had been cleansed."

But the bailiff had had the last word. "I know not John Shakespeare's beliefs about religion, but tomorrow we honor the bailiff."

The vicar had been in a quandary ever since. While he could not refuse to officiate at the burial, he had meant to show his disapproval by making the service as short and perfunctory as possible, but the official presence of the bailiff, the aldermen, and burgesses complicated the situation. Furthermore, the vicar was well aware that his patron, Sir Edward Greville, was opposed to Richard Quiney. Had Sir Edward been at home, he would have submitted his problem to him; in his absence in London, he prayed to God for guidance.

The vicar led the procession from the lich-gate to the grave, intoning, "I am the resurrection and the life, saith the Lord . . ." He had decided that, in view of the unexpected impressiveness of the gathering, he had better say a few words about the deceased, but he would not be a hypocrite and give praise where praise was not due; yet he must not give unnecessary offense to the living, especially when the family included such a godly woman as Mistress Anne Shakespeare; the widow too, and the son and daughter who lived with her, had all been zealous in church attendance. He had carefully weighed his words in advance and hoped he would be able to abide by them, but the temptation of a surprisingly large group of people around an open grave was hard for the spirit to resist.

He began conventionally enough. "We are gathered here to commit the body of John Shakespeare to the ground and his soul to God. I scarce knew the man because, for reasons known only to himself and God, he came not to church in my time, but the presence here of some of our leading citizens shows that he was honored in his day. He leaves behind a sorrowing widow and five children. Some of those too are unknown to me, for they have chosen to live their lives far from Stratford." He had meant to leave the reference to the London sons at that and to return to his favorite theme that the gaping grave should teach us to live every day as though it were our last, but he chanced to look at the youngest son, who, instead of standing with head bowed as was fitting for the occasion, was staring him full in the face, with even a hint of contempt and defiance. Vicar Byfield was challenged, and the spirit rose within him. "Yes, to live far from Stratford and from Stratford ways. This is a godly town and there is no place in it for those who make their living in ungodly ways. Let them ever remember this day. God is not mocked. To the grave we must come, and then begins the real life, the full life, of torment or joy, of burning fire or heavenly light, when we shall be judged for eternity by our lives here on earth. At this very moment John Shakespeare stands before his Judge. Now he bewails the fact that he scorned the haven of the Church. Be warned by his example all who stand here and do the works of the Devil, laying up for yourselves treasures on earth where moth and rust do corrupt."

A growing embarrassment had spread among the bystanders. Suddenly Mary burst into tears. Will put his arm around her to comfort her. The climax came when Ned, in whom anger had been mounting, violently threw his sprig of rosemary into the grave and stalked away. Richard called after him but he was deaf. The vicar was beside himself and shouted, "God will show you no mercy. Christ will turn his face from you. Be gone, back to the Sodom and Gomorrah where you belong."

Never had his congregation seen the vicar so uncontrollably upset. Richard Quiney moved to him, and grasped his arm to restrain him. Slowly he recovered, ashamed of his outburst, but not of his sentiments. He caught a look from Anne Shakespeare of understanding and pity, and it helped to restore him. Lifelessly he intoned the prayer of committal of the body to the ground, not even noticing the ironic description of the dead man as "our dear brother."

When the service was over and the family had cast their evergreens into the grave, the vicar moved to speak to the widow. He was grateful that he could not see her face—it was lost to sight under a thick black veil. He said, "You must excuse me, Mistress Shakespeare, but you will understand why I cannot come to your house now. But be assured of my prayers and sympathy. I will visit you tomorrow, when we can be alone together, and of course I shall expect to see all the family in church on Sunday." Then he walked away swiftly, his cassock and surplice billowing out behind him.

The funeral procession reformed irregularly for the return to the house. By the time they had walked the mile to the end of High Street and were about to turn into Henley Street it was well past nine o'clock. Those who had come out of respect to the family were looking forward to the meal that lay ahead and were relaxed into pleasant and scandalous chatter, chiefly deriving from the events at the graveside. Next to Richard Quiney's house at the corner of High Street was Atwood's Tavern, which had been busy for some hours. As the procession came toward it, the bailiff saw a group of about six already drunken rowdies whom he recognized as being in the pay of Sir Edward Greville, for they had caused trouble on his behalf before. The hostile men lurched into the road and barred the way. Their leader was a powerful ruffian known behind his back as Jack No-Good, but to his face as Jack; nobody knew his surname, but he looked foreign and spoke with an accent; Sir Edward Greville was said to have found him in the Azores, some of those foreign parts that were more mysterious to most Stratfordians than the moon. He held up his large, calloused, and begrimed hand and called out, "Stop! You are not bailiff. Take off gown and chain. We will take them to Lord of Manor."

While the family halted some way back, the rest of the procession broke up and gathered around the bailiff. They were joined by other citizens, from the tavern and elsewhere. Soon there were over fifty of them, and all opposed to Sir Edward Greville and his louts. The politician in Richard Quiney welcomed the confrontation, for the odds were on his side, but the magistrate in him had to preserve the peace. He said, "Know you the occasion you interrupt? It is a funeral. Your master would disavow this deed of yours, for there is a curse on those who disturb the dead."

Sir Edward's henchmen were considerably shaken by this argument, but one of them managed to say, "The funeral is over. Where is the parson?"

"The funeral is not over," said Richard Quiney with all the authority of his gown and chain. "Look there," and he pointed back dramatically. "Look at the widow and her sorrowing family. If you have complaints, come to the Guildhall and I will answer them. And now, be out of our way. On, Sergeant."

But the sergeant could not go on without bumping into Jack No-Good which he had no intention of doing; that foreigner was too handy with a knife.

It was the diffident Hamnet Sadler who resolved the impasse. He stepped forward to speak to the Greville men and displayed a confidence which surprised those who knew him. "Your quarrel is with Master Quiney, but I speak for Master Shakespeare of New Place. You insult him and his family and it will go hard with you. He has powerful friends at the court of the Queen, and Sir Edward Greville would not wish to offend him. Give way at once, and I will plead with him on your behalf; else, you and your master must take the consequences."

There was a pause of indecision. Richard Quiney began to speak, but Hamnet Sadler held up his hand to stop him, and to everyone's amazement he stopped. Hamnet said, "You must forgive me, Master Quiney, but this is a Shakespeare matter, and must be kept so." No one was quicker to grasp the cleverness of the stratagem than the bailiff himself, and he was anxious to avoid a brawl by any means.

Jack No-Good finally muttered, " 'Tis well. But Richard Quiney is not bailiff till Sir Edward say so." He turned to his followers. "We have no quarrel with Master Shakespeare. Come." And he led the way back into the tavern.

Several men began to congratulate this surprising, new Hamnet Sadler, but he stopped them and walked back to report to Will. The procession made some vague attempt at reforming, but they had not far to go. Many of them left forthwith to resume their daily labors, for they could not spare the time to take a meal.

By the time the family got to the house it was already full, and the loud and eager chatter was in sharp contrast to the muted voices of yesterday. Now that the dead was buried, life was resumed. There was a moment of comparative quiet when Mary lifted her veil to thank the bailiff for coming, but then she was led upstairs by Anne and Joan to return to her widow's bed, and the chatter began again.

The minds of the family were on one subject: Ned. All the way back from the churchyard Mary had moaned about him, and her anxiety was intensified when she found he was not at home awaiting their return. Richard had immediately gone out to the stable and had returned to report that Ned's horse was gone. Then he went up to the bedroom and was relieved to find that Ned's things were still there. Gilbert kept wailing, "He shouldn't have done it. He shouldn't have done it." But Will's private comment to his brothers was, "I think Father would have approved of what he did." This was the ironic truth: while he lived, John found little to commend in his youngest son, but he would have found pleasure in Edmund's action at the graveside.

As soon as he had left the churchyard, Ned regretted his anger; it would cause his mother distress at a time when she needed comfort. When he was reasonably sure that the feasting friends of the family had left he would go to her. Besides, he himself was getting hungry.

When Ned returned to the house, it was Will Hart who heard him stabling the horse and came hurrying out to him. He poured out a torrent of words. "Where have you been? Your mother is beside herself with worry about you. That was a terrible thing you did at the grave.

Everybody is talking about it. Some devil must have possessed you. I have never seen the vicar so angry. You must beg his forgiveness before we all go to church on Sunday."

Ned made no attempt to stem the torrent. There were neighbor voices in the living room, but chiefly women's and not too many of those. Ned gave them no chance for questions, but went straight upstairs to his mother, leaving the frustrated Will Hart at the foot.

Only Will was with his mother. Her joy at seeing Ned was so great that he felt guilty anew. He embraced her and felt her tears on his face.

He sat on the bed and said, "Will, I'm hungry, and I don't want to go down there."

"I understand," said Will, smiling, and he left the room.

Ned said, "I'm sorry about this morning, Mother. The vicar made me angry. He should not have said those things about Father. God is his judge, not the vicar."

"You must learn to control your temper, my son, or it will bring you into great trouble. Of all my sons, you are the most like your father. Perhaps that is why I love you so much."

Like his father? Ned was amazed. His father had been loud and opinionated and dominating.

Mary went on, "Your father could not abide Vicar Byfield. Whenever he came visiting the house, your father always stayed in the shop or went upstairs. He used to say, 'I cannot suffer fools gladly.' But the vicar had the last word, did he not? Now, what shall we do when you come to church on Sunday?"

"I cannot stay, Mother. 'Twill be better that way. The vicar would want me to beg his pardon, and for Father's sake I will not."

"Gilbert too says he must leave," Mary said sadly.

He said, "Tell me, Mother, that you forgive me for my anger at the grave, and I care not what others think."

"You did it for your father, and for that I would forgive anything."

He bent down and kissed her.

Will returned with a tray laden with food and ale, which Ned began to devour with gusto, stopping occasionally to force his mother to take a bite. There was deep happiness in the room, and Will shared in it.

Later in the day Ned spoke with Gilbert and they agreed to leave early on Friday morning, aiming to get to London on Sunday afternoon. Both would have liked to leave a day earlier but felt that this would have caused their mother unnecessary pain.

When Will heard of his brothers' decision to leave on Friday, he told Ned that he would make it easier with their mother by telling her that it was necessary for Ned to take urgent messages to the company since Will himself had decided to stay in Stratford. "And this is true," added Will. "We must talk at length tomorrow." He went on to say with a smile, "Let us meet at my house in the morning, since the vicar is expected here, and I doubt you want to see him."

It rained heavily and persistently the following morning, and Ned was drenched during the ten-minute walk to New Place. He was pleasantly astonished by Anne's concern for him; she was at pains to find dry things for him to change into. He could not resist sounding her about his insult to the vicar. "I am truly sorry for my anger at the grave, Anne."

"That I am glad to hear. I cannot understand you, Ned; nor could I understand your father. I think you are much alike." Again that puzzling comparison.

"Would you like me to beg the vicar's pardon?"

"What is it to me? It is between you and your God. The vicar too was angry. I pity you both."

Will had a letter for Ned to deliver to Augustine Phillips. "I have asked him to let you have my room."

Ned could only stammer his thanks. Then he said, "But are you never coming back?"

"Never is a long time. I do not know."

"Will you not write more plays?"

"That I cannot stop. I have asked Gus to send me some of my books by a carrier. At the last moment I left them behind because I could not make such a gesture of farewell to London."

"Is there a new play in you?"

"The beginnings of one, a bitter one, one that maybe I must write but which may never be played. I have come to the watershed of my life, Ned. The waters will flow to another sea from now on. *Hamlet* showed me the way. I see a vast ocean of endeavor that I may be lost in."

Ned stayed for dinner at New Place and it was a quietly happy meal. Both girls had been warned by their mother not to refer to the incident at the graveside. Susanna itched to talk about it and thought she had found an innocent way to open the subject. She said, "The vicar was supposed to visit Grandmother this morning, but perhaps the rain will keep him away."

Anne quickly scotched her. "It will take more than rain to keep a good man like the vicar from doing his duty, and it is your duty now to bring in the egg custard and the apples."

But Anne was wrong about the vicar. He did wait for the rain to stop before setting out on his parish calls, and so it was that when Ned returned home he was greeted by Gilbert with the news that the vicar was upstairs with their mother and had asked to see him.

"I don't want to see him," said Ned vehemently.

"But think of our mother; it would please her. And the vicar seems no longer angry. He said, 'Tell him not to be afraid. I would but speak to him for the good of his soul.'"

"I am not afeared of him; as for my soul, I doubt he is the man to do it good."

"I beg you to let him talk to you and not to answer back. It will please all the family. I will leave you alone with him."

As he spoke, the vicar came down the stairs, and before Ned could move, he had been seen. The greeting was almost affable. "Ah, Master Shakespeare. I hoped for a word with you. I have been speaking to your mother about you. Shall we sit down?"

Gilbert excused himself and, reluctantly, Ned sat on a bench at the table opposite the vicar. "Your mother has said that your disgraceful conduct at the burial was out of respect for your father. God has commanded us to honor our father and our mother. We were both angry yesterday, you for your earthly father and I for our heavenly Father. If I sinned, I have asked God's forgiveness. For the sake of your immortal soul, do likewise. I will say nothing of the life you live in London, though I believe it to be evil. I only pray that in the fullness of time you will be brought to see the error of your ways; there will be joy in Heaven when you do. And now may God's blessing be with you."

The vicar stood and left without another word. Ned had stood too, out of genuine respect for the man whom he was seeing for the first time. There had been no fire and brimstone in his voice; just a simple sincerity and concern.

Ned hurried upstairs to his mother. His face was happy with relief of an ordeal well past. "I spoke to the vicar," he said, which was not strictly accurate but it sufficed to light up his mother's face.

Now Mary tried hard to persuade Ned to stay to go to church with the family on Sunday, but she did not prevail. Then she said the family must have a farewell supper the following night. At that meal Will sat in his father's place, with Anne happily at his right hand. There had always been tension between her and her father-in-law. Now it was all over, and her husband had come home to her and her children. She suggested that, after the service on Sunday, the family should go to New Place for dinner; it would be the first time. Will was delighted by the suggestion, and it was taken up enthusiastically. Anne was sincerely regretful that Gilbert and Ned could not be with them; she had been made very happy by Mary's calculated-to-please account of Ned's meeting with the vicar.

With no competition or curb from John, Will Hart chattered endlessly, but nobody minded because it left them free to eat and not to listen. Ned's thoughts were all on London. Without Will there, he would really be on his own, and the prospect was exciting. He had been delighted by the promise of Will's room, but now he was not so certain. He could not really afford to pay for it, but they would let him have it because of Will. Everything was because of Will and always had been. The Phillipses had been good to him because of Will. As long as he stayed in their house, he would always be the young brother of Will Shakespeare. In the company too. He should and could stand on his own feet. That prospect made the future exciting, but frightening too.

Book Four

1603

THIRTY-THREE

It was a Friday, and the last day of the year 1602, nearly sixteen months since John Shakespeare had died. For a whole week the weather had been so rough as almost to paralyze life in London and in the countryside. Will had set out from Stratford early on Monday, December 27, and it had taken him until Friday morning to reach the Phillips home. Both he and his horse were exhausted. But he had insisted on adhering to the plans Augustine Phillips had already made for a reading of one new play in the house on that Friday afternoon and of another on Saturday afternoon.

Augustine Phillips had been deputed to travel to Stratford in mid-December to urge Will to return to London, for the Lord Chamberlain's Men were in desperate need of him. They had run into new and unexpected competition from two sources.

More than a year before, Edward Alleyn had returned from retirement as inevitably as Will was to return from Stratford, and he and Philip Henslowe had built a splendid new theatre, the Fortune, deliberately modeled on, but outdoing, the Globe. The Fortune was located in the fields northwest of the city, beyond Cripplegate, and there they were drawing the town.

To go to the Fortune the Lord Admiral's Men had forsaken the Rose Theatre, but it had not remained empty. A new company now occupied it, the Earl of Worcester's Men. There had long been a company bearing that name, but it had traveled the country and had never had a London home until the fourth Earl of Worcester had felt that his growing power at court would be enhanced if the players under his patronage successfully rivaled the two established companies. The new company had a fresh vitality and talent, and their very novelty was attractive to many people who took delight in seeing the established and well-known challenged with spirit and skill. The Earl of Worcester's Men had also found some new writers, notably one of their players, Thomas Heywood.

The new company provided an opportunity for ambitious young men in the other companies who were condemned to minor parts for several years after their maturing voices robbed them of the feminine roles. Chief among these was the aspiring Christopher Beeston who had joined the Earl of Worcester's Men determined to make the company his own in the fullness of time; and with him he had taken Ned Shakespeare.

Ned had wanted to escape the shadow of Will and the Phillips home. During the year 1602, he had succeeded in both aims, and had regretted both escapes. He did well as an actor in the new company, but life was made unbearable for him in the Rose by the leading player—William Kemp. Having been driven from the Lord Chamberlain's Men by Will Shakespeare, Kemp gained some measure of revenge by driving Will's brother from the Earl of Worcester's Men. Paradoxically, Ned found it easier to forgive Kemp than to forgive Will, who had prompted the clown's vindictiveness. Ned's dismissal had come after he had been goaded into physically attacking Kemp, a lapse for which he would never forgive himself, for Kemp had become a fat, old man.

After his dismissal Ned spent a wild two months, drinking and whoring until his money ran out. He had not even the rent for the sleazy room he had found in a shabby, rat-infested house, most of whose lodgers were Thames boatmen. Fortunately, Augustine Phillips had kept his eye on him, for Ned lived close by. He even tried to get Ned back with the Lord Chamberlain's Men, but this was strongly opposed by John Heminge—and by Ned. It was a dismal and worrying report about Ned that Gus had carried to Stratford—and yet another argument for Will's return to London. Then too, Gilbert had written to Will, reporting that his own effort to help Ned was angrily repulsed. The only man who had seemed able to deal with him was John Lowin, an impressive new actor in the new company. He was a few years older than Ned, and had only turned actor after spending eight years as a goldsmith's apprentice. A Londoner born and bred, Lowin was a large man whose impact on stage, both in comedy and tragedy, was commensurate with his bulk. He was first attracted to Ned because he had unbounded admiration for William Shakespeare, but he had got to like Ned greatly and learned much from him. Although he quickly proved himself at the Rose to be a player of remarkable talent, John Lowin had not served an apprenticeship in the theatre and Ned was very happy to pass on what he had absorbed from six years of training and playing. During Ned's riotous excesses after his dismissal from the company, John Lowin exercised a little restraint on him, and was the only one from whom he would take rent money.

Neither Gus nor Will had any delusion about the difficulty of helping Ned. If Gilbert's offer had been fiercely refused, how much more would Will's. In his cups, Ned had spoken bitterly against him to Gus. He had said, "He did not want to help me, and I did not want his help. Now he is free of me and I of him. Let him rot in Stratford, while I rot in London."

Will told Anne about Ned, hoping that the need to help his brother would be a stronger reason in her eyes for his return to London than the need to help a company of players. She made no comment, but he knew she was thinking that the Devil had but claimed his own. She accepted Will's going without undue stress; she had learned to be grateful that he had stayed so long this time. She was even gracious, if not cordial, to Augustine Phillips who had come to take him away.

Will had tried to dig his roots deeper into Stratford soil by the purchase of a hundred and seven acres of tenanted land to the north of the town, but they were powerless against the surprise visit of Augustine Phillips, and Will was able to leave with a better conscience than usual because he had arranged that the new town clerk of Stratford, Thomas Greene, and his wife, Letitia, should come to live with Anne and the children at New Place, until such time as they found a suitable home of their own. (It was such a mutually happy arrangement that it was a long time before they moved. Two of their children would be born there.) Furthermore, Will had bought a cottage for a gardener near the house, so now both family and premises would be well looked after.

The two new plays Will brought with him were such as he had never written before. He had hinted to Gus that they might not please, but he would not be drawn further on the subject. Now, as he rested in his room in preparation for the reading of the first play that afternoon, he found his mind more occupied by Ned than by *Troilus and Cressida*. He had moments of annoyance that it should be so and was fleetingly tempted to do nothing until his brother came asking for help.

Letty brought his dinner to his room; it had been thought wiser to spare him the chatter of the family board. With Letty had come Gus, carrying some mulled ale; it was too bleak a day for a cold drink. He tried once more to persuade Will to postpone the reading for a day to give him time fully to recover from his arduous journey, but Will would have none of it. He said, "I am as eager to read this play to them as they to hear it, but for different reasons."

"We all long for another *Hamlet*."

"Then you will be disappointed. This is such a play as Hamlet might have written in his bitterest mood." Seeing Gus's worried look, he added, "I think 'twill play well, for there are good parts in it."

"And the new comedy, *All's Well That Ends Well*. That gives a pleasant promise."

"But it too may not please. It tells of the love of a wonderful woman for an unworthy man."

"And he is redeemed by her love, as Bassanio was by Portia's?"

"I know not. It may be so."

"But your title says so."

"Then it must be so," said Will, smiling at the perplexed look on the face of his friend.

The sharers all arrived in high spirits and bearing gifts for the three Phillips children in honor of the morrow which would be New Year's Day. A son, proudly named Augustine, had been born the year before.

Will was much moved by the sharers' greetings to him: 1602 had been a bad year without him; never again must he stay away so long; but the new year was bright with promise, for he had brought back two new plays with him. Will was filled with apprehension and guilt, because he knew of the disappointment for them which lay ahead.

At last the room and the privileged audience were ready, the other members of the household having been dispatched upstairs. The sharers were delighted and surprised by the opening of the play; they had not expected so much fun, and Armin's part was clearly yet to come. Then there was the thrilling speech by Ulysses on "degree, priority, and place." Augustine Phillips glowed as he listened to it, for he felt sure it would be his. How could Will have had such doubts about this play? But soon he knew. Pleasure gave way to uneasiness and, by the end of the play, to consternation. Here there was no heroism in war, no truth in love, no retribution for evil.

Heminge was the first to speak. "I doubt it will please, Will. 'Tis a brilliant and honest picture of the world as you now see it—and these are dark days when many of us see little light ahead—but that is all the more reason why our patrons come to us for warm laughter, true love, and heroic sorrow. This will have the taste of a too salty caviar to the general. We had all hoped for another *Hamlet*."

"I too," said Will, "and it may yet come, but not now, not now. This is what is in me now. I know not whether my vision of the gods and men is clouded or clear, but I like little of what I see."

Even Henry Condell, Will's most devoted admirer, voiced criticism. "I cannot stomach that death of Hector, struck down by the brutal Myrmidons while he was unarmed, and Achilles looking on as they perform his vicious command. Homer tells us that Hector died in single combat with Achilles."

"Call you it single when the goddess, Pallas Athene, fought at the side of Achilles? Think you that the gods play fair? There was a man in Stratford, Richard Quiney. We grew up together. He was the bailiff and strove hard to make Stratford prosper. I doubt not that the prosperity of Richard Quiney was what mattered most to him, but there was much good in the man. He often led his fellows against the grasping lord of the manor, Sir Edward Greville. A few months ago there was a clash between Sir Edward's lackeys and some citizens. Richard Quiney was killed, but not by an enemy; by one of his friends; it was an accident. I heard the gods laugh."

"Then Troilus," persisted Condell. "At least let him kill Diomedes, who stole Cressida from him. They just go off fighting."

"That is life, Henry: all fighting and no conclusion. Be glad that I did not let Diomedes kill Troilus."

There was an uneasy silence. Will broke it by saying, "Let us not do the play. I had to write it, but we do not have to play it."

This was greeted by expostulation from several of the players, all speaking at once, though John Heminge and Richard Burbage significantly said nothing. When the shapeless clamor had subsided, Thomas Pope expressed the first positive view. "We must do it. There are those who will like it mightily. There is an abundance of excellent parts in it." He saw himself as Pandarus.

"Yes," concurred Robert Armin with enthusiasm. Thersites would give him great opportunities.

"It is full of good things, as good as you have ever written, Will," said Augustine Phillips. "It is just that the heart of it is sour."

"What think you, Richard?" asked Will, for Burbage had said not a word.

" 'Full of good things,' says Gus. 'Excellent parts,' says Tom. Yes to all of that; and yes there are those it will please, though I fear it will set the teeth of the groundlings and the merchants on edge, but that we can only know when we play it. But what do I play in it?"

This nonplused the whole company, for they had all assumed that he would play Troilus.

Burbage continued. "Say not to me Troilus, for I will not do it. He must be a youth and I am not."

This time there was general protest but he silenced it.

"Yes, yes, Romeo. I still play it and I suppose I must, but I long for parts, Will, that my middle age can carry. You helped me in *Hamlet* by making the prince thirty at the end of the play, and, after all he had gone through, I'm sure he felt thirty, but this Troilus is a hotheaded, hotblooded youth, not come to the wisdom of years, and I will not play him. If we do the play, Hector must be my part."

This categorical pronouncement by the leading player overshadowed any further general discussion of the play. No arguments would shake him, and Will admired this. Richard Burbage was right, and Will made a mental vow that never again would he write a play in which the principal character was a young man.

It was agreed that they would all meet at ten o'clock at the theatre the next morning in case a performance was possible, though it was considered to be extremely unlikely. Still, it was a Saturday, and there would be an audience if the weather gave them any chance; the groundlings could be admitted to the top gallery if the ground was deep in snow. If there were no performance, Will would read his other new play, *All's Well That Ends Well;* several of them expressed hope and comfort in the title.

The snow had stopped by the time the other sharers had left, but there was still the threat of more in the air. As the household gathered, hoping for news of the reading, Will disappointed them by asking Gus up to his room, for he had something to discuss with him.

As soon as the door was closed behind them, Will said, "This play may not prove popular, it may not even be performed, but, if it is, let it do some good. Why should not Ned play Troilus? He has the youth, the looks, the temperament, and enough experience." Augustine Phillips was so surprised by the idea that he said nothing, and Will went on. "He could not refuse such a part. But we would have to be very careful in presenting it to him. It must not seem like an act of charity. You would have to come with me and do the talking. I would insert a line in the play to show that Troilus and Ned are exactly the same age. Let me see: how old is that? Ned will be twenty-three in a few months' time. Pandarus could say of Troilus, 'he never saw three-and-twenty.' What think you of it, Gus?"

"It can never be, Will. John Heminge would never allow it. He cannot forgive Ned for leaving the company. Christopher Beeston was a different matter. He had been playing the female parts, but not Ned. And Christopher asked our advice about leaving, but not Ned. Only the other day, John said, 'I hear Will's brother has gone to the bad. I am not surprised. 'Twould have been better if Will had left him in Stratford. We are well rid of him.' "

Will was indignant, a rare state for him. "That is not true, and I shall tell John Heminge so. There is good in Ned, both as man and player. All his troubles come from his fierce desire to be himself, not his father's son in Stratford and not my brother in London. Is that evil in a man? He wants to be grateful, but he would give much to put me in his debt as he is in mine. I beg you, Gus, to help me to help him."

"But John Heminge?"

"I will speak to him tomorrow. I will ask it as a favor, but Ned must never know that. If I win John over, I will speak to some of the other sharers, then you and I can seek Ned out on Sunday. What say you?"

" 'Tis a good plan, but John will be hard to win over. You are right about Ned and he is wrong. Ned is going through the testing time of manhood, but he will stand the test. 'Twould be well if he would marry."

"By his age I had three children. I am the only one of four sons to marry. 'Tis strange. But Ned is still awenching and awhoring. 'Tis a miracle he has not caught the pox."

After a slight hesitation Gus said, "He has, but let him not know I told you. It was his good friend, John Lowin, who told me. 'Twas not a serious dose, and some hot salt baths soon cured him. Then it was he took to drink; he said it was safer than women. . . . But about this Troilus of yours. There is something else. I should have spoken of it at once, but I liked not to dash your spirit. John Heminge already has the other Troilus: Alexander Cooke."

"I remember him as an apprentice of John's."

"In this last year he has come on by leaps and bounds. He is a good player, and is capable of a wide range of parts. Once, when Richard was sick, he played Romeo and did passing well, even though he lacks the fire of a handsome lover. I am sure that every man's mind jumped to him when Dick said he would not play Troilus. I am sorry, Will. 'Twas a good plan."

"I shall still speak to John about it."

The family supper was a disappointing meal because the two sharers were uncommunicative; it was clear to Mistress Phillips and Sam Gilburne that all had not gone well at the reading. Mary, now in her ninth year, was the life of the table. Will could not help contrasting the latitude she was given with the strictness Anne imposed on her daughters.

Anne Phillips could no longer restrain herself from asking, "When will you see Ned, Master Shakespeare?" Her tone was unconvincingly casual, for she was genuinely concerned about the "boy," as she still thought of him; she was forever pestering her husband with questions about him. Gus now gave her a reproving look, but Will answered simply, "Tomorrow I hope. Gus and I will visit him."

AT THAT SAME MOMENT JOHN LOWIN WAS CLIMBING THE RICKETY STAIRS TO Ned's attic room. He carried food, ale, and news.

He came upon a triumphant Ned, for he had just caught and killed a large and long-troublesome rat; he was convinced that it was the one that had bitten him several nights while he slept. Ned displayed the rat gleefully, but it was a few moments before the visitor could clearly see either happy hunter or dead victim, for the only light came from a guttering and smelly tallow candle; there was but one small window space, and its shutter had been closed against the snow.

It was some days since John had seen Ned, and he found him dirty, unshaven, and unkempt. He still took some pride in his appearance when he went abroad, but the bad weather had kept him indoors. He had spent most of the time on the flea-ridden straw pallet which was his bed, his chief activity being to catch the fleas as they bit. He had not ventured out to get water and had lived on the food and ale left from John's last visit, the food having been carefully preserved from the rats in the room's most precious piece of furniture, a tin box. The only other furniture in the room was a small, rough table, two plain stools, a now most insanitary wooden bucket, and a trunk which contained Ned's clothes and all the rest of his possessions, including a few much-read books. He had pawned most of what would bring any money, but not the books; even the Lady Jane's ring had gone.

Ned dropped the rat into the full bucket, splashing some excreta on the floor. "That's where he belongs," he said vindictively. "Let him eat and drink that, if he can."

John, who knew Ned well enough by now, ignored his condition and the stench of the room; remonstrance must come later, and then it must be subtle and gentle. He said, "Come, let's eat. I am hungry." To suggest that it was Ned who must be hungry would have been wrong; never had he known a man who more resented his own needs for help from others.

"I'll tell you a secret, John: to reduce hunger, stay indoors. I have not been out for days; I know not how many. But I am glad to see you. Yet I cannot think why you ventured out in such weather. I hope 'twas not just to bring me food and drink."

"I like your company when I eat."

"Then you are welcome to it, but 'tis scurvy pay for such good victuals."

The main purpose of John's visit was to bring the news of Will's return and to prepare Ned for a probable visit of his brother, who he had heard was in London. He knew he would have to be very careful in broaching the subject.

When they had eaten and gossiped about their acquaintances, it was Ned who made the first unprompted and welcome move to improve their surroundings. "That bucket; it stinks," he said. "I'll take it down and empty it." He added with inspiration, "And I'll scoop up a bucketful of snow to give me water when it melts." He concluded, with comic dolefulness, "Though 'tis so cold in this hovel, that 'twill more likely turn to ice."

While he was gone, John, as usual, put the remaining food and drink into the tin box. This had become an accepted part of a visit. When Ned returned, John said, "It has stopped snowing and some daylight is left, so I will open the shutter. We will shiver, but the candle is almost spent." It took some effort to make the rusty and iced hinges respond, but at last some fading daylight and some much needed fresh, though cold, air came into the room.

As they resumed their stools, John said, "Ned, I hear that your brother is back in London."

"And I can guess where you heard it; from Know-All Beeston."

"Yes," said John, waiting for further reaction before he said more.

"So he's back again," mused Ned. "I knew he couldn't keep away. When Gilbert told me he had bought land in Stratford, I laughed. Gilbert represented him at the signing of the documents. Will belongs here, as much as I do."

"Think you he will visit you?"

"Why do you ask? Is it that you want to meet him? Is that what I mean to you, a way to my brother?"

It was hard for John Lowin to contain his anger at this biting accusation, the more so because there was some truth in it. He said, with a controlled impressiveness, "If you think that, I will leave now and never come back."

After a moment of tense silence, Ned said, "Forgive me, John. That was unworthy. Yes, I think Gus Phillips will bring Will to visit me, and, as usual, both of us will think much and say little."

"Let him not see you as you are."

"Why not? It may cause him pain, but it will give me pleasure. I am what I am and wish to be no other."

"That is not true, Ned," said John forcefully. "Your pride should not let him see you in a state to pity you."

"My pride is in being myself and free. I pity him. He is not free."

"He will want to help you. Will you let him?"

"No. That is all over, and deep down he will be glad that it is."

"But what will you do? You cannot stay here and rot."

" 'Tis an easy life, if the weather were only better," said Ned exasperatingly.

John stood and said angrily, "I see you are in no mood to discuss a subject that matters much to me, and that is your return to life, and so I will leave you. When next I see you, I hope you will look and sound and smell like the Ned I once knew." He turned and left the room abruptly.

Ned was taken aback by John's unusual conduct. He ran to the door to call after him, but John ignored him. Ned turned back into the room and slammed the door with such force that he dislodged a pile of snow on the roof and set unseen rats and mice scurrying. Then he crossed to the window and pulled the shutter fast. In the gloom he found his way to his pallet and threw himself down on it, his mood sullen, his mind confused. Suddenly it struck him that Will might be so disgusted by the tales he would hear of his brother that he would not come to visit him, and it surprised Ned to find that this idea was not pleasing. He wanted Will to see him as he was.

THIRTY-FOUR

THERE WAS NO FURTHER SNOW DURING THE NIGHT, AND IN THE MORNING the sun shone. The flag was run up atop the stage-house to let the public know there would be a performance in the afternoon. The top gallery would be opened for half price; the groundlings could not be expected to stand in the deep snow and slush.

Little was needed in the way of rehearsal to prepare for *Richard III*. Once John Heminge, who played Lord Hastings, had checked his costume and properties, he was free to talk to Will who had asked to see him in the privacy of the bookholder's room. Overnight Heminge had become partially reconciled to the company's doing Will's *Troilus and Cressida,* not least because, now that Burbage refused to play Troilus, it would give a much deserved chance to Alexander Cooke, who had been his apprentice but had long graduated into an excellent hired man. True he was not particularly handsome or spirited; it was his versatility and consistency that made him so valuable to the company. Besides, he was an admirable young man who never caused trouble and was always willing to lend a hand at anything.

As soon as the two men were closeted Will asked, "Are you for our doing my *Troilus and Cressida,* John?"

"Yes. 'Tis full of good things and excellent parts, though I still doubt it will be well received. We can only try. At least our players cannot fail to have pleasure. I hope, Will, you will soon see the world again with your old eyes."

"That cannot be, John. I too hope that my vision will change, but 'tis of Ned, my brother, that I would speak."

Heminge immediately assumed that Will was going to ask that Ned be taken back into the company, and he was strongly, even angrily, opposed to it. To him Ned was a worthless ingrate, whose real promise as a player was heavily outweighed by his disappointment as a man. He was sorry for Will in the matter, but felt that the best service he could render him was to advise him to have nothing to do with his brother.

Will continued. "I know what you think of him, but he is a good man at heart, John."

"You cannot see him clearly; he is your brother."

"That is why I know him better than you do. You see only his actions. I see what prompted them, and it is not all bad."

"He chose to leave the company, and that is that. Then he was dismissed from Worcester's Men for striking Kemp. He is finished as a player, Will. Nobody will hire him again."

"Ned bears my name. Cannot you imagine what this would do to Kemp, what taunting and torment he inflicted on Ned? It must have been beyond enduring for him to have struck Kemp. I am the cause of most of his trouble, John, because he owes so much to me. And do not forget that he thinks it was I who made Kemp behave to him as he did."

"Then since you cannot help him, 'tis better to forget him."

"That I cannot do, nor would you in your heart expect or want me to. Ned is my mother's last-born and her favorite, and I am now more father than brother to him."

"You would ask that we take him back into the company. It cannot be, Will."

"I would ask more than that. He would make an excellent Troilus and I want him to play it."

Heminge stared at Will open-mouthed.

"You must admit he is a good player, and Gus tells me that he won golden opinions with Worcester's Men."

The mention of Gus enabled Heminge to find words again. "Gus cannot want this. He says so to please you."

Will was quick to seize on this. "Then if he tells you that he would want it, even if I were dead, you would be persuaded?"

"No. It would be still to please you."

"Who would you have to play Troilus?"

"Alexander Cooke." Heminge said this almost defiantly, because he knew that Cooke lacked some of the qualities for the part that Ned possessed. "He is a good player, a worthy man, and deserves the part."

"But he is not my Troilus. Though 'tis true it is a long time since I saw him play, I cannot believe he is so transformed. There are many parts he can play well, but not Troilus or Prince Hal or Romeo."

"Will, I can never look on your Ned again with favor. It is because he is your brother that you seek him for Troilus, not because you want him as a player. 'Tis commendable in you, but I still think it is for your own good that you should forget him. Albeit, I promise to speak to the others at dinner; 'twould be better were you not there."

"You will tell them you are against it?"

"They will know that without my telling. I fear they may do it for your sake."

"Then beg them think of my Troilus rather than my brother, and I shall be content."

"There is one thing you have not allowed for. It may yet prove that I know your brother better than you do. It may well be that he will refuse to return here, even to play Troilus."

"That I know. The best way to get him would be for him to be asked not by me, or even Gus, but by you."

The absurdity of this idea made Heminge laugh uproariously, and they went their ways, the one laughing and the other smiling.

When the sharers met for supper, happy after playing to a surprisingly good house, Will was greeted with the news from several of them that Ned was going to be invited to play Troilus. He knew that the decision had been made largely to please him, and John made it quite clear that though he remained stubbornly opposed to the idea, he was happy to make Will happy. Then John came up with a surprising idea. "This John Lowin that is friend to your Ned. I hear very good things of him as a player. If we have to go on the road this summer, Tom Pope wants not to come. He was never one to welcome rough living, and he says he needs a rest. I am told this Lowin would make a fair Falstaff. And 'twould be sweet to steal him from Worcester's Men. I have whispered it to a few of our fellows and they liked it mightily. What think you?"

"I like it mightily too. Is he not a large man?"

"Yes."

"Then would he not make a good Ajax?"

"Excellent. Better and better. We can try his quality before committing ourselves for the summer. Who will speak to him?"

"Would it not be better if he came to us?"

"Yes, but how . . . ?"

"Ned. If you speak to Ned . . ."

"No, Will. That is too much. I will not go to him."

"How if he and John Lowin both come to you?" John hesitated and Will pressed home. "If they come to you, Ned will believe you when you say the sharers want him back. You can even say you are against his return; he will believe that too." Will smiled with those last words.

John smiled in response and said, "You are a wily one, but I like it in you. It shall be as you say. When shall I expect the two young men?"

"I know not. Tomorrow morning Gus and I will visit Ned. If we have good fortune, they may come seeking you in the afternoon."

This conversation had taken place in a corner of the supper room, ale in hand. Now the men were called to the table. The talk during the meal never mentioned Ned or Lowin; it was largely about the weather and future plans, but there was no hiding the eager anticipation of the reading that was to follow.

While *All's Well That Ends Well* disappointed the sharers in that it was not another *Twelfth Night,* they were relieved to find that it was more likely to please than *Troilus and Cressida.* It raised the problem of the Trojan play in a startling and critical manner. Again Armin and Pope were delighted, for the Clown and Parolles were rewarding parts, but what of Richard Burbage? When all looked to him to speak, he said, "There is nothing for me in this play. Even were I young enough to play your Bertram, I should not wish to do so. I begin to fear, Will, that you intend to drive me from this company as you did Will Kemp." He spoke with a wry smile, but the remark dismayed the company.

Will chose not to answer; it was unnecessary to protest in praise of the greatest player of the age. It was Heminge who protested. "A play without you is unthinkable; it would stand no chance. You say you cannot play the young man; then play the king."

"That is not for me. It was written for Gus. Am I not right, Will?"

"Yes," said Will.

Gus quickly said, "But you can have it, Dick, and give it much more than ever I could."

"No, Gus. This is one play that you will do without me. 'Twill be good for me to rest. And now I will bid you all goodnight, for 'tis fruitless for me to stay here longer."

After he had left, there was a brooding silence for a while, and then Henry Condell said, "Your year in Stratford has yielded a strange harvest, Will: rare and beautiful fruit but sour to the taste."

"Without Dick, I think we should not do the play," said Heminge.

" 'Tis a good and different play and must be seen," said his friend, Condell, and voices were raised in support.

"So be it," said Heminge with a heavy sigh. "I beg you, Will, to write plays for Dick."

To everyone's surprise, Richard Cowley spoke, for he rarely did. "These two plays are about the torment of love in the young; in the one, a man for a maid, in the other, a maid for a man. Older men have such torments too, and often worse." This sentiment was so unlikely from Cowley that it provoked smiles and laughter; after sustaining a long and quiet bachelorhood, he had finally succumbed to marriage a few years before and now lived in an apparent haven of connubial calm in Holywell Street, near John Heminge. Cowley persisted. "I know such a tale, Will. It was in an old play by George Whetstone, called *Promos and Cassandra*. It was the Cassandra in your play that reminded me of it."

"I know it too, Richard, but not as a play. He also put it in a book of tales. I shall read it again. Before I thought it too bitter a story; now it may better appeal to me."

"No, Will, no more bitterness, I beg," said Heminge. "Either noble sorrow, sweet pathos, or merry laughter. 'Tis time for us to go. Tomorrow in church let us all pray that Will's muse will smile on him again; now she makes ugly faces."

"The muse too gets older, John," said Will.

"So does Dick Burbage; let her remember that," Heminge replied.

That night Will and Gus decided they would go straight to Ned from church, in the slender hope that they might be able to induce him to return with them to dinner.

Ned's thoughts too that night were on his brother, and for once he was in desperate need of his help for he was under lock and key and in imminent danger of being lost to sight forever.

That Saturday, moved by a desire for reconciliation with John Lowin, he had ventured out to the Rose theatre; the flag was flying; there would be a performance. Cold, slush and snow quickly drove him back indoors, where he made a meal from the remains of what John had brought. Ned decided to please his friend. Tomorrow he would clean and spruce himself up as best he could and surprise John by meeting him at church. Now full of good intentions, he set about cleaning his room; there was a chance that John might visit him after the performance.

During the afternoon, he went out again to find John, wrapped in a blanket. He could not disgrace him by going backstage, dirty and uncouth as he was—besides, he would probably be denied admittance, being persona non grata with the company—so he took shelter in a doorway on a street down which he knew John would come. And there the pressgang men found him. They had orders to round up a hundred vagrants that day on the South Bank for service in Ireland or the Low Countries.

There were twelve armed men and a sergeant, and they were not in a good mood, for a day's work had netted less than half their quota. Ned saw them coming, with two hapless victims already roped together. He immediately jumped to their purpose and his danger. Once before he had brazened it out in such a situation, but then there were fewer men, and they not armed soldiers like these, and he not an unkempt vagabond as now. Instinctively he took to his heels, with two men in pursuit and the sergeant crying on him to stop. He was splashing through the slush when his blanket slipped and tripped him. Before he could get to his feet, the soldiers were on him, furious that he had made them mire themselves. One of them knocked him down again. The other said, "Easy, Joe. He's for the Queen's service. She will not want him harmed."

"This is a stubborn one; I can tell 'em."

Ned knew it was useless to protest or resist, and he submitted to being roped to the other two, one a starveling and the other a ruffian.

The troop stopped outside a brothel, the very one where Ned had caught the "French disease." Four soldiers remained outside to guard those already caught, and the sergeant led the other soldiers into the house. Soon there was a clamor of screaming and shouting, the clatter of booted feet on stairs, the banging of doors and of furniture being knocked about. Finally a struggling mass of men emerged; five had been caught, one proclaiming loudly against the affront to his status and dignity: could the officer not see he was a gentleman? Apparently the officer could not, for the worthy citizen was roped with the unworthy, and they were all pushed and dragged along to St. Margaret's, an old deconsecrated church which served as a temporary prison. A young apprentice, who could not have been more than eighteen, was roped to Ned. He was scared to tears. Ned said, with a world-weariness beyond his years, "Take heart, lad. You have just been saved from the pox."

As hunters and captives disappeared down the street they were followed by the maledictions on the soldiers of the cheated whores who shivered in the doorway and shouted. The ones that had not been paid for their services were particularly vicious in their curses.

The madam, well wrapped against the cold, stood behind her angry stock-in-trade and muttered, "May that sergeant rot with everlasting bone-ache, but without the pleasure that begets it. Come in, girls. 'Tis New Year's Day. God's bleeding body, what a beginning!"

THIRTY-FIVE

IMMEDIATELY AFTER CHURCH THE FOLLOWING MORNING JOHN LOWIN WENT
to Ned's. When he got to the room, he was surprised and delighted by its
cleanly state, and he congratulated himself that it was his rebuke which
had brought about the transformation. He was not perturbed by Ned's
absence; he may even have gone to church. He went to open the trunk to
see if Ned were wearing some church-worthy clothes. A quick examination showed that he was not. Perhaps he had just gone out to get some
water. John looked at the usually noisome bucket; it was empty and
clean. He sat down to wait for Ned's return.

Soon he heard footsteps coming up the stairs. The door opened, and
Gus and Will entered. John had already met Gus and had seen Will on
the stages of the Theatre, the Curtain, and the Globe, while he was still a
goldsmith's apprentice. He stood up with excitement.

"This is Master John Lowin, Will, a good friend of Ned's," said Gus.

"I am honored to meet you, Master Shakespeare," said John.

"Where is Ned, Master Lowin?" asked Will.

"I know not, sir." He suggested there were a few places he might go
and look for him. Will said he would be grateful and that they would
await his return—or Ned's.

When they were alone, Gus and Will exchanged complimentary remarks about John Lowin. Will was now delighted by Heminge's suggestion that they should recruit him for the company, and in particular to
play Ajax.

John Lowin had no clear idea of where to look for Ned. From the
clean state of the room he hoped that his friend might have washed and
even shaved. He was clearly still in his vagabond garb; he had not even
taken his cloak. If Ned had had money, John would have inquired for
him at two taverns and the brothel, but without money where could he
be? The searcher quickly and fruitlessly walked the nearby streets and
alleys, then decided to go to the taverns and brothel anyway in the hope
that somebody had seen Ned.

He drew a blank at the taverns and found the brothel fast shut; the
madam had decided not to risk opening on Sunday in case the sergeant
was a vindictive man and came back. John was about to turn away when
he decided that, since he had splashed his way there, he might as well ask
his question. He knocked loudly on the door; the sound reverberated as
through an empty house. There was no response. He knocked again; still
no response. As he began to knock the third time, a shutter above his

head opened, and a most unappealing young woman put out her head with its badly painted face.

The young harlot spoke in a gentle voice, ironically at odds with her appearance. "Cannot you see we are closed? What would you?"

"I seek a friend. 'Tis urgent. He may have been here last night."

"Then 'tis likely he's been taken for a soldier"; saying which, she closed the shutter.

That must be it, thought John. If the pressgang was out, it was most probable that Ned had been taken on the street; his destitute appearance would have been an open invitation to seizure. He decided to go first to Masters Shakespeare and Phillips, and then to St. Margaret's, the notorious way-station for unwilling soldiers and sailors.

Will and Gus were appalled by the possibility of Ned's plight; they had better assume that it was true and act at once. Will said that the surest remedy would be bribery; the ironic recollection flashed through his mind that Ned had been one of the comic recruits in the second *Henry IV*, in just such a scene, but now the situation was not at all funny. The three men pooled their resources, to see how much they could muster. Both Will and Gus, without prior conference, had brought substantial amounts in the hope they would be allowed to supply Ned's undoubted needs, and John, knowing it to be due, had brought along rent money in addition to money for a tavern meal. Altogether they were able to pool over thirty shillings; it should prove enough.

Gus too had remembered the recruits in Will's play. He said, "When Ned played Mouldy, he offered forty shillings for his release."

Will replied, "Falstaff would have taken less. Let us hope the officer will. Besides, Mouldy did not have you to ask for him." Gus looked his question. "Yes, it is you who must do the talking. What sergeant can resist a king?"

As they set out, John raised the question of Ned's appearance: how could they prove he was not a vagabond, and as such a fit subject for impressment?

Will said, "Let us hope the money will still such questions; if it needs help, we shall think of something."

When they got to St. Margaret's, still a formidable place of confinement in spite of its apparent decay, they found two guards outside the west door, in which there was a small wicket entrance.

Gus spoke to the guards in his loftiest manner. "Who is in command here?"

"The sergeant," was the sulky and reluctant answer.

"His name? And mend your manners in talking to me."

"Sergeant Gates—sir."

"Fetch him, and quickly too."

"Your name, sir?"

"That is for his ears alone."

Gus turned his back on the guards as if not doubting for a moment their immediate obedience. Will and John were filled with admiration for his performance. After some whispering, one of the guards went through the wicket door. Gus led his group slightly away.

Will said quietly, "Who are you that we may play our parts correctly?"

Gus said, "Just call me m'lord; 'twill suffice. And John, do you take this money; my hands should not be soiled with it. And take heed you do not laugh when I speak to the sergeant; I have a plan to excuse Ned's appearance."

After a while the sergeant emerged with the guard. He was in a bad mood; in spite of working late into the night, he had rounded up less than eighty men. He surmised the object of the callers, but he was determined not to release a captive—unless the ransom offer was far beyond his normal expectation. Taking a bribe was a dangerous business; one of his fellows had been heavily fined and lashed for it; and then sent to the wars; Ireland too, which was even worse than the Low Countries. Which of the pressed men had these come for? They were mostly a scurvy bunch. Maybe it was that whining fellow taken at the brothel who declared himself a gentleman; but any gentleman would have had the money for a better brothel; that was a poxy hole for sailors and soldiers and such.

He approached the visitors and said gruffly, "What would you?"

"To begin with, better speech from you," said Gus haughtily.

Will said quietly but loud enough for the sergeant to hear, "He knows not who you are, my lord."

"Is he so barbarous that he knows not blood when he sees it?" Certain that the sergeant was now off balance, Gus spoke to him again. "I have reason to believe, for I have good and loyal intelligence to serve me, that you have impressed my youngest brother. You are not entirely to blame, for I feel sure he appeared to you like a vagabond, though I doubt not his manner belied his rags." Gus was fairly sure that Ned would have put on a good act of outrage.

Which could it be, wondered the sergeant; that defiant young devil who refused to give his name? Pray God it was not, for he had been badly beaten. It was true he had spirit and a manner.

Gus continued. "I know not what name he gave you. It may be he gave you none. He was ever a rebellious young devil and disgraced his blood by his way of life, but I doubt he would defile his name. My man here," said Gus, with a slight inclination of his head toward John, "will go with you to see if indeed he is inside. If he is, you will release him forthwith. I will not be unmindful of the trouble you have been caused."

Again Gus turned away, followed by Will. John said, "Will you lead the way, sergeant?"

When he was about to comply, a sudden doubt struck the sergeant, who was no fool. With heavy sarcasm on the title he said, "Where's his lordship's coach or horses?"

Gus and Will heard this but felt they should not reply; they had to rely on John's inventiveness. He did not fail them. He said, "I hope for your sake that m'lord did not hear that impudent question. The news came to us while we were at church at St. Saviour's. The coach brought us here and then went back to take m'lady home." Sensing that the sergeant was still skeptical and that he might ask the guards if they had seen a coach, he added, "We got out in Maiden Lane; it was easier for the coachman to turn there."

Gus now made a play of chancing to look around and being surprised to find the sergeant still there. With astonished anger he said, "Did you not hear me? Be gone at once, or it will be the worse for you."

The sergeant hesitated no longer. Gus had raised his voice and the guards at the door had heard him; they were delighted by the sergeant's discomfiture.

The scene inside the church-prison was a dismal one. Most of the captives were sitting on the broken stone floor, some of them propped against a pillar; others were crowded for warmth around a brazier in the nave. There was a rough kitchen in the chancel, but the smell from its cooking was very uninviting.

John soon espied Ned, sitting by himself on the chancel steps. He jumped up as he saw his friend approaching, but before either of them could speak, the sergeant said, "Your brother has come for you. Tell me his name."

Mention of his brother clouded Ned's face, but he caught a warning look from John, who said, "His lordship is outside."

As soon as he had begun to speak, the sergeant tried to drown him with "Be silent!" But Ned had caught "His lordship." The sergeant spoke to Ned. "I ask you again: tell me your brother's name."

Ned replied with a hauteur to equal that of Gus. "I have already refused to tell you mine. Think you I will now disgrace my noble family by speaking it? Your minions have beaten and ill-treated me. So be it. Someday soon you will all pay for it. And so do your worst." He resumed his seat on the steps.

The sergeant was baffled. John took him by the arm and drew him aside. He said quietly, "For your sake, sergeant, I beg you to let him go. He was ever a rebellious youth and delights in causing trouble. You did right to take him, but he is not what he seems. I cannot tell you the family name, for it must never be known that the youngest son brought such shame upon it. But this I will tell you: the father is still alive and is much in the Queen's confidence. Here, take this to compensate you for all your trouble." With the skill of prestidigitators, the money changed hands.

The sergeant was finally convinced that he courted trouble in holding the objectionable young man. He turned to him and said curtly, "Come."

Will and Gus were relieved to see the group approaching, though Will was appalled by his brother's state. Even Gus had never seen him look as wretched as this.

The sergeant said, "Here is your brother, my lord." Ned was amazed that it was Gus who was addressed as his brother. How easily he might have spoilt the charade if he had not been quick to take John's hint, though even then he had assumed that the masquerade of nobility was Will's.

"I thank you, sergeant," said Gus. "You are well rid of him. He is an affliction to his family and all who know him."

Ned responded with a convincing performance of indignation; there was some truth in the impromptu play, on both sides. "I asked not for rescue. I asked not to share your blood. I asked not to be born."

"Enough of words. Come," said Gus, "and get cleaned and perfumed."

"This is not all dirt," said Ned defiantly. "These are bruises." He pointed to discolored patches, abrasions, and bumps on his face. It was hard for Gus to maintain his part, and the sergeant now feared his wrath, but Gus turned to him and said, "Have no fear, sergeant. The beating you gave him was well deserved, I warrant." He stalked away to hide his real anger. The others followed him, leaving the sergeant mightily relieved and richer by some thirty shillings.

As soon as the four men were safely out of sight, they stopped.

Ned said, "How did you know where I was?" He still addressed Gus, who replied.

"It was John." The shared adventure prompted the Christian name. "He heard of the impressment and guessed the rest."

Will spoke for the first time. "Are you hungry?"

"Yes; it was stinking swill they gave us for food."

"Then let us all to a tavern," said Will. "We need not only to eat but to celebrate."

"I cannot go like this," said Ned. "First I must wash and shave and change."

This statement made all three hearers happy. It seemed to mean the end of Ned's chosen squalor.

"And we must get some money," said Gus. "You forget we have none; the sergeant has it all."

"You bribed him?" said Ned with some bitterness. "I thought you had frightened him into releasing me by playacting."

"He was suspicious of us," said John. "The money helped to still his questions."

"It would be easiest for us all to have dinner at my house," said Gus.

"No," said Will quickly, sensing Ned's reaction. "This is a tavern occasion. You and I will go home, Gus, to get money, while Ned changes. We will all meet in the Three Bells in an hour."

"I will say goodbye. You will not need me," said John.

"Oh, but we do," said Will, "very much. And not just out of gratitude for helping us to find my brother. We came looking for you as well as Ned this morning. Come, Gus." And he strode away happily, followed by Gus, deliberately leaving the two young men puzzled.

John said he would go home to get some salve for Ned's damaged face.

"My body too," said Ned. "They spared no part of me. I took pleasure in baiting them and I paid for it."

Will and Gus were first at the tavern. They were able to get a cozy private room with a welcoming fire, and they ordered a sumptuous meal. Ned and John arrived together. It gave deep pleasure to the other three that Ned was restored to something of his old appearance; it would take time for his battered face to recover its good looks.

Will had already reimbursed Gus, against his protests, for his part of Ned's ransom money. He would insist on doing the same for John Lowin, but he would have to wait for a private opportunity. Ned would probably guess that it was Will who had bought his freedom and might even question John about it, but a public embarrassment should be avoided.

There was great elation as the four men ate, drank, and retold the morning's adventure; Ned had to hear about the first encounter with the sergeant, and Will and Gus about the scene inside; Ned was careful not to mention his first reaction to hearing that his "brother" had come for him; he was now heartily ashamed of it. He had not spoken directly to Will the whole time and wanted to. Rather lamely he said, "It has been a long time, Will, since I saw you. What is the news of Stratford?"

"Nothing bad and nothing you cannot guess; there will be time for that."

Gus, realizing that Will wanted to avoid a brothers' conversation, said, "This beating you received, Ned. What happened?"

John interpolated, "It was bad. There are parts of his body much worse than his face. 'Tis a wonder his bones were not broken."

"I deserved it all," said Ned. "My tongue earned it. It may be I wanted to punish myself. I have been a long time foolish and obstinate, and it may well hap I shall be so again, but now I want to thank you all for saving me. That I did not deserve."

"John is the one most to thank," said Will. "Without him we should not have found you."

"He has been a good friend," said Ned, feeling guilty about the unworthy thoughts he had sometimes harbored against John. He was now glad that, if John had in part clung to him as a way to his brother, he was at last rewarded. "But you said you had come looking for him as well as me this morning. We are both eager to know the why of that."

"It is not personal. We are envoys from the Lord Chamberlain's Men, so let Gus speak for us."

Gus explained the invitation to John Lowin to join the company, which fulfilled John's best hopes. And when he said it had been prompted by Master Heminge, both John and Ned were made even happier. Gus concluded, "So you see, Ned, if we are grateful to John for leading us to you, we are also grateful to you for leading us to him."

John had no hesitation in saying he would break with the Earl of Worcester's Men as soon as was necessary; there would be no difficulty as the company had not been doing well even before the bad weather; there had been much whispered foreboding backstage at the Rose yesterday.

"Have you seen me play?" John asked Gus.

"No."

"Has Master Heminge?"

"No, but your reputation grows and grows, and now we have met you. There are plans for you, but of those Master Heminge must speak, except for one. Tell him, Will."

"I have a new play, *Troilus and Cressida*. We want you to play Ajax in it. 'Tis a comic part, a beef-witted braggart."

The player in Ned was now envious of his friend. During his unhappy months with Worcester's Men, and still more since his dismissal, he had longed to return to the Lord Chamberlain's Men, especially with Will now apparently settled in Stratford. He knew it was a hopeless prospect; John Heminge would never forgive him for his defection. And his striking of Kemp would make him an undesirable member in any company; he had become a pariah, like Gilbert Spencer.

"And now your news for Ned, Will," said Gus.

"We want you to play Troilus," said Will.

Ned could not believe it; it must be a dream, hearing what he wanted to hear. He looked his disbelief.

Will smiled and said, " 'Tis true, Ned. I wrote the part for Richard Burbage, but he refuses any more to play young men. Troilus is exactly your age, and you have exactly the right quality for him."

Ned's reaction was unexpected. A year's inner turmoil, months of degradation, a hairsbreadth escape from cruelty and impressment, all to end in an invitation to play a Burbage part was too much for his control; he broke down into a wild sobbing that wracked his body. Will put his arm around him, but nobody said a word.

When Ned had become composed again, he said, "Will, tell me, and tell me true. Is Troilus mine because I am your brother, or because I am the player for it?"

Will smiled. "Troilus is mine too, and I would never give him to anybody but who could best play him. If not Richard Burbage, then Edmund Shakespeare. He will fit you and you him like one of father's best gloves."

"But John Heminge?" queried Ned.

"He has agreed, as have all the sharers. You must make your peace with him, and neither I nor Gus will be by. I suggest that, when we leave here, you and John both cross the river and go to him. He will not be surprised to see you."

"But my face; he will think I have been in some common brawl."

"Then tell him the truth. He likes honest dealing."

And so it was that Ned and John presented themselves at the Heminge home late that afternoon. They had first gone to John's room to make themselves as presentable as possible. Now, when he knocked at the door, Ned was filled with trepidation. And John was as much worried about Ned's reception as he was excited about his own; after all, it was the redoubtable Master Heminge who had first suggested his joining the Lord Chamberlain's Men.

The door was opened by Mistress Heminge, pregnant with her twelfth child. She did not recognize Ned—it was a long time since she had seen him—and she had never seen John before. Holding on to her skirts were three little children; the state of the streets made it impossible to take the brood for their usual Sunday afternoon walk. When Ned asked to see Master Heminge, he was told in a whisper that he was asleep; this accounted for the strange silence in a house full of children; the first commandment they had learned long before the Mosaic ten, was "Do not make a noise; Father is asleep."

But Father was not asleep. He had been lying on his bed upstairs but only lightly snoozing for he had been expecting the visit of the two young men, and was at something of a loss in how to deal with it, a rare state for John Heminge. He was eager to see this John Lowin, but not Edmund Shakespeare. The knock on the door woke him at once, and soon he was clumping down the stairs. His wife and several of the children took an anxious look at him, expecting thunder, but his face quickly reassured them.

As he approached he said, "All is well, Rebecca. I was half expecting these young men." He held out his hand to John and said, "You must be Master Lowin. I am glad to see you." John took the hand and mumbled thanks. Heminge did not offer his hand to Ned. He looked hard at him for a moment and then said, "What happened to your face?"

Ned had been much exercised about the manner to adopt to John Heminge. He expected to be greeted with hostility, but was determined not to let it rile him; after all, it was deserved. He must not be obsequious or even too contrite, for Heminge would not believe or respect it; on the other hand, he must be careful not to give added offense. In answer to Heminge's question he wisely said, "I was beaten."

"By whom?"

"By soldiers. I was impressed, and would not give my name."

"And your brother bought you out, I warrant."

Heminge's contemptuous tone made this a particularly difficult moment for Ned. John sensed it and said quickly, "I found him and went to fetch Master Shakespeare and Master Phillips."

"Well, come in," said Heminge. As he walked through the living room he gave forth the edict, "Make not too much noise, children. We have talking to do." He led the way to a comfortable back room, warmed by a good fire. As soon as he had seated his visitors, he went back to the door and called out, "Some ale would be welcome; let William bring it." As he sat down, he said, "First let me talk to you, Master Lowin. I will be frank. If we go on the road this summer, Master Pope will not come with us, and we look for one to take his parts; but if the gods are kind and we stay in London, there would be but small parts for you, and you are now a leading player at the Rose. What say you?"

"I would be content. It has always been my ambition to play with the Lord Chamberlain's Men. And Master Shakespeare spoke of Ajax."

"Ah yes, Ajax. Again I will be frank, for I want no disappointed and discontented player in the company." Ned could not help feeling that this was a reference to him. "Ajax you shall play, but I think not many times. *Troilus and Cressida* is so different that I doubt it will please. I would not say that to any other hired men, but 'tis well you should know it."

"The play is by Master Shakespeare; that is enough for me," said John.

"Well spoken. And now you," said Heminge, turning to Ned. "I need not to tell you how I feel."

Before he could say more, his eleven-year-old and eldest son entered, carrying a tray on which was a jug of ale and three tankards; the door had been left open for him. The boy was very serious and totally absorbed in the task of balancing his burden.

John Heminge said proudly, "This is my eldest son, William. I think he will be no player, but first I was a grocer, and there he may well follow me. Thank you, William. Now you may leave us and close the door."

The boy went out without word or smile, carefully closing the door behind him.

As the host poured the ale, he resumed his speech to Ned. "I was against your return to the company, but I was alone in this. I had thought that Alexander Cooke would play Troilus. I must in honesty admit that you will better him in the part, and so be it." He handed out the tankards. "Let us now drink to your future with the Lord Chamberlain's Men. May you both bring renown and profit to yourselves and to us." After they had put down their tankards, Heminge again spoke to Ned. "You have said nothing. Does my honesty offend you?"

"No, sir. I would have it no other. But I shall study to deserve your better opinion."

"Well said. And now we must talk practical matters."

It was agreed that they should both join the company for the first reading of *Troilus and Cressida*, which should be in two weeks' time. Then it came to payment. Heminge said, "I should discuss this with you separately."

"It matters not," said John. "We are friends."

Heminge looked dubious for a moment—money matters were to him a very private affair—but then Ned said, "I should not expect as much as John; he is already a leading player, and a sharer."

"And now he would become a hired man?" asked Heminge in pretended amazement; he already knew John's status with Worcester's Men.

"Yes," said John.

"I thought of eight shillings a week," said Heminge, prepared to bargain.

"So be it," said John with a smile, knowing how much his ready answer would surprise Heminge. "If and when you find me worth more, you will pay it."

"To whom will you sell your present share?"

"It matters not. I will get what I can for it."

"And you, Edmund," said Heminge, using the name for the first time, a sure sign of subsiding hostility, "you will come back at your leaving wage: seven shillings."

"I could not expect more. Indeed, it is generous, and I thank you."

"Well, that is all happily concluded, so let us drink to seal our agreement."

Soon Henry Condell and Richard Cowley dropped in—it was their Sunday afternoon custom—and a delightful hour of theatrical gossip and anecdote ensued. Ned was made to feel not only that he was welcomed back, but that he was more a fellow of these players than ever he had been before. As for John, the real fulfillment of his life began that afternoon.

THIRTY-SIX

THE FOLLOWING SUNDAY BOTH NED AND JOHN WENT WITH THE PHILLIPS household to church and then back with them to dinner. The whole expedition was a perilous one because the snow had been followed by a freezing and unremitting cold which turned the streets into rough sheets of ice. Falls and injuries were frequent. Very few horses were abroad, and they with hooves covered with sacking.

Anne Phillips was so overjoyed at Ned's return that she insisted on going to church. She went supported by Gus and Will, and at a timorous snail's pace.

The Globe had been open the whole week, but patronage had been small. The hardy spirits who ventured out sat huddled together and lost to sight under coverings. The players wore as many clothes as they could get on; even Richard Cowley looked fat.

Will had visited Ned in the middle of the week to carry him the Sunday invitation, and it had been a good meeting. He had been happy to find that Ned was moving to a room in the house where John lodged, and still happier when Ned had asked him for a loan of twenty shillings. Ned had also insisted on knowing how much the sergeant had been paid and on repaying it.

"Altogether I owe you fifty shillings, Will, and that you shall have in six months, but I owe you more than that, much more, and I can never repay it. Now at last I think I can accept the fact without letting it poison me."

"Your Troilus will put me in your debt," Will had replied.

The Sunday dinner was a very happy occasion, once Mistress Phillips had accepted the fact that Ned was not coming back to live in her house. The attention of the company was on the stranger, John Lowin. When Will and Gus pressed him for the reaction at the Rose to his news of leaving, he had only said, "Christopher Beeston was happy to buy my share. He will not be content until he owns both company and theatre."

"And Will Kemp?" asked Will.

"It would not be fitting at this Sunday table to report his words," replied John, smiling. "But I do not have to hear more of them; I left the company yesterday."

Anne Phillips took advantage of the first lull in the conversation to talk about a subject even more engaging to her than theatre: marriage. On Sunday, February 13, Robert Gough was to be married to her young sister-in-law, Elizabeth, at St. Saviour's, and the wedding was to take place from her house. The whole company was invited. Soon afterwards there was to be another marriage in the company, Will Eccleston to Anne Jacob, a very pretty girl, and she had heard that Christopher Beeston was soon to be married too—and yet here, at her table, there were three handsome bachelors with no thought of marriage.

"It may be they think too much about it, Anne," said Will slyly. "Marriage is like a deep sea. If you look at it too long, you will not enter it. 'Tis better to fall in, and then you learn to swim, or else you sink."

"Some are pushed in," said Ned. He regretted the words even as he said them, for he had not at first thought of their personal application to his brother.

But Will seemed unperturbed, for he said, in high good humor, "Better that than to stand fearfully on the dry shore."

Inevitably the subject of the new play came up. The copying of parts and the bookholder's copy was almost completed, and the cast list had been posted the day before. Sam reported that there had been much surprise and excitement among the hired men on reading the names of Master Lowin and Ned.

"Disappointment too?" queried John.

"No," said Sam emphatically. "They all know of you and long to see you play, and Ned was well liked before he left."

"But what did they say about my playing Troilus?" asked Ned.

"They know not the play yet. Since Master Burbage plays Hector, that must be the leading part. Julius Caesar has the title in his play, but not the leading part, and so it must be with this one. Is it not so?"

Gus quickly interposed, "The hired men and the apprentices will all know the play soon enough."

It was arranged that John and Ned should pick up their parts at the theatre on Wednesday. The play, if there was one, was to be *Romeo and Juliet,* and it was suggested that they might stay to see it, chiefly that Ned might watch the Juliet, John Edmans, who was to play Cressida.

There was a performance that Wednesday, and there was a fair-sized audience, for the sun shone even though it was very cold. Both John and Ned were warmly greeted by the company, and, after the performance, John was invited to sit at the sharers' table in the tavern. He was embarrassed to leave Ned, but was reassured when Ned said convincingly that he would prefer to sit with his former companions; the further he kept away from John Heminge for some time the better.

John Lowin was the center of attention at the sharers' table and the subject of much conversation among the hired men. Ned was happy to give glowing accounts of him both as a player and as a man.

But there was another subject of conversation at every table in the room, and probably at most tables in the city and many throughout the country, and that was the health of the Queen and the problem of the succession. Rumors were manifold: she was in constant pain, she could not sleep, she angrily refused any advice or medication from her physicians; she was kept alive only by her astonishing willpower, she would not yet accept the fact of imminent death and declare a successor. There was general fear about what would happen at her death. Only the oldest of her subjects had ever known any other monarch. It always amazed Ned to think that she had been firmly on the throne for years before even Will was born. Most assumed that the son of Mary, Queen of Scots, would succeed her. James VI of Scotland was not a dangerous Catholic like his mother, but a staunch Protestant, perhaps too staunch. But surely the secret but still powerful Catholic families would make a bid for the throne. Almost certainly their candidate would be the Lady Arabella Stuart, a first cousin of James of Scotland. Wild and contradictory stories were whispered about her: she was insane and in prison, she was secretly married and at large. Worst of all there was the possibility that the King of Spain himself might invade the country to seize the throne; after all, his father had been married to a queen of England. The old Queen should settle the matter by declaring for James. She must know she had not long to live. Yet the dying Elizabeth had yet a surprise in store for the Lord Chamberlain's Men.

The first reading of *Troilus and Cressida* took place in the tavern on the evening of Saturday. It was a particularly trying experience for Ned and John, but both acquitted themselves well. Ned read carefully and intelligently but in a deliberately low-keyed way. John might have been tempted to impress by giving a spirited reading, but he was so secure in his talent that he did not attempt to do so, and this, paradoxically, made a deep impression on the company. Ned was very aware of Alexander Cooke, for he had heard that he had been John Heminge's choice for Troilus. Now he was cast for Diomedes, and so was to steal Cressida from Troilus, after failing to take Troilus from Ned. All accounts of Alex were complimentary, and he himself had given a genuine welcome back to Ned. He had even said, "You will make a much better Troilus than ever I should have made."

The doubts about the play had spread and infected the company, but the reading largely dispelled them; the parts were so good and there were some wonderful scenes and brilliant speeches. Yet John Heminge's original judgment was not shaken.

The Sunday was to be free for study of the parts, and the first stage rehearsal was called for nine o'clock on the Monday; winter rehearsals were an hour later than summer ones. In spite of what, in a conversation with Henry Condell, he referred to as "the noisome spirit" of the play, Heminge did not anticipate any difficulty in getting it licensed for performance.

Will was to play only the Prologue, and was to be relieved of that and all other parts as soon as another play stirred within him; he longed to write again a part worthy of Richard Burbage, but the task was not made easier by the pressure to do so from other sharers.

The rehearsal began very well. Tom Pope showed such enjoyment of the part of Pandarus that Ned and John Edmans were encouraged to attack Troilus and Cressida with equal zest. Then came the wonderful speech of Ulysses which Augustine Phillips exulted in. John Lowin's first scene was with Robert Armin, and they were both caught by the unexpected excitement of the rehearsal; it was immediately clear that John was going to justify his reputation.

And then the Queen's surprise came. A messenger from the Lord Chamberlain arrived to command their appearance in a play before Her Majesty at her Palace of Richmond on Wednesday, February 2. She had heard that they had a new play in preparation and would like to see it.

The players were astounded by their good fortune and amazed by the fortitude of the Queen. Had the rumors of her approaching death been untrue, or was this yet another brave and brazen defiance of that last enemy she had kept at bay for so long?

John Heminge called an immediate meeting of the sharers and told the rest of the company to stand by. He was so certain that *Troilus and Cressida* would not please that he wanted to substitute *All's Well That Ends Well*. He was overborne. Will pointed out that the change was impossible, as the second play was not even copied yet; they would be hard put to it to get even the first play ready for a royal performance in two weeks and two days, especially if the weather allowed the theatre to be opened.

Henry Condell said, "Besides, John, a play without Dick Burbage in it would be certain to displease the Queen."

"Nor would she want to see a play about a sick monarch," commented Burbage.

"There is much to please her in the Trojan play," said Gus. "My speech on civil order will delight her."

Others, equally pleased with their parts, echoed his enthusiasm, but Heminge remained unconvinced. He said, "I fear. I fear. But if rumor be only half true, I doubt she will be able to take in what we say, and therein lies our hope."

Robert Armin said, "There will be many around her who will delight in the play."

"No one dare delight if she do not," said Heminge.

In the next two weeks, bad weather prevented seven performances, and for once all but Cuthbert Burbage were glad of it, for they needed every extra hour to prepare the new play for the Queen. They used the time to such good purpose that even John Heminge, who played Agamemnon, began to take heart.

Although Tuesday, February 1, was fine, no performance was given, for every minute was necessary to get the play ready for the next day's performance. Normally the Queen saw a play already well tried in public; this presentation of a new play before her was an infinitely more nerve-racking undertaking.

Then there was the complication of playing at Richmond, which necessitated a four-hour boat journey up the Thames, and that with the tide; it would be much longer if the oarsmen had to pull against it; to catch the flow they would have to leave no later than noon.

The royal household provided the necessary boats and barges, and they made a brave show as they set out. Although it was a bitingly cold day, a goodly number of people had gathered on the river bank to watch the departure. The news of the royal performance had quickly spread and the people were heartened by it; the Queen must be better in health.

The players responded to the cheers of the crowd as though they were on the stage, but, as soon as the boats pulled away, they were quick to wrap themselves up against the cold. On shore the wind was bad enough; on the river it was cruel. This served further to depress their spirits. The usual excitement of the first presentation of a new play was countered by doubts of the acceptability of this one, and by gloom about the Queen's health, for rumors had persisted that she was desperately ill; the most lurid recent accounts had her writhing in agony on the floor, unwilling or unable even to get into bed. Suppose she were unable to attend the performance; would it be canceled? Heminge had raised this possibility with the Lord Chamberlain's man and had been guaranteed payment, whatever happened. Moreover he had been promised some additional payment since the players were to stay at the Palace overnight and would not arrive home in time to give a public performance on Thursday.

Only Ned remained obstinately elated. Although he cringed with the others from the wind, his spirits danced. As his Troilus had grown in rehearsal, he had received casual praise from several of the players, and no commendation is more sweet than that of your fellows. Even John Heminge, in a friendly and jocular tone, had said to him that morning, "You are doing well, Ned. I begin to think that Will wrote this part for you."

Although he had not yet appeared with them in performance, John Lowin was already accepted and respected by the players as an established member of the company. If he was excited about appearing with the Lord Chamberlain's Men for the first time in a new play, and before the Queen, he did not betray it. Just over a year before he had been part of a royal performance with the Earl of Worcester's Men. He pointed this out to explain his calmness when Will commented on it, but others who had played before their Queen many times were very nervous.

When they got to Richmond, the players were conducted to a hall where blazed a large fire. There they huddled and thawed while Tom Vincent, Nat Tremayne, and their assistants unloaded and arranged the costumes and properties from the barges. Not to lose a minute, a word rehearsal was held around the fire. Then the company had an early supper before undertaking a detailed dress rehearsal in the Great Hall. All attempts to draw the Palace staff on the subject of the Queen's health were received with a blank silence. It was obviously among the most closely guarded state secrets, and everybody was expected to behave as though their royal mistress had the health and life expectancy of a radiant young woman.

The players were to be ready to perform at eight o'clock, awaiting the Queen's coming and pleasure to begin. At the appointed hour, the court and the players were in place. Two differences struck those used to these occasions: the muted conversation of the waiting audience lacked laughter, and the Queen's chair was almost in shadow. Usually she flaunted herself before her court, but tonight she wanted to escape their eyes.

The wait was a long one, and when at last distant trumpets sounded, there was an audible sigh of relief throughout the Hall. The players trooped out to stand in line, and the court stood. The second and nearer trumpets seemed unusually delayed; the Queen's progress was very slow. Finally, the trumpets outside the great doors sounded and the royal procession entered. Everybody bowed and remained so until the Queen was seated, but most contrived to take a surreptitious look at the person who was the center of their world. She moved slowly between the Lord Chamberlain and the Keeper of the Household, both of whom took the greatest care to make their support as unobtrusive as possible. Elizabeth was arrayed as gorgeously as ever, and her gown was a defiant white, trimmed with pearls. Her face was a painted mask.

When she was seated there was an embarrassing pause. All awaited her signal to begin. Was she so exhausted by the ordeal of the procession that she was unable to give it? At last there was a slight flicker of her hand, but it was hard to see it because the Queen was so ill lit. The Lord Chamberlain called out, "Her Majesty commands that you begin."

Again the players bowed and then withdrew, leaving Will to speak the Prologue.

For the first ten minutes the players were very uncomfortable because they could provoke no audible reaction. It was clear that all minds were on the Queen, and a laugh might be considered disrespectful. She must have become aware of this; it was contrary to her wish; everything should appear normal. At the height of Cressida's teasing of Pandarus, the Queen suddenly emitted a strained guffaw. The court took its cue and laughed heartily.

Now the Queen was determined to show that she had lost none of her powers. When Augustine Phillips had finished the long speech of Ulysses on "the neglection of degree" and Richard Cowley began to speak as Nestor, she did an unprecedented thing. Her voice, with all its old authority, rang out: "Hold! That speech. We liked it well and would hear it again. And do you, our lords and ladies, mark it."

There were four sharers onstage, and their relief and delight were obvious to all. The Hall was full of happy approval. When Ulysses ended his speech the second time it was received with great applause. Even Heminge began to regret his doubts about the play.

But the Queen had not ended her intervention. The play had less than twenty minutes to go to its end when her voice called out again, but this time it was tired and angry. Was the anger caused by the play or her pain? She said just one word: "Enough!" It followed a speech of Robert Armin as Thersites, and seemed to have been occasioned by it. He had just summed up his bitter view of men's conduct: "Lechery, lechery! Still wars and lechery! Nothing else holds fashion. A burning devil take them!"

For a moment there was a petrified silence. Then the Queen was helped to her feet. All stood. She rested for a moment, breathing hard. Then all bowed as she began to move painfully away, supported by the two lords and followed by an anxious train.

The court quickly dispersed in an ominous silence. The players gathered in an anteroom and waited in some trepidation, talking in whispers. Soon an emissary came from the Lord Chamberlain. His attitude immediately revealed the official position to be taken. He spoke haughtily. "Her Majesty is displeased by your play. She thinks it is not fit matter for her ears nor for those of her subjects." He walked away without further word.

The impact of his last words was clear to all. *Troilus and Cressida* was not to be played again. Ned was filled with a selfish fury; he was to be robbed of his first big success. Most of the others looked with sympathy at Will. He said, "You were right, John. The play did not please."

But now Heminge was angrily moved to the defense of the play. "No, Will. That was not it. She was in pain which got beyond bearing. That is why she cried out. But to hide her sickness from the world it must be given out that the play did not please."

"And now we must spend the night in this Palace of Despond," said Tom Pope miserably, cheated out of further enjoyment as Pandarus.

As they dispersed to go to their rooms, which had been pointed out and assigned before—there were four, five, or six to a room—Will came across to Ned.

"I am sorry, Will," said Ned, genuinely regretting his initial selfishness.

" 'Tis still a good play," said Will, "and it may be that someday men will know it. But you, Ned; it has served you well. Now all the sharers know your true quality. Be not too disappointed. In winning John Heminge, you have won a whole world."

THIRTY-SEVEN

THE FIRST READING OF ALL'S WELL THAT ENDS WELL TOOK PLACE ON Saturday afternoon, February 12. There was a gloom over the company as there was over the whole country, for there was a growing conviction that the Queen could not last much longer. Yet that very week she had received the Venetian ambassador who had come with a complaint against English piracy, and she had dealt with him in Italian and with all her old spirit; it was felt that such a display was but the magnificent spurt of a dying fire.

The players brought little enthusiasm to the new play; they doubted it would open, though nobody voiced this. Much could happen in three weeks. The Queen had not yet named her successor and might die without doing so. Then there would be chaos.

And there was a particular circumstance which made the reading a strange and unsettling occasion: Richard Burbage was not there. The chief merit of the play in the eyes of John Heminge was that it had a small cast, but he doubted the success of any new play by the Lord Chamberlain's Men without Burbage.

It did not help matters that several of the players were not happy with their parts. Henry Condell and William Sly were reduced to playing two lords at the French court; during the reading they were amazed and amused to discover that Will had made them brothers and that they now had a name, Dumain; their parts had been nameless when Will had read the play to them. John Lowin played a soldier, but he had an amusing scene with Tom Pope as Parolles. John was content to wait; there would soon come a time when Will would write a part with him in mind.

His Troilus had given Ned a new status in the company, and he was rewarded by being given the part of Bertram, but he did not like it. He himself had suffered from the disdain of nobility for commoners, and now he was called upon to play a young man who was the epitome of such disdain.

He and John had supper together and discussed Ned's disappointment. John pointed out that there must be something admirable in Bertram to make Helena fall in love with him: he was handsome, a brave soldier, much desired by the ladies of the court, and his prejudice against Helena was the inevitable result of his upbringing, which he finally overcame when he realized how deep Helena's love for him was.

Their talk broadened into a discussion of marriage, especially as they were both going to the wedding of Robert Gough the following morning. (The bridegroom had been thoughtfully left out of the cast of the new play. The hired men had joined together to give him a silver bowl. John had been deputed to buy it because of the knowledge he had gained as a goldsmith's apprentice, and Sam Gilburne was to make the presentation because he and Bob had partnered each other so often as boy players.)

"Will you ever get married, John?" asked Ned.

"I hope so; someday, but not yet. I am so much in love with the stage that I should make a poor husband. In this new play there is a line which struck me this afternoon: 'A young man married is a man that's marred.' Did that come from Will's own life?"

In spite of his close friendship with John, Ned instinctively resented this probe. He said, with perhaps too much assertion, "No. Will would never lay his life so open to the public gaze. It is not he that speaks those words, but Parolles, and he is a liar so there is no heed to be paid to him. Will has always loved his wife and children. Did he not spend the whole of last year with them? And did not Gus Phillips have to beg him to come back?"

William Kemp and Christopher Beeston came to the marriage service in St. Saviour's, but neither of them came back to the house; both of them spoke to Augustine Phillips but to no others of the Lord Chamberlain's Men. Kemp said, "I hear you have a new play in rehearsal. So have we. 'Tis a good one too, by Tom Heywood. *A Woman Killed With Kindness*. But there is nothing for me in it. I begin to feel, Gus, that the world is passing me by." He said it jocularly, but he could not disguise his real feeling.

There were many speeches at the wedding feast, but the one that gave most pleasure was Sam Gilburne's. He had taken great pains to prepare it. During it he said, "And so Juliet has become Romeo and Portia has become Bassanio. I will tell you a secret. Both Ned Shakespeare and I made eyes at the beautiful young lady who is now Mistress Gough, but she was blind to all but Bob, and she was right."

During the ceremony of the "Bride's Ale," when the new Mistress Gough dispensed tankards of ale from a cask to all the family and guests in return for a payment of silver, she coyly said to Sam, "Your speech was payment enough," but he still gave her a shilling, whispering, as he did so, "I wish Bob was giving this silver to Mistress Gilburne."

Prominent at the wedding was the father of Gus and Elizabeth, a hale and handsome old man of sixty-five who had come from Mortlake, where Elizabeth had been caring for him since her mother died a few years before. She and Robert were going to make their home with him. It would not be very convenient for Robert and there would be times when he would have to stay in London for the night, though since Mortlake was south of the Thames, he would not have to cross the river to get to and from the Globe.

Old Master Phillips had come from near Richmond Palace, and so he was pestered with questions about the Queen. He was surprising in his optimism. "She will not die yet a while. She will not go until she is ready to go, and she will not be ready until everything is in order in her kingdom. She will be Queen until the last, and only then will she name her successor."

To everyone's surprise the two new plays at the Globe and the Rose did open in the second week of March, and amid happy reports of improvement in the Queen's health, but the city was not in a mood to relax and enjoy itself. As if to contradict the Palace reports and rumors, there were ominous signs of imminent upheaval; in particular, the Lord Mayor and city council were taking steps to withstand a siege: stores of wheat were being laid up and the ditches outside the northern wall of the city were being cleaned and deepened to serve as moats. The king of France was now rumored to be among the contenders for the throne. There was no doubt that Protestant James of Scotland was the favored of the city, but Catholic voices were being openly heard against him.

It was not a time for theatre-going, but, even so, the Lord Chamberlain's Men were dismayed to find that their new play did not succeed as well as the one at the Rose. John Heminge was convinced that this was due to the absence of Richard Burbage from the stage, but others felt it was due to the nature of the plays themselves. Robert Gough had taken his bride to see *A Woman Killed With Kindness* and had reported that the audience was markedly different from the usual one at the Globe. Prosperous merchants predominated at the Rose where they went to see a highly moral tragedy about people like themselves; far removed from the court, the three principal characters lacked even a title. The faithful at the Globe came to see and enjoy *All's Well That Ends Well*, but the unsettled state of the country denuded the lords' rooms.

The success of the domestic tragedy at the Rose aroused an idea that had been long dormant in Will's mind. Over ten years ago he had been much taken with a Venetian tale about a Moorish general. He had come across it when he was living at the house of the young Earl of Southampton and had learned to read it with the help of the Italian scholar, John Florio, the earl's tutor. And now, above all, Will wanted a play for Richard Burbage. Then there was that tale that Henry Condell had mentioned, *Promos and Cassandra*. The audience, and the players too, had liked that twist in the plot of *All's Well* by which Helena had won her husband by a bed trick. Perhaps he could use it again.

Ned enjoyed playing Bertram more than he had expected to, more especially the scenes of soldierly comradeship with Henry Condell, William Sly, and John Lowin. Then, too, he had been given the part of Lysander in *A Midsummer Night's Dream,* and this kept him excitingly busy. John Lowin, too, was busy, but privately; he was quietly studying some of the parts of Tom Pope, but this fact was kept from most of the company.

The city, and with it the players, had become so used to living with news of a dying, yet not dying, Queen that they had been lulled into believing that such a state of things would continue indefinitely. And so it came as a shock when, on Saturday, March 19, all theatres were closed because of the parlous condition of the Queen's health and the consequent dangers to the peace of the land. The road to Scotland was busy with couriers carrying messages and gifts to James from those who sought to ingratiate themselves with him, and this intelligence was enough to prevent the proud and obstinate old lady from naming James as her successor. But the possibility of civil war was all too real; only that week a hotheaded young Catholic, Sir Edward Baynham, who had several times been fined for drunken attacks on the city watchmen, had loudly proclaimed that he was one of many thousands who would die before James should be king of England. He was promptly apprehended and imprisoned, but the fear of the "many thousands" remained.

The end came in the dark hours of the night on Thursday, March 24. With the dawn the news rapidly spread through the city. The Queen was dead and James VI of Scotland was King James I of England, Ireland, and Wales—and, said some, of France. It was assumed that at last Elizabeth had spoken in his favor, to secure the peace of her people. Gradually it became known that she had lost the power of speech days before she had died and so had never named a successor. The council, led by Sir Robert Cecil, had made the decision, and the vast majority of their countrymen were grateful to them. It was spread abroad that the Queen, although incapable of speech, had, in answer to a direct question, chosen James as her successor by holding her hands to her head to signify the crown; the skeptics smiled, but were glad to accept the fiction. Not least among the virtues of the new King was the comforting fact that he already had three children, and two of them boys. Prince Henry was nine years old and so past the initial dangers of childhood; Prince Charles was not yet three, and reputed to be sickly. It was considered a good omen that the princess who stood in age between the two boys was named Elizabeth.

Without being summoned, all the sharers and most of the hired men and apprentices found their way to the Globe that morning to discuss what the future held for them. From a confusion of reports and rumors they concocted a picture of their new monarch which in its contradictions was true of the man. He spoke in the broad Scottish tongue which nobody could understand; would they all have to learn to speak it? The man himself was said to be so weak in the legs that he could not walk any distance without support, and yet he was a daring rider and a mighty hunter, but a hunter who almost swooned at the sight of human blood. He was said to have a surpassing terror of death, particularly by dagger or sword, and was so fearful of assassins that he wore thickly padded clothes. His fears were not without good grounding; less than three years before he had narrowly escaped death by well-planned assassination on which occasion he had acted with courage and great presence of mind. Nick Dodman's leering comment on this fearfulness of King James was that, when he was in the womb, he had heard the screams of his mother as she watched her lover being viciously murdered; Ned vividly remembered Robin's ballad, and he scared himself with the traitorous thought that perhaps James was not his father's son; no one would now dare utter such a possibility. The King was known to be a very learned man who delighted in disputations with philosophers and theologians. He was a writer, too, of skill and authority. His book called *Daemonology* was in three parts, dealing with magic, witchcraft, and demonic possession, and was much quoted by scholars. There was one scandalous whisper about the Scottish king that was pounced on backstage at the Globe: he was very susceptible to the charms of handsome young men.

It would be more than a month before Elizabeth was buried, but her successor had no intention of being present at her funeral. Instead, he planned a very leisurely progress through his new kingdom, basking in the adulation of the people who would crowd his way and enjoying to the full the hospitality of the noble houses which would vie with one another in entertaining him.

The sharers agreed that the theatres would probably be closed for some further weeks of mourning after the Queen's funeral, so they could not expect to play again until some time in May. They had no doubt that they would open then, for they had received over the years reliable reports that James was well affected toward the theatre. In particular, he had given his royal favor in Scotland to a group of English players led by a Lawrence Fletcher. Presumably this gentleman would now return to London, perhaps to establish a fourth company, under royal patronage, to rival those at the Globe, the Fortune, and the Rose. John Heminge said that the new King was bringing with him a whole new age, and they must be prepared to adapt to it. There was no doubt that the other two companies would do all they could to secure favored treatment.

Mention of the new age brought a surprising and disconcerting announcement from Tom Pope: "It will indeed be a new age for the players, and I want to be no part of it." Received with a dumbfounded silence, he went on. "You already know that I had no wish to go on the road this summer, if we should be forced to do so. I know now that that was only part of it. I am tired. I want to play no more. John Lowin can take my place and will do so well. As for my part in the Globe I wish to retain it, but, with your approval, I would sell my share in our fellowship to Will Sly; he has served us well and I know he can pay the price."

He was pressed to postpone his decision until the King had seen him play, but he shook his head. Robert Armin said, "You will come back as Edward Alleyn did. Your feet will itch to tread the boards again. You will hunger for the applause of the crowd and thirst for their laughter. Without them you will die." But Pope still shook his head, and the others had sadly to accept his decision, John Heminge silently congratulating himself on his foresight in recruiting John Lowin.

Will had been deeply stirred by Tom Pope's determination to retire. Why could he not do the same? Playing meant much less to him than it did to Pope. Will asked, "Where will you live, Tom?"

"In London. Where else? This is my home, and I could not breathe outside it."

And so it was agreed that William Sly should replace Thomas Pope as one of the eight sharers in the Lord Chamberlain's Men. There was a feeling in the room that there was something far more significant about this change than when Henry Condell had replaced George Bryan and Richard Armin had replaced William Kemp. This was an end and a beginning; it was part of a Queen dead and a King to come.

On the Sunday, Ned and John Lowin joined the Phillips household at church and returned with them to dinner. The service at St. Saviour's was a sad occasion; it was a memorial to the late Queen whose body now lay in her Palace of Whitehall; on Saturday night thousands had watched from the banks of the river in silence and tears as it had been brought down the Thames from Richmond in a black-draped barge, followed by a line of barges filled with black-shrouded mourners, nobility and household attendants, the whole spectral scene made more awesome by the flare of innumerable funeral torches. Many in the church that morning had watched the spectacle the night before, and their minds were full of it. Although thanks were given to God that a new king had come to the throne peacefully, it was the old Queen who dominated the church. Ned's chief thought about her was that she had robbed him of his Troilus.

THIRTY-EIGHT

THE QUEEN HAD DIED ON MARCH 24. HER FUNERAL DID NOT TAKE PLACE until April 29. It was the Friday of Easter Week, and a beautiful spring day, with the new King happily enjoying himself well away from London. The black procession to Westminster Abbey was a splendidly sad sight, strangely at odds with the green rebirth of the fields and gardens and woods. The three companies of players were all represented by their sharers in the procession, though humbly placed, their long black gowns provided by their patrons. It was Tom Pope's last appearance with his fellows. Some irrepressible wag said later that it took the death of a queen to make Richard Burbage, Edward Alleyn, and Will Kemp appear in public together, but not even that event could make them talk to one another.

It would have been expected that all London would have lined the way to the Abbey in homage to their beloved Queen, but there were many who stayed indoors—from fear, not disrespect. The sudden spring had brought not only new life but new death; the plague had broken out. As yet it was not serious, but deaths were mounting.

Wednesday, May 11, was the great day of the new King's arrival in London. Terrified though he was of the plague, he could not avoid the ceremonial procession, but he was determined to betake himself as soon as possible to the safety of Richmond. There were still only four or five plague deaths a day, and most Londoners chose bravely to ignore them in order to give their new King a worthy welcome with bells and flags and decorated streets and music and noise. James managed to hide his fear sufficiently to make a good impression on his happy subjects. He was now in his thirty-seventh year and was seen at his best on his horse. He was noted to be gentle and scholarly in appearance, and more subdued than they would have liked in dress, probably the result of his upbringing among those niggardly, Calvinistic Scots; the brilliance and splendor of London would soon alter that.

While Ned and John went out to see the King pass and later to watch some of the fireworks, they were too busy to give their day wholly to celebration. The Globe was to open the next day and within the next week and a half John Lowin was expected to make his first appearance as Polonius in *Hamlet,* Shylock in *The Merchant of Venice,* Buckingham in *Richard III,* Sir Toby Belch in *Twelfth Night,* and Falstaff in both parts of *Henry IV.*

Hamlet had been chosen as the opening play out of compliment to James's Queen Anne, who had been a princess of Denmark. Will had agreed that it would be tactful to omit the line, "Denmark's a prison."

The plague deaths were now near the prohibiting number of forty a week, but no edict of closure had yet been issued, and it was confidently expected that the Globe would have a good house on Thursday. *Hamlet* was always a profitable offering, and the first opening of the theatre since the death of the Queen would be a continuation of the welcome to the new King.

There was an unexpected development during the rehearsal on Thursday morning. An ornately sealed message on scented paper was brought to Cuthbert Burbage. It virtually demanded a lords' room that afternoon and a conference after the performance with the sharers. It was signed, "Lawrence Fletcher, His Majesty's Player."

Cuthbert Burbage immediately brought the message to John Heminge, who said that Cuthbert should himself welcome Master Fletcher to the theatre and conduct him to the lords' room, assuring him that the sharers would be happy to meet with him afterwards.

It was at almost the last moment that Master Fletcher arrived, and at the stage door. He was accompanied by some half-dozen men, all of them handsome and most of them young. He himself was in his late thirties, but assiduously contrived to look ten years younger. One of his entourage informed the doorkeeper that Master Fletcher was expected. Cuthbert Burbage soon appeared and was ingratiating in his welcome. After he had conducted the party to their seats, he quickly sought out John Heminge to give his report: "A popinjay, but shrewd withal."

The house that afternoon was far from full but the performance was good and the audience enthusiastic. Many had seen the play before, but some of those had not seen John Edmans as Ophelia and James Sands as Gertrude, and none had seen John Lowin as Polonius. He was generally rated as not as comic as Tom Pope in the part, but the better judges realized that he compensated for this by being more credible as the chief counselor of the king. William Sly was appearing for the first time as a sharer in the company, and he celebrated the occasion by making his Laertes even more dashing than usual. Richard Burbage too was in a happy mood, quite recovered from the doldrums caused by *Troilus and*

Cressida and *All's Well That Ends Well,* for in the past week Will Shakespeare had confided to him that two plays had begun to form in his mind, both of them with parts worthy of Richard Burbage; one was a tragedy and the other a comedy, but a comedy of dark happenings; they should both be ready for the next season.

Word of the presence of Lawrence Fletcher had soon spread through the company. Several had seen his arrival and noted his reception by Cuthbert Burbage. The companions of Master Fletcher were also cynically noted. Ned had caught a fleeting glimpse of the peacock group, and had been astonished to see among them George! From behind the entrance door on the side of the stage, he had managed to take a surreptitious peep into the lords' room, and there indeed, in the second row, was George, right behind Master Fletcher and whispering in his ear, possibly telling him about his special relationship to the Shakespeares. Ned had been momentarily outraged that this player and his hangers-on should sit on the very benches where the Earl of Essex and his noble party had sat, and then he realized that he was indulging in the same contempt from which he himself had suffered.

After the performance, the Fletcher party trooped backstage. Master Fletcher himself was conducted to the bookholder's room by Cuthbert Burbage and there was entertained to wine and cakes until the sharers could join them. In the meantime, the other members of the party were introduced to some of the players by George. All but one of them spoke with a thick Scottish accent, and that one was a newly found friend of an older Scotsman, a satellite of a satellite.

George fluttered and sparkled. He assumed a patronizing intimacy with players to whom he had never spoken before and left behind him a trail of brilliant compliments and witticisms. Finally he caught up with Ned, who had been trying to avoid him. George bore down on him with the others in train. "Ah! Here he is at last; hiding from us, I'll be bound. This handsome creature is Edmund Shakespeare, brother to the renowned William and my own Gilbert. He spent his first night in London under my roof—though not, alas, in my bed. But I'll be sworn he has found his way into more beds since than there are in his native Stratford."

"My native Stratford. Yours too." Ned felt that this riposte was a fitting return for his discomfort; he knew that George liked to give the impression that he had been born and bred in the shadow of the royal court.

But George was in no mood to be so easily put out. "True, Ned, true. Fortune was blind enough to have us both born in Stratford beds, but, as soon as we could toddle, we made our way to London, our true home. But now let me introduce you to these gentlemen: Robert Urquhart, Ian Bruce, Gordon MacLaren, David Wylie—and this is a Londoner like us, Christopher Bagshaw; he was a friend of mine and, through me, became a friend of Master Urquhart."

All of them smiled as they were introduced and some of them spoke, but their Scottish vocabulary and pronunciation were largely unintelligible to Ned. Young Master Bagshaw seemed relieved to be able to speak to an Englishman, and his London tongue was as broad in its own way as that of his Scottish companion. He said, "I am pleased to meet you, Master Shakespeare. You were very good this afternoon; very handsome too. I wished you had been playing Hamlet; you would have been very good. But Master Burbage was very good too."

George said peremptorily, "Kit, be quiet. You are at your best when your mouth is shut." He turned to Ned. "Pay no heed to him, Ned. He means well and has his uses."

Ned burned with indignation on behalf of the snubbed young man, who surprised him by giggling and saying, "Oh, George, you are a monster," in acknowledgment of which compliment George smiled graciously.

In expectation of just such an encounter as this in spite of attempts to avoid it, Ned had asked John Lowin to rescue him, and now he appeared, dressed for the street. "Are you ready, Ned? 'Tis time we went." Then John turned to the others, "Forgive me, gentlemen, but the work of players does not end on the stage; we have much to do to prepare for the morrow. I play Shylock for the first time, and Ned is going to cue me tonight." John began to leave, saying over his shoulder, "Welcome to London, gentlemen. It was a pleasure to see you."

Ned followed John, saying, "Adieu, George, and gentlemen." He could scarcely forbear laughing out loud at George's deserved discomfiture.

In the bookholder's room, some welcome developments were taking place, quite unexpected even by the shrewd and farsighted Heminge. Lawrence Fletcher made a surprisingly good impression on all the sharers. Separated from his colorful companions—they had all been tailored by George, who owed this pleasant and profitable introduction to the new men of the new reign to a young nobleman who was heavily in his debt (George had thereby canceled his indebtedness) —Master Fletcher was a courteous, modest, intelligent gentleman, who neither sought nor bestowed empty flattery.

After the introductions had been completed, he complimented some of the players on their afternoon's performances in words that were both genuine and perceptive. Thus he said to John Heminge, "Your Player King was masterly; your performance did not belie Hamlet's description of it; your visage did indeed wan, and that is true playing at its best." Then he came directly to the point. "Gentlemen, I thank you for this meeting. It is ten years since I left London. The Lord Chamberlain's Men had not even been formed then. In that ten years a miracle has happened. Only someone like myself who has been away so long can appreciate what you have accomplished. I had heard of your reputation and had read such of Master Shakespeare's plays as had found their way to Scotland. When I knew I was returning to London with His Majesty, more than anything I yearned to see this afternoon's performance and to meet you like this. Both experiences have exceeded my high hopes. There are two other bands of players in London. I have not seen them yet, but I know that it is with you I would like to be associated."

"In what way, sir?" asked John Heminge, voicing the doubts of other sharers. They assumed that since Lawrence Fletcher was an actor he would want to play, and, since he was favored of the King, he would expect leading parts. They feared he might be an indifferent player.

With a charming smile, Fletcher said, "Be not fearful, Master Heminge. In Scotland I led my company, but I know that in quality I cannot compare with any of you in this room, or with others of your players who are not sharers; I was much taken this afternoon with your John Lowin. No, I do not expect to play, for His Majesty would not have me play less than the leading part. He has not yet seen Master Burbage, and so he has not seen true playing. But I would be a sharer with you." The puzzlement in the room was apparent; only players were sharers. "I shall willingly pay for my share, and some additional money might be useful, particularly if the plague grows as it threatens to do."

"But what would you do?" asked Heminge.

"Take a lively interest in all your affairs, and lend a word or a hand when it might be needful."

"But you are a player," said Burbage. "You will ache to play again."

"I think not. I was never good enough to satisfy myself. Playing brought me the King's patronage—and, in all modesty, I might say his friendship. I would not now jeopardize his high opinion of me as a player by putting it to a test I most surely should fail. Well, gentlemen, what say you?"

Normally John Heminge would have asked for time to consider the unusual proposition, but he sensed that all his fellows, in spite of initial prejudice, had taken kindly to this man. There seemed little to lose and might be much to gain by dividing their future shares between nine instead of eight, and, with a summer tour in likely prospect, the immediate cash payment would be useful. Heminge said, "I say aye."

This bald, unqualified statement, so unlike the cautious Heminge, but voicing their own feelings, so surprised the others that they echoed him and with joyous laughter. They all shook Fletcher's hand and uttered words of welcome, begging him to join them at the sharers' table for supper when they could welcome him with good canary.

He held up his hand to restrain their exuberant good fellowship. "Thank you, gentlemen, thank you. I cannot join you this evening, for I have friends outside who await me. But I hope to share your supper table many times. There is still something else I have to say. I deliberately left it unsaid until now." The sharers were taken aback. Heminge immediately blamed himself for being so precipitate. "I left it unsaid because it would have sounded like a bribe to admit me to your honored fellowship. I have already spoken of this to His Majesty. It is his wish that you will henceforth be known as the King's Men."

For a moment there was a stunned silence. No one had ever dared to imagine such an all-encompassing honor. Then Heminge stammered, "Did I hear aright?"

" 'Tis true. I vouch for it," said Fletcher, delighted by the sensation he had caused. "But I beg you to keep it a secret until it be formally promulgated. It will be but a matter of days, I think."

Near pandemonium broke out in the room. To the people waiting outside, it sounded like a hilariously drunken party. Lawrence Fletcher was overwhelmed by their gratitude and agreed he would join the whole company for a supper party on the day the great honor was made public. "But," he added, "I shall come to the theatre again tomorrow, for I want to be among the first to see Master Lowin's Shylock."

The following day he was accompanied by only one of his Scottish friends, and when he came backstage after the performance he was eyed with a new curiosity, for by this time all knew that he was to be a nonplaying sharer in the company, a strange status which led to much speculation.

While his friend waited for him, Lawrence first sought out John Lowin, who was already elated by the praises of his fellows. His Shylock had been even more disturbing than Pope's, for its villainous intent was too real to be laughed at and the reason for it more apparent and disquieting. Lawrence said to him, "I was deeply impressed. You revealed the man in the villain and without mitigating his villainy."

In the bookholder's room, the sharers eagerly wanted to know if there was any news from the court; Lawrence told them that he had been led to expect the announcement in about a week. Then he said, "I wish I could come to the theatre every day, but that cannot be. Yet I have a great desire to see your *Much Ado About Nothing*, for I hear 'tis very diverting. When do you play it?"

"On Wednesday," said John Heminge.

"That fits aptly. I shall be here. And by then I should have definite news."

Lawrence left the room with Will and asked, "Will you introduce me to your brother? I was much taken with him both yesterday and today."

Will was a little chary of the request, but he took him along to Ned, who was changing from his beloved Salanio costume.

After the introduction Lawrence said, "I bring you a message and an invitation from George and your brother Gilbert. On Wednesday they are giving a supper party to welcome me back to London. They and I wish you to join us." The day of the party had been left for Lawrence to decide.

Ned was intrigued because gossip had told him that this man had influence at the new court. He was also reluctant because he knew he would be uncomfortable at one of George's parties. He asked, "Is Will coming too?"

The answer came easily but there was a glint in the eye which showed that Master Fletcher was well aware of the implications in the question. "Master Shakespeare's time is much too important to waste on a frivolous party. We would not put him to the embarrassment of having to say no to us."

"Thank you, Master Fletcher," said Will with a smile. "That is most gentlemanly."

"Are you reluctant to come alone?" Fletcher asked Ned with comic surprise. "It is as the brother of Gilbert that you are invited. I will tell him that for some mysterious reason you cannot come." He began to walk away.

"No," said Ned hastily. "I will come. And I thank you, sir, for the invitation," he added.

After Fletcher had gone, Ned said, "I do not want to go to such a party. You know what they are like."

Will said, "Do not judge Master Fletcher too hastily. He is not another George. The sharers, and I among them, are much taken by him. Even John Heminge welcomed him."

"Only because he thought he had influence with the King."

"No, Ned; not 'only.' We still do not know how much influence he has, but he is now one of us. I shall be much interested to hear your account of him after Wednesday."

Much to everyone's surprise, Lawrence Fletcher came alone to the performance of *Much Ado About Nothing* on Wednesday. He first sought out John Heminge to whisper that the news he awaited would be made public the following day. Heminge quickly gathered the other sharers together to share his joy but warned them the news was to remain a secret; so must the arrangements for the party to celebrate it.

The theatre needed some good fortune, for the house that afternoon was a very meager one in spite of the fact that the sun was shining; the plague was clearly scaring the cautious from places of public assembly.

Ned was acutely aware of Lawrence Fletcher, sitting alone in a lords' room, and, while he chided himself for it, his performance was specially aimed at pleasing him. He had taken unusual pains to tune his lute, always a troublesome task. That morning he had debated much what he should wear for the party. His first instinct had been to dress drably, but he decided that this would have been a childish gesture, and so he went to the opposite extreme and took pains to look his best. John Lowin had been much amused by the tale of the invitation, and his comment on Ned's appearance as they walked together to the theatre that morning had been, "I see you are aiming yourself straight at the King's boudoir." It had been said with great good humor and Ned had replied in like manner, "In the hope that my arrow will land in the Queen's."

As they walked to the wharf after the performance, Lawrence Fletcher said, "You sing well, Ned, with an actor's feeling for a song."

"Thank you, sir," said Ned.

"That 'sir' again. I beg you to make it 'Lawrence.' I am of your company of players now. Yes, you sing well. But now I want to see you in your best part. Which is that?"

"Troilus, but alas! you will not see it."

Under interested questioning, Ned told the story of the court presentation of *Troilus and Cressida*. Lawrence said, "It sounds like a play the King might like to see some day. He is, above all, a man of peace, and will approve a play that exposes the ugly face of war."

"But the Queen said . . ."

"The Queen is dead, Ned, and the King is not bound by what she said or did."

Thus was a great hope born in Ned and with it the knowledge that he must make this man his friend. To begin with, he must hide his distaste for the party which lay unpleasantly ahead.

There was an elegant little boat, flying a royal pennant, waiting for them at the wharf. The boatman, in royal uniform, seemed imperturbably unaware of the many eyes that watched him. Ned could not resist a feeling of pride; he was glad he had decided to dress impressively.

When they came to George's house, there was no one in the shop, but the bell which the opening of the door had sounded brought George hurrying downstairs. He greeted his guests effusively, but it was clear that he was trying to hide something that disturbed him. As he led the way upstairs, he said, "Ned, I rely on you to entertain our distinguished guest for some quarter of an hour or so. Gilbert and I have still some tasks left in preparing the table. The cook was taken sick and could not come, and the one who came instead was not worthy of the occasion. We sent her on her way some hours ago. But all will be well. It is at times like these that I thank God for Gilbert. He begs you will excuse him a while, for he is as greasy as a kitchen wench. Now here is abundance of canary and comfits to stay you. The others will come presently, Robert with Kit and Ian with Andrew. Should I still be occupied, I beg you, Ned, to greet them for me." He hurried out, closing the door behind him.

The bell rang downstairs and Ned called out to the unseen hosts that he would attend to it. The other four guests arrived together, because Kit Bagshaw was the only one who had previously been to the house. Ned remembered him from the backstage meeting at the theatre; the two Scotsmen too, and he soon sorted out their names again—Robert Urquhart, who was about Lawrence Fletcher's age and, like him, trying to hide it, and Ian Bruce, a younger man. Ned had a feeling that he had also met the fourth one, Andrew Cotton, before, and he was sure of it when he saw the pleading and almost frightened look on Andrew's face, begging him not to recall their former meeting. Then Ned remembered: this was the young companion of the cynical Geoffrey, who had been with him at the battle of the chain on the morning of the Essex rebellion.

George's voice called out from the top of the stairs, "Come up! Come up! And welcome." Gilbert too had finally made an appearance and was talking to Lawrence. Soon there was a babel of talk while Gilbert poured and distributed canary. Ned seized the opportunity to take Andrew aside and say with quiet urgency, "What happened to Geoffrey?"

"Caught and executed. And Tyburn, not even the Tower. But I beg you to say nothing. They still might seize me. You too." Andrew's terror was very real.

Ned had long got over any such fear, and he laughed openly. "Nonsense," he said. "All that is long forgotten."

Gilbert handed them their glasses of canary and said, "I did not know you knew each other."

"We don't," said Ned. Then he added quietly, " 'Tis just that Englishmen find each other quickly amid so many Scots."

"Ned!" said Gilbert reprovingly.

Now that everybody had glass in hand, George called for silence to give a well-prepared toast of welcome. "Only a poem is fit for this occasion, and I have prepared one. Give ear.

> "We raise our glasses to our friends
> From far across the border.
> We'll do our best to make amends
> For long years of disorder.
>
> So welcome Lawrence, Ian, Bob,
> Our board and bed are yours
> To share, to use, but not to rob,
> Lest friendship not endures."

The leering bed implications caused some smiles and brought from Kit a shrill giggle which George silenced with, "Quiet, Kit. I have not finished. There are two more verses.

> "Already you have found new mates
> In lively London city,
> And that exceeds all other cates
> Else man were but to pity.
>
> 'Tis time to pledge our friendships bold
> In good and sweet canary
> And let our enemies be told
> That they had best be wary."

The recital was greeted with applause, particularly by the dutiful Gilbert and the unchastened Kit, but Master Urquhart, with a great rolling of his r's, said, "My name is Robert. You called me Bob. That is a barbarous practice of England."

Kit said, "I called him Bob, and he would not speak to me for an hour."

"A most pleasant hour, I am sure, Kit," quipped George.

Ned had been much embarrassed when it was inferred that he was a "mate" of Lawrence. He had been struck in the theatre by George's unbridled reference to the bedding of man with man, and here it was again. Was this one of the signs of the new times? Perhaps the stories about King James were true.

Lawrence won his gratitude and respect when he said, "Your verses were clever, George, but they went too far. Ned is no mate of mine, nor ever will be, I dare swear; but I hope he will be a good friend."

"I meant no more," lied George. "A poet cannot control what his words do when they touch the minds of others."

A handsome young man, almost a replica of the servingman Ned had seen there five years before, came to announce that supper was ready.

The sight of the laden table provoked delighted compliments, but Kit spoiled it all when he said, "George and Gilbert, you really are magicians. How could you do it all, when your cook was stricken by the plague?"

For a moment there was a fearful silence. Then George said, with cold anger, "Who told you that?"

"Is it not true?" asked Kit with wide-eyed innocence.

"It may be. The cook who came in her place told me so."

Lawrence asked, "Had the second cook been with the first?"

"They lived not in the same house. There is no danger. Come, let us eat."

"Drink and be merry, for tomorrow we die," added Andrew, but in a comic tone which did much to relieve the tension. Yet the conversation and the laughter during the sumptuous meal were strained, because everybody felt that the pestilence was presiding at the table.

Not one of the three men from Scotland had ever used a fork before, and Ned was full of admiration for the aplomb with which Lawrence accepted his lack of deftness with the strange implement. Finally he put the fork down and said, "I must practice this in private. Until I have learnt your skill, George, I shall use my fingers—as does the King."

That last thrust was gently delivered and with a smile. George responded to it gallantly. Putting his fork aside with a flourish, he said, "Then let us all eat in the Scottish manner." They all gratefully followed suit.

The meal lasted nearly two hours, and George was much put to it to prevent lapses into silence. Fortunately Kit was there to serve as the butt for his wit, and the young man seemed to enjoy being shot at. The Scotsmen added little to the conversation, for when either of them said something they had to repeat it to be understood, and even on occasion invoke Lawrence as translator.

As soon as the meal was over, Ned longed to leave. Although he had prepared John Lowin not to expect him, he now said he had promised to cue him because he played Sir Toby Belch for the first time on the morrow.

George said, "It appears this Master Lowin has mighty claims upon you."

Gilbert, who knew what a loyal friend John had been to Ned, said, "Master Lowin has done much for Ned."

"And we have not?" snapped George.

Lawrence forestalled Ned's sharp reply. "Ned is first a player, and he has a friendly duty to perform for a fellow player. I am sure he would prefer to stay with us, but his conscience would not be easy, and for that I applaud him. One more drink together, and then we will let him go. What say you, George?"

Grumblingly George said, "So be it. I know him well enough to know he might be a sorry companion if he stayed against his will. Had I but known he would want to leave so early, I should have found you a more congenial partner."

This conversation had taken place during the move from the table into the living room. As more wine was being poured and distributed, Andrew said, "Before you go, Ned, one song, I beg you."

Lawrence quickly interjected, "Players do not like to be asked to sing for their supper."

More and more Ned was finding that he liked Lawrence Fletcher. Now, to match his graciousness, he said, "I shall be happy to sing a song, if it will please the company."

"No," said George peremptorily. "That lute that hangs there looks well but sounds ill. 'Tis but for show—like Kit here."

Kit again enjoyed the joke against himself and then surprised everybody, including himself, by saying, "That is better than to sound well and look ill—like—but I dare not complete the comparison."

Even George laughed in amazement. He said, "Bless thee, Kit; thou art translated. Robert, I did you a better service than I knew."

Master Urquhart said, "If Kit become witty, 'twill bring me but mickle delight, for his tongue is too broad for my understanding."

"But it is well practiced in other uses," said George, who must always have the last and preferably dirty word.

When Ned had finished his drink, Lawrence said, " 'Tis time you went, Ned, while yet there is some light. I will come with you to the river."

"We will all go," said George, "lest you lose your way when you return, or fall in with thieves."

"The way is straight, I have a dagger in the use of which I am skilled, and I shall not be long away. Come, Ned."

Very soon Ned and Lawrence were walking together down to the Thames. Lawrence said, "You are ill at ease in such company. I am not; it amuses me. But I prefer the company of players and poets. Did you wonder why I wanted you there tonight?"

"It was you, not George and Gilbert that invited me?" asked Ned in surprise.

"Yes, it was I. George had someone else in mind for me. Be not alarmed. I seek your friendship only."

"But why?" Ned was now thoroughly puzzled.

"Time will tell. Suffice it now to say that you are a player of quality in my company, and you are pleasing to the eye and intriguing to the mind."

"And I am Will Shakespeare's brother," said Ned pointedly.

"Why do you use that tone? You should be proud to be his brother. But it matters not to me that you are related."

"It doesn't?" said Ned in some disbelief.

"Why should it? Your brother is my fellow. I wish you to be my friend. To prove it, I will tell you the secret of tomorrow, for I know you can be trusted."

When he had got over the initial excitement of the news of the imminent announcement of the royal patronage, Ned said, "The King. What is he like?"

"He is a good man, and has been generous to me and many others. In time I think you will meet him, and in circumstances when you can see the man, not the monarch. Then you can judge for yourself."

The King's scroll came to the theatre by royal messenger during the following morning's rehearsal. John Heminge called everybody onstage and made the announcement together with an announcement that a party would follow the afternoon's performance. Incredulity gave way to wild joy.

The audience was small, but not even this could impair the happiness of the company. Richard Burbage entered onstage, followed by the whole company who lined up behind him. An excited stillness grew in the audience as he said, "My lords, ladies, and gentlemen. We have just received very happy news, and we wish to share it with you. We have received a pronouncement from His Majesty, King James, and here to read it to you is our new fellow, Master Lawrence Fletcher."

Lawrence had not come on with the rest of the company. He now made an impressive entrance, carrying the royal scroll, the company making way for him. Ned felt a personal pride in him.

Lawrence said, "My lords, ladies, and gentlemen, I would first like to say how honored I am to be admitted to the fellowship of the greatest band of players in England." This was greeted with a burst of applause, for many of the company's most loyal adherents were present there especially that afternoon to see John Lowin's debut as Sir Toby Belch. "And now to the royal decree. I shall but read the first sentence, for 'twill suffice."

This tactic had been agreed on backstage, for the second sentence contained the ominous clause, "when the infection of the plague shall decrease." "Here then it is: 'Know ye that We of our especial grace, certain knowledge, and mere motion have licensed and authorized and by these presents do license and authorize these our servants, Lawrence Fletcher, William Shakespeare, Richard Burbage, Augustine Phillips, John Heminge, Henry Condell, William Sly, Robert Armin, Richard

Cowley, and the rest of their associates freely to use and exercise the art and faculty of playing comedies, tragedies, histories, interludes, morals, pastorals, stageplays and such others like as they have already studied or hereafter shall use or study, as well for the recreation of our loving subjects as for our solace and pleasure when we shall think good to see them, during our pleasure." He lowered the scroll and said, "And so, my lords, ladies, and gentlemen, you are about to see a performance of Master William Shakespeare's *Twelfth Night* played by the King's Men."

There was a long outburst of delighted applause. As the players moved offstage, one thought was uppermost in the minds of those among them who had not previously seen or heard the document: the first-named sharer was Lawrence Fletcher. This led to the conclusion that it was he who had brought about this great good fortune for the company. Ned felt that this augured well for his own future.

The performance began in a spirit of celebration, but it was not completed. When Augustine Phillips as Malvolio made his entrance in the letter scene, he had but spoken his opening line, " 'Tis but fortune; all is fortune," when a woman in the second gallery emitted a frightening scream. It was so startling that Gus stopped speaking. All eyes were turned in the direction of the scream. There they saw a middle-aged woman with her arm around a man, presumably her husband. He had vomited over her and was deathly pale. People near them began to draw away, and the terrifying whisper spread: "The plague!" In a surprisingly short time the theatre was empty, except for the couple in the gallery and the players onstage, where they had all gathered.

John Heminge took charge. "Cuthbert, get a cart. Some of you young ones come with me; only unmarried men must touch him."

When they got to the stricken couple, the woman was moaning and the man gasping. As the group approached, the woman said, "It is the plague. I have just felt under his arm; there is a lump there. He is a good man. He helped to bury a neighbor, and from him he caught it."

Soon Cuthbert called from below that the cart was waiting. It was John and Ned who took hold of the doomed man to help him down the stairs. Sam guided the woman and whispered words of futile comfort to her. When she stood up, she looked at her stained dress and, with the same pathetic whine, said, "My dress. Look at it. And 'twas a new one too."

It turned out that the couple lived but half a mile away and did not have to cross the river. They were made as comfortable as possible in the jolting cart, the man lying with his head in the fouled lap of his wife. Cuthbert paid the carter, one of the few men whose occupation throve during the plague. This particular one, an unsavory but cheerful specimen, said, "This is my third today, but the other two were dead already. Mark me, sir, this is going to be a heavy visitation," and he drove away, chuckling. The parsimonious Cuthbert had paid the carter out of quick compassion for the couple, but he was dismayed that they had ruined the performance and the word would soon spread.

A valiant effort was made to make the evening's party an occasion worthy of the company's great honor, but nobody could quite forget the pall that hung over the city. The hero of the evening was Lawrence Fletcher, and he saw to it that he met and spoke to every player, apprentice, musician, and stagehand. To Ned he said, "I am glad you left George's when you did. I enjoyed the rest of the party, but I don't think you would have. The wine even loosened Gilbert's tongue, and he was worth listening to. He even scored off George once or twice, and George was proud of him for doing so. But tell me where you live; I may need to see you."

As Ned gave him the address, he wondered what the "need" could be, but he now found Lawrence so likable that he saw no sinister purpose in it.

For the King's Men the new reign could not have started more auspiciously. But the pestilence spread so rapidly that, a week after the party of celebration, the theatres were closed. That was on Thursday, May 26. The Globe was to remain closed for the rest of that year, and more than thirty thousand Londoners were to die of the plague, among them some good friends of the company.

THIRTY-NINE

THE SHARERS MET AT THE THEATRE THE DAY AFTER THE CLOSURE. THE outlook was dismal. The season had been bad, and now they were faced with the necessity of a tour. They decided to set out on Monday, June 13. They would first go to Oxford, where they would stay as long as business justified, maybe as much as two weeks. That city was likely to prove the most profitable of the tour.

Will agreed to play with them in Oxford, but then he would leave for Stratford, where he would spend the summer in writing *Othello* and *Measure for Measure*. His outlining of the two plays did much to brighten the meeting.

Gus Phillips was particularly depressed by the threat of the plague. It was the menace to his new and only son which moved him as never before. He had lain awake most of the night and told Will the next morning that he had decided to rent out the London house forthwith—there was such a shortage of accommodation that there would be ready tenants, in spite of the plague—and would move the family to his father's home in Mortlake. Will would have to find new lodging when he came back from Stratford, for there was not an adequate place for him in the Mortlake house now that Robert and Elizabeth Gough were living there.

This was the first meeting of sharers that Lawrence Fletcher had attended. He endeared himself to his eight fellows by insisting that he would not take his share of the tour income; he was quite content and able to wait until they were profitably playing at the Globe again. Furthermore, he said he would keep them informed of any germane happenings in London, and if there was anything he could do for their wives and families left behind they had but to let him know.

While the sharers were meeting, John and Ned were also talking about the summer. It was almost certain that John would be engaged for the tour but it was unlikely that Ned would be. Ned was determined to earn money, not only to maintain himself but to continue paying his debt to Will; about half of the fifty shillings had already been paid. When John pressed him as to how he would earn money, he said he did not know; he did not tell John that he had decided to approach Lawrence Fletcher; there might be something Lawrence could find for him at court.

During the meeting of the sharers, Will made one request: if he could persuade Ned to return with him to Stratford, would he be allowed to play his parts in Oxford? It was readily agreed; even John Heminge was less opposed to it than Will had expected him to be.

As soon as the meeting was over, Will and Gus went to see Ned, who was in John Lowin's room. They brought the news that Gus was moving his family to Mortlake permanently, before he left on tour. Will said that he would not seek a new lodging until he returned from Stratford at the end of the summer.

"Will you write in Stratford?" asked Ned.

"Yes," said Will. "I have two plays in mind. And one of them will have a leading part for you, John—the villain."

Will regretted his words as soon as he had said them, for the sharers would fill all the other major roles. He began searching for an evasive answer to the question he knew would come.

"And me? Do you write another Troilus for me?" asked Ned.

"I should not have spoken about the plays at all," Will replied lightly. "Did you not see how Gus frowned at me? The giving of the parts belongs to the sharers, not just to the author. But come, Ned, let us go to your room, if these gentlemen will excuse us. I have family matters to talk about with you."

When they were alone, Will told Ned about the Oxford-Stratford plan. Ned was immediately wary. "Was it you who asked this favor?" he asked.

"Yes," said Will, "but the plan was welcomed. We want to give of our best at Oxford."

"And if I return to London from Oxford instead of going home?"

Will had not thought of this possibility. "There are many reasons why I want you to come to Stratford. First, there is our mother; she dotes on you, and she cannot have many more years to live. Then there is the plague here."

"But Gilbert will stay."

"He has to, but you do not. And there is more too. It would please me to have you there; I should be starved for London talk without you. Then there is Judith. She is eighteen now, and it distresses me that she cannot read and write. Perhaps you could persuade her to learn; you were always close to each other. If you liked, you could stay at New Place. Anne would welcome you; she has changed, Ned."

"Not as much as that, Will. She might endure me under her roof, but not welcome me."

"Let me not press you for an answer now, Ned. Let us go out to supper together."

Ned was caught in a dilemma. Will's plan was eminently sensible, and yet Stratford for a whole summer was a tedious prospect. He had no great fear of the plague; his destiny would not allow it to touch him, else why had the bullet killed Robin and not him? But he could not stay in London unless he found some work to do.

As if to resolve his dilemma, there was a knock at the door and Lawrence Fletcher entered. It was hard to tell whether the newcomer or Will was the more surprised to see the other.

Lawrence quickly recovered and said, "I had not looked for such pleasure: not one Shakespeare, but two. I had thought that Ned might be in low spirits to learn that he is to be left behind—unless, of course, he plays in Oxford—and I came to take him to supper to cheer him."

"That was part of my purpose in coming too," said Will.

"Then I will defer to you," said Lawrence.

"Cannot we all three sup together? And John too?" asked Ned.

After a slight hesitation, Lawrence said, "Master Will and I are both selfish, Ned. We want you to ourselves. You should be flattered. Tonight, your brother; tomorrow, your friend. I will come for you, and now I know where you live, it will be easier. Until tomorrow then, Ned."

As soon as the brothers were alone, Will said, "I wonder why he came."

Almost guiltily, Ned said, "To cheer me; that was all. You heard what he said."

"Yes, I heard," said Will. "Come, let us eat."

With the theatres closed and many people leaving the city, the tavern was almost empty. During the meal, Will said, "Ned, you are twenty-three and have true quality as a player, but you must be patient. You asked if I was writing parts for you in the new plays. First the sharers must be served. There would be little for John were it not that Tom Pope had left."

"And I must wait for Will Sly to leave or die," said Ned bitterly.

"You have already had good parts, and there will be others."

"It is I should play Romeo, not Dick Burbage."

"Even Dick might agree with you about that, but when the audience thinks of Romeo they think of Burbage, and while he lives they will have no other."

"By the time he dies I myself shall have become old. I shall never have my chance. I begin to loathe the theatre."

"No, Ned. You love it too much. I know that that is the kind of love that can turn all too readily to hate, but you must not let that happen. You are a player, much more than I am or ever was. It is the mystery of good playing that when you are another you are most yourself. You are that kind of player and would not be fully alive without the theatre. Just have faith that your chance will come, for your fellows now know your quality. Let us hope that we will be back at the Globe again soon after Oxford."

By this time Ned was in a bad mood. He said, "I do not want to go to Stratford, and I may not even want to go to Oxford." He felt he should keep his choice open until he heard what Lawrence Fletcher had to say.

"Not go to Oxford? I don't understand. What will you do in London?"

"What do other actors do when there is no work in the theatre for them? I shall live."

Will could feel himself beginning to lose patience, so he said he had work to do and they soon left the tavern. As they were bidding each other goodnight, he could not resist saying, "Let me know your decision about Oxford and Stratford as soon as you can. I suppose you must first talk about it with your new friend, Lawrence; maybe he has other plans for you."

With a hint of defiance, Ned said, "Yes; it may be so."

All the next day Ned was impatient for Lawrence to come. He had told John nothing about the expected visitor when they had eaten together at noon; he had not even said anything about Oxford, and was lightly evasive when John had asked him what he would do for the summer.

"Why don't you go home to Stratford?" John had asked.

"I might even do that," Ned had replied with a comic emphasis which implied that such a summer would be a fate worse than the plague.

Ned was delighted when Lawrence came an hour earlier than he expected him, and his obvious joy brought equal delight to the visitor. Ned had bought a bottle of canary to greet his friend.

"Such extravagance!" quipped Lawrence. "I feel honored indeed."

As they raised their pewter cups—Ned had no glasses—Lawrence said, "May we both have a very happy summer, in spite of the plague, and the tour." After they had drunk, he said, "What will you do, Ned?"

"I know not."

"Will you play at Oxford and then go on to Stratford with Will? That was the plan he had for you."

Lawrence's tone confirmed Ned's suspicions that Oxford was a bait to land him in Stratford, and he resented it, but he was careful not to show this. He said casually, "I may play at Oxford and then come back here."

"Have you told your brother that?"

"Yes."

"That must have upset him. Was he impatient?"

"No; he just pleaded with me to go to Stratford."

"He is a truly remarkable man. Already I know that I shall never know him. There are deep wells of bitterness and anger and sorrow in him but the surface is ever gentle. The unseen man is in *Hamlet* and *Troilus and Cressida*."

Ned seized eagerly on this last. "You have read *Troilus?*"

"Yes. You said it was your best part and had been intended for Burbage. As a sharer I can read all the plays, and that was the first I asked for."

"Your judgment? Will the King like it and allow it?"

"That is a whole quiver of questions," said Lawrence, amused by Ned's eagerness. "The play is much to my taste, and I would like to see it, especially since you would be the Troilus. As for the King, there is much in it that he would like too: the ancient heroes, the wonderful speeches, the dispraise of war—mark my words, he will bring peace with all the old enemies of England. He would not like the reduction of all love to lust, but he would applaud the true friendship of Achilles and Patroclus."

"Even though Patroclus was the catamite of Achilles?"

"Even so."

"Tell me, Lawrence, is the King so given?"

"If I knew that he were, I would not tell you or anybody, for that would be plain treason, but I do not know it. He likes the company of handsome young men and bestows time, favors, and affection on them, but he also likes to see them well married and is himself a good husband and a good father. Are you answered?"

"It still puzzles me."

"I too? Do I puzzle you?" Lawrence challenged with a smile.

Ned was embarrassed. "I must confess I cannot understand why you should choose me for friend."

"John Lowin is your friend. Does he puzzle you?"

"No."

"Then let it be so with me."

Ned was eager to change the subject. "But *Troilus*. Will the King allow it?"

"I know not. I have made inquiries at court. Most people think it was pain rather than displeasure which made the old Queen stop the play, but stop it she did, and the King might not choose to offend her memory by allowing it. And even if he did, I doubt it would please the groundlings, and as a sharer I must think of that."

Ned's disappointment was obvious. "I hoped not so much for the Globe as the King's Palace."

"How much would you give for such an opportunity?" asked Lawrence with amusement.

Ned answered impulsively, "Anything."

"That is a high price, and it is possible that the privilege might be bought for less." Now there was a mocking in the lightness. "But come. We must have a good supper. This is our first meal together."

"We ate together at George's and at the tavern party," said Ned with calculated innocence.

"Call you that 'together'?"

During the first part of the excellent meal, Lawrence was careful to avoid embarrassing Ned further. Instead he flattered him by confiding some of the secrets of the sharers' meeting. He was amazed, or pretended to be, that Will had not told his brother about the two new plays.

"He said that there would be no good part for me in them," said Ned bitterly. "I must wait for Will Sly to die."

"If I were Sly, I should tremble for my safety," joked Lawrence.

Toward the end of the meal, when they had both eaten and drunk too much, Lawrence said, "If you come back to London from Oxford, it would be foolish to pay rent for a room while you would not be earning; foolish too to risk contagion when you might escape it. Why not come and live with me? Wherever the King is, I shall have good quarters nearby. Now it is Hampton Court; it may be Windsor or Richmond; all pleasant places. And you would meet men of position and power, and much might come of that."

Ned had been so unprepared for this suggestion that he had let Lawrence run on. Now, his brain rather wine-befuddled, he said, "That is kind and generous, but what could I do for you in return?"

Lawrence looked at him appraisingly for a moment, and then said with a warm smile, "Friendship is not merchandise; it counts not returns. Your company would be all I ask."

"I fear I should be bad company, if I were not playing."

"I think not. You would find much to divert you. And it would not be amiss for you to learn the ways of those who haunt the court. But I do not need an answer now. Weigh it well: Stratford or the court?"

Ned reeled to sleep that night with a full stomach and a clouded brain. He awoke late the next morning. His head ached a little but his brain was clear, and he set about making his decision. He was convinced that, if he accepted his hospitality, Lawrence would ultimately expect him to become his bed companion. He was no longer revolted by the idea, but was certain he would find little pleasure in it, and he might find himself rejecting it; then the good friend could be expected to turn into a bad enemy. Yet he liked to be with Lawrence and was flattered by his attention; Ned knew many a young man who would desire above all to be so sought after.

He was tempted to discuss the whole matter with John, but could not. He knew what John would say: "If you are right about Lawrence

Fletcher, it would not be fair and honorable to accept his largess and then deny him your body."

Suddenly Will and the Earl of Southampton came to Ned's mind. There the position had been reversed; the patron had been the beautiful young man. Ned doubted that Will had lain with him, but it was possible, as it was possible that he himself would at last lie with Lawrence. There was even some excitement in contemplating the possibility, just because Ned did not know how he would react. Will was the one who could counsel him, but he could not raise the subject with him. From Will's remarks, he may even have sensed Lawrence's purpose. Then he would surprise both Will and Lawrence by going to Stratford. Yes, that was the wiser thing to do, until he knew Lawrence and himself much better. And if Stratford proved too intolerable, he could always return to London.

With his mind made up, and before he could change it, Ned went straight to the Phillips home to speak to Will. Without meaning to do so, he arrived just as the household was sitting down to dinner and was prevailed upon to join them.

Plans for the summer were the chief subject of conversation. It was clear that Mistress Phillips was leaving her London home against her wishes. "Gus is so frightened of this particular visitation; we have all lived through others." Nobody commented on this; it had been heard too frequently.

Ned gave to the whole table the news he had brought for Will. It was better that way, but Will's look across the table showed how happy he was.

Ned made it his business to be at the theatre the following Monday when he knew the sharers were meeting, for he had to give Lawrence his decision. He covered his going to the theatre by persuading John to accompany him for some sword practice on the stage.

Hearing the sounds onstage, Lawrence came out to see what was happening. Ned could not resist impressing him with a dazzling attack on John, who was both surprised and amused, knowing full well what had prompted the display. He parried as best he could but was soon laughingly calling out, "Mercy! I beg mercy!"

When they stopped, Lawrence came on to congratulate Ned and lead him aside. As soon as they were out of John's earshot, Lawrence said, "I hoped you would be here today. I thought you might be. Now tell me your decision. Are you going to spend the summer with me or at Stratford?"

Ned was quick to notice that the choice had changed from the court or Stratford; now it was Lawrence or Stratford. More than ever was he certain of his decision, but he had to soften the blow. "Will has persuaded me to go home after Oxford. My mother is old and cannot live long. I am her youngest and favorite son, and come September, it will be two years since she saw me; that was when my father died."

"That is the decision of a good son, and I cannot but applaud it."

There was a hint of coldness which Ned wanted to dispel. He said, "Mayhap I shall return soon; I shall quickly grow aweary of Stratford."

"Then I shall expect to see you. Where will you be staying?"

So the offer of hospitality was closing. Ned looked embarrassed as he floundered for an answer.

Lawrence said, "I fear my own house may be full by the time you return. So many people are crowding into Hampton Court that some are already living in tents. I have many friends; I cannot deny them room. . . . But John grows impatient; he is eager to repay that furious attack you made on him."

As Lawrence walked away, he said to John, "I am sorry I cannot stay to see you pay Ned back. I am sure you will do so. You must, for the honor of us older men."

Not for a moment had Lawrence lost his charm and poise, but ambition whispered to Ned that he had just kicked away a ladder; he was determined to regain it, but not by changing his mind about Stratford. That decision was now irrevocable.

John said, "Have with you. I must indeed pay you back." And he did so, and with ease, for Ned's mind was elsewhere.

Ned soon said, somewhat petulantly, "Enough. I grow tired of this." Then he added, "Forgive me, John. I am ill at ease."

"Master Fletcher?" queried John.

Ned looked him full in the face but said nothing. Then abruptly he left the stage, put his foil away angrily, and hurriedly left the theatre.

FORTY

SOON AFTER DAYBREAK ON THE MORNING OF MONDAY, JUNE 13, THE eighteen travelers gathered at the Globe. They knew they were bound for Oxford, but beyond that they did not know where they were going or how long it would be before they saw London again. Some of them were filled with anxiety for the wives and children they were leaving behind. The weekly death toll was steadily mounting; last week it had been over a hundred, but there was a fear that it might go to ten times that number, as it had in bad visitations in the past. Both Heminge and Condell had commissioned Robert Gough to find accommodations in Mortlake for their wives and large families if it seemed that the plague was going to be a major disaster.

There was promise of a beautiful day as the company set out to cross London Bridge. Cuthbert Burbage and Sam Gilburne were there to help them on their way and to bid them farewell, Sam striving to hide his sorrow at being left behind. The procession made a brave show. They were well aware that, by the time they crossed the Bridge, the streets would be busy and the King's Men had an obligation to their patron to look their colorful best when they paraded in public.

No one would be able to judge from their demeanor that probably many hundreds of tedious and painful miles lay ahead of them, all to be covered at a walking pace, set by the cart.

As soon as they had passed Tyburn, for once empty of corpses, Heminge and Condell rode on ahead to High Wycombe to secure beds for the night for the eighteen travelers. It would not be easy because many people were leaving London. Master Harry Lockett of the Stag welcomed them; yes, the inn was very full, but he would put them up somehow; they would have to sleep six a room, and the boys could sleep in the stables with the ostlers.

The players endured the discomfort of that first night with great goodwill. They ate at a table to themselves but in a crowded room. Most travelers had finished their meal before the players had begun, for the slow-paced cart had made them the last to arrive. The older sharers regaled the table with tales of previous tours, compared with which the present one was a royal progress; they told of the times when the only horse to be afforded was one to draw a cart, when the only roof to sleep under was a tree, when all their efforts were so profitless that to avoid starvation they had to sell their costumes and abandon their travels.

Heminge was quick to add that they might be confronted with unforeseen hardships on this tour, even though now they would be officially welcomed by the mayor and officially paid for one performance, "except in those puritanical cities where they will welcome the plague before a player." In most places, after the official performance at the Guildhall, they would have to play any further performances in an inn yard. Of course, there was always the chance of a performance and a night's hospitality at a great house; there were two near Oxford of which he had high hopes; those were the good nights: best pay, best food, best beds, and best audiences.

While they talked and listened they seemed to be oblivious of the other people in the room, but they were themselves the object of much curiosity and comment. Many of the people had never seen a play, but they had heard much of players, and none of it good. Yet these seemed worthy citizens, were excellently dressed, and were called the "King's Men." It was another of those strange things you chanced upon by traveling.

The next morning the King's Men were up at dawn and away soon after. This time Will and Gus joined Heminge and Condell in riding on ahead; apart from the accommodations to be found, there was the mayor to be seen.

Oxford was very crowded, not only with those traveling through, but with many Londoners who were wealthy enough to take up residence there until the plague had passed. Prices for supper and a bed had become exorbitant, but Master Davenant insisted on finding room for his "good friend, Master Shakespeare," and his three companions. The tavern existed to provide food and drink, not beds. John Heminge hoped to find accommodations for the other fourteen members of the company at the Cross Inn which was separated from the tavern by a common yard.

The cheery host of the Cross Inn was as unrelentingly grasping as he was heartily welcoming; after hard times he meant to make the most of a good one. The only thing which made him agree to squeeze in the fourteen was the fact that the yard would be used for the public performances of the plays, and for this he insisted on sharing equally in the money taken, in return for supplying a makeshift platform. John Heminge proved a match for him in bargaining; no one was to sleep in the stables, and after every performance the company was to be given a free supper with ale; if any of the players made music in the evening for the inn's guests, the host was to have only a quarter of the money taken, for he would benefit from the greater drinking of the guests who would linger to hear the music.

While John Heminge was dealing with the innkeeper, the other three men went to see the mayor. He was delighted to see them for he was an enthusiastic playgoer and had been rejoiced to hear of the great honor bestowed upon them by the King. He could not conceal the fact that he was also a harassed man, and finally confided the source of his distress, which was of great concern to his visitors. They were strictly enjoined to keep secret that a traveler from London had died that day of the plague. Fortunately he had been staying with a friend, a widower who lived alone, and so it was possible so far to keep the death a secret; the corpse would be buried without ceremony during the night.

Never had Oxford been graced with so many distinguished visitors as now; some foreign ambassadors with their retinues had taken up summer residence there, for the King seemed to be moving further west all the time; he was now at Windsor, having been driven from Hampton Court by an outbreak of plague among those who crowded the vicinity in hope of courtly favors. Were the news of the single death to leak out, Oxford as a place of refuge might soon be abandoned.

The mayor readily agreed to invite the King's Men to give a performance of *Hamlet* at the Guildhall the following evening after supper. He would pay them forty shillings. The players were much impressed, for this was more than they were likely to get for any such performance anywhere else. It flashed into Gus's memory that it was exactly the sum paid by the adherents of the Earl of Essex for the fateful performance of *Richard II*. The mayor would immediately set about inviting all the great ones in the city, but he feared that the heads of some of the colleges would not come as it might countenance the attendance of their students at subsequent public performances, and they would not be party to anything that would tempt the young scholars from their studies. "Besides," added the mayor, "one or two of them are of a puritanical persuasion and frown on all pleasures, but the city is not with them."

John Davenant invited the whole company to be his guests at supper that night. He was a changed man; he had almost learned to smile since he had found a new, young, beautiful, and buxom wife.

Ned was very disturbed by Mistress Jane Davenant. Was he right in believing that she looked at him invitingly? He readily agreed to sing after supper, but he was singing for her, and there was no doubt that she was aware of it. John Davenant had been a good friend to Ned, but what right did such an old man—he must be even older than Will, who was in his fortieth year—what right had he to marry such a handsome and healthy woman? And why had she agreed to the marriage when she could undoubtedly have had her pick of men of her own age?

That night Ned shared a bed with John Lowin and they discussed the new Mistress Davenant; they had to speak quietly for there were four others in the room: Alexander Cooke and Nicholas Tooley shared a bed and the two young boys, John Edmans and James Lands, were fast asleep on pallets on the floor. It was the boys that muted the talk; Mistress Davenant was the subject of conversation in both beds, for each of the four men was privately sure that he had received a special look from her which promised greater favors to come. All of them were to be disappointed, for Mistress Davenant could not resist making an attempt at conquest with every man she met, but she had no intention of giving anything to the conquered.

Once Jane knew she had touched their desire, while remaining friendly she kept all of them at a distance, all except one—William Shakespeare. It infuriated Ned to observe that Will was getting the attention from Jane that he wanted for himself. At times it seemed as if she was more affected by Will than he was by her—and John Davenant seemed at his happiest when his wife was dancing attendance on his friend.

The official performance for the mayor and Corporation was attended by many "great ones," but its success was marred by the whisper of a plague death, and when next day the news of two further deaths, both of Londoners, could not be suppressed, the attendance at the first public performance was scanty indeed. All these players had come from London, and it was their profession to mingle in public places with all and sundry.

In desperation the sharers held a council immediately after the performance. They would try *Hamlet* the following day, and Tooley would play the Player King to enable Heminge to visit the two great houses in the hope of securing a performance. If, as they dolefully expected, even *Hamlet* would draw but pennies, they would play no more in Oxford but press on to Bath and Bristol, hoping to secure a few shillings and a night's lodging at some houses on the way.

The Friday performance of *Hamlet* drew less than a hundred people and not enough money to pay for their beds that night. A depression settled on the spirits of the company, but Burbage led them gallantly through the performance.

Fortunately John Heminge came back with some good news. One of the great families had gladly agreed to pay twenty shillings for a performance of *A Midsummer Night's Dream*. Heminge had suggested the play when he noticed that there were four young children in the household. It delighted the lord and lady that their offspring would play the fairies. They had wanted the performance on that Saturday, but Heminge said it would be impossible to coach the children in their parts in such a short time. So it was agreed that the performance would be given on Sunday after an early supper; the children must not be kept up too late. Thus had Heminge secured two nights of comfortable and free lodging for the company; in return he had generously offered music for the family and their guests during supper on Saturday, with further music afterwards for dancing, should they so desire, and all at no extra cost.

The innkeeper was happy to hear that the players were leaving in the morning, for his share of the take on the two days had scarce paid for their suppers, players being mighty eaters. They ate little for dinner, for which they had to pay; they said they could not eat much before playing, but that was only an excuse to make them hungry for their free supper.

The great house to which the company journeyed on Saturday morning was only six miles from Oxford. It was new and elaborate, completed only ten years before. The owner, Sir Miles Talbot, had received his knighthood from Queen Elizabeth; he had been a shrewd investor in the adventures of merchant seamen, who had brought back rare silk and spices from the East as well as gold and precious jewels from the West, and he had been clever enough to allow the Queen to share in his profits at a rate absurdly incommensurate with her own investment; and on every possible occasion there had been an expensive gift to Her Majesty. Now Sir Miles, still under forty, was enjoying his wealth in a large mansion with extensive ornamental gardens, including a maze of which he was particularly proud. In Talbot Hall he lived with a beautiful wife, herself a prize, since she was the daughter of an earl, and four lively children, only one of them, alas, a boy.

Sir Miles was no uncultivated barbarian with a gift for making money. He was much given to music and poetry, and every one of his gifts to the Queen had been accompanied by some lines from his own pen. There was one poem he had composed to go with a magnificent pearl which had come from the Indies and was sent to the Queen for her sixtieth birthday. It was in acknowledgment of the gift of land on which his mansion now stood. Scarcely a day passed in which he would not find some excuse to recite its twelve verses. The first was,

> O virgin Queen, for such indeed art thou,
> Whom all men worship, as do I;
> On bended knee I proudly make this vow,
> For thee I'll live, for thee I'll die.

John Heminge had manfully listened to all twelve verses and had been appropriately laudatory.

When the company arrived on Saturday morning in time for a lavish dinner in the servants' hall, Sir Miles was genuinely excited to greet them, particularly because he had composed some verses to be spoken in unison by his children as fairies in the Sunday evening play. "You can insert them at whatever point in the play you think most suitable, but perhaps the very end, by way of epilogue would be most appropriate."

The lines began,

> We are fairies, one and all,
> Come to bless this noble hall,

and after another twenty such lines came the final couplet,

> Nobles, ladies, every wight;
> Thus we bid you all Good Night.

Sir Miles said, "With that last line I see them making a deep curtsy."

John Heminge saw it too and wished he didn't, but he knew that Will would be amused rather than annoyed by the addition to his play.

Preparations for the performance began that afternoon. It was to be given at the end of the magnificent long gallery, and it soon became clear that the fairies were to be the most notable ingredient in the presentation. When my lord and lady saw the dresses that Nat Tremayne intended to provide for their children they scorned them and Lady Talbot gave orders to her maids. "Set about making them becoming apparel forthwith, though it mean you sleep not tonight. And spare not my jewel chest. I would have my children dazzle the beholders."

Nat seemed to acquiesce humbly in my lady's contempt for his dresses, but inwardly he determined that Alexander Cooke as Titania should outdazzle the fairies, whatever they wore. He did venture to point out that the dresses should have some regard for the names of the fairies: Peaseblossom, Cobweb, Moth, and Mustardseed. But Lady Talbot soon dismissed that. "What arrant nonsense! Is Sir Francis Bacon a hog or Sir John Parrot a bird?"

Nat's determination to outdo the wardrobe of Talbot Hall grew and grew. Besides, Martin had been pressed into service as a player, and Nat had the pleasure in prospect of dressing him for the first time as Hippolyta; the usual costume for the Queen of the Amazons was splendid, but this time it should be such as had never been seen before. The maids were not the only ones who were likely to have little sleep that night.

All were busy. Gus Phillips was rehearsing the musicians who were to supply the supper music; they were himself, Ned, Cooke, Tooley, and the two boys. Tom Vincent and his assistant were solving the problems of presenting the play at the gallery end. Several players were making sure of lines they had not spoken before because of the new doubling of parts, which would become still more troublesome once the Shakespeares had left. Nat and Martin were feverishly sewing and Nat was saying something which he was to repeat with maddening frequency in the months ahead: "I knew we were going to need it. We should have had two carts, not one."

Will was rehearsing the children and enjoying himself. They ranged in age from ten to six—the boy was the last-born and would make an enchanting Mustardseed. They had already been drilled during the morning by their father in his own lines. Will decided that they should be spoken not only at the end of the play but after the King's Men had disappeared from the stage. He would explain to Sir Miles that nothing should be allowed to take attention away from the children as they spoke their father's lines, but he had the greatest difficulty in getting them to speak those lines with something other than the lifeless solemnity of church responses.

The evening passed pleasantly. Eight guests arrived for supper and to stay the night. Some two dozen more were expected the following evening. Ned's singing of "Who is Sylvia?" provoked some embarrassing laughter which made him stop. Then it was explained that the name of one of the guests was Sylvia. Ned was presented to her, and now it was his turn to embarrass her, for he sang it to her, though he thought her unworthy of the song.

The following morning all in the house except the younger children took Holy Communion in the private chapel; altogether over eighty people were present, and the service contained color and ritual that would have caused Stratford's Vicar Byfield to have delivered a whole series of sermons against idols and vain superstition.

The dinner was not inhibited by puritanical rules against cooking on the Sabbath, and the guests would have been glad to rest after it. However, their host insisted that before supper he should introduce them to the maze, where he would wager they would all get lost; yes, even those who had tried it before.

Even the dinner in the servants' hall was such as to make the players sluggish, and it was some time before the afternoon's rehearsal showed much sign of life. They all woke up when Nat paraded before their astonished eyes Alex and Martin in their guises as Titania and Hippolyta. When John Heminge began with, "But where did you get . . .?" Nat quickly stopped him with, "Ask not, lest my answer trouble you," and his smile suggested unutterable things.

The play, before an audience of more than a hundred, was a great success. The applause which the children received was not only dutiful to the host but deserved. They were delightful, even performing their dance with skill. The only marring incident occurred during the special epilogue. By that time little Mustardseed was very tired, and twice when he should have been speaking with his sisters their father's lines he emitted a great yawn. It provoked one or two embarrassed titters from the audience, but the players, safely hidden behind the doors leading to the gallery, were able to give more rein to their amusement.

The following morning Will and Ned left early for Stratford, and Ned was glad that there was no chance for drawn-out farewells. The wish of all was, "May we meet in London sooner than we expect."

Will and Ned left at a gallop and so they had no chance to speak until they rested their horses to a walk. Then Will said, "Do you feel sad?"

Ned thought for a moment and said, "I doubt I should like touring, for 'tis a hard and uncertain life, but I shall miss our fellows."

"Yes, 'tis so with me too. But if there had not been players who dared the hazards of the road—and 'twas much worse then than now—and if they had not come to Stratford, I should not have been a player or a playwright. Perhaps I should have been a happier man."

Ned answered forcefully. " 'Twas your destiny, Will. Had there been no plays or players, you would still have been a poet. You are what you must be."

"And you, Ned? Had there been no plays or players, what of you?"

"I know not. Stratford could not have contained me." He added wryly, "I doubt even the plague will keep me long from London."

FORTY-ONE

IT WAS JUNE 20 WHEN WILL AND NED TRAVELED TO STRATFORD, SO THEY arrived well before sunset. It had been decided that Will should go to New Place and Ned to Henley Street, whatever other arrangements might be made later. Now that the Greenes were living at New Place, there might not be a bed immediately ready for Ned there, whereas there would always be a place for him in Richard's bed.

Ned arrived to find the house in turmoil and distress; even as he stabled his horse, he heard a cry of pain from the Hart bedroom. Richard had heard the horse and come out. He seemed as delighted as surprised to see Ned, and very happy to learn that he might be home for the whole summer. He quickly explained the tense situation in the household: Joan was in the midst of difficult labor with her second child.

It was a hot night, but even so there was a dull fire burning in the kitchen, heating two pots which hung above it. Seated at an open window to catch an evening breeze was Will Hart, cradling in his lap his sleeping three-year-old son, William. The expectant father appeared glad to see Ned. He said, "Your coming this night is a good omen. 'Twill be a boy. They say 'tis a sure sign if an unexpected man enters the house while a woman is in labor."

Ned gathered that his mother and Anne, as well as the midwife, were with Joan. He could not go up to greet his mother, for it was an improper thing for a man to enter a birth room until the child was born, and then the first to enter had to be the husband.

Soon Will, who had heard the news, also arrived. As he entered the house, Will Hart's comment was, "Better and better. 'Twill be twins, both boys. That is why she is in such heavy labor."

There was general relief when footsteps were heard on the stairs. It was Mary, and she was crying. As soon as she saw her London sons, the surprise stopped her tears for a moment and then they broke out anew in joy as she hurried to take Ned in her arms.

But Will Hart cut short her flood of welcome and questions by insisting on knowing why she was crying; were things going wrong?

"No," said Mary. "It will be a while yet. It is a hard birth, but Joan is strong and with God's help all will be well. I came away because of the bickering between the midwife and Anne. Old Goody Carpenter has birthed more babies than she has years; she was with me for Richard and Ned; she learnt the skills from her own mother, and she was taught to put a piece of iron and a loaf of bread in the bed, the iron to give the mother strength and the bread for food for mother and child. Anne threw them out, and put instead a Bible in the bed; she said the iron and the bread were heathen superstitions. Goody Carpenter was so angry that she was going to throw the Bible out, but at that moment Joan's pains began again and she put it back. There is such enmity in the room that I fear it will bode ill for the child."

Will said, "Mother, go and tell Anne that I am here; then she will come down and you can stay with the midwife. I will ask Anne to come home with me, and Goody Carpenter can do as she will."

As Mary left to climb the stairs, Ned was shocked to see that she had become an old woman. He had been so thoughtless of her; one letter in almost two years. He forthwith determined that he would stay in this house, however newly gracious Anne might be.

When Anne came downstairs, Ned was surprised to notice that she seemed to have got no older; indeed, her face seemed less lined and grim than he remembered it, and there was no doubt of the pleasure, even warmth, with which she greeted her husband. She readily agreed with Will that she should go home; one of the men could fetch her, should she be needed. She said to Ned, "I am glad to see you, Edmund. I hope you will stay a long while to bring comfort to your mother; she takes great delight in you."

During the night the child was born. It was a girl, and by previous agreement she was named Mary, in honor of Joan's mother. The new Mary cried lustily, a good sign she would survive the hazards of infancy.

The bedroom had already been partially decorated in preparation for the inevitable flood of visiting neighbors. Susanna and Judith had eagerly promised to come to put the finishing touches to the room as soon as the baby was born. It was considered as tempting fate confidently to assume in advance the birth of a living child. After Goody Carpenter had left with a sense of double triumph—her iron and bread were still in the bed and a likely-to-live baby had been born—Will Hart insisted that his mother-in-law go to her room and try to sleep. He would stay with Joan and the baby until the morning.

But at first light Mary was up and in the Harts' room. Mother and child were asleep. In whispers Will Hart said he would take the news to New Place. Thomas Greene and his wife, Letitia, had agreed in advance to be the godparents. The baptism would take place in the church after the service on Sunday morning.

Ned had made Richard promise to wake him, and the brothers, before breakfast, went to congratulate their sister and greet their new niece, a red blob of unsightly flesh.

Then Richard quickly finished a meager breakfast and went into the shop to begin work. Ned would join him later, happy now to linger over his breakfast with his mother. She showed him his one letter which she always carried with her; it was now frayed from much handling. She plied him with questions, and Ned was richly rewarded by her happiness when she learned that he might be home for the whole summer and that he intended to work hard with Richard. It was inevitable that they should talk about the plague, and she revealed her deep anxiety about Gilbert.

"The plague could come here too, Mother," said Ned, meaning to comfort her, but it gave her the cue, which she was never slow to take, to tell about the visitation which had decimated Stratford during the summer of 1564 when Will was a newly born baby. "I trembled for him every day and every night. It was a miracle he survived when so many were dying."

While they were still happy in talk, Anne and her daughters arrived with Will Hart, explaining that Will would come later.

Ned was struck by the transformation in Judith. Susanna at twenty was little different from what she had been at eighteen, a charming and intelligent young lady. But Judith had changed from a lively and exuberant girl into a mysteriously disturbing woman, in whom there was a beautiful but unruly animal that she was forced to keep on a leash.

Both girls were glad to see their handsome uncle. Susanna said, "Happy though I am to see you, Uncle Edmund, this is not a morning for uncles, but for a new cousin, and I am eager to see her." And she hurried, but daintily, upstairs.

Judith had not run impulsively to hug Ned as was her wont, but she had not taken her eyes off him. Before she followed her sister upstairs, all she said was, "I am glad that you have come home, Uncle Ned."

Will Hart and Anne had preceded the girls upstairs, and Ned was again alone with his mother. "Are not the girls beautiful, Ned? Anne is an excellent mother."

"Judith is so changed," said Ned.

"Yes," said Mary, speaking quietly. "I worry about her. I sometimes think she is jealous of Susanna, whom everybody praises. And she misses her grandfather. Perhaps it will be better for her now that her father has come home."

Ned left to return his horse. As he passed the Hornby smithy a sight astonished him into stopping. Two men were at work, neither of them Master Hornby. One was clearly the elder son, Roger, but the other? He looked much older than Roger, was toothless and almost bald, his skin a mass of unsightly blotches, and he had a wooden stump for a right leg. The wretched creature looked up and stared at Ned with eyes that burned with a strange fire. He called out, "Ned Shakespeare!"

Could it be his old friend from long ago? Tentatively Ned said, "Francis?"

"Yes, Francis, but a changed man, Ned, not only in my ruined body, but in my saved soul. The Devil tempted me to run away to sea, Ned, and I listened to him. I lusted after foreign women in heathen lands, I did all the works of the Devil, and God punished me with every disease of the flesh, but he saved my soul, and I have come home a happy man."

"You talk too much," said Roger curtly. "There is work to do."

"I testify for the Lord; that is all. Roger has been good to me, Ned. Our father can no longer work, and Roger has made place for me. It was not easy, with only one leg, to shoe a horse, and often I fell down, but always Roger picked me up and helped me. Now I manage well, do I not, Roger?"

"Well enough sometimes, but you talk too much always."

"And you, Ned, have you given up the works of the Devil and come home a saved man?"

"I go back to London, Francis, when the plague is over."

"London is an evil place, Ned, and God punishes it with the plague." Acutely uncomfortable, Ned began to lead his horse away, but Francis called after him, "Repent, Ned, before it is too late. There is no happiness of the flesh like that of the soul."

Ned was deeply disturbed. The prospect of a daily encounter with Francis in his present state was not to be borne. He would try to avoid him. After he had returned the horse—the metal tab it carried showed that it had been out four days, for which the charge was six shillings and sixpence—Ned went to New Place. He found Will in the orchard with the gardener; they were estimating the crop of apples, pears, and plums, which promised to be good. Will proudly displayed to Ned the many new trees which had been planted the year before. Then he said he would return with Ned to pay his respects to Joan and the new Mary, but before they left Ned must meet Letitia Greene; her husband, Thomas, had already gone across the street to Guildhall; after successfully representing the Corporation in a number of actions in London, he had recently been appointed Town Clerk.

Mistress Greene was busy in the kitchen. She and her husband, as godparents, were giving a christening feast on Sunday for the new baby; altogether they expected some twenty people, so there was much to be done in advance, and this was a good opportunity to cook and bake in Anne's absence.

Ned was much taken by Letitia Greene. She combined the apple-cheeked health of a country woman with the poise of a lady of the court. He soon found out that she came from West Meon in Hampshire, but had made frequent visits to London where she met her husband. She surprised Ned by saying she had seen him at the Globe. "It was in that play about Beatrice and Benedick and the comic constable; you sang beautifully. We did not know you then, and Will was not in the play, so we did not seek you out. I wanted to. After all, you and Tom are cousins."

This was a surprising piece of information to Ned. He looked for enlightenment to Will, who said, "Tom is a great one for searching out families, and he says that his great-grandmother was sister to my grandfather. I am happy to believe it."

"Tom is a poet too, like Will," said Letitia. "It must be in the blood. And while he studied at Middle Temple, he played in the Twelfth Night revels." She added, with a smile, "We only talk of such things in private here. Anne frowns upon the theatre, even though she lives by it. But she is a dear and good person, and Tom and I count ourselves fortunate to share her home. And now that Will is home, it will be even better."

As the brothers set out for Henley Street, Ned questioned Will about Thomas Greene. Will was full of praise for the man who lodged in his house; he was pleasant in person, lively in mind, sound in judgment, and honest in all things.

"Does Anne like him?" asked Ned.

"How else would he be in our house?"

"Then is he a Puritan like her? His wife is not. They went to plays in London. He writes poetry too. Is it religious?"

"No, but I am sure he does not read it to Anne. Tom has a gift for pleasing those he wants to please, out of friendship, not weakness. He is a strong advocate in law. With me he talks about poetry and the children; with Anne he talks about the Bible and the children. He is a good friend to Michael Drayton, the poet, and also is at ease with Vicar Byfield."

When they got to the house, neighbors had already begun to pay their visits, and Ned was glad to escape to the shop. In a very short time he had set to work as though he had never been away. Richard was particularly pleased to have his help for he was behindhand with orders for the morrow's market. Now that the delicate and elaborate work of decorating the gloves had fallen to him, he could produce twice as much with help to prepare the leather.

There was one great difference between the shop Ned had fled from and the one to which he had temporarily returned: his brother hardly spoke at all; his father had never stopped. Even when Ned questioned him, Richard's replies, while friendly, were exasperatingly brief. But Ned was glad of the freedom to let his thoughts roam, to John Lowin and the players, to Lawrence Fletcher, to Ben Jonson. Yet he readily welcomed an interruption when someone came into the shop; it was Judith. She seemed to have no particular purpose in coming, and there was a diffidence about her in sharp contrast to the vigor and exuberance Ned remembered.

After a few moments, Richard said, "Did you come for something, Judith?"

"No," she replied. "I just wanted to see Uncle Ned again." She said this as though it were a shameful confession.

In an attempt to restore the old Judith, Ned struck a comic pose and said, "Well, here I am. Behold me!"

Judith gave a nervous smile and moved toward him. Quietly she said, "How long will you stay?"

"Until the plague is over and the King's Men return to London."

"The King's Men?" asked Judith, puzzled. The surprising name had even caused Richard to pause in his work. Ned's explanation awed both his listeners and made Richard even more dubious about the general Stratford condemnation of plays and players.

Judith said wistfully, "I always wanted to see the Queen, but I never did, and now she is dead and buried. I wonder if I shall ever see the King." Her tone implied that she knew she never would.

Ned said jocularly, "Soon you will marry and have children, and then you will have no time to think about kings and queens."

But Judith was not to have her mood changed so easily. With a hint of anger that Ned should treat her so playfully, she said, "I doubt I shall meet in Stratford the man I would marry." Abruptly she turned away and walked out of the shop.

Ned asked Richard, "What has happened to Judith?"

Richard shook his head and said, "I know not. There is a deep unrest in her. Had she been a man, she would have gone to London, like you and Will and Gilbert." He added with a smile, "You should understand her better than I can. Suppose you had been a girl and forced to stay here in Stratford."

Ned remembered what Will had said about teaching Judith to read and write. That was not what he had meant at all. He had sensed the discontent in her and hoped that Ned might be able to help her to accept her lot.

In the next few days he did not see her. Although she came to the house, she did not come into the shop, and there Ned stayed and worked with an industry that surprised and pleased even himself. Nor did Ned see Will; he must already have settled down to his writing. But a dozen times a day his mother found an excuse to come into the shop—to bring him a tidbit to eat, to tell him something amusing that a neighbor had said, to beg him to take a rest. ("Even your father never worked as hard as this.") Every time the look of happiness on her face amply repaid him for his efforts, but for once he was grateful for the Stratford Sunday which stopped all work.

It was a beautiful day for the christening. Joan had been up for two days and was well able to go with the family to church. Will Hart was troubled. He had calculated that this baby was the thirteenth to wear the christening robes. They had been made for Mary's first child, who had died soon after wearing them. Then they had been worn in turn by her seven other children. Then there had been Will's three children and his own William. Of the thirteen, four were dead, two in infancy and two in childhood. It boded ill for his Mary. Finally he confided his superstitious fears to his wife.

She smiled at him and pointed out that he had made a mistake; Hamnet and Judith being twins had been christened together, and a second makeshift gown had had to be made; Joan who was sixteen at the time had helped to stitch it.

"Which of them wore the family robe?" asked Willikins.

"The boy, of course, Hamnet."

The christening feast at New Place was a happy occasion, and it was attended by the vicar and three aldermen with their wives. The vicar greeted Ned warmly; the past was to be forgotten, but he could not forbear pointing out that the plague was divine punishment for man's sins and saying several times, "God is not mocked."

Thomas Greene fulfilled all that Ned had been led to expect. He was a perfect host, effortlessly charming. He said to Ned, "At last I meet you, though I have seen and admired you as a player. I regret what has driven you home, but I cannot help hoping that it will keep you and Will here a while, for you bring a welcome breath of London to my wife and me."

Judith was busy with the other women of New Place in keeping the guests supplied with food and drink, but Ned felt her eyes on him several times. She was obviously making up her mind to say something to him, and finally she did so. "When they have all gone, will you take me for a walk, as you used to?"

It was not a casual request, but Ned treated it as though it were. He said lightly, "I shall be honored. Will Susanna come too?"

"No," said Judith vehemently. Ashamed of her tone, she added limply, "We used to go alone before."

"So be it," said Ned, deliberately ignoring the seriousness that was in Judith.

When the others had all gone, Ned stayed to walk and talk in the garden with Will and Tom Greene; Judith had to take her part in cleaning up after the party, though, since it was the Sabbath, as much work as possible would be postponed to the next day. Soon Ned espied Judith waiting for him, and he said, looking very directly at Will, "I am going for a walk with Judith."

Will said, "I am glad."

Tom Greene said secretively, "She has moped much lately. I think 'tis her coming to full womanhood."

There was no question of which way Ned and Judith would walk; as of old custom, they turned toward the river. Still trying to avoid any seriousness, Ned joked about the christening and the party, about how the baby had started to cry so that the vicar had had to raise his voice to be heard, about how much the fattest alderman had eaten and drunk. Judith neither laughed nor said anything. Finally Ned's efforts to entertain her petered out, and a silence ensued.

It was Judith who broke it. She said, "I do not want to call you Uncle any more. I am eighteen and you are twenty-three, and that is less difference than between my father and mother."

"But what will your mother and the others say?" asked Ned.

"When we are with them, I shall call you nothing, but when we are alone together, I want to call you Ned."

Still trying to keep the conversation light in texture, Ned said, "I doubt we shall be much alone together. I expect to be very busy, helping your Uncle Richard in the shop."

"Don't you want to be alone with me?"

"When time allows, I shall enjoy having walks with you. I always did." Then he added something which he hoped would keep a distance between them. "Is there not some young man you want to be alone with?"

Judith stopped, forcing Ned to stop. She looked full at him accusingly, and there was hurt in her eyes. She said nothing, but Ned knew that she desired him. The suspicion had grown in his mind in the last few days, but he had refused to face the possibility; he could refuse no longer, and it would be cowardly and cruel to pretend that he didn't understand.

Other people were taking their Sunday afternoon walk along the river. All of them knew Judith and some of them knew Ned. There were greetings and smiles. Ned had wanted to get away from them, but now he was glad they were in a public place.

Judith began to walk on again, looking grimly ahead as Ned spoke quietly to her. "It cannot be, Judith. You know it cannot be. I am your uncle, and nothing can alter that. I want to be friends with you, but it can never be more, and unless you can accept that, we cannot even be friends."

There was silence for a while, then quite abruptly Judith turned around and ran away. Ned called her name, but decided not to run after her. He was relieved to see that she turned up toward her home.

Never had Ned known such a dilemma. He began to walk home too, but not past New Place. What should he do? He would have to explain to Will why he couldn't spend time with Judith. Now more than ever he hoped he would not have to stay too long in Stratford, and he thanked God that he did not feel any stir of desire for Judith. Still, when he got home, he could not resist finding an opportunity for a private peep into the family Prayer Book, where he read as number 25 in the Table of Kindred and Affinity that "a man may not marry his brother's daughter."

The next day he was glad to return to his work in the shop. Judith came every day to the house but never once to the shop. Nor did Ned see Will until the following Sunday when the whole family went after church to New Place for dinner.

Conversation was lively at the dinner table, so Judith's taciturnity was not remarked, but Ned noticed that she avoided looking at him. After the meal, Will said he wanted to see him in his room. There he showed Ned a letter he had received from Gus Phillips. It had been sent from Bristol, and while it tried to minimize the difficulties the players were encountering, it was clear that they were earning just enough to keep going; they intended to work their way north to Shrewsbury.

After Ned had read the letter, Will said, "Are you going to take Judith for a walk again this afternoon?"

"No; she has not asked me," said Ned.

"And will not you ask her?"

"No, Will."

"I think I know why. She believes she is in love with you. Is that not it?"

"Yes, and I know not what to do. I wish I could leave Stratford."

"Ned, you have done no wrong. Between us we must try to help her. She longs to leave Stratford and cannot. You are the only young man she knows from that other world. You and London are one in her mind, and she dreams of you all the time."

"Have you spoken to her?"

"Not about what troubles her."

"Does Anne know what she feels?"

"No, and she would never suspect the truth. She worries about Judith and wonders why she cannot be as happy as Susanna. But Judith is a good and obedient daughter to her." Will got up and walked to the window, where he stood looking out into the garden. He called Ned to him and pointed. Judith was with Tom Greene, and she was laughing heartily. Ned was very relieved to see it. Will said, "Go down and ask her to go for a walk with you."

"No, Will. I don't know what to say to her."

"Ned, you have to arrive at an understanding with her, or life will be impossible for both of you here in Stratford. You must learn to talk with the new Judith. Say whatever comes to you, but make no pretense. Honesty sometimes works its own purposes."

As Judith saw Ned approaching, her laughter stopped. Tom Greene said, "I have been telling Judith about some of the comic people I have seen in London. She always likes to hear about London, but I doubt she would like to live there. Her father and I are always glad to get back to Stratford."

"Uncle Ned is not. He only comes here when he must," said Judith. Ned was glad to hear the "Uncle." "I should be like him; I should not want to come back."

"Then you two Londoners talk about the great city; I have work to do," said the town clerk.

Judith, in her old playful mood, said, "It is the Sabbath. You must not work."

"I am but going to read. Is that work?"

"Yes, if it be not the Bible."

"How if it be papers that the vicar has asked me to read?"

"Then the sin is his, and God will punish him."

It was all so lightly said that Tom Greene went away laughing.

"Shall we go for a walk?" asked Ned pleasantly.

Judith hesitated. She had become serious again.

"I beg you to come, Judith. We must be friends again."

Judith looked up at him with a nervous, tentative smile, then by way of answer began to walk. Ned fell in by her side.

"You have avoided me all this past week, and I was glad of it, but we were both wrong, Judith. When I learnt how you felt toward me, I was shocked, but now I am grateful for it."

Judith stopped and looked at him, her face alive with hope.

Ned grasped her arms, looked at her with great compassion, and then went on. "We cannot be lovers, but we can be friends as never before. Whenever I think of Stratford now, I shall think of you."

Judith said, "Is there a woman you love?"

"No, Judith. But I have loved, or thought I did. It could not be. She married another, and now I never think of her."

"I shall never forget you."

"Nor I you, and that is good. Ours is a friendship that will endure. Now, come. Let us go down to the river as we used to, and you must tell me all about Stratford while I tell you all about London."

Judith was not her old self that day, but she gradually relaxed enough to laugh once or twice, and Ned had a great sense of triumph. As he walked home alone to Henley Street after taking Judith back to New Place, he had a strange sense of having become a much older man. Many women of Judith's age were wives and mothers, and he had been treating her as though she were a generation younger than he. Always he had been afflicted with the sense of being the youngest. This strange experience with Judith made him feel as old as Will.

The next day Judith came into the shop, and she was smiling. Richard was surprised and pleased to see the change in her. She had a message for Uncle Ned from her father. "He said to say 'thank you' but he didn't say for what. Was it something about London?"

"Yes," said Ned. "He had lost something and I found it."

FORTY-TWO

As the weeks passed, the news and rumors of the London plague began to frighten the whole country; the weekly death toll was said to be moving from the hundreds into thousands. All semblance of Christian burial had disappeared; cartloads of corpses were being thrown into hastily dug deep pits. Letters from the players told Will that their patronage everywhere was poor; the fearful saw them only as travelers from the plague-stricken city, who might be carriers of death.

At the end of July Will received a letter from Cuthbert Burbage which told him that Tom Pope had died of the plague. Ned was overwhelmed by the irony of the news: if the first Falstaff had not resigned from the King's Men to enjoy retirement, he would have left London with them and escaped the plague.

Ned too received a letter; it was from Lawrence Fletcher. Lawrence had rented the house of Augustine Phillips in Southwark, "at a plague price." The letter said, "With the court continually on the move, I grow dizzy and must take root. What better place than the Phillips home, near the Globe? It was quickly and amicably arranged with Robbie Gough, who had power to act for his brother-in-law. I am sure your brother will learn of it from Gus, but I wanted you to know first. Do you grow tired of

Stratford? Then return to the house that was your first home in London. Think not of the plague. Death will come when it will come and how it pleases, and may as soon call upon you in Stratford as here. Say the plague take one in ten; be confident that you and I belong to the living nine."

While Ned was disturbed by the letter, he was also pleased to know that he had not permanently lost the friendship of Lawrence Fletcher, but still he doubted he could ever bring himself to pay the price he instinctively felt was necessary to retain the friendship. That Lawrence had left the neighborhood of the court might mean that he had lost favor. After much pondering, Ned decided to show the letter to Will.

When he had read it, Will handed it back without immediate comment.

"Think you his influence with the King wanes?" asked Ned.

"I know not. We must wait until we return to London to find out."

"We?"

"Yes, Ned. As long as I write plays, I shall continue to take them to London, but I doubt I shall play more. That pleases both Anne and me." Will's final comment on the letter was, "I am happy that Lawrence is in Gus's house. Much good music was made there, and Lawrence is worthy to inherit the echoes."

Two weeks after the receipt of the letter which had told of the death of Tom Pope, Gilbert arrived in Stratford without warning. George had died. It was hard for Ned to realize that the plague could touch such an exquisite creature, and that his venomous wit was forever silenced. Gilbert himself was very ill, and almost incoherent with fever. A makeshift bed was made for him in an empty room in Henley Street, and his mother nursed him with devotion. There was an unspoken fear that he might have brought the plague to Stratford. Fortunately he had arrived late at night, and every member of the family agreed to keep his arrival secret. If indeed it were the plague and Gilbert died, the secret was necessary to ensure a decent burial for him and to protect the others in the house from being treated as pariahs.

After two days in which Gilbert showed no improvement, Will Hart could no longer contain his fear. At supper he said, "I tremble for my children. We must call in a physician."

Mary's eyes blazed. Never had Ned seen her so angry. "'Tis for yourself you tremble, Will Hart. Gilbert is my son and I will nurse him alone. If you bring a physician here, you leave this house, you and your family."

Nobody, not even Joan in defense of her husband and children, made answer to this. After a lengthy silence, Mary left the table and went upstairs to her sick son.

But it was not the plague which afflicted Gilbert, and slowly he began to recover; the slowness was largely due to his lack of will; he was constantly low in spirit, and it was considered wise that someone keep him company as often as possible. He said very little, but it was Ned to whom he spoke most, for no one else in the house really knew and could understand his relationship with George. Gradually Ned was able to piece together the macabre story.

With the first painful swellings in the groin, George knew his fate was sealed. Gilbert knew it too. While George was still lucid, he insisted that nobody be told. Only Gilbert was to see the deterioration of his body. To spare himself the sight, George made Gilbert drape the mirror. The shop was to remain open. Fortunately, there were very few customers, and they were told that George was out on business; soon no one came to the shop. George had made no will, and his first concern when he knew the end was inevitable was to ensure that Gilbert was his sole legatee. He said with an attempt at a smile, "I do it not for you, Gil, but to cheat my brothers." He dictated with characteristic comment the simple formula. "I, George Smith, being sound in mind and body—a liar to the last, Gil—do give and bequeath all I die possessed of to my dearly beloved friend, Gilbert Shakespeare, to whom I owe the best that life has given me." Gilbert wept as he wrote. "No tears, Gil, or I shall change 'the best that life has given me' to 'the worst.'" Now came the problem of the witnesses to the signature, and they had to be found quickly while George could still write. It happily chanced that Kit Bagshaw came to the house to bring the news of Lawrence Fletcher's move to Southwark. Gilbert decided to confide in him, and his trust was not misplaced. He readily agreed to witness the signature and to seek out Lawrence Fletcher, who he was sure would come at once. When George heard about it, he said, "I cannot believe that Kit can write his name; I shall die happy, having witnessed a miracle."

Ned asked, "Why did you not get Tim the Tailor to witness the signature?"

"The plague had claimed him the week before. I sometimes think it was he George caught it from. Anyway, Tim could not write."

Lawrence Fletcher came readily, but by the time he and Kit arrived, only Gilbert could make out what George was trying to say. It was that he wished they could be blinded like the mirror. Thereafter Lawrence and Kit came every day. Altogether it took George nearly a week to die and during that time Gilbert ate and slept little. Much of his time was spent in keeping the bedroom sweetly perfumed, to purge the air of pestilence. As he watched the painful and delirious end when all communication with George had ceased, his chief concern was to secure Christian burial for his friend. Every day the heavy cart rumbled through the streets to the accompaniment of the heartless cry, "Bring out your dead." Somehow he had to save George from anonymous and prayerless burial with unknown bodies piled in heaps. George died in the night. Gilbert lovingly shrouded the corpse in the best linen they had in store; then he painted the face to hide the ravages of disease. When he had completed his task, he took down the covering cloth from the mirror, as though he wanted George to see his work and approve.

In the early morning he went to see the vicar of the parish, but that frightened man said he could only give Christian burial to those a physician, in person, warranted had not died of the plague. When Gilbert got back to the house, he was horrified to see a cart full of dead bodies stopped outside the door, which was open. Two bearded ruffians with clubs were on guard to prevent any members of the tainted household from escaping. Gilbert guessed later that some suspicious neighbor had informed the authorities and they had broken into the house and found the body. Gilbert was first stopped from entering the house, but, when he explained that he lived there, he was pushed inside and told to stay there. Fearing what was happening, he was already becoming hysterical, and when he saw the shrouded body being roughly handled down the stairs by two men who were making jeering remarks about the painted face and the beautiful linen, he screamed at them and tried to tear their hands from their burden. He heard one of them say, "This linen is too good for burial. 'Twill fetch a good price." Unable to deal with the corpse and Gilbert, they called for help from the guards. They came in and one of them clubbed Gilbert into unconsciousness.

Some hours later he was dragged back into awareness by heavy knocking on the door and loud calling. It was Lawrence Fletcher. Gilbert tried to answer but could not make his voice heard. He tried to rise but could not. Lawrence had arrived to find the red cross of warning fixed to the door, which had been nailed shut, for want of a watchman to guard it. The door now bore the words, "Lord have mercy upon us." As he pondered what to do, Kit Bagshaw arrived. To their eternal credit, and Ned was deeply impressed by it, neither was scared away by the sign on the door. It was clear that the plague had been discovered in the house, and it was probable that George was already dead.

They decided to defy the ban and open the door. Both carried daggers, and they used these to dig the nails loose. As they worked they were aware of fearful and incredulous glances from the rare passersby. When they got inside, they closed the door, leaving the mark of death on it to ensure that they would not be disturbed. Quickly they moved to Gilbert who lay exhausted on the floor, moaning and crying. They lifted him and made to take him upstairs, but he resisted; he did not want to see the bedroom. They sat him down on a stool and gradually gathered from him the story of what had happened earlier. By now Gilbert was very weak from lack of food and sleep, frighteningly feverish, and in utter despair. Finally he consented to lie on the daybed in the living room, and, soon, under the soothing words of Lawrence, he was asleep. Kit would stay with him, but first he would seize his chance to slip out through the back of the house without being seen, to get some fresh food. It was evening before Gilbert woke, but Lawrence and Kit were still there keeping watch. When the realization of what had happened came to him afresh, Gilbert burst into a wild fit of crying. Lawrence cradled him in his arms. Kit had prepared a cold meal in the kitchen, and all three ate. Gilbert seemed better; the burst of crying had done him good. Above all, he wanted to go home to Stratford, and it was agreed that Kit would stay in the house, to protect it from plundering. Kit had no qualms about sleeping in the bed where George had died, for an astrologer friend had assured him that he would live to be an old man; besides he wore an amulet which gave him sure protection from death by the plague.

Lawrence agreed to bring Gilbert a horse the following morning. It would have to be his own, for there were no more for hire in London. Only later did the implication of this sacrifice on the part of Lawrence occur to Gilbert.

His journey home was a dreadful experience. Because Gilbert looked ill, and became progressively more so, no inn or tavern would give him shelter or food. Fortunately the weather was dry and he was able to sleep under trees and hedges. Once he awoke to find that his horse had broken its tether and was nowhere to be seen—and he was still some fifty miles from home. But a kindly, nearby farmer had found and fed it, and then come looking for the owner. When he saw Gilbert, he took pity on the sick man and fed him too; it was the only meal Gilbert had during his three days' journey.

It took Ned several days to get the whole story of what happened in London from Gilbert, and one of the abiding impressions he gained from it was of the goodness and courage of Lawrence Fletcher; he decided to write and tell him so.

Gilbert's future was the subject of much discussion in the family. First, George's eldest brother, Francis, had to be told of the death and about the will. Francis was a bachelor and a successful haberdasher. He was well thought of in Stratford as an industrious and sober citizen. He was often spoken of by the vicar as a "model godfather," for he sedulously cared for the spiritual well-being of his numerous godchildren. Francis and George had disliked each other from boyhood, and the dislike had grown with the years into a mutual detestation; this had been one of the forces which had driven George out of Stratford. Francis decried his brother's "worldliness," and for his part George had frequently told Gilbert that Francis was really like them in desiring men but was too afraid of the Devil to acknowledge it even to himself. He had shocked Gilbert once by saying, "If God prefers Francis to me, he shows poor taste." He had also said, "Francis condemns us the more because he is jealous of our love." As a part of George's reprehensible life, Gilbert was anathema to Francis.

It was first decided that Richard should take the news of George's death to Francis, but Will had a better idea: he would ask Tom Greene to take it and show Francis the will, declaring his legal opinion that it was valid and unassailable. The town clerk agreed to do this. He knew something of the relationship between Gilbert and George, and, from what he had heard of the dead man, felt that Gilbert had well earned every penny that might come to him.

The first comment Francis Smith made on hearing of the death of his brother was, " 'Tis the judgment of God." Tom Greene could not forbear saying, "The plague is no respecter of persons; it takes good and bad alike." Francis had no reply to this, but his look suggested that such an opinion was almost heretical. On the subject of the will he was surprisingly amenable. He said, "George shunned his family in life, and we shun him in death. Whatever property he left was tainted with sin, and we want no part of it. 'Twill bring no good to his paramour." He relented sufficiently to hope that his brother had received Christian burial. When he heard of the common grave, he said, "Now I pity him. He was buried as shamefully as he lived."

Ned took great pains in composing his letter to Lawrence. His admiration and gratitude were genuine, but he did not want to make promises he might not keep, nor yet close doors that should remain open. He said he was glad that Lawrence now lived in the Phillips house, which had been his own home for nearly six years, and he would be happy to return to it "should circumstances allow."

The letter was carried by a young man who rode Lawrence's horse back to London. He longed to see London, even in time of plague.

Gilbert had also sent a letter of gratitude to Lawrence, asking that it might be read to Kit. The writing of the letter had forced Gilbert to consider the future. While the plague lasted, he would stay in Stratford, but he could not stay forever; London was as necessary to him as to Ned. He decided to leave all decisions until he returned to London, which he would do as soon as it was safe. He asked Lawrence to see to it that Kit had all he needed, "and thus you will add to the already immeasurable debt I owe to you, and which with all my efforts I shall never be able to repay."

It was a summer of letters. Almost every week Will heard from one or other of the sharers. After Shrewsbury, they were working their slow way east to Cambridge, Norwich, and Ipswich. Their most profitable engagements had been at private houses, now filled with relatives and friends driven from London. But a doleful letter from John Heminge in early September said, "This dreadful plague bids fair to finish the King's Men before they have begun." He also said that his wife and family and those of Henry Condell had moved to Mortlake; he would be ever grateful to Robert Gough for his good offices in the matter.

During the summer Ned received three letters from John Lowin. The first came from Bristol and set the dismal but humorous tone of the others. It said, "There is much talk here of the Indies and Virginia. It may be we should set sail to play there, for there are but few who come to see us here. The Indians would not understand us, but they would pay with precious stones to see us on display, as we pay with pennies to see them in London."

In mid-September Will was surprised to receive a letter from Ben Jonson. It read:

My dear Friend:

I write to you because you can understand my sorrow. I have lost my little Benjamin. The plague has taken him. I was not even with him when he died, and I was spared the horror of seeing him thrown into a death-cart and from there into a pit.

With my old schoolmaster, William Camden, I am living in Huntingdonshire under the noble and generous patronage of Sir Robert Cotton, recently and most worthily knighted by the King. One night my Benjy came to me in a dream, the red cross of the plague on his forehead. I awoke in terror and was assured by Sir Robert and Master Camden that my dream was but my fear. Then came a letter from my wife with the horrible news.

Benjy was but seven years old, and each day of those seven years was more precious to me than all the words I have written or shall ever write.

When I first met you, I learnt that you had lost your only son. I sympathized, but could not fully enter into your sorrow. Now I know. There is an emptiness in the lives of both of us that nothing can fill.

> *Your desolate friend,*
> BEN JONSON

Will replied immediately. His letter read:

My dear and sorrowing friend:

Your loss brings mine to me afresh. I cannot give you the comfort that time will heal, for 'tis false. Every day I see and hear my Hamnet, as you will see and hear your Benjamin. Both of us were not with our sons at the end, and you, I know, will feel guilty for this, as I did. But it is a mercy that our memories of them are as they were before Death's cruel hand marred their beauty. Our wives were alone, without us to aid them, as they watched the young life ebb painfully away, though for my part I fear I should have given but sorry aid.

There is one comfort for both of us, and this I can avouch. The Muse has power to distract us even from our greatest sorrow. We have lost the sons of our bodies, but to save us from despair there are the sons of our pens crying to be born.

Others will speak to you of God's will, but that is a mystery beyond my understanding. They will urge you to trust His mercy and goodness, and I do so too, but I know you not well enough to know what comfort those words bring you. I write only as one bereft father to another, and it is good to know that one is not alone in this desolation; our common loss will provide a new bond between us when next we meet.

> *Your friend in grief,*
> WILL SHAKESPEARE

By October, London seemed far away to the three Shakespeares who had left it, and the news was that the plague showed little sign of abating. Mary rejoiced that all her sons were home, and she lived for the Sunday dinners when the whole family was together, alternately in her house and at New Place. But the three brothers longed more and more to return to the city, Gilbert because he could never be at ease again in the restrictive atmosphere of Stratford, Ned because he ached to act again, and Will because he had almost completed the two promised plays.

Gilbert was a shrewd man of business, and he did much to improve the affairs of both Will Hart and Richard; the one had been too rash in his dealings and the other too cautious. It was not long before neither would make a purchase or accept an order without Gilbert's approval. Gradually, under his tuition, their own powers of judgment improved; he had to make them independent of him that he might be free to leave as soon as the plague subsided. It had been agreed that all three brothers would return together, but not until it seemed safe. A new resolution had formed within Gilbert; he would reopen the London shop on his own and see what happened.

Ned was happy most of the time, but only because he knew his stay in Stratford was temporary. On Market Days he usually met a readily obliging maid, for the handsome and gallant young Londoner was the subject of many a whispered speculation and unspoken hope, but none could catch his heart.

Will was so eager to share his *Othello* and his *Measure for Measure* with the company that he hungrily gathered all news and rumors from London. By mid-October it was reliably reported that the weekly death toll was down from the thousands to the hundreds, but even so it was still too dangerous to return. Ned and Will were a boon to each other during their isolation from the theatre. They took many a walk together and remembered with affection and laughter plays and players. Ned sensed that Will wanted to read his new plays to him but was not suggesting it to avoid the frustration of Ned's hearing parts that he would crave but which would be given to William Sly. Still, there would be the satisfaction of hearing the plays before the sharers did, in itself a sign of the new bond between the player brothers, and when Ned finally asked to hear them, Will readily agreed. He did not even pledge Ned to secrecy, because he knew there was no need to do so.

When he had heard *Othello*, Ned's disappointment that Cassio could not be his part was balanced by his excitement that Iago had been specially written for his friend, John Lowin. He was transported with admiration of the play itself. Richard Burbage would be magnificent.

Measure for Measure amazed Ned, less for itself than for the glimpse it gave of the secret Will. Could a poet write with such power of the torment of unsatisfied lust who had not felt it? And yet Will gave no hint in his life of such experience. Ned longed to question him but could not. Instead he talked about the play.

"I cannot understand why Isabella did not lie with Angelo to save her brother's life."

"In the story I borrowed she did, but I wanted to write about other things. With so much death in the air, it fills my thoughts, and I am led to ponder about the afterlife."

"Do you believe there is one?"

Will smiled as he replied, "Even to question it is heresy. Claudio believes, but when he is faced with death he is terrified, which proved to Isabella that he did not believe. Her belief was a sure knowledge in her, so that death was not an end but a beginning. That is why I made her a novice. The marriage she saw for herself was with Christ. When she sees her brother's fear of death she is surprised into anger by his hypocrisy; he had believed with his tongue and disbelieved in his heart."

"And you, Will?"

"I long to be as Isabella, and am not quite as craven as Claudio, but that is perhaps the natural and merciful acceptance of the inevitable that grows with years. What about you, Ned?"

"I never think of death. It is something that happens to others. I have felt fear, as when I was wounded in the Essex rebellion, but I have never really faced death. Thus far, this world is enough for me."

At the end of October came a disturbing letter from John Heminge. Although the plague still raged in London, they were abandoning the tour in Ipswich, for their financial plight was desperate. They would return to Mortlake and there wait until the Globe could open again, though there was now little hope that that would happen this year. They begged Will to meet them in Mortlake by mid-November, for some drastic decisions had to be made. Besides, if he brought them two new plays, it would go far to restore their spirits. John Heminge put much faith in Lawrence Fletcher, that he might intercede on their behalf with the King.

Ned made up his mind to go with Will to Mortlake. Richard had insisted that he receive five shillings a week throughout the summer and he had hoarded most of it for just such an emergency as this.

Gilbert's quandary was much more difficult to resolve. If he returned, it must be to his home in London. For nearly two months he had received no news, but he assumed that Kit Bagshaw was still there. During those months it had been virtually impossible to get letters to or from London. As the period of silence lengthened so did Gilbert's anxiety deepen. It was the desire to have done with doubt and uncertainty that finally determined him to travel with Will and Ned, even though he would go alone on to London. The whole family did its best to dissuade him, but he showed unsuspected strength of purpose. To his crying mother Gilbert said, "I tended George to the end and did not catch the plague. Surely that means it is not meant I should do so. And if I find I cannot open the shop, I shall return. But go I must to learn how things are. 'Tis cowardly in me to let another risk death in caring for my house and shop."

The three brothers were to set out on Monday, November 14. Reliable news had arrived from London that the weekly death toll was now down to about five hundred, but even that was a fearful number, and among the recent and notable victims was Will Kemp. Both Will and Ned were saddened by this last news. They talked about it, and Will said, " 'Tis certain he died cursing all Shakespeares. It seems we cannot be true to ourselves without causing pain and making enemies. We can only hope there was no evil in our hearts. Will Kemp was a good clown who made many people happy, but he was an unhappy man himself."

The last Sunday dinner took place at the Henley Street house. It was a depressing occasion, with everyone making a determined effort to make it cheerful. Even Will Hart's habitual garrulity was strained; he would grievously miss Gilbert. For once they were all grateful that the baby was troublesome and demanded much attention and the little boy, who bid fair to be as talkative as his father, tiresomely practiced his expanding vocabulary.

After the dinner, Ned went for a walk with Judith; it had become part of the Sunday ritual. The walks had become progressively more pleasant, so that both looked forward to them as the one event of the week that never disappointed.

"It will be a long time before you come home again," said Judith.

"How can you know that? I may be back very soon. I cannot stay in London unless the theatre opens."

"When Grandmother dies you will come."

Ned was shocked. "You must not talk like that. My mother is not sick. She may live for many years. I may die before her."

"Would you come home if I got married?"

"Yes, I would, if only to warn your husband what a teasing devil he was wedding. But tell me; is there a man?"

"No," said Judith lightly, "nor sign of one. I do not like the young men of Stratford; they think only of cows and corn and buying and selling. It may be I shall never marry. The Shakespeares are not good marriers. There's you and Uncle Richard and Uncle Gilbert: all single."

"But it is not right for a woman not to marry."

"Then why do you not marry one?"

" 'Tis different for a man."

"Because if he lies with a woman, no one need know, but the woman may bear a child. But God's commandment, 'Thou shalt not commit adultery,' is for the man as much as the woman. Have you broken that commandment, Ned?" There was an embarrassed silence. Judith persisted. "Have you, Ned? You said friends like us should have no secrets."

"Why do you make me say it? You know I have lain with women."

"Often?"

"Yes, often." said Ned angrily.

"I'm glad."

This remark took Ned completely by surprise. "Glad? Why?"

"I like people who break rules. I shall break some too."

"What do you mean? What rules?"

"I know not yet. Even talking with you like this is breaking the rules of seemly maiden conversation, and I like it. I shall miss you, Ned. I always did. But this time it won't be so bad as before. I was silly and unhappy about you. Now I see you clearly, and myself too, and it is good. Why do you frown?"

"I worry about you, Judith. I fear life will hurt you."

"It cannot hurt me worse than it hurt my mother. She is now content, and so shall I be."

The revelation that Judith knew something of the painful relationship between her parents stunned Ned, for he was certain that Anne would never have spoken ill of her husband to her children. Did Judith and Susanna know, for instance, that Susanna was conceived before her parents were married? Ned longed to probe, but decided it was wiser not to. He was glad that it was time to turn back for supper at New Place.

The supper table was dominated by a piece of news from Thomas Greene. His wife, Letitia, was pregnant. If the baby was a boy, it would be named William; if a girl, Anne. Will made a promise that, come what may, he would be home for the baptism and would stand godfather.

FORTY-THREE

THE THREE TRAVELERS TO LONDON WELCOMED THE COLD, BRISK WEATHER, not only because it spurred their horses to a good pace, but because it would surely hasten the end of the plague. They had made an early start and rode well, but, even so, the day was so short that it was almost dark before they arrived at Oxford. The city was still crowded—there had been plague deaths there throughout the summer, but not enough to scare many people away—but Master and Mistress Davenant were delighted to greet the three brothers and to give them a room.

Again Ned noticed the extravagant attention the hostess paid to Will. He was particularly interested to see how she would behave to Gilbert. She had not met him before, because by the time he had got to Oxford on his unhappy ride home he had given up all hope of receiving shelter. Rather to Ned's surprise, Mistress Jane was immediately very warm toward Gilbert, and he toward her. Perhaps it was because she sensed that he would never challenge her favors.

There was no doubt that in coming to Oxford the travelers had moved from the bucolic concerns of Stratford to the political orbit of the court, which was now at Winchester. All the talk was of the "conspiracy." Vague rumors of arrests of notable men had filtered through to Stratford some months before, but, since there had been no talk of armed insurrection, they had been dismissed as the result of the inevitable jockeying for power in the new reign. Now, it seemed, the prisoners had been moved from the Tower of London to stand trial for treason before the Commissioners of the King at Winchester. A most ill-assorted group of Catholics and Puritans was accused of conspiring to seize the King's person and even to dethrone him, some said in favor of the Lady Arabella Stuart and others the King of Spain. The most incredible accusation was against Sir Walter Raleigh, a lifelong and implacable foe of Spain, but a man who made enemies easily.

The Davenants were relieved to know that Will and Ned were going to Mortlake, not London, for, although the plague was declining, last week's death toll had been around four hundred. They begged Gilbert to stay with his brothers in Mortlake until it was quite safe to go to the city. They warned him that one minute with a plague victim was enough to bring death. Gilbert nodded, grateful for their concern, but he thought of the week he had spent with the dying George.

As the three brothers rode together to High Wycombe the next day, they were not very communicative even when their horses walked or when they stopped for dinner; they were each lost in his own thoughts of the future. As if to emphasize the bleakness of their prospects the road was deserted, the sun did not shine, and a cold wind bit at them. Master Harry Lockett was glad to welcome them to the Stag Inn, but he was clearly a disturbed and unhappy man. It was Will who guessed that Master Lockett's distress might be prompted by sorrow that among the arrested men awaiting trial at Winchester were some notable Catholic priests. Whatever happened to Lord Cobham, Lord Grey, Sir Walter Raleigh, and the other "conspirators," there was no doubt that the priests would be horribly executed.

Gilbert's comment was, "And I suppose Vicar Byfield would have been burnt when Queen Mary reigned. The Catholics and the Puritans cannot both be right. Where lies the truth, Will?"

"They both have truth, Gil, and both will die for it. It seems that truth is too big to be contained in one man."

Ned said, "Yes, they will both die for it—and kill for it too."

"Not all, Ned. Remember Ben Jonson's priest. He would not kill. And on the other side, my Anne would not kill either."

Before they went to sleep, Will and Ned, after much effort, persuaded Gilbert to travel with them to Mortlake the next day and spend the night there; he had planned to part company with them and ride straight home to Blackfriars. It was Ned who used the winning argument. "First you should see Lawrence Fletcher, and he is certain to be with the other sharers at Mortlake."

But he was not. The sharers had a warm welcome for Will, though some were surprised that Ned was with him, for there seemed to be no immediate prospect of playing. Will had expected difficulty in finding a place for the three brothers to stay, but there was none; those refugees from the plague who could afford it had long fled further west, and a few people had, in the last few days, ventured back to their London homes. The company was waiting for their immediate future to be decided and that depended on Lawrence Fletcher. John Heminge had sent him letters of mounting desperation, and when the company had arrived in Mortlake on the previous Saturday—it was now Wednesday—a message from Lawrence awaited them. He had gone to see the King in Winchester on their behalf. They expected him back any day.

John Heminge had been awaiting Will's arrival for a crucial meeting of the sharers. There was no need to detail their parlous financial state, but Heminge had a surprising suggestion to make. He said, "From the beginning we were only eight sharers, and now we have nine, though the ninth has shared nothing yet. If nine, why not more? The purchase price would give us much needed money at once. 'Tis true our shares would be thereby diminished. Those of you who have no part in the Globe would most suffer, and you it is who must say yea or nay to my idea. I propose that we invite two more sharers to join us: John Lowin and Alexander Cooke. I have made discreet inquiries and I think they can pay our price. When Alex was my apprentice, he always seemed to have more money than I did."

Henry Condell was the first to speak. "My own need for some immediate money is great, for it has been costly to maintain my wife and family here in Mortlake, and there is no knowing when we may move back with safety or when we shall play in the Globe again. For my part, I welcome John's proposal."

So did the others and there was much testimony to the worthiness of Lowin and Cooke both as players and as fellows. John Heminge was deputed to transmit the invitation forthwith.

The unmarried members of the company all stayed at the same inn, and there Heminge found them telling tales to Ned of their adventures on the road. Gilbert too listened, but his mind was on London and what he might find there the following day; he was annoyed that he had allowed himself to be talked into staying the night at Mortlake, especially since the most telling argument had been that he would see and get a report from Lawrence Fletcher. Insofar as he was capable of anger, he had angrily denied the pleas of his brothers that he should stay with them at Mortlake until Lawrence returned from Winchester; come what may, he would go home tomorrow. As he used the word "home," the thought of the place without George suddenly overwhelmed him, and he walked away quickly to hide his tears.

The unexpected appearance of Heminge puzzled the gathering, as did his request for a private word with "John and Alex," rather than the more formal "Master Lowin and Master Cooke." He took the two men into a small private room of the inn and came to the point at once.

"I need not to tell you that the King's Men are royal in name but not in purse. We must find new money and quickly too. I am thus honest with you because you would wish me to be and are men worthy of the truth. Though the sharers hold you both in high esteem, our invitation would not have been made at this time had we not needed the money. We ask you to join us as sharers. The price for each of you is sixty pounds."

It was hard for the two players to believe their good fortune. They had thought they would have to wait years until a sharer died or retired. For a moment neither spoke and then both blurted out their happiness together. The price was high but fair; almost three years' wages, for there had been many weeks when they had earned nothing. Both had made quick calculations about the money and had found ways of getting it as soon as they could get back to London.

John Lowin wanted to go at once to tell Ned his good news, but Heminge said, "No, John. In all matters relating to our fellowship, the sharers must first be told. Besides, it will not be wholly good news for Ned; he is but human, and while we rejoice in the good fortune of a friend, we often wish it could be ours."

Later that night, after the first welcoming celebration of the new sharers had quieted, Will found occasion to speak to John about Ned.

"This will make a difference to your friendship with Ned, John. He cannot but be jealous of your good fortune, even though he is younger than you and much less important to the company. And from this time forward you will have secrets that you cannot share with him."

"But I know he will be happy for me."

"And unhappy for himself. Patience does not come easily to Ned."

Ned was up early the following morning to see Gilbert off. He begged him to return to Mortlake as soon as he could with a report of what he found.

John Lowin was up early too, looking for Ned, whose first words to him were, "What happened last night? I waited for you."

"I was very late at the Phillipses'. Ned, I am a sharer."

A rush of thoughts filled Ned's mind: complete surprise, delight at his friend's success, the realization that it would set something of a barrier between them, the long and perhaps hopeless wait before he himself could become a sharer. It was this last thought that prompted him to say, "Alex Cooke too?"

"Yes," said John, disappointed that Ned's first reaction had not been one of happy congratulations.

Somewhat cynically Ned said, "I wish I had been apprenticed to John Heminge instead of Gus Phillips. But then Alex has money too."

"And he is older than you," said John with some annoyance.

"Only two years." Ned became aware of his friend's disappointment and hastened to make amends. "I'm sorry, John. It was just that I was so taken by surprise. I am truly delighted for you. No one deserves it more. Whether they made you a sharer or not, you are already a leading player. Let us drink together."

While they shared their drink of celebration, John told Ned that as a sharer his first privilege would be to hear Will's two new plays, *Othello* that afternoon and *Measure for Measure* the next afternoon. Ned longed to tell John the good fortune that lay ahead for him in the tragedy, but knew that he must not.

Ned's thoughts that day were full of Lawrence Fletcher. John Lowin's advancement made Ned more than ever determined to improve his own status in the company, and Lawrence might be the way. The result of Fletcher's present mission to the King would certainly indicate the extent of his influence.

But Lawrence did not come that day or the next, and the resulting anxiety impaired the full enjoyment of Will's reading of his two plays. Everybody was excited about *Othello*, particularly since Richard Burbage would have a part worthy of him, and all the sharers were happy that John Lowin would play Iago, the first part Will had written with him in mind. *Measure for Measure* was well received too—Richard Burbage was fascinated by Angelo—but a few of the sharers could not hide their disappointment that Will had not returned to the mood of the happy comedies.

All their immediate plans depended on Lawrence Fletcher, though no one knew exactly what they expected him to produce, and it was decided to postpone all arrangements for the new plays until he arrived, but hope had begun to dwindle. It was only failure that could have so delayed him.

John Lowin tried hard not to tell Ned his Iago secret, and Ned had great private enjoyment from the struggle because he knew what it was that John could not tell him. Ned teased him.

"John, you look like Sarah must have looked when she was ninety years old and knew she was with child for the first time. Is that what being a sharer does to you?"

"There's more than that."

"What could be more? Have you come into a fortune?"

"I cannot tell you, Ned, but I want to."

And finally he did tell him, in the greatest secrecy, and Ned was very glad to be told, if only because it gave him a sense of superiority over John, for Ned had kept his private knowledge secret from John and continued to do so.

Gilbert returned briefly on Saturday, as he had promised he would. He was beaming with happiness. He had found everything unbelievably well. Kit Bagshaw was still in the house, and he had changed everything around as much as possible so that it would seem to Gilbert a different place from the one in which George had died. Then, about six weeks ago, he had brought a friend into the house, Simon Middleton, a young man of good breeding who had been intended for the law, but whose delight, much to his father's disgust, was in tapestry and needlework. Kit and Simon together had set about overhauling the shop's supply of clothes, and, with the help and encouragement of Lawrence Fletcher, had actually sold a few suits to some men who, like themselves, had stayed in London and dared the plague. They had kept a careful account of their transactions and had spent only such money as they needed to live. For the last month they had not had to ask Lawrence to advance them any money.

And so a threesome had been established to live and work together: Gilbert in charge, Kit to bring in customers and buy and sell, and Simon to design and make the clothes. Neither Will nor Ned could ever remember seeing Gilbert so happy.

Ned could not resist asking, "How do you sleep?"

"Well," replied Gilbert mischievously.

"Yes, but how? Who gets the bed, and who is on the daybed?"

"At the present the nights are cold, so the three of us share the bed." And Gilbert's eyes twinkled in a way that belonged more to George than to him.

It was Sunday afternoon when the anxiously awaited Lawrence Fletcher finally arrived. With him was Andrew Cotton, the young man whom Ned had met twice before, in the yard of Essex House on the morning of the rebellion and at George's party. Each time Ned met him he seemed to be on intimate terms with a different companion: first there was Geoffrey, then Ian Bruce, and now Lawrence. Ned wondered if Andrew held the place in Lawrence's house that he had been invited to take and he was disturbed to find that his reaction to the probability was one not exactly of jealousy, but of having been cheated.

Lawrence had no opportunity for more than a happy wave to Ned because he was immediately gathered by some of the waiting sharers and borne off to the Phillips home. On the way Lawrence was informed by John Heminge of the election of the two new sharers.

Lawrence's reaction was unexpected. He said, "That is a major decision, and, since I am affected, I think you might have awaited my return. Am I a sharer or am I not?"

Heminge was flustered. "But we needed the money," he said.

"Was that not the reason for my mission to the King? Were you so certain that I would fail that you could not wait?"

Condell, who was also walking with them, said, "John Lowin and Alex Cooke are worthy of our fellowship. They were sorely tested and found true this summer. For that, as much as the money, I wanted them to be sharers."

"I might want them too," said Lawrence, "but my opinion was not asked."

"I'm sorry, Lawrence. We did wrong," said Heminge. "It was my fault. We should have waited. Forgive me."

Lawrence's victory was complete; never again would John Heminge act as though he were a sharer in name only. During the exchange, Lawrence had displayed no anger, but this had made the cold steel of his objection more impressive, and with Heminge's rare and genuine apology he quickly resumed his gracious manner and amusingly refused to allow his companions any knowledge of the result of his mission or any reason for his protracted absence until all the sharers were present. He quipped, "What concerns all must wait for all," and the implication was not lost on the contrite Heminge.

As soon as all the sharers were present, Lawrence spoke: "I have good news. I understand it was usual for the late Queen to command your presence for the performance of a play during the Christmas season. That will not suffice His Majesty, who is eager to see more of your quality, which I have commended to him in the highest terms. He commands you to perform for him five plays on five succeeding nights, the last being on New Year's Eve." Stunned silence gave way to a babel of happiness and a confusion of excited questions. Lawrence smiled and held up his hand; he had much more to say. "The plague diminishes weekly and Christmas is more than a month away. His Majesty hopes to be at Hampton Court for our plays." Again Lawrence was forced to hold up his hand for silence. "I have more good news, something quite unexpected. You may wonder why I was so long away. While I was at Winchester I received an invitation to visit the Countess of Pembroke at Wilton, which was a day's journey away. I was as surprised as you must be, for I had never met the greatly honored and learned lady, nor do I know how she found out that I was at Winchester, but later I discovered that she knows everything. She must be the most remarkable woman now alive. For reasons of her own she wishes to entertain the King lavishly before he leaves Winchester, and to this purpose she thought it appropriate that he should first see his own players under her roof. Accordingly, we are invited to play *As You Like It*—yes, she named the play too; 'tis her favorite comedy. We are to play it at Wilton on Friday, December second. That will give us ample time."

While, like his fellows, John Heminge was thrilled by this extra piece of news, he was also instinctively cautious; it would be an expensive engagement. He said, almost apologetically, "But 'tis nigh on a week's journey away."

Lawrence looked at him and smiled. "John," he said, as though he were talking to a beloved child, "you will soon learn that I am as aware of money as you are, else I should not have lived so well for so long. The countess and her two sons are all lovers of plays and players, as was her late husband. I had no need to tell her of the hardships the plague has caused us, nor of the cost of the journey to Wilton. Tell me, John, what payment would satisfy you?"

Heminge made a quick calculation, and the result was beyond what could be expected; still, there were benefits other than money to be gained from the performance. He said, "I would hope for fifteen pounds."

The others were surprised by the amount, but Lawrence smiled and said, "The payment will be exactly twice that."

Again he had amazed the sharers. There seemed no end to the miracles this man could work. He was subjected to a bombardment of thanks and congratulations, which he received with a cool enjoyment.

Gus Phillips jokingly said, "Have you brought us any more news to astonish and delight us?"

"One thing more, but 'tis not yet certain, and I pray God it be not necessary. I debated with myself whether I should even tell you this yet, but I know you need as much comfort as I can bring you and that I can trust you all to bury this last deep within you. It may yet be some months before the Globe is open, and I told His Majesty it would go hard with us, should that be so. He promised that, if the theatres remain closed throughout January, he would come to our aid with thirty pounds."

Now their cup of joy overflowed. They were the King's Men indeed and were generous in their acceptance of two other court secrets: by the end of the year, the Admiral's Men would have the patronage of Prince Henry and Worcester's Men that of Queen Anne.

It was time for Lawrence to ask a question. He addressed it to John Heminge. "What have you done while waiting for me?"

"We needed something to buoy our spirits. I hope you will understand and pardon us for proceeding without you. Will read us his two new plays."

Lawrence smiled and said, "In such a case you did right not to wait for my return." He turned to Will. "May I have the privilege of reading them?"

Will replied, "I fear my scrawl would give you a puzzle not a play, but I should be happy to read them to you."

Heminge suggested that it would give them all pleasure to hear the plays again, but Lawrence said, "I should be the more honored if Master Shakespeare read them to me alone, as he has offered to do."

While the meeting of the sharers was taking place, Ned was having a long and revealing conversation with Andrew Cotton who knew most of what Lawrence was saying and had no qualms about sharing it with Ned. But Andrew was much more interested in court intrigue than in plays and told Ned something Lawrence had not seen fit to tell the sharers.

It was Friday morning before he and Lawrence had started out from Winchester, to which they had returned from Wilton. They had waited to hear the verdict of the trial of Sir Walter Raleigh, which had taken place the day before. He had been found guilty of treason and was to be hanged and quartered, not even being granted the dignity of being beheaded. "And thus it is that you will play *As You Like It* at Wilton." Ned looked his complete bewilderment, which Andrew enjoyed. He went on to explain. "Sir Walter's life now lies within the King's mercy. The Countess of Pembroke admires Sir Walter greatly. Lawrence told me she described him as being as brave in mind as in body, and thus the envy of lesser men. She will entertain the King at Wilton that she may plead for Sir Walter's life."

Ned wanted very much to know the relationship between Andrew and Lawrence. He asked with deliberate casualness, "Will you come with us to Wilton?"

"I want to, but Lawrence says no"

"Is he not coming?"

"Yes, but he requires me to stay at home. He says he will have time for none but the players."

Ned wondered if he should read a personal meaning into that. He said, "Stay at home? You live, then, with Lawrence in the old Phillips home?"

" 'Twould be nearer the truth to say I stay there for a while. Lawrence's affections are fickle, but he is a kind and generous man."

That evening a grand supper with wine was given at the inn for the whole company to announce the news about Wilton and Christmas and to honor Lawrence Fletcher; the cost was borne by the senior sharers. As Lawrence's companion, Andrew was also invited and made very welcome.

Ned was pleased to find that Lawrence looked for him as soon as he came to the inn and took him aside. He said, "I am sure you know my news, for Andrew is loose of mouth, and for once I do not regret it. I should have told you myself, if John Heminge had given me any chance. Is it not good?"

"Very good. The sharers must be very happy."

"Are you not happy too?"

"To be sure I am. I long to play again."

"I go to London on Tuesday—your brother reads me his two new plays tomorrow—but I shall be back, for I shall travel with all of you to Wilton on Friday. I look forward to much of your company."

Knowing the answer to his question, Ned could not resist asking, "Will not Andrew be with you?"

"Your question surprises me. I would have taken an oath that he would have told you he would not be coming, for he has pleaded with me for days to let him. He is happiest when he can be near noble people in noble places. But this time I shall not need him, and 'tis not wise to leave the London house unguarded too long."

Further conversation was interrupted by John Heminge who came to drag Lawrence away; the supper was about to begin. It took place in a private room and was a memorable occasion with speeches, jokes, reminiscences, music, and some comic acts by Robert Armin, all aimed at the guest of honor, whom Will described as "Our good angel from the North, who brought with him no less than a king to aid us."

In bed that night Ned asked Will where he would live when they returned to London.

"I shall look for a place in Cripplegate, near John Heminge and Henry Condell. I shall not want much for I am likely to be more in Stratford than in London from now on. I doubt I shall ever play in the Globe again. And you, Ned. Will you live with Lawrence Fletcher?"

"What would you say if I did?"

"I would wish you happiness, Ned, and hope you would not be hurt."

"How could I be hurt? I am not a boy."

"You are right, and Lawrence seems to be a good man."

Ned lay awake longer than usual, wondering if Will saw Lawrence as Ned's Earl of Southampton. Ned only hoped that Lawrence would prove as valuable to him as the earl had been to Will—whatever hurt resulted.

FORTY-FOUR

THE KING'S MEN SET OUT FOR WILTON, NEAR SALISBURY, ON THE MORNING of Friday, November 25. They delayed their start some two hours, waiting for heavy rain to stop but finally had to set out in it. Luckily no one was walking; the roads were already a quagmire. Lawrence had returned from London the night before, bringing with him the horse that Andrew had ridden. Ned knew that he meant it for him but was grateful that the intention was not obvious.

Altogether there were twenty in the soon rain-soaked and mud-bespattered party. Only fifteen miles were covered on that first day, for they had made a late start and were glad to make an early stop.

By the morning the rain had given way to a thick frost which dominated the rest of the journey and made the going so slow that it was midday on Thursday, December 1, before they arrived at Wilton. Lawrence found several opportunities to speak to Ned during the journey, though he was careful to avoid embarrassing him by singling him out for too much attention. Ned wanted to know if there was any possibility that *Troilus and Cressida* could be included in the plays to be presented to the King at Christmas.

"No," said Lawrence. "That can only happen when the King has got to know you and like you; then he will want to see you in a leading part. But it will take time, and much will depend on you. Two of the plays he is likely to see at Christmas will give you a good chance to show him your quality: *Much Ado About Nothing* and *A Midsummer Night's Dream*. The sharers have been discussing what plays to present, and it has been practically decided that the *Dream* should be given on New Year's Eve as the last of the five plays. The first will certainly be *Hamlet,* in compliment to the Queen."

On the day before they reached Wilton House, Lawrence finally raised the subject that Ned had been expecting with confused feelings. He said, "The sharers, all except Gus Phillips, who has settled in Mortlake, now talk of returning to London after the Christmas plays. They are certain that the lessening of the plague will continue, though they know it will be weeks and may even be months before the Globe can open. I spoke to your brother. He hopes to find a place in Shoreditch. Will you stay with him?"

Ned smiled and said, "Did you not ask him?"

Lawrence returned the smile. "Yes."

"What was his answer?"

"He said, 'Ned believes that brothers are for time of need, not for daily company.' Will sometimes even talks in pentameters."

"I owe him much."

"You said that as if you wished you did not. Are you worried lest friendship with me may make you my debtor?"

"Perhaps. I do not know."

"Ned, you know I want you to come and live with me. Will you? You must have thought about it."

"Yes, I have. 'Tis best to be honest. I think you know my desire is for women. Why then would you want me in your home?"

"I too have lain with women, and with pleasure, but my greater delight is in men. The King and I have one thing in common. There is a Pygmalion in both of us. He will favor a young man and teach him the lore of scholarship and government. I wish to favor you to further the career of the player you have it in you to be. But I confess that both the King and I can only be interested in a handsome young man, though he must have a mind and a quality that match his body. And now is the game of truth fully played between us?"

"Fully enough for now, and I thank you. And I do accept the invitation to live in your house, and I thank you for that too."

Ned felt a great need to let two people know his decision as soon as possible: Will and John Lowin.

Will said, "I am not surprised. In your place I should have done the same. Tongues will wag, but pay them no heed. Strive to deserve a good judgment of yourself; none else matters. 'Tis only yourself you have to live with always, and we both know ourselves are often our own sorry companions. Be kind to Lawrence. Whatever he gives you or does for you, remember that there is one thing you have he has lost forever: youth."

John Lowin made light of it. " 'Twill not last, Ned, but while it does, make the most of it. Lawrence Fletcher can do you much good, but I beg you to remember your old friends."

A constant subject of conversation among the players throughout the journey had been their patroness, Mary Herbert, Countess of Pembroke, famous as Sir Phillip Sidney's sister, and herself a poet and friend of poets. Ned gathered so much information about her that he longed to see the great lady.

It was Lawrence who shared with him the gossip picked up at the court. The Earl of Pembroke had died two years before, and now it was whispered that the widow was enamored of a famous physician, Sir Matthew Lister. Some even said she was secretly married to him.

But it was the countess's son, the third Earl of Pembroke, that most interested Ned. He had been one of the adherents of the Earl of Essex, but a personal trouble had saved him from deep involvement in the rebellion. He had gotten with child a favorite maid of honor of Queen Elizabeth, Mary Fitton, who attracted men as a magnet does metal, but he had refused to marry her. A boy was born in the very month of the Essex rebellion, but he was stillborn, which perhaps was fortunate for himself and his parents. The Queen was always outraged when one of her ladies was sullied by a courtier, and imprisonment was the inevitable result; this had been the case with the Earl of Southampton, even though he had happily married the deflowered lady. She was much more irate with the young Pembroke because he had adamantly refused to wed the pregnant Mary Fitton. After a short imprisonment in the Fleet Prison he was banished from the country, but the Queen's death was the signal for his quick return from the Continent. Now, Ned learned from Lawrence, he was much in favor with the King, who was amused rather than scandalized by his treatment of Mary Fitton. She herself bore him no ill will and was said to be pregnant again by an unknown father. Some gossips even dared to suggest he was a commoner. Ned was delighted to know that the young earl was almost certain to be in the entourage of the King at Wilton House, as was his younger brother, Philip, who was also much favored of the King. Lawrence said wryly, "I need not tell you now that the two brothers are very handsome young men, and both seem to have inherited the mind and wit of their mother."

The company was well received at the magnificent Wilton House, one of those noble residences built in the days of Queen Elizabeth to display grandeur and magnificence when the strength and security of castles were no longer necessary. The chamberlain of the house himself welcomed the players and saw to their disposition. They were entertained to a sumptuous meal within an hour of their arrival. The King and Queen had been in residence for nearly a week, and with them, in addition to numerous courtiers and servants, they had also brought the nine-year-old Prince Henry.

The chamberlain brought several messages: Master Lawrence Fletcher was to wait on His Majesty after dinner; Master William Shakespeare was to wait on the countess at the same time; some entertainment with music was to be provided in the Great Hall after supper. Not one of these commands was a surprise, and the sharers had spent many a supper hour on the journey in preparing for the last of them. It had been decided that the entertainment should consist of three parts: some songs and madrigals; some clowning by Robert Armin; and, to conclude, a lively dance by some members of the company.

Ned prepared, with even more than usual assiduity, for his part in the evening's entertainment. He was to sing "Who is Sylvia?" and "Sigh no more, ladies." It would be the first time the King would see and hear him. Nat Tremayne had brought along a few extra costumes for just such an occasion, and he was happy to make Ned look his best.

Will and Lawrence were back to join their fellows at supper, but Ned was seated too far away from them to hear what they reported of their afternoon audiences. Will brought an unexpected request from the countess. She was not content that only Robert Armin of the sharers should appear before the King that evening. She thought it would be appropriate if Master Burbage and Master Heminge played the scene between the new King, Henry V, and the Lord Chief Justice. When Will had objected that they had not the appropriate costumes with them, she had said she would explain that to His Majesty, and she had added, "Master Burbage could still play a king, even in rags." But she wanted Will himself to appear too and speak some of his own lines; her choice was Portia's speech on mercy from *The Merchant of Venice*. Will had privately thought this was too obvious a ploy in her campaign to save Sir Walter Raleigh's life, for the King was already famous for his quick and subtle mind. The same thought occurred to others at the table, but nobody expressed it; such matters were wiser left unsaid.

The three sharers who had not expected to perform left the table early to rehearse their speeches. As Will rose to go, he said, "I never thought it would chance that I should play Portia," to which John Lowin, who now played Shylock and had during the past week overcome his initial reserve in the presence of the other sharers, replied, "A Daniel come to judgment, in very sooth."

As the company broke up after the meal to get ready for the entertainment, Ned saw to it that Lawrence had a chance to speak to him, though he knew that it was absurd to expect that he would already have spoken to the King about him.

Lawrence said, "I hope the King notices you enough tonight to question me about you, but be patient. If not tonight 'twill be at Hampton Court. After the performance tomorrow, I have to present the sharers to him, but not, alas, the hired men and apprentices. His Majesty is in a good mood and was most pleasant with me."

With that Ned had to be content. Never had he been so nervous as he dressed; he was even irritable with Nat who sought only to beautify him with costume jewelry. He snapped, "Leave me alone," to which Nat replied as he flounced away, "Hoity-toity! Leave you alone I will and gladly."

There were so many guests, nearly a hundred, including the Lords of the Council, that dinners and suppers were served in the Great Hall at tables placed to form three sides of a square, and it was in the space between them that the entertainment was to be given. The play too was to be similarly presented the following evening, thus avoiding any redisposition of the seating arrangements.

Ned was one of the eight players who entered to sing the opening madrigals. As they came through the great doors at the far end of the hall, Ned's eyes were glued to the top table. He was not yet dressed in all the finery he would wear when he sang his two solo songs, for it had been decided to sandwich the play scene between the madrigals and the songs, and this would give him ample time to change his doublet and put on the jewelry.

The King was better-looking than Ned expected. He was only two years younger than Will but his complexion was as fine and pink as that of a child; somehow his square, reddish, chin beard and well-trimmed moustache seemed incongruous, as though a child had put them on to ape a man. His forehead was as impressive as Will's, but the most notable feature in his face was his eyes; the candlelight made it hard to determine their color, but they were large, dark, and alive with a shrewd intelligence. As he sat, his figure seemed to be somewhat dumpy but this could be the effect of the padded doublet he wore.

There was a sharp contrast between the ladies who bracketed him. Queen Anne on his left seemed vivaciously younger than her thirty years while the Countess of Pembroke on his right seemed sedately older than her forty-odd years; indeed she seemed much the more queenly figure.

On the countess's right was undoubtedly the third Earl of Pembroke, a handsome and almost dandyish figure, from whose left ear dangled an elaborate jewel. (Ned forthwith determined not to wear his, as he had originally intended, lest he be thought to be imitating the earl.) The King wore a stiffly starched ruff, but the earl wore a collar of delicate lace.

On the Queen's left sat a young man, not yet twenty, who was clearly the other son of the countess. He too was handsome, and he exuded a boyish gaiety which was obviously much to the Queen's liking.

The whole feeling in the room was one of happy celebration; there was lively conversation and hearty laughter, and nothing austere in the royal presence inhibited the people's relaxed enjoyment.

After the players had made their initial obeisance, they had to wait a full minute before there was sufficient quiet and attention for them to begin. The madrigals were well sung and well received, and the players backed out bowing from the royal presence with a grace that any courtier would envy.

The scene between Burbage and Heminge was received with such great applause that Ned was made all the more nervous. Just before he was due to enter for his songs, Lawrence came to him. He did not speak any conventional words of good wishes, but grasped Ned's shoulders, smiled, and nodded confidently.

Ned was in good voice and acquitted himself well, but though he sang for the King, his songs were instinctively aimed at the Queen, and she acknowledged it by giving him a delightful smile at the end of each song. Between the songs, Ned was aware that the earl whispered something to his mother, who in turn whispered to the King. Ned longed to know what it was. Just before he made his bowing exit, he smiled and looked the King full in the eyes. Was he fooling himself in thinking that the King responded with a look of interest?

Then it was Will's turn. The sight of him drew warm applause, for in recent years he had not often been seen. As he spoke Portia's plea for mercy a tense excitement gripped the room; everybody knew that the countess must have arranged this. The boldness of the choice of speech was made more startling by the fact that only two days before, two priests, Watson and Clarke, had been brutally executed at Winchester for their part in the plot against the King, and their severed heads and quarters had been put on public display. The purpose of the speech was made all the more apparent when it stopped after fourteen lines and before the direct appeal to Shylock; it dealt only with the theme that, in showing mercy, a king is most like God. It was over before the audience had time to absorb the daring of the incident, and, almost without their being aware of it, Will was bowing and withdrawing in silence. Now no one could applaud unless the King did. All looked at him. His face was inscrutable, and then suddenly it relaxed into a smile and he clapped his hands, which released the assembly into energetic applause just in time to gratify Will before he disappeared from sight.

Will's relief at hearing the applause was shared by those waiting for him in the anteroom, and most of all by Lawrence Fletcher. He knew the King would approve the sentiments of the speech, for he was a merciful man; indeed, there was no part of royal power he seemed to enjoy more than its absolute prerogative of pardon. But Lawrence was worried too, for the King had a contrary face which he occasionally displayed. There had been that incident on the journey from Scotland when he had ordered the summary hanging of a cutpurse without any show of a trial.

This event had caused many a whispered misgiving among the English-men in the royal train, yet on the same day and in the same place, Newark in Nottinghamshire, he had ordered the release of all prisoners held in the castle.

As the twelve who were to perform the concluding dance were getting into order for their entrance, a King's attendant came from the banqueting hall; His Majesty wished to speak with Master Shakespeare. Will, and through him the whole company, seemed about to receive a royal reprimand; the Christmas plays might even be canceled.

Will reentered the hall in another silence, this time eager rather than anxious, for the King was smiling, and there was no twist in the smile. Everyone strained to hear the forthcoming dialogue, if indeed the player was given a chance to speak, in reply to a direct question.

The King said, speaking with a strong Scottish burr, "Master Shakespeare, ye have penned many a thousand line. Why did ye choose the ones ye spoke to us?"

James knew the answer to his own question, and so did everybody else in the room; some could not even forbear a quick glance at the countess, but Will was not among them. He said, "They are favorite lines of mine, and I hoped they would find favor with Your Majesty."

"They do. From which of your plays do they come?"

"One called *The Merchant of Venice,* sire."

"Ah! We have read it. Master Fletcher gave it to us in Scotland. 'Tis about a cruel Jew, and those words are spoken to him. Are we to you the cruel Jew, Master Shakespeare?"

"You, sire, are the fount of all human mercy, and I hoped you would honor the words as being worthy of your own lips."

"Well spoken. We are pleased with your answer, and so is the countess." As he referred to her he looked straight at the countess, who returned his gracious smile but could not hide her embarrassment. "Master Shakespeare, you and your fellows who are now our players, are to provide us with entertainment at Christmastide. Let one of the plays be *The Merchant of Venice.*"

Will bowed and withdrew. As he did so, he received the greatest applause of the evening.

The players had managed to catch all the King's words but none of Will's, for his back had been to them and his voice had been respectfully modulated, but there was no doubt that he had done well, and he was greeted with broad smiles and handgrasps.

The dance, a lively galliard, was introduced by a comic jig performed by Robert Armin. As the twelve dancers cavorted, the King expressed his pleasure by clapping the rhythm, and soon the whole room was clapping so that the music was drowned. The climax was achieved when, in response to a request from the King, the Queen, nothing loath, joined in the dance, partnered by the Earl of Pembroke; unlike his predecessor, the King himself had not the legs for dancing, but enjoyed looking on.

The players went to bed happy, with a sense of achievement. Lawrence did not return with them to their quarters; he had to attend on the King.

In the morning Lawrence happily reported to the sharers that the King was mightily pleased with his players and looked forward to the play that night and even more to the five that he was to see at Christmas. Since one of those was now to be *The Merchant of Venice,* the order was finally determined as *Hamlet, The Merchant of Venice, Much Ado About Nothing, Twelfth Night, A Midsummer Night's Dream.* The King had wanted them to begin on Christmas Day, but had finally been dissuaded from this as being against custom; he had agreed only because this year Christmas Day would be a Sunday, and if the first play were given on December 27, the fifth would be on December 31, and New Year's Eve for a Scotsman was the time of greatest rejoicing.

As soon as his meeting with the sharers was over, Lawrence sought out Ned. He had good news for him: the King had asked about him, and had been told that he was Will's brother. So that was what the whispering was about, thought Ned; again it is that I am Will's brother that matters; but he said, "Did you tell him that I am to live with you?"

"Not yet," smiled Lawrence; "it is too early for that."

Preparations for the evening's performance kept the company busy all day, though they only had access to the hall itself for two hours between dinner and supper; the countess had provided a large tapestry of a woodland scene which she thought would provide a suitable background for the play.

They were in the middle of the afternoon rehearsal when they were interrupted by Lawrence Fletcher, whose usual self-control failed to hide the fact that he was disturbed. All the sharers were on hand and he called them into quick consultation. Without any preliminaries he delivered his bad news.

"I fear the performance may have to be canceled. It has come to His Majesty's ears—how I know not—that one of our company has come from plague-stricken London."

"Sam Gilburne," said Gus Phillips, "but . . ."

"For the King there are no buts. He is deeply angry that we should have exposed him and his court to such danger. He has sent me to find out the truth."

"There is no danger," began John Heminge.

"A physician must judge of that. How long is it since the young man left London?"

"Fully ten days," said Heminge.

"Let me speak with him," said Lawrence. Sam was called over. Lawrence, whose manner had been grave, smiled at him. "Tell me, Sam, have you become friendly with a young woman here?"

Amazed, Sam said, "How did you know?"

"News travels fast at court, even from the lowliest and most hidden corners. Who was she?"

"Martha, a kitchen wench."

"Did you talk of London?"

"Yes. She said she had never been there and would be afraid to go."

"Because of the plague?"

"Yes, and many other things."

"You told her that you had been there all the summer and the plague had not touched you. There was nothing to be frightened of."

"Did she tell you everything?" asked Sam, astonished and embarrassed.

"I have not spoken with the wench. Come with me."

In a complete daze, Sam followed Lawrence, who turned to say, "I shall return as soon as I can. In hope of the best, continue with the rehearsal."

But it was a worried troupe that had no spirit to rehearse a comedy. There was much speculation as to why and where Lawrence had taken Sam, and it was half an hour before Sam returned. Now his mystification had given way to guilt; never again would he trust a woman; but he had not even realized that he was telling her a secret.

Eagerly he was seized on for a report, but before he would answer any questions, he said, "I am grievous sorry, Master Heminge. I did not know I was doing wrong."

With a compassion which surprised most of the company, Heminge said, "It was we who did wrong, Sam. Now tell us where you have been."

"Master Fletcher took me to a physician, who examined me and questioned me and did all manner of things to me. I told him I had not touched one dead of the plague, nor been in a house where one had died, nor had I been sick one day this summer."

"Did he say you were to be confined?" asked Gus.

"No," said Sam, as much in terror as in answer.

"Where is Master Fletcher?" asked Heminge.

"I know not. He told me to return here and that he would come as soon as he could."

It was another half-hour before Lawrence returned, and he still looked serious. He said, "I went with the physician to His Majesty. The physician said that Sam is well and there seems to be but slight danger, yet it will be another two weeks before he can be considered safe. The King is still angry."

"Do we play tonight?" asked Heminge.

"I do not know. We must prepare as though we will."

"And Christmas?" asked Gus.

"I do not know."

With little zest, the company resumed the rehearsal. A messenger came from the countess; she wished to speak with Master Shakespeare.

Will did not return before the rehearsal had to be stopped so that the hall might be prepared for the supper, and the players waited miserably in their quarters for sight of Will or some decision of the King. Confidentially Lawrence told a few of the sharers that it was a characteristic of the King to keep people in suspense; it was a prerogative of royal power that he seemed to enjoy.

The company was already at supper before Will joined them. With many household servants in evidence he would not give a full report to the whole company. He contented himself with smiling broadly and saying so that all could hear, "We play." The relief in the room could be felt.

Will sat down between Heminge and Fletcher, and to them he quietly gave an account of his interview with the countess. She had not shared the King's anger; her sole concern was that he might now be in no mood to consider clemency for the condemned Raleigh; the fate of the other doomed men seemed not to concern her. The earl was even then with the King, attempting to alleviate both his fears and his anger, and she wanted Will to remain with her while she awaited her son's return.

"What did you talk about?" asked Lawrence.

"My two new plays. When I told her about *Othello,* she told me about the Moorish ambassadors who were in London three years ago. She had seen them. They were not barbarous in behavior as she had expected; indeed they were arrogant in seeming to despise all Christians as lesser people, but they were always courteous. They would not eat our food, nor touch ale or wine. Above all, they could not understand that we would choose a woman to rule over us."

"But the earl?" asked Heminge impatiently.

"He came back smiling. The King had agreed that the play should go forward, but he would not promise to stay and see it. Moreover, he would not grant us an audience afterwards, as he had told Lawrence he would."

"Any word about Christmas?" asked Heminge.

"He would not discuss that with the earl," said Lawrence. "He will tell me of that tonight."

"He will not see us. Mayhap he will not see you," said Heminge.

"He will," said Lawrence confidently. "I shall make a solemn promise that no member of the company will visit London even for an hour between now and Christmas. I shall even suggest that as soon as we have returned to Mortlake to make our arrangements there and to pick up our costumes and properties—it is providential that the plays we are to perform were all out on tour with you—we should be ready to move to wherever the King will spend Christmas as soon as his messenger comes to inform us. 'Tis most likely to be Hampton Court! Thus we can eat and sleep at the royal expense."

A thought suddenly struck Will which they all had missed in their concern over Sam Gilburne. "How comes it, Lawrence, that the King is so distressed about one of our players who came from London ten days ago when you . . . ?"

Lawrence smiled and said, "Quiet, Will; walls have ears. The King does not know I have lived in London this summer. He left me in Windsor and there he thinks I still reside."

"Think you the King will stay to see the play tonight?" asked Will.

"For a wager, I would say yes. The Queen will want to stay, and she will plead courtesy to the countess."

Lawrence would have won his wager, for it turned out as he said, but the King sat rather severely through the first part of the play and the rest of the audience had to act accordingly. When the Queen ventured a titter at an early witticism of Touchstone, the King glanced at her reprovingly. It looked as if the evening were going to be a trying ordeal for both players and audience but the first song of Amiens caused the King's face to show the ghost of a smile of approval. Was it the song or the singer that pleased him? Ned dared to hope that it was the latter, and he led with gusto the second verse which was sung as a chorus. From there on, the King gradually allowed himself to enjoy the play, and when John Lowin as Jacques said the speech on the seven ages of man he held up his hand to stop the action and he said, "That speech again, Master Jacques." This was approval indeed, and from now to the end of the play the audience made up for the previous royal restraint with abundant laughter and applause. Almost immediately after the repeated speech of Jacques, Ned had to sing his favorite song in the play, whose two verses ended with the line, "This life is most jolly." His happiness was so infectious that the King smiled broadly and called to hear the song again.

So complete was Ned's success that when he made his brief appearance at the end of the play as the rustic clown, William, a rustle of whispers ran through the room as everybody told his neighbor that that was the handsome young singer beneath the comic disguise.

The applause at the end of the play was hearty and genuine; even the King seemed to wish to atone for his earlier disapproval.

After the players had made their exit, they anxiously waited to know if the sharers would be called to the presence as had been originally promised, but a chamberlain come to express His Majesty's approval of the play and to ask for Master Fletcher only; it was clear that the King meant still to show a modicum of disapproval.

But none of the company could go to bed until Lawrence returned from the King; in any case, they were too happy and excited to sleep.

Lawrence's report was exactly what he had foretold; they were to be the King's guests, probably at Hampton Court, as soon as they could get there after his messenger had come to Mortlake. He had a particular piece of news that delighted Nat Tremayne. Lawrence had pointed out that the players wanted to look their best in their performances at court and were debarred from replenishing their costumes from the stock at the Globe; they had taken a minimum of requirements with them on the road. The King had said they could draw on the wardrobe at Hampton Court. But Lawrence stressed that under no circumstances was a member of the company to go to the City until the new year.

As they all dispersed for the night, Lawrence drew Ned aside for a special message: the King had been so taken with him that he wished to see him in private at Hampton Court. Ned went to bed with a heady feeling of triumph, tempered by a vague sense of apprehension. He shared a bed with Will, but he did not share his news with him.

FORTY-FIVE

THE COMPANY ARRIVED BACK AT MORTLAKE ON THURSDAY, DECEMBER 8, after a journey only slightly less unpleasant than the outgoing one. In spite of the hardships of the weather, they were happy with accomplishment and promise. Andrew was waiting for Lawrence.

What passed between them Ned did not know, but the following morning Andrew took Ned aside before leaving for London. His manner was cold and cynical. He said, "So you are coming to take my place with Lawrence."

"No," said Ned hotly. "I may be coming to live in the house, but not to take your place."

"You are either the wiliest man I have ever met, or the most foolish—and I do not think you are a fool."

"Did Lawrence say you are to leave the house?"

"Such things are not said: they are implied."

"I shall tell him I will not come unless you stay."

"He will have an answer for that too. Lawrence always has an answer."

As soon as Andrew had left, Ned went looking for Lawrence. Impetuously he asked. "Why should Andrew leave your house if I come to live in it?"

Lawrence smiled imperturbably and said, "So Andrew has been speaking to you. I knew he would, and I knew what he would say."

"Is it not true?"

"Andrew will not share me with anyone. It is his decision to leave the house if you come to live in it. He is welcome to stay; he is very useful."

"I do not want to drive him out."

"Tell him so, and try to persuade him to stay."

"I cannot; he has already gone."

"Then plead with him when you next see him, though I fear he may leave the house before we return. Andrew will never stay long with anyone; he demands too much."

Ned was thoroughly confused and looked it. Lawrence grasped his shoulder and said, "You worry too much. Let happen what will, and make the best of it."

But Lawrence soon had something to worry him, too, though he tried to hide it: the King's messenger did not come. Ten days passed and there was no word. Lawrence did his best to relieve the mounting anxiety in the company, and insisted that they spend their time in rehearsing the five plays, in all of which there was some reallocation of parts from the touring versions, for now Will, Ned, Robert Gough, and Sam Gilburne were included.

Two relevant items of news came to Mortlake during the days of waiting: the titled men among the condemned had had their sentences commuted to imprisonment (plain Master George Brooke had been beheaded), and the premature return from the country of Londoners to their homes had doubled the deaths from plague, which had been reassuringly diminishing.

Lawrence encouraged the players to feel that they had something to do with saving the life of Sir Walter Raleigh. Will commented, "Then we must also be blamed for failing to save the life of Master Brooke."

Lawrence smiled and said, "There are limits to the King's mercy, else he would stand accused of weakness."

Privately with Ned, Lawrence discussed the character of the King he was going to meet, as it was exemplified in the dramatic stories of the pardons. "I could have told you how it would be. One by one the men were brought to the block, and one by one they were returned to their cell on some pretext, such as to give them more time to pray. Finally they were all brought out to the scaffold together and then told of the King's pardon. I cannot tell what it is in him that makes him enjoy the cruelty of delay."

"Is that why his messenger has not come to us?"

"I think not. It is the increase in the plague deaths that makes him reluctant to return to Hampton Court. Death acts strangely; it ignored thousands who stayed in London, yet bided its time for some who fled it and then returned. You cannot evade Death when it decides to call on you. Does it frighten you, Ned?"

"I never think of it."

"I do; often. I hope I shall greet it with a mocking smile. There is something in me that wants to dare Death, else why would I have chosen to live in London this summer?"

"Will you ever tell the King that you did?"

"It may be, when the danger has passed. Then he may even praise me for it. He once said to me, 'The only free man is he who does not fear Death.' He himself lives in daily terror of his end."

It was Monday morning, December 19, before the King's messenger came asking to see Master Lawrence Fletcher. His Majesty was in residence in his palace at Hampton Court, and he desired the presence of his players there forthwith. Lawrence had been right again: the delay of the call had been due to uncertainty about the King's whereabouts at Christmas because of the temporary increase in the number of plague deaths; last week's toll was less than eighty, and the King had decided to adhere to his original plan.

There was a great and happy bustle at Mortlake, hasty farewell family dinners, and at two o'clock the company set out on their two-hour journey. As if to crown the day, the weather was beautiful: bright sunshine and the air sufficiently cold to make energetic walking enjoyable. Those who owned horses rode them, but no extra mounts were hired; those without them preferred to walk.

The King's Men looked their best as they set out, for they were determined by their first appearance to make it clear to the servants of the royal household that they were prosperous gentlemen from the city, not indigent vagabonds from the road. There was much waving of hands and calling of good wishes from families and friends left behind, together with the inevitable tears from Anne Phillips, in which her three children dutifully joined; in sharp contrast, the numerous Heminge children were vociferously happy at the departure of their father; even William, the sad-faced eldest son, was smiling.

The King's messenger had been persuaded to stay for dinner and return with the company, and he in his royal livery rode at the head of the procession with Lawrence. Ned was proud and happy to see that Lawrence was readily awarded the right of leading the King's Men to their patron. He had fully earned the honor.

As he walked along with Sam Gilburne, who was garrulous with happiness, Ned found it hard to listen, for his mind was full of the exciting possibilities that lay just ahead.

"You are not listening to what I'm saying," said Sam.

"Yes, I am," lied Ned.

"Then answer me."

"About what?"

"There you are," said Sam in triumph, "you were not listening."

"You were telling me about that lusty wench in Wilton."

"That was minutes ago. I was talking about Master Fletcher. Everybody has noticed that he favors you; all that talking quietly together in corners. We think he's after you for his bed."

Ned's instinct was for a strong denial, but he realized in time that that would be the wrong tactic. What did the Queen say in *Hamlet?* "The lady doth protest too much, methinks." Instead he smiled and said, "Then you know that Master Fletcher is hunting the wrong animal."

"That's what I said," commented Sam with a vigorous nod of the head. More soberly he added, "Then what do you talk about?"

"Mostly about Will and Stratford," was the glib reply. This seemed to satisfy Sam, who changed the subject to the ways of women, about which he felt Ned had a lot to teach him.

As they approached the bridge to Hampton Court, Ned was dazzled by the magnificence of the Palace, its myriad towers and turrets. He had heard that the walls of the great chambers were hung with tapestries of gold and silver thread, and that some of the ceilings were fretted with jewels; there was said to be a small presence chamber that was so gilded and decorated with precious stones that it was known as Paradise, but he was certain that no player would get a peep at that.

Everything was sumptuously ready for the disposition of the company. Will and Ned shared a small bedroom overlooking the river. Ned wondered about Lawrence; later he discovered that he alone of the players had a room to himself and some distance away from the rest of the company.

Most of the players were well used to the Palace for they had played there for the Queen, but, fortunately for Ned, Lawrence, too, was new to it and had sufficient influence to ask to be taken to see the Great Hall, where the plays would be given. He invited Ned to join him and graciously agreed that John Lowin could join them too.

The Great Hall looked from the outside like a vast chapel, but inside it was more like a large banqueting hall. As a theatre, it was the most impressive that John and Ned were ever likely to perform in and they both longed for the plays to begin.

As they walked back to the hall where they were to have supper, Lawrence said to John, "I understand you are a good friend to Ned."

"The best I ever had," said Ned warmly.

"Then," said Lawrence, "I am sure you have told him that you are coming to live with me."

"Yes," said Ned reluctantly, wishing now that he had told no one.

"And what was your comment, John?" asked Lawrence.

"I cannot remember," said John, who remembered very well. He added with a smile, "Ned has never welcomed comment from me or anybody else."

"But I welcome it. What say you?"

Ned said angrily, "I cannot bear to hear myself discussed," and he walked away quickly.

"So," said Lawrence quizzically.

" 'Tis best we say no more, Lawrence," said John, and they completed their walk in silence.

After supper, Lawrence took Ned aside. He found him still smoldering with anger. He said, "Ned, I do not want you to be hurt. That is why I asked John's opinion. He is your friend. If he thinks ill of your coming to live with me, what about the others?"

Ned was now livid with anger at the underlying assumptions. He said, with a defiant loudness, "I care not for anybody's opinion. And to share your house is not to share your bed. Keep Andrew for that." Before Lawrence had chance for a word, he ran out into the night.

As soon as he found himself in the courtyard he began to berate himself. While he had come to like and admire Lawrence more and more, and to bask in his friendship, Lawrence was, above all, a means to an end. Now he had denied himself the end by cutting off the means, for Lawrence could never forgive his cruel outburst. On the other hand, perhaps Lawrence had had the sinister intention of provoking John into some comment which would have set Ned at enmity with his old friend. Ned had seen no trace of that kind of man in Lawrence, but it was the man that Andrew had hinted at.

In his miserable perplexity, Ned avoided company and went early to bed, but not to sleep. He was still awake when Will came up some two hours later, happy with wine. He asked, "What is wrong, Ned?"

Testily Ned replied, "Nothing is wrong. I was tired; that is all."

"I wish you had been with us downstairs; the talk and the music were good. We are to provide entertainment for the King after supper tomorrow. You must sing again, but different songs. The evening is to honor the Earl of Pembroke. He has been invested with the Garter in gratitude for his hospitality at Wilton. What a happy turn of fortune: exile one year, the Garter the next. May the wheel turn so for you: tonight the clouds, tomorrow the sun. Lawrence whispered to me that he thought you were troubled about something, but he did not know what. He said to give you a message, Horatio's words to Hamlet: 'Good night, sweet Prince.' "

Ned said nothing. He did not even return Will's own goodnight to him. Long he pondered the message and finally decided he would make no approach to Lawrence. What had his advice been? "Let happen what will, and make the best of it."

In the morning there was a meeting to announce the program for the evening and to set it in rehearsal. It was to have practically the same form as the one given at Wilton, but with different material. The main item was to be the wooing scene from *Henry V*, played by Richard Burbage and John Edmans. Augustine Phillips would read three sonnets written by the King. (Lawrence had supplied a copy of these, but he had to explain some of the Scottish words to Gus.) Will was to read the first nine verses of his *Venus and Adonis* and Ned would sing two songs from *As You Like It*. There was to be clowning by Armin, more madrigals, and a concluding dance. All of this meant a day of hard work.

At the morning meeting, Ned avoided looking at Lawrence, the more so because he knew that Lawrence was frequently looking at him; and, to emphasize that he perversely felt no regret for his conduct last night, he was determinedly happy, making merry quips to his neighbor, Sam Gilburne, when opportunity afforded.

After the meeting, Ned stood waiting with Sam for the three musicians, when Lawrence approached. He said, "I should like to speak to you for a moment, Ned."

Sam made to move away, but Ned grasped his arm and said, "Go not away, Sam. Master Fletcher has nothing to say to me that you should not hear." Ned could not tell what prompted him thus to make a difficult situation between him and Lawrence still more difficult. After all, it was he who had offended, and here was Lawrence attempting a reconciliation, only to be rebuffed.

It was Sam who saved the situation. Walking quickly away, he said, "I need to make water, or I shall burst in the dance."

Lawrence, as charming and collected as ever, said, "Ned, you may wonder why I continue to seek your friendship, when you make it clearer day by day that you dislike me. I begin to wonder myself. Know this: I shall pursue you no further. I should not wish you to live in my house, feeling as you do; nor would you wish to. But if you learn to look on me with truer eyes, come and tell me so, and I shall be happy to hear it. Now 'tis time for your dance."

As he walked away, those who had observed but not heard the conversation, would have assumed from Lawrence's manner that it had been of pleasant inanities. Ned was determined to maintain the same appearance, but he was deeply disturbed. Lawrence had been his way to the King, and the King his way to the top. And suppose he had been wrong in his suspicions of Lawrence; everybody else in the company seemed to hold him in high regard.

Before the afternoon rehearsals began, Ned asked Will with as much casualness as he could muster where Lawrence was. Will had sensed from the previous night that the two were at odds, and Ned's manner did not succeed in hiding from his brother his genuine concern. He said, "I know not where he is. He said he would not see us until the entertainment this evening. I should have thought you would have known more about him than I."

"No," said Ned lamely. He had an impulse to tell Will that he would not be going to live with Lawrence, but checked it; it might not yet prove so.

Before the entertainment, Lawrence came to join the players as they waited in an anteroom of the Banqueting Hall, but he remained exclusively with the sharers. Now it was Ned's turn to look frequently at him, but without any acknowledgment.

The entertainment was an even greater success than at Wilton. The audience was much the same, but larger. This time the King and Queen shared the center of attraction with the Earl of Pembroke, who was wearing for the occasion the collar and garter of that most coveted and illustrious order of knighthood, with which he had recently been invested.

In compliment to the King, the reading of his sonnets by Augustine Phillips drew prolonged applause, though the sonnets were not entirely intelligible to many present. Ned looked and sang well, but he did not make as marked an impression as he had at Wilton. He blamed this on the songs—he was at his best when his songs were addressed to ladies or about them—but he knew his mind and spirit were divided in their concentration and that this marred his performance; if Lawrence had but come to him before he went on to sing, as he had at Wilton!

It was the only entertainment the King's Men were to give before their performances of the five plays the following week. They discovered that theirs were not to be the only diversions of the Christmas season: the Queen was much given to elaborate masques, and her first Christmas in this new and lively kingdom after dour Scotland was to be marked by two magnificent displays, the preparation of which kept the whole court busy. One masque was to be presented by the King's cousin, the Duke of Lennox, and the "Queen's Masque," in which she herself would appear as Pallas Athene, was to be presented by the Countess of Bedford, herself, like the Countess of Pembroke, a patroness of poets.

The players, with feelings ranging from pleasure to apprehension, expected that Ben Jonson would arrive any day as the poet of the Queen's Masque, if indeed he were not already hidden away somewhere in the vastness of the Palace; but they decided that no palace, however vast, could keep Ben hidden. They were surprised to learn, some with disappointment and others with relief, that Ben was not to be the chosen writer on this occasion; it was to be Samuel Daniel, a charming poet, now in his forty-second year who had long been favored and supported by the Pembroke family; for years he had been lost to sight in the writing of an apparently endless epic poem on the hundred years of dynastic strife in England; the first four books had been published eight years before, just in time to be of service to Will in his writing of *Richard II*. Now the Countess of Pembroke and her son, the earl, had brought Sam Daniel out of his study to write the masque which was to be called *The Vision of the Twelve Goddesses,* this in spite of the fact that a masque by Ben Jonson had already delighted the Queen on her journey from Scotland. Such was the reward of influence at court.

Will said, "I would give much to be there when Ben hears the news. I should not be surprised if he comes to make his protest in person."

During the week of luxurious waiting between the entertainment on December 20, and the performance of *Hamlet* on December 27, there were leisurely rehearsals and much good fellowship. Only Nat and Martin, his assistant, were feverishly busy; a sight of the costumes being prepared for the masques, some of which were more valuable than the whole wardrobe of the King's Men, spurred Nat to dazzle both players and audience with the results of his industry, artistry, and ingenuity; some of the clothes he was allowed to borrow from the Palace wardrobe he refurbished unrecognizably. But Tom Vincent had a frustrating time of it; rarely could he get into the Great Hall, for most of the time it was closed to prying eyes as the machines and scenery for the masques were installed; there was talk of a mountain and a cave and a temple such as had never before been seen. Tom had to be content with the promise that, once they had been constructed, they would be removed the day before the plays were to begin.

Ned longed to make his peace with Lawrence but did not know how to. Lawrence joined the sharers for most meals and occasionally watched a rehearsal, but he gave no sign that he was aware of Ned's existence; nor did he give him an opportunity to approach him. Ned made a valiant attempt to hide his despondency, and laughed frequently with John Lowin and Sam Gilburne, particularly when he thought there was a chance that Lawrence might be watching. But he started to drink too much in the evenings, and this made him cantankerous and hostile. On Friday evening he became so generally obnoxious that John Ieminge took Will aside and told him that, unless he could do something about his brother's conduct, he was going to ask Ned to leave the next day; Sunday was Christmas Day and he was not going to allow a bad-tempered wine-bibber to spoil the holiday for the company.

Will looked across at Ned. Only John Lowin was sitting with him. Even to Ned's befuddled mind, it was clear that he was being ostracized. Thickly he said, "Go away too. Go away with the rest of them. I don't want you; I don't want anybody."

John Lowin got up reluctantly and walked away. He feared that Ned was about to embark on another wild bout of self-destruction, as he had a year before. Then the cause had been clear; his expulsion from the Earl of Worcester's Men. But what was it now? He sensed it had something to do with Lawrence Fletcher, but it could not be the pangs of rejected love, for he knew that Ned was incapable of such love for a man, and Lawrence must know it too.

Will was in a quandary. Ned had to be talked to, but any attempt to do it while he was growling in his cups would only make matters worse. He suddenly decided to seek out Lawrence Fletcher, for he was certainly the key to the situation, and Will was sure he could rely on Lawrence's understanding and discretion.

Will went to Lawrence's room but hesitated at the door, because he heard a low male voice inside; it would be very embarrassing if he were interrupting a bed meeting.

The voice stopped, there was a slight pause, and the door was opened by Lawrence whose happy surprise seemed genuine. He asked Will in and closed the door. There was no one else in the room. Lawrence smiled at Will's puzzlement. "You heard a voice. It was mine. I was reading your *Midsummer Night's Dream* and could not resist trying on my tongue your beautiful lines. This is the one play of the five we do here that I have not seen, and so I borrowed Tom Vincent's copy. It is fitting that this is the last of the plays the King will see, for it will delight him beyond measure; the Queen too. But sit and take a glass of wine with me."

Within a minute, Will came directly to the purpose of his visit. He spoke of Heminge's threat and of his fear that Ned, if he were dismissed from the company, might return to the desperate life of a year before, which he described in some detail.

Lawrence said, "I might ask why you come to me, but such an evasion would be unworthy of both you and me. I know not how much Ned has told you about us."

"Little, and nothing of what has gone wrong. He told me he was going to live with you."

"That is now in doubt, because of things he said, though in saying them he hurt himself more than me. I tried to approach him again but was rebuffed. Now he must come to me."

"That will be difficult for him; I know of no one in whom pride is so much a disease."

"His pride is one of the qualities that makes him so attractive, like a spirited horse."

"It is always sad when a fiery mount is brought into submission by the spur and the lash."

"Life provides the spur and the lash for all of us, Will. We are what we are and life is what it is, and therein lies the pain. I would not hurt Ned; I would do much to spare him hurt. He came here with high hopes, which I planted in him. I told him he might find favor with the King, for so I believed. He may yet do so, for the King sees with his own eyes, not mine. But Ned thinks that in losing me he has lost the King. That is it which sours and enrages him."

"The King will not see him unless we can sweeten and calm him, for John Heminge meant what he said, and he was right."

Lawrence got up and moved to a side table on which lay a few gaily decorated parcels. He picked up one and gave it to Will. He said, "You see that this was ready, so he need never know that you spoke to me. It is a Christmas present for him, my last attempt at a reconciliation. Put it where he can see it when he wakes in the morning; he may think I stole in and put it there. He will have it a day earlier than I meant him to, but John Heminge will not wait. There is a message with the present. It may have the opposite effect to the one we want, but I know not what else to do."

"You are a good man, Lawrence."

"Nay, Will, I only do what pleases me."

When Will got to his room, he was relieved to find that Ned was deep in a drunken sleep. He put Lawrence's gift on the floor on Ned's side and got into bed beside him.

Ned was still asleep when Will got up quietly in the morning. There was a rehearsal of the *Dream* at ten o'clock and the decision as to whether Ned was to be replaced would have to be made by that time. Will did not want to stay in the bedroom, waiting for Ned to wake, and so be present when Lawrence's parcel was opened. He dressed warmly and went for a walk by the river.

When he returned to the bedroom, he knew immediately that all was well, and a wave of happiness swept through him. Ned was dressing. As soon as he saw Will, he stopped and said excitedly, "Look what Lawrence has given me." He hurried to show Will an exquisitely wrought silver medallion. Embossed on it in letters of gold were the words, *"Non sanz droict,"* the motto of the Shakespeares.

Will said, " 'Tis beautiful. He must have had this made in London some time ago."

"And I have behaved cruelly to him. It is I who should give him a gift to beg his pardon. He must have come here last night while I was asleep. Did you see him?"

"No," said Will, thinking it wiser to lie.

"Will, I had a terrible dream last night: I dreamt I struck you and John Heminge, just as I had struck Will Kemp. Lawrence stood by and laughed at me. I turned to strike him, and it was not Lawrence; it was the King. But I could not stop my hand in time, and I knocked him down. I was taken away to be hanged forthwith—no prison, no trial, nothing. And there was nobody there but the hangman and the soldiers, not even a priest. I kept calling for Vicar Byfield. I was made to climb a ladder, the noose around my neck. The ladder was taken away. I could feel the rope strangling me; it was terrible. Then I woke up."

"That was the end of a bad few days for you."

"I was drinking too much, and I know I behaved abominably—even to John Lowin."

" 'Twill be easy to make amends."

"Lawrence sent a message with the gift. I should like you to read it."

Will read: "This gift will surprise you. I hope it will please you. I know you are sorry for your angry words to me; your conduct has proved that. I still want to be your friend, and wish only good for you. You have nothing to fear from me. If you believe this, come to my room after church on Christmas morning that we may renew our friendship before we join our fellows for the holiday dinner. He who would be your good friend, Lawrence Fletcher."

As Will returned the letter, Ned said, "I do not deserve such forgiveness; it makes me so ashamed. I want to go to Lawrence at once."

"You have no time. There is a rehearsal of the *Dream*. It mayhap that Lawrence will be there. Now finish dressing. I have things to do before the rehearsal."

Will left to find John Heminge. He quickly assured him that Ned was himself again and contrite for his bad behavior.

"What happened?" asked John.

"There was a misunderstanding, but now all is well."

"That brother of yours is a bushel of trouble."

"But a good player, John."

"I grant you," said Heminge.

Before the rehearsal Ned went to John Lowin and begged his pardon. "I get these bad spells," he said. "None knows that better than you. I cannot think why you remain my friend."

"Nor I," said John, smiling.

Ned, as Lysander, was involved in the first scene, which had already begun before Lawrence arrived to watch. As soon as the scene was over, Ned walked straight to him; he cared not who saw. He whispered, "Thank you," but his face was such an open plea for forgiveness that Lawrence was much moved. He whispered in reply, "Then I shall see you after church tomorrow." Ned nodded vigorously and moved away. As he did so, a quick smile passed between Will and Lawrence, though Will was involved in the scene taking place, in the part of Peter Quince.

Ned was in such good spirits for the rest of the day that it was as much remarked on as his bad mood had been. Sam Gilburne said, "You must have found the woman you thought you had lost."

"Something like that," agreed Ned, laughing.

Only one thing marred Ned's happiness that day. He had to take a present to Lawrence the next morning, and where could he find one at court? After dinner he broached the subject to Will, who told him, "What you give will not be as important to Lawrence as the message that accompanies it. Remember those verses you used to write for father's gloves? Compose such a verse for Lawrence. Make it true and he will treasure it."

"Will you help me?"

"No," said Will. "When Lawrence asks if it is your own work, you must be proud to say yes."

Ned toyed briefly with the idea of giving Lawrence the Taurean amulet which he still wore at every performance, but he decided that he should not part with a lucky charm; and he did not know what Lawrence's birth sign was. With some difficulty he found the court jeweler, but that harassed and bitter-mouthed worthy laughed to scorn his request for a jeweled ornament. "Ever since His Majesty arrived I have scarce slept, nor have my three assistants, though, to speak truth, awake or asleep they are equally useless. Here I am, with every great one in the land bringing me gems and pearls to turn into gifts for His Majesty, and you, a mere player, dare to ask me to make a gift for you, and you do not even bring the precious gems for the purpose. What do you take me for? A peddler? Not all the ill-gotten gains of all your players would serve to secure my handiwork. Be off with you, sir."

Ned was proud of the self-control which made him hold his peace; he was determined not to cause any more trouble at Hampton Court.

Will solved the problem of the gift. He had with him a book which he had intended to give Ned for Christmas; now it could be given to Lawrence. Will handed it to Ned before supper, when he was in the bedroom, struggling with the poem for Lawrence. The book was *Love's Martyr*, and it was handsomely bound.

Ned had never heard of it, and before he opened it he asked, "Did you write it?"

"No, but there are some lines of mine in it; some by your friend, Ben Jonson too. The chief poem is by Robert Chester. I think Lawrence will like it. The others of us wrote lines on the same theme, *The Phoenix and the Turtle*. We did it to honor Robert Chester, who is a pleasing man, and his noble patron, Sir John Salisbury."

Ned was delighted by the book and said so. He began to leaf through it; then, handing it to Will, he said, "Here; show me your poem." Will did so, and it was so short that Ned read it immediately. He looked puzzled and said, "I do not fully understand it, but I like it, yet 'tis sad for Christmas. It speaks of a strange love: two in one, yet never mated, and both are dead. Who were they?"

" 'Tis an allegory of the ideal union between love and constancy. They should be one, but, alas, our love is often marred by lust and selfishness and our constancy is too easily broken."

The evening was a joy. John Heminge found occasion to say to Ned, "I am glad to see you merry again. I had begun to think you were going to turn Christmas into Good Friday for us. Your brother must have worked a miracle on you."

Ned was completely mystified by the reference to Will, but decided to let it pass. John Heminge was beaming at him, which was all that mattered. In another mood he would have been offended by the suggestion that he owed every good thing to Will.

Lawrence was not at the supper or the Christmas Eve party which followed it; presumably, at the King's command, he was present at a much more illustrious gathering. His absence made Ned all the more eager for their meeting in the morning, especially since he was rather proud of the poem he had concocted.

The Christmas morning service was memorable. Never before had Ned worshiped God in company with a king, a queen, a prince and all the great nobility of the land. And the bishop and priests were robed for the occasion with a splendor that would have horrified Vicar Byfield. During the service Lawrence stood with the sharers—there were seats for only the greatest. His eyes searched out Ned, and he nodded to him with a slight smile; he had already heard from Will about the success of his gift and message. He was delighted to see that Ned was proudly wearing the medallion.

There was long, low bowing and deep curtsying as the royal procession left the chapel; then there was a merry flurry of Christmas greeting and admiring comments on the appearance of the royal party and entourage. Lawrence quickly disappeared, but Ned was detained by his friends.

It was Sam who commented on the medallion. He said, "That is beautiful; costly too. Did Master Shakespeare give it to you?"

"No," said Ned with such a smile as he knew would mean only one thing to Sam.

"You pass all belief," said Sam in admiration. "Every other man is beggared by giving gifts to women for their favors, but it is they who shower you with good things. Some wealthy merchant's wife, I'll be bound."

"Imagine what you like; my lips are sealed."

"But I'm your friend," said the disappointed Sam.

"Sam, learn this about women; be generous with your body but miserly with your speech."

John Lowin approached. He said, "Will you come for a walk, Ned?"

"Later, John. I have something to do first."

Sam, pointing to the medallion, said, "He has to return fitting and private thanks for that gift."

"'Tis handsome, Ned, and deserves good thanks." John smiled exasperatingly. Had he guessed the identity of the giver?

In spite of his good resolutions, Ned could not avoid a little testiness. "Sam is wrong, as ever. What I have to do has nothing to do with this gift. I will see you later."

Lawrence was waiting for Ned. As he opened the door for him, he greeted him with "Merry Christmas."

Ned responded with "Merry Christmas" and entered the room. As Lawrence turned from closing the door, Ned began, "I am very sorry, Lawrence, for . . ."

"I know how you have been feeling. Say no more about it. I am happy that you have come here this morning—and wearing my gift too."

"It is beautiful beyond my deserving. I cannot understand why you are so good to me."

"Nor can I," joked Lawrence. "I only know it pleasures me to make you happy. But let us take a Christmas drink together."

"First, I have a gift for you. 'Tis a book. I hope you do not already have it."

Lawrence's delight at the gift was obvious. *"Love's Martyr.* No, I do not have it, but I have heard well of it. And 'tis handsomely made. Thank you, Ned. But what is this?"

"Some lines I wrote for you."

"You wrote?"

"Yes, I. I am no poet, but I once wrote jingles for my father's glove-trade. I want you to read the lines aloud. The letters at the begining of the lines spell your name."

Lawrence happily agreed. He read:

"Let peace and joy abound this Christmas Day,
And let it long abide in friends held dear.
When anger, spite and cruelty held sway,
Rejoice that you alone remained clear.
Enough of contrite words can ne'er be said,
Nor can the tongue express what heart doth feel.
Consider only this, when I am dead:
Erring Ned to me this day did kneel."

There were tears in Lawrence's eyes, which surprised Ned, for he had thought of him as a man always in control of himself. Impulsively and without a word, Lawrence embraced Ned. After a flicker of hesitation, Ned returned the embrace warmly.

As they released each other, Lawrence turned to the table on which stood a jug of wine and two goblets. With his back to Ned he said, "And now for our drink."

Ned had a moment to take stock of the room. It was bigger and grander than the one he shared with Will and was dominated by a magnificent carved, canopied, and curtained four-poster bed.

Lawrence handed a goblet to Ned and then raised his own with the words, "May this be the first of many a Merry Christmas we shall share."

Ned was annoyed by something in himself which was wary of this toast, but he quelled it and said with apparent conviction, "Amen."

Lawrence moved to sit on a daybed and invited Ned to sit by him. When they were both seated, Lawrence said, "I shall long treasure your poem, but there was one idea in it that must have been dictated by the rhyme. 'When I am dead.' I am so much older than you that 'tis almost certain I shall die first."

"Maybe not. Death does not always wait for age. 'Tis true the word 'dead' came to mind to rhyme with 'said,' but, when it did, I had the strongest feeling that it was true, that I shall die young. But there was more than that. I felt that I, the youngest brother, will go first, and Will, the eldest, will go last."

"You must not think like that."

"I did not choose to think it, but I am not frightened."

"Did Will see the poem?"

"No. He said it should be for you alone."

In response to this, Lawrence put his arm around Ned and hugged him. Ned smiled, a little nervously, and quickly introduced the subject most on his mind: would he see the King, and when?

"I cannot tell. I can do little until His Majesty first shows an interest in you. You caught my eye as Rosencrantz, and may well catch his, in which case he may ask about you the following day and look for you thereafter. But if you are nervous about this, you will not give of your best. At the entertainment last Tuesday you were not the same as the singer at Wilton."

"That was because . . ."

"I know the reason. I wanted to see you before you went on, but was not certain I should have been welcomed, and then fresh anger would have made your performance even worse."

At this point they were interrupted by a knock on the door. Lawrence went to open it and admitted a young and handsome groom of the King's chamber.

"His Majesty wishes to see ye, Lawrence," said the groom with a Scottish lilt.

"This is Ned Shakespeare, and this is Gavin Carmichael."

"Ah, I remember ye, Ned. You sang the other nicht. But come, Lawrence. There isna much time; soon he will go in to dinner, and 'tis such a meal as ye have never seen—boar's head and peacocks and I know not what."

Gavin bustled out followed by the other two, Lawrence telling Ned that he hoped to see him later in the day. Ned decided to put aside all anxieties about the week's plays and give himself entirely to the enjoyment of the day, for which there was no better company than his fellow players.

Lawrence was to ask the King whether the players should present the shortened version of *Hamlet* which had been given on tour or the longer one they now gave in London, though this latter was still considerably shorter than the original play. At dinner Lawrence returned with the gracious reply, "We cannot have too much of Master Shakespeare and Master Burbage." And the royal audience, which had been canceled at Wilton, would be granted after the performance, "no matter how late the hour." This served to complete the Christmas merriment, and Richard Burbage asked that a speech he loved but had not spoken for two years might be reinserted.

"Done," said John Heminge, already at noon flushed and happy with drinking, "if you can speak it here and now without conning it."

As Burbage rose slowly to his feet, Heminge commanded the room to silence and explained the wager. It seemed such a long time before Burbage began that everybody thought he had lost without beginning, but then he began quietly:

> "How all occasions do inform against me
> And spur my dull revenge!"

He had no difficulty with the lines, for every time he had looked through his part before a performance he had mouthed them with loving regret; his pause resulted from his desire to do them some justice at such short notice. When he finished the thirty-five lines, he remained standing for a moment in a Christmas room of silence, and then he sat down quietly. There broke out such an ovation of homage from his fellow players as made the incident memorable for him and for them. Never had Ned more admired Burbage. Ambition burned in him anew.

After the prolonged dinner, most of the senior sharers went to their rooms for rest, to prepare themselves for the evening of eating, drinking, and jollity. Lawrence took the opportunity to tell Ned about an exciting plan. In reading *Hamlet* again he had discovered a speech of Rosencrantz which had not been spoken since the first performances. It would appeal mightily to the King for it dealt with the awesome responsibilities of kingship. Lawrence was going to try to get it reinserted; the inclusion of Burbage's usually omitted soliloquy would give him the excuse, especially since the speech was only thirteen lines. If the sharers agreed, then on Tuesday, the day of the performance, he would tell the King beforehand, and this would most certainly make him aware of Ned.

When Ned was alone, he upbraided himself because all he could remember of the speech was his angry sorrow at having lost it, now more than two years ago. How different from Richard Burbage, who could easily recall a much longer speech he had lost at the same time! When John Lowin approached him to join a group which was about to indulge in some Christmas music, he excused himself briefly and hurried to his room to get out the part of Rosencrantz and learn the speech forthwith.

His entering the bedroom awoke Will who was taking a rather noisy snooze. Ned begged his pardon, hesitated for a moment, and then decided to tell him Lawrence's plan; it was as well to warn him so that he would be prepared to support it at the supper table.

Will was amused by the way Lawrence meant to use the precedent established by Burbage.

"Do you remember the speech?" asked Ned.

"No, but I remember its substance, and Lawrence is right: the King will like it."

"Will you support Lawrence?"

"To be sure I will. Not only am I your brother, Ned, I am the author of the play. I should like all the lines restored, though that will never happen."

Ned soon found the speech. It was a good one, and he would make the most of it. As he settled down to learn it, Will suggested that he should postpone doing so until the morrow.

"Because you think they'll not agree?" asked Ned in anguish.

"No; because this is Christmas Day, and your fellows will miss your company. You owe it to them," Will said, with a smiling reference to Ned's conduct a few days ago. Reluctantly Ned had to concur, and he left.

It was Will who was deputed to tell Ned after supper about the speech to be restored. Lawrence had been so persuasive in his knowledge of what would please the King that there had been no difficulty.

The evening was a happy one, but all were prepared to go to bed early because most of the players had a deal of relearning to do, since they were not to play the touring version of *Hamlet* to which they had become accustomed.

A platform had to be built on which to present *Hamlet,* in order to accommodate the grave into which Hamlet and Laertes had to jump. Again Lawrence's influence was effective. Tom Vincent had supervised the preparation during the week of the parts of the platform-stage, and he and some court carpenters were in the hall early on Monday. Since the stage had to be built for *Hamlet,* it had been decided to use it for all the plays, and so it had become a somewhat elaborate structure, made to approximate the Globe stage, with side and center entrances.

Sour-faced Tom Vincent was made almost to smile by the enthusiasm of the players when they saw the stage for the first time. Nat Tremayne also had worked wonders with the costumes; never had the Court of Denmark looked so splendid.

The Great Hall had been made ready for the audience too. At the upper end was a richly canopied dais on which stood two thronelike chairs. Other chairs and benches in two rows were on the floor on both sides of the dais and along the side walls; there were also two rows of benches in the gallery. John Heminge instinctively counted the seats and found there were well over two hundred all told.

The players were too excited for supper. It was true that the King had already seen them, but there had been an impromptu atmosphere at Wilton. They had the same feeling as at that memorable first performance of *Hamlet,* except that this time the trumpets would not be theirs and would signal not the beginning of a play but the entrance of a real King.

It took a dozen servants a full hour to light all the candles and lamps. At last the noble audience began to arrive, and their happy buzz as they were shown to their appropriate seats by the Court Chamberlain and his men could be heard by the waiting players and heightened their nervous excitement. It seemed an endless time before the first distant trumpet was sounded. The players could sense the standing and silencing of the audience they could not see. That was the moment Lawrence chose to approach Ned and whisper, as he grasped his arm, "All will be well." The series of trumpet calls was climaxed by a fanfare in the Great Hall itself; the King and Queen were entering.

The players could visualize the deep obeisance of the whole court; then they could hear the audience sitting again, after the King and Queen were seated. The Court Chamberlain came to the players and said, "Their Majesties command your duty and attendance that you may entertain them with your quality." The sixteen players made an orderly procession onto the stage, and, when they were all in place, made a deep bow. The Court Chamberlain, having received a slight nod from the King, said, "His Majesty is pleased to command that you begin." The players made a well-rehearsed bowing exit, leaving only Sam on stage as Francisco; his halberd had already been placed onstage. He moved to pick it up and shoulder it, and, with his cold pacing as a guard, the play began.

His brief glance at the august and glittering assembly had unnerved Ned. It was impossible that the hub and center of that world could be interested in him. All confidence oozed out of him. He began to grasp for the words of the reinserted speech; he could not even remember the first line. He looked around him in dismay. There was Will in ghostly armor waiting to make his entrance. Will seemed to sense his eyes, for he looked around and smiled at him. Suddenly the words came to Ned:

> The single and peculiar life is bound
> With all the strength and armor of the mind
> To keep itself from noyance . . .

From beginning to end the play went flawlessly. Burbage had never been better, and his best drew their best from the other players. At the end the applause was like that from delighted groundlings, and it was led heartily by the King and Queen. This was no decorous acknowledgment of a royal entertainment, but the spontaneous tribute to excellence.

Lawrence led the other ten sharers to the dais to introduce them to the King and Queen. Everybody in the hall strained to listen to what the King might say. Burbage was the first to be presented. The King said to him, "We welcome you, Master Burbage, as a king without rival among players." Will was next. To him the King said, "You have a rare gift, Master Shakespeare. We thank God that you serve us—and so should Master Burbage." This joke was greeted with appreciative smiles; laughter would not be seemly, for the King was already receiving Augustine Phillips. He spoke to only one more player, and that was the last, Alexander Cooke. He was the only one to whom he asked a question.

The King said, "Were you not Guildenstern?"

"Yes, your Majesty," said Alex as nervously as though he were confessing to a crime.

" 'Tis strange to see you without Rosencrantz. Why did you leave him behind?"

Alex was tongue-tied in unreasonable guilt, and it was Lawrence who came to his rescue. He said, "If I may be permitted to make answer, your Majesty. Master Cooke is a sharer in the company, and Master Edmund Shakespeare is not—yet."

"Yet we think he deserves to be presented to us, as do the others who have pleased us much. Let them approach."

The Chamberlain called to the six players on the stage, "His Majesty commands you to approach."

Ned was transported with happiness as he led the others to the royal dais. After all, it was he that had been mentioned, but he was glad that the others had also been called. They bowed low to the King. Lawrence presented Ned.

The King said, "Another Shakespeare. Are you not brother to the poet?"

"Yes, your Majesty."

"Are you a poet too?"

"No, sire. I am but a player."

"But a player? We think 'tis enough, for 'tis the players that give life to the poet's words. You spoke some tonight that pleased us much."

The King had no words for the other players but was gracious to them all. Led by Lawrence, all the players bowed and stepped back three paces. The King stood and with him the whole assembly. The trumpets sounded. He held out his hand to the Queen, who also rose and the royal couple went out of the room.

Thus did the King's Men become his indeed.

The hour was late and a busy day lay ahead, but the players were in no mood for sleep. In their own dining room they made such a noise of celebration that a senior member of the household staff came to bid them be quiet. Servants in a nearby building had been awakened and they had but few hours of sleep when the court was in residence. The steward was irate and obviously had little respect for players. In appearance, mood, and speech he brought to mind Malvolio's interruption of the midnight caterwauling in *Twelfth Night,* and, as soon as he had left the room, Gus Phillips, who played Malvolio, could not resist quoting, in comic whispers, "My masters, are you mad? Or what are you? Have you no wit, manners, nor honesty, but to gabble like tinkers at this time of night?" This was enough to set them off·again, but John Heminge uttered an imperious "Hush!" He went on to say, "We must to bed. This has been a great beginning, but much remains to be done. Our last words and thoughts this night must be for Master Lawrence Fletcher, to whom we owe much. *Hamlet* was the first play of ours he saw, and it brought him to our fellowship. *Hamlet* tonight has sealed him in that fellowship. Let us drink to him in gratitude and friendship."

All raised their goblets or tankards and, with muted voices, saluted Lawrence. He responded by saying, "I thank you all, but it is your merits, not I, that have won you the King's favor. I am proud to be part of this fellowship."

As they all broke up for the night, Ned waited till Lawrence was free of the sharers to say to him, "Thank you for everything."

Lawrence smiled and said, " 'Tis but the beginning."

THE MERCHANT OF VENICE WAS WELL RECEIVED THE FOLLOWING EVENING, but for the players it was an anticlimax after *Hamlet.* There was no commendation beyond the applause and no player was presented to the King. They all went quietly to bed and to prepare themselves for *Much Ado About Nothing* the next day. Ned was especially disappointed. Surely there might have been some word from somebody about his appearance in his eye-catching Salanio costume. Lawrence had complimented him before the performance, but he had not seen him afterwards.

The spirits of the troupe revived the following day, and they rehearsed *Much Ado* with a fresh zest. Ned's Balthasar had won him so many notable conquests in the past that he was determined to be in best voice. "Sigh no more, ladies," had never failed, nor should it tonight.

Nor did it, though it was not until the following morning that he found out. Ned was sitting, rather dejected, at a rehearsal of *Twelfth Night* when Lawrence came to him. Lawrence had interrupted the rehearsal for a private conference with a few of the senior sharers and Tom Vincent.

Lawrence smiled as he approached Ned. He said, "I have good news. His Majesty was well pleased by your singing last night and wishes you to entertain him in private this afternoon. You have been given permission to leave the rehearsal and prepare yourself. Come."

Giddy with happiness, Ned left with Lawrence, without word or look to the others. As they walked to Ned's room, Lawrence reported, "The King said that if you please him as much in private this afternoon as you did in public last night, he wishes to see you even more privately after tonight's performance." While this news was what Ned had been waiting for, it struck a note of alarm in him. Lawrence swept on, "I have a plan for this afternoon. Could you learn a song the King has written? 'Twould please him mightily."

"Yes," said Ned eagerly, "if 'tis a measure to which I know a melody."

" 'Tis easy; each verse has six lines with four beats each. 'Tis like that song of spring you sang, but without the refrain."

When they were in Ned's room, Lawrence gave him a piece of paper on which he had written out the three verses of the King's song. "I have made it more English in the spelling for your greater ease. 'Tis said he wrote it while he was yet a boy, but methinks that is a fable to flatter royalty."

Ned read the poem slowly to himself and was amazed by its content. Here was no flight of fancy, no delightful conceit, no lofty sentiment, no pious invocation. It was a poem of crafty, worldly wisdom. The first verse read:

> Since thought is free, think what thou will,
> O troubled heart, to ease thy pain.
> Thought unrevealed can do no ill,
> But words passed out come not again.
> Be careful aye for to invent
> The way to get thy own intent.

The other two verses contained such maxims as "Let none know what thou dost mean," "Let wit thy will correct," and "Make virtue of a need."

Before Lawrence left to find Nat Tremayne and decide upon a suitable costume for Ned for the afternoon, Ned had a few questions for him.

"How many songs should I prepare?"

"The King's appetite for things that please him is insatiable. Prepare as many as you can. Surprise him with his own after three or four others."

"How many people will be present?"

"Some half dozen or so of the most favored."

"Any ladies?"

"No; no ladies." Lawrence's parting smile again made Ned apprehensive, not from fear but from doubt of his own behavior.

Ned did not go down to dinner. Will brought him some food and drink and since he had no part in *Twelfth Night,* Will was free to stay and hear Ned's songs. When Ned asked him for his opinion of the King's song, he said, "If he abides by his own advice, he will prove a skillful king."

Ned decided to confide in Will the possibility of the meeting with the King after the performance; his tone made his doubts clear.

Will said, "Is not that what you have most wanted?"

"Yes, but now I . . ." His words trailed off.

"Remember this, Ned. You have talent as a player—much more than ever I had—and the King's favor cannot improve or impair that."

Further words were prevented by the exuberant entrance of Nat and Martin, carrying a costume borrowed from the royal wardrobe. It was perfectly chosen to avoid an unbecoming flamboyance while fully displaying Ned's excellent figure. As Nat made the final adjustments to the costume, he twittered, "I want to hear all about it, who was there, what they said. I am sure the Earl of Pembroke will be there, and his brother, both so handsome. The Earl of Lennox too, I'll be bound. He is son to that earl that it is whispered was the King's lover in Scotland and was driven into exile in France by those barbarous Scottish noblemen. Noblemen, forsooth: Brigands is nearer the mark. And in France that beautiful earl died. This is the son, brought back by the King to Scotland while he was yet a boy. Handsome too, like his father. Still, none will surpass you, Ned, none."

Lawrence came for Ned all too soon. As they walked to the royal quarters, he reminded Ned that he was only to speak when asked a direct question.

The first thing that struck Ned when he entered the richly decorated, private audience chamber was that a young boy was present. He was sitting on a low, upholstered stool at the foot of the King's exquisitely carved and cushioned chair. The boy must be the nine-year-old Prince Henry, and for some reason Ned was filled with relief by his presence. As Ned bowed low he was aware that he was standing on such a beautiful carpet as he had never before seen.

There were some half dozen courtiers present, as Lawrence had forecast. Ned immediately recognized the Earl of Pembroke and his brother, and the Earl of Lennox, who at thirty was the oldest man present, apart from the King and Lawrence. He did not know the others, but saw that wine was being served by the Scottish groom who had come to fetch

Lawrence. The wine was served in Venetian glass which was as casually handled as pewter tankards.

As Ned and Lawrence entered, the King was completing an anecdote; his Scottish tongue was as broad as that of the groom. ". . . and we said, 'We like not that name "Saul"; the Apostle was called "Paul" after he was converted.' And the sweet rascal said, 'An' it would please your Majesty, my name should be Dung, could I but manure your fields.' " There was a climax of laughter, in which Lawrence thought it seemly not to join. As for Ned, he was so overwhelmed by the occasion and amazed by the words he had heard from the royal lips that he had no wish even to smile.

The King was now free to notice Lawrence and Ned. He said, "Ah, Lawrence. You have brought the comely young man to sing to us." Following Lawrence, Ned now stood up straight. " 'Tis Master Shakespeare, we think. But that name rightly belongs to your brother, whose pen does it much honor. We would have a more familiar name for you. By what name were you christened?"

"Edmund, your Majesty."

"Then we shall call you Ned." Ned had a sudden wild desire to say, "Call me Dung if it please you," but restrained himself.

"Lawrence," said the King, "we have brought the Prince here because we thought he should share what entertainment we have by day since the need for sleep robs him of that we have by night. What say you, son Henry?"

"Your Majesty promised I should stay up late on Saturday to see the New Year in."

"We promised, but we wager you will be asleep long ere midnight."

"No, sire. I shall command a groom to keep me awake, and, if he fails, I shall punish him."

The King commented to his noble audience, "Such are the pains we inflict on ourselves and others in pursuit of pleasures that always disappoint us."

This piece of royal wisdom was greeted with dutiful and appreciative smiles.

"Now, Lawrence," said the King, "come and sit by us and let Ned begin."

Lawrence moved to sit on the floor near the King. Ned strummed his lute to test the tuning, when the King said, "Wait. 'Tis likely your mouth is dry. Gavin, some wine for Lawrence and Ned."

Gavin Carmichael poured wine into two beautifully cut glasses and gave them to Lawrence and to Ned, who was in a nervous quandary. What did he do? Just drink it? The King solved his dilemma, but in a way that petrified Ned.

"This is the first time you have drunk in our presence, Ned. We would like to hear a loyal toast."

To make matters worse, everybody in the room except the King—even

Prince Henry—rose and looked toward Ned. He groped wildly in his brain for something he said in one of the plays that would be appropriate, but nothing came. He looked to Lawrence for help but received only a steady, confident smile, and then he remembered his faculty for rhyming lines; he had always prided himself on being able to do them on the mere prompting of a name. He raised his glass and began tentatively, but gradually his old facility returned and he gathered speed and ended triumphantly.

> "To James, our sovereign lord and king,
>   Ourselves, our lives, our all we bring,
> To do him ease, to save him harm,
>   To be for aye his shield and balm."

After they had all drunk the toast, not even the presence of the King, who alone should speak, could prevent an outburst of delighted chatter of compliments. Ned had undoubtedly passed the test. He caught a gleam of pride in Lawrence's eyes.

From then on Ned could do no wrong. At the King's command, he launched happily into his first song, and the obvious pleasure he gave was only exceeded by the pleasure he felt. He kept the King's own song for the fourth, and the surprise of it transported the author. Only he, the Earl of Lennox, and Lawrence knew who the poet was.

The King said to the Earl of Pembroke, "Know you who penned that, William?"

The tone of the question gave the earl a strong hint of the answer. He said, "A poet as wise in the ways of men as he is skillful with words."

"Mark you that, our son Henry. 'Twas your father who penned that poem when we were little older than you."

Lawrence avoided Ned's eyes at this remark lest a smile should reveal his amusement that the poet became younger with every telling of the tale.

The King went on to say, "We shall have much to teach you about government, Henry, when you get older, but we think it fitting that you should learn that song e'en now. Lawrence, see to it. But tell us, Ned, how came you by it?"

"Master Fletcher brought it to me, your Majesty."

"Then 'twas not your own idea to sing it to us," said the King with a trace of disappointment.

"I liked it, sire, when I read it, and wanted to sing it."

"Then come. Some more of your quality. We are much pleased. But first, our song again, so that the Prince may have further understanding of it."

Ned repeated the song and sang three more. Then the King glanced at an ornate clock that stood on an inlaid side table. He stood speedily, followed by all the others, and said, "When time passes pleasantly it passes too quickly. The Princess Elizabeth and the Prince Charles expect us, and our own pleasure must not deprive them of theirs." He moved to the door with Prince Henry. The groom hastened to open it while the others bowed. At the door the King stopped and said, "A word with you, Lawrence." He left the room and Lawrence followed him. The courtiers waited a discreet moment, then they also left the room, all of them smiling at Ned as they did so but not saying a word to him.

Gavin smiled at Ned, who awaited Lawrence's return, and said, "Ye did richt well. Ye're a bonny minstrel; a bonny man too." As he spoke he collected the glasses, draining with enjoyment any wine left in them. "His Majesty likes ye fine; I can tell. Here; let's tak a wee drap o' wine. Come; dinna fash yersel'. What the eye doesna' see, the heart canna grieve over." He poured two glasses of wine and handed one to Ned. "Here's to ye; I like ye fine. But be carefu' wi' Jamey. He can be a vera guid friend, and a vera bad enemy. And remember this: he never forgets he's King, and dinna ye either."

Ned longed to ask questions but was dumb with relief that his ordeal was over and with shock at Gavin's intimate use of "Jamey."

His silence prompted Gavin to say, "Canna ye speak, or do ye only sing?"

Ned smiled and said, "Please forgive me. I am still overcome by the afternoon."

"Ye'll get used to it. Tell me. Did ye mak up that poem to the King in your head as ye spak it?"

"Yes," said Ned. "I've always had a gift for quick rhymes."

"Ye're a vera clever man, and ye'll need to be wi' Jamey. He's too clever for his ain guid."

Further conversation was interrupted by Lawrence who was in high spirits. He grasped Ned's arms and said, "I'm proud of you. I knew I would be." Then, aware of Gavin he said, "Has my Scottish friend been entertaining you?"

"He has been very kind," said Ned.

"Did you understand him?"

"Better than he understands ye, Lawrence Fletcher. I'll tak my oath on that."

Lawrence laughed this away, but Ned noted it and pondered it later. "Come," said Lawrence. "You must change before supper and get ready for the play."

As they walked back to Ned's room, Lawrence said, "The King wants to see you after the play tonight. Tell not the others. Say that you are tired from the afternoon. Put on your own best suit and I will come for you and take you to the King."

"But Will must know; he will see I am not in the room."

"Yes, we must tell him," said Lawrence reluctantly, "but he is discreet and will understand."

When they got to the room, Will was there, writing. Lawrence launched into an enthusiastic account of Ned's afternoon triumph. Then, moderating his tone to a confidential one, he told Will of the further meeting with the King that night.

"Will you be present too?" asked Will. Ned had not thought of this possibility. He had assumed he would be alone with the King. He might be worried about nothing. He remembered what a pleasant surprise the sight of the young prince had been that afternoon.

In a somewhat hesitant reply to Will's question, Lawrence said, "It will by my part to take Ned to the King; after that, I know not His Majesty's pleasure."

Lawrence went to tell those players who were finishing the *Twelfth Night* rehearsal about Ned's success, for they would all feel they were involved in it; so when Ned came to supper with Will he was greeted with acclamation. For the first time, Ned was the hero of the hour, and it was a good feeling.

It was just as well that Ned had little to do in *Twelfth Night,* for he was in such a turmoil that concentration on a part would have been difficult. He pleaded tiredness at the end of the play; after all, tomorrow's rehearsal of the *Dream* would be the most exacting for him.

Alone in his room, Ned dressed with a nervous care. The evening had made him feel that he now bore the responsibility of cementing the favorable attitude of the King to the whole company. Before, he had been merely concerned with his own advancement. He was ready when Lawrence came for him, as ready as he ever would be.

This time they went to a small boudoirlike room in the royal quarters. The King was alone. He was dressed in a long, thickly padded, brocade gown and velvet slippers, and was lolling on a comfortably cushioned daybed, sipping wine from a glass which he himself replenished from a decanter. There had been two guards in the anteroom, but no sign of a groom. The guards had obviously recognized Lawrence and must have expected him for they had made no attempt to stop him when he had quietly knocked on the door and entered.

Lawrence and Ned bowed low. The King said to Lawrence, "You have done your mission well. We will call you when we need you."

Lawrence bowed and went out, closing the door behind him. He had studiously avoided looking at Ned, who was completely at a loss. He had foreseen with apprehension the probability of finding himself alone with the King, but not as suddenly as this. In spite of himself, he began to feel a deep resentment welling up in him. He was being taken for granted, like a whore, and Lawrence was the pimp.

The King smiled at him and said, "You seem afeard. Here, have some of this good wine; 'twill give you ease." And he poured a glass of wine for Ned. This was overwhelming: the King himself serving him wine! It had been drilled into him that he should only speak in answer to a question, and then as briefly as possible. He took the glass and bowed by way of acknowledging it. "Sit and drink," said the King, indicating an upholstered, square chair.

Ned did so. The wine was good, the richest he had ever tasted.

The King said, "'Tis right and fitting that you should be awed at finding yourself alone with us for the first time, but we shall find little pleasure in your company until you gain some ease. You have much to commend you: your looks, your talent, and your mind, for we think you to be quick of apprehension. But tell us first about that toast this afternoon. Was it indeed an extempore creation, or did your skill as a player but make it seem so?"

Ned's indignation at the implied trickery made him momentarily forget his situation. He said with some heat, "No, your Majesty. 'Twas new. I had not expected such a request."

"We thought that Lawrence might have anticipated it. He is a clever man, and your good friend. Come now. Prove your quality to me. Some lines on Lawrence."

Desperate to prove himself, Ned drained his glass while feeling for rhymes. What came surprised both him and the King.

> "You say in sooth he's friend to me,
>   A friend indeed is Lawrence;
> But yet it still remains to see
>   If love will turn t' abhorrence."

Taken aback, the King said, "You seem to have little faith in mankind. Why should you doubt Lawrence?"

"Mayhap 'tis myself I doubt, sire," Ned tried to justify himself with an apologetic smile. "'Twas the first rhyme for Lawrence that came to mind."

The King smiled in return and said, "We doubt there is another. Come; some more wine. You have earned it."

Ned stood and held out his glass to the King. He felt there was something wrong in his position, and with theatrical aplomb dropped to one knee to receive the wine.

The King was amused by this move and pleased by the grace with which it had been accomplished. He smiled as he poured the wine and said, "Had we a sword at this moment, we should knight you. Rise, and sit by us."

The King moved to make room, and with some return to his earlier unease Ned sat by him; but the mention of a knighthood, frivolous though it had been, had dazzled his mind.

The next question took Ned completely by surprise. "Tell us of your brother, Ned. Is he papist or Puritan?"

"Neither, sire. He is a good churchman. He cannot be both Puritan and player."

"Then a papist?"

"No, sire. He is a true Englishman. I do not think he gives much mind to such matters."

"He does, Ned, he does, else he could not have written *Hamlet*. And you, Ned. What think you about religion?"

"I do not think about it, sire."

"Then you should. We must instruct you, for we are the Head of the Church as well as of the land." As he said this, the King's bejeweled hand, for emphasis, patted Ned's thigh and then remained there. "But not tonight, we think. There will be time for that, if you continue to please us. Lawrence tells us that you will live with him when we return to London."

For some reason Ned was infuriated by the knowledge that Lawrence had discussed this with the King, and for one wild moment was tempted to say that Lawrence already lived in London and had done so throughout the plague. It was fortunate that he had not been asked a direct question.

The King went on. "It will be pleasing to have you near our court. After the troublesome work of ruling the realm, a quiet hour like this brings sweet refreshment to us." The hand moved from the hip to encircle Ned's shoulders, and the King moved closer to him. "Drink up, Ned."

Automatically Ned obeyed. The King also drained his glass, then put it down, but Ned held on to his. "Set down your glass." Ned did so. The King cupped Ned's face in his hands. Ned averted his eyes. "Look at us." Reluctantly Ned obeyed. The King chose to interpret Ned's desperate look as one of natural and becoming embarrassment, and he kissed him full on the lips.

Ned's body went rigid and he pulled away. Now there was no mistaking his look of outrage. The King's manner responded. With an imperious coldness he said, "We were mistaken in you. Leave us."

Ned stood, bowed awkwardly and stumbled out of the room. The King had rung a bell which was near at hand, and as Ned opened the door, he almost collided with Lawrence, whom he brushed roughly aside. Quickly the guards seized Ned. Had there been an attempt on the King's life? They awaited word from the room. Ned stood in their firm grasp, breathing heavily. Within a minute, Lawrence emerged and said with a coldness to rival the King's, "Let him go." Then he reentered the room and closed the door.

The guards had not missed the tone of Lawrence's command, and they pushed Ned roughly away. Somehow he found his way out into the freezing night and, in his confusion, felt an urgent need to confide in his brother, Will. Ned went to their room and poured the whole story out. Then he asked, "Will this make a difference to the company? Will the King favor us less?"

"No," said Will with smiling confidence. "I do not expect a good reception tomorrow night, but that will have nothing to do with you. The minds of the court will be full of the masque that is to follow us. To the company you will be still the minstrel that pleased the King this afternoon. They will know nothing about tonight, nor ever will."

"And Lawrence?"

"I think he will avoid you for the rest of the time we are here. The King will blame him for what happened tonight, and he will be at pains to make amends. You say he had told the King that you were to live with him. 'Tis certain, in my judgment, that he will now promise that that will not happen."

"Will, I meant to act differently, to hide my feelings."

"You tried to be false to your nature and you failed. If you had succeeded tonight, there would soon have come a time when you would have failed. 'Tis an honorable failure."

"I expected so much from the King's favor."

"And now you are disappointed. But are you not relieved too?"

After a moment, Ned said, "Yes; mightily."

"Where now will you live in London? Would you choose to live with me?"

"No, Will. 'Tis better I live alone."

"Until you get yourself a wife."

Ned made no answer to this, but after a slight pause he said, "Think you I shall ever be a sharer?"

Will said lightly, "If you live long enough and another sharer dies soon enough."

Ned said seriously, "When I wrote that poem for Lawrence, I had a strange certainty that I should die young."

Will thought for a moment and then said, "I sometimes think we live as long as life has need of us—and you have much to give."

Ned pondered that for a moment, and then he started to chuckle and said, "That's two pentameters. You write plays even when you speak." Still chuckling, Ned added, "Think you the King will tell Lawrence that I rhymed his name with abhorrence?"

By this time they were enjoying themselves, and Will said, "I hope he does, for 'tis a rare rhyme, and someday I think they will savor it again, and laugh together over it. And now Ned, goodnight, for we have the *Dream* tomorrow. Dream happily tonight, for all will be well."

Book Five

1607

FORTY-SIX

As Ned cradled his sleeping son in his arms, sitting in the garden of the house which was the child's but not the father's, his mind was full of failure and death.

It was the first Sunday in July of the year 1607, and the plague had come again. Yesterday had seen the last performance at the Globe for the season. Tomorrow the company would set out on tour again, and again without Ned. The sharers must first be provided for, and there were now ten of them who were active players, quite enough for the male parts in the truncated touring versions of the plays. Ned felt that he would never be a sharer, and his ambition to be another Burbage had gradually given way to an acceptance of his work as a supporting player. The need for money after the terrible plague of 1603 had induced the sharers to admit another to their ranks, Nicholas Tooley. The theatre had not been able to open until the spring of 1604; the additional capital had been needed even though the King had come to their aid with a gift of thirty pounds, as Lawrence Fletcher had said he would. Ned had not even felt hurt by Tooley's promotion, for at that time he was numb from his personal debacle with the King and the resulting loss of Lawrence's friendship and support. And when Augustine Phillips had died a year later, in 1605, it seemed only right, even to Ned, that he should be succeeded as sharer by his brother-in-law, Robert Gough.

Poor Gus! He had lived less than a year after the death of his too much beloved son, who had died at two years old. His father had protected him from the plague by moving to Mortlake, but death had found the little boy there. He had been almost the same age as Ned's own son now was. Ned had begun by hating the child because his birth had caused the death of the mother. Now he loved the child intensely.

Ned's sad musings were interrupted by the approach of Rachel Ponsard, Marie's devoted servant, who held the house and estate in trust for "Monsieur Neddy." It was time to take the child for his afternoon meal at the breast of his wet-nurse; he would not be weaned until he was three.

With Rachel was a man whom Ned was surprised to see. It was Jack Barnet, now Sir John and married to his Lady Cynthia. He was one of the three men who knew the full story of Ned and the child; the other two were Will and John Lowin.

As they approached, Rachel began to talk in French to Sir John. When Sir John chastised her for this, she answered, "Madame de la Motte would have spoken French to her son if she had lived."

"Alas, she did not. I am the guardian of all she left, and the most important thing she left was Neddy, and I say you speak English to him."

As Sir John greeted Ned, Rachel bore the child away to be fed, pointedly crooning to him in French.

Sir John said coldly to Ned, "I knew you come here every Sunday afternoon, and I had to speak to you though I no more wanted to see you than you me. I could not rid myself of the idea that it was your child that killed Marie. That was foolish, but none of us is free from folly. I or one of half-a-dozen others might have been the father, as you cruelly told Marie. Do you have doubts about the boy now?"

"No," said Ned curtly. The child sometimes looked uncannily like his father and sometimes like his grandfather, but always a Shakespeare.

Sir John proceeded. "Did you really believe Marie was the wealthy widow she pretended to be—Madame de la Motte? I still cannot quite understand how she succumbed to your charms, for she sold her favors dearly. What could you give her?"

Ned could keep silent no longer. Words poured out of him angrily. "I had nothing to give but myself. I loved her and she loved me, but she would not marry me because you rich and noble gentlemen had made her used to a life of wealth and ease that she could not forsake. And so my son—yes, my son—was born a bastard."

Sir John answered, " 'Tis clear that you meant something more and something different to Marie from us other men; she told me so when she was in her last month. I wanted to fetch you to her, but she would not let me."

Won over by the change in tone, Ned said, "We had quarreled bitterly. When she told me about the child, I said she should prove it was mine by marrying me. She refused. Month after month our quarrels got worse. I left to play with the King's Men at Oxford and then to go on to visit my family in Stratford. When I came back she was dead."

"Tell me how you met her, and how you found out the truth about her life. She told me much, especially in those last months—she seemed to know she was going to die—but about you she would say nothing, except that you were the father of the child, and if it was a boy it was to be named Edmund Shakespeare."

"I met her first at the Mountjoys' in Silver Street, not far from here. My brother was lodging with them and still does when he is in London. I stay in his rooms when he is not there. She mistook me for an apprentice. My dignity as a player was offended, and I spoke to her haughtily. She laughed, and it was that laugh that won me; it was so free and so warm, and there was no scorn in it. I went home with her that very day, and soon every day on which we could not meet was an agony of emptiness."

"How did you find out about her?"

"I shall never forget that terrible day. Master Mountjoy told me when he was in his angry cups. He was raging against all women when I came in, and he told me to beware of them, and particularly that whore, Marie Boulanger. At first I didn't know who or what he was talking about, but he soon made it clear; too clear. I went mad; 'tis a miracle I did not kill him. Then I rushed out and to Marie's. Rachel tried to stop me, but I forced myself into Marie's bedroom; she was there with a man. I screamed the word 'whore!' at her, and rushed out again. I was vaguely aware that the naked man had scrambled out of bed and was making for his dagger. I sometimes think it would have been better if I had let him kill me then."

"But you went back to Marie."

"Yes. For days I was in a fog. I went to the theatre and to rehearsals of the Christmas Revels, but I don't know how I got through it all. Every day a message came from Marie; they were true messages of love and at last I went to her; I could not keep away. She told me all, but she loved me as I loved her. Then came the day when she told me she was with child by me, and the quarrels about marriage began. When I said we could not let our son be born a bastard, she said, 'Why not? I was born so and it has not hindered me. I was nobly if ill begotten. My mother was a serving wench but my father was the count of the chateau.'"

"Even I did not know that. . . . But I have come today about Neddy. I wanted your opinion. The plague has come again, but 'tis not expected to be severe; hundreds of deaths perhaps, but not thousands. Should we arrange for Neddy to leave London?"

"I was pondering that very question when you came."

"Rachel says, like a true Huguenot, it is God's will whether the child live or die, plague or no plague. She also says, truly enough, that Neddy was not touched by last year's plague, so why should it be different this year?"

Ned replied, "More and more I feel that death has his own time for each of us, else why does one in a household die and the others live, why does a bullet fired wildly kill one man and spare those standing next to him, why does lightning strike one tree in a forest? And I know that Rachel will take every possible care of the child."

"So be it. Neddy stays. And you?"

"I know not yet. The company goes on the road, but without me.

Maybe I shall go home to Stratford for a time. It would please my mother; she is old and cannot live much longer."

As they walked to the house, Sir John said casually, "Your friend, Ben Jonson. Have you seen him of late?"

Immediately wary, for Ben, still a papist, was always in trouble and always miraculously out of it soon after, Ned said, "No; not for a long time."

Sir John smiled. "You need not be so cautious. I like Ben. He is noisy, but harmless. I am sure he has tried to convert you to Rome, and I am equally sure he has not succeeded. I thought of you, Ned, when he was called up last year on charges of seducing youth to popery."

"Why me?"

"Ever since his *Volpone*—a very good comedy and I like your Bonario in it—ever since that, you became very friendly with him again. Yes, we keep our eye on Ben; he often leads us to interesting people. But let us make our adieux to Rachel and Neddy."

Soon they were out of the house and walking together along the street, in something of their old friendship.

At home, Ned found a letter which was as much a surprise as had been the meeting with Sir John Barnet. It read: "It would give me great pleasure if you would take supper with me at my .house this evening. With the company leaving London tomorrow without you, it may well be that you feel in need of some company, even mine; it is most certain that I should welcome yours. There are things to be said between us and things I would impart to you. I write to you at such short notice because it may well be that you will take a sudden whim to go to Stratford, and I should be greatly disappointed not to see you before you left. In spite of all, I pray that you will believe I am your friend, Lawrence Fletcher."

Ned was much intrigued. He immediately decided to accept the invitation, and to look his sprucest for the meeting. He would shave—he had not done so for two days—trim his neat beard, wash, and change. As he made his elaborate preparations, he mused over all that was implied in Lawrence's phrase, "in spite of all."

It was now more than three and a half years since the contretemps with the King, and in all that time Ned had had no private meeting with Lawrence. There had been casual and polite encounters at the Globe and elsewhere, and whenever Lawrence entertained the whole company Ned naturally was included. After the night of Ned's refusal of the King's caresses, Lawrence had left the Phillips home in Southwark and returned to the vicinity of Hampton Court. Time must have performed its healing for within a year Lawrence had returned to Southwark, to a house in Hunt's Rents in Maid Lane, where he had lived ever since. His return to royal favor had become increasingly apparent to the King's Men and had been climaxed in the summer of 1606 by the performance at Hampton Court, in the presence of two kings, James and his brother-in-law, Christian of Denmark, of the new play, *Macbeth*. Lawrence had done much to encourage Will to write the play, but other sharers had been opposed to the project on the grounds that a Scottish play might cause trouble at the Globe. During the years that followed the King's accession there had been an endless and deeply resented influx of Scots into London. But the power of the play itself had overborne all possible opposition, and the players had been careful to avoid any suggestion of a Scottish accent.

Macbeth had been important for Ned too. Will had begged that his brother might be allowed to play Malcolm—the small part of the King of France and some nothings had been all there was for him in *King Lear*—and Heminge had twitted Will that he had written the scene of Malcolm's testing of Macduff just because Ned was to play Malcolm. But the importance of the part for Ned was that it had resulted in his reconciliation with the King, at least to the extent that he was among the players presented after the performance at Hampton Court; His British Majesty had even bestowed a smile on him, but not a word.

As he dressed for the evening, Ned had a momentary impulse to wear the medallion that Lawrence had given him so long ago. Instead, he decided to take it with him in his pocket.

Almost as soon as Ned knocked on the door, Lawrence opened it for him and the obvious delight of his smiling welcome was very warming. He said, "I am so happy that you have come. I was afeard you might not, and I should not have blamed you."

As Ned entered the house, he looked around expecting to see some other person, probably a handsome young man, but Lawrence smiled and said, "There is nobody else here. I live quite alone now. There were a few others after Andrew Cotton, but they all taught me I am wiser to live alone, and seek for an evening's company when I need it. I have a good widow who comes in every day except Sunday, for she is not only good but godly. It is I who have laid out the supper for us this evening. But come into the garden, where 'tis cool in the shade of the trees."

When they were seated in the garden, Ned, in response to the friendliness of Lawrence, said, "I was glad to receive your letter. I have always regretted the trouble I caused you."

"'Tis I who should feel guilty. I should have known how it would be with the King, and I should have prepared you for it. I had hoped you would have endured his kisses; he would not have asked for more. Jamey is always and every moment the King. His caresses are royal favors, and 'tis almost treason to reject them. But the same majestic dignity would prevent him from uncovering his royal nakedness except to his Queen, however much his flesh might crave otherwise. 'Tis all past now, and, I thank God, well past."

"I acted foolishly. My mind said one thing and my body another. But I regret only the harm I did you."

"I deserved it, because I can confess now that I sought you for my own bed. That would have made us enemies, whereas now I hope we may be friends. 'Tis strange that it has taken us over three years to have this talk."

"I have often wanted it."

"For long months it was impossible. We were angry with each other, and I had much ado to regain the King's favor. Then those months of angry silence built a wall between us. It is good to know that you as well as I wanted to scale that wall or breach it. Often I wanted to comfort you when I knew you were unhappy—when Nick Tooley became a sharer and then Robert Gough. There was something else too: I knew about Marie and Neddy."

Ned was dumbfounded. "But how? Who told you?"

"Marie entertained several courtiers, and one of them, Sir Timothy Littleton, thought he was in love with her and was very jealous. He had her spied upon and found out about you. When he found she was pregnant, he tortured her into telling him the father. She could so easily have told him a lie but she was brave enough to tell him the truth."

"I'll kill him," said Ned with a deadly intensity.

"Too late; it has been done for you. In his first fury Sir Timothy happened to meet me; the court was at Whitehall at the time. He wanted to challenge you to a duel but could not because you were not worthy of his sword; nor was I, though I should have been happy to have undertaken for you. But I told him I would find a worthy opponent for him who would willingly stand in for you."

"Jack!"

"Yes; Sir John Barnet. He easily dispatched Sir Timothy, and I know not any who wept for him."

"But why was I not told?"

"To what purpose? Not even Marie was told. When she asked where Sir Timothy was, Sir John told her he had died of a fever in the country."

"I begged Marie to marry me."

"She was wiser than you. She would have made a poor wife, especially to one who lacked riches, even though she loved you, as I do not doubt she did."

"But now Neddy is a bastard."

"Be not so hard on bastards. Pope Clement VII was a bastard and he was a much more handsome man than his legitimate cousin, Pope Leo X. And your Neddy has such well-favored parents that he cannot fail to prosper. Besides, consider how well your brother writes of bastards—Falconbridge in *King John* and Edmund in *King Lear*."

"I think rather of what Cyril Tourneur says of them in *The Revenger's Tragedy*. Every time I hear the lines spoken they burn into my mind and I cannot rid me of the sear:

> "Oh! what a grief 'tis that a man should live
> But once i' the world, and then to live a bastard,
> The curse o' the womb, the thief of Nature,
> Begot against the seventh commandment,
> Half damned in the conception by the justice
> Of that unbribed everlasting law."

"Consider it not so crossly. Your brother has the right of it. 'Tis only the Puritans that would condemn a man for a fault that is not his. But come, let us to supper. I am happy, and when I am happy I am hungry. And we must drink a toast to our coming together—and to Neddy."

First, Ned excused himself and used the opportunity to take out the medallion and pin it on his doublet; he was eager now to please Lawrence, the return of whose friendship he welcomed heartily.

The sight of Ned wearing his gift deeply affected Lawrence but all he said was, "I'm glad to see you still have the medallion. I often wondered about it. I thought you might have sold it, pawned it, given it away, or even thrown it away."

Ned responded in a similarly light-hearted tone. "I might have done so, but it had the family motto on it, and I could not get rid of it without bringing shame to my family."

"Why else would I have had the words put on it?"

During the meal of celebration, for it had such quality and proportions, Ned asked, "Why, after all this time, did you send the letter to me today?"

The answer surprised him. "Because this past week the King spoke to me of you. Now he can afford to be generous, for he has found his beloved Robbie Carr. He said you were a brave man to have been true to your nature when to be false might have brought you into royal favor. He also said that the next time you were presented to him with other players, he would speak to you."

"I should have thought he would have forgotten me long ere this."

"For men like the King—and me too, Ned—you are not easy to forget. Besides, he has seen you play many times since, and never, I am sure, without remembering."

"This Robert Carr. The whole city talks of him."

"And well it might, for if he is as shrewd as I think he is, he will become one of the great ones of the land and with a swiftness that will dazzle all beholders. Already the knowing ones are paying court to him as though he were a great earl, and he not even knighted yet."

"Is it true he was but a page?"

"Aye. He came with us from Scotland. He was but a lad then, and too young by English custom to be in the King's service, so he was let go, a stranger in a strange city. But one so handsome in body and beguiling in manner soon found good service. When he first came to the King's notice—and that was not yet four months ago—he was in the service of Sir James Hay."

"He that was married last Twelfth Night when we played the comedy at Whitehall to celebrate the occasion?"

"The same. In March there were the joustings to mark the fourth anniversary of the King's accession. I think it will be known henceforth as the first accession of Robbie Carr. In the tourney, Master Carr, who was in attendance on his master, fell off his horse and broke his leg right before the King; never was limb broken to such good purpose. The King's natural compassion was stirred, but when he heard the young Adonis moan in the broadest of Scots tongues, his heart was lost. He ordered his own physicians to have care of the injured page, and began to visit him every day. As soon as the limb began to mend, Robbie limped to the King every night. When the King discovered that Robbie's father had been devoted to Queen Mary of Scotland, Jamey's ill-starred mother, the bond was complete. Now the King has undertaken Robbie's education; 'tis whispered that Robbie is as slow in acquiring Latin as he is in learning English, but I think his slowness to be shrewdly well judged. Robbie's Scottish tongue is so thick that he and the King can tell secrets aloud, even in the presence of English courtiers."

"If the King advances Robert Carr as swiftly as you expect, 'twill be hard for the young man to keep his balance."

"Aye, but he is a canny one and vastly likable. I judge he will ride high and long before he fall. And I judge his downfall will be a woman. They are his pleasure, and the King knows it."

"Tell me truly, Lawrence; did you see me as a Robert Carr for the King?"

"I know not what I saw, but I hoped that the King would favor you in ways of your choosing. Tell me what you hoped."

"I was foolish and dreamt I would lead a new company of players, or at least that the King would insist that I become a sharer and play big parts, like Troilus. But now such foolishness is past and done with."

"And you are still a hired player, waiting for a sharer to die. 'Tis strange and a marvel to me that you have not become more bitter."

"Sometimes to me too, but when I loved Marie, the theatre was but a place to make a living, and now Neddy means more to me than any part. I suppose I lack the strength of purpose and ambition that drives Chris Beeston; I hear he is soon like to be the John Heminge of the Queen's Players."

"But your talent is much greater than his."

"I am content to play; Chris must govern players."

It was almost dark before Ned left Lawrence's, with the promise that he would come again to supper on Wednesday, a promise readily given because Ned had thoroughly enjoyed his evening. Now there was no barrier between the men of deviousness on the one part and suspicion on the other. As Lawrence had said during the evening, "When you rebuffed the King, you rebuffed me too. Now I know where I stand with you, and am content to be your friend."

FORTY-SEVEN

NED ARRIVED TOO LATE AT THE GLOBE TO BE OF ANY HELP IN PACKING THE cart for the tour, but his appearance, rare on occasions of tour departures, surprised and cheered several of the players, particularly John Lowin. Only Ned knew that John had fallen desperately in love with a married woman, Joan Hall, whose husband was a good man, to whom she felt bound in loyalty.

Ned moved to bid farewell to Nat, who was in a bad mood. "Mark my words, Ned. We'll be back within a month. The plague won't last longer. And we are taking out five plays. Two or at most three would have been enough. And what plays! Only two by Master Shakespeare, and one of those about a mad old man, and the other about a Scotsman who will be booed and hissed everywhere. Then there's *Volpone,* a pack of horrible old men. The people want youth and gaiety. And *The Revenger's Tragedy,* all rape and incest and murder, not prettied by a line of poetry. As for *The Devil's Charter,* 'tis well named, for the author is an escaped murderer, though he be the son of a bishop, and I care not who hears me say it. We have seen our best days. The light is all gone and we are in the dark. If you would do us all a favor, Ned, and yourself too, go home to Stratford and persuade your brother to write us another *Dream.* The world is tired of nightmares."

Ned moved back to the players. Wives and children were gathered to say farewell, and soon the cavalcade set out due west, avoiding the Bridge and the City. Ned took a boat to cross the river to visit Gilbert, whom he had not seen for some months.

Prompted by the family farewells he had just witnessed, Ned pondered the problems of marriage. What would have happened if he had persuaded Marie to marry him? It probably would have been hell for both of them most of the time, and Neddy would have suffered. Happy bastardy was better for the child than unhappy legitimacy. But Will and

Anne had made Susanna legitimate, and she seemed not to have been touched by the torment at the heart of her parents' marriage. And now Susanna herself was a month married—well married too—to an eminent physician, John Hall. Ned had not gone home for the marriage; he had pleaded that he should work as much as possible in face of the likelihood that he would be out of work for the summer. He knew Will had been hurt by his decision, but all he had said in a letter was, "Had it been Judith I know that you would have come, so we will wait for that. Besides, though John Hall is an admirable fellow and will be a better husband to Susanna than I have been a father, he is an unrelenting Puritan. It irks him as much as Anne that I am of the theatre. Perhaps he will be relieved not to have another player at his wedding."

Ned supposed that the happiest marriage he had known was that of the Phillipses. Anne had been desolated by the death of Gus, but a year later she had married a worthless spendthrift, John Witter. They had moved back to the Southwark house, and his first action as her husband and the legal inheritor of her possessions had been to attempt to raise a mortgage on the Phillips's holding in the Globe.

Gilbert too had had a kind of marriage, with George, and in its own way a happy and successful one, but an astonishing change had taken place in Gilbert now that he was forced to stand in his own light. Kit Bagshaw had long left him but Simon Middleton remained, and they had formed a most prosperous partnership unencumbered by sexual or emotional involvement; each sought his own bodily pleasures elsewhere. The unexpected development was that Gilbert had become the dominant and sometimes domineering partner. The ideas and the designs were all Simon's but the buying and the selling were all Gilbert's, who was even becoming quoted for his wit, as George had been. When one malicious young gentleman had said in the presence of others, "Gilbert, you remind me much of George for you have borrowed his wit even to the very words," Gilbert had retorted, "Borrowed? Nay, I do but claim my own again, for it was always my pleasure to hear George say at noon what he had heard me say at nine."

WHEN NED GOT TO THE SHOP, A YOUNG MAN HE HAD NOT SEEN BEFORE WAS dealing with a disgruntled, middle-aged customer whose dyed hair, painted cheeks, and youthful clothes failed to disguise his age. The young man was saying, "But I tell you, sir, that Master Shakespeare is not here, nor Master Middleton either."

"When will they be back?"

" 'Tis hard to say; maybe not for some hours."

At this point Gilbert gave the lie to his hired assistant by entering the shop from the street. He was flurried, and, without noticing Ned and with a cursory "Good morrow, Master Carey," he disappeared into the back room.

Master Carey called after him but to no purpose, and he sat down grumpily on a stool to wait. Soon Gilbert emerged, carrying delicately an exquisite lace collar. It was then that he noticed Ned and, ignoring the plaints of Master Carey, crossed to him and said, "I am happy to see you, Ned, you unfeeling rascal. How could you stay away so long without coming to hear about the wedding? I have much to tell you but you have chosen a bad morning." Bending close to Ned he whispered, "Master Carr comes." Then he resumed a conversational voice. "But wait and I will return anon. With the Globe closed you have naught to do, and I have much."

All this while Master Carey had been trying to gain his attention, and before disappearing again into the street, Gilbert said to him, "I know what 'tis, Master Carey; the new doublet is too tight. I warned you. Now you cannot breathe in it. Well, you must choose between breathing and eating."

Flustered and furious, Master Carey stalked out of the shop. The assistant laughed decorously; it would not be fitting for Master Carey to hear him. Then he crossed to Ned and said, "You must be Master Shakespeare's brother; I have heard much of you. My name is Mark Garfield."

As they shook hands, Ned asked, "Where has he gone now?"

"But next door. Two old tailors work for us there. They are brothers, twins, John and James Weston, and I cannot tell one from the other; they are both so bent and withered that you would think they are half in the grave, but their skill with the needle is a wonder to behold; their gnarled fingers are as busy as ants."

Gilbert returned and, as he entered, he said, "We must have a door cut through from the back room so that we can come and go without old ninnies like Master Carey seeing us. Come upstairs, Ned. We are ready for Master Carr now, and Mark will tell us when he arrives." With a kindly sarcasm he added, "That much it is safe to entrust to him. But he is good to look upon and honest, two necessary virtues." As they climbed the stairs he continued, "I want you to meet Master Carr, for his sign is in the ascendant. The King shows good judgment in him too; but you will see. Then, when he is gone, we will go to a tavern for dinner and I will tell you of the wedding." When they got to the living room, Gilbert flopped onto the daybed. "Zounds, Ned, I am tired. Never have we been so busy. 'Tis such that I am almost grateful for the plague, for 'twill drive many away. As for me, I fear it no more; I have lived through many visitations now. Death will come when it will come. I marvel it stays so long for our mother. She is old now, very old, and talks most of her mother and her childhood. She was very sad that you came not for the wedding. In spite of all, she kept saying 'He will come; he will come; if not for Susanna then for me.' You must go home to her, Ned. There is naught to keep you here."

Gilbert did not know about Neddy, and Ned changed the subject. "This Robert Carr. 'Tis great good fortune that he comes to you. How did it happen?"

" 'Tis a case of 'Cast your bread upon the waters and it will return to you after many days.' When Carr was a page to Sir James Hay, someone brought him to the shop. I took a vast liking to him, for he is as pleasant in manner as he is handsome in face and figure, though I confess that at first it was hard for me to understand his speech. He came again and again, but he spent more time with Simon than with me. He loves beautiful clothes and made many good suggestions for their making. At last we made him a present of a suit of his own design, and so he has never forgotten us. Now the King wants to see him in a different suit every day, and many tailors are kept busy. This morning he comes for three suits and cloaks, and his patronage brings us much more."

Ned commented on the further changes that had been made since his last visit in the furnishings of the room where they sat, and added with a smile, "But the room is not more changed than you, Gil."

"Metamorphosis is the word, Ned. 'Tis one of the new long ones. The King is so learned that everybody uses long words, no matter their meaning so you speak them with confidence. The King is the fount of all wisdom and knowledge. He disputes with men wise in the law, in philosophy, in poetry, in religion, in science, in all subjects, and 'tis said he betters them all, but I suspect that, in arguing with King James, 'Discretion is the better part of valor.' Has he ever spoken to you, Ned?"

"Yes; at Hampton Court."

"What said he?"

"He commended my playing."

At this moment Mark called up to say that Master Carr had arrived.

"Then ask him to come up," Gilbert called back, as he moved excitedly to the top of the stairs.

Ned stood up to greet the newcomer, who was a striking young man, still only about twenty but carrying his new importance with ease. He was of medium height, his well-groomed hair flaxen, his carefully tended beard golden, his complexion a delicate red and his richly lashed eyes a light blue. With him was a young attendant whom Gilbert addressed as "Bart"; it was his function occasionally to interpret for Master Carr, whose Scots speech was still as thick as when he had left his native land over four years before.

After Gilbert had made the introductions, he begged to be excused while he went to fetch Simon and the clothes.

"I have seen ye, Master Shakespeare, at the Globe. 'Twas when I was page to Sir James Hay, and I look forward to seeing ye many times when ye play at the Christmas Revels. But I thocht the players had left the city because of the plague."

"They have, but they did not need me; they do not travel with the full company."

"Then I shall speak to His Majesty for ye, to gain ye employment at the court until the players return."

"I thank you," said Ned, secretly amused at what the King might say in reply to such a request, "but I shall go home to Stratford-on-Avon to visit my mother who is sick and aged."

"Ye are too young to have an aged mother, but now I remember me, your brother, William, is much older than ye."

"Sixteen years."

"His Majesty said the other day that late children are either verra bricht or verra dull, and ye prove the point, Master Shakespeare."

"Am I so dull?"

Robert Carr laughed heartily at this and his laugh was delightfully infectious for Ned and Bart found themselves enjoying it with him.

"Nay, Master Shakespeare—I like not that name; it belongs to your brother. I would call ye Ned. Am I so permitted?"

"I should be honored."

"And I to ye am Robbie. Ye are older than I but I feel we are of an age. So Ned and Robbie. How say ye?"

"So be it, Robbie."

"Then thus I would say: ye are the bricht late child. I dare swear ye can even con the Latin."

"A little."

"Your little would be my much, for 'tis a mystery and a puzzle to me. Why should a table be feminine, its leg neuter, and its foot masculine? It maks no sense to me and never will. But the King is verra patient and laughs at my mistakes; I gi'e him much to laugh at. I like it better when he talks to me of English books. He was telling me of *Macbeth,* which your brother wrote. I long to see it. The King was michtily taken wi' it. He said your brother changed history to please him, something about changing an ancestor of his from a villain to a hero. I said that was dishonest and lying, but he said—let me recall it now—'A poet twists facts to tell truths.' I canna understand that. Can ye?"

Ned was prevented from making answer by the bustling entrance of Gilbert and Simon, laden with clothes. Ned had met Simon several times and liked him. He was only a few years younger than Ned but looked even younger than Robbie. He was short of stature and slight of build, of obviously good breeding, with a pleasant but undistinguished face, and a quiet manner. He rarely spoke and then usually to agree, except in matters of design and color, on which he held firm and staunchly defended opinions.

All attention was focused on the clothes, about which Robbie was enthusiastic. He said, "Simon, ye are a true master, for always the results are better than ye lead me to expect. The fit is always perfect, but I maun try on this blue doublet with the crimson cloak. While I do so, do ye, Bart, go with Gilbert some other where and pay for the clothes; 'tis a miracle that base money can produce beauty but they should never come face to face."

When Robbie and the attendant Bart had left, the happiness the visit had engendered remained in the shop, and Gilbert was in the best humor to deal with two waiting customers, both of them glad to wait to see the already famous Robert Carr. One was a wealthy merchant who expected to be able to buy himself a knighthood and was already behaving with the peremptory authority of an earl, and the other was a smooth-tongued rascal who knew where Gilbert could purchase some fine brocades cheaply. The merchant came at the suggestion of his wife who wanted him to dress more elegantly and youthfully. He said, "I want to look like yon Master Carr."

"So do I," said Gilbert, "but, alas, God has decreed otherwise."

"Be not so glib," barked the merchant. "I mean in dress."

"Sir, I do not think we could please your wife with our clothes for you, for we do not look on you with the same eyes, and so I bid you god den."

"This is monstrous. I came here to buy and you are here to sell. I will pay you a good price, and now I am firm-minded that you supply me. Let me see your wares."

"Alas, sir, they are not for you."

The merchant was flabbergasted. "Are you not a merchant like me? Do you not sell where there is good silver to pay? Or are you some lord who dispenses favors?"

"No lord, sir, but honest workman who will not paint a barn pink."

Gilbert held the door open, and the merchant had no choice but to leave, fuming. As soon as the door was closed, they all broke into hearty laughter, all but Simon who was always embarrassed by such altercations; the most he could muster was a doubtful smile.

Then Gilbert turned to the rascal, whose laughter at the discomfiture of the merchant had been the heartiest. "And now you, sir. I can guess what you have come for, and the answer is no. It always was no and it always will be no, and so good den to you too."

"But these brocades are honestly come by."

"Then I am Queen Elizabeth."

"In the old days, George . . ."

"Soil not his name with your tongue. And the old days are past, long past. Be gone, and do not return."

When the door was closed again, Ned said quietly and with a smile, "Metamorphosis indeed!"

Gilbert smiled in return and said to Simon and Mark, "My brother and I have family matters to talk over. We will go to the Three Pheasants, but I shall be back within the hour."

After they had ordered their meal in the tavern, Gilbert launched into an account of the wedding. "The new vicar, John Rogers, would have been happier to bury Susanna than to marry her. He's more of a merchant than the one who just came to the shop; money and goods are all he cares for. Susanna was one of the few who had the courage to stay away from Easter Communion last year because the offering would go to the greedy vicar. She is a young lady of spirit."

"It must have been bitter for her mother and John Hall to have her labeled a recusant, for that usually means papist."

"The Corporation knew better and did not even fine her. I am sure most of them admired her but lacked her courage. She was not alone. The Sadlers, Hamnet, and Judith, were also recusants."

"Does Vicar Rogers have no supporters?"

"Many, for he is a jolly man with ever a quip although he is a good Puritan, and he is powerful in the pulpit. Besides, he is zealous in visiting the sick and full of good advice to merchants and farmers. But he would graze sheep in the churchyard and build a pigsty against the church wall if they would let him."

"How did he behave at the wedding? Did he come to the feast?"

"He would not miss a feast even if Satan were the host. And the bridegroom, Physician Hall, is already a man of high and wide repute. I am sure he tends the vicar's wife and family for no fee. Indeed, Judith reported to me in great glee that Susanna had said to John, 'You mend all the Rogers family for nothing; let him marry us for nothing in return.' But John Hall is such a dutiful Christian that he would willingly give more than his tithe to the church, believing that it goes to God, not to John Rogers. It is amazing, Ned, how much respect is already accorded our physician-nephew, and he but yet barely seven years in Stratford."

"But is he a solemn Puritan?"

"Strong, but not too solemn. He admires his wife's wit, but is himself quiet. I think he prizes words above gold and silver."

"Anne must like and admire him."

"Aye indeed, and he her. In him she has found the son she lost. To be sure, he is much older than Hamnet would have been; he is even eight years older than Susanna."

"Then he is five years older than I."

"And he looks it, Ned. He has the sort of serious face that gets lines young."

"They are living at New Place, are they not?"

"Aye, and the Greenes too. I told Will it would soon be named New Place Inn. Little Anne Greene is three years old now, and the life of the place, and Letitia is pregnant again. I sometimes think little Anne loves her godmother more than her mother. It will be wonderful when Susanna gives her mother a grandchild."

"When? Better say if."

"Oh, come Ned, come. If a physician cannot be trusted to beget a child, who can? I pray it be a boy, even though he bear not our name."

Ned could not escape the thought that their own mother had a grandson, his son, who did bear the family name, but she was cheated of ever knowing about him or ever seeing him.

"I thank God our mother has two grandsons, even though they be Harts. William is now seven and as emptily talkative as his father. The little Thomas, who is now two, seems to cry all the time. As for Mary, I fear she is a sickly child. But Ned, one last word. I beg you again to go home to Stratford this summer. Our mother cannot live much longer, and you will never forgive yourself if you stay away until it is too late to see her. Why not leave this week?"

"I cannot."

"I smell a woman."

Ned smiled but said nothing. He was glad that Gilbert was in a hurry to get back to the shop, for he had decided to visit Neddy, even though Rachel would probably be put out by his unexpected appearance; Rachel liked rules to be observed and Sunday was Ned's day. She was still deeply hostile to the man whom she thought of as having killed her mistress, though this was slowly being tempered with gratitude to the man who had given her Neddy, for she considered the child to be hers rather than his.

When Rachel answered Ned's knock on the door, she did not move aside for him to enter. What could he want on a Monday?

Ned said, "I want to see my son."

"He is asleep and must not be waked."

"Where is he?"

"In the shade of the garden."

As Ned said, "I want to see him," he pushed past Rachel. She was taken aback for a moment and then fluttered after him, protesting. When they got to the garden, Ned turned to her and said with a muted incisiveness, "Quiet! You will wake Neddy." Rachel pulled up short, snapped her mouth shut, and glared at him.

Neddy was not asleep, but was struggling to get out of his crib; he had been awakened by the buzzing and tickling of a large bluebottle fly. His delight at seeing his father made Ned glow with pride. He picked the child up and held him high in the air where he gurgled with joy.

Ned said to Rachel in a tone which brooked no gainsaying, "Leave us for a while."

After a flicker of rebellion, Rachel flounced away, muttering in French.

There followed the happiest half-hour father and son had ever spent together. They walked hand in hand; Neddy toddled after a butterfly and with his father's teaching managed to call it a buff-eye. Ned lay on the grass while the child crawled over him. They were soon both exhausted, and Neddy went fast asleep again. Ned reluctantly returned him to his crib. When he entered the house, he said, "He is asleep, Rachel. I shall come again soon," being careful not to specify Sunday. He did not wait for a reply but left the house.

Since he was so near home, Ned decided to go there and take a brief rest. He was greeted by the rare sight of a letter from Stratford awaiting him. It was from Will. It read: "My dear brother. I grieve to tell you that little Mary, Joan's child, is dead. 'Tis no great surprise for she was always weak and ailing. The sorrow of her parents is natural, but I fear for the effect on our own mother, for the child was her special care. Little Will is too boisterous and noisy for her, and the child, Tommy, too querulous. Quiet Mary was her darling, and she is gone. I write to you rather than Gilbert because this is to beg you to come home for our mother's sake, but I know you will give Gilbert the sad news. I too would be much cheered by your coming, and I shall look for you daily. Your loving brother, Will."

Ned went up slowly to his room, deeply disturbed by the letter. He had just come from Neddy, and here was yet another proof of the fragility of children's lives. Oh God, was he right to leave Neddy in London? But his son was strong and healthy, while Mary Hart had always been sickly. Her death was somehow more poignant because he had seen her in the first hours of her life. Then there was his mother; he had to go home to see her, and soon. He felt sad about leaving Neddy and then decided that tomorrow he would see the child again, and the next day and the next; six more romps with his son in the garden and then briefly home to see his mother. The best feeling in the world was to be needed by people. How ridiculous now seemed his disappointment at being left behind by the players! People were more important than plays, especially a beautiful son and a loving mother.

FORTY-EIGHT

On Tuesday Rachel was again surprised by Ned's arrival but again gave way to his insistence on seeing Neddy, but he told her he proposed to come every day, and so she was prepared for him on Wednesday. She spied his coming from a window and was determined not to open the door to him. Ned went around to the back, found the garden gate open, and went straight into the house to confront Rachel.

"Why did you not open the door to me?" he asked with seething anger.

His scarcely suppressed fury was so frightening that even the imperturbable Rachel was shaken and she said, "I did not hear you." The act of lying in itself weakened her inner confidence.

"You lie. You are not deaf. And do not be so careless again to leave the back gate open. You are responsible for the safety of my son, and even your God cannot save you from my wrath if anything happens to him. Remember this, Rachel. Neddy bears my name in law. He is mine, not yours, and if need be I shall take him from you."

This last threat was more than Rachel could bear for she was already in too uncertain a state to challenge it and she broke down and cried, a rare sight indeed. Ned made no attempt to assure and comfort her but walked out to Neddy, who fortunately was wide awake and wriggled with glee at sight of him. Ned's sense of triumph lent particular enjoyment to the afternoon, and it was completed when he found Rachel waiting for him with a new respect and deference when he returned to the house after leaving the happily tired Neddy asleep in his crib. She said, "Master Shakespeare, I shall expect you tomorrow, and I am sorry about the gate."

Ned was in the same high spirits when he had supper that evening with Lawrence, whose pleasure in the evening made all the stronger his disappointment that Ned had decided to leave London. He said, "I see that you must go to Stratford, but 'tis sad to lose you again so soon. I had hoped that this supper meeting would take place at least once a week, and perhaps more often. But you must promise me that you will come again on Sunday. You will need company that evening, for you will have said goodbye to Neddy in the afternoon."

"I shall be happy to come, and when I return from Stratford."

"How long will you stay there?"

"I cannot tell; perhaps a week, perhaps a month, perhaps longer. If the plague gets worse, it will be hard to find a reason for returning, and my brother Richard will be glad of my help."

"And your brother William of your company. It may well be that he has finished writing his *Antony and Cleopatra,* and 'twill be your secret privilege to be the first to hear it. He must long for an appreciative ear from London when all the ears around him are filled with talk of harvests and swine fever and enclosures and Sunday sermons. But I hope this *Antony* is not another *Timon.*"

Quick in the defense of Will, Ned said forcefully, "You know 'twas done against his will. Even John Heminge wanted to do it, and there were those who praised it highly. Ben Jonson said, ' 'Tis foul-tasting medicine, but strong medicine is necessary for such malignant diseases as afflict our times.' "

"That is true, but we had only the foul taste and not the cure."

"Will told me the play had gone sour in his hands. He had started it before *Lear* and abandoned it. When he was pressed for a new play for this spring he finished it. He said he was glad to finish it, for it would always have troubled him, but he cared not if it was ever played. 'Twas like a purgative of his spirits, he said, and he felt the better for the clearing. I am sure that *Antony and Cleopatra* will be a very different matter. I am a player and what I most wonder is what there will be for me in it; little, I fear. Oh, Lawrence, 'tis hard to wait for a man to die, and there are times when I long for it to happen. Is that very wicked?"

With a warm and understanding smile, Lawrence replied, "Yes, very wicked, but very human. I think there are few who have not sometimes caught themselves in guilty hopes that one, even very dear to them, might die. But you, Ned, are still young, and some of the sharers are getting old."

"I no longer feel young."

The Sunday, as if to remind him that life could not be pleasant for long, was full of disappointments. To begin with, the sermon at the morning service disgruntled him. It was filled with such sentiments as "It hath pleased God to visit us again at this time with the pestilence, for we have sinned against Him most grievously. And if it be God's will that some now listening to these words shall die of this visitation, let them die in full repentance, secure in the knowledge of God's everlasting mercy. And some there be who will lose loved ones to the plague. Let them gain courage in their grief by remembering that life is but a fleeting moment, and that time is but the gate to eternity."

As Ned walked to Marie's house, recollection of the sermon again tormented him with doubt about leaving Neddy in London. Even Rachel's welcome which was meant to please him had the opposite effect, for it made him feel he was deserting his son. She said, "This is the last time Neddy will see you before you go away. He will miss you."

Then, to add to Ned's frustration, Neddy was fast asleep. For half-an-hour Ned paced the garden waiting for him to wake. Finally, when he did not, Ned woke him, but not without a feeling of guilt which was increased when the child sniveled petulantly at being disturbed. Gradually the boy's happiness at being with his father asserted itself, and they played together, but the usual joyous zest was missing and the child welcomed being cradled to sleep in Ned's arms sooner than usual. By the way of compensation to himself, Ned held his son for quite a while before setting him down.

At last Ned felt he had to leave. He took a long goodbye look at his sleeping son, admonished Rachel unnecessarily to take good care of him, and stalked away from the house in a bad mood, feeling guilty as he went that he had not been more gracious to Rachel, who as the week progressed had become almost friendly.

Even supper with Lawrence proved to be a disappointment, for he was not alone, and while his happiness at seeing Ned was quite genuine, Ned soon sensed that he would be happy to see him leave early that he might be alone with the young man he introduced as "Cyril Parton, whom I met a few days ago and who surprised and delighted me by appearing here only a few minutes before you did."

Ned did not take kindly to young Master Parton, and not only because his presence robbed him of the private conversation with Lawrence to which he had looked forward. The newcomer obviously exulted in the power his well-made body and handsome face gave him over men like Lawrence. He said little but abided his time with an insouciant and arrogant confidence. Ned was moved to pity for Lawrence who in most matters had wisdom and authority but seemed to be at the mercy of Master Parton, whom his mind must judge to be worthless. It was an awkward supper at which Lawrence did almost all the talking, most of it a nervously witty account of trifling court gossip. Ned laughed dutifully and Cyril Parton smiled patiently. Lawrence was guiltily grateful when Ned made an excuse to leave early. As Lawrence accompanied Ned to the door, he whispered, "I am sorry, Ned. I did not expect Cyril this evening, but I had told him to come at anytime, so I could not turn him away, could I?"

Ned was keenly aware of Lawrence's embarrassment, and he said, with true sympathy, "I understand, Lawrence; it could not be helped. I will see you as soon as I return."

Ned slept badly and was stirring at first light. The horse he had hired was good and sturdy but his pace was somewhat reduced by his burden, for Ned had left few of his belongings at the Mountjoy House. Even so, he was determined to get home in one day from Oxford. During his night there at the Crown Tavern he had a vivid dream that his mother was dying and calling for him, and he had arrived too late for her to know him. This was probably caused by his perpetual guilt about his neglect of his mother, coupled with the enormous supper the Davenants insisted on his eating. They were supremely happy, for a year ago Mistress Jane had borne her busband the son for which he had longed. The child was christened William, for his godfather, William Shakespeare. Ned, mindful of the mother's assiduous attentions to Will, could not escape the momentary, wicked speculation that Will might be more than godfather to the child, but he would have been outraged if he had lived to see that child later, when he became the famous Sir William Davenant, man of the theatre and Poet Laureate, not disavow the wicked whispers about his parenthood, but smile knowingly.

It was dark on Wednesday night before he got home. He stabled the horse as quietly as possible, hoping that the back door was unlocked—his father's unnecessary precaution had always irked him—and that he could steal in quietly and sleep on the kitchen floor until the morning.

The back door was unlocked, but, as he opened it carefully, he heard a slight creak on the stairs; somebody had heard his arrival and was coming down. It was Will Hart. He explained that he was awake because little Tommy had been crying and he had to get up to nurse him back to sleep.

Ned felt that this was surely Joan's function, but said nothing. Instead he asked, "How is my mother?"

"Well, for a woman her age. She spends much time in bed now and talks of her childhood. She has changed since Mary died."

"I was sorry to hear about that; Will wrote to me."

" 'Tis sad, and I miss her sorely, but I still have two sons and maybe God will bless us with more. Joan is not yet forty, indeed not yet thirty-nine, and is healthy and still fruitful. And now, will you go up to join Richard in bed?"

"No, I would not wish to disturb him. I shall sleep down here."

"Then I bid you goodnight." Will Hart started to climb the stairs, but stopped and turned to ask, "Why have you come home? I hope not bad news."

"I was free and wished to see my mother; that is all."

FORTY-NINE

NED WAS VERY TIRED AFTER HIS HARD RIDE FROM OXFORD, BUT EVEN SO HE was awakened by someone coming downstairs at the first glimmer of light: it was his mother. As soon as he recognized her form—it was not yet light enough to see her face—he scrambled up and hurried to embrace her. She was so taken aback that she cried out in fear. Ned strove to assure her, "It's Ned, Mother, Ned," but he seemed unable to quiet her fears for she struggled feebly against him and whimpered in distress. Ned was completely at a loss. Fortunately he heard some movement upstairs; the cries had awakened somebody. Richard was hurrying downstairs closely followed by Joan.

Joan took their mother from Ned and led her to sit down while she spoke quietly and soothingly to her as if to a child. Richard opened the back door to let in more light.

Ned began to fear that his dream had been true, that he had indeed arrived too late for his mother ever to know him again. As the light grew and he could see her face he was appalled at how old she had become in two years. He hovered helplessly while Joan continued to talk to her and Richard busily stirred the fire to heat some milk for his mother.

At last Mary spoke but in a bewildered way, saying, "Dinner. I must get the dinner. John will be angry if dinner is late."

Joan said, "No, Mother. 'Tis too early. Look, the sun is not full up yet."

Richard came to Ned and said quietly, " 'Tis Market Day, and I must be busy. See to the milk. Let it not be too hot and soak bread in it and sugar." And he went into the workshop.

Ned was glad to have something to do. He tended the fire, being careful not to make it too fierce for it was going to be a hot day, and stirred the milk and crumbled bread into it. The description by Will's Jacques of the last age of man came sadly to his mind: "second childishness and mere oblivion." Now what mattered most was that his mother should know him again and be glad to see him.

When the sweetened bread and milk was ready—how he had loved it when he was a child!—Joan took it from him and began to feed their mother with it, saying as she did so, "Look what Ned has brought you. You remember Ned. He's your son, your baby. He has come all the way from London to see you."

Mary nodded and smiled vaguely but was too intent on her breakfast to pay much attention to anything else. Ned could stand the sad scene no longer and he went into the shop. As he spoke to Richard, he began automatically to help him to get things together for Market. "How long has she been like this?"

"Some days she is better than others. Your coming shocked her, but when she gets up early, 'tis always a bad sign. And then to be hugged by some strange man in the dark. 'Twas enough to make the sanest of women scream." Richard said this with a smile. "Be not too distressed, Ned. She will know you. Joan will take her back to bed and get her to sleep, then when she wakes 'tis like she will be almost her old self again. The past and the present are strangely jumbled in her mind. There are times when she will talk of naught but her mother and busy herself to get ready for her mother's coming. But you will see."

"Does she know you and Joan all the time?"

"For the most part, but then she sees us every day."

Richard intended no criticism of his brother by this remark, and Ned knew it. He asked, "And the others; does she always know them?"

"Some days she does and other days she doesn't. Sometimes she calls Will, John, and little Willie Hart, Ned. But then if Tommy comes to her at the same time she gets confused, because you were the youngest, and Tommy is the youngest. But tell me, Ned; how long will you stay?"

"I know not. Much depends on Mother. If I can do her any good, I shall stay longer. The plague has come to London and the players have left. While I am here I will help you, Richard."

Richard smiled and said, "Your company will be more welcome than your help, for there is little to do. The times are bad. The harvest is poor and the riots against enclosures have done much harm and left much bad feeling. Stratford is not a happy place this summer, Ned."

Ned insisted on helping Richard to carry the goods to market. As they left the house he commented on his surprise that Will Hart was not yet up and about; it was Market Day for him too.

Richard said, "Ofttimes he is up much of the night with Tommy, else none of us could sleep."

"Why does not Joan get up to quiet the child? Is it not the mother's part?"

"What with Mother and the house and the children, Joan has much to do and Will has little. In times like these, trades like Will Hart's and mine are the first to suffer. And I fear Will surrenders to adversity too easily. I sometimes think he is glad of the child's crying in the night for it gives him good reason to sleep late in the morning."

"But this is Market Day," protested Ned. Richard made no further comment. "Will Hart heard me last night and came downstairs. Before he went back up again, I think he wanted to say something to me. What could it have been?"

"Likely something about his trade. Could you lend him some money, or did you know somebody who would? Or mayhap about London. He sometimes talks as though going there would solve all his problems. He is envious of Gilbert's success."

"Gilbert belongs to London; Will Hart does not. He would be lost there."

"Fear not; he will never leave Stratford. Here he has a good home for which he pays no rent. And I think Joan is as frightened of London as Anne is."

There was nothing Ned could do to help Richard at the stall, and he was eager to get back to see his mother in the hope that she would know and welcome him, but Richard advised him to let her sleep a while, and first to visit New Place. As Ned was about to leave, Richard asked, "Did you bring a wedding gift for Susanna?"

Ned had forgotten all about it. At the time of the wedding he had thought of sending something by Gilbert, but had put it off until it was too late. He had to take something with him now, for Will's sake even more than Susanna's. Richard said that, under the influence of John Hall, she had become almost as religious as her mother, so anything vain and merely decorative would not be welcomed. Ned wished that the new Bible which the King had ordered had been published. He had heard much talk about it in London, but the translators were still busy and the end was still some years away.

Richard suggested "something for use in the home." Then came Ned's inspiration: forks! Susanna might have become very religious but she certainly would not have lost her ladylike gentility, and what better evidence of her new standing as a notable physician's wife than to learn the use of forks and probably be the first to introduce their use to Stratford? They were fast becoming a sign of good breeding in London. Richard had never seen one, but said that sometimes there was a silversmith from Coventry at the High Cross and Ned should look for the man on the western side of High Street.

Ned soon found the silversmith, for already his display of silver goods had caught the morning sun and its gleam had attracted some gazers, though the intensity of their interest in the display was as nothing to that of the smith's in their possibly predatory fingers.

As casually as if he were asking for cups, Ned said, "Do you have any forks?" Few of the bystanders had ever heard the word except as an instrument of gardening, and they looked at Ned in bewilderment.

The smith stopped and looked appraisingly at Ned; the young man was well enough dressed and spoke like a gentleman. "Yes," he said with a slow drawl, as if a confession were being unwillingly extracted from him. "Yes, I have forks, young sir, and beautiful ones too; but not here. Who could have expected to sell forks in Stratford? As yet there is little sale for them in Coventry, but the Earl of Warwick has some, and of my making. I had not expected to return here for a fortnight, yet at your request will come again next Thursday, if that be to your liking."

Ned thought quickly. He was now determined to get the forks, despite their probable cost and the delay. He said, "So be it. Next Thursday then," and he began to walk away.

"Wait, young sir," called the smith. "We have not talked money. 'Tis like that your purse is full and you care not for price, but 'tis well to settle it now. And how many forks do you need? And should they be engraved with a crest or initials?"

"Some half dozen with just one initial: H," said Ned grandly.

None of the audience recognized Ned but the mention of the letter set minds awhirring and tongues awhispering.

"How say you to a round pound for a price? And that is a true bargain, for it may well be that the use of forks by a family of standing in this town could lead to further selling."

A pound was double what Ned had intended to give; such a sum he would willingly have parted with for Judith, but not Susanna. Still the presence of the audience had led him to adopt a pose which he must now maintain. He said, "A pound be it"; he added, lest the audience, and the smith too, think he was a gull with money and no brains, "provided the workmanship merit my good opinion." Then he walked away, followed by staring eyes and gaping mouths. He did not hear a hostile comment he left in his wake: "I wager his father waxes rich from enclosures. They rob us of food to have money for baubles."

As a quick afterthought it came to Ned that Will Hart might assume

from the gift that he was a man of money and pester him. He felt he had
to return to Richard to report the result of his quest but he did not want
to be followed by the curious and thus lose his impressive anonymity. Not
for the first time, he had been trapped by playing a role. He made the
return to Richard circuitously, and there at the stall was Judith. She
often came to help Uncle Richard on Market Day and was now sufficiently expert to enable him to go home for a quick meal.

Richard had told her of Ned's homecoming, and her joy at seeing him
was unbounded, though the public place forbade more than a decorous
cheek kiss from uncle to niece. Richard suggested that Judith should
walk with Ned to New Place so that they could talk together. When Ned
reported about the forks, Judith came up with an excuse for the week's
delay. "You ordered them two months ago in London, in time for the
wedding. You thought of sending them with Uncle Gilbert but knew you
would be coming home yourself later and wanted to give them to
Susanna with your own hands. You had asked the silversmith to keep
them for you but when you went back for them on Saturday he had sold
them to somebody whose name also began with H; say Hornby, like the
smith here. You had not told him when you would come for the forks
because you didn't know. Now he is making and engraving a new set,
and it will come by carrier."

"Judith," said Richard in mock reproof, "you sound practiced in
making up tales. Do you often do it?"

"Yes, Uncle Richard, I do," was the smiling reply. " 'Tis the best way
to give mother peace of mind."

As they walked away from the stall toward New Place, Ned said, "H
for Hornby and Hall. Have you learnt your letters?"

Judith said slyly, "I have long known enough of them for my need but
have no desire to read and write."

As they walked to New Place, Ned questioned Judith about John Hall
and the marriage. "He is a gentle man, but serious and stern. And very
clever. He even speaks French and reads French books. He learnt his
doctoring in France. Everybody comes to him; they say they feel better
even from talking to him."

"But the marriage. How goes that?"

"Well; very well. Susanna is so proud of her husband. Mother is proud
of him too."

"And you, Judith. Are you not jealous of your sister?" asked Ned
lightly.

"No; not at all. I could not be married to the doctor. I need for a
husband someone more lively and less perfect." She added banteringly,
"Someone like you, Ned."

"And have you found him?"

"I doubt I shall, but I keep looking, and there is fun in the search. In
the meantime I rejoice in Susanna's marriage because it gives me a bedroom to myself."

"With three families in the house, it must be getting crowded."

" 'Tis a big house; there is still room for more."

"Your mother. How is she?"

"I cannot remember her happier. Father is home, Susanna is married to a man that Mother would have chosen for her out of all the world, little Anne Greene, now three years old, is an abiding joy, and only last week it was discovered that Letitia is with child again; if it is a boy, it will be named William for Father."

"And soon your mother should have a grandchild all her own, and then her happiness will be complete."

"No; she won't be fully happy until I am married. She says little about it but I know she thinks of it all the time." With an abrupt change of subject she said, "Did Grandmother know you?"

"No," said Ned sadly.

"Be patient; she will. Some days she thinks I am her sister, Elizabeth, who was long dead before I was born; then other days she knows me full well, and talks of how much Grandfather loved me."

When they got to New Place, Tom Greene and the new husband had already left. Anne welcomed Ned with more warmth than he had ever known from her, and she made a comment which in former times would have sounded harsh, but now had a lightness that was almost witty. She said, "It takes the pestilence to make you mindful of the fifth commandment. But to speak truth, Ned, your coming will do your mother much good."

At this moment a sprightly little girl ran into the room and ran, gurgling with happiness, to Anne who picked her up with great joy and said, with careful enunciation, "Good morning , Anne."

"Good morning, Godmother," said the child, with delight at successfully completing her part of the morning ritual.

Anne set her down and said, "This is Master Edmund Shakespeare." Seeing the child confused by the difficulty of the name, she added, "You may call him Uncle Ned."

The child tried it—"Uncle Ned"—and was pleased to find it easy, and the gentleman was smiling at her, so she smiled back.

"Now say good morning to him and curtsy." Anne held her hand while she accomplished the difficult feat.

Ned saw in little Anne Greene Neddy a year from now. What happy times they would have as he taught him new words and fine manners!

Letitia Greene came into the room, delighted to see Ned, and longing to get him apart to hear news of London. And then Susanna came. She had always been ladylike but now she was a full lady. At twenty-four there was no doubt, in the presence of the other three women, that she was the queen of the household, but there was nothing pompous in her mien; she was gracious, charming, and light in manner. Ned began to stammer excuses for being absent from her wedding, but she put him completely at ease by saying, "It would have been wrong for you to come when, by so doing, you would have breached your duty to your fellows."

Judith could not refrain from saying, "He has brought you a beautiful gift; or rather, it is coming. Tell her, Uncle Ned." She had remembered the "Uncle" just in time.

Ned, embarrassingly conscious of the presence of Judith, told somewhat haltingly the story she had made up for him.

At the mention of silver forks, Susanna was elated. She said, "What a generous and fitting gift! Only the other day my husband was speaking of them; he said their use was very cleanly."

Judith said, "I remember that Grandfather scoffed at forks. He said, 'Next they'll be drinking ale with spoons.'"

Now Ned remembered it too. But it was so long ago. Judith could only have been a young girl at the time. Did children remember so well? Then he must be careful of what was said in front of Neddy as he grew up.

When Ned said that he wanted to see Will, Anne said, "But he is working and likes not to be disturbed."

Ned was glad to note that Anne referred now to Will's writing as work, and was even protective toward it. He reassured her with a lie. "'Tis about his work I have to see him." He went upstairs to Will's room.

Will was not writing but reading, and he happily set aside his book to greet Ned. Will moved to the door and looked out. Then he closed the door and came back to Ned. Even though no one outside could hear him he spoke quietly when he said, "Your little son. How fares he?"

Ned launched into a happy account of his good times with Neddy, of his victory over Rachel, of Sir John Barnet's duel on his behalf, but he ended with the worrying question that would not leave him. "But the plague, Will. I fear for him."

"You tell me he is a sturdy child and has good care. If you took him away from London, the journey might expose him to the danger more than leaving him at home. And if you had stayed in London and visited him every day, and then he had caught it, you would never forgive yourself. There are those who carry it to others while remaining unharmed themselves. No, Ned, 'tis better as 'tis. You can but pray for Neddy's safety. And now think of our mother instead. Go to her. She may know you have come and be waiting."

"But we have not talked about you. How goes the new play?"

Will smiled and said, "There will be time to talk of that and much else. Now go."

As Ned walked back through High Street and past the Market Cross, the way was thronged, for even though times were too bad for most people to buy more than necessities, there was no charge for looking and there was a great need for meeting and chatting. But Ned was aware of a difference. Instead of the usual loud talk and boisterous laughter, the chatter was muted and there were many sidelong glances. Only the sellers called out as of yore, and their blandishments went largely unregarded. Small wonder that the Coventry silversmith had agreed to make a special journey to sell six forks. Ned had heard much talk in London about the riots in the Midlands against enclosures. It had been said that there had been thousands of insurgents in his own county of Warwickshire alone, all bent on destroying the fences and hedges and filling up the ditches which they felt had wrongfully deprived them of their rights of common pasture.

Some of these very people had probably been among the rioters and now they feared to speak aloud for every stranger might be a spy; Ned had heard that some of the leaders had been imprisoned, and that others were being sought.

Mary was downstairs and dressed and waiting to welcome her best beloved son. When she had awoken, Joan had gently tested her awareness and gradually made her understand that Ned had come home to see her. Ned's relief at being recognized was as great as Mary's joy at seeing him. They embraced a long while, murmuring endearments, and there were tears in Ned's eyes as well as his mother's. Finally she said, "Why did you not wake me when you came home last night?"

He said only, "I did not want to disturb you."

"How long will you be staying this time?"

"As long as you need me."

"Then you will never leave. But come; let us go into the garden; the children will give us no peace."

As they walked out to their garden seat, Ned took stock of his mother again; she was old and frail indeed, and he had a feeling that her grasp of present reality was very tenuous.

But for a while all was well. She spoke with tears of the death of the child, Mary Hart—"She was to me like the first two little girls I lost so long ago"—with admiration, even awe, of Susanna's husband—"They say he can cure everything but old age"—with anxiety about Will Hart—"I fear he is not a good provider; in bad times like these, hats are not enough to live by in Stratford"—and with affectionate hope that Judith, like her sister, would find a good husband—"That is a woman's greatest blessing, Ned, and I was richly blessed in your father."

The talk seemed to have tired her and she fell silent. Suddenly she stood up and said, "What am I doing here? Mother is coming and there is much to be done, and your father will be home for dinner from the Corporation meeting." She moved toward the house, then stopped and turned to Ned with a painfully puzzled look. "Why are you not in school?"

"I left school long ago, Mother. I am a man now."

She shook her head, trying desperately to understand, then went slowly into her house. Ned did not follow her. Instead he went back to Will, who eagerly set aside his book again to hear Ned's report on their mother. In reply to Ned's distress he said, "Let us be glad that she knew you and was her old self again, even for a short time. Sometimes her mind is wholly in the past and then she is happy. It is only when her mind is a puzzling mixture of past and present that she is unhappy. I still believe your coming will help her to live more and more in the present. Be patient and brood not on it, for 'twill do no good. And one thing more: be grateful to Joan. I know not what we would do without her. There are times when our Mother is incontinent of body, like a baby, and Joan is then as loving and gentle in care of her as if she were indeed her own child and not her mother."

Ned left Will after a while, but was reluctant to go home and face his mother again. He was near the Swan Inn and he decided to go there to see his old boyhood hero, Dick Dixon, the champion archer.

Although it was Market Day, the inn was not crowded and there was an almost conspiratorial tone to the conversation. An occasional laugh was quickly broken off as if guiltily. When Ned entered, he was immediately appraised by all eyes. It was not until he hailed Dick Dixon and was recognized by him that conversation was resumed. What a change had come over Dick Dixon! Still in his middle thirties, he was bald and rapidly becoming fat; the lithe bowman had become a stout boniface, though he was as gentle as ever. When Ned asked him if he still kept up his archery, he said, "No, Ned. 'Tis all gone, with much else. 'Tis all powder, shot, and shell now; the bow has become a child's toy. Besides, the King has brought us days of peace."

"Peace abroad but war at home," said an aggressive voice. Ned saw that it came from a rough-looking man of about forty who was clearly not a Stratford tradesman or artisan; his clothes, his skin, his smell proclaimed earth and animals.

"Take care now, Hugh. We know not who this young gentleman is," said an older man among the half dozen who were drinking ale as they stood together near Ned.

"I reck not. Be he the Devil, I care not."

Dick Dixon quickly interposed. "This is no devil, but a fine young man of Stratford, newly returned from London. He is Master Shakespeare."

"Shakespeare?" said Hugh suspiciously. "Kin to the Shakespeare who has land in Old Stratford and Bishopton?"

"His brother," said Dick.

"Then he is in league with the Devil to take the bread from the mouths of children and the roofs from over their heads."

Ned angrily replied, "I know not what you are talking about, but if you speak of my brother, I say you lie."

For answer, Hugh threw what was left of his ale into Ned's face. Infuriated by the act itself and by its injustice, Ned attacked the man savagely. After an ill-aimed blow or two, the men grappled. Powerful Hugh seized Ned in a bear hug while Ned tried to throttle him. All the while other men tried to separate the assailants. As Ned felt his chest being crushed, his grip on the throat began to weaken. Suddenly Hugh released him and, as he did, kneed him in the crotch. Ned bent double in pain and Hugh dealt him a blow to the head which sent him stumbling to the floor where his head hit sharply against the square edge of a table leg. Ned lay momentarily stunned and, while Dick knelt down to tend to him, Hugh was hustled out of the inn by his companions.

Dick called for a hand to raise Ned and help him to the kitchen. There he was cared for by Mistress Dixon while Dick went back to tend to his customers. One of them said, "What can a man from London know? There they eat what we grow and wear what we make, and know nothing of what we have to bear to feed and clothe them."

"But they have the plague," objected another.

"Which is better: to be robbed quickly of life or slowly of living?"

Ned was soon restored, his clothes put to rights and brushed clean of the rushes into which he had fallen. But there was a large lump and cut on his head, and it took many cold compresses to stop the bleeding. The while she tended him, Mistress Dixon jabbered away, her garrulity in sharp contrast to her husband's reticence. "Oh, Master Shakespeare, you are well out of Warwickshire; there's naught but trouble here. To my mind, it all comes from those terrible days when the sun was darkened and then, but days later, the moon too. 'Twas a sign from Heaven of God's wrath with man. That was nigh on two years past now, and things have gone from bad to worse ever since. Those riots some weeks back were terrible, and, mark my words, they are not over yet. I don't know the right and the wrong of it, but I do know if poor people like Hugh Grover have no place to graze their few animals, they cannot live."

"What has my brother to do with it?"

"He owns land, and that is enough for men like Hugh."

"But has my brother enclosed land that was of custom open to everybody?"

"I know not." But the answer sounded evasive. Mistress Dixon added, "Time was when all land was open to grazing after the harvest and in the fallow years, and it did the land good, for it needed the dung of the animals. Now they fence it off against all animals but their own. And worst of all, they fence off the common land too."

Dick, who had come in, said gently, "Take care, Sarah, lest you be counted among the rioters."

Sarah replied defiantly, "I say naught but what is right and just, and there are few in Stratford who do not say the same."

Ned became increasingly anxious to find out Will's position in the matter of enclosures. He bade a hasty goodbye to the Dixons and hurried to New Place.

Will was in his orchard, inspecting the fruit trees with the gardener. After welcoming Ned, he said, "Not a good crop this season. I can but hope the Globe will prove more fruitful than the orchard."

When they were seated in the shade, Ned took off his hat and disclosed his injury. This prompted an account of the incident in the Swan Inn.

Will listened gravely. Ned ended with a direct and accusing challenge. "Tell me Will, and tell me true; do you enclose against the people?"

"I do not enclose, because I do not farm the land I bought. The tenants are Thomas Hiccox and Lewis Hiccox, as they were when I bought the land."

"And do they enclose?"

"They have in part and would do more."

"And cannot you stop them?"

" 'Tis they that pay me rent for the land, and should I stop them from making the best use of it?"

"But what of those like Hugh Grover who suffer?"

"I do not know the answer to that. I feel their need and I feel the need of the future too. The people multiply and the land shrinks, and so the best use must be made of the land to feed and clothe the growing crowds; there are twice as many people now in London as when I first went there. And I believe that enclosures are making the land more fruitful. It has always been like this. Fences and hedges and ditches have crept across the land from untold time. While there was much land and few people, all was well. But now there are many people and little land. And think not, Ned, that I own the county; 'tis but a hundred and seven acres for crops and twenty for pasture."

"I cannot think it right for the Hugh Grovers to starve."

"Nor do I. Their rights to the common pastures must be preserved, but I doubt they will be content with that."

"And are not even the commons being enclosed?"

"They are indeed, and to my mind 'tis shameful. But in this, as in all things, there are not heroes and villains but only selfish and one-sighted men. Both sides speak of the rights of many but think only of their own. Even the Corporation of this town is loud in protests against enclosures but sells the common lands in time of need. We are all frail mortals, Ned, and it seems the innocent will always suffer—as did you this day."

They both smiled at the reference to Ned's injured head, and Will continued, "My next play will be about the needy Hugh Grovers, and of wily politicians who take advantage of their need, and of one incorruptible man whose gigantic pride and contempt for people leads him to destruction. His name is Coriolanus. I was reading about him again when you came to me this morning."

Ned's thoughts, now happily deflected to the theatre, said, "And *Antony and Cleopatra*. It is finished?"

"Yes, and I think it will find favor." Ned was silent, but Will went on to answer the question that the actor's silence implied. "There are many parts and most of the sharers will play at least two. I shall read the play to you some day soon, and if there is a part which appeals to you I will try to get it for you. But you will not be jealous of Will Sly this time; even he will have to play more than one part. The play will belong to two people, Burbage as Antony and the boy as Cleopatra. I think every player will want to be that boy, and no one player can ever encompass her infinite variety; I think she is my fullest and truest woman."

"What will John Lowin play?"

"Enobarbus, a good part he will make the best of."

After a slight pause, Will spoke as if in answer to Ned's secret dream. "But Ned, there is something I would say to you. When next the opportunity affords, I would buy you a share in the King's Men." Ned was so surprised that he could say nothing, and Will misinterpreted his silence; he assumed that the old resentful independence was rising again in his young brother. He quickly added, "Be not offended. 'Tis high time and right and proper that you become a sharer. And you can pay me back the purchase price as and when you will. Think of me as selfish in this matter. I shall spend less and less time in London, and it would be good to know that there is a Shakespeare at the meetings of the sharers."

"Oh, Will, I . . ." Words failed Ned, but his gratitude was obvious.

"I am relieved that you take it so. For a moment I feared the old Ned had come back between us."

"Never, Will, never. He was a foolish young man and he died long ago, else how could I have told you about Lawrence and the King and Neddy and much else? It was only that I did not know how to thank you enough, for it has long been my dream to become a sharer. But how can it happen? Must I wait for a man to die?"

"Not of necessity. That would be a grim prospect, and each day in the theatre you would look hopefully at the sharers for signs of death." Will said this lightly and Ned laughed at it, but both knew there was truth in it. "No, Ned, 'tis not so dismal. Only one sharer yet has died while he was a member of the fellowship: Gus Phillips. Three others have resigned: George Bryan, Will Kemp, and Tom Pope. It may well be that another will grow tired of playing and be happy to sell his share. And if my pen grows weak and dies, I shall resign, for I think I shall never play again. 'Tis some years now since I trod the stage, and I miss it not at all. There is much I miss here in Stratford—above all, the company of my fellows— but not playing. That proves I am not a player as you are. But be not too hopeful that it is my own share you will inherit, for as yet my pen shows no sign of dying in my hand. And now, go back to our mother."

Before he left Ned managed to say, "Will, you have always been a good brother to me, and never more than now. I shall try to be worthy of your trust."

As Ned moved cheerfully away, Will called after him, "Tend well that bump on your head. I thank you for it, for 'twas on my behalf you got it. Were you married, I should think you were growing horns."

When Ned got home, his mother was alone in the house; he learned later that Joan had taken the children for a walk through the market and to their father's shop.

As soon as she saw him, Mary said, "Ned! I was just thinking about you. Where have you been? To see Will?"

She was sitting in the chair. Ned knelt down beside her and she became aware of the injury to his head. Immediately she was all solicitude, but he assured her it was nothing to be concerned about. "I slipt and hit my head against a wall."

"Are you sure you were not drunk?"

They laughed together, and never had Ned found laughter so blessed.

FIFTY

NED HAD A GREAT SENSE OF TRIUMPH. ON FRIDAY AND SATURDAY HE had determinedly stayed near his mother, even when she did not know him, mistook him for someone else, or was confused by his presence, but gradually the periods of her real awareness of him lengthened, and on Sunday morning it was judged that she was well enough to go to New Place for dinner. Joan said, "If she becomes uneasy or unhappy, we can always bring her home again, and it will do us all a power of good to get away from our own table." Mary herself was delighted by the prospect of the excursion and even wanted to go to church, but this was ruled out by Joan. Mary was placated by being told that Ned would hurry home, as soon as the service was over, to accompany her to New Place.

For once, Ned was eager to go to church, not so much to worship God as to see two people: Vicar John Rogers and Doctor John Hall, the one because Susanna had clashed with him and the other because Susanna had married him. Both men proved worthy of his interest.

The vicar was a jolly-looking man, pink and fat. He seemed to take God for granted, but not his congregation. His bright, little eyes were forever darting over his flock as if looking for missing sheep or ready to pounce on those present who were caught in some misdemeanor such as nodding asleep. Not that his sermon was likely to induce slumber: he had a remarkably energetic delivery and he battered his parishioners with words. This morning he was bent on denouncing "Those double-damned twin sins of the flesh—gluttony and concupiscence." Ned felt that the speaker was a living warning against the first and was ready to believe that he knew the second from experience too; but Ned liked the man, and could understand why Susanna didn't. This man's preaching was the fulfillment of a professional duty whereas Vicar Byfield's had resulted from an inner compulsion. Vicar Rogers preached against the Devil because he was paid to do so, and the greatest sinner in his eyes was he who failed to come to church or pay his dues, whereas Vicar Byfield would have preached against the Devil even if he had not been ordained to do so. Ned supposed that Byfield was the more laudable man, but Rogers was certainly the more likable.

Ned was much impressed by his first sight of John Hall. As Judith had said, he did indeed look older than his thirty-two years. He was tall and spare, and had an air of quiet dignity and natural authority. As he entered the church people watched him with respect; small wonder that Susanna was proud of him. Even the vicar's darting eyes seemed to stop for a moment on him with approval and almost as if to thank him for coming.

When the service was over, Ned stayed only long enough with the greeting groups for a brief introduction to Doctor Hall. It was Will who introduced his young brother to his older son-in-law. Ned mumbled some conventional words; the physician smiled graciously at him but said nothing. Ned excused himself, saying that he had to fetch his mother to New Place. This time he received in response a slow nod of the head but again no words.

Ned was the more eager to get away to avoid the return company of Will Hart. As he had feared, the hatter had whined his way to church with accounts of his financial distress and implied appeals for help. "I fear the folk around here care not for fashion," he had complained.

"They must buy some hats," Ned had replied testily. "They cannot go unbonneted in the sun or the rain."

"True, Ned, true. But they make do with what has served them for years and those with money are either like our niece, Susanna, who thinks it ungodly to spend money on a fine bonnet, or else prefer to buy their hats in Coventry or even London. Ah! London. That is the place for men of skill like me."

"There are more poor people there than there are rich, as there are everywhere, and far too many hatters. Methinks you would do well to suit your wares to your market; hats must fit pockets as well as heads."

"Well said, Ned, well said. And I do my best, Ned, to earn an honest penny, I do my best. But the times are against me."

As Ned hurried home, he was fearful lest his mother's mind might have lapsed again, but she greeted him happily and was dressed and ready for the walk to New Place. Mary's body had not suffered the same degree of impairment as her mind, and she took her son's arm in pride rather than from need. Several people greeted them in passing, but Ned avoided stopping.

Both the doctor and Will had warned the families to show no undue excitement over Mary's visit, but she said, " 'Tis good to have the family all together again, all but Gilbert. It has been a long time." It was noted with relief that she did not refer to those who were absent through death.

When they arrived at New Place, all were there except the doctor who had been called for urgently to attend a young boy who had been bitten by an adder while blackberrying.

While their elders ate, the three children played together in the garden, though Anne was not happy about even this desecration of the Sabbath; she compromised by insisting that they play quietly. Willie Hart, at seven, was happy to be given the responsibility of keeping the two little ones out of harm, and Anne Greene, at three, was more able to entertain the usually miserable two-year-old Tommy Hart than were any of the elders.

Conversation at the dinner table began as always on Sundays with discussion of the sermon. Tom Greene said lightly that, in view of the vicar's denunciation of gluttony, the women had put before them not a meal but a temptation.

Susanna's comment was, "To be tempted is not to fall."

Judith asked, "What is gluttony? Eating too much? Then the vicar has sinned over and over again."

Anne had frequently been pained by having to hear in her own home criticism of the new vicar, particularly when it had led to the charge of recusancy against her own daughter, Susanna. She said now, with something of her old sharpness, "The vicar's sins are between him and his God. 'Tis our own sins that should trouble us. And Vicar Rogers brings us the word of God with truth and power."

Tom Greene, ever the mediator, said, "And surely, Judith, gluttony is not just eating too much, though that is a sin against the body as well as the spirit. Nor is it taking pleasure in food, else why would God have given us good appetites and the sense of taste to enjoy good food? No, gluttony is the sin of making a god of eating—when all our thoughts are filled with the next meal. Think you not so, Will?"

Will answered with a quiet reflectiveness which for the moment changed the atmosphere at the table. "When our lives are governed by any of our appetites, we sin and suffer for it."

Judith surprised the table with a question to which she fully knew the answer. "What is concupiscence?" No one answered, so she directed the question to Ned with a mischievous innocence. "Do you know, Uncle Ned?"

Looking straight at her, in reply to her playful challenge, and speaking as if to a child, Ned said, "It means lust, Judith."

"As you very well know," said her mother reprovingly.

Judith wasn't to be so easily put in her place. She said with the same apparent lack of guile, "But what I don't understand is that all the preachers speak of it as a sin of men only. Are women free from it?"

Three of the four wives present were embarrassed, but Susanna retained her self-possession and took it upon herself to resolve the awkward situation. "Judith, you know that it was Eve who tempted Adam, and any woman who does so to a man is guilty of a grave sin."

It was Mary who ended the subject by saying, "This cold ham is very good. Who baked it?"

"I did," Letitia Greene said.

And Will Hart quickly jumped into the conversation. "'Tis indeed good, Letitia, passing good. Joan too is a rare baker of hams, but alas! they do not grace our table at Henley Street now."

Richard, who rarely said anything, was shamed by this parade of poverty. He said with spirit, "They will when we have a sow ready for the slaughter."

"Ah, Richard, you are a prouder man than I. I confess my weakness. I cannot pretend that things are better than they are."

"We lack nothing," said Richard forcefully.

"And for that I am grateful," said Will Hart. "But if the house depended on me, we should lack much, and that is not right, for the children are mine. If only I could get out of debt and start again, I feel all would be well, for no one can gainsay my skill in the craft."

Will chose to ignore the bait as he had frequently before. He would always take care that the family lacked for nothing, and he knew that Richard was a model of thrift and industry. He tolerated his brother-in-law with a sympathetic amusement as a man with no real vices who seemed to make Joan a good husband and had given her two sons and his mother two grandsons.

The dinner lasted over an hour, and, just before the gathering was about to break up, John Hall returned. Immediately Susanna busied herself in making a place for him at table and ministering to him.

Will asked, "How is the boy?"

"He is in no danger," replied the doctor. "His mother had opened the bite and sucked out much of the poison. She was too late to get it all, but the lad should be well in a week." He added in a lightly serious tone, "I think the boy will never again gather blackberries on the Sabbath." Then he addressed himself to Ned. "'Tis good to meet you at last. I find it difficult to call you Uncle, as my wife most rightfully does, for I am older than you by some years."

"I should be happy if you would call me Ned."

"So be it. Tell me, is the plague a severe visitation? I ask because my father, who is a physician, lives in Acton, and many were stricken there in 1603."

"When I left London, the deaths were not yet one hundred a week."

"Then we can but pray that it will not get worse."

"John, what think you causes the plague?" asked Will.

"I know not. It is a sickness of cities and may well be bred by sin."

"But it comes only in the heat of summer, and sin never ceases. Besides, cities are not alone in having sinners," objected Ned.

"It is true that summer is the time of greatest plague," said the doctor, "but it has killed people in the coldest weather too."

Thomas Greene said, "If it is God's punishment for sin, why should children die and wicked men escape?"

"God's mysteries are hidden from man; it is part of His divine plan that the innocent should suffer with the guilty. As a physician I try to cure and to save, but my work is in God's hands. I am often amazed when a strong man dies and a weak child lives. God's providence is greater than man's skill."

Judith asked, "Why should a physician try to heal the sick if God decides who shall live and who shall die?"

"Your sister will answer that question."

Susanna was glad to do so at the bidding of her husband, else she would not have ventured to speak. "Christ himself healed the sick, and St. Luke was a physician. In all fields of endeavor, man must strive to do his best, then pray for God's blessing on his labors."

Ned wondered how Will could stand such pious talk Sunday after Sunday, and possibly on weekdays too. How could he love the life in Stratford so much after London? Perhaps it was because his most real life occurred when he was alone in his study, pen in hand, and that life flourished best away from the distractions of the great city. Ned had no such compensation. Apart from the happiness he might bring to his mother, he could not even feel useful this summer because Richard did not have enough work to need his help.

The conversation had drifted to the poor fruit crop, but Ned was paying little attention. He broke into it by saying, "I think I should take Mother home."

All now looked intently at Mary; since John Hall had returned, they had been watching her less closely. It was immediately clear from her look that she did not quite know where she was.

"Would you like to go home, Mother?" asked Joan.

"Yes," said Mary with relief and eagerness.

"Come on, then," said Joan as she began to get up.

"No," said Ned. "Stay with the children. I will go."

Mary said nothing on the way home, but she smiled frequently and Ned could but hope that, wherever her mind was, it was in a happy time and a happy place.

When they arrived home, Mary sat beside the fire and began to nod to sleep. Ned decided it was safe to leave her for a while and went out into the garden to sit and muse in the shade. He remembered that his mother had pleaded with Will, in this very same spot, to take the young Ned with him to London. Only now did he realize the full extent of her unselfishness in begging to have her favorite son taken from her.

Ned did not know how long he was lost in his musings, but he was aroused by a shout from the house. It was Joan's voice. Ned hurried in. He was horrified by what he saw: his mother was on her knees and her skirt was on fire; Joan was doing her best to crush the fire in the folds of the skirt, while her mother was nursing her already burnt hands and whimpering.

Joan cried, "The carpet. Quick."

Ned seized the precious carpet from the table and used it to smother the flames.

As soon as she saw that there was no further danger, Joan fetched some butter and bandage to tend her mother's hands and took her upstairs to bed.

Joan had said not one word of reproof to Ned, but he waited for her in an agony of self-reproach, unable to fathom what had happened. The fire had been out. To occupy himself he examined the precious carpet. Years of taught respect for it had led him to expose the underside to the flames. There was a little searing but nothing to impair the appearance of the face. He restored it to its Sunday place on the table. He thanked God that Joan had come back in time. She must have sensed that their mother might need her.

It seemed a long time before Joan came downstairs, and when she did her chief concern was to give Ned some peace of mind. "She will be all right. I gave her a potion and stayed with her until she was sound asleep. You must not blame yourself, Ned. When she is in the past she tries to do all the things she used to do, like cooking and cleaning and knitting, but her fingers have lost their skill."

"She was asleep in the chair—I did not know how to get her to bed— and I went out to sit in the garden for a while."

"She must have waked, seen that the fire was out, and got down on her knees to try to light it. Then sparks from the tinderbox caught her skirt." All this while she had been examining the damage to the skirt. "It's beyond repair, but I can use what's left of it to make something for the children."

"I'll never leave her alone again, Joan."

"I try not to, but sometimes it cannot be helped. Just remember that she went out today with you and was happy."

"Are her hands sorely burnt?"

"'Tis hard to say yet, and she is slow to heal now; the slightest bruise leaves a mark for months." Seeing Ned so unhappy, she said, "Why don't you go back to New Place and join the men?"

"No; I should have to tell them about the accident." Then he remembered Judith. "But I could take Judith for a walk; we used often to walk by the river on Sundays."

"She had already left before I did; some young man, I suppose. I worry about her, Ned, and I know her mother does."

"But why? Is it not right that she should seek a young man to marry her?" asked Ned, who was surprised to feel a slight stab of jealousy that Judith no longer needed his company on Sunday afternoons.

"I think she seeks not a husband. 'Tis certain that no man comes to ask for her hand. She told me once that maids marry too young, that I was wise to wait until I was nigh on thirty." She added wryly, "As though I waited from choice." She went on, "I think Judith finds it easier to talk to me than to her own mother. She is a good and warm-hearted young woman, but too lively and playful for her mother. I warned her that some young men might not be mindful of her good name. She laughed and said, ' 'Tis for me to be mindful of that.' But Francis Hornby frightened her."

"Francis Hornby?"

"Oh, you know not about that. His religion turned to madness. They say it only happened when the moon was full, but I tell them that is nonsense for he was just as mad by day when the fit was on him. He began to see the Devil in every young woman, and he would attack and beat her, cursing the Devil the while. He attacked Judith but she got away from him and picked up a stone. When he caught her again she hit him on the head with it and ran away."

"Did she kill him?" asked Ned in horror.

"Oh no, but it might have been a mercy for Francis if she had. Soon after, they put him in chains and took him away to some place for mad folk where they chain them to the wall so that they can do no harm."

At this point Will Hart returned with the children. He was in a bad humor because he had wanted to stay much longer with his distinguished relatives, but Tommy had begun to cry for his mother and would not be appeased.

Ned could not face the prospect of a session with Will Hart, so he decided to go for a walk. He had been much upset by the story about Francis Hornby, and he needed privacy to assimilate it. Besides, he was concerned about Judith and might chance to meet her; he would like to see what company she now had on her Sunday afternoon walk.

As Ned walked down toward the Clopton Bridge black thunder-clouds gathered overhead. People out for their afternoon walk were hurrying home to avoid the inevitable rain. After a moment's hesitation Ned continued his walk; he would find shelter somewhere if need be.

There was a startling flash of lightning followed quickly by a loud crack of thunder. A little girl cried out in terror, and her father picked her up and hurried faster. With the first spatter of large drops of rain, people began to run and Ned did too, to the Swan Inn. As he ran he assured himself that it was unlikely Hugh Grover would be there; he was almost certain that the laborer lived outside Stratford and came in only on Market Days.

Ned got inside just as the downpour came. The place rapidly filled with shelter-seekers, most of whom made no gesture of buying a drink in return for the protection of the roof, but Ned ordered a tankard of ale. Dick Dixon was glad to see him and was relieved to hear that the lump on the head had almost disappeared. Then Ned saw Judith. She was among the last to run in and was already well drenched, but was laughing merrily at the adventure. With her was a young man, and Ned took good stock of him before Judith espied her uncle.

Her companion was clearly some years younger than Judith; Ned judged him to be about eighteen. The thought suddenly struck him that that was the age at which Will had married a woman years older than he. But this young man was no Will; there was an animal exuberance about him. Ned had a feeling that the couple was well but dangerously matched.

Judith spotted Ned and hurried across to him gleefully. The young man followed, wondering with hostility who his handsome rival was. He was relieved to be told that he was Judith's uncle. Judith introduced him as "Tom Quiney."

"Richard Quiney's son?" asked Ned.

"One of them," was the jaunty reply. "My father was as busy in bed as elsewhere. He had eight sons and three daughters, though three of the sons died as babies. Men are supposed to be stronger than women, but more boys die at the breast than girls."

"Not always," said Ned. "My mother's first two children were girls and they both died."

"Judith here is the strong one; it was her twin brother that died."

"Enough talk of death," said Judith. "I am wet outside and would be wet inside too." Looking mischievously at Ned, she said, "My uncle is rich. He buys silver forks for my sister, so I am sure he will be happy to buy ale for us, Tom."

Ned smiled and ordered the ale. He noticed that many eyes were watching them without seeming to do so. He wondered if Tom were accepted at New Place; if not, he was sure Judith's being with him would be reported to her mother and father. He must find out more about the young man. He said, "Do you know Judith's parents, Tom?"

"Everybody in Stratford knows them."

"Uncle Ned means do you come to New Place? No, Uncle, he does not, because he chooses not to."

Tom explained, defiantly. "I would not enter a house where I should not be welcome. I seek not Judith to wife . . ."

"Nor do I wish to marry Tom," quickly interposed Judith.

". . . but if I did so seek her, Master Shakespeare would judge me not worthy. I have no skill, nor do I wish any. I am content to enjoy each day as it comes."

"But you must do something to earn a living," said Ned, feeling strangely old and paternal as he did so.

"I am healthy and strong, and there is always some work to do."

"But have you no ambition?"

"Yes; to have an inn like this."

"You would drink all the ale," quipped Judith.

Tom changed the subject. "Judith has told me about you. You are a player in London. It sounds mighty wicked to me. The people here say bad things about plays. I have never seen one, nor ever will in Stratford. But Judith says you have played before the King."

"And before the old Queen too," added Judith proudly.

"Do you dress up as a woman?" asked Tom.

"No," said Ned, smiling. "The women's parts are played by boys before their voices have changed."

"I hear that sometimes they are castrated," said Tom with horrified awe at the possibility.

"There are none such in the King's Men," said Ned with some embarrassment on Judith's behalf.

But she surprised him by saying lightly, "That would be a high price to pay even for playing before the King."

The rain stopped as suddenly as it had begun, and the sun beckoned people outdoors again. "Come, Tom," said Judith, "the sun will dry us sooner than this inn." And with hasty farewells and thanks for the ale they left.

Ned was intrigued by Tom Quiney, and not a little worried too. He decided to go to New Place in the hope of a private conversation with Will; surely by this time the men had finished their after-dinner chat and Will had repaired to his study.

He found things at New Place as he had hoped. When Ned went up to Will, he was sleeping in a chair, the book he had been reading fallen from his hands to the floor.

Will woke guiltily at Ned's approach and said, " 'Tis a sign of my forty-one years to fall asleep after dinner. I saw our mother was lost in her own world before the end of the meal. How is she now?"

Ned had to tell about the fire, and his distress caused Will to say, "There have been other such happenings; that is why Joan did not upbraid you, because she has felt guilty so often. I try to comfort her, as I do you now, for it ill becomes any of us to say aught when we have not the day-by-day care of our mother. It is only Richard who has eased the burden for Joan, and then only in the evenings and on Sundays, for he works hard at his craft. Richard should have been called Peter, for he is indeed the rock on which our old home stands. Judith spends much time with Mother too, and Joan tells me that Judith is better than anybody else when Mother is reliving her childhood, for she asks her the right questions and makes up the right things to tell her. Judith has told me some surprising things she has learnt from her grandmother, but then Judith is full of surprises herself. She worries me, Ned. She should have come to London with us. Here she sometimes reminds me of a wild beast in a cage, or rather a peacock in too small a pen. I fear she will come to harm by dashing herself against the sides of the pen."

"She might have come to greater harm and sooner in London, and her presence there would have interfered with your work."

Will smiled and said, "I fear my work would not have brooked such interference, any more than it did from you. The Muse is a tyrannous mistress, Ned, and sometimes I think she is glad that Anne is as she is, for if my wife and family had come to London, she would have had a rival. Look at Ben Jonson; the Muse took him away too from a wife and family he loved."

"But you have come home to Stratford and are happy here."

"Only because I have this room and Anne has accepted what I do here. I sometimes think Judith understands; there are moments when there is a strange and unexpressed bond between us, and then there are times when she exasperates me beyond measure."

Ned told of the meeting at the Swan. Will said, "I have heard of the young man, and have repeated what I have heard to Judith. He is spoken of as a menace to virgins, but Judith only laughed at that."

"They say they do not want to become husband and wife."

"And I hope they never will."

"Do you think Judith will marry?"

"I suppose so, though I think it will be rather to have children than a husband. Anne is always looking for the right husband for her, but I'm sure that Anne's choice will not be Judith's. But tell me what you think of Susanna's husband."

"That he would never have suited Judith." They both laughed. "But to speak sooth, he awes me."

"John is a good man, Ned, and I am proud to have him for my son-in-law. Although he is serious of mien, he has brought much happiness to the house."

"Can he laugh?"

"I remember being surprised when I first heard him do so. And it was on the Sabbath too! It was at something Judith said. Letitia was complaining that her baby was not taking her breast well, and Judith said, 'Small wonder. How would you like to have no food but milk, and that without sugar?' Even Anne smiled, but only because John had laughed."

FIFTY-ONE

THE FOLLOWING WEEKS PASSED PLEASANTLY. NED SPENT MUCH OF HIS TIME with his mother, and her happiness in his company when she knew him and her reliance on his presence when she didn't made him fearful of what would happen when he left. Somewhat to the family's surprise Joan became pregnant again. This jolted her husband out of his despondency and he began to work with a will; in his new-found energy and enthusiasm he made and sold more hats in one month than he had in the previous six.

The silver forks were delivered as promised, and their initial use at a Sunday dinner at which the whole family was present was a notable occasion. The forks were to be used by the Halls, the Greenes, Will, and Ned. The two Londoners were fairly adept in their use, and this made forks a dubious appurtenance in the eyes of Anne and an enviable one to Will Hart, who became determined to acquire the use of Ned's when he had left again for London. Judith found them as unnecessary as reading and writing—there was much of her grandfather in her—and was unduly amused by Susanna's initial ineptness. In the privacy of Henley Street, Joan commented, "There are those who can pick up things with their toes, but God gave us our feet to walk on."

Apart from some good hours with his mother, Ned's best were spent with Will. It was a memorable afternoon when Will read to him his *Antony and Cleopatra*. Ned was so dazzled by the poetry and the wonder of Cleopatra that he found he was no longer just listening for a worthwhile part he had some chance of being given. After he had tried to express his admiration for the play, Will said, "And what part in it would you like?"

The surprising answer was, "It matters not, so I be in it somewhere."

With an amused doubt Will asked, "Do you speak truth?"

"Yes, Will. I am not as I was. I am content to wait now, like a soldier in time of peace who polishes his arms ready for the day of battle. My time will come, and I shall be ready. As you said before, most sharers will play more than one part in this play, so what can a hired man expect? But there is one small part at the end that would please me: that man of Caesar's who brings the truth to Cleopatra."

"Dolabella; I had already thought of that for you."

"Will, you must read this to the sharers as soon as may be."

"I shall, but John Heminge tells me in a letter that this tour is doing well; and the plague may yet get worse."

"Antony is a wonderful part but Burbage will long to play Cleopatra."

"As he did to play Juliet. He once asked me why I wasted the best parts in some of the plays on boys."

"But Will, this Cleopatra. How do you know her? There is little of Anne in her."

Will refused to be drawn. He said enigmatically, "My Muse showed her to me." With that Ned had to be content.

In early August Ned received two letters. The first was from John Lowin, who said that his beloved Joan's husband had died of the plague and that he and Joan hoped to get married as soon as they could make arrangements. He looked for Ned to stand by his side at the ceremony. The other letter was from Lawrence. It said in part: "I regret our last evening together was spoilt by Cyril Parton, as the latter part of the evening with him was spoilt by thoughts of you, for he proved to be a sorry companion in all but body, and even there he was less pleasing than I had anticipated. London is a dull place without the players, and the plague seems determined to be only bad enough to keep them out of town."

THE WORLD CHANGED FOR NED ON THE MIDDLE SATURDAY IN AUGUST. THE day had begun very pleasantly, especially as Richard needed Ned's help in the shop to taw some leather and compose some verses; their mother was a little tired and had been persuaded to stay in bed for a few hours, which she agreed to the more readily because Ned had brought her breakfast of sweetened milksop to her and stayed with her while she spooned it up, amusing her with his insistence that she leave not a drop.

In the middle of the morning Susanna came with the exciting news that she was pregnant. Now there were three expectant mothers in the family circle: Joan, Susanna, and Letitia Greene. Judith accompanied her sister and shared her joy.

Joan went upstairs with the two sisters to Mary, who, when she heard the happy news, said, "So I shall have a great-grandson!"

"I think it will be a girl, Grandmother," said Susanna.

"Then will you name her Mary for me?"

"No, Grandmother," replied Susanna with a genteel firmness. "She will be named Elizabeth for my husband's mother, for so he would wish it."

Dashed for only a moment, Mary said, "Then Judith must have a daughter named for me."

"That would make me very happy, Grandmother, except that I have to find a husband first."

Joan couldn't resist saying, "You don't look for him in the right places."

Judith responded without any rancor. "It mayhap that Stratford is the wrong place. Both you and Susanna found husbands who were born elsewhere."

Mary returned to the subject of names by saying, "I am sure that if Judith has a son he will be named John, for she loved her grandfather."

"And because I loved him he will be named not John but Shakespeare, for that name meant much to Grandfather, and it seems now that his sons will not give him a grandson."

"To be sure they will," said Mary. "Even if Anne is past bearing, there is yet Gilbert and Richard and Edmund."

Susanna said, "Your husband will determine your son's name, Judith."

"I shall not wed a Doctor Hall, Susanna," said Judith mischievously.

"Nor would a Doctor Hall marry you," said Joan.

After dinner Ned took his mother into the garden, and she got him to tell her about the King and the court, but in the mid-afternoon they were both surprised by the approach of Will, who never came in the afternoon. After a greeting he said, "I have come to take Ned away for a time, Mother. I need his help, but must show him something first."

Mary said, "More of these mysterious London matters, I suppose, beyond the understanding of us simple Stratford folk."

As soon as they were outside the house, Will said, "We have a visitor from London. Lawrence has come to see you."

"But why?" asked the dumbfounded Ned.

"It's bad news, Ned, and he felt it was too private to entrust to a letter."

Ned stopped and in a strained whisper said, "Neddy!"

"The plague," Will said quietly.

Some people had paused at sight of the stricken Ned. Will took his arm and said, "Come, Ned. I have told them at the house that Lawrence has come with important and private news about the King's Men. To impress them, I have said that he comes with a message from the King, and to still Anne's fears I have said that it does not mean that I will have to return to London, but that you may have to go; I thought that the need for secrecy here in Stratford might be too much for you to bear."

Ned said not one word in reply to Will. When they got to New Place, Lawrence was being gracious to the four women, all of whom, even Anne, were impressed by him. Apart from his personal distinction, they thought of him as the King's Messenger. His mission, the nature of which they were resigned to never knowing, was so urgent that he had not stopped on the way for dinner, and so they plied him with all the good things the larder had to offer, Susanna seeing to it that he was also supplied with a fork.

At the door Will had made an urgent plea to Ned to try to hide his grief from the women. Ned had nodded in a dazed way, but his efforts were not very successful; the most he could manage was a sad, lifeless smile. The women showed their concern and Will hastily gave them an explanation: "I have told Ned he may have to return to London, and he is distressed at having to leave our mother now that she has come to depend on him so much." Judith alone was not deceived.

At their first sight of each other, Ned and Lawrence had shaken hands and looked wordlessly at each other.

Will, with artificial bustle, said, "We must confer without delay," and the three men went up to Will's study.

As soon as the door was closed and they were seated, Lawrence began his tale. Will had already heard the substance of it, so he watched intently the effect on Ned. "It was on Tuesday, Ned. He did not suffer long. It seems that the healthier they are the sooner they go. Jack visited him last Sunday, as he had done every Sunday since you left. This time he took me with him. I had never seen Neddy before; he must have been a bonny lad. He was very sick and Rachel was beside herself with grief. There was no doubt it was the plague. Rachel was sure the wet-nurse had brought the pestilence to the child; one had died of it in the house next to the nurse's, but Rachel had found out about it too late. I went to get a physician who told us what we already knew. Jack and I were both with Neddy when he died. Our first thought had been that I should ride posthaste for you, but the physician assured us that it was impossible you could be brought in time."

Still Ned said no word.

After a pause, Lawrence took out a letter and handed it to him, saying, "This is from Jack."

Ned took the letter and looked at it uncomprehendingly.

Will put his hand on his shoulder and said, "Ned, I know how you feel. I lost Hamnet, and he too was dead and buried without my seeing him."

Ned began to fumble with the letter, but he failed to break the seal, and he handed the letter to Lawrence with the unspoken request that he should read it aloud. Lawrence opened the letter and read: "My dear Ned. When you read this you will be stunned by the news that Lawrence has brought you. Rest assured of this: despite the plague, Neddy was given proper burial at the Church of St. Giles on Wednesday. Lawrence is riding straight from the church to you. One thing more: blame not Rachel. She is tortured by guilt, though it is none of hers. All her devotion to Marie went to Neddy, as did yours. I have assured her you will not blame her. It would be empty words for me to send you the consolations of religion, for my faith, and I suspect yours, goes not deeper than church-going; this is our loss. But I can send you the consolations of friendship, and this I do with all my heart. In spite of the plague you may choose now to return to London. If you do, there is one who will be eager to see you: your friend, Jack Barnet."

When he had finished reading the letter, Lawrence folded it again and handed it to Ned. He had to hold it out a moment before Ned became aware of it. As he finally took it, he seemed to come to himself with an effort. He looked at Lawrence as though trying to bring him and his surroundings into focus. Then he said in a trembling voice, "Thank you. Thank you for everything."

"What will you do, Ned?" asked Will.

"Do?" echoed Ned blankly.

"Yes. Will you return to London with Lawrence or stay here until I return?"

"I know not yet."

Will decided it was better not to question Ned further for the moment, and so he addressed himself to Lawrence. "How long will you stay?"

"Not later than Monday morning. I have slept but little of late and should welcome two nights of rest."

"We must think of some explanation of the urgency of your visit, and one that involves Ned."

For the moment they had ignored Ned and so they were the more surprised when he said, "I shall tell them the truth."

"No, Ned," said Will sharply.

"Why not?" challenged Ned, his grief turning into belligerence. "Bastards are as well known in the country as the city, and I was proud of Neddy. Why should others be ashamed? Had my blood been noble, he would have been honored by all."

"It can do no good now," pleaded Will. "It can only hurt innocent people."

"I care not what your Anne and your Susanna and her pious husband think. If they shun me, so much the better."

"And our mother?"

Ned was silent, and then abruptly stood up and left the room violently. Impelled by the fury of his sorrow, he stormed out of the house. Judith, who from the moment of Ned's arrival at the house had sensed that Master Fletcher had come with bad news for him and was now convinced of it, called out "Ned!" The other three women looked at her strangely, for never before had they heard her omit the word "Uncle." She ran upstairs, ignoring protests from her mother, determined to find out what was wrong.

Judith almost ran into her father in the doorway; he had come to close it after Ned had flung it open. She had collected herself sufficiently to remember the proper mode of address, and she said, "Uncle Ned. What is wrong?"

Will said, "Come in, Judith," and he closed the door after them. As they moved to sit, he glanced at Lawrence and their eyes shared their quandary. They had not had time to decide on a tale for the family, and, if Ned carried out his threat, whatever they made up now would be proved to be a lie.

Will began cautiously. "There are certain things we cannot tell you,

Judith, things that are so secret they could not even be entrusted to a letter; that is why Master Fletcher had to come all the way from London."

"But it's about Uncle Ned. Is he in danger?"

This last question was directed at Lawrence who replied with smiling assurance, "No."

Judith turned back to her father. "When Uncle Ned went out he looked angry. Was it against you or Master Fletcher?"

"No, Judith, not against anybody. If you want to help him, you will not ask him any questions; that would only make him angrier. Rest assured that he is in no danger and that all will be well. And now leave us, for Master Fletcher and I have much to talk about."

Judith left the room, dissatisfied and still worried.

Ned was in the woods beyond Clopton Bridge, where he had often gone in turmoil of spirit, usually after a clash with his father. He remembered a time, one of many times, when he had irritated his father, and had provoked the comment: "There are sons who are blessings and sons who are curses, and a son who is a curse is worse than the seven plagues of Egypt." Anne had been unable to refrain from saying, "There were ten plagues in Egypt," which had prompted the quick reply, "Then the other three are daughters-in-law." Ned smiled at the memory. He had begun by thinking his own Neddy a curse for causing the death of his mother, but oh how he had grown to love him!

A beautiful butterfly alighted on a nearby bush. As Ned gazed at it he heard again Neddy's delighted cry of "buff-eye." The recollection suddenly overwhelmed him, and his body was racked by an onslaught of sobbing. As he recovered from it, the words of Will's Constance in *King John* came to his mind, "Grief fills the room up of my absent child," and he remembered how Will had stolen out of the theatre not to hear them after the death of Hamnet and how little he, Ned, had felt his sorrow at the time. Now he knew. Then Ben Jonson had lost his only son, and Augustine Phillips. It was natural for sons to lose their fathers, but not fathers their sons.

Ned felt a strong need to visit the church where the body of his son lay. Perhaps it was folly to return to London in time of plague, but feelings were stronger than reason. And he also knew that he would not carry out his impulsive threat to tell the family about Neddy; his private life was not theirs to share. The disclosure would pain his mother, though he believed that she would be more upset by the death of Neddy than by his illegitimacy.

His mind made up, he got up from the ground on which he had been sitting, and set out to tell Will and Lawrence of his decisions, and to settle with them the story that was to be told to the family.

By good fortune, Ned chanced on Will and Lawrence as he crossed the Clopton Bridge. They had decided to take a walk so that the visitor could see something of Stratford. They had already been to the church and were walking by the river before turning left up the Causey to go to the Henley Street home.

The three men now found a convenient place and sat on the river bank. Ned began by telling them that he had decided to return to London with Lawrence, "at least for a short while."

Lawrence said, "I want to leave on Monday morning."

"The sooner the better," said Ned. Then, without referring to his change of mind, he said, "We must decide on a story to tell the family, and it must concern me more than Will, for it was I who was upset and am returning to London. Have you thought of anything yet?"

"No," said Will. "We were waiting to know your decision. Tom and John will be home for supper, so we must have our story pat by then. Will you come too, Ned?"

"No; I will stay with Mother and try to prepare her for my leaving. But I must tell the same tale to the Harts and Richard as you tell at New Place."

"I think I have it," said Lawrence. "We will say that Ned has been offered a post at court, as other players have, which would involve his ceasing to be a player, and this he will not do in spite of pleas from Will and me; it was our words that made him angry. But he has to come back to London to explain his position."

There was a moment's silence while they watched the swans on the river, then Ned said, "All this making up of tales is so far from Neddy; it somehow seems false to him."

Will said, "Think of it rather as protecting him. I was just thinking of Neddy too, and regretting that I had never seen him. I think of him as looking like my Hamnet."

"They say he looked like me, especially when he smiled."

"Alas! I never saw him smile," Lawrence said, "for he was already sick unto death when I saw him, but I could still see a resemblance to you, Ned. You two have both begotten sons and lost them. I have been barren. In some ways it is a worse fate."

Each was rapt in his own sad musings. It was Will who roused them by saying, "Let us go."

They found the Henley Street house in distress. Mary was whimpering in the chair; she had been scolded by Joan who had caught her with a sharp knife in a dangerous attempt to cut up some meat for stew. Ned was able to comfort her, though she did not know him. Will told Richard that Ned would be returning to London on Monday with Master Fletcher; he would leave it to Ned to explain the reason.

"Will he return soon?" asked Richard. "Our mother will miss him."

"Ned knows that," said Will, "and he will be troubled at leaving her. I beg you not to stress it to him. She must get used to being without him again, for his life lies in London, not here."

When Will informed the supper table at New Place of Ned's leaving, the vague terms in which he had couched the agreed explanation had satisfied all but Judith, and had indeed transformed their estimate of Ned, both because he had been sought for to serve the King and because he had the temerity to refuse the call.

After the supper, Will took Judith aside and told her that her Uncle Ned would like to walk with her the following afternoon. Judith was both flattered and intrigued by the tone of her father's voice, which suggested that there were things her uncle would tell her that could not be told to the rest of the family.

AFTER THE SUNDAY DINNER NED SET OUT TOWARD THE RIVER WITH JUDITH, who jolted him into awareness of the purpose of their walk by saying, "I don't believe that story about the King's service. Master Fletcher brought you bad news, and it was news that could not be trusted to a letter."

Ned felt himself put on his mettle to maintain the fiction. "You must not tell anyone what I am about to tell you. Master Fletcher brought me a message from Sir John Barnet. He is high in the secret service of the King. I met him over six years ago, at the time of the rebellion of the Earl of Essex. He wants me to leave the King's Men and join him on some secret mission. The rewards are high, but 'tis against my nature and I will not do it."

"But why were you so sad when you came to the house? I knew 'twas not because of Grandmother. You looked as if somebody you loved had died."

"You are right, Judith. Somebody had died, somebody very close to me. The plague had taken him." Judith could not doubt the truth of what Ned was now saying. As Ned relived his grief, they walked on without speaking. Then, feeling a traitor to his sorrow, he used it to quell Judith's doubts. "It was he whose place Sir John Barnet wanted me to take."

For a moment Judith said nothing and, when she spoke, it was to change the subject. "Master Fletcher. Is he married?"

"No," said Ned, unable to hide a slight embarrassment.

"Why not? Is he like Uncle Gilbert?"

The baldness of the question unbalanced Ned. "I know little about Master Fletcher except as a sharer in the King's Men. Not every man marries. I am not married, or your Uncle Richard."

"Uncle Richard puzzles me; I have never seen him even walking with a woman. But you are different; you will get married. Have you ever loved a woman, Ned?"

Relieved to be able to speak honestly again for a moment, Ned said, "Yes, twice. One was beyond me and married a nobleman, and the other died."

"Of the plague?"

"Yes," said Ned, forced to lie again, and again covering his discomfort by changing the subject to Judith. "And you? Will you marry?"

"I suppose so," said Judith without enthusiasm. " 'Tis a maid's destiny. I sometimes wish I could be like Queen Elizabeth who died a virgin, but she was a queen, and what was accounted virtue in her in London would be accounted a scorn to me here in Stratford."

When they got back to New Place, Ned went straight up to Will's room. He was amused to catch a slight flurry of papers; the interrupter might have been one who disapproved of the reading of a play at any time but particularly on a Sunday.

Ned apologized for spoiling the reading of *Antony and Cleopatra*, but Will and Lawrence assured him that they were glad to see him, Will only asking that he might finish the scene; the reading could be resumed after supper. But Lawrence said, " 'Tis a measure of my regard for you, Ned, that I can brook your calling pause in the reading of his magnificent play; Will has never written better."

Will set the manuscript aside at the point where Caesar was consoling his wronged sister. The last words of the scene were "My dear'st sister." Having said them, Will turned to Ned and said, "And now, my dear'st brother, we must talk about where we shall live in London. Old Chris Mountjoy has seen the last of you, and me too. We can tell him we must live nearer the Globe, for that is where I would find my rooms now. I thought you might look for a good place when you get back. The plague should make one easier to find, and cheaper. If you decide to stay in London, you could use it until I come."

"And until you find it, I should be happy if you would stay with me," said Lawrence.

" 'Tis good and considerate of you both," said Ned. "I accept your kindness and I thank you, but when the players return, I shall find a place of my own again."

"So be it," said Will. "And now about our mother. I think it would be better if you stole away tomorrow without seeing her. If she were in her right mind, your leave-taking would but grieve her, and if she were as she now is, it would grieve you."

And so it was decided. Lawrence said he had come by way of Aylesbury and Banbury, and the inns had been good, especially the King's Head at Aylesbury. Ned had never traveled by that route, and readily agreed to travel the new way because it would avoid Master Davenant's questions to account for his returning to London in time of plague.

FIFTY-TWO

IT WAS STILL DARK WHEN NED AWOKE THE NEXT MORNING, BUT AS HE came downstairs he heard Richard's quiet voice. He was talking to their mother, trying to persuade her to go back to bed. Again she had got up in the dark and come downstairs to busy herself dangerously in preparing for a day that was long since past. Mary was proving obstinate. Richard could not persuade her that it was still the middle of the night. As Ned appeared she said with the triumphant logic of a child, "If 'tis still night, why is he up and dressed?" "He" was no longer her best beloved son, but a stranger pounced upon to win an argument.

"Tell her, Ned," said Richard.

Ned said, "Richard is right, Mother. 'Tis night. I was just going to undress to go to bed when I heard you downstairs and came down to see what 'twas."

Completely baffled, Mary allowed Richard to lead her toward the stairs. She stopped and turned to Ned. She looked at him with a worried questioning. "Ned?" He came to her eagerly and said "Yes, Mother." He longed for a last moment of recognition, and, as if to help her to see him, there was the first hint of the coming light of dawn. But with a slow and sad shake of the head she turned and began, with Richard's help, to climb the stairs.

Ned was deeply hurt by his mother's inability to know him in this unexpected moment of farewell, and he wanted to get away from the house as quickly as possible. He gathered up his baggage and hurried to the stable. But before he could get away, Richard came out to him.

"Were you going away without a word?" asked Richard.

"I'm sorry, Richard. I wish I could have got away without seeing Mother like that again."

The sky was lighter; the first rays of sunlight would soon appear. Ned said, "I must away." He grasped his brother's hand and arm. "Thank you, Richard."

Somewhat embarrassed, Richard said, "I merit no thanks. I am but what I am."

Ned smiled and said, "It is for that I thank you."

Although he was early at New Place, Anne, Will, and Lawrence were waiting for him. Anne had insisted on preparing a breakfast which was more like a dinner, so that they could get to Banbury with ease before nightfall.

She was cheerful because Will was not leaving, and by tacit agreement the others made no mention of his doing so later. Anne's insistent hospitality delayed them, and before they were allowed to get up from the breakfast table all the other members of the household, including little Anne Greene, were downstairs. Everybody was made to partake of the lavish breakfast, and there were the inevitable jokes about "crumbs from the rich man's table" and "the horses will not be able to carry the extra burden."

But at last Lawrence and Ned were in the saddle. Will remained outside for final words with them, and Lawrence was now free to express once more his enthusiasm for *Antony and Cleopatra*. He begged Will to anticipate the players' return to London that he might be there to welcome them home with this "rich gift." As the horses moved out into the street, Will called out, "Find a good home for us, Ned."

It was a bright morning with promise of a warm day, and people were already astir in the streets. Ned was quiet, and Lawrence, assuming that the journey to London was bringing back thoughts of Neddy, did not obtrude upon his silence. After a time, Ned, wanting to avoid questions and yet to appear sociable, said "Tell me about Banbury, Lawrence."

"My chief impression was that the food was good there: excellent ale and cheeses and cakes. 'Tis a Puritan stronghold, and they tend to like good food, though simple. Five years ago, while the old Queen was still on the throne, they destroyed the famous cross in the market square, saying it was a sign of popish superstition. I am surprised your Stratford did not follow the example. If the Puritans had their way, they would destroy all players too. 'Twill be a sad day for us if the country is ever ruled by one of their persuasion."

Lawrence knew that Ned had heard *Antony and Cleopatra* and so they could share their enthusiasm for the play; it was going to be hard to remain mum about it in London until the sharers had heard it. Will had also told Lawrence about his plan to make Ned a sharer at the first opportunity. Lawrence now reported that his first reaction had been "Why not now? Four years ago the number of sharers jumped from eight to twelve. Why not a thirteenth?"

"That would make me the Judas of the company," said Ned lightly, though he himself had wondered why he could not be the thirteenth.

"If there were a chance, Will would press for it, and so would I."

"And John Lowin," added Ned.

"But Will told me that the older sharers are already complaining about the number. They would not speak to me about it because I am one of the newcomers. As soon as a share is available, they want to buy it and reduce the number. John Heminge and Henry Condell, with their growing families, would like it back to eight again. When Will told me that, I felt guilty. I don't even earn my share by playing."

"If you never did any more for them—and you will—you have earned your share, and they know it."

"But perhaps I should play again."

"And risk your reputation and standing both with the company and the King?" quipped Ned, and with a laugh he spurred his horse away to forestall a rejoinder.

They took but a brief rest at midday, chiefly for the sake of the horses, and arrived in Banbury around four o'clock. They had no difficulty in securing a comfortable room to themselves at an inn, and as they disposed their baggage, an awkward silence occurred between them, occasioned by the confrontation with the bed.

It was Lawrence who first spoke, and with a sad lightness. "At last we are going to spend a night together, but I will not embarrass you as did the King; I could not bear the rejection. Besides, I prize your friendship, Ned. But we had better not share a bed; such a temptation would give me a sleepless night, and 'tis a long ride to Aylesbury tomorrow. Let's see if there is a truckle bed." He looked under the four-poster and pulled out the single low bed. "Now which of us shall sleep in this?"

"I will, of course," said Ned, overwhelmed by Lawrence's solution of their dilemma.

"No, no," said Lawrence. " 'Tis my base desires which make the truckle bed necessary, so I should sleep in it."

Ned spluttered in protest and Lawrence laughed and said, "Then we shall toss a coin for the lowly privilege. 'Twill be most fitting, for this is an age of gambling."

To his great joy Ned won the toss. He had a longing to express his gratitude to Lawrence but was tongue-tied; all he managed was "Oh, Lawrence."

"Enough. 'Tis settled now between us. There will come many a time when I shall feel regret, but at the moment I feel relief. Come; let us see Banbury and then eat a supper to celebrate our friendship."

They were away early the next day, because the long ride to Aylesbury lay ahead. They stopped for dinner at Bicester, where they talked little and listened much, chiefly to the garrulous host, whose subject was how good things had been in the days of the old Queen and how bad they had become since her death. There were only three other travelers having dinner. One was a young man of good breeding, possibly a student at one of the Inns of Court. The other two were a substantial lady, painted and bewigged to hide the ravages of time, and her serving man who accompanied her for protection, though she seemed formidable enough to need none. She alone of the five at the table occasionally interrupted the host's disquisition with a commendatory response, though when he referred to the days before the Armada she kept a discreet silence, as though she had not been born then. Although her ears and words had been given to the host, with an exaggerated air of patronage, her eyes had been summing up the three gentlemen at the table.

Lawrence and Ned were the first to arise and, as they did so, the lady spoke to them. "You must pardon me, gentlemen—for such I perceive you to be—which way do you travel?"

"To London, ma'am," said Lawrence.

"But for tonight?"

"Aylesbury."

"I too, and 'tis a goodly ride. Moreover, I am given to understand that there may be highwaymen on the way. My man here is a doughty defender, but if we traveled together there would be less likelihood of an attack. What say you?"

Lawrence and Ned had no desire for her company on the road, for her pace was like to be very slow, and they had no great fear of highwaymen for they both wore swords and could handle them well. Lawrence said, "Your company would pleasure us, ma'am, but we are in great haste; you will note that we ate but little dinner and you have scarce started." Indicating the lone traveler, he added, "If this young gentleman is going your way, I am sure he would be glad to accompany you." Without waiting to know the outcome of the suggestion, they bowed and left.

As they mounted their horses and rode away, they speculated that the painted old lady was probably the wealthy proprietress of a brothel and gaming house. They differed as to the reasons for her journey: Lawrence decided that she was returning from an expedition in search of country fillies for her city stables, while Ned thought she had been visiting a son or daughter, who had been richly nurtured by her illicit earnings but carefully sheltered from their source.

They got to Aylesbury without untoward incident and with more than an hour of light left and were given a room at the King's Head Hotel. It was fairly full with travelers from London, a sign that the plague was increasing, but the weekly death rate was reported to be still well under a hundred.

As they sat at supper, Lawrence and Ned were amazed to see the arrival of the trio from Bicester. They had been certain the old lady would have traveled too slowly to complete the journey by evening, especially since she had obviously intended to enjoy a full and leisurely dinner. As soon as she saw Lawrence and Ned, she gave instructions to her man to see to her room and her baggage, and she sailed across the room to them with the young traveler now in tow, exclaiming as she arrived, "I am so happy to see you again, for now I know you." Her voice and appearance were such as to silence the room; there were ten diners scattered at two long tables and seated on benches. Lawrence and Ned said nothing, completely taken by surprise and awaiting her further disclosure, but instead she said, "But my secret will keep until I join you at supper. I must first wash off the dust of travel. This is Simon Frisby, a student at the Middle Temple and a very pleasant traveling companion, who has graciously agreed that my man may use the truckle bed in his room tonight. Come, Simon." And away she sailed like a great galleon.

Her disappearance was followed by some titters in the room, and Lawrence was irritated because they seemed to be partly at his expense. He was eager to finish the meal and go to their room before the Gorgon came back, but Ned was amused by her and wanted to find out what she knew and how she knew it. Simon soon joined them, but his enthusiastic accounts of the extraordinary old lady proved too much for Lawrence. He begged to be excused and left the table.

Simon told Ned that not the least of the wonders of "Mistress Mountjoy" was her horsemanship. He had found it hard to keep up with her. He had also been impressed by the strength and devotion of her man, Tim. He was a mute, who had been a sailor, had been captured by the Spaniards in the Indies, and had had his tongue cut out before he could escape. Ned recalled something coarse about his way of eating but had ascribed it to ill manners. Tim had been in Mistress Mountjoy's service for ten years. As they were talking about him, this fearsome creature joined them. He was still only thirty-five years old, and his plain but well-made clothes did not disguise his elemental power, but his manner was quiet and diffident. He smiled at Ned when he was introduced, but his eyes assessed him deeply, as a watchdog might a second-time visitor.

Both Simon and Tim waited to begin supper until Mistress Mountjoy arrived. Her entrance drew all eyes to her. The three men awaiting her stood, and, as if magnetized, so did all the other men in the room. She had a raddled magnificence, as though she were impersonating Queen Elizabeth without having the taste or the wealth to do so properly. When she spoke, she cared not who heard her, and most strained to do so.

As she sat, she said, "Where is Master Fletcher?" Ned was taken aback that she knew the name, and, before he could make some excuse, she said, "It matters not. I am glad he is not here, else we should have been thirteen." Everybody who heard her quickly confirmed her arithmetic. She had seated herself next to Ned and across from Tim. "I am sure, Master Shakespeare, that Simon has told you about Tim, the most fortunate find of my life." And she beamed at her man. "But I see you are drinking ale. No more. We must have wine."

She had clearly given orders that the newcomers were not to have the ordinary supper, for a variety of dishes began to appear, so appetizing that Ned regretted that he had already eaten. He was happy to have some wine and he gallantly toasted the lady with the first goblet, standing to do so; her very presence called for the theatrical. "To Mistress Mountjoy, a goodess among women, for she has more than mortal knowledge."

The old lady loved the tribute and laughed uproariously at the quip. She said, as they settled down to the meal, "So you think my knowledge of your names is more than mortal. 'Tis but my memory, Master Ned, for that is what I shall call you. In return you can call me Mistress Sophie, for so do all my friends—and all my enemies too, and sometimes I do not know which is which. I have often seen you at the Globe, and always with pleasure."

"But Master Fletcher? He does not play."

"I was there that afternoon when the Lord Chamberlain's Men became the King's Men, and when Master Fletcher read his own name out first, I wondered and wondered, and asked and asked, and found out much." Her old eyes wrinkled with cunning as she looked straight at Ned.

"But that was four years ago."

"In my life I have learnt to benefit by remembering a man's name and face." Again her eyes suggested layers of meaning beneath her words. "I have learnt to make quick judgments too, and I have rarely been wrong. Take Tim here. Ten years ago he took a dagger to me to rob me. I looked at him and said, ' 'Twill pay you better to protect me.' "

Tim smiled in embarrassment as he heard the story.

"But how did you find out his history? He could not tell you himself."

"Nor can he read and write. But when I want to find out something, I have my ways. In Tim's case it was easy; at that time he had a woman, but she is long since gone; she was not worthy of Tim. He had met her in a tavern and she had heard his story from one of his shipmates."

"Mistress Mountjoy," Ned began but she laid her hand on his arm and said, "Nay, 'tis Sophie to you, but let me whisper, Mountjoy is not my true name. 'Tis so long since I have heard my true name that I have forgotten it myself." This caused her to laugh so infectiously that everybody in the room smiled though only Ned had heard the whispered joke.

"Then, Sophie, I must leave you now."

"Nay, Ned. Let Master Fletcher cool his heels. I knew he would not wait for me and that you would. I'll be sworn he hurried his supper to avoid me."

Ned's look of amazement showed that she had been right, and again her laughter filled the room. When it had subsided enough to allow her to speak, she said, "Sing to us, Ned, as sauce for our supper."

"I have no lute."

"The inn will have one."

"But 'twill be ill tuned, and it takes time to tune a lute."

"Then sing without one, as the lark does." Before Ned could demur further, she addressed the room. "This gentleman here is a minstrel beyond compare. I would have him sing for us. What say you?"

The starved performer in Ned reacted to the call to sing as a hungry boy to the call to eat. He stood up, moved to a good position, and gave them song after song to increasing applause. In the middle of the fifth song, Lawrence appeared. Ned was immediately aware of him, and his awareness made Sophie turn to see him too. Ned continued his song but with somewhat less vitality for even as he sang he wondered why Lawrence had come.

As Ned ended the song, Lawrence clapped and called, "More, prithee, more," but Ned sensed a sarcastic edge to the request, and hesitated to comply with it. But Sophie said, "You hear Master Fletcher, Ned. He speaks for all of us. Come, one last song."

Lawrence moved to take Ned's end seat on the bench, next to Sophie, bowing to her graciously before he sat. He was resentfully certain that Ned had told her his name.

Ned had already sung "Who is Sylvia?" but he ended by singing it again, and, as much in defiance of Lawrence as praise of Sophie, the song became "Who is Sophie?" The room was delighted, all but Lawrence, who smiled and bowed to Sophie with acid, which was not lost on the lady, though she seemed amused by it.

At the end of the song Ned approached the table to most warming applause, and none was more vigorous than that of Lawrence, determined to cover the nakedness he knew he had revealed to Sophie. He stood up and said, "That was delightful, Ned. But come; 'tis time for bed. We must make a very early start in the morning."

Sophie said, "No matter how early, 'twill be dark before you get home. 'Tis too long for a day's ride, except with fresh and unburdened horses."

"The morrow will tell us that," said Lawrence, "and now I bid you goodnight, ma'am."

"My name is Sophia Mountjoy, Master Fletcher."

"Then goodnight, Mistress Mountjoy." Lawrence bowed and walked away, but, as he did so, she called after him, " 'Twas not Master Shakespeare that told me your name."

The uncanny insight which must have prompted this parting shot caused Lawrence to stop for a second as though she had actually hit him with a thrown pebble. She was a witch, a dangerous witch.

Sophie turned to Ned. "Goodnight, Ned. Sleep well." She gave even that conventional wish a mischievous implication. "We shall meet again," and she obviously meant it.

Ned was baffled but intrigued. He said, "But how . . . ?"

"Don't ask me how, when, or where. But we shall meet again; I know that. Unless you do not wish to see me again."

"But I do," protested Ned, and he meant it too. "Where do you live?"

"In sundry places at sundry times," she said with twinkling evasion. "Fear not; we shall find each other again."

Ned was most reluctant to leave this fascinating creature, but he bade goodnight to Simon and Tim. As a last gesture Sophie held out her beringed and food-greasy hand for him to kiss. He did it with consummate courtesy, thinking she is indeed a queen; Hecate, queen of the witches, but lovable.

As Ned entered the room, Lawrence, who was almost ready to get into bed, looked at him for a moment. Neither said a word. Even after they were in their beds, the silence continued. At last Ned said, "Goodnight," and received a cold "goodnight" in return. Ned was asleep long before Lawrence.

Ned was amazed to be awakened by warm sunshine. Lawrence was asleep. Ned called to him, and Lawrence jumped into full awareness when he realized how late it was. He said, without measuring the effect of his words on Ned, "Damn that witch. She put a spell on me to keep me asleep so that her prophecy would be proved true. But she shall not win. We'll get home, no matter how late the hour."

Ned thought it wiser to say nothing. They hurriedly dressed and packed. Finally Lawrence, in a placatory voice, said, "Can you do without breakfast?"

"Yes, and without dinner and supper too, if need be. But I ate much more last night than you did."

Lawrence did not reply, but just as they were about to leave the room he put his hand on Ned's arm and said, "I'm sorry that I allowed that painted old harridan to upset me. 'Tis over now, and we shall not see her again."

Ned smiled and said, "Come. Let us waste no more time."

Before they left the inn, Ned found out that Sophie, Tim, and Simon had already left—more than an hour ago. Remembering how fast a pace Sophie set, he did not think they would overtake the trio.

They pushed the horses too hard, especially in the August heat, and after two hours they began to falter and had to be rested by a stream, where they could drink and crop the grass, but they could not be allowed to indulge themselves to their stomachs' content or the most that could be got out of them would be a slow walk.

Ned sat on the bank of the stream in the shade of a tree, but Lawrence paced restlessly. Ned looked up at him questioningly, causing him to say, " 'Tis such a waste of good time. We could be eating too, and I must confess to hunger now. I believe 'tis not far to King's Langley, and we can have a quick dinner there and perhaps let the horses have a few oats."

"Would it matter much if we stayed the night at an inn?"

"I am stubborn, Ned. I cannot let Mistress Mountjoy win. Does that surprise you?"

"It puzzles me."

"It puzzles me too, but so it is."

At King's Langley where they stopped for dinner Ned found opportunity to inquire discreetly about the trio. Yes, they had stopped at that very tavern, but had left more than an hour before.

As they rode on into the evening, going ever more slowly, it became clear that they would not get to the City before dark, and that was dangerous. Ned began to be irritated by Lawrence's unreasonable stubbornness so that when he was told "I think we should press on without supper," he said, "You press on, Lawrence. I have a mind to stay the night at the first inn we come to."

"You are bewitched; I knew it," was Lawrence's angry comment.

But before they came to an inn they approached a horseman who waited at the side of the road. The light had begun to fade and the statuesque figure seemed menacing.

Ned was the first to recognize the waiting man, and he cried out happily, "Tim!" and urged his horse forward. By the time Lawrence had come up to them, Ned was reading a message that Tim had handed to him; there was still light enough to see it, and Sophie had written in a large hand as if to allow for the fading light. In his own excitement Ned did not think of the effect his words would have as he said, "Sophie has a house nearby. She invites us for the night."

By way of reply, Lawrence angrily spurred his reluctant horse into a gallop. For a fleeting moment Ned wanted to ride after him and forget about Sophie—he had an obscure feeling that this was a crisis in his relationship with Lawrence—but his independence determined him to accept Sophie's invitation; Lawrence was being very unreasonable and subsequently might acknowledge this and all would be well between them again. He told Tim to lead the way. Tim nodded his head happily and smiled; his mistress had foretold that only the young man would return with him.

Near where Tim had waited there was a path hidden by trees. About half a mile in from the road they came to a new brick-and-stone building, about the size of New Place but enclosed by a high wall. The entrance to the yard, which contained a fish pond and beds of flowers, was guarded by two heavy doors, one of which now stood open. A stable boy was in attendance to close and bolt it as soon as the horses were inside.

Sophie was standing at the top of the five semi-circular steps to the open front door. She was dressed in a loose silk gown, caught in at the wrists to hide her aged arms. Her neck was also hidden by a high collar, studded with jewels which caught the rays of the setting sun as did the pearls which trimmed her gown. She wore a high-piled red wig, in which more jewels glittered. Again Ned thought of Queen Elizabeth as she might be imitated by a courtesan.

Ned dismounted, leaving his horse and baggage to the care of Tim. Sophie said, "Welcome to my country home; I knew you would come."

"And that Lawrence would not?" ventured Ned with a smile.

For answer Sophie laughed and extended her hand. "Come in," she said. "Simon and I have finished our supper. Yes, he is here too, but you will not have to share a bed with him, or with me. There are rooms aplenty, and all of them empty for the nonce. Are you hungry?"

"Famished."

"I expected so."

Simon greeted Ned effusively and was garrulous in praise of Sophie's hospitality. "I cannot think why she would be so gracious and lavish to two strangers."

Sophie smiled and said, "Master Fletcher would tell you that it was for some nefarious purpose."

"And is it?" challenged Ned jokingly.

"Time will tell," replied Sophie laughing. "Now let us eat, drink, and be merry, for tomorrow—tomorrow you go to London and its plague."

"You will stay here?" asked Ned.

"Until I know how bad the plague is going to be."

"You know so much. Do you not know that?" questioned Ned, half seriously.

" 'Tis only man and his ways I know. The ways of God pass my understanding."

"And the ways of the Devil? Know you those?"

"Man has taught me those."

The supper was lavish and the wine pleasant and plentiful. It was served by two maids, neither of them beautiful or young; Ned would have expected handsome young men. Although she had already eaten, Sophie amazed Ned by sampling most of the dishes again. His astonishment must have been apparent, for Sophie said, "I like eating. My body has brought me most of my pleasures, and now that the only one left is food and drink, I make the most of it."

Simon did not eat again, but he did drink, and he was soon in a state in which even he was incapable of speech. Sophie asked one of the maids to fetch Tim, whom she ordered to carry Master Frisby to bed. He did so literally, and with ease.

"At last we are alone," Sophie said mischievously.

"And I am glad of it," replied Ned gallantly and truthfully.

"Let us go to the music room, not that I want you to make music but so that Joan and Nellie can clear away and go to bed. They are good women who have served me well."

The music room was richly furnished with woven mats on the floor, a large tapestry opposite the window wall depicting a delectably naked Susanna spied on by some lascivious elders, a brocade couch, two large chairs, and a number of cushioned stools. There were several small tables on each of which was a lighted and perfumed candle.

As she sat down on the couch, Sophie indicated that Ned should sit by her. She offered him a dish of marchpane and other comfits, and chose one herself with almost childish glee, for it was an especial pleasure to eat something that melted in the mouth. She had long lost all her teeth but her gums rendered her yeoman service, and what she couldn't bite she swallowed, trusting her iron stomach to deal with it.

She said, "Simon was good enough company until better came along. You caught my eye and my ear long ago. But tell me, why do you return to London now, with the Globe closed and the plague at large?"

"I have my reasons," said Ned, making it plain that Sophie should probe no further.

"I shall wait until you want to speak, and that time will come. But tell me this: what mean you to do until the players return? I ask because if you need to earn money, I may be able to help you—and help myself at the same time."

"How?"

Instead of replying, Sophie seemed to ignore the question. She said, "Tell me, Ned, what think you of me? And I do not ask for idle praise. Who and what am I?"

"A wonderful woman, and wealthy."

"Is it my wealth that brings you here tonight?"

"No," Ned protested vehemently.

"And whence comes my wealth?"

"I know not. It does not concern me."

"You speak not sooth, Ned. Ever since you saw me, you have wondered, and I now reveal to you that your basest thoughts of me, which you blush to disclose, are true." Here she gave vent to a deep chuckle to which Ned responded with an embarrassed smile. "I keep a fine house for gaming gentlemen. Yes, I will admit none but gentlemen; if they have a title, so much the better. But I give not a fig for these new titles that the King bestows to gain money for such as Master Robert Carr. That handsome lad will come to a bad end, for none can resist the poison of sudden and undeserved favor."

"The games you provide are cards and dice?"

"Ladies too, for that is the oldest game."

"And the biggest gamble."

"You speak of the pox. 'Tis worse than the plague in my business. But I do my best to keep the ladies clean of it, and once 'tis found in man or maid, the door is closed to them until I am assured they are cleansed."

"But where is the place for me to earn money? I hope not you think of me as a male whore."

"Nay, Ned," said Sophie, genuinely shocked. "I have not such doings in my house. Nor do I think you would be party to them, though they are much in the fashion of the new day. I would have you sing in my house every evening, and will pay you more than you get at the Globe. You could still play there in the afternoons. What say you?"

Ned didn't know what to say; he floundered. "But where would I sing? The gamesters would not listen to me; nor do I think I would be welcomed in the bedroom."

Sophie laughed. "I see you know not my house. There is a large room where the gentlemen and ladies meet, and there they drink wine together and talk. My ladies give more than the companionship of their bodies. Some of them are skilled in foreign tongues and are much sought after by the noble ambassadors who come to the court. In that room—it is already called the Music Room as if it were waiting for you—you will have a better audience than you have ever known."

"Why is it called the Music Room, if no one sings there?"

"Sometimes a courtly gentleman likes to sing to his lady, for sometimes she becomes his lady in all but name, for he returns to her again and again."

"Sophie, I thank you and will be happy to do what you ask. Where is it and when do I start?"

"Not so fast; doubt should not so quickly turn to eagerness. What will Master Fletcher say?"

"I care not. He is my friend, and no more."

"But a good friend, I think, and they are rare."

"I shall be earning a living by singing, and to noble folk too. What harm is in that?"

"I think Master Fletcher will find some; he likes not me. But to answer you. My house is on the river between Queen Hythe and the Bridge. You may have noticed it. There is a lawn, between ivy-covered walls, that slopes to the river where there is a landing for boats. Many gentlemen come by way of the river."

"I know the place," said Ned with excited recognition.

"This is Wednesday. Come and join me for dinner there at noon on Saturday. By that time I shall better know my plans. August is a bad month, with the King away hunting; soon there will not be a deer or a hare left in the land. Far better if they hunted foxes that kill the chickens, but 'tis part of a gentleman to hunt only what is good to eat. A pox on such gentility! But no King, no court; and only the younger sons of younger sons left in London, all name and no money. There's the plague too. Yes, August is a bad month."

"Then is the house closed?"

"No; there are always some gentlemen who remain, and there are others who fill the breach, poor in name but rich in pocket." Suddenly the indecent significance of her metaphor struck her and she laughed uproariously as she repeated it. "Fill the breach. Fill the breach." When she had recovered, she continued. "When the King comes to Hampton Court in September, and to Whitehall in October, the merchants will have to go elsewhere for their pleasure; then will be seen in my house none but noblemen and ambassadors—and a handsome minstrel."

"Your name, Sophie. Why did you choose such an unlikely one as Mountjoy?"

"Unlikely, forsooth!" retorted Sophie, bridling. "And choose! 'Tis mine by right, if not by law. The knave who owed it to me wouldn't give it, so I took it. I have just returned from a journey to his grave. I used to go there to spit on it; now I go there to laugh, for he is dead and I am alive, and there is no greater difference than that."

" 'Tis much to take such trouble for a laugh."

Sophie looked at him hard for a moment, and then her tough face sagged into an aged sadness. "I go not just to visit his grave. I go to see my daughter. She is blind and has an infirmity of the mind too, but she is dear to me and is well cared for, and she will be so cared for after I am gone."

Ned was deeply moved, not least because it was the first time in their conversation that this old woman had ever shown that she thought of death. Now that her defenses had crumbled at remembrance of her daughter, she suddenly looked pathetically old. He wished she would cry—he was near to tears himself—but instead her face gradually firmed again and she smiled, as she said, "You are privileged, young man, to know so much, but I know my secret is safe with you."

Wanting somehow to express a sympathy and equal trust, Ned was impelled to tell her about Marie and Neddy, and the tears which would not flow for her own sorrow soon flowed for Ned's. Again she fought back to a smile, as she used her sleeve to dry her eyes, and she said, "I told you you would tell me why you returned to London now."

"I'm glad I did," said Ned.

"This Marie of yours. I knew about her, though she was out of my welkin. She did right not to marry you, Ned. And for Neddy, remember the happy hours you had together, and know that they would not have lasted. And now to bed. Tim is waiting outside to show you the way. I shall not see you in the morning. After a long journey, I spend a day in bed; my old bones need it. But I shall see you at dinner on Saturday. Goodnight, Ned." She extended her hand to him as if to tell him that their relationship was now restored to one of pleasant companionship, their secret selves again safely in custody.

Ned kissed the hand with a new warmth. "Goodnight, Mistress Mount-joy, and tell Sophie that I am bound to her with hoops of steel."

"That's from one of your brother's plays; I remember the phrase."

"Yes, they are his words but my feelings." Ned turned to go, but stopped and turned. "One last thing. This Mountjoy. Did he owe you his name as a father or as a husband?"

Sophie was her old self again as she replied, "You want to know too much, young man," and she wafted him away with her hand as she chose a last piece of marchpane.

Ned went out of the room laughing and was greeted with a smile by the waiting Tim who now strongly approved of this young man because he made his mistress happy. He led the way to a richly appointed bedroom which contained a massive four-poster. Ned must ask Sophie who used it, but as the question formed in his mind he heard her comically imperious voice saying again "You want to know too much, young man." He was still smiling as he fell easily asleep.

FIFTY-THREE

THERE WAS NO NEED FOR AN EARLY START IN THE MORNING, AND NED indulged himself by staying in the comfortable bed an hour after waking. His reluctance to get up was partly caused by a wish to postpone what would inevitably be an awkward if not unpleasant meeting with Lawrence. He would cut it short by saying that he wanted to go to Neddy's grave and to see Rachel.

He had a leisurely wash in perfumed water before dressing himself and going down to an excellent breakfast. Simon had already left. Ned doubted that he would ever see him again, for he was fairly certain that Sophie had not given him an invitation to her London house. Ned's horse had been thoroughly groomed and looked better than when he had first set out from London, now more than a month ago.

It was just before noon that Ned arrived at Lawrence's house. As he dismounted and tethered his horse, he half hoped that Lawrence would not be in. He knocked at the door. He had to knock a second time before the door was opened by a genial, gray-haired, dumpy, little woman who must be Lawrence's "good widow." The fact that Lawrence had described her as not only good but godly had led Ned to expect a much more dour person. She was not at all surprised to see a handsome, young man at the door, and told him pleasantly that Master Fletcher was away in the country and had not yet returned.

"But he returned last night," said the puzzled Ned.

"No, he did not. Please give me your name and when he comes I will tell him that you called."

Automatically Ned replied "Edmund Shakespeare."

The housekeeper repeated the name to make certain she had it correctly, wished him good day, and closed the door.

Ned was perplexed and worried. Something must have happened to Lawrence. Even if he had been forced, after all, to spend the night somewhere, he should have been home by this time. Ned decided to postpone his plan to visit Rachel and the Church of St. Giles; first he must find Lawrence.

He was so near the Globe that he decided to go there first. Even if Lawrence were not there, he might have called earlier. But the theatre was locked fast and there was nobody inside. He decided to return to tell the housekeeper of the reason for his concern; he should have done so at first.

As he rode through the busy streets he kept his eyes open for signs of the plague, but saw only three houses with the fatal sign on the doors.

When the housekeeper answered the door to him again, she was surprised to see him back so soon and said, before he had time to question her, "He hasn't come back yet, Master Shakespeare."

Ned commended her silently for remembering his name. He said, "When I was here before, I should have told you, Mistress . . . what is your name?"

"Russet, sir, Russet. And I remembered your name as soon as you had gone, because Master Fletcher mentioned it when he asked me to prepare a special supper for you once."

"Well, Mistress Russet, it was I that Master Fletcher came to visit in the country. We set out on the return journey on Monday morning, and we traveled together until last night, when I stayed with a friend and he rode on alone. It was getting dark and now I fear some mishap."

Mistress Russet's immediate concern was shown by her saying, "Oh, come in, sir."

When they were seated inside, they agreed that somebody should stay in the house until Master Fletcher returned or some news of him came, but Mistress Russet would have to leave as usual around four o'clock, "for I have three children: two girls who go out to work and come home hungry for supper, and a boy of twelve who would get into mischief if I did not come home to keep him indoors."

Then Ned revealed that it had been arranged that he was to stay with Master Fletcher until he had found a place of his own, and he suggested that he should move in at once.

After a flicker of hesitation, Mistress Russet said, "I believe you are an honest man, Master Shakespeare, so let it be as you say."

"Thank you, Mistress Russet. I will bring in my luggage and stable my horse in the back."

"I will prepare your room for you, but there is no food in the house; it would all have spoilt in the summer heat."

"I will eat out; I know this district well."

The house was a small one. It had two stories, but was only one room wide and two deep. The room that was to be Ned's was in the back, overlooking the neat garden which contained some fruit trees and berry bushes. It was furnished more as a study than a bedroom, but there was a daybed which reminded Ned of the first night he had spent in London in George's house.

When horse and luggage were settled, Mistress Russet brought Ned some fruit from the garden, "to stay your stomach till supper." As he ate it they wondered afresh what could have happened. Mistress Russet was certain that all was well, but Ned wasn't. To comfort him, she said, "He is in God's hands." When he had previously heard this sentence, it had usually sounded to Ned like an invocation of doom, as though the deity were bent on destroying his creatures, but from the mouth of cheerful Mistress Russet it was a simple utterance of a reassuring fact.

Hunger took Ned out of the house for an early supper, but he did not linger over it. When he came back he wished he had taken more time, for there was no sign of Lawrence or a message. Now he had to face a lonely evening, just waiting. He remembered seeing some books in his room; one of those would pass the time. He climbed the stairs to examine them. As he had expected there was a goodly number of plays, some of them Will's, some books of poems, some of tales, books on courtly behavior such as he had seen at George's, and most notably, because they were the best bound, a set of books written by the King; Ned was surprised that he had written so many. He picked up one that had a bookmark sticking out of the top. The book had a Greek title which passed Ned's comprehension. Idly he turned to the page already marked and there his eye was caught by the word "sodomy" which the author listed among "horrible crimes." Why was the bookmark inserted at that page? Was it because it provided Lawrence with a ready disclaimer when the morals of the King were impugned? Ned found he was not deeply interested in finding answers to his questions, as he might once have been. He returned the book to its place and took instead Thomas Lodge's *Rosalynde;* it would be interesting to see how Will had used it for his *As You Like It.*

He took the book into the cool of the garden and settled down to read it in the remaining hour of light, but he could not concentrate and soon abandoned the attempt and went indoors again. He lit some candles before there was need. Time and again he opened the front door and looked up and down for sign of Lawrence. Before he went to bed he bolted the door so that he would have to be awakened to let anybody in.

Ned slept fitfully. Twice he came downstairs because he thought he had heard a knocking on the door, but it was Mistress Russet he had to unlock the door for the following morning. She had brought him some ale and bread and cheese, and there was still some fruit left from the night before. She said, "Now, Master Shakespeare, you must stop worriting. I can see you scarcely slept at all. It may well be that Master Fletcher won't come back for days, or even weeks. He may well have gone to join the King ahunting."

"He likes not hunting."

"Aye, but the King does, and there are many servants who do much against their grain to please the master."

But Lawrence returned that morning—stretched out in a cart, his head, left leg and shoulder all heavily damaged, his face unshaven and wan from loss of blood. His coming was heralded by a knock on the door by a pixielike old man whose energy of body and speech belied his years and whose stench proclaimed his trade: he was a pig-farmer. As happy as if he had won a great prize he said, "I've brought Master Fletcher home! But I'll need a hand to get him off my cart; my wife helped to put him on, but she is sturdier than you. Ah, there's a likely young man behind you. Come, sir, but you must be careful; he's still in pain. Those dastards nigh left him for dead."

At sight of Ned, Lawrence smiled feebly but said nothing. Ned was relieved by the smile; he took it for a sign of reconciliation. He and the pigman managed to unload Lawrence, though not without causing him pain, until he stood on his right leg with his right arm around Ned for support; he was unable to use his left arm. The little farmer danced behind them, never stopping giving advice, as Lawrence hopped into the house.

Mistress Russet had quickly sized up the situation and had readied a chair and stool with cushions to receive the injured man. As soon as he had been deposited, Lawrence said, though he was still suffering from pain caused by the movement, "Thank you, Master Gimble. I think you have saved my life, and 'twill not be forgotten. Ned, I have been robbed, but if you have a gold piece for Master Gimble for his pains I shall be bounden to you."

Ned hurried upstairs where he did have a few gold pieces and quickly returned with one. The pigman took it naturally, without effusive thanks or simulated reluctance. He merely said, "I thank you, sir," and resumed his interrupted conversation about pigs. "Yes, delicate creatures they are, delicate, and as likely to die without warning as to live. Pigs and children are the same; they make you wonder if the ones that live are worth the trouble of the ones that die."

Mistress Russet was pouring wine for the three men. As Master Gimble took his glass, he said, "Ah, wine! A rare drink for me. And in a glass too. Here's to your health, sir."

Ned raised his glass to Lawrence and said, "I thank God you are home safe."

Mistress Russet said, "Amen."

"And I thank God you are here to welcome me," said Lawrence, which made Ned very happy.

Ned went outside to see the little man off and to thank him again. When he returned, Lawrence told him to leave the door open, and, although it was mid-morning, Mistress Russet was lighting candles. Lawrence said, "A good, little man, but a stinking one. I reek of pigs, and it will be a while before I can change my clothes and bathe my body. I trust that the fresh air and the candles will sweeten the room."

Both Ned and Mistress Russet were obviously waiting to hear some account of what had happened, but Lawrence said, "My tale can wait. They brought a surgeon to me—it must have been yestermorning—but I doubt he was a good one. I have faith in Barber Sims. Fetch him, Ned. Tell him a broken crown and a broken leg are more urgent than the cutting of hair or the trimming of a beard."

The barber's shop was not far away, nor was he busy. Master Sims liked the patronage—because he liked their company—of players and courtiers, though most of the latter who came to him were smooth-tongued hangers-on who often paid him with witty words, salacious gossip, and specious promises rather than coin of the realm. Now that both players and court were in the country, the barber had to content himself with ordinary citizens who always paid but usually bored him. Nor had his routine been broken by calls on his surgical skill, except for the extraction of a few teeth most days.

After Ned had explained to the best of his limited knowledge what was wrong with Lawrence, the fat barber waddled around gathering up splints, bandages, instruments, and medications, all the while delivering a cheerful commentary on the dire results that might have befallen Master Fletcher if he had been kept from the ministrations of Master Sims a day longer.

When the barber saw his patient, he beamed at him as though it were a delightful occasion. "Well, Master Fletcher, 'tis good to see you again."

Lawrence said wryly, "I could wish the reason for the visit were other than it is."

"You were set upon by a highwayman, I think."

"Not one, Arthur; four."

"Then 'tis a wonder you are alive. But let me start with the head. A man can do without his arms, he can do without his legs, but without his head he is finished." He giggled gleefully at his wit as he unbandaged Lawrence's head, which he did with a deftness surprising in his podgy hands. Mistress Russet had prepared a bowl of warm water and some towels, knowing they would be wanted. Lawrence's head had been shaved in patches which were now dark blobs of coagulated blood. Arthur decided to investigate all the areas of damage before dealing with one. At sight of the uncovered head he said breezily, "It looks as if they meant to kill you; they knew not what a hard head you had." His solitary enjoyment of this joke lasted while he unbandaged the shoulder to reveal a large black-and-blue swelling. The surgical fingers probed deep, causing Lawrence to wince with pain, which prompted Arthur to say, "It takes pain to kill pain," a homemade quip of which he was particularly proud, and frequent use had not robbed him of its pleasure. Now it was the leg's turn. When it was disclosed, in addition to the discolored swelling it was apparent even to Ned's eye that the leg was misshapen. Triumphantly Arthur proclaimed: "I knew it! The bone is broken and some numskull fastened it without straightening it aright. You should have sent for me at once!"

Ned said, "But, Arthur, it happened miles away."

Arthur swept away this objection: "Trust those highwaymen. They know how to choose the right spot." Then he stood back a few paces as if to survey the field of his operations. Finally he gave forth his judgment with a ponderosity comically at odds with his usual vivacity. "Ye-es. I think we shall clean the head wounds first to see how deep they are. Then we shall anoint the shoulder and bandage it. Your shoulder was pulled out, but 'tis back in place, more by nature I dare swear than the blundering fingers of the surgeon who tended you. But then there's the leg, which we will have to straighten. I shall give you a potion to lessen the pain but, even so, I think we should get you upstairs before we work on the leg. With your right leg and Master Shakespeare's help I think we can manage it. There I must stand aside, for when I mount the stairs, there is room for no other." This quip at his own bulk restored his breeziness. As he washed the head wounds he kept up a running commentary, being particularly enthusiastic about one of the cleaned gashes. "A goodly blow indeed. Who dealt that had a strong arm. But it was a wooden weapon he used, else he would have cloven the skull." This last remark had an air of anticlimactic disappointment. "Now I'm going to hurt you," he said brightly. "Some bite their lips to blood, others swear and lash out, while still others swoon. Which will you do, Master Fletcher?"

"Time will tell," said Lawrence.

Arthur fetched a phial from his bag. "This will burn," he said as though bringing a Christmas gift.

Lawrence held out his right hand and grasped Ned's forearm tightly. Arthur carefully poured the liquid into the wounds, one after the other. With each dose of pain, Lawrence's body tensed and he squeezed Ned's arm, but he did not cry out. Arthur said, with reluctant admiration, "Such bearing of pain. 'Tis a wonder. I should have swooned at the first burn, and not felt the others. But not even you will bear the straightening of the leg," which anticipation compensated Arthur for his first disappointment.

When the head and shoulder were again bandaged, Lawrence took a glass of wine to fortify himself for the climbing of the stairs. Arthur accepted one too, saying that he always needed extra strength to climb a stairs; this he thought particularly funny, and it seemed not to matter to him that the others did not share his laughter.

With some difficulty and pain the transition to the bedroom was accomplished, and, while Lawrence rested, Arthur filled in the time with praise of the room's furnishings, which were sparse but rich. Then the pain-killer was administered, and during the minutes Arthur allowed for it to take its effect, he instructed Ned on the help he would need from him. Ordinarily the assistant's function would have been to take a firm grip under the patient's arms, but the injured shoulder made this impossible, and so Ned was to lie alongside Lawrence and encircle his lower chest with both arms, holding him tight against the pull of the leg.

All was ready. The fat fingers had carefully assessed the damage to the leg—both the tibia and the fibula were cracked but not severed—and Arthur had kept watch on Lawrence's reactions to the pressure of his touch, noting the progressive effect of the analgesic. With a nod to his assistant, Arthur pulled, and, in spite of the drug, Lawrence cried out. Mistress Russet stood by, muttering a prayer. After a further examination, Arthur felt another slight adjustment was necessary: another nod, another pull, another cry, another prayer. It was over, and all four were perspiring freely. With the help of Ned and Mistress Russet, Arthur quickly and firmly bandaged the leg to splints. Then he said that he was going to give Lawrence a potion which would put him to sleep for some hours.

Lawrence was exhausted but managed to thank all three, and was deeply reassured to learn that Ned would be staying in the next room. After the sleeping drug had been administered, the three went downstairs. Arthur was easily persuaded to take another glass of wine, and laughingly gave it as his opinion that it would be six weeks to two months before Master Fletcher would be able to get about, and then with the aid of a walking stick.

It was nearly noon before the barber left, promising to come again the following day, "no matter how many heads go unshorn," and Ned and Mistress Russet discussed their plans for the day. They had been assured that "not the trump of doom will awaken Master Fletcher for four or more hours." Mistress Russet would use the time to buy some food and then cook and bake; she had a secret cache of housekeeping money and needed none from Ned. He would use the horse to make some calls before returning it, and should be back well before Mistress Russet had to leave. While they talked, Ned ate bread and cheese, postponing his main meal until an early supper time, when they hoped Lawrence would be awake and well enough to join him. It was Friday, so it would be a supper of fish.

The sky was clouded when Ned set out and it had started to rain before he got to "Marie's house." When Rachel opened the door to his knock, her petrified face showed how much she had dreaded the meeting. Ned smiled at her and said, "Let me in, Rachel. I am wet."

Hastily she made way, saying, "I am sorry, sir. I meant no offense. It was the surprise of seeing you."

"But you knew I would come."

"Yes, sir." She burst into tears, and Ned led her to sit down. Incoherently she babbled on about Neddy's death and how she wished she had been taken instead, but gradually she was comforted by Ned's assurance that he did not blame her. Then she went on to say she would willingly give up to Ned the house and all that had been left to her, but Sir John Barnet would not let her.

"Nor will I," said Ned.

"Then, sir, it would please me mightily if you would come to live here so that I could wait on you, for now I have nothing to do, and that is not good."

This idea had never occurred to Ned. He said, "Did you speak of that to Sir John?"

"Yes, sir."

"And what did he say?"

Rachel hesitated before saying, "He doubted you would want to do it."

Ned wondered why. Did he think that Ned would not want to live with reminders of Marie and Neddy? The very question made Ned realize that he had now fully accepted and absorbed the two deaths.

Rachel had kept silent, waiting for Ned to speak. He drew himself out of his reflections to say, "I thank you, Rachel, for your invitation. I shall think of it, and it may be I shall come for a time. But first I must speak with Sir John."

"He wishes to speak with you too. He has been to see me twice since . . . since the funeral. He said he would come again on Sunday afternoon."

Sunday was Mistress Russet's day off, and he would have to stay in to care for Lawrence. "I cannot come on Sunday. I have to tend a friend who is sick. But Sir John knows him. Please ask him if he has the time to visit us. The name is Lawrence Fletcher, and he lives in Hunt's Rents in Maid Lane in Southwark. I shall have to stay there until my friend is able to get about again."

Rachel remembered Master Fletcher very well and very gratefully. Ned had forgotten that Jack had brought Lawrence to the house and that he had stayed there for Neddy's last days. Now Rachel was full of solicitous inquiries about him and said she would be happy and honored to take care of him, and though it was not necessary at the moment, Ned stowed the idea away in his mind. He was particularly thinking of the nights he would be at Sophie's, which in turn made him think of the inevitable scene which would develop with Lawrence. Ned said, "I want to go to the church. 'Tis not far, and the rain has stopped, at least for a while. Would you come with me, to show me where Neddy is buried?"

"Gladly. I will put on a shawl and bonnet."

"And I will go into the garden for a few moments."

Ned was not as strong against the past as he had thought. The garden, empty of Neddy, brought tears. A crowded five weeks shrank to yesterday. He saw and heard the child again, sleeping, laughing, gamboling, learning to talk.

Rachel came out into the garden to tell Ned she was ready, but she went in again and waited discreetly. At last Ned came in and they set out together, but without a word.

The little grave on which the mound of earth had not yet fully settled to ground level was shaded by a yew tree and covered with flowers. Rachel said, "I bring him some flowers everyday. He liked pretty flowers. I brought him some this morning."

Ned managed to say, "Thank you, Rachel."

"They wanted to bury him away in a corner, but Sir John stopped that."

"How is his burial registered?"

"Under your name, sir. They only wanted the name of the father."

"I should like to see the record."

When they found the sexton, he was in a bad temper. He had had little sleep the night before, because there had been two illicit after-dark burials of plague corpses for neither of which had he received what he considered to be satisfactory largess, and then there had been an early morning burial of a man killed in a duel, which had also provided him with scant reward. Although he was obviously doing nothing, he made it quite clear that he was too busy to show them the burial register. A coin changed his mind. He was an appropriate attendant on death, for it seemed a wonder that he was still alive; he shuffled at a snail's pace and his head was sunk so low into his body that his bony shoulders reached his ears from which sprouted bushes of gray hairs. As the three made their slow way to the vestry, he grumbled in a wheezing voice which was aimed at his own ears, for he had for many years talked to himself more than to others. "The world is in a parlous state. No more decent funerals. Plaguey corpses that should be cast into a ditch. Or men killed in duel that should be denied Christian burial." When he was opening the drawer which contained the records he asked, "What was the day of the burial?"

"Wednesday, August 12."

He muttered this over and over as he turned the pages, moving the book away after each examination, for his long nose had to touch the page before his squeezed-up eyes could read what was written on it. "Ah, here it is. What was the name?"

"Shakespeare."

"Shakespeare . . . Shakespeare . . . Ah. 'Edward, son of Edward Shakespeare, player. Baseborn.'" The last two words were croaked with mounting scorn.

Ned said, "The names are wrong. They should both be Edmund." He looked accusingly at Rachel.

"I don't know, Master Shakespeare. All I ever heard was Ned and Neddy."

"Change it," said Ned to the sexton.

"Nay; never," was the reply, as the book was quickly shut and returned to the drawer.

"But 'tis wrong."

"Records cannot be altered. You must be the father. Your shame is writ large here as it is in the Book of Heaven. And a player too. Double shame to you. Be off with you and mend your ways." And he creaked away, muttering dire forebodings to all sinners, but especially to players who begot bastards.

Rachel was frightened by Ned's mounting fury. She laid a hand on his arm, silently beseeching him to control himself in the House of God. In response, he moved angrily away and out through the vestry door. He went back to Neddy's grave and stood there, still seething. It was when the rain started again that he became aware of Rachel, standing patiently a few yards away. "Come," he said.

When they got to the house, Rachel gave him some mulled ale to ward off any fever that the wet clothes might give him. But rain or no, Ned could not stay long. He had to get back to Lawrence's before Mistress Russet left.

After he returned the horse to its stable, he got caught in heavy rain during the more-than-a-mile walk home, but he hurried on to the amazement of those taking shelter. He arrived home with half an hour to spare. Lawrence had not awakened. He lay motionless in deep sleep. Ned was moved to great pity by his friend's unusual lack of grooming and by the exhaustion from his suffering and loss of blood which made him look old and very sick.

Mistress Russet had prepared an excellent cold meal and she hoped Master Fletcher would be able to enjoy some of it. Master Sims had said that Master Fletcher should be able with help to sit up, propped by pillows. She had put a table bell at the bedside, but if Master Fletcher did not wake in time to have enough light to see it, perhaps Master Shakespeare would go up and sit with him and wait for him to stir.

Ned settled down to wait for the bell or the dark to summon him upstairs. He arranged and rearranged the supper on two trays, taking an occasional nibble to stay his hunger. After a restless hour of casting around for something to do he remembered that there was a table with paper, pen, and ink in his room. He would write to Will. Quietly he climbed the stairs again, though he had to fight an impulse to climb noisily in the hope of waking Lawrence.

The letter took a long time to compose because of the need for discretion in case others at New Place should read it. By the time it was finished, the daylight had begun to fail though there was yet a good hour before candles need be lit. Ned went into Lawrence's room without excessive caution but he did not wake nor did the sleeper seem to have moved an inch since Ned had seen him some hours before.

At long last Lawrence moaned softly and stirred slightly, and a few moments later his eyes opened in pain. Ned was quickly standing at his side. As he became aware of him, Lawrence managed a wan smile, and in a weak voice he said, "My head aches."

"Would you like to eat something?" Lawrence shook his head slightly and slowly. "I have waited supper for you," pleaded Ned.

"Bring it upstairs and I will watch you eat, and take a glass of wine with you."

"First, let me raise you a little and prop you up with cushions."

With the greatest care Ned accomplished this, causing Lawrence only one moan of pain. Then he lit some candles. As he did so, Lawrence said, " 'Tis good to have you here. 'Tis almost worth the misadventure." Ned smiled and hurried downstairs. When he returned with supper, he first poured some wine and they drank together, Ned wishing Lawrence a speedy recovery, to which Lawrence replied, "My head still aches, and other parts too, but I begin to feel hungry; 'tis the sight of the food." Ned was delighted to cut up whatever Lawrence could not manage with his one hand, and they shared a happy meal, though Lawrence ate little. Ned gave an account of his visit to Rachel and the church, the highlight of which was his impersonation of the crusty old sexton. He made no mention of Rachel's invitation to him to stay at the house, but did speak of her earnest offer to nurse Lawrence, who commented, "Unless you leave me, I wish no other nurse than you."

Ned said lightly, "Why should I leave you?" Then he hurried on to say, "But tell me what happened to you. I know little yet."

"There were four of them. They were on foot, lurking among the trees where I suppose they had hidden their horses. My horse was tired and slow. Two sprang out and seized the bridle, causing the animal to rear, while the other two dragged me violently to the ground; that was how I damaged my leg and shoulder. Although I was in pain, I struggled to free my sword. Then two of the ruffians attacked me with heavy sticks and I knew no more until early the next morning. Some travelers to London— a merchant and two of his men—saw me and at first took me for dead, but they managed to revive me. They decided they had better find a cart to carry me, and one of the men went in search of one. He found the pigman. While they took me back to his farm, the pigman took one of the horses and went for a surgeon. He bandaged me and botched my leg, and said I should not be moved for twenty-four hours. The rest you know."

"You lost everything?"

"My horse, my baggage, my sword, my rings, my wallet—everything."

"Oh, Lawrence, if I had been with you, it would not have happened."

Lawrence smiled and said, "Or if I had been with you." After a pause he said, "Tell me about your evening with the witch and about her house."

Ned restrained himself to saying simply, "She is no witch." Then, realizing the danger of any further conversation on the subject in Lawrence's present condition, he said, "But that can wait. You have talked enough now and should rest. And I should take these supper things downstairs."

There was a somewhat uncomfortable silence as Ned collected his load, but just before he left the room Lawrence said to him, "Tell me just one thing. Are you going to see Mistress Mountjoy again?"

Without any elaboration Ned said, "Yes," but then changed the subject. "I forgot to tell you that Jack Barnet is like to visit us on Sunday. He is going to see Rachel and hopes to see me. But I cannot leave you alone so I think he will come here."

"I shall be happy to see him, and, if Mistress Mountjoy is what I think she is, he will know her and tell me what you are so reluctant to tell me."

"How would Jack know Mistress Mountjoy?"

"I believe her to be the mistress of a brothel, and, since she obviously is wealthy and gives herself the airs of a lady, albeit a vulgar one, her brothel is like to be for gentlemen and such. I see from your face that I am right so far. Now I do not mean that Jack is a frequenter of brothels, but the expensive ones are places of much information. There is nothing a beautiful and clever whore cannot wheedle from a man when he has drunk too much. And it may well be that Madame Mountjoy's is a place where ambassadors are taken, for they too must relieve their flesh even in foreign lands. In such a place some of the wenches, gifted in tongues as in other matters, are good servants of the state, and that is what would give Jack knowledge of Mistress Mountjoy—if I am right about her."

Ned smiled in admiration. "Lawrence, you are a devil."

"Poor Ned! Now he is torn between a devil and a witch." He began to laugh but stopped suddenly because it caused a pain to shoot through his head. He smiled wryly after a moment and said, "The subject is a painful one. One last guess. I have heard of just such a place right across the river from St. Saviour's. Do you know if that is the one?"

"Yes, it is," said Ned.

"And will you go there?" asked Lawrence.

"Yes; I go there to dinner tomorrow." He added quickly, "Mistress Russet will be here to look after you, and I shall be back long before she leaves."

"Feel free, Ned," said Lawrence with an ill-disguised coldness. "I wish not to be a burden to you. I can always find someone to look after me."

FIFTY-FOUR

NED WAS AWAKENED THE NEXT MORNING BY MISTRESS RUSSET TALKING TO Lawrence. He hurried in to Lawrence's room to find that he was already eating some breakfast.

"Did you have a bad night, Lawrence?" asked Ned.

"It was made worse by knowing that you had a good one."

Mistress Russet laughed at the witticism, quite unaware of the barb it contained.

Ned left the room and dressed in readiness for the dinner at Sophie's. When he was ready, he went straight downstairs to avoid comments by Lawrence. Mistress Russet was full of compliments on his appearance.

He was still eating breakfast when Barber Sims arrived. That worthy began his visit with a joke and raucous laughter. "How is Master Fletcher? Still alive?" He was glad to join Ned in a tankard of ale before going upstairs, happily informing him that the plague showed some signs of getting worse. Ned did not accompany him when he went upstairs; he took the opportunity to tell Mistress Russet that he would be out for dinner, asking her to see to Master Fletcher's meal and promising that he would be back well before four o'clock.

Master Sims was a long time upstairs. He had taken up hot water to shave the unbearded parts of Lawrence's face. "If he sees himself in a mirror now, he will die of grief." They could hear the laughter which punctuated the barber's jokes, but were mercifully spared the jokes themselves. The barber-surgeon at last came down to deliver his report on Master Fletcher. "I find him somewhat melancholy this morning for he did not sleep well. Here is a draught that will bring him sleep. This is enough for three nights. Tomorrow I shall not come. 'Tis the Sabbath: church in the morning and good-fellowship for the rest of the day. I shall come again on Monday morning, but I fear my head will be worse than Master Fletcher's then, after all that Sabbath good-fellowship." And away he went, delighted as ever by his wit.

As soon as they were alone, Mistress Russet gave Ned full instructions for the Sunday meals; she had prepared plenty of food until she came again on Monday. The bell rang and Mistress Russet hurried to answer it. She soon came back downstairs to say it was Ned Master Fletcher wished to see.

Lawrence looked better for the barber's services, but still pale and weak. Ned said, "Good morning, Lawrence, though I did come in to see you before."

"I had forgotten. You said that Sir John Barnet might visit us tomorrow." The use of Jack's title emphasized what had been apparent from the first word, Lawrence's remote coldness, barely covered by a smile. "I would write a letter to the King which Sir John will know best how to see delivered. I should be grateful if you would get me the wherewithal." Then, as Ned placed the writing things on the side of the bed, Lawrence said, "I have done much thinking, Ned, as I lay awake in the night. I shall be laid up like this for many weeks. It is unfair to expect you to tend on me all the time. I think I should find someone who will do it for payment. What say you?"

Ned knew that Lawrence was just tormenting them both. He longed to agree so that he would be free to sing at Sophie's in the evenings, and yet regard and pity for Lawrence, as well as gratitude, made him say, "I shall be happy to stay here until you are well, and to tend on you."

"But you have a private life."

"I shall find the opportunity to live it." On a sudden impulse, Ned decided to break down the barrier between them. He sat on the bed and said, "Lawrence, what is it that you have against Sophie?"

"Sophie?" said Lawrence in apparent bewilderment.

"Very well. Mistress Mountjoy. I beg you, Lawrence, do not pretend. Your friendship is precious to me and this coldness may well freeze it to death. 'Tis true I have a private life, but so have you; that need not affect our friendship. I want to stay with you, but not if my presence will be painful to you. Again I ask: why does my liking for Mistress Mountjoy distress you?"

After a moment of hesitation, Lawrence's manner changed to one of moving sincerity. "I do not know, Ned. I had hoped you had seen the last of her, and then to hear that you are going to her house to dinner today! I had expected you would eat with me."

"But I shall be back for supper, and we shall have dinner many days together."

"I know. It's just that, in the first conflict of loyalties, she won."

"But I made the promise before I knew you would be like this, and were not Mistress Russet here, I still would not go."

"I know I am unreasonable, Ned, but I do not like or trust the woman. I am sure she pursues you for some purpose of her own. Tell me this. That student who traveled with her. Did he spend the night at her country house too?"

"Yes, he did," said Ned in triumph. "It was a large enough house; we each had a bedroom."

"And will he be at dinner with you today?"

"I know not," said Ned lamely. Lawrence smiled. Ned blurted out, "I will tell you all. 'Tis true that Sophie had a plan for me, but now 'tis postponed. If the plague did not close down her house, she wanted me to sing there in the evenings, and she would pay me more than I get at the Globe. I shall not do it now until you are well. One thing more. You do not know Sophie. I do, and I like her, and I cannot think why I should not. If you would see her as I do, you would like her too."

There was a short silence before Lawrence spoke. "Ned, I am a foolish man. I have lost other friends by demanding too much. I will not lose you. But I cannot allow you to forgo the money Sophie offers."

"I tell you 'tis settled in my mind. And speak to me not of payment in our friendship. I shall wait until you are mended. Sophie will understand, and approve."

"Even though she dislikes me?"

"Her dislike is your own seen in a mirror."

"It may be so. Go now to her and tell her that someday I hope to meet her again." Then he added with something of his old wit. "I am not like to be one of her patrons, though I suspect that she already knows that."

Ned first deposited his letter to Will at a carrier's and then had no difficulty in locating Sophie's house. It was the only private residence on that stretch of the river, its three stories standing prim and dignified in a crush of shops and warehouses. Almost as soon as he had knocked, the door was opened by a handsome and sturdy young footman, clad in a rich livery. He kept his hand firmly on the door and barred the entrance.

When Ned asked if the house was Mistress Mountjoy's, he received for answer a question: "What is your name, sir?"

"Edmund Shakespeare."

"Come in, sir. You are expected."

Ned entered into a small hall. Facing him was a narrow staircase, bracketed by rich and heavy curtains. In each of the two side walls was a door. The footman bolted the front door. Since the house was within the city walls, it was under the jurisdiction of the city fathers. Though the eminence of Sophie's patrons would be likely to curb their moralistic urges, still, it was as well to keep the front door bolted. Just as Ned arrived, Tim came bounding down the stairs. His welcome of Ned was wholehearted, if wordless, and without any preliminaries he took Ned into the room where Sophie was waiting. While she had not yet put on her evening finery, it was hard to conceive how she could outdo her present garish magnificence. She sat on a thronelike chair, and Ned kissed her extended hand, but the formality ill concealed their delight at the reunion.

"Ned, you have made a conquest not only of me but of Tim too, and that is a much greater compliment. So, Tim, let us have some wine." Tim happily fetched a silver tray which stood waiting with a flask and goblets of Venetian glass. "Now let us drink and talk a while before we eat. But first, a toast. May this be the first of many meetings."

"But it is already the third."

"You mistake; it is the fourth. We glanced each other at Bicester, met at Aylesbury, got to know each other at my house in the country, all of which was preparation for this, our first real meeting."

"Then I happily drink to many more such meetings with the most remarkable person I have ever met."

"Person? I like not that, for it might well betoken a man, which I assure you I am not."

"Then the most wonderful woman I have ever met."

"Woman? I should prefer lady, but even at woman you go too far, for I think you are not without a wide acquaintance with my sex. But enough of compliments. I have much to hear. Tell me of Master Fletcher."

Ned told her the tale of what had happened to Lawrence and added, "Sophie, he said he wanted to see you sometime. I am sure you would take much delight in each other's company."

She smiled and said, "For your sake we would both try. Did you tell him about coming to sing here?"

"Yes, but I cannot do so now until he is mended."

"That is well, because I know not what will happen to my house if the plague gets worse. We must wait—but not for dinner. Come, let us eat."

Ned escorted her to the table and Tim soon appeared with the first of a succession of succulent dishes, all of them carefully chosen and prepared for easy mastication by her age-hardened gums.

During the meal she enlightened Ned about some of the secrets of her trade; in spite of his experience with women, he was essentially innocent about the mysteries and aberrations of the flesh. In particular he wanted to know how Marie, who had lain with many men, could have been certain that Neddy was his son, although he had no doubt about it.

"She cherished your seed and spurned that of other men."

"But how?"

"Again you want to know too much. I have to teach my ladies how to stop or kill or cleanse themselves of unwanted seed. They do not always succeed. And men are stranger creatures than you know, Ned. The way to the womb is not the only way into a woman's body, and many men want not to use it. Indeed there are men who need only a woman's hand, and some whose only desire is to caress a woman's body with their hands, and others who need no more than a woman's comforting words for all their complaints and distresses. But my house is simple compared with some I could tell you of, houses of racks and whips and chains and the pleasure of pain; that I would never abide. There was a certain Spanish nobleman who gagged and bound one of my ladies and then lightly carved on her belly the letters IHS, *Jesu Hominum Salvator*. The poor lady was not mortally hurt but I did not cease until I had accomplished the recall to Spain of the villain. When the lady had recovered, she was much in demand to reveal the wonder on her belly. Thus we benefit from our misfortunes." She smiled slyly as she added, "Tell Master Fletcher that story."

Ned then surprised her by asking, "Do you know Sir John Barnet?"

Sophie's reaction was astonishing; she was frightened. Her mouth was full of food and she took a couple of great gulps of wine before she spoke, to say with a cold caution, "Why do you ask?"

Completely baffled, Ned said, "Lawrence thought you might know him. He's a friend of mine."

This last statement produced clear hostility in Sophie, and she shocked Ned by saying, "Then you are no friend of mine."

"I don't understand."

"Tell me of your friendship with Sir John Barnet."

Ned told her the whole story, from his first meeting with Jack in the oyster house to the duel fought in his behalf and without his knowledge, and Jack's good offices at the time of Neddy's death.

As she listened, Sophie gradually relaxed and her suspicion that Ned might be a minion of the highly placed spy disappeared, and when Ned had finished his tale, she grudgingly conceded that Sir John Barnet must have some good in him.

"Why are you so opposed to him?" asked Ned.

Before she answered, Sophie resumed eating, wondering how much she should tell Ned. She could tell him the essential fact because Sir John already knew it. "Ned, I am a good Catholic. Does that surprise you?"

"No," said Ned, but it did.

"I have a secret chapel in my house in the country, and a priest too. Your friend, Sir John, knows all about it, and it gives him power over me. He uses my ladies, especially those who can speak foreign tongues, to find out things for him."

"But 'tis for the safety of the state. I cannot believe you are a traitor or would harbor such."

"You are right, Ned. I do but worship God in my own way. I can no other. Tomorrow I shall go to the English church and I shall obey the law of the land by taking communion, but I shall not listen to the lies of the parson and as I take the bread and wine I shall know it is not the true Body and Blood, and shall say to myself there is never any harm in taking a morsel of bread and a sip of wine." As she said this, she drained her glass, which Tim quickly replenished; it was clear she had no secrets from him. She was her old self again as she said, "Your Sir John is not all bad, even to me. He wants to keep this house open and has helped me when trouble threatened from the city fathers, and he it was who helped to get that vile Spaniard recalled. But I cannot trust him, and where I do not trust, I fear."

"Does he ever savor the delights of your ladies?"

"Again you ask too much. It is the pride of the house that who dallies here does so in secret."

"But Sir John knows."

"Not all. He often brings here the very men whose secrets he would ferret out, and he and I would often seem to be the best of friends, but 'tis not so." She looked penetratingly at Ned before proceeding. "I trust you, Ned, and to prove it I shall tell you something that Sir John would give much to know. Yet 'tis all so long ago that perhaps even he would laugh at it now, for 'tis a good story. Do you remember the escape from the Tower of Father John Gerard and John Arden? But how could you? Only Catholics have such long memories."

"But I do remember, because I was questioned about them."

"You?" exclaimed Sophie.

"First your story, and then I will tell you mine."

"While they scoured all London for the priest on that first night, he was here in a room with Dorcas, one of my most lovely ladies, and in case of search he was ready to jump into bed with her. Indeed he had to do so, and naked too, for they searched every room, but knowing the priest for a devout man, they could not take him to be the man in the bed, especially when Dorcas screamed and cursed them out of the room. They deemed it only natural that the naked man should seek to hide his face from them. But I suffered a grievous loss that night, for by the morning Dorcas had been converted from her evil ways by the priest and had become a better Catholic than I, for nought would do but she must leave my house forthwith. I have never seen her since."

Ned burst into laughter, heartily joined by Sophie. Tim was clearing away some dishes at the time, and his body shook with an almost sound-less mirth.

It was Ned's turn to tell the story of Clement, and his account still further endeared him to Sophie.

At the end of the meal, the talk turned to practical matters. Sophie asked Ned to come again to dinner on Friday, for she would return to the country on Saturday and stay there until it was clear which way the plague was going. She asked Tim to show Ned the Music Room and the Gaming Room, "but no more." Her parting words to Ned were, "Tell Master Fletcher that I look to see him here at my table with you as soon as he is mended, and remind him that the last time he spurned my invitation he suffered grievous bodily harm."

The Music Room was entered by the other door in the entrance hall. It was the same size as the room Ned had come from, and had two couches and several cushioned chairs. The couches were occupied by two couples, each lost in its own intimate conversation. The ladies were indeed such, as far removed from the harlots Ned had known as Richard Burbage was from Robin. Both the men were much older than their companions and clearly indicated that this was Sophie's off season; they reeked of money and Cheapside rather than manners and Whitehall.

From the Music Room they went into the Gaming Room. Only one game was in progress, though there were tables for eight. The four men playing cards were doing so with a silent intentness, though they were merely entertaining themselves until men capable of higher stakes might arrive. They themselves were of the "younger sons of younger sons" variety, of good breeding and, for the most part, of good looks, who miraculously managed to maintain an impressive front on most slender means.

In one corner of the room, away from the gamblers, two attendants sat in quiet and desultory conversation, waiting for a demand for a game of cards or dice which would require their services, and ready at all times to intervene in disputes and deal with unruliness. They were such men as Sophie might be expected to employ, handsome and strong and devoted to their mistress because of some service she had been able to render them. All six men looked up at the two newcomers, but a shake of the head from Tim returned them to their occupations.

Ned arrived home soon after three o'clock in great good humor, which was amplified by the wine he had drunk. Mistress Russet said that Lawrence had asked that, whether he was asleep or awake, Ned would go up to see him as soon as he returned. Ned bounded up the stairs, and was greeted by a welcoming smile. Lawrence wanted to know everything and Ned told him a great deal, omitting only the story of Father Gerard since that had been a confidence and test of trust.

"Lawrence, she wants to entertain us both at dinner as soon as you are well. Will you come?"

Ned's question was so eager that Lawrence smiled and said, "Yes, for now I want to see her again. A good Catholic cannot be a witch, but I'm sure Sophie needs a priest all to herself because she keeps him so busy with her confessions."

FIFTY-FIVE

AS A RESULT OF THE BARBER'S DRAUGHTS LAWRENCE SLEPT WELL. HE awoke to find Ned spruce and dressed and ready to have breakfast with him. They could enjoy the morning all the more because they could ignore the clamant calls of London's hundred churches; Lawrence's crippled state was ample excuse for omitting the obligatory attendance.

Sir John Barnet came to call, as he had promised, soon after two o'clock. He and Ned looked at each other for a while without speaking. The sympathy of one and the gratitude of the other were too deep for words.

Jack spoke first. "Rachel told me you had been to see her and that you went together to the church. She was worried because the name in the register was wrong."

"Oh, it matters not. I have often been called Edward."

"And I Bartlett. But worst of all is to be called Sir John Beldon, after my wife's family."

Both men laughed and they sat down to share a flask of wine. Ned said, "Jack, I can never repay you for all you have done for me, but if ever you need me, please call on me."

"That's a dangerous invitation, young man."

"I would trust you."

"Your friend, Mistress Sophie, doesn't."

Ned was dumfounded. "But how did you . . . ?"

"I was there last evening. I had heard that a strange young man had had dinner with her."

"Who told you?"

"That is a question I never answer. For once Sophie had no hesitation in telling me about her visitor, for you had said you were a friend of mine, for which I thank you. No, Sophie need never fear me. I wish you could get her to believe that. I like her too much; she is a wonderful woman. Besides, a word in your ear: when my lady wife is in the country, as she is now, and sometimes when she is not, one of Sophie's ladies is much to my liking. I'm sure Sophie never told you that."

Ned said, "Lawrence told me about the man you killed for me. I have forgotten his name."

"So have I. He lies not on my conscience. I did the world a service to take him out of it, and I was in no danger. I should not have killed him if he had not taunted me at the last with cruel words about Marie. And, Ned, there is one thing you forget. I knew Marie longer than you did, and anything I did for you or for Neddy or for Rachel I did for Marie."

"Why did you tell Rachel I would not want to stay in Marie's house?"

Jack looked straight at Ned as he replied. "It was not that I thought you would find memories too painful; in most men the heart heals quickly. It was that I could not bear the thought of your lying in Marie's bed with some other woman. It may be foolish and sentimental of me to be so affected toward Marie, but so it is."

"And I honor you for it."

"When you get married it may be different, for it would be a kindness to Rachel to have a family to care for."

Ned told Jack then of Lawrence's injury, and after he had heard the story they went upstairs to see the invalid. In Lawrence's room, the three men drank wine together. Their first toast was to the King and they fell to discussing him. Jack was eager to learn from Lawrence all he could about the Scottish James before he had come to England. In particular, he wanted to know how far the King might go in his indulgence of favorites. "This Robert Carr, for instance. Think you he might be advanced to a position of power?"

" 'Tis possible," said Lawrence.

"Lies the King with Master Carr, think you?"

"No; I'll take my oath he does not," replied Lawrence rather too heatedly.

Jack smiled and said, "Restrain the fervor of your loyalty, Lawrence; remember you are a sick man. I make no moral judgments; a man can be no other than he is. I seek but to find how powerful Master Carr might become. In one sense I wish the King did lie with him, for then I think he would not remain long in favor."

Lawrence said, "The King condemns sodomy. Ned, there is a book in the other room. It is called . . ."

"Basilikon Doron," said Jack. "I have studied it carefully. I can even quote the passage you would have me read, it has been pointed out to me so often in defense of His Majesty. 'There is some horrible crimes ye are bound in conscience never to forgive: such as witchcraft, wilful murder, incest (especially within the degrees of consanguinity), sodomy, poisoning, and false coin.' But, Lawrence, I pay little heed to that. They are

counsels of perfection to the Prince who will succeed him. All men recite the Ten Commandments on Sunday, and break them in the days that follow."

"But the King need not have mentioned sodomy," said Lawrence.

"And set many tongues awagging by its omission."

"Not more than wag by its inclusion."

"You say true, Lawrence. And I confess that I know this Master Carr to delight in the beds of women. What think you of these matters, Ned?"

Ned had become increasingly embarrassed by the conversation. It was clear that Jack knew Lawrence's proclivities, and he felt it urgently necessary that Jack be told that Ned did not lie with him.

Ned replied tritely, "Appearances often deceive," hoping that the formula would cover more than the King's relationships.

"True," said Jack, smiling, "but 'tis my function to unmask the deceit. We are all strange creatures, and none more so than the King. He abhors the sight of human blood and yet he delights in the chase, where I am told he has been seen to rip open a deer and bathe his hands in the bloody entrails as though he were happily washing them in perfumed water. But enough of the King. Let us drink a toast to Lawrence's speedy recovery."

Lawrence said, "I thank you both, but one more thing about the King. I have here a letter I have written to him. Would you see that it is delivered for me, Jack?"

"Happily. Last time it was you who bore a letter for me. 'Twas to Ned, and it brought you back to London together." He added, "I am puzzled, Lawrence. Why didn't you accept Mistress Sophie's hospitality, as Ned did?" Lawrence glanced at Ned, assuming he had told the tale but Jack was quick to notice and said, "It was not Ned who told me, but Sophie."

Lawrence commented, "Then I'm sure she enjoyed the telling."

Jack said, "You are wrong about her, Lawrence. Your judgment is clouded, for what reason I know not; perhaps because of her trade. She can be as hard and glittering as a diamond, else she would long have been broken by life and died, but she can be compassionate and wise too. When Sophie told me about you, it was with sadness for your mishap, nothing other."

Lawrence said, "I marvel you speak so well of her. Is she not a dangerous papist?"

"A papist but not dangerous. And even if she were, I should still feel warmly affected toward her. I admired the Jesuit Garnet, while I sought his capture and death. But Sophie is harmless and useful. She has nothing to fear from me, for she has no secrets I know not."

Ned felt excited by his own knowledge of the escape of Father Gerard, and wondered how many more such secrets Sophie had kept from Jack; he hoped there were many, and then felt shocked because that was the hope of a traitor. Jack's next words alarmed him.

"You are now Sophie's good friend, Ned. If she should ever confide in you something you think I should know, I charge you on your promise of grateful friendship to let me know; and it will be your duty as a loyal Englishman."

"Knowing me to be a friend of yours, she is not like to trust me with secrets," said Ned.

"Women are often indiscreet; I thank God for it," said Jack. "And Sophie is a woman, albeit now old and worn."

THE BARBER-SURGEON CAME EARLY ON MONDAY, SOON AFTER MISTRESS Russet. He took the bandages off Lawrence's head and shoulder, and reluctantly admitted that the injuries were healing. He put on fresh medication and clean bandages, but he said he would not touch the leg for another week. When Lawrence complained that the itching of the leg was sometimes hard to bear, he said with a surprising sourness, "Scratch the splints." He quickly added, "I beg your pardon, Master Fletcher. 'Tis my head. 'Tis in sore distress this morning and it poisons my tongue."

When the barber had left, Ned went to visit Gilbert. After a brotherly greeting, Gilbert said, "Let us have dinner together, but you must pay. . . . Can you?"

"Provided we have the ordinary."

The brothers laughed together and then Gilbert said to Mark, "If we have a customer, which may God grant, no matter who or what he is, sell him something to the full size of his purse."

On their walk to the tavern Gilbert was much more ready to talk about himself than to listen beyond the call of dutifulness to Ned's reports of Stratford. As soon as the minimum civility of listening was over, he said, "Times are bad, Ned. I know not what to do."

"Have you lost patrons?"

"No; it would have been better if I had. There is abundance of work for handsome young men, but they have no money to pay for it. And when they get some money, they gamble it to make more, and lose all. I am owed countless pounds, and still the smiling rascals come to order more clothes."

"And still you let them have them."

"I confess that to some I cannot say nay; they are such beguiling devils. I swear they mean to pay when they can, and sometimes they come in with a few shillings."

"What of Master Robert Carr?" asked Ned.

"His reckoning is the longest, but he pays something when he can. He yet has received no regular pension from the King, but he vows 'twill come, and with it my money. Ned, when the players come back to town, I beg you to bring them to me for clothes."

"They cannot afford your prices."

"I will cut my cloth to suit their pocket."

"Are players such honorable payers of debts?"

"Bring me only such as are. And methinks you meet others than players who might be good patrons. Tell me—for only now does the thought strike me—what are you doing until the players return? And why did you come back to London before they do, and in a time of plague too?"

Ned smiled mischievously and said, "I have my reasons."

"Some woman, I'll be bound. A lady? One with gentlemanly and wealthy acquaintances who could be brought to my shop?"

"Such ladies as I know, I know only in secret."

"But how do you make money to live?"

"I sing, do I not?"

"But where? I would come hear you."

"For then you might find new patrons. No, Gil. When and where I sing is most secret and private, for then is the pay highest."

"You are a teasing devil, and behave not like a brother," said Gilbert peevishly. "You know all about me and I know nothing about you. I dare swear that you tell Will everything."

"He doesn't want to know things I don't want to tell him."

It was not a satisfactory meeting. Ned was glad when it was over, and Lawrence was happy to see him back.

After Ned had told Lawrence about the visit to Gilbert, he asked, "Think you that he is in dire trouble?"

"I know not, but many who depend upon the vagaries of the court are. The King is extravagant. He distributes largess widely and expects rich gifts in return. After the parsimony of Scotland, England, by compare, seems to have the wealth of the world. The courtier's life has become a gamble; he gives all he has to the King, and sometimes more than he has, in order to win rich favors. Soon it will be that anybody with the money to pay for it will be knighted. 'Tis small wonder that those without the money go to gaming houses to try to win it. But about Gilbert. Does he know you are staying here?"

"No, I told him nothing about you. It would have led to too many questions."

"He will find out about my injury, and may even come to visit me. What will you say when he sees you?"

"I know not, but I hope he comes if only to see his surprise. He will imagine the worst about us."

"Yes, but he will deem it the best."

They laughed together, and Lawrence was relieved to find that laughter had become less painful.

IF LAWRENCE STILL HAD RESERVATIONS ABOUT SOPHIE, THERE WAS NO SIGN of them on Friday, when Ned was leaving to dine with her. He said that he looked forward to the time when he could accompany Ned to Sophie's, and in the meantime he looked forward to an account of what he was certain would be a happy meeting.

But when Ned arrived at Sophie's house, it was only to be greeted with the news that Mistress Mountjoy was in the country, sick with a fever. No, Master Shakespeare could not see her. When she was sick, Mistress Mountjoy allowed no one to see her but the priest and Tim and Joan and Nellie. Was a physician tending her? No; Mistress Mountjoy would never see a physician; she said she knew more about her body than they did.

As Ned walked back, he was tortured by the fear that the plague might be claiming Sophie. What a gap in his life her going would leave. He was led to musing on the ironies of the plague: people would flee from the city to escape it only to be caught by it on their too-early return, or even to have it find them in the country; people would welcome the onset of cold weather which was supposed to kill the plague, only to find that it would claim an occasional victim on the coldest day. It seemed to be a malicious as well as a deadly presence.

Lawrence was genuinely distressed by the reason for Ned's return. Assuming that Sophie's sickness was the plague, it vividly brought home the fact that the official weekly tally of plague deaths had now risen to a hundred, and was expected to rise higher. While this was still a mild onslaught compared with the devastation of 1603, it led Lawrence to beg Ned to return to the comparative safety of Stratford, but Ned would not hear of it. He shared the attitude of Lawrence, "If 'twill come, 'twill come," but agreed that he would not visit Sophie for at least a week.

On Saturday the house received a surprise visitor: Robert Carr. He had come as a personal messenger from the King in reply to Lawrence's letter. When he saw Lawrence, the lively and handsome visitor said, "Well, well, I'm sorry to see ye sae crippled, but 'tis guid to see ye are out o' bed. And I ha'e brought ye some guid news; nay, 'tis better than news; 'tis money. His Majesty has sent ye a gift in the hope that ye get well soon. Here 'tis."

Robbie handed Lawrence a braided leather pouch, which Lawrence accepted graciously and gratefully, asking Robbie to convey his appreciation and thanks to the King, and saying that he would, of course, write to His Majesty.

Lawrence set aside the pouch, but Ned longed to know how much was in it, and his curiosity was satisfied by Robbie, who said, "Are ye not going to count how much is in it? But ye needna, for I ha'e done it mysel'. 'Tis forty golden pounds."

Ned was astonished; it was enough for him to live on, and like a lord, for a year.

Lawrence said, "His Majesty is, as ever, generous."

" 'Tis no more than ye desarve. But isna money a slippery thing? I never ha'e enough." Ned thought of Robbie's debt to Gilbert. "But soon

I shall ha'e a muckle o' money. Let me whisper it to ye, but dinna ye spread it." Ned wondered with amusement to how many more Robbie had whispered what was coming, and with the same injunction to secrecy. "Before Christmas, Jamey—I mean, His Majesty—is going to settle on me a pension of six hundred pounds a year and a knighthood to go wi' it. Aye, I shall be Sir Robert come Christmas, but to ye and all my friends I shall still be Robbie."

Ned and Lawrence glanced at each other, and they both knew what the other was thinking. But Ned discovered that he had no feeling of jealousy. Even were higher honors heaped on Robbie, Ned knew now that his independence was worth any prize that would make him the lackey of another man.

Robbie said, "I verily believe that King James is the most generous man that ever lived. D'ye know he has even granted a monopoly to his jester, Archie Armstrong? It's for the clay from which smoking pipes are made."

"But the King abhors all tobacco," said Lawrence in surprise.

"That's the jest of it. Now every man that smokes a pipe will make payment to a fool! His Majesty has a rare wit."

It was decided that Robbie would take dinner with Lawrence while Ned would eat downstairs, to provide company for Robbie's attendant, Bart. They would not linger over the meal, because they wanted to get back to Hampton Court by nightfall, and the journey was upstream.

Ned found that he liked Bart. He was as reserved as Robbie was outgoing, and, when Ned tried to draw him on the subject of Robbie, all he would say was, "Master Carr is not a private man. You know him almost as well as I do."

In the meantime, Robbie was describing to Lawrence with great distaste the number of tents that were being erected near Hampton Court to house the "hang-bys." "Any man with good looks and a good mien passes for a courtier these days. And in this time of pestilence 'tis right dangerous. I warn Jamey about it, but the bigger the court the happier he is." Robbie said that he would arrange for a royal barge to bring Lawrence to Whitehall as soon as he could come in October so that the participation of the King's Men in the Revels could be arranged.

Mention of the royal barge reminded Robbie that he should be on his way, "and I should be gratefu' for some of this guid food, for 'twill be well past suppertime ere we get to Hampton."

Food and drink was packed for them, and for the four oarsmen and it required Ned as well as Bart to carry the provisions down to the waiting barge. Robbie said, "We ha'e enough provender for a voyage to that New World that His Majesty is always telling me about."

Some twenty or so bystanders had gathered to watch for the passengers in the barge; the royal pennant always attracted gazers. None of them knew who Robbie was but they caught his Scottish tongue and it grated on their ears. As the barge pulled away the roughest and boldest of the onlookers spat into the river in the trail of the barge and said, "Another of them foreign peacocks come to rob us of our land and living. I knew how 'twould be when we fetched a king from Scotland."

But any hostility to the Scottishness of the King was wiped out by great compassion when, on two successive days, Thursday and Friday, September 17 and 18, two of his children died. The Princess Mary was twenty-nine months old, and the Princess Sophia was fifteen months. Everybody whispered of the plague, though it was seriously thought that such a vulgar intruder could not invade a royal bedchamber. It was given out that the little princesses had died of a disease of the lungs. It was known that in a time of plague people died in this manner without any of the bubonic swellings which were alone thought to betoken the plague; moreover, such affliction was always mortal and speedily so, whereas recovery from the bubonic plague was possible, though rare.

Ned had postponed his going to Sophie's from day to day because he was certain that he would find she had died and been buried, but on Saturday he went at the urging of Lawrence. As he rode he prepared himself to find a mourning house, or perhaps even one closed and empty.

But Sophie and the house were very much alive. She greeted Ned with "Where have you been? I began to fear the plague had got you. Oh! I see from your face how it is. You thought the plague had claimed me." She laughed uproariously at this. "No, Ned, no. Death can never be counted on. It plays strange tricks. It takes royal babes and leaves old women. But come. A drink before dinner, and today 'tis not fish."

The joy of seeing Sophie alive and well made the visit a particularly happy one, and the time to leave came all too soon, but Ned was eager to tell Lawrence the good news about Sophie, and Lawrence was genuinely happy to hear it. He was now rather proud of himself for his generous acceptance of Sophie.

FIFTY-SIX

ON THE LAST DAY OF THE MONTH, WHICH WAS A WEDNESDAY, CAME A letter from Will, saying that he was setting out on the first Monday in October and hoped that Ned would have found a new lodging place for him. He would come straight to Lawrence's to be guided by Ned to his new address.

Except for an occasional procrastinating thought, Ned had neglected his promise to find Will a place to live on the South Bank. His life had settled into such a pleasant and comfortable routine that he had not even faced the time of his leaving Lawrence, though leave he must; both men would need to resume those parts of their lives in which the other had no share and for which they both needed privacy. Already there had been one occasion of unspoken unpleasantness when Ned had not returned for supper from an afternoon he had spent with a young lady. She lived very conveniently in Southwark, and, still more conveniently, her husband had but recently left on a mission for the King to Venice. The very sight of her had kindled in Ned a burning urgency. He had accompanied her home, where they were happily alone, and with remarkable speed they were lying together. Agnes, for that was her name, had been seriously thinking of leaving London to flee the plague; the meeting with Ned had made her decide to stay. As she had said, " 'Tis cowardly to leave when others must stay."

Ned's breezy excuses for being late had left Lawrence in no doubt of the reason for the delay, and he had been unable to control his reaction of cold fury to it. Ned did not allow subsequent meetings with Agnes to make him late for supper; still, he must leave Lawrence as soon as he could fend for himself, if only to preserve their valued friendship.

On Thursday, October 1, Ned set out to find a lodging for his brother. He knew that Will would spend as little time as possible in London from now on and would not want to waste money on a commodious home; one large room would be enough, or two smaller ones. He and Lawrence agreed that he should inquire of Cuthbert Burbage and Arthur Sims; the first would know the best bargains and the second the best places.

Cuthbert reported that he had received two letters from Cambridge, one from his brother Richard, and the other from John Heminge. The players were coming home on Friday, October 9, even though they knew that the plague would keep the Globe closed. They had had an unusually successful tour and wanted a rest before starting rehearsals for the Christmas Revels.

"And Will. When comes he?" asked Cuthbert.

"On Wednesday or Thursday."

"Excellent, i' faith, excellent."

Cuthbert gave Ned the names and addresses of two widows who maintained themselves by renting out rooms in their houses and who had both come to ask him to recommend players for lodgers, "but only such as are sure and certain payers of rent, and not roisterers."

Ned went to both houses. He did not even look at the rooms in the first house, for the widow was a shriveled and whining woman whose slogan seemed to be "No food!" and furthermore she would not think of having players in her house if the times were not so bad. The other widow was much more promising as a landlady, but there was an unpleasant smell in the house, which was explained when the widow said that all her lodgers worked at the bearpit. "I have only one room, the best one, upstairs in the front. Master Carter, 'e that was the best bearward the pit ever 'ad, took old and died. Come up and see the room." The briefest sight was enough, for their approach caused a scuttle of rats, and the stench was as strong as if the dead Master Carter had not yet been removed. Ned made an excuse and hurried away to Arthur Sims, who greeted him happily.

" 'Tis good to see you, Master Shakespeare." His face lit up as he said, "Did Master Fletcher try to come downstairs too soon and fall and break his leg again?" Ned smiled and shook his head. The disappointed surgeon turned barber said, "Then 'tis but for a haircut and beard trim you have come. 'Twill be a pleasant change from lousy heads, filthy beards, and fetid mouths of rotten teeth."

" 'Tis about a private matter I have come," said Ned.

Before he could say more, Arthur quickly interposed, "If 'tis an abortion I will not do it, for I like not to meddle with the bodies of women."

When Arthur heard Ned's request, he told him of the "one and only place." It was a two-story house nearby which belonged to a childless couple, the Forresters; he was the chief tapster at the White Hart Inn— Ned knew the man by sight—and she was a seamstress who sometimes did work for the Globe. They lived on the ground floor of their house.

Ned took the address and went straight over. It was a neat and trim little house tucked between two large three-story ones. Mistress Forrester was as neat and trim as the house and such a jolly, matronly little body that it seemed an absurd waste that she had not borne a houseful of children. She said that the Forresters liked the theatre but they weren't able to go often. She had seen Ned and heard him sing in *Much Ado About Nothing* and *As You Like It* and would be honored and happy for Master William Shakespeare to live in the house.

Ned was first struck by the cleanliness of the rooms. They were comfortably enough furnished, though sparse and simple. The big double bed in the back room, innocent of carving or decoration, seemed sturdy, and Ned was urged to try it. He did so and proclaimed it good. He was certain that Will could be comfortable here. Ned felt that all arrangement about the provision of meals could be decided between Will and Mistress Forrester, but he was glad to sample a tankard of her ale because it was well known that a housewife who brewed good ale kept a good kitchen. Her ale was very good.

As they were about to part, it became evident that Mistress Forrester had assumed all along that Ned would be staying with his brother, and her disappointment that he would not was very genuine. "Two are as easy to care for as one," she pleaded. She was partly mollified when Ned said he might well stay there when his brother went home to Stratford.

Will did not arrive until late afternoon of the Thursday, a day after he had been expected. He was surprised by the anxiety that had been felt for him. He had just not hurried. Ned's wicked suspicions turned to Mistress Davenant. He asked, "How was Master Davenant?"

"I did not see him," said Will. "He had gone to Southampton to buy some Spanish wine."

"And Mistress Davenant?"

"Full of the pride of her little son, William. He's eighteen months old now and very lively."

Will stayed for supper before going to his new lodging, and was pleased by plans for his reading of *Antony and Cleopatra* in Lawrence's house on Sunday.

As Ned and Will walked to the Forresters' Will talked about their mother, who was becoming more frail and living increasingly in the past. Ned's chief report was on Sophie, and he was surprised to find that Will knew of her.

"Have you been to her house?" asked Ned.

"I like not gaming; my money has been too hard come by."

"And Sophie's ladies?"

"Ned," said Will in comic shock, "I am a husband and father!"

Will liked both Mistress Forrester and her house. With a quick survey of his new premises, he decided that the backroom would be his study; it was always easier to write with trees to look at. With the help of Master Forrester and Ned on the morrow he would move the big bed to the front room. As for his meals, Mistress Forrester would be happy to provide whatever he needed, but was not so happy to hear it would be but a scant breakfast every morning, and that for the most part he would eat his dinners and suppers with his fellows.

When Mistress Forrester had gone downstairs, Will asked how long Ned intended to stay with Lawrence.

"Only until he is quite mended. This time with him has been pleasant, and I am glad to have been able to help, but soon I must leave, for his sake as much as mine."

"And will you come here? There are two rooms and you will be most welcome."

Ned smiled as he said, " 'Tis brotherly of you to say that, but 'tis safe, for you know I will not come, except, maybe, when you are in Stratford."

Will asked if Ned needed money, and was told he did not. This led to an account of Sophie's munificent offer for his services as a minstrel.

Will laughed outright, and Ned's annoyed look made him hasten to explain. " 'Twas bad enough for stern-faced Stratford to be shamed by one Shakespeare who works in a theatre, but now another is to work in a brothel!"

Ned felt free to join in the laugh. "We shall say I am a court minstrel, for my audience will be all courtiers and courtesans."

"And no man of Stratford will ever find you out, for when they come to London to do business and secretly to savor the delights of the town, they will be content with cheaper ladies than Mistress Mountjoy's. Her prices would rob them of the ability to perform the act for which they had paid."

After dinner together the following day, the brothers went to the Globe. Tom Vincent, Nat Tremayne, and Martin were just finishing their unpacking of the cart. Nat was in a buoyant mood, for, as he said, "London with the plague is better than any place else without it." Tom Vincent undertook to inform all the sharers of the dinner and reading at Master Fletcher's on Sunday.

When Ned returned to Lawrence's he was surprised to find John Heminge there. He had come straight from the theatre to see Lawrence, even before going home to his family. Ned guessed he wanted to assure himself that Lawrence was well enough to make arrangements for the Christmas Revels. He must have received that assurance because he was in a cheerful mood and showered compliments on Ned for the good care he had taken of Master Fletcher. He even went so far as to say that, in reward, Ned should be present at the reading on Sunday.

But Ned was not to be cheated of Agnes, especially as he had already heard the play, and he said, "Nay, Master Heminge. 'Twould not be seemly, but I thank you for the kind offer."

"Well spoken, Ned, well spoken. I hope there is a good part for you in the new play."

"Master Burbage will play Antony, and I doubt you will give me Cleopatra."

John Heminge guffawed and made his own addition to the jest. "Nay, lad, that is for me."

Lawrence and Ned laughed heartily, more in happiness at Master Heminge's mood than in commendation of his joke.

FIFTY-SEVEN

THE SHARERS, STILL HAPPY IN THE AFTERGLOW OF THE SUCCESS OF THEIR tour, gathered at Lawrence's house for Will's reading on Sunday, October 11. They were delighted to welcome Will again and to see Lawrence almost completely recovered from his misadventure.

After dinner the hired servingman cleared the remains of the meal from the table, replenished the jugs of beer, and put out additional bottles of wine. As the sharers settled down happily and expectantly, Will said, "You are all in such high spirits I think you would even find *Timon* pleasing this afternoon."

"I stoutly maintain 'twas a good play," said John Heminge. "But I will wager that your *Antony and Cleopatra* will please us all mightily. My only fear is that after such a wondrous dinner we shall all fall asleep, so read well, Will, read well."

The audience was held from the opening lines, and so absorbed did both reader and listeners become that the tragic tale was told headlong from start to finish without a break. There was a silence as the exhausted author closed his manuscript, and then John Heminge said quietly, almost as if to himself, " 'Tis a miracle." Even this did not open the floodgates of praise that all felt the need to express; any conventional words would belittle the mightiness of the scope of this play and the depth of its humanity. It was Will who restored normality by saying, "I should like a glass of wine." So many hands reached out to get it for him that laughter released a torrent of overlapping words.

Finally John Heminge restrained the exuberance to discuss practical matters. In the morning Will would set the copying in train, and they would meet at two o'clock at the theatre for a preliminary discussion of the casting and other matters. The most important other matter was raised by Will's question, "When think you the Globe will open?"

John Heminge replied, "I have discussed it with Cuthbert. This is a strange visitation, worse now than in the heat of summer. Although it begins to decline, it is far from allowing us to open. We must be patient, perhaps for a number of weeks. But we have a glorious new play to rehearse, so let us not lose heart. And soon we shall be preparing for the Christmas Revels. When, think you, Lawrence, you will be able to go to the court on our behalf?"

"Arthur Sims thinks in a week or so. I cannot come to the meeting tomorrow, but I know I can rely on Will to report it to me; he lives close by now."

As they took their leave, the sharers in turn said something about the new play to Will. Two, in particular, impressed him.

Robert Armin said, "I began to think there was nothing for me in the play, and then came the clown at the end with the asp, a necessary and wonderful part in a perfect place. Oh, that line! 'Those that do die of it . . .' How goes it, Will?"

" 'Those that do die of it do seldom or never recover.' "

Armin went away, muttering the line and chuckling at it.

Richard Burbage said, "Again you have given me cause to thank you, Will. Antony is a part to exult in, but Cleopatra! She is the greatest of all your women. How I wish I could play her! No boy can compass her. But I have a thought, Will, I have a thought." Will looked his question. "Nay, more of that tomorrow. I must first sleep on it."

Things had not gone as expected for Ned, and his return was delayed. He had seen Agnes at church, but her maid had been with her. Ned had heard much of the maid, but had not seen her before. She had been chosen by the husband and the sight of her showed why; she was a forbidding guardian rather than a lady's servant. Agnes had caught Ned's eye long enough to see his slight nod of the head, the sign that he was free for the afternoon.

Ned decided that Agnes might be able to steal out of the house after dinner, so he would take an ordinary at a tavern and then he would go to the riverbank and wait where they had sometimes sat together and fed the swans.

The dinner was not only bad but led to an unpleasant altercation. Ned had chosen a cheap tavern, and the cold mutton he was served had maggots in it. When he protested, the tavern-keeper, who could not deny the presence of the insects because they were all too writhingly obvious, said, "Pick 'em out if you don't like 'em. But they won't do you no 'arm. Meat is better and tastier when it's gone off a bit. Nobody else 'as complained." And nobody had.

Ned had already paid his groat for the meal, and he knew it would not be returned. In his fury he exclaimed viciously, "Your food isn't fit for swine."

But the host had the last word. As Ned stormed out he called after him, "Then don't eat it, Master 'Igh-an'-Mighty Swine!" and Ned heard the retort received with laughter by the contented maggot-eaters.

The last rays of the sun were burnishing the Thames as Ned returned without having seen his Agnes. He hoped Will had stayed with Lawrence, but he hadn't, and Lawrence was already in bed. Again there was that cold and hurt reception which made Ned determine to find a place of his own as soon as possible; the difficulty was that he was earning no money and had no assurance of when he would begin to do so, either at the Globe or Sophie's.

Lawrence said, "I am relieved to see you. I began to fear something might have gone amiss." But his tone betrayed reproof rather than concern.

Ned asked, "How did you get upstairs?"

"I managed somehow. I was tired; it has been a long and tiring day. I must learn not to rely on you, Ned." He tried but failed to hide the barb, and Ned reacted accordingly.

"Then if you need me no longer I shall leave as soon as I can find a place of my own."

"I beg you not to hurry." Lawrence covered the quick appeal with a smile as he added, "I have not even been out of doors yet. There is a sharers' meeting at the theatre tomorrow but I dare not try to attend it; I should fear to cross a street or climb those theatre stairs. Oh, Ned, I wish you could have been here at the reading. Will excelled himself. The play seemed even better than when he read it to me. He's going to urge that you be given Dolabella, and so will I."

The following afternoon Lawrence and Ned eagerly awaited the return of Will from the theatre. They had not expected the meeting to be a long one and so were surprised that they were already at supper before Will arrived. He readily agreed to join them while he gave them the news. Ned was flattered that no caution was imposed by his presence, nor was any reference made to the need for secrecy.

After the normal business of the meeting had been happily concluded, preliminary discussion of the casting of the new play was begun. It had been assumed by all but two of the sharers that Cleopatra would be played by John Edmans, but Richard Burbage questioned it. When it was thought that his objection was because Edmans might be getting a little old for the part, he surprised them by saying that the boy was not old enough. He had called on Will to quote the phrase, "wrinkled deep in time," Cleopatra's own description of herself, and had said that a mature player was needed. He wanted Robert Gough for the part, a player who had not played a woman for ten years, but had once been a beautiful Juliet and Portia. Pandemonium, led by John Heminge, broke out, much to the embarrassment of Robert Gough, now present as a sharer. He stood up and walked out, and this brought a momentary lull in the noisy meeting. Richard Burbage took quick advantage of it to appeal to Will, who dumbfounded John Heminge and others by saying that the very same idea had occurred to him. The meeting broke up shortly thereafter with no decision made.

Lawrence said, "I shall be there next Monday. I never saw Bob Gough play a woman, but if you and Dick want him, Will, he has my vote."

And so it was decided the following Monday, Heminge giving in gracefully because the welcome presence of Lawrence had turned his mind to the Christmas Revels. Bob Gough had stayed outside until the question was settled. Will went to give him the result and to fetch him back in. With his usual quiet modesty all Bob said to the meeting was, "I thank you, sirs. I am honored. I shall do my best." The rest of the casting was settled amicably, though it was an intricate process because some forty parts were involved. Will had conferred with Tom Vincent in preparation for the meeting, and some of the sharers were assigned three parts each. It was Lawrence who proposed that among Ned's parts should be Dolabella, and it was readily agreed to. The only sour note in the meeting was the bleak prospect for the opening of the Globe; the plague toll for the previous week had been one hundred and thirteen, far above the forty which would allow the theatre to open. But this was forgotten in the happy announcement that Lawrence was to go to Whitehall by river the following day to make the Christmas arrangements. He expected to be back on Thursday or Friday, and another sharers' meeting was called for Saturday morning to hear his report. The first reading of *Antony and Cleopatra* would take place at the theatre on Monday, October 26.

Lawrence was eager to bring Ned the happy news about Dolabella, and to report on the whole meeting to him. They had a delightful supper together, but, since Lawrence was leaving on the morrow for three or four days, Ned felt it imperative to raise a subject both had been avoiding. He said, "While you are away, I shall look for lodgings. I want to move before rehearsals begin next week."

After taking a moment to absorb the news, Lawrence said, "I knew it had to come and I shall not try to dissuade you. Your friendship is very precious to me, Ned. Whenever you need a home, for a short time or a long one, mine is yours. One more thing. I talked to Will about it on that Sunday when we waited for you after the reading. If I should die before you, as is most likely, my share in the King's Men is to be yours, and without payment."

Ned said, "Lawrence!" and was unable to say more. Impulsively he got up, went around the table, knelt by Lawrence and embraced him.

Neither spoke for a time and then Lawrence said with a forced return to his customary witty manner, "Now get up, Master Shakespeare, or you will be leading me to expect from you what you have no intention of giving."

Ned broke the embrace but remained on his knees to say, "Lawrence, I deserve not such friendship. When I think what . . ." Ned could not utter the unworthy thoughts he had held about Lawrence.

"When you think what?"

Ned smiled and said, "Nothing. Some day I hope you will need me so that I can show my gratitude."

"Gratitude is a base coinage between friends. Come now. Let us drink to the success of my mission tomorrow."

Ned arose and they drank together. Then Lawrence said, "Promise me one thing. Be here when I return, if 'tis only to hear my news before the sharers do."

"That is a promise as easy to keep as to make."

Ned accompanied Lawrence to the river the following morning, carrying two heavy bags. He was astonished that so much luggage was needed for two or three days, but Lawrence explained that never must he appear twice in the same clothes. He said, " 'Tis a strange irony of the court that the wealthier a petitioner appears to be, the more is he like to get. 'To him that hath shall be given,' as Will would have said if the Bible had not said it before him."

While he was now walking easily, though with the aid of a stick—he had borrowed a richly ornamented one from the theatre for the occasion—Lawrence explained to the bargemen that he would need their help in boarding and disembarking. As soon as he was safely and comfortably settled on a cushioned seat in the bow, the boat pulled away.

One of the knot of idlers who had watched the departure asked Ned, "Oo's 'e?"

Ned looked straight at his grimy questioner and with impressively muted voice said, "The Earl of Essex returned from the dead!"

The inquisitive one stepped backward as if to ward off a blow, and Ned stalked away. He heard another spectator say, " 'E's Bedlam mad."

Ned decided to set about finding a new lodging immediately and went to Will's to ask the landlady, Mistress Forrester. He was certain that any room she suggested at least would be clean.

Will was out, probably at the theatre having conferences about the new play with Tom Vincent and Nat Tremayne. It was difficult for Mistress Forrester to understand why Ned could not stay with his brother; the bed was big enough. But she had heard that players were strange people, and perhaps the desire to be alone was one of their crotchets. Yes, some friends of theirs, the Barkers, did have a room; it used to be their only son's, a shipwright, but he had got married and gone to live in Bristol. Sam Barker, the father, was a mason and a fine man, and now like to become a wealthy one because by the new proclamation all house fronts had to be made of brick. Mistress Forrester would take Ned over at once.

The Barker house was bigger than that of the Forresters, with three storys and a stable at the back big enough for a horse and cart. Mistress Barker was a quiet, dignified woman, beginning to show the frailty of age.

Ned liked the room she showed him at the top of the house, but he had been predisposed to like it by noticing that the stairway which led to it gave a fair privacy of access; one, of course, could be seen, but only by a deliberate watcher, and he did not think that Mistress Barker was such a person. Terms and conditions were easily settled; they were very reasonable; it was clear that the Barkers were in no need of money. Ned arranged to arrive on Sunday evening and was urged to join the Barkers for supper, as Master Barker would be eager to meet him.

As Ned left the two women happily chatting together, he felt a great elation of spirit; this new home was a happy omen for the season that was about to begin. He went to the theatre to tell Will his good news, and there, too, his good fortune held, for Will invited him to dinner. It enabled Ned to discuss with him Lawrence's promised legacy of his share.

"Lawrence is a good man," said Will, "and an honest one. He told me much at supper after the reading, though he was not at ease, for every sound made him think you were returning. You are right to leave him, for your presence is both a joy and a torment to him. Cherish his friendship, Ned. He is a worthy man, and I pity him in his loneliness."

It was late on Friday afternoon before Lawrence returned from Whitehall, and Ned was very glad he was in the house to welcome him. Lawrence was in a jubilant mood; it was clear that things had gone well, but how well was almost unbelievable. The Revels were no longer to end on Twelfth Night. Their Majesties so loved them that they were to be extended to the end of January, and perhaps even beyond, and, as usual, the lion's share of providing the entertainment was to fall to the King's Men; it would mean ten or a dozen plays; perhaps more. The first three evenings of the Revels were to be provided by the King's Men, beginning on December 26 with *Antony and Cleopatra*, followed by *Much Ado About Nothing* and *Macbeth*.

The shared excitement of the news had occupied them during supper, and, when the meal was over, Ned told Lawrence he had found a new lodging.

Lawrence smiled sadly and then said, "That has somewhat dashed my spirits, though I knew 'twas coming. When will you move?"

"I should like us to go to church together on Sunday, then have dinner together, and I would move in the afternoon. Rehearsals begin on Monday, and it would be well to be settled by then."

"So be it. But Ned, be not a stranger, I beg you."

Ned smiled and said, "I promise to wear out my welcome." Then he told Lawrence that he had also arranged to start singing at Sophie's on the first Monday in November. He wanted Lawrence to be there.

"I shall be ill at ease in a brothel, no matter how elegant and expensive it be," said Lawrence, in a bantering tone.

"But to please me, Lawrence. And we could have supper with Sophie. I long for you to meet her."

"You forget we have met." The appealing look on Ned's face caused Lawrence to say, "I do but jest. Sophie and I have not really met, and 'tis a pleasure I look forward to. But tell me, how can she open her house in time of plague when the theatre must remain closed?"

"I suppose because her house is private and the theatre is not. Besides, she has powerful friends."

The next afternoon, to Ned's surprise, Will came back with Lawrence from the sharers' meeting, and they had both drunk themselves into particularly high good spirits. The meeting and dinner had been joyous, and had quite obliterated any despondency over the fact that the plague deaths for the week were one hundred and ten. Lawrence had suggested to the sharers that, if there were an eleventh play during the Christmas revels, it should be *Troilus and Cressida*. He had argued that it was a fine play which had never been given a fair showing and that its classical tale and characters would much appeal to the King, but everyone in the room had guessed that Lawrence's real purpose had been to further Ned's career. They had been in a mood to grant Lawrence anything, and accepted his suggestion as a most welcome inspiration. John Heminge had gone so far as to say, "I long to play that Agamemnon again. Aye, and to see Ned Shakespeare's Troilus. 'Twas a fine piece of work, and 'twill be four years better now."

Not for the first time, Ned could not express his gratitude, and Will made it quite clear that it had all been Lawrence's doing.

Sudden doubt struck Ned. "But think you there will be an eleventh play?"

"The Master of the Revels gave me to believe so."

In his inability to find words, Ned stood up and his whole body thrilled as he uttered "Oh!" several times. Then he spoke. " 'Tis better than hearing I had become a sharer. Oh, Lawrence, you had it planned all the time. Why did you not tell me last night?"

"It would have been too big a disappointment if the sharers had not agreed."

"I will be such a Troilus as will make you proud, and it will be all because of you, and for you."

Lawrence and Will had already drunk too much and they now joined Ned and drank more, and soon it became apparent that Lawrence could not climb the stairs without great danger to his leg. It was decided that, while he was sober enough to do so, Ned would hoist him over his shoulder and carry him upstairs. This feat was accomplished with boisterous laughter, Will climbing the stairs with some uncertainty behind Ned in an absurdly futile gesture of being ready to give help should it be needed. As soon as they were safely in the bedroom, Ned went downstairs again to fetch wine, for they thought it right to congratulate themselves on the physical achievement of getting upstairs. While he was down Ned thought it prudent to put some supper on a tray for he might have difficulty in carrying it up later.

They ate a little and it sobered Will enough to say with a giggle, "We are drunk. 'Tis a goodly thing for friends to get drunk together once in a while, for it matters not what friends hear when the brain reels and the tongue is loose."

At last Lawrence, fully dressed and sprawled on the bed, was fast asleep and snoring. Ned, still the least drunk of the three, caught Will by the arm and tried to get him to stand up. "Come, Will," he said, 'tis time to go home."

Will pulled his arm away, almost falling out of the chair with the effort, and quoted his own Sir Toby Belch. "Nay, 'tis too late to go to bed now. And mark you this, Ned, Mistress Forr-Forres-Forrester is not my keeper. There will be other nights too when I shall not go home." Chuckling to himself, his head sinking on his chest, Will too was soon fast asleep and snoring.

FIFTY-EIGHT

WILL WAS THE FIRST TO WAKE IN THE MORNING, BECAUSE HE ACHED IN ALL his joints from sleeping in the chair. It was dark. Painfully he stood up, his head trying to burst and his furred tongue to choke him. Carefully and slowly he groped his way to the stairs. Lawrence grunted and groaned in his sleep. With infinite caution Will felt his way downstairs. He needed fresh air. Why was there no moonlight? It was almost full moon. When he got into the street, he knew; it was raining, not heavily but blissfully. Will stood in the rain, his face upturned. He remembered it was Sunday; he would have to go to church. He went inside to sit down and collect his thoughts.

There had been something the previous evening about the three of them going together to St. Saviour's. He preferred the old pre-Reformation name, St. Mary Overies, St. Mary-over-the-River. He could not go to church as he was; he would have to go home as soon as the first gray light began, to spruce up and change.

Lawrence was the next to wake, but it was some time before he returned to full consciousness and remembrance. It had been a memorable evening, well worth the dreary aftermath which he was now experiencing. He got out of bed, lit a candle, looked at himself in a mirror, was appalled by what he saw, blew out the candle, and returned to lie down until it was lighter. When it was, he got up again and stole in quietly to see if Ned was still sleeping. But his opening of the door knocked over a stool which Ned had moved, and Ned woke with a start. Lawrence apologized; he had not meant to wake him.

"Then what did you want?" asked Ned, irritated and fuzzy.

"I know not. I wanted to know if you were still asleep."

"I was, but now I am not. Where is Will?"

"Will?" asked Lawrence blankly.

"He was fast asleep in the chair in your room when I went to bed."

"He's not there now. He must have waked and gone home. I'm sorry I woke you. I shall dress. 'Tis Sunday."

By the time they had both washed and changed their clothes and gone downstairs for breakfast, they were in a condition to recall the previous evening with happiness. The first bells began to ring, giving worshipers a half-hour's notice of the service. The clangor of bells from churches near and far would have waked all but the dead, and before they had stopped, Will arrived. He showed no sign of the evening's debauch, and they chatted happily together as they awaited the final call of the bells. Ned needed to be assured that he had not dreamed about the possibility of *Troilus and Cressida*. His comment was, "Then eleven is to be my magic number in the year 1608."

As soon as the bells started their last call, they set out for St. Saviour's. It was the twentieth Sunday after Trinity and the Epistle for the day contained St. Paul's admonition to the Ephesians, "And be not drunk with wine, wherein is excess." This provoked some self-conscious smiles between the three men.

Ned saw Agnes in the church, but she studiously avoided looking for him; not only was the Gorgon with her, but also an older and forbidding-looking man, presumably her husband. She had told Ned previously that she had had no say in the marriage; her parents had produced six daughters who lived and two sons who died, and any man of position who looked with desire upon one of the girls was zealously pursued by the parents for a son-in-law.

Ned dreaded the dinner that day, with its inevitable emotional undertones, but he need not have worried, for Lawrence seemed determined to make the parting easy and casual. He even insisted on accompanying Ned to his new home and carrying one of his bags. He was most gracious to the Barkers, who were much impressed by his gentlemanly appearance and behavior, and complimentary about Ned's room, where he left him to settle in, saying that he would see him in the theatre in the morning.

At the excellent supper, the Barkers were full of questions about Master Fletcher, though they avoided being annoyingly inquisitive, and Ned was happy to flaunt Lawrence's connection with the King. It turned out that Master Barker was one of the many masons employed on the new Hall at Whitehall. He said, "The City is paying for it. I wish it had been the King; he would have been more generous."

Ned slept well and was early at the theatre in the morning. It was good to welcome and be welcomed, and Ned was flattered to find that, apart from the two boys who would play Charmian and Iras, he and one other were the only hired men who had been called for the first week of rehearsals.

The distribution of parts was a lengthy and complicated business. Ned found himself with three: a messenger from Rome at the beginning of the play, then the Roman officer Silius, and finally Dolabella.

It was a whole hour before the reading began, and it was a very tentative one because the knitting together of the parts was a slow process. Richard Burbage was, as always, a very hesitant first reader and this encouraged Bob Gough to be so; while he was excited by his unexpected opportunity, he was made nervous by the responsibility.

There was one notable break during the days of rehearsal, when the whole company attended the marriage of John Lowin to his Joan. Ned stood at the groom's side, and the wedding filled his thoughts with Marie. On impulse he decided, on a free afternoon, to visit her grave. He had rarely done so. Even when he had gone to Neddy's grave he had avoided going to hers, which was some distance away. In the haste and confusion of the burial of a plague victim, it had not been made clear that the child Shakespeare was to be buried near Madame de la Motte, the name Rachel had insisted that she be buried under.

As he stood beside her grave, Ned realized that two years had not dimmed the effect that Marie's death had on him. Sometimes his body ached to embrace her again, and at other times he was filled with a frustrated fury at a fate which robbed her of life in giving life. And now the child whose birth had killed her was himself dead. He felt bitterly cheated, and walked away angrily, not even going to Neddy's grave.

He needed distraction, and he went home and settled down to relearn the lines of Troilus.

The weekly death toll was still more than twice what it would have to come down to before the Globe could be opened, and so the Saturday rehearsal finished in time for Ned to go home and freshen his appearance before setting out for Sophie's.

When he arrived, though he was expected, Sophie was not immediately available. He was taken into the usual room and Tim, as welcoming as ever, served him wine. Tim pointed to a lute which was lying on a small table. It was so long before Sophie appeared that Ned picked up the lute and idly tuned and strummed it.

When Sophie did appear she was less elaborately dressed than usual, and she looked tired; she failed to disguise this even though her face lit up at sight of Ned. She was very glad to sit in her chair and almost slumped in it, like an exhausted old woman.

"Are you sick?" asked Ned, deeply concerned.

"No," she answered with some of her old spirit, "just a little weary. There has been much to do." She took a drink or two of the wine which Tim proffered, sighed heavily, and said, "Esther died. I have a new lady in her place. Her name is Amy. There is so much to teach her, and so little time before Monday."

"How did you find her?"

"They find me. Yesterday and today I have seen a dozen. Somehow they had all heard of Esther's death."

Ned longed to meet Amy. "May I see her?" he asked.

After a moment of amused hesitation, Sophie said, "It may be." Then, more thoughtfully, she added, "Yes, it may well be. But first supper. Conduct me to the table." And she was her old imperious self again.

During the meal Ned was urged to give a full account of his recent doings. He told of the move to his new lodging, of the rehearsals of *Antony and Cleopatra*, of the wedding of the Lowins. He carefully refrained from mentioning *Troilus and Cressida*, since it was still so doubtful. But he had come with something on his mind. He said, "Sophie, I want to talk to you about the payment for my singing. 'Tis too much you offer."

"Too much?" echoed Sophie in disbelief. "I think I hear Lawrence speaking. Was it not he that first said it was too much?"

"Yes, but I thought so too and had beforehand decided I could not accept so much."

"Why not?" and the words were more challenge than question. "Are you afeard I might want you to do something more than sing? Do you not trust me?"

"Verily I trust you. I have told you things I have told no one else."

"Then why cannot you let me be generous to you?"

"That is it. 'Tis generous, a gift, charity, not payment for work."

"So be it then. I will pay you nothing. When you have finished singing, you can take your cap around the room, like a minstrel at a fair."

"No!" said Ned appalled.

"The choice is yours."

Ned, in spite of himself, began to feel angry at being played with, at being trapped. He said, "There is another choice: I do not sing."

"So be it," said Sophie, apparently unperturbed, as she picked up a rabbit's leg to gnaw on it. "The house needs not a minstrel." Ned ate in vicious silence for a while. Then Sophie asked, as though she had no particular interest in his reply, "Well, do you sing?" Ned still vented his anger on his food. Sophie smiled benevolently and said, "Anger is ever a bad counselor, Ned, so let us wait a while and talk of other things. You wish to meet Amy; you shall. When we have finished, I will send for her, and perhaps you will sing for us. I have it! If you like Amy, let her be the price of your singing on Monday, and afterwards we can talk of future payment." Now Ned's mind was whirling. Although he had not met Amy, he longed for her, and yet he was disturbed by the thought of buying her body, even though the coinage was his voice. And another unsettling thought came to him: was Sophie just using him to try out a novice? But she was still speaking. "Both your brother and Lawrence were coming here to supper with you on Monday, to be present when you sang. Will you disappoint them, and me?"

Ned knew that Will would not be disappointed if he did not sing at Sophie's and Lawrence would be relieved. It was Ned himself who would be disappointed, and all because he was too proud to accept Sophie's generosity.

Sophie said to Tim, "Ask Amy to join us for some wine. She is waiting."

Waiting! So Sophie had intended for them to meet, before Ned had asked to see her, and even before he had known of her existence.

Again Sophie seemed to read his suspicions. "I wanted you to meet Amy. You will like her."

It all seemed straightforward, but Ned would make one thing quite clear. "I do not want to lie with Amy unless she likes me."

"She will like you," said Sophie with a kindly smile. "But, Ned, I beg you, for both your sakes, not to like her too much; she is here to make a living, and a good one. Already she has known men. She loved one and he hurt her; that is why she is here."

Tim returned with Amy. Ned stood up and Sophie said, "Amy, this is Ned. He is a friend of mine, not a patron. Sit at the table with us."

Amy was beautiful—a few years younger than Ned, auburn-haired, pale-skinned, of medium height, with proud breasts and elegant hands. She was dressed in flowing and filmy silks which seemed to symbolize an elusive, ethereal quality about her. It was a sense of strange contradiction in her which first struck Ned, a powerfully attractive bodily presence coupled with an almost forbidding remoteness of spirit, as if she were saying at once, "Embrace me but touch me not."

When Tim had supplied Amy with a glass of wine, Sophie said, "I think you should toast Amy, Ned. She is about to begin a new life."

Ned thought for a moment, raised his glass and said, looking at Amy, "May you have all the success and happiness your beauty deserves."

"Thank you," said Amy, with an appraising look at Ned. "I consider myself very fortunate to be chosen by Mistress Mountjoy."

"Very featly said, both of you," said Sophie. "Ned will sing for us shortly, and I hope you can persuade him to sing in the Music Room on Monday. He had promised to do so, but now he has some doubts."

"But why?" Amy asked Ned. "You sing well; I have heard you."

"You have?"

"You are a fine player too. I saw you play Troilus and was angry when the Queen stopped the play, but she was sick nigh unto death. I long to see the play again; there is much truth in it."

Now Ned was completely at a loss. What was this woman doing at Richmond Palace more than four years ago? And her endorsement of the bitter mood of the play was a sad commentary on her young life. But she was speaking again.

"Tell me what happened to Troilus. Did he die in battle?"

"No. The last we see of him is vowing vengeance for the death of Hector."

"He loved an unworthy one; that can ruin a life."

"Enough of this sad talk," interposed Sophie. "You are both young, with the best of life yet before you. No matter what has happened before, you must make the best of what comes."

With his old affection for her, Ned said, "As you have done, Sophie."

"Yes, as I have done. But come, some music."

Ned fetched the lute and soon began his songs. After he had sung three or four, he thought he caught a look between the two women. It might have been a signal, because after the next song Amy stood up and said, "I beg you to excuse me. I have some work to do. I am not fully settled in yet. I hope to hear you sing again on Monday."

Ned stood and said, "It has been a pleasure to meet you, Amy."

Amy smiled, bowed her thanks, and left the room.

Sophie said, "Will she hear you sing again on Monday?"

"Yes," said Ned. Then he smiled and said, "You are a wily one, Sophie. But we will talk about payment again after Monday."

She made no comment, merely saying, "Sing my song." Ned sang "Who is Sophie?" and the question had never seemed more puzzling.

FIFTY-NINE

THERE WAS A NEW AND WELCOME SENSE OF URGENCY AT THE REHEARSAL ON Monday morning. The doleful likelihood that the Globe might not open at all before the Christmas Revels had given way to the optimistic possibility that, if the plague continued to decline at the previous week's rate, the theatre might well open in three or four weeks. There was a great need to submit *Antony and Cleopatra* to the general public before presenting it to the King.

But Ned's mind was on the night. Will and Lawrence were to accompany him to Sophie's for supper at six o'clock. It was not until the afternoon that the play began to take life as both Burbage and Gough showed glimpses of their Antony and Cleopatra. It was well past five before a halt was called, and then, after a conference, Will came to the impatiently waiting Ned to ask to be excused from the evening at Sophie's as both the principal players wanted to work with him on their parts; he would come to Sophie's another evening, very soon.

Ned contained his angry disappointment as best he could and strode away. Lawrence was waiting for him and was quick to justify the prior claim of the theatre on Will; he was sure that Sophie would understand. The important thing was for Ned to calm down, else he would not do his best that night. Ned said nothing.

Lawrence was already dressed for the evening and went with Ned to his lodgings where he assisted him in dressing to make his best appearance. His genuine solicitude finally succeeded in turning Ned's thoughts to the evening, and as a final gesture of appreciation to Lawrence he put on the medallion. The evening that lay ahead would be exciting: there was the meeting of Sophie and Lawrence now not cushioned by the presence of Will, there was the performance itself, and there was the promise of Amy. But how would he get rid of Lawrence, who would certainly expect to accompany him home?

When they arrived at the house, Ned sensed a difference. This was the first time he had been there when it was in evening action. The entrance hall was empty of all but the doorman, though voices and laughter could be heard from other rooms.

Ned and Lawrence were asked to wait, and when Sophie did finally appear, she was so bizarrely resplendent that her guests were momentarily bereft of speech. It was astonishing that she could carry herself so regally under such a weight of jewels or that her face could reveal any animation under such layers of paint; and how could she keep that high-piled wig, a hillock of pearls and gems, balanced on her head?

She spoke first. "Master Fletcher, 'tis good to welcome you at last, and fully recovered I see. But where is your brother, Ned?"

"He has been delayed by rehearsal at the theatre and cannot come. He is very disappointed and hopes you will invite him again."

"Most assuredly I will. His absence will allow Master Fletcher and me to become better acquainted, though I feel we know each other well already."

Lawrence had not yet spoken. He decided that this extraordinary woman would appreciate a show of honesty. "When first we met, 'twas not in friendship, but in the more than two months since then, I have learnt to admire, respect, and be grateful to you, and now I am honored by this invitation and delighted by this second meeting."

"And I too am pleasured to welcome you to my table, Master Fletcher. Nay, since we now are friends, let it be Sophie and Lawrence." She extended her hand for him to kiss and he did so gallantly, though it was difficult for lips to find flesh to touch, it was so guarded with large rings and trinkets. "But now to supper. We cannot dally over wine tonight, as I have given it out that Master Edmund Shakespeare will delight us all in the Music Room at seven of the clock."

Ned said and ate little during the meal. Not only was he nervous about the imminent ordeal in the Music Room, but he was happily content to enjoy Lawrence's entertainment of Sophie, for he was at his witty best. Only once was Ned drawn into the conversation. Sophie said, "That medallion, Ned. 'Tis beautiful. I have not seen it before."

"Lawrence gave it to me for Christmas a few years ago."

"It has words on it. What are they?"

"*Non sanz droict*. It is our family motto. It means . . ."

"I know what it means, Ned—even with your vile pronunciation of the French. 'Tis a good motto, and you should bear it in mind when we discuss payment for your services here. Lawrence shall judge between us. Will that content you?" She turned to Lawrence and asked, "And what, think you, would be fair and just payment for Ned?"

" 'Tis hard to determine," Lawrence answered. "Your patrons do not come here to hear a minstrel."

"Nor is this a common brothel, Lawrence," said Sophie suavely. "I have long thought to regale my gentlemen and their ladies with music. Think not that, in employing Ned, I am finding some excuse to give him money. But he must be paid. I think now it should be by the night and not the week, for there will be nights when he cannot come. And bear in mind this: he cannot forever sing the same songs; he must learn others, and that will mean much work away from here. And if I find that, after a while, few people stay to listen to him, his being a friend of mine will not stay me from saying, 'No more.' "

Both Ned and Lawrence were bowled over by this sudden practicality. At a loss, Lawrence said, "What say you now, Ned?"

" 'Twas all much about nothing."

"Nay, Ned; money is never nothing," said Sophie.

"You are right, as always," replied Ned. "I am content to leave the payment to you."

The time had come. Ned was left to tune his lute while Sophie, on the arm of Lawrence, went to see to the disposition of the audience and to introduce Ned. When all were properly seated and served with wine, Sophie said, "My lords, ladies, and gentlemen. To mark the reopening of our house, we have engaged a minstrel to entertain you. He is Master Edmund Shakespeare of the King's Men. If his singing pleases you, he will come again and again, for as his brother has written, 'Music is the food of love.' "

Laughter at the final innuendo and applause for the much beloved Sophie followed as she signaled to the attendant and then sat down next to Lawrence in the most imposing chair in the room, which had been reserved for her as her queenly due.

When Ned entered the room he was surprised by the number of people present, nearly fifty altogether; later he learned that Sophie had closed the Gaming Room while he sang. Amy was sitting next to Sophie, but was otherwise unaccompanied, though she drew many men's eyes on this, her first appearance. The whole atmosphere of the room was so courtly that Ned was reminded of the times he had sung before the King. Sophie had told him that there would be "several titles" present.

He began nervously, but Sophie came to his rescue. After the first timid verse, she broke the formality and tension by saying, "Now, Ned, you have tuned your voice as well as your lute, so begin in earnest." The tone was so friendly that Ned was grateful rather than embarrassed and from then on his acceptance grew from song to song. When there was a nonsense refrain like "hey, nonny nonny," it was taken up more and more until the room was ringing with song.

When he had completed the eight songs he had decided to sing, Ned said, "My lords, ladies, and gentlemen, I shall sing a song that many of you will know, but I shall sing it with a difference."

As soon as they heard the words "Who is Sophie?" the song was interrupted by approving laughter and applause, but Ned had a surprise in store even for Sophie herself; he had composed an additional verse and he arose from his stool as he sang it and bowed to her.

> "Then to Sophie thus I rise
> And my devotion tender.
> Ne'er did lady meet men's eyes
> To equal her in splendor.
> Hers I am till Death's surprise."

The last line was sung with such sincerity and the last two words were so unusual that for a moment there was silence. Ned began to walk out of the room. The movement released the audience into wild applause. Ned stopped and bowed, and the informality of the occasion asserted itself. Some quickly crowded around him to congratulate him, while others went to Sophie to thank and praise her for such a pleasant addition to the charms of her house.

Never had Ned felt such a sense of triumph, for he did not have to share it with anyone. It was so heady that he wanted to be alone to savor it. Somehow he broke away from his admirers, hurried across the hall and into Sophie's room. There he put down the lute, closed his eyes, and breathed deep in ecstasy. He was glad to have those few moments to himself before the door burst open and Sophie entered with Lawrence, both beaming. Sophie so far abandoned her regality as to embrace Ned against an uncomfortable crush of jewels. "A triumph, my minstrel, a triumph," she trumpeted. When she released him, Lawrence embraced him and whispered, "Troilus next."

Sophie moved to her chair, Tim appeared, and wine and comfits were served. As Sophie and Lawrence vied with each other in describing the reactions of notabilities to Ned's singing, his mind gradually focused on Amy. He had no doubt that she was waiting for him somewhere, but there was equally no doubt that Lawrence was waiting to walk home with him.

Lawrence said, "The whole evening has been memorable, Sophie, and I am grateful to you, as Ned most assuredly is, but we must be going now; Ned has rehearsal in the morning."

"I have something further I must discuss with Ned; some private matter. But I cannot let you walk home alone; my man Tim shall accompany you."

"But Ned . . ." Lawrence floundered.

"Do not worry. Tim will be back and shall accompany Ned home too. You must come again, and soon. You will always be welcome." She held her hand out to Lawrence. He kissed it graciously but when he turned to Ned it was obvious that he was both puzzled and irritated. Ned managed to look bewildered while secretly exulting at Sophie's maneuver, and soon Lawrence was gone.

When he was safely out of hearing, Ned gave a whoop of laughter and embraced Sophie, saying, "You are the cleverest creature in Christendom."

"You mean the infidels have someone cleverer? But you had better be clever too when next you meet Lawrence. He will want to know what I wanted to see you about. But now let us briefly talk payment."

"Whatever you say, Sophie."

"Then I say three shillings a night for the time being. Tomorrow night will be a true test, for I shall not close the Gaming Room. You are always welcome to supper here, and most often in this room, though there will be times when I shall have some other private guest."

"Sophie, you suddenly sound like a merchant."

"I am a merchant, and you are now in my employ, while yet remaining a friend. And now for tonight: three shillings or Amy?"

"Amy."

Sophie smiled. "You have chosen well. She goes not so cheaply to others. And so, a very good night to you." She held out her hand and he kissed it. Then he looked at her with wonder and gratitude. She said, "Until tomorrow at six. Supper, song, three shillings, but no Amy. Mark me, Ned, no Amy."

He smiled wickedly. "Then I shall make the best of my bargain tonight."

Tim conducted Ned to Amy's room with a smile of warm hospitality, without a trace of any leering suggestion. The room was in the back on the second floor and overlooked the lawn and the Thames.

Amy was in the large bed and waiting with a welcoming smile such as a loving wife might give to a husband returning after a successful voyage. As he crossed the room to her, Ned was vaguely aware by the light of one candle of its spaciousness, of a large mirror and handsome furniture; it was the room where a lady lived, not where a whore worked. Ned sat on the bed and gently took Amy in his arms. Her right hand caressed the back of his head as she said, "You were wonderful tonight. I was as proud as if you belonged to me. This is my first day in the house. It was as if Mistress Mountjoy had arranged it to welcome me. It makes me very happy that you are my first."

That last sentence made Ned sharply aware that tomorrow night there would be another man in his place, and then another until she found a wealthy one who enjoyed her so much that he preempted her for his exclusive use. Ned would not lie with Amy again so he must make the most of his opportunity. He disengaged himself, quickly undressed and got into bed.

They were equally matched in sexual adroitness and surprised and pleased each other until they lay back deeply satisfied. Then they began to talk in words of endearment that both knew were temporary but part of an enjoyable game. And soon the hands began exploring again and desire mounted. When next they spoke, Ned tried to question Amy about her past, but she would have none of it. She said, "Spoil not this beautiful night by making me remember the past."

"Tell me one thing: how came you to see my Troilus?"

"Suffice it that I was there, and that an evening which began full of promise for both of us ended sadly. But no more of that. Tell me of your life as a player."

As Ned began to answer, he had a sudden compulsion to tell Amy about the possibility of his playing Troilus again, a secret he had kept from Sophie. But then Amy had seen him play the part and this created a special bond between them. At last Ned had found someone with whom he could share his dreams. Their conversation turned to intimate endearments, and both felt a new sincerity; they knew now that this would not be their last night together.

It was some hours before they were blissfully exhausted, and faltering words trailed off into sleep.

Ned had hoped to wake in time for a moment of final enjoyment, but he overslept so that rehearsal was in progress at the Globe before he was even out of bed. Lawrence had gone to call for him at his lodging and, when he had learned that Ned had not come home, his old suspicions began to plague him.

Ned was more than an hour late, and he arrived at a time when he was not needed on stage, but it chanced that John Heminge was offstage too. Accusingly he said to Ned, "Why are you late?"

During his rush to the theatre, Ned had prepared an answer for this inevitable question. The simple truth that he had overslept would only have added fuel to the fire. He had decided to rely on vagueness and mystery. "I cannot tell you, Master Heminge, but 'twas none of my doing. I am in honor bound to say no more."

"Some wench, I'll be bound."

Ned looked unutterably hurt. "If you choose to think so, I cannot prevent it."

"Then 'twas not so?"

"I beg you, sir, to say no more. I am content to pay my fine."

"Content or no, 'twill be taken from your wages this week." John Heminge stalked away.

So, thought Ned, two shillings fine and three shillings at Sophie's: five shillings for Amy. She was worth it.

Ned's second evening at Sophie's was as infuriating as his first had been exciting. When he arrived, the doorman told him that Mistress Mountjoy regretted she could not have supper with him; unexpected visitors had come with whom she had private business. Ned was asked to wait while Tim was fetched. He was as affable as ever, and took Ned to a backroom where an excellent but solitary supper awaited him. After the meal, with many gestures and pointing to the lute, Tim indicated that Ned was to stay there and tune his lute until he was sent for.

It was the doorman who came to tell him that he was awaited in the

Music Room. When he got there, he was disappointed by the numbers present, only about half of the night before. As he settled on his stool he looked for the faces he knew. There was no Sophie to introduce him, and he could hear some voices in the Gaming Room behind him, though they were not loud. Worst of all was that Amy was there with a strange man. While she smiled at her companion, she looked at Ned with longing, and anger mounted in him.

He vented his resentful feelings by launching into a vigorous old ballad which told of love betrayed and bloody revenge. He had sung it the night before, but as his sixth song. Its effect this time was startling, for the audience not only listened to a gripping tale but seemed to see the betrayed man himself. At the end of the song Ned paused to decide what to sing next and became aware of a silence in the room and then a burst of applause of such intensity that he was dazed by it. He responded with surprised smiles of thanks, and was further gratified when some men came in from the Gaming Room, drawn by the noise which proved that they were missing something good.

From then on all went well. He sang the same songs as the night before, except that he omitted "Who is Sophie?" For a moment he was tempted to sing the original "Who is Sylvia?" but decided that this would be petty. Sophie must have been prevented by some good reason from not being there. Or perhaps she had wanted the evening to surprise him, to test his quality. Well, if such were the case, he had passed the test, and gloriously.

When he arrived next evening, two courtly gentlemen were at the door and were being refused admittance. Ned thought he recognized one of the men from the Monday night audience, but he was not in turn recognized because the two were intent on a muted and puzzled conversation. When the door was opened to Ned, he was quickly admitted and asked to go to Mistress Mountjoy's room. There he found her anxiously awaiting him and in obvious distress.

"Oh, Ned," she said, "they are closing the house."

Any coolness Ned had meant to show toward Sophie vanished. He put his arm around her and led her to her chair. Tim hovered helplessly in the background, suffering with his mistress. Gradually Ned was able to piece together the story.

Two court officials she had never seen before had come to the house the previous evening. They had shown no evidence of hostile intention and Sophie had entertained them to dinner, even daring to think that they might have come as envoys for some highly placed lord who might have required one of her ladies to be sent to him for a secret rendezvous. They wormed out of her much information about the nature and scale of her operation, though she was as sedulous as ever in disclosing no names. When she had stressed the high standard of her patrons it had but served to confirm them in the rightness of their mission. Some of the city fathers who were supplying the money for the new Hall in Whitehall Palace were using this as a lever to secure court approval of their puritanical prohibitions. One of their targets was Sophie's house, and they had seen to it that the King himself had been informed that certain of his courtiers were frequenting a place of ill fame in a plague-infested city. It was not moral indignation that had angered the King but fear of contamination by the pestilence. When the two officials had heard the applause from the Music Room, Sophie had been hard put to it to stop them from joining the audience to find out who was there.

"They were not evil men," Sophie stressed, "but true gentlemen called upon to do an unpleasant task. They were sure my patrons were powerful enough to defy the city council when the plague was down enough for the theatres to open."

"Theatres and brothels are the same to some Puritans," commented Ned savagely, seeing his new success and source of extra income so quickly stopped. But there was the compensation that Amy was temporarily free from strange men.

The very telling of the story to Ned had done much to soothe Sophie, and while they had supper together they buoyed each other with the certainty that the house would soon be open again. They could even laugh together as Ned recounted his singing of the gory ballad. Sophie had received enthusiastic reports of the recital. It was also clear that she had received from Amy an account of Ned's prowess in bed.

Without any rancor, Ned said, "Was I some kind of test for Amy?"

"No," said Sophie, but with a smile that made it hard to believe her fully. "I wanted Amy's first night in my house to be a happy one, and I was sure you would supply that. She paid you the greatest compliment a lady of her trade can pay a man. She said, 'I should have done it without payment; nay, I should willingly have paid him.' Oh, Ned, Fate was cruel to separate us by so many years!" She said this with a heavy comic sigh which ended in a loud belch, at which they both laughed uproariously. Tim joined in, delighted that his saddened mistress was her happy self again.

At their parting Sophie gave Ned six shillings, and, when he began to protest, she said, "Amy was a present. Three shillings could not have bought her."

SIXTY

It was not until the last week of November that the plague's death toll was sufficiently low to enable the theatres to open, and now the weather was such that only sporadic performances were expected. Still, it was announced on bills and much bruited abroad that a new tragedy by William Shakespeare, *Antony and Cleopatra,* would be presented at the Globe Theatre on Tuesday, December 1, "in full splendour, as it will be performed before His Majesty at his Palace of Whitehall on St. Stephen's Day."

On the last Friday in November Sophie, who had gone to the country when her house was closed, came back to town. When Ned returned home after supper that night, he found a message awaiting him. It read: "I am back and look to see you soon at supper, when your rehearsals permit. The house will open again on Monday and would be graced by your presence and delighted by your voice. Your friend and employer. S.M."

Ned longed to see her, but he had promised to have supper with the Lowins after rehearsal on Saturday and dinner with Lawrence after church on Sunday. Then it would have to be supper with Sophie on Sunday, and that was the meal he most looked forward to.

After the Saturday supper with the Lowins, now snugly ensconced in their new home, John and Ned cued each other in their parts, as they had so often done in the past.

The Sunday dinner with Lawrence was very pleasant. Ned had not been to the house for two weeks, though they had frequent and friendly conversations at the theatre. Lawrence had wonderful news for Ned, and he wanted him to know before the sharers. The day before, he had received a message from the Master of the Revels that there would definitely be an eleventh play, and a twelfth, and possibly even more, so sometime before the end of January Ned would play Troilus.

"Do you remember the part?" asked Lawrence.

"I could play it tomorrow. Ever since you told me that it might be the eleventh play, I have conned it and conned it."

"Then after dinner, go and fetch the part and let me cue you. I have never heard you say the lines, and it would pleasure me greatly to do so."

It was a blissful afternoon for both men, and when Ned said the lines,

"I am giddy; expectation whirls me round.
The imaginary relish is so sweet
that it enchants my sense,"

it was not of Cressida he was thinking.

When it was time for Ned to leave for Sophie's, he was glad to know that Lawrence expected company for supper, "a young man I should be happy for you to meet, for he aspires to be a poet, and already writes well; moreover he wears his youth and good looks easily and without arrogance."

When Ned saw Sophie, it was clear that the slightest movement caused her pain. She said, "My old bones ache; I fear 'twill rain, and heavily. So warm me with your good cheer, Ned, and ease my joints."

Ned confided in her his exciting January prospect, explaining that not even the sharers knew it yet. He told her the tale of *Troilus and Cressida* and spoke for her many of his lines.

"You are Troilus," commented Sophie. "You would have been angry and bitter like him if your Cressida had proved faithless. Oh, Ned, I pray that you will find someone worthy of your love." Ned's thoughts raced to Amy, but for once Sophie had not read his thoughts, for she said, "But now tell me: when can you start singing here again?"

"I must wait until *Antony and Cleopatra* is played. Cannot you come to see that?"

"Alas, Ned, no. I cannot sit in an open theatre except in the warmest of weathers, but you will tell me all about it and I shall imagine I was there."

Sophie's bones proved true prophets. Heavy rain closed the Globe day after day, and it was not until Monday, December 7, that *Antony and Cleopatra* was presented to London. The new play was a disappointment. While it was well received, it did not kindle the expected excitement, and at the subsequent supper, celebration soon gave way to analysis. All the spectators—and the theatre was full—had to splosh their way through streets of ankle-deep mud, and the groundlings had to stand in it for the performance. By constant repetition without full performance the lines had staled, and in the morning there had not been a full run-through because the time was taken up with rehearsal of the complicated groupings and movements on the stage from which rain had banished the players for a week; and then it was very cold. The audience sat and stood, bundled up in furs and wools, and beating their bodies with gloved hands to keep warm; although it did not rain, the sun did not shine. Nat Tremayne had tearfully pleaded with players not to cover up their costumes with extra protection against the cold but in most cases he failed; only Robert Gough dared the cold in the silks and satins Nat had prepared for him, and there were times when he was seen to shiver on the stage, to the amusement of some wags in the audience. Indeed their too ready laughter was the most disconcerting element in the afternoon.

It began with the line of Lepidus, "Your serpent of Egypt is bred now of your mud by the operation of your sun." The very mention of mud was enough to cause more laughter than the line merited. But a particularly insensitive groundling dared to snigger loudly when Richard Burbage, as the despairing Antony, said, "O sun, thy uprise shall I see no more." There were angry protests at the barbarous reaction. Burbage seemed to ignore it, but his astounding rage against Cleopatra which followed immediately may have been fed by the unwitting groundling. Once Antony was dead, the wags felt released to enjoy every possible misinterpretation of a line. Bob Gough suffered most. Cleopatra's line, "Rather on Nilus' mud lay me stark-naked" drew many guffaws, and few protests. The fact that the play was long and that the weak daylight had begun to fade robbed Iras of all pathos when John Rice spoke the line, "The bright day is done, and we are for the dark." But the worst was reserved for Cleopatra, blue with cold, when she took farewell of her handmaids with the line, "Come, then, and take the last warmth of my lips."

Yet, in spite of all, the applause at the end had been enthusiastic, perhaps as much in tribute to the players' overcoming of obstacles as to the new play. And there was no doubt that some unexpected and insensitive laughter had not seriously dimmed the triumph of Robert Gough's Cleopatra, and both Will and Burbage had been quick to assure him of this immediately after the performance. As Burbage said, "They even laughed at me!"

The sharers decided at the supper that they would not show the new play to the public again until the spring, and Will agreed to make some cuts in the text before the royal performance.

As Lawrence walked home with Ned, it got colder and colder, and he said, "I fear there will be few in the theatre tomorrow to hear you sing 'Sigh no more, ladies.' " And he was right, for Londoners awoke to a frozen world.

The Great Frost began on Tuesday, December 8, and it lasted well into January, with one brief thaw. Overnight the deep mud turned into thick ice, and within a few days the Thames was frozen and the Globe was closed.

A crisis also occurred at Sophie's on the day the Globe had been forced to close. The house had no more coal. There was a dearth throughout the city because ships from the north were prevented by the frozen river from replenishing the exhausted stores, and the excessive demand for firewood had soon put that in short supply. Tim jealously hoarded all the fuel that was left in the house and all he could buy in the city to keep a fire burning in Sophie's bedroom, from which she did not stir; even her food was boiled or warmed on the bedroom fire; the kitchen fire was out as were all other fires in the house. While the house was not explicitly closed, the Gaming Room was empty. Only the most libidinous patrons chose to stay in the cold bedrooms, and even they did not undress to conjugate with their warmly gowned ladies. It was obvious that Ned would have had no audience in the Music Room, and Tim conducted him to Sophie's palatial bedroom, the heat of which, by contrast, hit him like a blast from a furnace. Sophie was in bed. He wondered how she could endure the extra heat of the blankets, but she seemed to be comfortable, out of pain, and in good spirits.

Ned said, "You must be so hot that I think you will be happy in hellfire."

"Only if you are there, Ned, and I doubt not you will be."

They laughed together and enjoyed an excellent stew boiled by Tim on the fire. Ned longed to ask about Amy but dared not arouse Sophie's suspicions. The time would come when the successful player could declare his interest in Amy. Now, all he said was, "I cannot remember if I ever had a hot supper before."

"At least your mother's milk was warm. But today I fear that babes have sucked on frozen breasts with icicles for nipples."

By the time Ned had become accustomed to the heat of the room, he dreaded the walk home because a bitter north wind had begun to blow. While there was no hope of an audience in the Music Room until a thaw had unlocked the Thames, Sophie begged Ned to visit her, and he promised to do so. "I shall make some skates of bones and skate across the river." There had been much skating on the Thames in the last few days.

"Nay, Ned, unsay that at once, else if you do not come I shall think you have broken your legs, your arms, and whatever else about you is breakable."

When he left, Ned was so wrapped up in additional garments provided by Tim that he could not be recognized, but even so the wind found its way through to bite him sharply, and it continued to do so all the way home.

Mistress Barker had been anxiously awaiting his return. Her husband did not like coal in the house, but they had an ample supply of wood and she had kept a good fire going in Ned's room all day, but she would not let him go upstairs until he had thawed out by her fire and warmed his belly with a tankard of mulled ale.

When Ned woke the next morning he was both hot and shuddering. He realized he had a fever. The fire had gone out, but he decided to stay in bed and not to rekindle it. He would wait until Mistress Barker came.

But it was the master of the house who finally appeared, carrying a bundle of firewood. He was home because the weather made it impossible to work on outside masonry. He was immediately struck by the feverish look of Ned and, after questioning him, went downstairs to get his wife to prepare one of her "powerful possets that will drive out any fever." He soon returned and set about lighting the fire. In due course Mistress Barker came upstairs with a steaming mug. She said, "Make yourself drink this, Master Shakespeare. 'Tis unpleasant but potent medicine. I learnt it from my mother, and it has stood us all in good stead."

Ned made a wry face at the first taste of the concoction, but persevered until he had drunk it all. No, he did not want any breakfast, nor did he want Master Barker to go to tell Will that he was sick; he was certain he would be quickly well.

When he was alone Ned realized gleefully that his fever brought one consolation: it was Sunday, but he would not have to go to church. But the Barkers went and told the Forresters about Ned's condition. The Forresters told Will, who in turn told Lawrence, when they met in church, and both men, muffled against the cold, though the wind had dropped, carefully picked their way over the rutted icy roads to see Ned.

He was still very feverish but quite normal in mind and speech. While he was cheered by their concern, he assured them he would be at rehearsal in a day or two. This raised the whole question of rehearsals in the weather which was colder than anyone could remember. Work on the open stage would be impossible and yet rehearsals every day were imperative because the opening of the Christmas Revels at Whitehall with *Antony and Cleopatra* was less than two weeks away, and at least six other plays must be readied by then. The only play that would need intensive rehearsal would be *Troilus and Cressida,* and they would not begin on that until January. It was presumed that rehearsals would take place in the tiring room; there was a fireplace there, but it was rarely used because of Nat Tremayne's fear for the safety of the costumes, but Will said, "Even Nat will want a fire lit tomorrow, else his frozen fingers cannot ply his needle."

Mistress Barker surprised the three men by arriving with a large tray of dinner for them. It was cold, for nothing could break the Sabbath injunction against cooking, but she suggested that the Lord would forgive them if they warmed their ale by dipping into it a poker heated in the fire. She said, "God sent us the frost, but He also gave us the fire to withstand it." She felt Ned's forehead. It was still fevered, but she smiled and nodded her head reassuringly.

What had begun as a brief visit to the sick turned into a pleasant dinner for the three men. Ned ate very little, and that only at the urging of the other two. He told them of his visit to Sophie and of the cruel change from the overheated room to the cold street and the north wind. They decided that it was this that had caused the fever, and that he must be doubly cautious about not venturing out into the cold again until he was fully well and strong.

A six-days' thaw set in on Wednesday, the sixteenth, and on that Thursday Ned was at rehearsal again. The theatre would not be reopened until after the Revels, which were now expected to go well into February; all the time was needed for rehearsals and preparations.

Ned was both flattered and embarrassed by the welcome he received on his return; it seemed out of all proportion to the length of his absence and the severity of his illness. Perhaps it was due to the fact that all now knew that *Troilus and Cressida* was to be played, and Ned was already being accorded a new status in the company. His mind was awhirl with his future: first Troilus, then Romeo, and, after a few years, Hamlet.

The thaw continued through the Monday, allowing the new Hall to be completed in time. Friday would be Christmas Day and the Revels would begin on the Saturday with *Antony and Cleopatra*. The King had overridden the old objection to holding a Revel on a Sunday, and *Much Ado About Nothing* was to be given that evening, with *Macbeth* following on Monday. So on this prior Monday excitement and bustle and frayed tempers were everywhere at the Globe.

Both Ned and Lawrence were glad to get away from the theatre. They had come prepared to go straight to Sophie's that evening, because they knew the rehearsal would drag on. They crossed the thawed river by boat, to save time and avoid mud, but they still arrived so late that Sophie had given them up and started dinner; her joy at seeing them was thereby enhanced.

She was her old self. There was now abundance of coal in the house and one of her ladies had found for her a magic unguent which made movement bearable. Before supper she had gone to test the Music Room and had found it warm enough, so that she would be able to sit with Lawrence at Ned's performance, "as on that first time, exactly seven weeks ago."

Sophie insisted that Ned come close to her so that she could really see how he was, "for my sight gets mistier every day, but that is no loss, for there is much in this world that 'tis better to look at with misty eyes, and I shall not need them in the next."

At her request, Ned knelt by her chair and she peered at his face closely. She was not satisfied by what she saw, especially when she pressed down an eyelid and saw that the inside was pale. She said, "Now that you are here you shall sing tonight, but not again until after the Christmas Revels. You must promise me that you will go straight to bed after supper every night. You are not yet in full health, Ned."

"But I feel well," Ned protested, though in fact he had known for some days that he lacked something of his usual energy, and had seemed to feel the cold more than his fellows.

"Promise me," Sophie insisted, "else I will not even let you sing tonight."

Reluctantly Ned promised, and was allowed to return to his place at the table.

"And think not you are missing much. This is Christmas week and we shall close the house on Wednesday until after Twelfth Night. I shall stay in London, though I look not to see you until the King's Men have a gap in the Christmas Revels."

There was a gratifying audience for Ned's performance, and he acquitted himself well. Amy was there with another stranger. To Ned that was better than her being with the same man. He had begun to have dreams of such success as a player that he might be able to afford to reserve Amy for himself alone. Even the word "marriage" had flitted teasingly across his mind. Sophie, sitting with Lawrence, had not introduced Ned, but she interspersed his songs with comments, most of them unnecessary for her audience, and some of them incorrect. Thus when he sang, "Blow, blow, thow winter wind," she said, "You do not well, Ned, to remind us of winter winds and freezing skies. Still, 'tis a good song." To the room she said, "It comes from his brother's play, *Twelfth Night*."

"Nay," said Ned. " 'Tis *As You Like It*."

"Then, if 'tis as I like it, it still comes from *Twelfth Night*."

Ned ended his recital with his song to Sophie, including the special verse, but later in Sophie's room where she insisted that Ned and Lawrence take a tankard of mulled ale "to keep out the cold," she said, "I like my song but not the last two words of the extra verse, 'Death's surprise.' "

" 'Twas the first rhyme that came to me."

"Then think of another. Lawrence, cannot you help him?"

"Even if I could, he would not wish it. Once he wrote a verse for me and in that too he spoke of his death."

"His death?" said Sophie with genuine amazement. "Tell me, Ned, in my verse who was Death going to surprise? You or me?"

"Me," said Ned, equally amazed that there was any ambiguity in the line.

"Oh," said Sophie, "then it can stay." And they laughed together.

When the two men got out into the street, the weather had turned intensely cold again. They hurried down to the river, and the muffled boatman cursed his way across because he was certain that the river, and with it his livelihood, would be frozen again by the morning.

And he was right. The Great Freeze had come again, and worse than before. Rehearsals could not be suspended, and it was decided to transfer them to the warmth of Lawrence's house, though his largest room, even when divested of all furniture, was cramped and inadequate. Lawrence was always eager to provide some extra service for the players; his conscience was never fully reconciled to being a sharer without playing.

Ned found he was exhausted by rehearsal, and could not understand this, because he had comparatively little to do. He was glad to keep his promise to Sophie, and he went to bed on Tuesday and Wednesday immediately after supper, of which he ate little, much to Mistress Barker's disappointment.

On Thursday they rehearsed *As You Like It*, in which Will's part of Adam was now played by Nicholas Tooley. It was a great effort for Ned to venture out into the frozen street even for the short walk to Lawrence's, and when he arrived he was breathing so fast that his fellows were disturbed and insisted that he rest by the fire for a while. Lawrence even wanted him to abandon thought of rehearsal and go upstairs to lie in the bed, but this he refused to do and soon felt well enough to join in the rehearsal.

He sang the songs of Amiens without accompaniment and with apparent ease, but when he came to William's scene near the end of the play, he had just spoken with a broad Warwickshire accent the line, "Aye, sir, I have a pretty wit," when his face went suddenly ashen and he staggered. His breathing was now alarmingly fast. Simultaneously Will and Lawrence hurried to him. Each took an arm and took him into the kitchen in the back where Mistress Russet, busy with preparing dinner for the players, was frightened by his appearance. Surely young Master Shakespeare could not have caught the plague? This was not the season or weather for the pestilence.

The same fear had seized Will and Lawrence as they helped Ned to sit on a settle by the fire. They longed to know if there were any swellings under the arms or in the groin, but they did not want to terrify Ned by probing either with their fingers or questions.

He asked, "What ails me, Will?"

Will said, "The fever you had before has returned. You ventured out too soon." But Will did not believe his own words. He went back into the front room to reassure the players.

John Heminge voiced the general fear. "What is it, Will? Is it . . . ?"

But Will cut him off quickly. "I know not. Haply the return of the former fever."

Mistress Russet had abandoned her cooking to brew a herbal medication. When Will returned to Ned, Lawrence was softly speaking words of comfort to him, but the breathing had not slowed down. It was Lawrence who said, quietly to Will, "I think we should get him to my bed and I should go for a physician."

Ned made no protest this time, and as they began to help him toward the stairs, Mistress Russet said she would soon follow them with the medicine.

Each step required a herculean effort by Ned in addition to the help of Will and Lawrence, and halfway up the narrow stairway the sick man was taken with a violent fit of coughing, which seemed to tear his lungs until finally some sputum dribbled on his chin. It was stained with blood.

By the time Ned lay on the bed, all three were exhausted, and the two helpers rested for a moment. Then they partially undressed Ned and put him under the blankets. As they worked on him Will managed to feel under his arms; there were no swellings. Ned had not failed to notice the examination. He looked at Will and weakly shook his head.

"The groin?" Will asked.

The answer was another feeble shake of the head.

Mistress Russet appeared with the hot herbal infusion, and while she waited at the bedside for it to be cool enough to drink, Will and

Lawrence conferred quietly in a corner. Lawrence would go for a physician he knew who lived nearby. Will would stay with Ned while Mistress Russet served dinner to the company.

The first sip of the potion brought on another bout of coughing, and again there was blood in the mouth. Mistress Russet prayed, without knowing that she had spoken aloud, "Dear God, our Father in Heaven, spare him!" It was decided that no further attempt should be made to get Ned to drink the medicine until the physician came. Lawrence and Mistress Russet went downstairs.

For something to do while he waited, Will tended to the fire, though it needed no tending. His thoughts were in a turmoil. It looked as if Ned had caught that fatal fever of the lungs which attacked some in time of plague. This it was that the little princesses had died of in September. There was no plague now, and yet he had heard it said that there was never a day on which the plague could not find some victim. In two days' time *Antony and Cleopatra* was to be presented at Whitehall, but how could he leave Ned? Ned was saying something. He hurried to the bedside.

Very weakly Ned said, "The rehearsal. Go. The rehearsal."

"They are having dinner, Ned. There is no hurry. Lawrence has gone for a physician."

Lawrence had omitted to explain to the physician about the rehearsal so the little man was taken aback when he entered a roomful of men, speaking with muted voices while they ate. The entrance of the physician caused a silence while Lawrence led the way upstairs.

The physician wasted neither time nor words. After a brief examination, he picked up the medicinal potion which stood on a stool, smelled it and said, " 'Tis too late for this. I will bleed him." Lawrence gave him a bowl and very quickly it contained more than a pint of blood taken from Ned's arm. The physician used a salve to stanch the flow of blood and bandaged the arm. Ned's eyes were closed but his mouth was open and his breast was heaving almost once every second. The physician moved to a corner to speak quietly to the anxious men. "The bleeding should ease the fever but he is beyond the help of all but the Divine Physician. I can but counsel you to pray."

"Is there no hope?" Will asked.

Reprovingly the physician replied, "There is always hope in prayer."

"Is it the plague?" Lawrence asked.

" 'Tis not the common plague; there are no swellings. 'Tis a plague of the lungs, and I have known none to recover from it."

"How long before the end?" said Will.

"Some days; three, four, perhaps five."

Lawrence took the physician downstairs, paid him and quickly returned. He found Will looking down at Ned with infinite sadness. Thinking it would be best to be practical, Lawrence motioned Will away from the bed. Speaking quietly he said, "I think it best to send the players away. Tomorrow is Christmas Day; I had almost forgotten. We meet again at the theatre at eight o'clock on Saturday for the procession to Whitehall."

Will nodded but said nothing. Lawrence went downstairs. Somehow the players had sensed the worst. Their conversation had almost stopped, as had their eating. They looked anxiously at Lawrence. He had meant to speak privately to John Heminge, but was prompted by the looks to address the room. He said, "I fear Ned is very sick. We cannot rehearse more today."

It was not his place to announce future arrangements, so he looked to John Heminge, who said, "So be it. I think we are ready for the Revels. Tomorrow is Christmas Day. We will all go to church and pray for Ned's recovery. Then on Saturday we meet for Whitehall at eight of the clock." He turned to Lawrence and said, "We thank you, Master Fletcher, for your hospitality."

"There is something else," said Lawrence. " 'Tis certain that Ned cannot play on Saturday and 'tis a new play, so his parts must be given out now."

"I had thought of that," said Heminge, "and hoped to talk to Will about it."

As if in answer, Will appeared in the room. He had thought of the same problem and now said openly, "I think it best that Sam Gilburne play Ned's parts in *Antony and Cleopatra,* and we can make the other dispositions on Saturday. Sam will come with me now to Ned's lodging and we will find the parts. Besides, I must go to tell the good lady of the house what has happened, for Ned cannot be moved back there."

Soon the company had all departed, except for Sam and John Lowin. The shock and distress had been so deeply felt by all that nobody had spoken conventional words of sympathy and hope. John had lingered to know the truth. When he asked Will, the answer was, "Go, see for yourself."

"I too, Master Shakespeare?" asked Sam.

Will nodded, and the four men went upstairs.

The sound of their coming must have stirred Ned's awareness for he opened his eyes. When he saw John and Sam, a trace of a smile slightly changed the shape of his mouth, which was gasping for breath. John managed to hide the shock he felt at the sight of Ned, who in so short a while had become a man clearly marked for death. Sam was not so successful in hiding his reaction. With a great effort Ned spoke but all he managed was "John. Sam." In return they said nothing but nodded and smiled encouragement.

In the meantime, Lawrence had whispered to Will, "I shall fetch Rachel," and he left the room.

Later, as Sam walked with Will to Ned's lodging he said, "I shall scarce be able to speak Ned's lines on Saturday when I think of him."

"Nor I to hear them."

"Will you be there?" asked Sam, unable to hide his surprise.

"I must; 'tis a new play. And duty is a good antidote to sorrow when you are helpless."

"Master Fletcher. Will he come to Whitehall too?"

"He can do nothing for Ned and much for his fellows. But I shall return to Ned at first light on Sunday, for the players will not need me after *Antony and Cleopatra*."

After Sam had been dispatched with the parts and Will had given the dire news to the distressed Mistress Barker, he went to tell Mistress Forrester that he would not be home for the night. Although he had not discussed it with Lawrence, he knew that they would alternate in keeping watch over Ned. When he told his landlady about Ned, she said, "Be not so dismayed, Master Shakespeare. Your brother is young and strong."

"I have known Death to have a special appetite for the young and strong."

When Will returned, he found that there had been no change in Ned, nor had he attempted to say anything. John Lowin left and Will sat down to watch, helplessly, his dying brother. Three, four, or five days, the physician had said. Will felt he had to be with the boy at the end, though it would do no good. Strange he should think of him as a boy again. The thought of having to leave Ned on Saturday to go to Whitehall was hard to bear. Ned would have to be left to Rachel and Mistress Russet. No. Gilbert! He would go to fetch Gilbert tomorrow afternoon.

When Lawrence came into the room with Rachel, Ned did not stir. When she saw him, Rachel could not restrain a burst of tears, and she left the room abruptly.

Lawrence told Will that he had decided not to go to Whitehall on Saturday; he would wait until Will returned. "His Majesty will not miss me. If he should send for me, do you go in my stead and tell him the truth. There is no one who better understands the claims of friendship than the King."

"But tomorrow I shall fetch Gilbert to take our place."

"That is as you wish, but he cannot take mine until you return."

Both men went downstairs for dinner, leaving Rachel with Ned. When they went back, they were amazed to find her sitting with a satisfied smile on her face, and Ned apparently asleep, his mouth more closed and his breathing a little easier and slower. Rachel had given him a potion. The change seemed miraculous and their hope renewed. In whispers they discussed plans for the night. Will and Lawrence would rest in turns on the daybed in the study.

And so began the first night of the deathwatch. Ironically it was Ned who seemed to sleep most that night, for Rachel's potion had contained an opiate.

Will was with Ned at dawning of Christmas Day. He thought of his reference in *Hamlet* to the legend that cocks crew all night long to herald the birth of the Savior. They had not done so this night. It had been eerily quiet, because the world outside was frozen into complete stillness; so quiet that the labored breathing of Ned had sounded ominously loud. Once or twice he had stirred in the night and had even muttered some words, but neither Will nor Lawrence had understood them.

The Christmas clamor of church bells awoke Ned from his deep sleep. Almost immediately his breathing became faster. With an effort he said, "Sunday?"

"No," said Will, shaking his head. "Christmas."

Ned closed his eyes and Lawrence went down for Rachel. Soon they returned. This time she had two liquids, the herbal medication and some warmed milk containing honey. She handed one each to the two men and she sat on the bed and with surprising skill and strength gently raised Ned to rest against her. She took the milk from Lawrence and said to Ned, "First you must take something to stay your stomach." Carefully she began to pour the milk into his mouth, but most of it trickled out. Yet Ned gulped and swallowed. The watching men tensed in anticipation of the coughing, but it did not come until after the third swallow, and even then it was not too violent, yet soon some blood dribbled from the mouth. Rachel desisted from trying to feed him more milk. She crooned to him and rocked him as though he were a baby, cleaning his chin with the corner of a sackcloth apron she wore. When she deemed that Ned was ready, she began to feed him the medication. Again much of it spilled out but he took several swallows without coughing. She continued to rock and croon to him until his eyes closed and the opiate took effect. Then she gently laid him down again. Quietly she said, "He will sleep now. 'Tis the best we can do."

Will told Lawrence he had to go to see Gilbert. He went back to his lodging to get his horse. It was too long a walk to Blackfriars on the icy streets and the horse, its feet thickly padded in sacking, would be more surefooted than he.

The streets were almost deserted, though there were a few skaters on the Thames. It was past two o'clock when Will got to Gilbert's, and as he dismounted and tethered his horse he heard laughter from the second floor; Gilbert was holding a Christmas party.

Will had to knock a few times before the door was opened by Mark Garfield. He knew Will and asked him in. Will said he did not want to join the celebration; he needed to see Gilbert alone.

As Gilbert came down the stairs, already happy with wine, he greeted his brother. "I wish you a warm and joyful Christmas, Will, in spite of the frost." Will did not return the greeting, and his serious mien changed Gilbert's tone. "'Tis our mother, I know. Well, 'tis a happy release for . . ."

"No, Gil. 'Tis Ned. He is dying, I fear."

"Ned?" Gilbert struggled to absorb the news. "Some accident? A duel?"

"Nay. A disease of the lungs. There is no hope. 'Tis but a matter of a day or so."

"But he is the youngest of us, Will. How can it be?" Gilbert felt behind him toward a stool and sat on it.

Will ignored the unanswerable question, and went on to tell of his own duty to be at Whitehall on the morrow. He wanted Gilbert to take his place at Ned's bedside.

"I will come at once." said Gilbert, rising from the stool.

" 'Tis not necessary, Gil, and can do no good."

"I cannot stay here to rejoice." Gilbert went upstairs to explain his mission, and laughter gave way to silence.

When they got to Lawrence's house, Gilbert was appalled by Ned's appearance, even though he was still asleep. The healthy cheeks were now sunken and ashen; even the lips seemed to be tinged with gray. Gilbert tried to restrain his tears.

Lawrence had been much worried about the strain on Will of a strenuous day at Whitehall following two nights of inadequate sleep, and now he insisted that Will go home for a night's rest. Gilbert and Rachel added their pleas, and finally Will consented, with the strict condition that he would be fetched if there were a change in Ned.

But there was no change. Will came the following morning before going to join the company at the theatre and all Lawrence and Gilbert had to report was that Ned had made some indistinguishable mutterings in the night. Gilbert thought he had heard the word "varlet" and Will said, "You did. He was saying his first line in *Troilus and Cressida*." He looked at Lawrence. "It will never be played now. It belonged to him. Troilus would have been Ned's true beginning as a player. He had it in him to perform wonders."

Lawrence and Gilbert had passed part of the night in court gossip, particularly about the new knight, Sir Robert Carr, but Lawrence gave no indication of the dream he once had of Sir Edmund Shakespeare, and Gilbert was more concerned with Sir Robert's substantial pension than with the title, for the young knight was honorable and had already fully paid his debt and ordered more clothes. Lawrence was glad he would not be going to Whitehall in the morning as the inevitable celebration of Sir Robert Carr's investiture would have been hard to participate in with a mind filled by Ned's approaching death.

Fortunately there was no need for the usual colorful procession from the Globe to the Palace; there were no bystanders, and the players dressed for warmth, not display. The company was in a somber mood, but grateful to Will that, in spite of his sorrow, he had come to help them through the ordeal of a difficult new play to be presented to the King without sufficient trial before public audiences.

And he amazed them that day. As if to take his mind off Ned, Will worked with an unusually dominating energy. It was clear that he had thought much about the play since that first performance, and during his vigil over Ned, he had come to some drastic conclusions, all designed to speed up the action. He was ready with ruthless cuts which were so bewildering that the company worked right through the day, with scarcely time to eat, but in the final run-through they captured the excitement of Will's first reading, and they longed to share it with the King, the Queen, and the court.

The result was wonderful. Robert Gough's Cleopatra surprised not only the other players and the audience, but himself. Ned was forgotten during the performance, even by Sam Gilburne as he played Dolabella. He confessed this to Will afterwards, and was told, "Feel not guilty, Sam. You did right and well. Had your places been changed, Ned would have done the same, for he too was a player."

Sam noted the "was" and turned away to hide his emotion.

As expected, the King did send for Master Fletcher, but Will asked Richard Burbage to go and explain the absence; he himself could not face the ordeal. Burbage was to say that Master Fletcher would be there to wait on His Majesty's pleasure tomorrow, and for the rest of the Revels.

Will was exhausted after the performance and some of his older fellows saw to it that, after a light supper, he went straight to bed. But he slept little. If it had been possible he would have risen and gone to Ned's bedside. He felt an unreasonable compulsion to be with him at the end. Perhaps it was to make up for not having been there when Hamnet died.

It was granted to him to be with his brother at the end, for Ned did not die until the early hours of the Tuesday morning. In his last minutes, his struggle for breath eased, and it was the absence of the sound that roused Will who was half dozing in the chair. He got up and stood over Ned. There were several lighted candles in the room. Ned opened his eyes and recognized Will. He spoke his name and smiled faintly, and then said two words which mystified Will; they had been spoken with remarkable clarity. Almost immediately he was siezed with a giant convulsion and a small flow of blood came from his mouth.

Will ran in to get Lawrence, forgetting for the moment that he had gone to Whitehall. It was Rachel who now lay in the daybed, taking turns with Will in the vigil. By the time they returned to the bedside, Ned was gone.

Later Will told Lawrence of Ned's words, and he learned from him their context and significance. The words were, "Death's surprise."

TO SPARE WILL AND GILBERT, LAWRENCE WENT TO THE CHURCH TO ARRANGE the funeral service. The chief sexton readily agreed to a gentleman's burial at ten of the clock on the morrow, which would be the last day of the year. Would the gentleman require the bell tolled?

With sudden inspiration Lawrence said, "Aye. The great one."

The sexton was taken aback, for this was an expensive privilege reserved for the noble and the wealthy. "A forenoon knell of the great bell is costly."

"It matters not how much."

" 'Tis twenty shillings."

"So be it," said Lawrence, and he took from his pouch two golden pounds and a golden angel, munificent payment for all the services of the church in the burial.

And so there was entered, in the register of St. Saviour's Church, "Edmund Shakespeare, a player, buried in the Church, with a forenoone knell of the great bell. XXs."

POSTSCRIPT

WILL SURVIVED HIS THREE BROTHERS AND WAS THE LAST MALE TO BEAR
the family name. He died in 1616 at the age of fifty-two. Gilbert had died
in 1612 at the age of forty-six and Richard the following year at the age
of thirty-nine.

The women of the family were hardier, for all survived their husbands:

Mary died within a year of her youngest son, having outlived John, her
husband, by seven years.

Anne, too, survived Will by seven years. She was sixty-eight at her
death.

Joan outlived Will Hart by thirty years. She died in 1646 at the age of
seventy-seven. Two of her three sons also predeceased her.

Susanna survived John Hall by fourteen years. She died in 1649 at the
age of sixty-six. She did not live long enough to see her daughter, Elizabeth, become Lady Bernard by her second marriage.

Judith lived as long as her Aunt Joan. She died in 1661 at the age of
seventy-seven, having probably outlived her husband and certainly her
three sons. Some two months before her father's death she had married,
when she was thirty-one, Thomas Quiney, of whom her father showed
disapproval in a hastily altered will. By Quiney she had three sons:
Shakespeare died in infancy and Richard and Thomas within weeks of
each other, Richard being twenty-one and Thomas eleven.

He was not a member of the family,
but it may be noted in
this postscript that
Lawrence Fletcher
died within a
year of
Ned.

ABOUT THE AUTHOR

PHILIP BURTON WAS, FOR A LONG TIME, PRESIDENT and director of the American Musical and Dramatic Academy, and before that, had a distinguished career in the theater and with the BBC. He has taught many of the leading performers in Europe and in America how to act, particularly in Shakespearean drama. Among the distinguished actors who have benefited from his wisdom is Richard Burton, his adopted son.

Besides being an important figure in the theater, Mr. Burton is an eminent scholar, writer and lecturer. His previous books are *The Sole Voice: Character Portraits from Shakespeare* and his autobiography, *Early Doors: My Life and the Theater*. Mr. Burton now lives in Key West, Florida, and in Asbury Park, New Jersey.